LENGTH OF DAYS TRILOGY

Doris Gaines Rapp

LENGTH OF DAYS TRILOGY Copyright 2020 Doris Gaines Rapp

Daniel's House Publishing
P.O. BOX 623
Huntington, Indiana 46750

Contact Daniel's House Publishing at
www.danielshousepublishing@gmail.com. To send a package or
envelope, email - a package was mailed to P.O. Box 623 for pick up.

This book is a work of fiction. Names, characters, places, and
incidents are either products of the author's imagination or are used
fictitiously. Any resemblance to actual events, locales or persons,
living or dead, is entirely coincidental.

Biblical Passages:
THE HOLY BIBLE, NEW INTERNATIONAL VERSION®,
NIV® Copyright © 1973, 1978, 1984, 2011 by Biblica, Inc. ™
Used by permission. All rights reserved worldwide.

LENGTH OF DAYS TRILOGY ISBN: 978-0-9988590-9-5
Copyright 2020 Doris Gaines Rapp

**To purchase one book of the trilogy at a time or its eBook,
they each have their own ISBN.**

LENGTH OF DAYS – THE AGE OF SILENCE
Copyright © 2011 by Doris Gaines Rapp /2nd Edition released in 2014

Library of Congress Control Number: 2014934058
ISBN: 978-0-9637200-4-7 (eBook)
ISBN: 978-0-9637200-2-3 (paperback)

Cover Art: Photo by Robert A. Clayton

LENGTH OF DAYS - BEYOND THE VALLEY OF THE KEEPERS
Copyright © 2015 by Doris Gaines Rapp

Library of Congress Control Number: 2015902254
ISBN: 978-0-9915033-5-3 (paperback)
ISBN: 978-0-9915033-6-0 (eBook)
Cover Art: Great Smoky Mountains from Morton Overlook
©Jeremy Edwards/Thinkstock
Gypsy Woman photo © Paul Hakimata/Thinkstock

LENGTH OF DAYS – SEARCH FOR FREEDOM
Copyright © 2016 by Doris Gaines Rapp

Library of Congress Control Number: 2016903959
ISBN: 978-0-9915033-9-1 (paperback)
ISBN: 978-0-692-66397-4 (eBook)
Cover Art: © <u>Daveallenphoto</u> | <u>Dreamstime.com</u> - <u>North Carolina
Blue Ridge Parkway Autumn Sunrise Mountains Photo</u>
(eyes) Gypsy Woman photo © Paul Hakimata/Thinkstock
The oval inset: A photo the author took while horseback riding near
Dripping Springs Ranch, New Mexico, later painted by a friend. I
took a photo of the painting and cropped it.

The Trilogy

The current state of our country prompted my decision to bind the
three Length of Days novels into one book. One trilogy will be less
expensive for the reader to purchasing than three separate books. Now
is the time to think about what the future could be if we don't stand
up and protect our wonderful nation. Read all three novels. They are a
fictional glimpse of what could be if we remain silent.

Dedication

I **Dedicate** this trilogy to my family and my parents. Daniel and Mildred Gaines taught me to go after what I believe in. My husband, Bill, supports me in my efforts as do our children. God has blessed me abundantly.
Doris Gaines Rapp

ACKNOWLEDGMENTS

I thank God for giving me Christiana Applewait and her story in the *Length of Days Trilogy*. A reverence for life is a reverence for the giver of life.

Thanks to Bob Clayton (Robert A. Clayton) for his wonderful picture of the snowy mountains on the first cover. Your gift of photography blesses us all.

To Bobbi Ray Madry, "Thank you! Thank you!" With more than thirty-five years of experience as a published author and Senior Editor of Novels, Textbooks, Teaching Guides, and Audio-visuals, I value your belief in me and *Length of Days - The Age of Silence.* For your friendship, again, I thank you.

To our Writers Group (SDG), thank you for your encouragement. I value you all as writers and friends.

I give a loud shout-out to Debi Lindhorst of The Type Galley in Warren, Indiana. You took my ideas and made a great cover design.

Thank you to Victoria Borgman for reading the Length of Days Trilogy books, and to Debbie Wilson for reading *Length of Days – Beyond the Valley of the Keepers.* I appreciate the helpful suggestions.

DORIS GAINES RAPP
LENGTH OF DAYS
THE AGE OF SILENCE
A Novel

LENGTH OF DAYS
THE AGE OF SILENCE

Doris Gaines Rapp

The first novel in a series of three

Daniel's House Publishing

Copyright © 2011 by Doris Gaines Rapp
2nd Edition released in 2014

Table of Contents

Prologue		13
1	Capitol City, Central Zone, USA	15
2	The Sanctuary	21
3	The Spot	27
4	Silas Drummond	31
5	The Doctor	35
6	The Note	43
7	Grand-mère and Grand-père	47
8	Inspector Stoner	59
9	The Horrors in the Note	64
10	A New Way of Being	67
11	Seeable but Unheard	75
12	The Precious Document	77
13	Ward Stoner Found a Solution	85
14	Covered Her Tracks	87
15	The Demitasse	89
16	Cameras in the Capitol	97
17	A Cache of Books	99
18	Stoner's Encounter	104
19	Dahlia's Secrets	109
20	Chalky Boone	115
21	Christmas – A Word from the Past	118
22	The First Christmas Carols	123
23	Forbidden Singing Heard	128
24	The Spirit inside the Book	131
25	Stoner Challenged	136
26	Silas is Taken	138
27	Formation of the New Society	141
28	Stoner Demands Answers	150
29	Gracie's Grief	154
30	An Invitation and a Discovery	158
31	Stoner Waited	166

32	Many Had No Joy	168
33	Thackery and the Blue Guard	171
34	Story Checking	178
35	A Dance in the Snow	180
36	Warmth from a Distance is No Warmth at All	183
37	Eyes in the Apartment	185
38	Ice Cream as an Alibi	192
39	The Shadow	194
40	The Evil at Howard Mountain	197
41	Stopped	205
42	Surveillance	208
43	Rebecca's Husband Michael	211
44	A Little Understanding	216
45	Michael Was Saved	225
46	The Capitol at Night	228
47	Chasing Phantoms	234
48	A New Emotion – Rage	237
49	Stoner Panics	244
50	The Eyes on Christy Are Closed	251
51	Christy's First Christmas	257
52	A Referendum, Some Petitions and Christmas Joy	261
53	Unlawful Entry	267
54	The March to Freedom	273
55	Accusations Turn to Revelations	279
56	A Holy Night	287
Epilogue		293

Book 2 – *Length of Days – Beyond the Valley of the Keepers*   299

Book 3 – *Length of Day – Search for Freedom*   581

PROLOGUE

I had no idea what Silas Drummond wanted from me.

He seemed to appear everywhere. In 2112 people didn't approach Legacy Citizens, but Silas continued to interrupt the tranquility of my days.

It was Gift-giving Season, during *The Age of Silence.* The emergency policies established during the crises of the previous century were still in place. That meant my dear grandparents would soon enter the never-ending-sleep, terminating their *Length of Days.* Even though there were atrocities all around us, none of us knew the evil at the core of our society.

No one saw the gathering darkness. It came slowly, like a fog that shimmers on the horizon before the dense veil overtakes the light. But then, few people were free to seek the glow of truth. In my day most walked in muted tones of gray.

Had I known what evil lurked in the shadows, I would have sought the light. If I had paid attention to my books, I would have seen when the flame began to dim. The last spark of truth was a dying ember, buried but not snuffed out.

Maybe if Silas had explained the true activities at the mountain, a little at a time, I would have braced myself for the horror. Had I known the depravity that forced the silence on our people, I would have listened for the angels' song. But powers stronger than I could imagine, controlled the darkness, and closed our hearts to the light.

Indifference can silently steal our will and freedom. Sometimes, when life is too much to bear, we simply turn our eyes away. Had I known what Silas was trying to tell me, I would have been terrified, unable to stop the terrible fate that awaited us all. I had until the end of December to find a way to overturn the despicable law. Will the solution come in time?

Lady Christiana Applewait

Proverbs 3:1-2 (NIV)　　　My son, do not forget my law but let your heart keep my commands, for length of days and long life and peace they will add to you.

CHAPTER ONE
Capitol City, Central Zone, U.S.A.

8:00 a.m. Friday, December 23, 2112

Only seven days left! How could that be? I knew that my loss would be coming soon, but I had avoided thinking about it for a long time. Now, I felt overwhelmed. My heart ached as I struggled with words to explain what I was feeling. Feeling words had vanished from our vocabulary decades ago. No one felt anything anymore, good or bad. I simply couldn't bear to think about what was coming, so I decided to bury myself in the library, the one safe place where I could always hide ... where books had the power to release me from the gnawing pain inside that I could not expressed.

As I hurried up the steps to the main entrance to the library, a strange little man charged into my path. "Christiana ... Miss Applewait ... My Lady, I must talk to you!"

"What?"

"Please," he begged as he touched my arm.

"Do yourself a favor, Buddy—move along." The Blue Guard Officer assigned to my protection reached for his prodding stick as he boldly studied the man who appeared to be about forty years old.

"Please My Lady ..." the man tried to speak again.

"You are free to go, Ma'am," the officer waved me on. "This man is finished here."

From behind me, I could hear a struggle but I didn't look back. The man called out my name again as I dashed into the building. I slipped past the front desk and went directly to the forbidden back room of the library. I felt safe in there. Marge Cummings, the curator, and I were the only ones permitted access to the books, files, and documents locked away there.

I closed the door behind me, leaned against it, and caught my breath. *Why did the man on the steps frighten me so? What did he want?* I trembled as I latched the door to the back stacks before I went to my favorite brown leather chair. The smooth worn armchair reminded me of the old ones—my grandparents. They had a leather sofa. But it hurt too much to think about them.

This month of December 2112 had come too soon. It was the month of Grand-mère and Grand-père's final birthdays, when authorities would force them into the never-ending-sleep, terminating their Length of Days. Why should my dear grandparents be part of the discarded, the forsaken? Why should they be among the unwanted, defective and overpopulate infants and children? They certainly weren't unproductive adults like some. No! Not my grandparents. I, Christiana Applewait, was one of the Privileged Legacy Citizens. But, what could I do?

"Christiana, dear, though we are Legacy, your grandfather and I have accepted this edict," my grandmother had assured me.

"You should fight it, Grand-mère. You have the power."

"Power, yes, but we are no better than others."

From beyond the inner door of the library, I thought I heard another scuffle and loud shouts. Did that odd little man call my name again? I recognized the fear in his voice, an emotion everyone still possessed. What was he trying to say? The very thought of discord startled me out of my world of books. Then—I heard nothing more. The man must have managed to get away from the officer and sneak into the building. When discovered again, they forcibly ejected him.

I tried to concentrate on my books, but foreboding thoughts kept tugging at my mind. I knew the chaos of the previous century had set the world spinning into social collapse. In the current era, it was becoming more obvious that life no longer had valued, and empathy had ceased to exist. What remained after the whirlwind of global chaos was an amoral society in which Grand-mère and Grand-père would soon be terminated and cast aside into the chamber portal to the great sleep.

"Grand-mère, please," I had begged her, "do something."

"It wouldn't be proper, Christiana. We're not above the rules."

"Acceptable principles of conduct and rules no longer exist, Grand-mère. I know —"

"What do you know, Christiana?"

"You know I practically live in the library. I—just know." What could I say? I didn't know how to respond to her calm acceptance of the Length of Days laws or the unexplained never-ending-sleep in which no one could visit or know if they would ever return.

One day, around Grand-mère's warm kitchen table, it all seemed so clear. I knew, one-hundred years ago, those in power erased thousands of years of history from our books with the stroke of a pen. The leaders of the revolution had banned everything written before that point. Only rewritten and newly crafted, politically conforming, texts remained. I could still see Grand-mère's sad eyes in my mind, as if she felt she had let me down.

What did that man want? Why couldn't I shake the sound of his pleading voice?

"Lady Applewait!" There was urgency in his voice that had made my body tense with fear.

Doesn't the man know how dangerous it is to stalk a Legacy Citizen? What does he want from me? Then, I had to reassure myself. *You're safe, Christiana. With the door locked, no one but you and Marge can get in.* Now, that strange, frightened man had drawn me into an intrigue by simply calling my name. Somehow, the world from beyond the library walls had found me.

Until now, I had flooded my mind with images from the books I had been reading so I wouldn't have to think about my grandparents' fate any longer. Today, too many questions had intruded into my thoughts and wouldn't let me escape, as I longed to do.

I wanted to save my grandparents, but I didn't want to be brave.

I felt like a walking contradiction, and didn't know the real *me*. I wanted to be counted on, to help my grandparents in some way. I had thought about it all year, then I had procrastinated for months and now it was December already. I had done nothing but bury my head in my books. Here in the library, in my secret place, I had always been able to lock myself away from reality and the staring public. But, today, reality had found me.

Here in the back stacks, in a place far removed from everything else, I could be alone with the feelings I experienced while reading. Once beyond the maze of closed, locked doors, the dark, dimly lit hallway led the way to a mysterious inner sanctum. This part of the library testified to the secretive nature of the old volumes but revealed nothing about the reason for the labels of *evil* and *forbidden* they had acquired. I had wondered about all the secrecy concerning the old books and why they banned them as *corrupting literature*. Then, I thought of the little man. Was someone trying to reach me because I have access to illegal material? *No, I must not allow such thoughts to upset me.*

Here, inside the back room, it wasn't dark or sinister at all. December morning sun streamed through the high, crimson and blue stained-glass windows that faced the east and sent dancing rainbows across the floor. I settled down in my chair and soon became engrossed in the characters in the novel. Chills ran down my back, not from the coolness of the dawn, but from the warmth of the words and excitement of the images that flooded my thoughts as I read. The beauty the images created in my mind mesmerized me as I devoured the vivid descriptions and strong characters on each page of the books now locked away and forbidden.

"I know you have been reading a lot," Grand-mère had ventured cautiously that day in her kitchen. "What books do you enjoy the most?"

"Oh, I love to read everything I can find—but the novels—they are wonderful! People had such deep feelings."

"And religion and philosophy, Christiana?"

I hadn't responded to that question. I'd rambled on about a novel I'd read and didn't really answer her properly. Starved for the love and affection that the books of fiction had described; they were the ones I had been devouring.

The world inside my books and the reality I tried to avoid, were nothing alike. The present era was so different from anything the books of times past described. I knew that few people had read the wonderful old volumes. Most people had never learned what had happened before the current epoch. Initially, I had only been interested in the everyday lives of people, as played out in the wonderful old stories. I didn't know what I should, or what I could have known, about history or governments and the rest.

I didn't have an excuse. I was privileged to be able to explore all the knowledge hidden here; yet, I had squandered the opportunity my special position had given me.

Like royalty of old, I had inherited a favored place in society, not earned it. I was a Legacy Citizen.

"My dear," Grand-mère had cautioned, "you were given a wonderful chance to be of service the day you were born."

"I know Grand-mère," I had mechanically agreed.

She had taken both my hands in hers. "Christiana, look into my eyes. You were born a Legacy Citizen, not a better person. You were born for service, dear, not entitlements. Do you understand?"

I did. Had I not been born a Legacy Citizen, it would have been impossible to have achieved anything significant enough to merit a place in society in the present age. They kept the masses of people in a controlled state, satisfied with the most mediocre existence possible. Currently, there was no incentive for hard work, no merit pay, only everything equal in every way, including nothingness.

Having access to the forbidden areas of the library, I had soaked in all the knowledge and emotions written on the secret pages of many of the books stored here. For fear of detection, I had to hold the mysteries close to my heart. That morning, I hadn't even told Grand-mère anything more about what I had been reading.

I had recently earned my Master's degree in Library Science and that, coupled with my Legacy status, had qualified me to carry a master key to the library when I began my research. Members of the

Blue Guard escorted me around campus but, once alone in the library my master key gave me access to rooms that held the old texts, documents, and novels of ages past. Even though the old books were not on the bibliography of my University-approved thesis topic, *An Argument for a New Form of Cataloging Books,* there was no one who really knew what I was reading while tucked away in the back recesses of this old wing.

Oh, to have lived in those olden days talked about in the books of fiction, to have experienced those emotions: desire and hope, expectation and surprise. The more I read about the past, the more I longed to be truly alive as the characters seemed to have been then.

Why didn't I know I had not been living to the fullest of my emotions? Why hadn't I noticed that others seemed even flatter in their feelings than I? I had begun to realize that my experience was different from most. I had been living my life inside the pages of books other people never saw or read.

I wondered about the people who lived in my building. They seemed to feel joy, in spite of their drugged state, and I wondered if I was every really happy. What I had read about in the books was more joy than I, and probably others, had experienced.

I was learning about passion and commitment, of people living and learning into advanced old age. People died of natural causes in the arms of their family, not as my beloved grandparents, doomed to leave me, locked away in endless sleep.

As I sat there in the library trying to sort out what to think and do, a little pull on the back of my blouse interrupted my thoughts. *That spot on my back is catching again.* I reached over my left shoulder and scratched at the snaggy spot. *A vaccination isn't supposed to tear at your clothing.* Tossing my hair to one side, I reached back again so I could feel around on my old scar. My vaccination was years ago, but there was a tiny, hard piece of something protruding from my old inoculation site. *I'll have it checked,* I promised myself.

I tried to take my mind off my shoulder. But I had read too many stories about the illnesses in the old days to stop worrying about it. *There is definitely a lump. What could it be?*

CHAPTER TWO
The Sanctuary

"Christiana Applewait, what are you doing here so early?" Marge smiled as she breezed into the room, as if the morning had just occurred to her.

"What ya readin'?" Marge asked as she glanced at the book I was holding.

"*A Woman of Substance,*" I answered. "In this novel, Emma Harte falls in love, makes mistakes, works herself out of them and lives to an old age, with all her memories gathered around her like a down comforter on a winter morning." I closed the book and inserted Grand-mère's old pink-and-white crocheted cross bookmark in the place where I had left off. I remembered asking her once what the cross meant. She said she would tell me sometime.

"Very romantic, I know. I've read Bradford's books," Marge paused. "Did you hear all that ruckus earlier, out there in the entry hall? Someone was all agitated and looking for you."

"I'm sure it must have been a mistake." I pretended I knew nothing about the man who had tried to get my attention.

Marge leaned in toward me as if someone might hear her. "It was no mistake. He was calling out your name. Then the guard threatened to lock him up if he didn't go away."

"I don't want to think about that now."

"Okay," she agreed. "I've found something you will be interested in though. No one else knows this stuff even exists."

Marge inserted a key into a massive wooden case nearby and removed a small, metal box.

"What is that?" I asked as she placed the box on a stand.

"It's an old operating system of some sort that runs on electricity. Since our generator supplies the alternative energy we need for some of our older devices, I imagine we're one of the few places that would be able to play something like this ... our library and the hospital." She plugged the box in and inserted a disk of some sort into the opening. A moving picture burst forth on the surface with a lilting musical accompaniment.

"I've never seen anything like this before," Marge whispered. "Our telecommunications messages are so stiff. '*What to do in case of an emergency.*' '*How to rear your children.*' You know, the same old stuff."

"And all the games, Marge, thousands of games. People don't even see the buried images in the game grids." I threw up both hands, trying to express my disgust with the kind of censorship and indoctrination now forced on the population.

"One book I just finished reading," I remembered, "described news programs with dozens of commentators, who talked all day. If people weren't informed back then, it wasn't from lack of a messenger. It was because they didn't want to know."

"That's why the society stopped all those broadcasts," Marge nodded. "They said people were restless all the time and anxious about things they didn't need to think about. The Lawmakers thought no one should spend time worrying about finances, scandals, or the workings of government. They also banned programs that filled the mind with frivolous fluff and programs that told stories."

"Christiana," Marge interrupted, "that's what I found, one of those programs."

"Marge, you mean a story on film?"

"Watch," she restarted the little machine.

We sat in front of a small screen and soaked in all the joys and sorrows of the family in the teleplay. The brothers and sisters walked to a friendly grocery in their bare feet, but no one complained. The parents stole a kiss or a hug as they passed each other, just living their lives. My heart stung with unexercised empathy and longing. Stretching it hurt. No one in 2112 demonstrated affection in public.

I shook my head in disbelief. I'd never seen anything so poignant before. "Six children, a mother and father, and two elderly grandparents all lived on a meager income at the foot of a mountain during the Great Depression of the previous International Chapter and yet, they seemed so happy. And, Marge, the old ones! How could they have lived so long?"

"People just lived until they died." Then Marge shook her head. "What a terrible financial drain they were on their families and the country's economy. They were too selfish to get out of the way so the next generation could live comfortably." I knew Marge was speaking out of rote memory, not out of understanding for the dignity of people, or a reverence for life.

"Marge, my grandparents will soon be seventy-five years old. You know what that means."

"The never-ending-sleep," Marge said with an indifferent tone. "My parents reached the end of their Length of Days when they turned sixty years old, not seventy-five like the Council members."

"It isn't fair," I whispered, even though I knew I was one of the lucky ones. I would one day be on the Council of Elders, the Wise Ones, like my great-great grandparents before me. Our Length of Days is longer than the rest of the population. But it still isn't fair.

"What choice did society have, Christiana? When they made the decision, health care costs were astronomical, insurance was out of reach and the cost for housing prisoners was beyond the average citizens' imagination. Massive public-funded feeding programs, although well intentioned, had swallowed up a huge portion of the national treasury. Our nation's debt had surmounted any ability to repay. So, they decided to allocate to each person a Length of Days, based on their worth to society. Then, they entered into the never-ending-sleep. My job as curator is unique, so I'm more valuable than some others. I get to live longer than many."

"But Marge, how can people's lives be judged this way? We don't even celebrate birthdays after a child turns ten years old. A kind of grief sets in. Since people know when they will pass on, they have no hope for a brighter future. There are no surprises in life, only a ticking of the clock. And, my own grandparents' birthdays are in a few weeks."

"I know, Christiana, but let's talk about it more after Gift-giving." She stood up and bent over to give me a hug. "What's that?" Marge winced. "I scratched my hand on your shoulder." Marge pulled her arm back and inspected the small surface-wound on her finger.

"Oh that," I shrugged it off. "There's something caught in my vaccination scar. It catches on my clothes. I've snagged several shirts on that little piece that is sticking out."

"Christiana, you must have that looked at. It could be serious," Marge turned me around and ran her fingertips around the spot.

"I suppose," I admitted.

"No 'suppose' to it. There's a new doctor in town and he's taking patients."

"Capitol City needed another doctor? With no stress, no worries, and no outliving the energy of our bodies, we were all to enjoy good health." I felt the hair on the back on my neck bristle. "We weren't even supposed to need health care providers."

Marge shrugged. "They thought they could handle the costs of illness for a limited number of years per person, so the weaker, flawed ones are sorted out at birth. But it's nothing we should think or worry about."

Heaven forbid that we should think. I thought it, but didn't say out loud. "That's only if the flawed baby is not your older brother," I mumbled, then added. "My parents never got over their loss."

"They didn't have to limit themselves to one child. They could have had another baby after you were born," Marge stated dryly. "Families are just prohibited from having more than a total of two children and must abort other fetal masses that may form."

I shuddered as I listen to her. "My parents' case was too

complicated." But I didn't want to share the story. There was too much suffering wrapped up in that one little boy. "Though my family had the privilege of living beyond most other people's Length of Days, they had to terminate the life of a dearly cherished child. It was too hard for them."

Marge jumped to her feet and smiled, oblivious to the family pain I was feeling. "Well, I hear there is someone in town that is not too hard to deal with, the handsome new doctor I told you about. You start on over to his office, and I'll call and tell them you're on your way. As a future Legacy replacement to the Council of Elders, you'll receive preferential treatment."

I dutifully grabbed my shoulder bag, red hat, and my green cloak and headed out to do my civic duty by keeping my body healthy.

Outside, the air was crisp, and the earth still clung to the memory of the fall season. It was a glorious winter day. As I walked mechanically up to the corner transit platform, I heard my name again.

"Christiana," a voice rang out behind me. It was the small man who had tried to stop me this morning. As he hurried toward me, another Blue Guardsman stepped between us and pushed the man aside. He fell to the sidewalk and scrapped the side of his face on the concrete.

I thought I should hurry on until I noticed blood dripping into his eyes. There was something familiar about the man I hadn't noticed before.

"Lady Applewait," he called out as he tried to get to his feet.

"Stay down," the Blue Shirt ordered roughly.

I finally recognized the man. He lived in my building, although I had never spoken to him. "Silas, is that you?"

"Yes, My Lady," he whispered.

"I'll keep him down, Ma'am. You can move along," the Guardsman spoke with authority.

"Wait, please," Silas begged. "I wrote it out for you." He pulled a piece of paper from his pocket and started to hand it to me. When the officer reached for it, Silas snapped it back. "No, no!" Fear was in his eyes. "It's only for Lady Applewait."

I saw the urgent look on his face. The same fear that had gripped me when I heard him calling to me rose up between us. Just as the uniformed man touched the paper, I snatched it out of his hand. "Thank you, Silas."

"It's just a few notes about gift giving in the building you had asked me for the other day, Ma'am." Silas's trembling voice threatened to give away his lies. "Tell this Guard he's overreacting, please."

"Let me see that," the Guard insisted.

"No Sir," I assured him with as much royal privilege as I could muster. "I have it." I could see panic in Silas's eyes. I didn't know what he was talking about or what was going on, but I immediately grasped the grave situation Silas was in. He risked his life to get a message to me. I was sure it wasn't a Gifting list.

"Thank you. I'll check it over later. I have an appointment now." I shoved the folded paper in my bag and hurried up the transit steps.

I quickly forgot the note as my thoughts turned back to the video Marge and I had seen. The happy family's expectation of good things to come was intoxicating. Their hope was contagious. I just couldn't accept the fate of my grandparents. The Length of Days policy was new in the larger pattern of history. I was one of the few who knew that life had been different in the past.

My mind churned as I thought of the possibility of overturning the law. I didn't know where to begin. I had read something curious a few months back while I was rummaging through the old files doing research for my thesis. In one of the books, there was something about "inalienable rights." *When I get back to the library from the doctor's office this afternoon, after I have seen my grandparents, I'll find the old manuscripts and see if I can understand what I know is there. I have already read it. Maybe wisdom will be gifted to me before the passage of time.*

I had no idea that within another day, I would be facing my rebirth, where wisdom would unfold rapidly.

CHAPTER THREE
The Spot

10:00 a.m.

I knew I had to have the spot on my back checked. I didn't want to go to the doctor, but it was the responsibility of a Legacy Citizen to take care of their health. I sat on a quiet bench in the Public Transit waiting area, in the warm sunshine, and tried to make sense of what this day had meant so far. I would have preferred going most anyplace other than the doctor's office. Just as my books allowed me to escape the reality of my grandparents' fate, I also chose to avoid addressing health issues. As a Legacy Citizen, society cared for and over-protected me. I didn't have to face life as most people experienced it. That was just the way life was. Now, I needed to protect the lives of my grandparents by finding a way to use my legacy status to save them.

I'll think about that tomorrow. But the truth was, I was running out of time, and so were Grand-mère and Grand-père.

Just as the inverse trolley pulled to my stop, I heard the piercing wail of a Blue Shirt's strata-car. I thought of Silas Drummond and shuddered. I couldn't remember ever having been frightened before within my bubble. I hurried on board the Public Transit where I felt safe. Riding above the streets on the P-T felt serene and peaceful, up in the quiet above the fray. The transit cars floated on electrified steel ribbons, silently crisscrossing the city on a grid that covered the entire metropolitan area. Riding across town with other people, even though they kept their distance from me, was usually pleasant, but my thoughts overwhelmed me with my grandparents' situation and this spot on my shoulder.

Maybe I have cancer, I worried. According to my books, people used to have a disease that destroyed healthy tissue in the body. It often started with a lump.

When the Transit reached my stop, I bounded down the steps from the disembarking area, pretending there was nothing wrong. I had learned a long time ago that Legacy Citizens are constantly under surveillance, not in a threatening way, but I knew to present myself to the public as calm and organized. That day, I felt like I was fooling no one.

As I walked up the broad steps of the medical center, I kept thinking about my grandparents and the old ones in the program Marge and I had watched. The actors looked much older than Grand-mère and Grand-père. How amazing it must have been for them to go on living as long as nature allowed.

Once inside the office, a woman looked up from her work. "Yes?" The woman at the reception desk, in the physician's suite, questioned in shorthand. She reached in my direction with a detection wand.

"I am Christiana Applewait. Someone called —"

"Yes, Ma'am. I have your information right here. You can come on back."

I saw other patients already waiting for their time with the doctor, but I still accepted my place at the head of the line. It had always been that way. I watched as one mother cradled her sick daughter in her arms. The child's cheeks were red with fever, and her eyes glazed over with pain. I looked away. My parents taught me—it is best to not fill your head with other people's pain. After all, there was nothing I could do about it.

"Come along, Miss Applewait. Let's not expose you to germs unnecessarily." The nurse hustled me out of the waiting room, down the hall and into examination room number two.

I recognized the nurse. She was Dahlia Zoobamba. We lived in the same building, but we had never spoken.

"This is nice," I said as I looked around the small examination room. I had rarely been sick, and I didn't realize that Society had redecorated the entire Medical Complex the previous year. The pictures were somehow different from those usually displayed. "The animal photographs are wonderful, especially the farm scenes," I remarked.

"Doctor wanted people to remember the animals as they used to be. The government slaughtered many to reduce Carbon Dioxide levels. Look at those brown eyed cows. Can you believe people used to eat those beasts?"

"Thank goodness for chemically processed food," I mumbled. "This picture of the dog is great. Dogs are so rare now."

"The government thought they used up too much of our food supply."

"I saw one the other day," I reminisced as I remembered the happy, frisky little dog peering at me from a window I had passed.

As the nurse prepared her charts, I noticed the newness of the equipment and the room. Perhaps I could ask a question I had wondered about while she methodically went through her routine. They said this building needed major renovation as a normal part of maintenance. There was a rumor that other motives were at the bottom of the paint cans. "Is the epidemic over?"

"Epidemic? There's been no epidemic." Nurse Dahlia's answer was flat and crisp.

"A friend said two of his cousins needed to be in the hospital but there were no beds. It sure sounds like an epidemic to me." I knew what I heard.

The hospital had filled with people so distraught; they couldn't function. Marge and I had looked in an old medical book for symptoms we had heard about. Depression met all the criteria. Endorphin boosters in the water supply controlled the old disorder, until nearly eradicated.

"I've noticed people arguing in the library, and I've seen people crying for no apparent reason," I told Dahlia. "My friend told me that six young women had made a suicide pact, but the superintendent in their building had discovered their plan and stopped them before it was too late."

"Suicide? That's an archaic term," Dahlia bristled. "People just don't do that any more. We ... never mind." The nurse straightened her glasses and turned to leave. "The doctor will be with you in a moment."

She bowed out of the conversation with a dismissive tone I didn't appreciate. I stood there for a moment and wondered if I should leave, but I felt my shoulder again and reconsidered. I gazed out the window and watched the morning move toward noon day. Beyond the building, in the park below that fronted a small, old-fashioned shopping village, a young woman hurried along the sidewalk, then disappeared over a little rise near a wooded area by a fish pond.

Just then I caught sight of a man as he jumped out of his red car. He started to cross the street in the direction of the Medical Center but a Blue Shirt swung his baton with a blow to the back of the man's knees. As he buckled to the ground, his body turned and I could see his face.

Oh no ... it's that man. It's Silas again. Fear suddenly gripped my heart. *Why has he followed me? What is so important he would risk his life to touch mine?* I fumbled with my bag until I found the note. It was still there.

CHAPTER FOUR
Silas Drummond

Earlier that morning - Before Sunrise

No one saw Silas Drummond around town in the daytime. What had happened that morning to cause him to risk danger to talk to Christiana Applewait? He had never dared speak to her before.

Just hours before he had suddenly appeared in town, Silas Drummond was deep in the bowels of Howard Mountain, going through the routine of his despicable job. He had shuffled as rapidly as his aching legs could carry him, along the sterile tile floor that led back to his post. The bell had rung announcing another delivery for the furnaces. There were arrivals almost around the clock, every day of the week. Silas was warned not to leave the place or reveal anything he knew, or about his duties there. Some bodies arrived already deceased. Silas discarded those. The cases that were hard for Silas were the breathing ones who seemed to expect a bed and pillow to rest on, for their never-ending-sleep.

Dark smoke rose from the peak above the vast tentacles of crematorium chambers buried in the caverns underneath the once majestic mountain, miles from Capitol City. While death stalked below, purifying snow draped a blanket of white across the slopes above. Death had become so common place the few people who lived near the sickening foulness paid no more attention to what was going on, than those who had lived near the Nazi death camps, more than a century and a half ago. It didn't matter. Silas had become accustomed to the stench long ago. The year 2112 was a new time, but an old evil lurked below the mountain like a putrid mold, while seasons came and went on the surface above.

A wide desolate road ran at the base of the mountain and stretched several miles to the edge of the city. One of Silas Drummond's jobs was to check the driver's list of end-travelers as they emerged from luxury vehicles, much like the limousines from the previous era. The list contained the names of those who had reached the age for entering the long sleep that ended their Length of Days. Silas knew that the end-travelers thought they were riding in luxury, like sophisticates of old, to a restful place to sleep for a while, but Silas knew it was their journey's end.

Blackened clouds from the mountain top blocked the morning light, as another driver pulled his black stretch limo to the gate and hopped out.

"Watch your step folks," the driver cautioned. "You don't want to sleep away your days with a broken leg." He chuckled to himself but lost the humor on his passengers.

The tall iron gate swung open and two white-coated burly men helped the travelers into several small electric cars that would deliver them to the processing center.

"You got time for coffee, Silas?" the limo driver spoke into the gate speaker.

"I'll be able to take a break in a few minutes, Harry. Come on in with the group and then have a seat in the lounge. Be sure to take the back hallway as usual, not the main one. No one's allowed in that part of the complex."

"Then why do they call it the main hall?" Silas heard Harry mumbled to himself, but said no more.

Silas stepped away from the communicator and waited near the elevator for the newest arrivals. He longed to leave, to get away from the wretched place, but he would have to process the new group of end-travelers immediately, before reality had time to register.

The huge ornate doors opened, allowing the citizens to enter the pleasant reception room where Silas was waiting to check them in.

"Silas, I didn't know you worked here." A petite blond girl who appeared to be about twenty recognized him. She walked with a severe limp with the aid of crutches.

"The leg still bothering you, Mari?" Silas asked. He knew what that kind of disability meant.

"Some. On rainy days it's the worst. My medical counselor said it would be best for me to get a long rest." She smiled as she hobbled along after Drummond's scuffling steps. "It'll be okay. It's not like the endless sleep of the aged. It's like ... a long nap."

Silas was speechless as Mari and the group followed behind him like sheep. Bitter bile rose in his throat where it mixed with fear and anger. "But ... but," he stammered and then saw the guard at the enrollment station glare at him.

Silas had little contact with the travelers as he escorted them to the door from which no one returned. His main responsibility was to make constant rounds, checking all of the gages in order to keep the furnaces firing at the right temperature. He wanted to know nothing and to see even less.

I could not strap her to the tray. He shuddered at the very thought of it. *Much less keep the flame under her young body at a steady, even temperature. I know her ... I like little Mari.*

They have lied to her. He screamed inside his mind. *And, she's not the only one.*

Later, safely concealed inside a locked restroom, he grabbed his pocket knife and scratched another inch-long jagged red mark on his already scarred arm. His dark blood dripped into the bowl then pooled near the drain as he blindly carved on his own body until the knife penetrated deeply enough that he could feel again.

Control yourself, he demanded. If he complained to his superiors about putting his young friend in the furnace, they might place a stripe against him in his employment jacket. If caught giving out information, it would mean certain death. He knew the attendants would take Mari's time piece, belt buckle, and shoes. They took jewelry and anything of value and promised to store it. That was something, this time with Mari, he could not accept.

The long nap is a lie. It's not temporary. It's permanent! And, the never-ending-sleep is not a gift. It's extermination. Silas knew, little Mari, these elderly citizens, and many others, duped by lies, were totally unaware of the real process they were facing.

Silas returned to his desk to pick up his belongings as eerie music lilted through the subterranean lair. Those despicable chambers were the only place left in society where music still played, intended to quiet the victims' fears. Silas muttered to himself, "It's not a lullaby. It's a dirge of death." The ghastly songs were not just for the end-travelers, but also for those whose job was to carry out the daily procedures or suffer elimination, along with their families, if they didn't.

"Silas, there you are." The limo driver looked up as Silas hurried toward the exit.

Gotta get out of here. Silas hardly knew he was muttering to himself. *Gotta tell her. It has to stop. I know I'll be in trouble for leaving early. If I don't clock out, maybe I can claim I forgot to have my time card punched. Maybe I can be gone long before they miss me.* Then he rushed out, leaving the driver alone in the lounge.

She is the one person who might be able to stop this madness. Lady Christiana is a Legacy Citizen. She was the only person he knew who might listen to him, and perhaps believe his story.

Silas hobbled to his car, always bent in a hurried stance. He deposited something large and wrapped in the old blanket from his resting chamber in the back seat, got in and sat in silence while he fumbled nervously with the car's ignition. Then he whispered, "It'll be okay. We'll get to my sister's place before everyone starts stirring."

He would leave the mountain and the stench behind him. As he drove along the road toward the city, he was unaware that another vehicle had pulled away from the mountain at the same time and cast a long shadow behind them. Silas was not alone.

CHAPTER FIVE
The Doctor

I stood and watched Silas Drummond through the medical office window as I waited for the doctor to come in. I was unable to stop studying the little man. He surely knew what would happen if he continued to pursue me. He had been warned more than once that very morning. I had seen him in the apartment building a few times but we had never even shared a glance. It would not have been proper. In fact, it was unthinkable for someone to try to step into the space of a Legacy Citizen.

Suddenly, my attention shifted from Silas and back into the doctor's examining room. "Good morning," a friendly voice, the texture of warm chocolate, greeted me from behind.

Startled, I spun around to see a tall, athletic man enter the room. I jammed the paper Silas had written more deeply to the bottom of my tote. My heart was pounding. *What does Silas want with me?* "Good morning," I said as the attractive, white coated man came toward me.

"I'm Dr. O'Reilly," he nodded but didn't extend his hand. "I'm happy to meet you."

I knew I was trembling from the events of the morning. My world was usually cushioned with the cotton of quiet solitude, above the stratum on which others lived. My bubble had been invaded many times that morning. I tried to control the anxiety that gripped me.

Dr. O'Reilly smiled. His expression was soft as he studied me. "Have we met? You seem familiar to me."

I didn't remember having met him—and I would have remembered. There was something in his eyes that was different. He exuded an appeal I could not identify.

Dr. O'Reilly motioned to the examination table. "Jump up here, please. It's your shoulder that's bothering you, right?"

I slipped up on the table and removed my outer jacket. "My shoulder, specifically ... the vaccination site." My voice sounded shaky to me. *Get control of yourself!* I didn't want to have to explain the reason for my anxiety ... the Blue Guard ... or the note Silas Drummond had passed to me.

Doctor O'Reilly moved in closer to examine my shoulder. I could smell a faint scent of aftershave, something that had nearly gone out of custom.

"Let's have a look." He raised his arms as if ready to help remove my blouse but he didn't touch me.

I realized he was being respectful of my station in life, so I slipped the sleeve down by myself. I unbuttoned the top of my garment and slipped it off my shoulder. I twisted and turned again but I still couldn't see the spot.

"You would have to be a pushmi-pull-yu to see the back of your own shoulder," he smiled.

"A what? A push-pull-what?"

"Just a fictional animal from a book I read. Dr. Doolittle," he smiled.

"But if the animal was not real, it was not a book of facts or a book of science. I know books. You had to have read a book of fiction, Doctor."

"Fiction books were banned a long time ago," he protested with that special tone of authority that medical people often use to claim an expertise on more subjects than just medicine.

"What books have you been reading, Dr. O'Reilly?" I was impatient. I had to know. He would not intimidate me with his education. "Which ones?"

"Oh, you know, just the usual," he offered lamely, avoiding the topic and redirected the conversation to the examination.

I could feel my heart pounding inside my chest. There was another stash of books somewhere, outside of the library. He would not dissuade me.

Dr. O'Reilly paused near my ear. "I know this could be risky, but since you know about books of fiction, you may have read some. Books seem important to you." He paused and looked at me. "It's not necessarily a secret but few people know the old wing of the hospital has a library."

I felt my heart catch in my throat. How did he know I lived for my books? "You read them ... the books?" I kept my voice low and tried not to show any emotion.

His fingers rolled over the lump on my shoulder. "I can feel the sharpness beneath your skin."

I would not let him change the subject that easily. "Do you read the books, Dr. O'Reilly?" I knew I sounded somewhat demanding and I didn't want to draw unusual attention to myself, but I had to know. "Please ... do you read the books?" I couldn't believe there may be another stash of novels somewhere.

Dr. O'Reilly paused. "They are wonderful," he whispered.

The door handle rattled and Nurse Dahlia reentered the room. The conversation returned to talk of the bump under my skin. Discretely, Dr. Riley pulled back slightly while still examining the lump on my shoulder.

"Do you need any help Doctor?" the nurse questioned politely but had a puzzled look on her face. "Your voices were not clear over the room monitor."

"We are fine, Nurse." Dr. O'Reilly dismissed any concern Dahlia may have had by involving her in the exam. "Come here and take a look at this?" He stepped back and motioned for Dahlia to examine my mysterious lump.

Dahlia looked at me and I sensed by her expression that she recognized me too. Suddenly, I was aware of all of the apartment building neighbors I had never spoken to. They talked and joked between each other but I was always on the outside. Since laws forbid others to speak to a Legacy person first, my isolation was of my own making.

"Ma'am, have you fallen or been hit by something?" Dahlia's questions were professional, and she was careful not to actually touch me. "I haven't heard of any injury you may have sustained."

She was right. If a Legacy Council member, or those who would inherit that position through benefit of their birth, had tripped over a curb, all of the people would have heard about it. We were watched, emulated, guarded, secretly envied, and were socially positioned within the circle of the elite, set apart from the masses.

"No, Nurse Dahlia, never. I know I haven't had any kind of accident, unless I was sleepwalking and didn't remember it."

The nurse stepped back quickly and stared at me. She seemed to be surprised that I used her name.

"I know who you are, Dahlia," I reassured her. "You live in my building."

"Yes, Ma'am. But I didn't know —" She caught herself before she completed that thought. Then she added, "It is a great neighborhood building, isn't it?"

"It's nice to finally speak to you." I looked directly at this woman I saw every day, but had never been in her world of friends and neighbors.

"Yes, Ma'am." She looked back at my shoulder. "Actually, it doesn't look like an injury. It looks as if something is trying to work its way out of your body."

"Oh Dahlia, that sounds awful." I recoiled at the thought of a foreign body under my skin, trying to emerge to the surface. I thought of the alien beings that possessed the bodies of Earthlings in the old science fiction books I had read.

"You're right, Nurse," Dr. O'Reilly concurred. "I found that very curious."

"Yes, Sir." She turned and started to leave, "Oh, I reviewed her chart, Doctor. Miss Applewait is twenty-four years old now."

"Thank you, Nurse." He turned back to me and patted my shoulder. "Let's carefully remove that sliver. It shouldn't leave any more of a mark than the original vaccination did. Then we will address the issue of your age."

"What issue?" I asked. When Dahlia closed the door again, I whispered, "Tell me about the books."

Dr. O'Reilly's words and his gestures suddenly didn't match. His mouth said, "Well, your age isn't an issue so much as a milestone," but his hands were pantomiming another message. He put his index finger to his lips and then opened his hands like he was holding a book.

I nodded and added. "I had a birthday recently but I didn't know it was any major event."

"Do you need any instruments?" Dahlia intruded over the room's two-way monitor.

Dr. O'Reilly muffled a chuckle. "Thanks Dahlia. No, I have what I need." He applied a cool gauze pad over the site and waited a second. "It will be numb in a moment." He pointed to his watch, threw up six fingers and mimed sipping a cup of coffee. Then he pointed out the window to the low row of buildings across the street beyond the park.

I knew the little coffee shop. I had been there several times. I especially liked the quaint, old-fashioned design of the entire cluster of businesses. I nodded and smiled that I understood.

Dr. O'Reilly covered the spot on my shoulder with an anti-bacterial solution and draped the area in order to keep it sterile. As he approached me with the scalpel, I turned my eyes away. He made a tiny incision and skillfully removed a small piece of something from my shoulder.

"Well, there it is," he offered as he held the object with tweezers. "Are you sure you weren't accosted by a communications monitor? It looks like a little component of some sort."

"No attacks or encounters of any kind." I studied the strange, tiny piece in the doctor's hand. "It looks like a bitty chip, doesn't it? Why on earth would that be in my shoulder?"

"Perhaps your parents had you tagged when you were a small child, to ensure a measure of protection against kidnaping."

"Tagged?"

"It evidently is the usual practice with children. I was talking to a pediatrician at lunch the other day. He said he had tagged six babies that morning." Dr. O'Reilly shrugged. "Not being in pediatrics, I wasn't aware of the practice." He started to throw the chip in the hazardous waste container and then stopped. "Do you want this thing? It could be an interesting souvenir."

"Sure. I'll ask my parents about it. It's nice that they may have wanted to keep me safe. I could have it mounted. It'll be a conversation starter. Goodness knows I could use one." I knew my face had become red because I could feel my cheeks grow hot. My books called it blushing.

Dr. O'Reilly cleaned the chip quickly and wrapped it in a clean tissue. "There you are, My Lady." He bowed slightly.

Few people addressed me as Lady Applewait. Silas had. Most people, however, didn't speak to me at all. It was illegal to intrude on the privacy of the Council of Elders and those, like me, who would ascend to that position. I put the tiny piece in my tunic pocket. "Now, what is this about my age?"

"Oh yes," Dr. O'Reilly remembered. "None of us in this practice has treated a Council member before, but bulletins have come through regularly to remind us of the protocol. When Legacy members turn twenty-four, they are to begin a regimen of fresh water, eight glasses a day. Since we have additives in our water system, to purify it and to add necessary nutrients, you are to begin diluting your water supply, flushing out the additives. It seems that Legacy Citizens are not to ingest chemicals of any kind and the little pills will turn your tumbler full into fresh water."

"How?" I asked. "I was never told about this." It all seemed incredible to me. With all the books I have read, I should have read something about diluting the water.

"With every glass of water, you must drop in a highly soluble tablet. This is a fairly new process. It was only begun a few years ago." The doctor went to the cabinet and unlocked a small compartment. "Once you start the pills, you are to get them from the same source, so there is a clear record of your taking them. You will need to come back to see me for refills. They are tiny, so there are a lot in each package." Dr. O'Reilly handed me a small paper envelope full of infinitely small, white tablets.

"What is this all about?" I was beginning to wonder if I had reason to mistrust the doctor.

"As I said, the practice is rather new to this office. I've heard not everyone agrees with the policy. Alister Bedlam is not in favor of the detoxification process."

"Alister Bedlam—the wealthy man who thinks he's the Master of the Universe? How is he involved in all of this?" I was confused. Bedlam was neither Legacy nor a governmental official.

"It is my understanding Alister Bedlam is not in favor of the detoxification process for anyone. So far, his protests have been over ruled by the Council of Elders." The doctor patted my arm.

"Bedlam is always behind the scenes, pulling the strings. That's what great wealth can do for those who are power hungry. At least, that's what I've heard from my grandparents. Bedlam may be the richest man in the world but he isn't Legacy."

"Apparently, the Council of Elders wants to ensure that none of the side effects of the additives in the water we all are supposed to drink, affect your body. The Legacy Citizens of your parents' generation began the detox process about four years ago. Even I ..." Dr. O'Reilly stopped abruptly, then continued. "Bedlam wants everyone to continue with the chemicals, the water additives. He says it is a fair and equal treatment. Up until now, the Council's support of the detoxification program has kept it going." Again, he put his finger to his lips. "Just make sure you put a pill in every glass of water."

I knew the gesture meant that the tablets were important. While I may not have known why I needed to take them, I would follow the doctor's orders. There was something about his manner that caused me to sense the seriousness of the tablets.

"Nurse Dahlia will check you out," Dr. O'Reilly instructed. Then, he tapped his watch and pointed his thumb over his shoulder in the direction of the shops.

I didn't hesitate. I returned the gesture with a nod and a smile.

Before I had time to hop down from the table, Dahlia breezed back in the room. "Here, My Lady, drop one of those tablets in this glass of water before you leave. We are supposed to make sure you begin detoxification immediately." She handed me the glass and added, "Drink all of it. The full effects of the pills build up quickly. You will soon reach the therapeutic level. And, make sure you take them regularly. There can be no drug holidays with these pills. The full detoxification process takes time, so drink it all."

All? Detoxification? I thought to myself and then mumbled, "I didn't know I was *toxified* in the first place."

CHAPTER SIX

The Note

10:30 a.m.

It was a short walk back to the transit stop from the doctor's office. I didn't mind. I had a lot to think about—detoxification—coffee with the young doctor—and Silas Drummond. I was afraid Silas would pop up again, and I looked around anxiously. I didn't see him anywhere and felt some relief. As I sat on the transit waiting bench, I pulled Drummond's note from my bag.

> "Dear Miss Applewait,
> I must talk to you immediately. Be very careful.
> They linked us together since I tried to contact
> you at the library. I'm sorry. Now, we are both in
> grave danger. You may be the only person who can
> help expose this evil. The entire endless-sleep program
> is a sham!"

What is he talking about? I jammed the paper back in my tote. *I'll read the rest of it later.* Fear crept in again, like a mountain lion that stalks the shadows, waiting for a weakened prey. I had to think. My mind raced in circles, from my grandparents, the doctor, the note, the mountain people from the old video Marge and I had viewed—to the beautiful day.

I looked out over the city below the transit platform and drank in the beauty around me. We were well into December and snow was beginning to cover the distant mountain peaks. The frost that had covered the ground earlier in the morning lingered in the lower spots.

I had missed many seasons while buried away with research for my thesis. Now, I only wanted to enjoy the holiday Gifting lights, and the colors that dance off the glittering frost.

My thoughts went to the video we'd seen, because it had taken place around this time of year. That family had celebrated Thanksgiving and gave thanks to their favorite Deity. Yet, they had so little to be thankful for ... except love. In November 2112, we too had celebrated what Society has provided for us. So, you see, in some ways, we are the same ... and yet.

I was surprised by the glorious December day. The bright morning sun was warm. I took off my tunic and laid it over the back of the bench. It was not possible that cold weather was upon us ... but it was.

Lost in my own daydreams, I thought of Dr. Jason O'Reilly and smiled. *Don't be silly,* I admonished myself. *I just met him. We're not even friends, not yet.* When the cross-town transit car arrived, I jumped to my feet and boarded quickly.

"Ma'am," the driver commanded softly, "you didn't pay."

"Pay?" I was confused. No one ever asked me to pay for a bus ride. Then I remembered my cloak. "Oh, wait, I left something on the bench." I jumped off the bus and grabbed up my tunic, then skipped back on.

"Oh, I'm sorry Ma'am," the driver corrected himself. "I thought. ... Please, just have a seat."

I moved past the currency exchange as an older woman quickly got out of her seat. "Here, take my place," she offered. "I'll be getting off soon." With a drawn expression, her color seemed pasty white.

"Thank you." Surprisingly, a feeling of gratitude stirred within me. "Are you all right?" The woman seemed frail. Perhaps she wasn't well. Maybe she was the one who should be sitting.

"Yes, dear," she smiled briefly and then her face fell again as if she remembered something sad.

I started to sit down, then asked again, "Are you sure you're okay?"

"I am sure, thank you," she added, but this time her face was flat, expressionless.

"Maybe you'd better go home and rest. What are your plans today?"

"Plans? I haven't had any plans since my Harold died." The little woman's eyes were empty and distant. I studied the old woman as she moved toward the exit and waited.

At the next station, the woman got off and a young man bounced up the steps. He moved quickly with a spring in his steps. I thought him odd. He had more energy than most people my age. *Everyone else lacks zip, why not this fellow?* The man's eyes met mine, and he didn't look away. Why? People always averted my gaze. It was protocol. Why was he different? He looked familiar but his stares made me feel uncomfortable. I turned to the passing scene beyond the window. The calcium reinforced stone on the passing buildings glistened like jewels as the sun bounced off the surfaces. Regardless of what was out there to see, Silas's words whispered in my ear, "Danger ... danger!"

I tried to focus on my destination, not the people inside or outside the tram. The trip to the stately old homes on the other side of the city wound past sleeping gardens tucked behind white fences. Red and green Gifting lights, that replaced the orange and yellow mums of the past season, peeked out from brightly decorated windows.

Many of the homes had two stories, a tradition banned in newer construction. Recent structures, designed to occupy a minimal footprint, stood tall against the city's skyline. The multi-family buildings lacked the beauty of the rambling homes that lay on both sides of this street. The old houses reminded me of the home I had seen in the teleplay, large and roomy with space for everyone.

My parents had a single-family home that was more modest than these. Mother and Daddy had one large gathering room, a kitchen and eating center, three sleeping cubicles, and two bathing areas. It was quite adequate for them. They both worked long hours. Mother was the Chief of Staff to the Center Chair of the Council of Elders and Daddy was the Director of the Schools. While most people spent their spare time after work at the Social Centers around town, where they played games and listened to lectures, Mother and Daddy spent quiet evenings with friends and family.

When Legacy Citizens turn twenty-one, after we graduate from University, we move out of our parents' home and into our own apartment where we can begin to live independently and solve our own problems. We're supported by our trust; still, we must work or go to graduate school before taking up a career. It never occurred to me to be thankful for all I had. I was simply entitled.

As the transit passed through the Victorian subdivision of Oakwood, the lines dropped down to ground rails, like a trolley of old. People on wraparound porches smiled and waved at us. Surprisingly, the driver waved back. I guess he felt free to be friendly there. These were my people, Legacy and Council of Elders members. I closed my eyes and enjoyed the renewed sensations of warmth and neighborhood.

"My Lady," the driver prompted, "I think this is your stop."

It was the end of the line. The stop had to be mine. As I walked along, I had the eerie sensation of watchful eyes. I had led such a sheltered life, I was not prepared for this intrigue, and I was frightened.

In my grandparents' block, no one was in adjoining yards that cuddled up to the sidewalk, but the street out front was busier than usual. In the time it took me to walk from the bus stop to my grandparents' front door, two Blue Guard strata-cars drove past slowly. They seemed to be searching for someone as they scanned right and left. With Silas Drummond's letter stuffed in my pocket, I thought of his desperate warning. We were seen together earlier and that had frightened him ... and me. The officers looked right past me and then looked back again. Were they looking for Silas? Or, were they looking for me?

CHAPTER SEVEN

Grand-mère and Grand-père

11:30 a.m.

When I arrived at my grandparents' sidewalk, I just wanted to be inside, away from whatever was happening outside. The neighbor's yard had a pair of stuffed dogs that barked and wagged their tails when I passed. Except for the prowling Blue Guard cars, the stuffy dogs were the only movement in the neighborhood. Even with the warm winter day, no one sat on their porch at the houses around my grandparents' home.

As I walked up the sidewalk, the old house I loved so much seemed wrapped in goose down, all soft, comfortable, and warm. The heavy wooden door, with its beveled glass panes down both sides, let light flood the entry beyond. I tapped on the door then opened it with a shove of my hip.

"Christiana!" Grand-mère sang out and threw her arms open to welcome me. She was just crossing the entry hall from the kitchen when I walked in. "I didn't know you were coming."

"I took the chance that the Council of Elders wasn't meeting today Grand-mère. I wanted to visit the two of you. Where is Grand-père?" I looked around the familiar room where the family had gathered each December for Gift-giving. It was a joyous holiday when we thought of ways to please other people rather than cater to ourselves. Gifting Day was full of promise and joy.

"Come, Baby, sit here with me." Grand-mère patted the sofa beside her as she sat down. "Grand-père is puttering in his garden out back, clearing away the dead plants that gave up blooming several weeks ago."

I snuggled close to her. She always smelled like flower petals or cinnamon and other spices, a sign that her cookie jar was full. For me, that cookie canister was a symbol of Grand-mère's love for her family and neighbors.

"Now you stay right here and I'll bring us some lemonade and a plate of cookies. I just made some this morning." Grand-mère patted my hand and hurried toward the kitchen.

Sometimes, I felt a little guilty for being closer to my grandparents than to my own mother and father. But, Grand-mère was able to demonstrate so much more love than Mother did. I guess Grand-mère had memories from the old ways that Mother never experienced, just like the story I had seen on the small screen that morning. Grand-mère's love oozed from every love pat and hug.

I am sure Mother felt loved as she grew up. Grand-mère was always Grand-mère. But Society was severe in their edicts on demonstrations of affections. During those years, when Mother was a child, the instructions, "Drink plenty of water," was the norm. I thought about that as I waited for the cookie tray. But Dr. O'Reilly said the detoxification tablets began only four years ago. So, Mother was exposed to the water everyone drank all of her life, into middle-age. If the pills dilute the additives, I wondered what the chemicals did to people's bodies, including hers. When I was small, my mother and father would have been fully medicated. Now, there was evidently a reversal of thought, at least for Legacy Citizens. According to Dr. O'Reilly's timetable, my parents would have probably undergone that transformation in the last few years. They would have begun detoxification after I was already out of their home and on my own. As I think about it now, I guess I had noticed a change in my parents. They were warmer, more loving, more interested, and attentive.

As a child, I had my grandparents, the unmedicated generation. I know how fortunate I was. None of my friends still had their grandparents. Most of the older generation had already gone into the never-ending-sleep, which made me think of Silas Drummond again.

What was his note trying to tell me?

"What brings you way over here?" my grandmother asked as she came back with the treats, eager to entertain. Those in her neighborhood rarely had drop-in visitors.

The Oakwood area wasn't banned, but casual sightseeing in the neighborhood was discouraged. All of the Council of Twelve lived in that section of town. Their privacy was strongly protected. Among my grandparents' neighbors were high-ranking government people, bankers, all those, whose Length of Days extended beyond that of the common person.

"I've been thinking Grand-mère. At the end of the month, right after Gift-giving Day, you and Grand-père turn seventy-five."

"Yes, dear ... seventy-five."

"How old were your great-grandparents when they died?" I was cautious. I wasn't sure how she felt about the inevitable which was to come.

"Christiana, you're worried about the never-ending-sleep, aren't you?" Grand-mère moved closer and took my hand. "It is a natural occurrence. It's not something to worry about."

"It is not natural. I've read enough books to know there is nothing natural about it. Today, someone called it a sham."

"A sham? What on earth are you talking about?"

"Oh, I don't know. Somebody just ..." I hadn't finished reading Silas's message, so there was little more that I could say. "Grand-mère, it's important to me. Truthfully, do you know how old your great-grandparents were when they entered the sleep?"

"The truth? Honey ... well, some day you will be a member of the Twelve. I guess there are things you need to know. Let me see. Both of my great-grandparents were still living when I was small. Great-Grandma died when she was, ah, eighty-seven and Great-Grandpa was ninety-one."

"Died? I've read about dying. That's when they just ... pass on, isn't it? My friend Rachel fell from a top terrace and ceased to live. She must have died too because she didn't enter the permanent sleep chamber." I knew Rachel's passing was different from most. People my age, sheltered and protected, rarely died an accidental death, and science eradicated most diseases.

"Yes, Honey, but back then, when they just ... died, sometimes people suffered with physical maladies and serious illnesses. They may have been in pain and ... no one would want that."

"Grand-mère, would you rather have no pain or live more years with Grand-père?"

"Sweetheart, I would rather be unable to walk or be in constant pain, than to lose one precious moment with your dear grandfather." My grandmother's eyes glowed as they often did when she spoke of Grand-père.

"I'm going to research the never-ending-sleep. It's new to society. I have ... well ... I've read many books. Across eons of time, there was never something like the never-ending-sleep. Imposed only in the last one hundred years, it's not natural. It's calculated murder."

"Christiana!" Grand-mère gasped. "Don't let anyone hear you say such a thing."

I could see the fear in her eyes. "I cannot just wait for you two to be ... terminated, Grand-mère. I have to do something."

"It won't be in time, Honey. We will be seventy-five in two weeks, after Gift-giving time."

"It has to be in time! You have a right to live as long as you can. I saw an old document in the library Grand-mère. It read in part, *We hold these truths to be self-evident, that all men are created equal, that we are endowed by our Creator with certain inalienable rights that among them are life, liberty, and the pursuit of happiness.* We have a right to life, Grand-mère, an inalienable right, a right that cannot be repudiated. Our *creator* gave us that right. Now, Grand-mère, please tell me, who is the creator? I will contact him." I picked up her hand, pressed it to my lips and silently pleaded for the answer.

"Christiana, it is forbidden, dear. I ..."

"But, I'm Legacy, Grand-mère. I'm supposed to grow in wisdom and wisdom requires as much knowledge as can be learned in a lifetime."

"Christiana, I ... it's been so long since Great-Grandpa told me about God." She seemed to search for words again. "He said ... if you seek God, he will come in and make his home within you.

"He said that the creator is ... God, the Holy One, he who created everything, even you and me. God is *other*, not anything within our understanding. He is the all-in-all and his most precious gift to all of us, is a reverence for life, for he is Life."

"Where can I find him Grand-mère? Maybe he will tell me how to reverse this terrible edict of Society." I had to know where he lived. God may have been the only one who would have known how to accomplish what seemed impossible.

Grand-mère smiled sweetly. "He lives in the *other* place, Honey, just as he is *other*."

"Other what?" I couldn't fit it all into my unstretched, unpracticed, untouched mind.

Overwhelmed with all the new information, still, I wondered if I already knew. Something or someone had been tugging at my heart for months as I read the old books. It was a force that was strong enough to call to me from the pages of man's writing and move within my being, like a fog that overtakes a meadow of wild flowers and blankets it, while doing no harm, then leaves a light nourishing mist on the surface of all that lives there.

"What more did Great-grandfather tell you," I pressed.

"Great-grandfather taught me about the ways of the Lord. He told me—" Grand-mère hesitated but she seemed to want to tell me all she knew. Finally, she went on, "There is a special book about him—God—but all those books were destroyed, their contents long forgotten. Great-grandfather had much of it memorized and quoted from it often." Grand-mère looked away from me. "No," she began again quietly, "that's wrong. They weren't all destroyed. Society had entrusted a copy of the book with Great-grandfather since he was the great philosopher, the Wisest One."

"Grand-mère, if he was so wise why did he vote to institute the Length of Days policy?"

"He did not vote for it, Honey. He cast a black ball, not a white. But the *yeas* won out. There is nothing that can be done now." Again, Grand-mère seemed to accept the inevitable.

"Maybe there is, Grand-mère. What about the book you talked about and the old Bill of Rights? I just know there is something." I could not accept the required sleep. Exposed to life through the old volumes and the harmless teleplay I had watched earlier in the day, hope had begun to take root in my heart. I felt an awakening of my spirit that somehow felt familiar, but I couldn't remember having experienced it before. I felt surrounded by a sweet life-force that I neither understood nor could describe.

"Let's go into the study, my dear," my grandmother offered as she rose and steadied herself. Large wooden pocket doors, which vanished into the wall and reappeared with a pull on the recessed ring of a brass plate, parted for the two of us to enter. "Over here," she directed.

I followed her into the wonderful old office with its elegant oak desk. Shelves of books that reached from floor to ceiling stretched around the entire room. "You haven't let me come in here very often," I whispered in awe.

"Now that will have to change, won't it, Christiana."

"Why now, Grand-mère? I have been Legacy since I was born."

"Yes, dear, but now you are twenty-four years old. You've started your detoxification process, haven't you?" She asked as though she already knew.

"Yes, in fact, I came here from Dr. O'Reilly's office. I had this thing on my shoulder."

"What *thing* on your shoulder?" My grandmother seemed concerned. My health and well-being were important to all.

"There was something in my vaccination site. It turned out to be no big deal. More curious than anything. Dr. O'Reilly removed it." I reached in my pocket and pulled out the tissue containing the small piece he had returned to me.

"Christiana, that looks like your chip. That was not to be

removed." Grandma Constance picked up the piece from my hand and turned it over. "Jason O'Reilly should have known better than to remove the chip. He's Legacy too. This little chip contains the proof of your linage."

I was surprised and amused. The doctor almost bowed in my presence and all along, he was Legacy too? "Dr. O'Reilly is a Privileged Citizen? Why didn't he tell me?"

"With you, Legacy identifies your position. With Jason, his occupational title hides his privileged status. Rather than Lord O'Reilly, he is by education and examination, Dr. O'Reilly. As a physician, he should have known not to remove the chip."

"Have all physicians been trained to know about the device?" I folded the little piece over in the tissue and replaced it in the pocket of my cloak.

"Well, perhaps I'm wrong. I may have been too harsh on Dr. O'Reilly. I imagine only the pediatricians would need to know, since the chip is implanted in an infant immediately after birth." She paused for a moment in her conversation while she searched the upper book shelves. "I only know that everyone is supposed to have one. It's like a permanent census card." She stopped and held the back of her neck as she craned to see the books on the top shelf near the ceiling. "There it is. Christiana, would you climb up there and fetch it down? It's a little beyond my reach these days, my dear."

"Sure." I pulled over the library ladder attached to a track that ran along the ceiling, in front of the shelves of books. From the higher elevation as I climbed the rungs, another thought struck me. "Grand-mère, how does it happen that you and Grand-père were both of Legacy Linage?"

"Well, I don't really know," she responded slowly. "Over a little to your left, dear. It's that black leather book between the two red volumes." I fingered the book spines and then she exclaimed excitedly, "That's it." She watched for a moment then added. "Your grandfather was the only man I was ever attracted to. Just Oliver Richly. He made my socks droop."

"Grand-mère!" I gasped and laughed until I nearly dropped the book.

"Christiana, have you never met a man who absolutely turned your heart into a field full of butterflies?"

"Not yet, Grand-mère." Then, the face of Jason O'Reilly flashed before my eyes and I began to giggle. "Why are we talking about this?" I laughed out loud. As I descended the ladder and handed the book to my grandmother, I felt the warmth of a blush.

"We're discussing this topic, because you asked ... sort of." Grand-mère took the book to the brown leather sofa that sat in front of the window. I smiled as I thought of my cozy spot in the library.

"Yes, this is it. I've never read it but Great-grandfather told me it had been a very popular book at one time." She took a handkerchief from her pocket and dusted off the cover. After patting it for a moment, she handed it to me. "Now you must protect it. Great-grandfather said it is sacred. This is the one book that Alister Bedlam has not only banned but has also attached the punishment of imprisonment on anyone who possesses it."

"Bedlam? Grand-mère, he's not in the government. What does he have to do with decisions that impact all the rest of us?"

"Oh, Christiana, he has never been elected but he pulls the strings. He's like the supreme head of a shadow government that influences all aspects of life without ever holding office."

"You said, *prison,* Grand-mère. One could go to prison for just possessing this book. I don't like the sound of that. Besides, I thought the prisons had been emptied a long time ago."

Grand-mère leaned toward me and lowered her voice. "There is one prison, outside of our zone, that houses ... political detainees."

"Political prisoners? You mean, owning this book could threaten the very fabric of our government?" My mind raced. "As docile as people are in this Age of Silence, how could anyone be a threat? Besides, you've had the book a long time. You and Grand-père have been safe."

"That's what I am hoping, for you," she whispered. "It is absolutely necessary that this book lives on. I am so sorry, my dear, that I have to pass it on to you. But you're the only one I can trust. Besides, no one else in your world will know of its importance."

"Thank you Grand-mère, for your confidence in me. I'll protect it." I thought for a moment. "I'll need to find a safe place for it."

"It may be safe out in the open but above or below eye level, as we have stored it."

"Did Grand-père read the book?" I wondered out loud.

"No, I —"

A familiar voice joined the conversation from the door. "Yes, I have read the book, several times, and replaced it in the same spot after each reading." Oliver Richly removed his wide-brimmed gardening hat and slapped it across his leg.

"Oliver, dear, the dust," Constance scolded softly.

"I'm sorry, Honey. *Dust to dust,* some people say. If people were really passing through on dust beams, I guess we would all have to stop using the vacuum cleaner." He smiled and winked his eye. Then his voice softened and his eyes shone with a spirit of light.

"Christiana, dear," he began as he took my hand that cradled the precious book, "promise that you will read it word for word, chapter by chapter, cover to cover. And, when you've finished, read it a second time, for a clearer meaning and greater understanding."

"I will, Grand-père. I promise." His words charged me with the power of purpose.

"Oliver? Why didn't you tell me you read the book? Would I have liked it?" She sounded surprised, hurt, as if her love had betrayed her heart.

"Oh Connie, you would have loved it. But you saw me reading it many times. Since you didn't say anything, I didn't push it on you." Grand-père was taken aback. "I never intended to leave you out."

"Perhaps, I should leave the book with you Grand-mère, until you've had a chance to read it." I was embarrassed. It felt like I was taking something of great value from my own grandmother who had only weeks to live.

"No, no, Christiana," Grand-père corrected, "you must take it. And, you cannot reveal anything about what I'm about to say."

"Of course," I said as layers of intrigue piled up like cordwood around me.

"My dears," Grand-père's voice lowered to a whisper, "I made a copy of the book a few years ago when we still had access to personal copy machines."

"You mean you actually had a copier here in the house? I don't think I remember that. Why are those things no longer available to everyone?" I asked.

"When the country converted the energy source from electricity, they said it wasn't fair that everyone should have to buy a new computing machine and printer. And, since everyone's personal space is much smaller than it used to be, they decided to have computing centers for communication and use the home models exclusively for gaming. It seemed reasonable at the time."

"And now?" I couldn't imagine why anyone would consider decreased reading and communication, something one would praise.

"I don't know any more. It seems like people have lost interest in life, in each other, in everything," my grandfather admitted, but had no explanation for the phenomenon.

"*They* said? Grand-père, who are *they*?"

"The government, honey. The Council of Elders only advises the government. The decisions belong to the governmental officials unless it is a constitutional issue."

Then his eyes brightened again and he added, "You take this one." He patted the leather-bound book in my hand with reverence. "And, I have something for you, dear." He pulled a manuscript from a high shelf and handed it to Grand-mère. "You may have this one Connie."

I cradled the book in my arms and drew it to my chest. It seemed precious to me, at least that's the impression I got from my grandfather and I believed him. "I'll have a safe installed in my apartment."

"No!" both of my grandparents admonished me at once. "They will suspect you're hiding something."

"They?" Their sudden outburst startled me.

"Society ... the government. It would be best if you put it in a grocery sack and simply carried it into your building along with vegetables and fruits. You can remove it from the sack and put it somewhere in your apartment. When you move over to this end of town, they won't be curious. They wouldn't dare. The homes of the Council of Elders are off limits."

Grand-père gave me a hug and kissed my forehead. It felt like he was anointing me as I ascended into the Lower Council where future members are exposed to the vast wealth of knowledge available to the few.

"Gotta run, Sweeties. I have an appointment," I chuckled and started toward the door.

"A meeting?" Grand-mère questioned.

I thought for a moment and wondered if I should reveal my afternoon coffee time with an interesting man. "I'm meeting Dr. O'Reilly in a while for a cup of coffee, and I want to take this book home first."

"Here's a little shopping bag, Honey." Grand-mère offered one from the corner of the desk. "I brought a new pillow home in it. Put the book in here," she offered. "We'll get some celery and apples to put on top of it." Then she smiled mischievously, "You're meeting Jason O'Reilly for coffee?"

"I'll get the food camouflage while you two have some girl-talk," Grand-père winked.

I studied the impish look on my grandmother's face. "Now, don't make something out of this," I laughed softly. "It's just coffee."

"Yes, dear," she agreed but it sounded like she was only humoring me. "I'll try not to ask any questions."

"There isn't anything to say, Grand-mère. I just met the man this morning," I protested.

"But you're having coffee with him already, my dear. It seems to me like there is something to say. If nothing else, you could say, 'He seems like a very nice man.'"

"Okay Grand-mère—Dr. O'Reilly seems like a very nice man." As we laughed together, the giggles warmed my heart. I knew how much I will miss our time together once Grand-mère enters the sleep.

"Here you are." Grand-père returned with the food and placed it in my sack. Then he did something he had never done before. He placed his right hand on the top of my head. "Now, may the peace and safety of the Lord go with you, my child."

I felt blessed and overcome with awe. I didn't want to leave. I wanted to stay in the glow I was feeling. But time was moving on. I breezed back through the house with the musical laughter of my grandparents tickling my ears from the warmly paneled office. *Those two Rascals, they are probably in their hugging and laughing with the sheer joy of life. I have so much to learn.*

As I stepped out onto the porch and started down the walk, another strata-car pulled to a stop and then the driver-side window opened. "Excuse me Ma'am. We're looking for a man in a red car that has darkly tinted windows. Have you seen the vehicle or the man?" The Blue Guardsman asked.

"No," I answered but that one word caught in my throat like a seed and I could scarcely breathe. *They are talking about Silas Drummond. They're looking for him. He's in danger. I may not be safe either.*

There was something to fear and I didn't know what it was. As the squad car moved on, I turned for one last look at Grand-mère and Grand-père's stately old home and wondered where my family would gather next year on Gift-giving Day. I had to find a way to save them. *I want them around forever, and if not forever, then when their bodies wear out, not when they wear out their time.*

CHAPTER EIGHT
Inspector Stoner

Out on the streets, other forces bustled about the city. It was the season that brought most people out of their little apartment cubicles and into the world of shops with holiday trappings. Extra police were on patrol. The masses needed supervision.

An official Blue Guard, four-wheeler strata-car, with a unique black stripe down the side, passed by one of the many transit entrances. The strata-car windows, tinted black, made the whole thing have a dark, menacing look, like a rolling crypt. But the strata-car was no burial place. The vehicle had multilayers of assault and defense technology that made it nearly impenetrable and unstoppable.

Busy, busy, busy little people, the strata driver mocked. Inspector Tombstone was what his men called him, never to his face, but he knew it. Inspector Stoner would never have permitted it. He stared blankly at the holiday shoppers as they passed. *A bunch of rusty robots, every one of them,* he mumbled to himself. *How can they drag about like lazy mice in a maze?*

He had been driving around all morning. With Gifting Day not far off, there was an increase in security in town. And now there was this business of Silas Drummond going AWOL at work. Drummond had to be found. Everyone, from boot officers to Ward Stoner, the Chief Inspector of the Blue Guard, was on the streets.

Most people were afraid of the Blue Guard and crossed to the other side of the street when they encountered one. The officers' behavior was just too unpredictable. One day they might help a child up the steps to the transit platform, another day they might not be helpful at all and could even be abusive. If the walk-paths were congested, a member of the elite division thought nothing of jabbing someone in the ribs with a prodding stick to move them aside. If accused of a crime, a handcuffed person could arrive at Guard Headquarters bloody and broken. Now, during the holidays, even the Guard had joined with the regular police patrol and Inspector Tombstone didn't like it one bit. He was above having to deal with babysitting women in shopping cart brawls.

He gripped the steering wheel tightly and stirred restlessly on the seat. He saw a young family begin to cross the street and turned on the siren, as much to scare them, as to hurry them along. *That's right—take your time,* he groaned sarcastically. *There's always somebody dragging their sorry carcass across the street, getting in everybody's way. Why don't they stay at home in their tired little apartment if they can't move about the streets with more power than that?* The chief inspector of the Blue Guard sneered at the world around him.

"Inspector?" His communication device interrupted his thoughts.

"Of course," he snapped back.

"I'm sorry to break into your patrol, but there's no one else to send. There has been some sort of situation on a Public Transit car this morning."

Stoner sighed and pulled away from the curb. As he listened to the details, he headed toward Capitol Square.

When he arrived up town at the City Transit office, Ward Stoner—skilled detective and Chief of the Blue Guard's entire investigative division—burst through the door with the might of one who had no problem seizing authority. He had no time to waste and was in no mood for nonsense. He was a man ruled by his own power. Power was his master and he controlled others by the strength of that small Kingdom of Stoner, his own world, his own power, his own rules. No one got in his way.

Stoner burst through the door of the transit system office. He would make the frivolous stop but he didn't have to like it. "What is all of this about?" His question was crisp. His tone sounded bored.

"Yes, Sir." The woman in the outer office jumped to her feet. "Follow me, please," she said as she led the way through a swinging gate that separated the inner rooms from the public space, then down a hall to the manager's office. The woman entered the room first and attempted to introduce the Chief to the transit line manager. "Mr. Munson, the Inspect—"

"Stoner," the Inspector interrupted. "We are nearly upon Gift-giving Day and you have me running around chasing a—a what—a ghost?" Stoner laughed rudely as though he would rather spend his time somewhere else, doing almost anything besides talking to Munson.

"I don't know what it was, Sir," Munson whispered as he shooed the woman out of his office. He checked the hall for eavesdroppers and motioned to a chair for his guest.

Stoner waved him off and remained standing. "I have no time to get comfortable." He squared his shoulders and tried to remain calm in a situation that was making him more irritated by the moment. He blinked his eyes three times, tilted his head to the side and worked his jaw with gritting anger. "Again, speak up Mister. What is this all about? Invisible intruders? Maybe it's the jolly Gift Giver." Once more, his jaw tensed and he ground away at apparently nothing, except Munson's tired explanation.

"Sir," Munson stood up, leaned his knuckles on the desk and stared the inspector in the eyes. "I do not know what was there. I am reporting a ... situation."

"Well now," Stoner drew out his words in mocking disbelief. "Why don't you tell me about the ... situation?"

"My driver on the midtown line called in a strange ... situation. I'm sorry, Sir. I don't know what else to call it."

"Go on ..." the inspector's boredom was evident in his voice. He wanted information, not irrelevant details, and he wanted it fast.

"The driver reported that a woman boarded a bus this morning and didn't set off the buzzer, just a ... swish ... you know ... a ... swish ... like when a cat passes in front of a sensor."

"A cat ..." Stoner could feel his pulse beating behind his eyes and knew his blood pressure was rising. He was wasting time. He still had a few Gift Day presents left to buy and time was running out.

"Sir ... you are making me feel a little foolish. I was ordered to report any irregularities." The manager stood as tall as he could. What power he didn't have in authority, he seemed to be trying to make up for in height.

"Go on," Stoner moaned. His jaw flexed as his eyes darted from the window to Munson and back again.

"A cat ... or a dog ... anything other than a person makes when it passes." Munson cleared his throat. "The driver said that a woman got on the bus and didn't set off a buzz, just a swish, and then got off to get something she forgot. When she got back on, the buzzer sounded like it was supposed to. He didn't think anything more about it, but he thought he'd better report it when he got to the end of the line." Munson said his piece and waited.

Stoner's eyes snapped back at Munson. "Did he check the mechanism? Was it defective? There has to be a more logical answer than a *swish*."

"He pulled the bus into the garage so we could check it out. There was nothing. The tone trigger worked just fine." Munson crossed his arms. "We have done our job here, Sir."

"Did he say who the passenger was?" Stoner didn't acknowledge Munson's unspoken message. *Now you do your job* seemed buried beneath the surface. The Inspector didn't take orders from anyone.

"The driver said he was busy this morning and couldn't say for sure who it was."

Inspector Stoner gripped his hat in his hands several times, then, controlling himself again, he smoothed it with his fingers. "It happened only one time and yet, he was too unobservant to notice who the patron was."

"He noticed that it happened but not who it was, Sir. That's why he reported it." Munson's teeth sounded clenched.

Stoner ignored the man's mounting anger and walked toward the door. "You did the right thing, Munson. I'll look into it." He started to leave without looking back, then turned and shook the man's hand. Stoner respected a man who could hold his own in a good argument.

He shook his head and tried to clear his thinking. *No guilt here. Toughness is what's needed, what's always needed,* he thought. He had to remain hard and rigid on the job. He was sure, if he didn't use fear to intimidate others, he would lose the power that came with his office. He battled with himself daily. One side of his head was at war with the other, as if good whispered in one ear and evil writhed in the other. *Chatter on—I will win this battle.*

CHAPTER NINE

The Horror in the Note

1:30 p.m.

After leaving my grandparents' home, I rode the transit back to my apartment, but I couldn't focus on the city as it passed. *There is that same man again.* I was very uneasy with his constant presence. *He was on the bus earlier today. His stares make me feel uncomfortable. He didn't even look away when I caught him looking at me. Does he know I'm carrying the secret book?* A chill over took me, and I shuddered. I could not appear anxious or secretive. No one could have known that I was carrying a banned volume. I had to make sure my behavior and attitude didn't create suspicion. I tried to ignore the man and maintained an empty gaze out the window.

Rather than being concerned with the scenes as they passed, or the penetrating gaze of the other riders, I thought of the words and images I had just experienced at my grandparents' home. I was determined to do whatever I had to do, to find a solution for overturning the Length of Days policy that would seal their inevitable fate.

As I thought of the Length of Days policy, I pulled Silas's note from my bag and picked up reading where I left off.

> "The entire endless sleep program is a sham!
> Lady Applewait, people either reach their allotted days,
> are ill or injured, and then told they will enter into
> an endless sleep. Some people actually believe they will
> awaken sometime in the future. Some have even

> left a wake-up-call for a specific date and time. They
> thought they were staying in a fine hotel. The saddest
> people, My Lady, are the ones who would have healed
> on their own but are told they will heal more quickly if
> they take a long nap. All of those people, the timed-out,
> the sick and the tricked, have the same fate. Ma'am, they
> take them alive to the mountain and place them in
> the furnaces, and their ashes are disposed of."

I gagged on the words and fear rose in my throat like vomit. I wanted to scream, but I knew people would be watching me. I had to hold myself together. The man on the front seat stared at me intently as I tried to control the waves of sickening nausea. I trembled at the thought of the danger the information had put me in and the fate awaiting Grand-mère and Grand-père. I had to finish reading the note, but I also had to control myself. I breathed in and out slowly several times. I wasn't finished with the letter. What more could Silas have written?

> "Their bones," Drummond continued, "are ground into
> calcium powder that is used in the mortar of our
> buildings and epoxied into large chunks for carving
> statues and other works of art. Please, My Lady, I
> didn't know anyone else I could tell. You are the only
> one who can stop this abomination. I will contact you at
> the apartment building soon.
> Respectfully,
> Silas Drummond"

No, I whispered bitterly. *It is all a lie!* I had to regain composure. *Control, calm, peace*—I repeated it over and over. Suddenly I felt a light touch on my shoulder. The little boy who sat with his mother on the opposite seat patted my shoulder.

"Don't cry, Miss," he soothed. "It'll be all right."

I buried the note in my tote again and wiped my eyes. "Yes, honey, I think it will be." I jumped up, eager to get away where no one would observe me. I patted the boy on the head with a sincere, "Thank you." Then it was my stop, and I bounded quickly from the transit.

I know it's not true. It can't be true. I will get to the bottom of it. I'll track Silas down. He'll pay for this. If I find it is true, if this evil exists, I'll absolutely do something. What? I don't know ... but something

CHAPTER TEN

A New Way of Being

2:00 p.m.

I ran from the transit and down the platform staircase with Silas's note in my bag and Grand-père's precious book held tightly in the sack with the vegetables. Near the entrance to my residential building, I heard a faint whimper coming from the shadows under a low bush near the door.

"Well, what's this?" The little puddle of fur was not much larger than my hand. "A real kitten," I marveled as I stroked the fur. For a brief moment, I was transported from the danger I was in. "I never noticed any of you little mouse patrollers before. Where did you come from?" As I picked her up, I looked around, but no one was nearby.

I walked to the corner and looked down the side street for a possible cat owner in search of a kitten. No one.

"Amazing," I purred to the little creature in my arms. "I never knew your kind would be so soft and cuddly." I had never held a kitten before. Her fur was as smooth as the silkweed from the grassy meadow behind Grand-mère's house. As I petted the kitten's head and belly, a quiet calmness came over me.

I knew the kitten's ancestors had been feral for decades, but I wanted to keep it. "I don't think you'll eat much. Would you like to come home with me?" I whispered. The little creature nestled in the crook of my arm, balanced on top of the grocery sack with the precious book inside. Carefully, I carried her into my building.

My mind raced, one thought canceled out the other. The kitten was soft and cuddly, a stark contrast to the rage that coursed through my body. A new purpose flooded my mind. Emotions I had never known before collided and demanded my full attention. I felt terrified and energized at the same time. Despite the vileness of the information Silas had passed on to me, a feeling of joy mingled with fear and disgust. Courage had ridden in on the back of all that anger. I was determined. I would do something to help my grandparents.

As I walked through the apartment lobby, I felt exposed. Maybe I had been reckless, drawing attention to myself with the kitten. I felt sure the people around me could see the entire contents of my bag with x-ray vision. I knew that made no sense, but my insides knotted like a Gifting bow. I was relieved when everything in the lobby seemed cheery. Colored lights and a festive wreath hung from the walls. Everything looked brighter, more vivid. The biggest change must have been within me.

How can so many opposing feelings survive in one mind? Tender feelings, fear, anger, hope, courage. And just as amazing, I have a new energy. It felt as if I could actually fly or I'd fly apart from the tornado of emotions within me.

"Hi, Mrs. LaGassi," I sang out as I passed a longtime resident of the modest building.

"Good afternoon Ma'am," the woman responded. She appeared startled that I had noticed her along the way.

"How is your son, Tony? He was sick, wasn't he?" I stopped for a moment with my foot in the elevator door and continued to enjoy my contact with the middle-aged woman.

"Yes, he was, but I wasn't aware that you knew. He is much better now. Thank you for asking," Mrs. LaGassi added with an air of surprise.

"You tell him, I like the hat he had on the other day. They used to call those, ball caps." I stepped onto the lift and continued to hold the door with my foot. "Baseball was a game they used to play, on teams, with other players ... outside ... in the field."

"Oh," was all the woman could say as the elevator door closed.

All the way up to the tenth floor my mood was erratic. It was a strange experience. My insides rattled. I understood the fear and anger, but they were mixed with good feelings as well. Pounding waves of emotions rolled within me. *I'll research these symptoms when I get back to the library. My books will tell me what I need to know.* I looked at my timepiece. It was already a little after 2:00 p.m.

I pushed the door to my apartment open and entered my sanctuary, my sweet solitude from the world. The kitten scampered playfully around the kitchen when I put her down. The white furry ball of fuzz wrapped her body around, in and out and through my legs.

"I think I'll call you Shakespeare," I said. "No one now knows who Shakespeare was, so you'll be my own private bit of culture in a dull and drab world." I poured her a little saucer of milk as my mind darted to what the events of that day could mean. *First, I must hide this book.* But the other ... *I don't know what to do with Silas's note.*

Gripping fear clouded the outer edges of my mind, as I went to my desk and research area. *Where should I put this strange Bible? My friends have never understood about me and my love of books. They thought I was nuts for having any of them. Now, I'm even crazier for bringing a banned book into my home. A banned book, a banned cat, and a note that could inflame a revolution. Citizens' lack of interest may be the very thing that will protect me from the danger I could be facing.*

My collection of books was innocent enough. Many of them were a group of uninteresting volumes about rules and policies of the Populous. Yesterday, I felt privileged to have four rows of unimportant books. Now, they had become the very camouflage to conceal the book that held such mystery and danger.

My communication instrument flashed its blinking light. "Hello?"

"Christiana, dear —"

"Grand-mère! Twice in one day, how wonderful!"

"My dear, I have been so worried about you since you left."

"Worried? Why?"

"The ... the box of candy we gave you today, dear. Possessing chocolate is very dangerous for you—it could draw in neighbors you don't even know." She spoke in code and faked a little chuckle. "Have you hidden the box as we said?"

My mind raced to catch up. Grand-mère was talking about the Bible. The communications line—it may not be secure. We would not know who could be listening. "I was just about to."

"Where, Sweetheart?"

"Well," my stomach started to tighten and my heart pounded. Where was I going to hide the Bible and how could I tell Grand-mère, to ease her mind, without revealing much? "I was just going to shelve it in the pantry. Maybe I'll wrap the box in brown paper and put it behind Great-grandpa's favorite cereal. No one would see it or know it's there."

"Yes, yes ... no, wait —"

"Grand-mère, you're frightening me."

"I'm sorry." Her voice became low and full of regret. "Maybe we shouldn't have given the candy to you."

"No, it'll be all right. It will be well hidden behind my other foods."

"But what if someone finds the box wrapped in paper? If it's discovered, then they'll wonder why it's so important that it needed to be camouflaged and concealed."

"Oh, Grand-mère." Fear gripped my chest like a vice. "What's in that candy?" I couldn't believe my grandparents would have had anything vile or sinister.

"Christiana, it is a box of chocolates full of love and promises."

"Love? What's so subversive about love?" Fear and joy clanged inside me, both at the same time. All of my new emotions were bombarding my mind with contradictory messages.

"Love, my dear, can change the world, even more surely than the arms of war. You must be careful. Chocolate is the stuff that inspires revolution." Grand-mère tried to sound light and bubbly but there was an intensity in her manner that let me know her concern.

"Mutiny? Grand-mère ... anarchy? In that box of chocolate?" I laughed nervously.

"A revolution of the heart, sweetheart. Just hide it well. Perhaps out in the open is still the best place to put it. Just another box of food among many. Besides, most people have no interest in sweets anymore. Anyone who visits won't even see it."

I wanted to ask her more about the never-ending-sleep. But it wasn't safe to talk about such things over the communication lines. I decided not to question her but imagined what Grand-mère would say.

"Sleep dear. Just a very long sleep," is all that she would say. I dared not ask her more.

"Well okay, Grand-mère. It was nice talking to you. I'm fine. Everything will be all right. Bye-bye."

Grand-mère didn't know the horror that Silas wrote about. *It must be a lie*, I told myself.

I sat down in front of the large window and watched the day. Some of the Gifting lights were on even though it was the middle of the day. Still, they were beautiful. I sat there and allowed my mind to empty of all of the evil images Silas's note had imprinted on my mind.

• • • • •

I have no idea how long I had napped. But I felt a little better when I awakened. Still, I had to hide the book.

I looked over my shelves of books for a good spot to place the leather edition. On the top shelf, to the left, was a series of leather-bound philosophy books my great-grandfather had written. I had been so proud of the volumes. I had always thought of them as objects of beauty or artful room decorations. Now, something had changed within me.

"I'll devour every page right after Gifting Season, Shakespeare," I mumbled to the scampering toenail tapper in the otherwise silent room. "I want to know the legacy he left to me, and not just to me. He had willed it to all of us."

I pushed the book shelved beside the set of six, farther down the shelf, and placed the precious one I had just brought home on the shelf beside them. At a quick glance, it looked like a cluster of seven, rather than six, and would go unnoticed, certainly by the uninterested eyes of my friends who usually passed unaware. It had to go unseen.

Possessing revolutionary materials would have meant an indictment for treason. Although no one is allowed to violate the privacy of a Legacy Citizen or enter their living space without the written consent of a zone judge, they often did. My hands trembled as I thought about the gravity of the situation I was in. I had to know what threat waited within its pages. Why was it banned? What made it precious? *I'll begin reading it later,* I promised myself.

Even while Grand-mère's frightening words still hung in my mind, I felt I had to avoid facing them as I always had. *I'll quickly splash some water over my face and apply a small dab of lip rouge. At least I'll feel refreshed.* I started toward the sink and then I thought of Dr. O'Reilly and decided to apply a little color to my cheeks as well.

I fumbled with the compact that refused to open. "Oh, stop it, Christiana," I snapped at myself out loud, but my hands would not stop shaking. Their trembling only made me more anxious—I was anxious over being anxious. In my usual form, I tried to ignore my fear.

"You are being melodramatic," I admonished myself. Life simply isn't that deep or complicated. "Who do you think you are— some international spy?" I grumbled into the mirror. "Don't make yourself that important at a time like this. Fear won't be your credentials, but it may be your undoing. Snap out of it. Get some courage." Trepidation continued to fight a battle for my mind, so I chose to focus on happier thoughts. As I applied the lip rouge and brushed some color over my cheeks, I remembered blushing in the doctor's presence without the help of cosmetics, and for a moment, I smiled to myself. Then, I remembered the seriousness of my task.

I'll hurry over to the library and begin researching the subject of death. I also want to review the change made to our laws regarding the Length of Days policy. There will still be enough time to meet Dr. O'Reilly at 6:00 at the Demitasse Coffee Shop. I grabbed my tunic and darted out the door, relying on my name and position alone to protect the Bible book. *No one is allowed to violate the privacy of a Legacy Citizen—yet rules have been broken.*

CHAPTER ELEVEN
Seeable but Unheard

3:30 p.m.

On board the Public Transit again, I moved to the first seat, sat down, and resumed my gaze out the window. The scenery that passed outside was very different in that part of town from the picturesque, old section where Legacy Members and the Council of Elders lived. A tired looking woman of nondescript age sat down beside me.

"It's not as colorful in this part of town is it?" I said but didn't expect her to answer. The woman glanced in my direction then back to nothingness.

"The buildings are all the same, one apartment building after another."

She said nothing, but I noticed her breathing had changed.

I tried again. "It seems we have high taxes for infrastructure, community centers and parks, but nothing to brighten up people's homes."

She leaned slightly in my direction and whispered, "People have no money left to personalize their own homes—just sameness everywhere. That's why I love the lights at Gifting time." She then faded back into the vacant space from where she had just come. Like the surroundings, she had merged her *self* with the masses.

When we got to the woman's bus stop, she started to get up, then turned back to me and whispered. "Funny how those in the government and other professionals can maintain a measure of uniqueness for themselves, isn't it My Lady?" Then she was gone. I rode on in amazement. The woman had learned to move in and out of mob dullness at will.

The transit bus stopped again at the corner near the library. As I disembarked, I stepped into a day that seemed brighter and more glorious than any December afternoon I could remember. It was as if I were seeing the world through new eyes. How could anyone be in danger in that bright world? The colors were more vivid and sparkling than I had ever seen them. Why? Why was the sky so high? Why did it have such a vast expanse? Why did the whole world suddenly come alive? All of that beauty had the power to lift my spirits higher than I had ever known.

On a mission, I hurried into the building. "Good afternoon, Frank." I breezed past the guard stationed at the portal, near the archive room.

"Afternoon, Ma'am," he smiled back without looking up from his row of monitors. "Funny, I didn't see you come in," he remarked dryly.

"I am invisible today, Frank," I teased.

"Most likely," he yawned. "Or in-hearable," he added.

I didn't know what he meant, but I didn't linger around to ask questions. I floated through the swinging gate and stopped at the Reference Desk.

"May I leave my bag and stuff here, Mary?" If I had to leave the back recesses of the library in a hurry, I didn't want to leave anything behind. Mary, the Research Librarian, was always helpful.

"Sure, Christiana, just stash them under there." Mary pointed to a low shelf in the checkout desk, out of vision and out of touch.

"Thanks," I added and moved on through the outer reading room and into the back stacks. My shoes clicked and echoed on the concrete floors. I had left my purse behind and had taken only a small pencil, some paper to take notes, and my keys. Unlocking the side door, I slipped into the archival room. It was a tense adventure into my beloved books, since I knew I would only have a few minutes before someone would come to check on me. After all, I had already checked out of the library for the day when I left for the doctor's office in the morning. I had been thinking of an excuse that I could use for being in the room if someone came back. The only thing that came to mind was an explanation about having left something in the room when I was researching other materials. The misplaced item could not be my tunic I decided. No, I had left it with my purse. *I'll have to think about it as I look through the papers and texts. Maybe it won't matter. It could be anything. No one else knows what's in the room anyway.*

I couldn't help thinking how I had amazed myself. Where had I gotten the nerve to be on this dangerous quest in the first place? Silas's note, if true, was motivation enough to speak out, but it was also reason for fear. Now, suddenly, I felt new strength to follow through, to find the truth, to do something about the terrible policy of termination, even though I didn't know yet what to do. Did I really grasp the seriousness of the cause and the danger I was in? Would I succeed ... and at what cost?

CHAPTER TWELVE

The Precious Document

4:00 p.m.

The long rays of afternoon light were still streaming through the western window of the library when I walked into the back sections. The light was so beautiful I didn't need the lamps. Besides, I preferred natural light to the dreary blue haze cast by energy efficient lamps. I moved directly to the document case I had noticed when I had been in the archives before and stopped in front of a large glass-covered display box. I paused and listened for the guard to come to see who had gotten too close to the case and had activated the sensors. No one came. I was still alone.

The document was clearly visible through the glass, in spite of its faded condition. It was considered to be one of the few copies made of an original document. School children no longer filed past to view the archive. The top of the case had only gathered dirt. No one studied its contents. Few people were even aware of its existence anymore, but still it remained, sealed up in an environmentally controlled case, safe in its own cocoon.

I pressed as closely as I could, wiped the dust of the ages from the surface, and read the words that I had only glanced at before. An odd sensation overtook me as I began to read. Excitement and awe bathed me like anointing oil.

IN CONGRESS, JULY 4, 1776

The unanimous Declaration of the thirteen

United States of America

When in the course of human events it becomes necessary for one people to dissolve the political bands which have connected them with another and to assume among the powers of the earth, the separate and equal station to which the laws of nature and of nature's God entitle them, a decent respect to the opinions of mankind requires that they should declare the causes which impel them to the separation.

So, when the people decided to make their own country, under the authority of their God, they believed they should list the causes for their decision to separate.

We hold these truths to be self-evident, that all men are created equal, that they are endowed by their Creator with certain unalienable Rights, that among these are Life, Liberty, and the pursuit of Happiness. — That to secure these rights, governments are instituted among men, deriving their just powers from the consent of the governed. — That whenever any form of government becomes destructive of these ends, it is the Right of the People to alter or to abolish it, and to institute new government, laying its foundation on such principles and organizing its powers in such form, as to them shall seem most likely to affect their safety and happiness.

Wow! Everyone is equal—there are no elite—no Legacy Citizens, and everyone has a right to live, to be free, and to pursue their own happiness. These people are to govern themselves, and when the government interferes with the right of the people to self-govern, that government should be abolished. It is their responsibility to do so. It is all here—every bit of it—especially my grandparents' right to life.

Prudence, indeed, will dictate that Governments long established should not be changed for light and transient causes; and accordingly, all experience hath shown that mankind are more disposed to suffer, while evils are sufferable, than to right themselves by abolishing the forms to which they are accustomed. But when a long train of abuses and usurpations, pursuing invariably the same Object evinces a design to reduce them under absolute despotism, it is their right, it is their duty, to throw off such government, and to provide new guards for their future security. —

It says when a government, even a long-standing one, becomes tyrannical and their abuses are evident and numerable, it is the duty of the people to abolish that government and create a new one. The colonists had reached the limit of their patience. They would act. And we have reached the limit of ours.

Such has been the patient sufferance of these Colonies; and such is now the necessity which constrains them to alter their former Systems of Government. The history of the present King of Great Britain is a history of repeated injuries and usurpations, all having in direct object the establishment of an absolute Tyranny over these States. To prove this, let facts be submitted to a candid world.

My heart leaped within my body. I grabbed my chest and felt the beat of it. Self-evident truths. *Our Creator ... our Creator ... God. God is the Creator*! I couldn't stop rolling the thought around in my head. A sweet cloud of Presence filled the room, and I knew ... I knew. I read it over and over, until I had satisfied my soul that I had buried the words in my heart.

The *truths*, that we are all created equal, that we have inherited from God—the right to life, liberty, and the pursuit of happiness—took my breath away. *We are guaranteed the right to life, the right to live. Why did they change it?* With mood altering additives in our water there were fewer disturbed individuals and fewer still who disturbed others. People rarely got angry. But then, they rarely felt anything at all.

The people were to be self-ruled. If they were not and those who governed, repeatedly abused their authority, that government should be taken down and replaced by one that will govern by the will of the people. The colonists listed their grievances for all the world to see.

I had to move on. The other materials I wanted to see were

further back in the room. No one went into the old manuscript room, not even the cleaning staff. The books within that space were forgotten.

I walked freely through the room. Books and papers were shelved haphazardly everywhere. It looked as if someone had shoved the last bit of knowledge away from sight, slammed the door and locked it. Nearly a hundred years later, I had unlocked the rooms full of old novels, and the history, philosophy, and religious texts banned years ago. Newer versions of those books had been cannibalized beyond recognition. The new editions, re-written texts, no longer spoke truth but were rendered utterly impotent with their lies. Marge had alluded to a time when information flowed like honey from the hive, then its comb was cut down and thrown behind locked doors where it buzzed in silence, still living but unheard.

I checked my time piece. There was still time to do more research before going to meet Jason at the coffee shop. Against the back wall was a long series of history and legal volumes. *Let me see*—I fingered my way through the books until I found historic references that were previous to the last one-hundred years. I leafed through the index. *The New Bill of Rights.* It was right there. On page 384 I began comparing the old with the new first ten amendments to the United States Constitution. The first and fourth amendments tugged at me more strongly than the others. I wasn't able to let go of those two.

1. Freedom of Speech, Press, Religion and Petition.

4. Right of search and seizure regulated.

What I read seemed unbelievable compared to the policed restrictions of the new society. Citizens used to have the right to speak their mind in public, get accurate information from newspapers and news outlets, and were free to worship their God. There he was again, the Creator, God. What on earth had happened?

Then, the *New Bill of Rights* glared at me from the pages. During the upheaval of one-hundred years ago it was determined, in order to control the people, there had to be fewer citizens and a smaller territory. So, they separated the country into four political zones/states, each with their own government and president, which was all controlled by a central government and Prime Minister. A new government was established with a new set of rights. *Let me see, Preamble to the New Bill of Rights.* I read on:

> "The Constitution of the United States made certain introductory statements that can no longer stand in a modern thinking society. In particular, individuals have a right to life, liberty, and the pursuit of happiness. An enlightened society recognizes that life is a privilege and should be available to those viable souls who participate the most, for the greatest good of all. In light of the cost of living, education of the masses, health care, incarceration of those in opposition to society, and financial entitlements and support for those who will not be productive, it is evident that each individual's Length of Days should be planned and terminated before the cost of care begins to be a burden on society. No one has a right to expect society to care for an individual for an undetermined and lengthy period of time. Therefore, an individual's Length of Days will be calculated as follows:

> twenty-two (22) years to graduate from college

> two (2) years beyond education to form a family unit

> two (2) years from the beginning of the family unit to the arrival of the first child

> two (2) years until the second child is born and thus replace the two parental units

> twenty-two (22) more years to rear the youngest child and support them through four years of college

> six (6) years to give ample time for the youngest child to be reared, educated, construct a family unit, and have their first and second children

> four (4) years until the youngest grandchild is established in a society supported preschool

> A total of sixty (60) years equals an individual's Length of Days, with the exception of certain professions that require additional education and length of service, such as medicine, space, and politics. Those professionals will live until age sixty-five (65), in order to serve society with their knowledge.

The members of the Council of Elders will live until age seventy-five (75) to take advantage of their wisdom.

In addition to these citizens, families who initiate fetuses over the allotted two per family will terminate the gestation of the third and any that may follow.

In the event a couple may want to swap out an existing child for another, the first child will enter the sleep chamber by eighteen months of age, thus keeping the family unit to three or four in total.

I was stunned. It was all there, a planned termination of each individual citizen into the endless sleep. With a few strokes of a pen a century ago, people had moved from a right to life, to a right to a speedy termination, with no suffering, just a simple sleep. Some people called it *putting a citizen down*. Silas Drummond's message didn't confirm the long sleep however. He called it extermination.

According to the older documents, life was not all we had a right to. People had a right, given to them by God, to liberty or freedom, and the pursuit of happiness. Now, it was becoming clear to me that society had translated the last right, to a guarantee that all people would be happy. In order to guarantee happiness, our ancestors who were in control of society had started putting additives into the water supply. The antidepressants and chemicals that restrained people's behavior through mind control were loaded daily into the water supply. It had a less than desirable effect on everyone however. While people would not say they were sad, they couldn't say they were happy either. Their emotions and energy were flat. They were neither unhappy, nor happy, just maintained.

Of course, this explained why their need for intimacy and sexual contact was without desire. It was just strong enough in the early years of the formation of their family unit, that they were able to consummate and create a pregnancy to ensure the next generation. The chemicals were modified for each couple through the conception of a second child. By eliminating the sex drive, society thought they could control the root cause of violence and successfully eradicate competition and aggression.

But, why was a free press so important? The writers listed it early in the document, right up there in the first Amendment. Then, it came to me. *When people are informed, they'll not allow their freedoms to be stripped from their grasp. But, their televisions dispensed news all day long. Had the news casters lied to the people?* It hardly seemed possible.

My mind whirled around my *new understandings*. I had studied the New Bill of Rights in school and had always had an innate sense of there being something more, something beautiful, energetic. The novels had also taught me about romance, love, a fuller life.

I was aware of my time in the back stacks and felt panic overtake me as I tried to read all I could. The Original First Amendment stated:

> "Congress shall make no law respecting an establishment of religion, or prohibiting the free exercise thereof; or abridging the freedom of speech, or of the press; or the right of the people peaceably to assemble, and to petition the Government for a redress of grievances."

So, under the original Constitution, the government could not set up a National religion or keep the people from exercising the religion of their choice. I would need another book to pursue my second question.

I got out the dictionary. "Abridge: to reduce or lessen in authority; to deprive, cut off." *That's easy. An abridged dictionary is shorter without changing the definitions and meanings.* So, the government could not shorten or change the free speech of people or the press. Then I continued on to the fourth amendment:

> "The right of the people to be secure in their persons, houses, papers, and effects, against unreasonable searches and seizures, shall not be violated, and no warrants shall issue, but upon probable cause, supported by oath or affirmation, and particularly describing the place to be searched, and the persons or things to be seized."

That means, the Blue Shirts simply cannot come into my home and take out books and papers without good reason. That includes the Bible book and Drummond's paper. I looked at my time piece again. I had to be careful in the library. I wouldn't go undetected for very long. Someone would remember seeing me come back to the Library later than usual. I quickly turned to the page that contained those two amendments in the New Bill of Rights.

"When in the lives of a free people, it becomes evident that the speech of a gentile society has slipped into an inflammatory, prejudicial, and threatening treatise, it becomes necessary to limit the ability of that society to express itself openly. Under penalty of punishment by incarceration and fine, there will be no speech that is prejudicial with respect to age, social class or occupation, nationality, race, sex, sexual orientation, political affiliation, or religion. Within the press and media, there can be no inflammatory words written or spoken in respect to the above classifications. All written and verbally expressed media will first seek governmental approval of their proposed texts, and then file for position equivalence time, so that all represented opinions can be presented at the same time and in the same venue, whether that be private or public, on television or radio programming, in religious locations or public institutions."

I knew I must speak up and speak out, but how was I going to stop them? I wasn't a public speaker or a particularly brave person. It would be easier to look the other way. But, I couldn't. My grandparents' lives were too dear to me.

I finally knew the truth. There was a glorious time in a blessed place, when Freedom had stepped onto the stage of life, inspired the world with her words and gifts and actions, then, like a bored, tired, careless actor, forgot her lines and silently, willingly, drew the curtain closed, turned off the lights, and went home to sleep.

CHAPTER THIRTEEN
Ward Stoner Found a Solution

Ward Stoner walked briskly into the main lobby and thumped his knuckles on the desk. In his mind, as the muscle behind the Blue Guard, it entitled him to fast service. Everyone else could go to the back of the line. A woman and two small children had come in ahead of him to return a stack of books and Stoner was losing his patience. The boy and his sister bounced back and forth arguing over who would carry the books.

"Madam, control your children," he snapped.

"Certainly, Inspector." The woman led both children through the portal. The curly haired five-year-old looked back at Stoner and stuck out his tongue. Stoner deemed the boy a good judge of character.

Stoner took pride in being a part of an elite department of the national police. People considered the Blue Guard a necessary evil. They took their orders from no one and their actions were under the scrutiny of no one. At one time, they had the power to protect the citizens from abuses from the government. They were originally established to derive their powers, not from the government, but from the people. Now, they were too often the source of abuse against the people. Stoner was one of those who perpetrated some of the most heinous abuses, especially in the last year.

Something had been working in Ward's life. His attitudes and behavior vacillated back and forth, from somewhat considerate, to wholly inconsiderate. One day recently he woke to find himself changed. A shroud had lifted from his eyes, and he could see again.

That day, he hesitated before lashing out and thought before applying force. Other days, he bent his personality around his old principles as he searched for more power. He was a jagged riddle unto himself, never knowing which side of his personality would emerge at any point during the day, until the day acted upon him. But he had a job to do. He had shopping to complete ... and he did not like waiting.

"Thank you, Ma'am," he mumbled and tipped his hat at the woman as he went through the library gate.

"May I help you, Sir?" Frank, the portal monitoring guard asked as he watched the inspector approach.

"No, I know the area I'm looking for. I spent many hours in here as a student." Stoner pushed through the gate brashly and covered the length of the hall with great strides. He rarely asked for assistance in anything. He depended on no one.

Science, here we are, he mumbled to himself. Stoner studied in those stacks as an undergrad student intent on becoming a renowned scientist. Then he met Miriam, the counterbalance in his life. But now she was gone. All he had left was his mother and his son. His true balance had died with his wife.

He walked through the stacks and slowed at the A's. *Astronomy.* There was a large section of books, astrological charts, and other related materials. He ran his eyes rapidly over the bindings until he found what he was looking for. He took the volume to a nearby table and flipped it open to the index.

There it is, Pluto, Discovery. He ran his finger down the page, speed-reading the text and then snapped the book closed. *I knew it,* he sneered as if he had been walking his trap lines all morning and had just caught an unsuspecting animal.

CHAPTER FOURTEEN
Covered Her Tracks

All of the books and papers I had taken off the library shelves, I carefully replaced, so no one would know I had been in the room should someone venture in. My ability to move about in the back section of the library and linger as long as I had, was a stroke of good luck. Earlier, I had logged out for the day and this time I hadn't signed back in. Security guards could have seen me enter, checked on me, and then thrown me out.

I walked cautiously from the back room and locked the door behind me. Even when I hurried along the corridor back to collect my things before leaving, there was no one in the hall or around the next corner. I stopped at Mary's desk to pick up my bag and tunic before I left the back area. I had Dr. Jason O'Reilly on my mind.

"Oh, Christiana, I've been so anxious to get out of here, I had forgotten you were back there." The reference librarian looked up from her work. "I didn't hear you. Wonder why I didn't?"

"What do you mean?"

"Every time someone comes or goes, there's a faint buzz. Nothing happened this time."

"How odd," I agreed then retrieved my belongings and put the paper and pencil into my pocket.

As I hurried down the library's main hall, I saw a Blue Shirt approaching from the left. I could feel my heart beating faster and wondered if my fear was obvious to the officer as well. I had hidden the book at home, but I still carried Silas Drummond's desperate note in my bag. Upset with myself for displaying such a reaction to the guard's presence, I tried to cover my surprise with a comment.

"I see someone else is spending the near holidays in the library." I wondered if I sounded as panicked as I felt. *Christiana, get a grip on yourself!* I was surely going to dissolve into helpless fear or giddy giggles. I didn't know which. I only knew I was nearly out of control.

"Yes Ma'am," the blue-shirted Chief Inspector murmured gruffly, tipped his hat, and moved swiftly past me. The clip, clip of his shoes sounded just as rigid as he had appeared.

I exhaled and darted past Frank with a merry smile. "In a hurry—sorry."

"Certainly, My Lady." He glanced up and waved me on.

I panicked again but resisted the urge to run out of the building. My leg muscles ached. I felt as if I were fleeing down a marathon course on the inside, while crawling to the finish line in reality. *Did the Blue Guardsman know me? Do I have to jump and run every time one comes near? Will all of this never end?*

CHAPTER FIFTEEN
The Demitasse

5:30 p.m.

By the time I got to the transit, I felt calm and more in control, until I boarded. I was both amazed and irritated. That strange man who had ridden the bus before and stared at me was still on the bus or maybe he had boarded again. Was I being stalked? The thought made my skin knot in fear. My feet were ready to run while my body was forced to remain still. Finally, I took a front seat where I didn't have to look at him. I tried to clear my mind by thinking about the little shops that flanked the medical complex.

The old books would have called the buildings quaint. I liked that word, and I loved the shops. They reminded me of something I couldn't recall, an old picture, or a description from a romantic novel I had read. Each small shop was slightly different in architectural style and painted an array of colors that fed my spirit. They seemed to greet everyone like assorted bobbles on a charm bracelet. Their ambiance of comfortable steadfastness helped to wipe away the anxiety I had felt in the library and on the transit.

6:00 p.m.

Once at my destination, I smiled with anticipation as I entered the *Demitasse*, the popular coffee shop. I was surprised to see Doctor O'Reilly waiting for me at a corner table.

"You're early." I laughed. "I've finally met a physician who is willing to be kept waiting. It is usually the other way around."

"I was able to leave early." Dr. O'Reilly smiled. He stood and pulled out my chair for me.

I stared at him for a moment. It was unusual to see a man with the old manners most men had forgotten years ago or never had. "Thank you, kind sir." I sat down and wanted to bluster out with question after question. *Tell me about the books. How many have you read? Do you know anything about the Length of Days process?* I decided I had better know a little bit more about the man before I asked too many questions.

"How long have you been here in Capitol City, Dr. O'Reilly?"

Before he could answer, the serving girl came to take our order. My questions had to wait.

"What would you like, Miss Applewait?" Then, he turned to the waitress. "I'd like the steak sandwich and coffee," Jason said.

"Um, I don't think I have eaten all day. I had just a few of my grandmother's fresh baked cookies. That sounds good. I'll have the same." I sat back and looked around the delightful room.

"Right," the serving girl jotted down the order and bustled away.

We dissolved into casual conversation, *small talk,* one of my books called it. It felt natural and comfortable. We packed even the silent parts, while we took time to eat, with a closeness that was growing. I was surprised that I was enjoying myself so much.

"You've had a busy day?" I said as I watched him relax and enjoy his food.

"Very busy," he admitted. "Hospital rounds took longer than usual, which put me behind schedule seeing my office patients. Luckily, the hospital would discharge those there in time for the holidays. But there were a lot of them."

"What with the epidemic and all," I teased, reverting back to the morning's conversation I had with Dahlia in the medical office.

"I wouldn't call it an epidemic in the same sense as an illness or communicable disease. But, Christy ... is *Christy* okay?"

"Sure Jason." I felt comfortable using his first name. He was rapidly becoming more Jason than Dr. O'Reilly.

"It's not like we have an outbreak of an old illness, like influenza, or something. It's ... I probably shouldn't talk about the office."

"You're not talking about your patients. You're talking about the non-epidemic. You don't have to give me their names."

"True," he paused again. "Christy, I am seeing suicidal young people ... so many of them. Medicine had eradicated depression and suicide when they put additives in the drinking water. And, there's another curious thing. All of these young people expressed a fear that I would take them back to their previous feeling level, of flat and bland emotions. They wouldn't consider returning to a life of nothingness. Their new found joy of living was worth the possibility of their death."

"Did they have a wound on their shoulder at their inoculation sight, like I did?" Something inside of me was trying to pull together all of the mysterious threads that were emerging in my life.

"No, they had no complaint of itching or something tearing their clothing. A general exam didn't reveal anything either?" He looked intently at me, a curious expression on his face. "What do you know, Christy? I feel I am getting answers to questions I never knew I was supposed to ask."

I reached in my pocket and pulled out the tissue Jason had given me earlier. "Grand-mère said this small coded particle was not to be removed. She said it was my identification chip that has everything on it, including my DNA code."

"I knew we used to tag people, but I had no idea ..." Jason shook his head. He seemed bewildered. "Why didn't I know that? I'm a physician. I'm sorry, Christiana. I didn't mean to —"

"Jason, I guess I understand your anger. A few hours ago, neither of us knew anything about tagging children nor the true reality of this world in which we live. Of course, a doctor should be told about all aspects of their patients' health, like removing the chip from my shoulder. How would you know how to treat any of us if you had not been trained or informed about the I.D. chips?"

He looked at me as if a few of the missing pieces had suddenly fallen into place. "That's what the pediatricians were talking about." He shook his head. "Why didn't I ask?" He stared out the window in silence for a minute. "I am embarrassed. I should have known. Why didn't I?"

"I think the important question is why did they keep the secret from you? Especially, since you're a Legacy Citi—"

Jason's eyes snapped up to meet mine. He didn't seem angry, just surprised.

His eyes squinted and he smiled quizzically. "Now, how did you find out about that?"

"Grand-mère told me." I lightly touched his hand. "I am sorry. I didn't mean to let your secret out."

"Don't worry about it, Christy," he said as he took my hand in his. "It isn't a secret. It's just something I don't tell people. I'm already treated differently because I'm a doctor. If people knew I was Legacy as well, they would be spreading laurel wreaths in my path. I don't want any part of that."

"I like that in you," I whispered, then wondered if I should have spoken so honestly. Why was I feeling such a strong and immediate attraction to this man? I changed the subject. "Jason, do you think the chip could have other functions besides identification?"

"I don't know, but I'll tell you this, I'm going to find out." Jason picked up his cup and made a face. The coffee had obviously grown cold. He motioned for the server to come and freshen up our cups.

After she left, I whispered, "If the suicidal kids had a missing or damaged chip that might have told us something. You have removed mine, what if I don't have it put back? What effect would that have?"

"I guess you won't be identified. After I gave you the detoxification tablets and you left, Dahlia told me she had found a lot of pills missing. She couldn't tell me exactly how many since we have never dispensed them before, they've just waited there, locked away in storage. We have no idea who could have taken them."

"Why would someone want to go through the detoxification process? What would they get out of it? What do I get out of it? What is this all about, Jason? Should I put the tablets in my water or not? What about you?"

"Since doctors don't prescribe for themselves, I get my detox pills from another physician. I take them. I advise you to take them too. After you've used the packet of tablets I gave you, I'll give you a second amount with a higher dose, gradually increasing the amount, while you slowly detoxify. Think about it. If these kids used the tablets in a non-prescribed way, I have no idea what the outcome would be. They may have taken larger initial doses than they should have."

"One would think that pure water would be a good thing."

"Christy, it is a good thing. But, we're not really sure what is filtered out. Maybe pure water isn't the only goal."

A spark of insight flashed through my mind. "Jason! The antidepressants that are in the water ... maybe the young people are filtering out too much too fast. That may explain the suicide tendencies. They could experience a ricochet of reverberating emotions, bouncing all over the place."

"That is it, Christy! That has to be it. But, why are they using the tablets, and why are they using such a high dose?"

"Well ... what are some of the side effects one would experience with antidepressant medication? The side effects would be gone too." It made sense to me to see what they would gain back, if they eliminated the medication from their system.

"Sex!" Jason whispered excitedly. He had obviously been too loud when others turned to stare. He lowered his voice and added, "Christy! They would get their sex drive back."

"Sex drive? You mean that I'll get a sex drive? Jason O'Reilly, you tell me the truth and you tell me right now." I blushed at the very idea that we were sitting in a quiet coffee shop talking about sex. Not that it was taboo. It wasn't. In fact, no one seemed to care about sex anymore. Maybe the additives in the water were the reason everyone stopped caring.

"Christy, I think you may have hit on the cause of several situations, the etiology of the *epidemic* as you called it and the reason for the low libido in everybody else. As I read the old books, I wondered what they were talking about when they spoke of passion and longing. As I explained, I began my detoxification several years ago, but I was never attracted to anyone before. Now, Christy, with you —"

"Jason, I'm attracted to you too and I've only had one dose of the detoxification tablets. It's all happening so fast." I sat back in my chair but could not take my eyes off his handsome face.

"Maybe, as we detoxify, we become drawn to others who are also medication free, or at least have begun the process. In that way, Legacies are attracted to each other." Jason leaned in even closer. "Did you just say you're attracted to me?" His smile was mischievous and compelling.

There was an amazing excitement I had never experienced before. It made my heart rate increase. I actually thought I was beginning to perspire ... in December!

"Christy?" Jason murmured lowly. He cupped his hand under my chin so my eyes would meet his. His warm smile spread from his eyes across his face.

"Yes, you heard correctly, Dr. O'Reilly." I blushed and then cooled my passion by turning the conversation to the books he had talked about. "Wait a minute. What do you mean you read about passion in the old books? You were going to tell me about those books."

He hesitated. "You switched tracks on me pretty fast that time." Then he smiled, "The books ... okay." He lowered his voice and looked around to see if anyone was close. "I'm feeling a little paranoid talking about the books in public."

"I know what you mean. When I am in the back rooms of the library, I'm afraid someone will come in unexpectedly. I am constantly looking over my shoulder."

"Is that a bad thing? Is the library a dangerous place?"

"The back rooms, the ones all the way down the back hall, are totally off limits to everyone else, except Marge, the curator of old books and documents, and me."

"What's back there, Christy? The Constitution?" Jason smiled as if he had just made a joke. "Christy?"

"Among other things ... yes." I patted his hand, hoping we could move on. "Your books? Let's talk about your books."

"Well, they aren't my books. Maybe ... I guess they are *like* mine," Jason said. "No one else knows they are kept there. That must make them mine. And, I'm the only one who brings them home."

"Home? Jason, where are they?" I needed to know about other collections of books, those outside the library, in case there were books there that I hadn't read.

"Christy, they're in the hospital library. People used to read while they recuperated. I take them home, one at a time, and then return them later. They sealed off that wing of the hospital many years ago. Since it also houses the DNA file banks and bears the Bradford family name, our strongest benefactors by the way, that section remains open, even if it isn't open to the public."

"How many books are in there? What kind? Who are the authors? Can I see them?"

"Slow down, Miss Applewait. Drink your coffee." He wasn't ordering me. It was a tease rather than a command.

I watched Jason closely. There was so much to learn about him. "You know I'm going to see those books eventually, don't you? Sooner or later." Just then the server brought fresh water, and I remembered the little white tablets and took them out of my bag. "Every glass of water?" I asked as I paused over the water before releasing the pill.

"Every glass," he agreed, then smiled mischievously. "And, let's not forget the side effects, or the elimination of them in your case."

I couldn't believe he had just said that. I had only known him half a day. What I had learned so far, I liked. Admittedly, there was an attraction. I had no idea how to handle the new emotions I was feeling, except to avoid them. So, I changed the subject. "Could we go to the hospital library Jason, so I can see the books?"

Jason looked at me and the corners of his blue eyes crinkled softly. "Yes, I guess that would be all right. There wouldn't be anyone in the DNA lab at this time of day, given the upcoming holiday. We can go there from here, if you have the time."

"Do I have the time? I'll carve time out of my imagination if I have to," I laughed. "But I have just one more question." I scanned the room for safety and then whispered, "My grandparents will be seventy-five in a few days. What is the process with the never-ending-sleep?"

He looked surprised that I was asking about the Length of Days law. "The sleep? Everything we have been taught tells us that it is just that. When a person gets to the end of their Length of Days, they are put into a state of perpetual sleep."

He wasn't confirming what Silas said at all. "Where are their bodies then?" I asked.

"There are storage areas for sleepers within some of the mountains around here." He looked at me carefully. "Why the questions?"

"I read some very disturbing information recently. But we can talk about it later." I knew I shouldn't get the note from Silas out of my bag where someone else might see us exchanging something that appeared secretive.

We left the restaurant and stepped out into the wonderful late afternoon air. The wind from the northeast was chilling, so I drew my tunic around me. A light frost crunched under our feet and the aroma of espresso coffee from inside the Demitasse hung on the cold air like perfume from a fine crystal bottle. It was breathtaking and it was December, nearly Gifting Day. Snow would certainly follow in a few days. The Gift-giving season was upon us and I hadn't even noticed the passage of time. In spite of the frost in the air, I felt strangely warm as Jason took my hand in his.

CHAPTER SIXTEEN

Cameras in the Capitol

In the heart of the city, Ward Stoner pushed his way into the Capitol Building and flashed his badge at the guard. His attitude of entitlement to authority was enough to command domination. He stormed past the entry portal, elbowed an elderly woman out of his way and made a straight path back to the Capitol security office.

"Yes Sir," the duty officer jumped up and snapped to attention. He kept his eyes focused forward like the royal guards of old.

"We may have a small glitch in our security around town." Stoner paced back and forth, both impatient and somewhat bored with the smallness of the task. "Only one incident has been reported. It's rather an odd situation. It may be an anomaly but we're not going to error on the side of laziness."

"No, Sir," the duty officer agreed.

Stoner glanced at the guard. The officer's rigid, fixed gaze irritated him. How could he intimidate someone who never blinked? "Someone has accessed a secure area without setting off a buzzer," Stoner sneered. "While the reported incident happened on a transit bus, we are not going to wait until it happens in a more sensitive area. I will be stopping at the courthouse, the banks, the hospital, and the communication headquarters with a system to get things started before the holiday."

The duty office said nothing. He simply maintained attention.

"Are you hearing me, Mister?" Stoner growled, with his face

aggressively thrust out toward the guard.

"Yes, Sir," the security officer shot back with bullet report speed. "The Capitol will be locked up tight during the holiday weekend. No guards will be on duty because no one can get it."

"I'm taking no chances," Stoner snapped. "Then, on December twenty-fifth, while the buildings are closed, I will view the tapes and see if we've caught anything or anyone. The little *swisher* will not get past me."

"The twenty-fifth, Inspector Tomb— ... Stoner? That's the holiday."

"Yes, it is the holiday." Stoner worked his jaw in impatient anger. He had heard the slip and chose to ignore it. "We cannot wait until we have a serious breach of security before we begin investigating."

"Yes Sir."

Stoner pushed the security guard's papers to the corner of the office desk, plopped his bag down in the middle and unzipped it. "I have some old motion sensor video cameras we're going to use to catch this guy."

"Really Sir? Those haven't been used in years." The officer's interest peaked as he studied the camera. Such stop action picture equipment was no longer available.

"No, they haven't. But we have a well-stocked arsenal of weapons and instruments, both new and vintage. We use the best weapon for the kill and in a case like this, one of these. I'll set up a camera here at the portal to the Capitol, a few throughout the building, and at the other major locations I mentioned. I'll put second camera ten yards past the security check to catch anyone we missed with the first images. We will see anyone who walks through the portal, even if we don't hear a buzz. It won't matter if it's an animal, human, or specter."

CHAPTER SEVENTEEN
A Cache of Books

7:30 p.m.

After leaving the café, Jason and I walked across the street to Memorial Hospital where he would sneak us into the private library. It was dark outside by that hour so the building glowed with glittering lights, an oasis in the dimly lit city. By contrast, the other neighborhoods only had an eerie glow, from the energy-efficient, non-heat producing bulbs that cast a pall over the city. The Gifting lights provided a colorful break from the drab.

"You walk in first, Christy," Jason whispered. "I'll follow behind you and we'll meet by the elevators. We'll ride up to the second floor, then get off and walk up two more flights. That way, it won't be obvious that we're going to a closed area of the hospital." Jason kissed my cheek and guided me in through the front door.

In the middle of the open hallway on the main floor, a marble topped information desk and communication station commanded a presence. A pleasant looking, middle-aged woman looked up and smiled as I walked past but since I kept on going, she said nothing. I reached the elevators just as the doors opened. Looking back, I didn't see Jason and didn't know what to do next. Another woman, in a green uniform, stepped onto the elevator and stared at me. "Well, Ma'am, are you coming?" Then she seemed to recognize me and looked away.

Up two floors. I rehearsed Jason's instructions and stepped into the car just as he hurried around the corner and slipped onto the lift. I started to smile, when the woman in the green uniform spoke to him.

"Dr. O'Reilly, why are you here at this hour?" She didn't really look at him but faced forward and watched the floor numbers tick off above the door, as people tend to do who need assurance and control.

"I'll just be a little while," he explained, then stepped to the side as the doors opened on the third floor.

I hesitated. He wasn't getting off.

"Ma'am?" the lady groaned again obviously irritated.

"Oh," I feigned absentmindedly, "sorry."

I stepped off without looking back at Jason, and walked toward the drinking fountain. A moment later, Jason darted through the door that led from the stairwell, out of breath and beaming.

"That was fun!" He whispered hoarsely as he touched my back.

"Jason, what happened?"

"I thought I'd better not make a display of getting off the elevator with you, so I rode up to the next floor, waited to the last second, then pretended I'd been daydreaming and nearly missed my floor. I squeezed out through the closing doors. Right or wrong, it was still exciting." He took my hand and led me back into the stairwell so we could walk up two additional flights. Jason paused at the stairway door, checked to make sure no one was in that wing of the hospital and then eased us silently into the hall. We darted through the double doors to the left and into a darkened passageway. "If we stay close to the wall, we can make our way into the back recesses."

We turned at the next cross hallway. A little beam of moonlight was sneaking in through the window at the end of the hall, just enough to lend light to the next turn. Once around the corner, Jason guided us through a windowless door into a room on the right. "We can turn on the overhead lamps in here. The room is in the heart of the building. None of the walls have outside exposure. No one will look in and see us in here."

"Ah!" I gasped as the lights snapped on. I found myself in a richly veined gold mine of precious books. "Oh Jason, look at all of them." I ran my fingers over the first few shelves and moved on around the room. "How many are there?"

"I don't know. I've never counted them."

"How many have you read?" I saw titles of many wonderful old stories from the last centuries. I had read some of these books before, their words strung together like pearls on a string that created a beautifully crafted work of art. Over the years, the language, attitudes, and vocabulary changed, but in these books the underlying message was always the same: good won over evil, and love was the redeeming and saving emotion of all time.

"There are hundreds of them locked in here," Jason said. "I've had the ability to safely get them out of the hospital, and since I don't have much to do in the evening, I read." Jason's voice trailed off. I thought it might have been a sad testimony to his loneliness. "We shouldn't take too long," he hurried me along "I usually hear a beep if someone comes through that outer door."

"A beep? Someone else said something about a beeping sound as people passed certain points. I haven't heard any tone."

"Oh sure, there's always a sound. You just get used to it after a while." Jason pulled a book from the shelf. "Here's one I like, *Autumn of Love.*" He opened the small leather-bound book and leafed through a few pages and read:

> "Autumn's richest golden days
> held love's promise within their grasp,
> and sending leaves upon the wind,
> whispered, "Death won't win. Love will last."

"Jason," I gasped, amazed at the beauty of the words from lives lived long, with promise and togetherness. "I don't know what to say. I can only feel."

Jason pulled me to him and kissed me tenderly. "I've waited so long," he whispered. I knew what he meant, even though I didn't know I had also been waiting until I found Jason's arms.

He held me close. I could hear the beat of his heart against my chest. I felt safe and at home. I never knew that *first love* would surpass the love I'd read about between the pages of my novels, and the dreams I had dreamed. We lingered in our embrace only a few minutes.

"We'd better go," Jason said. "There are no sensors in this old part of the hospital, but they'll soon be aware that X-number of people came into the building and there are two unaccounted for."

"Sensors? The rest of the hospital has a ... what? Like a census system? They can count people as they come and go in here? Jason you mean they ..."

"They trace our every move, not just in the hospital. There are sensors everywhere." Jason put the book under his jacket and took my arm.

"Then, there are sensors in the library too?"

"Sure, everywhere, except the oldest buildings. There are only three structures that are so old they probably don't think sensors are needed: here in this original hospital wing, the old sections of the library that you're aware of, and the archival rooms of the Capitol."

"Jason that must account for the buzzing noise we set off as we pass. Maybe that is the key. They are numbering the citizens and checking each person's activities."

"Probably. They used to do a census, now I guess we just buzz." He turned off the lights and guided me out of the room.

"Could I borrow some of those books? There have to be some that aren't in my library."

"Sure, we'll come back another day or if you know the title of a particular book or a favorite author, I can pull several from the shelves and bring them to you."

Our whispers hovered in the hall and seemed to echo off the walls. I thought of that buzzing sound again. "You know, when I was in the library this afternoon, they didn't even know I was there. And, the transit driver thought I had to pay. Then, when I went back and picked up my tunic, he apologized. Jason! It finally came to me ... The chip! The chip that you removed from my shoulder was in the pocket of my tunic. When I didn't have the wrap with me, I went about unnoticed. Now, I guess, we know why infants are tagged," I gasped. "Jason, they track our every movement, from the time we're born until we reach the end of our days. The DNA code etched in our chip lets them know exactly where we are and who we are. It's like we have an old-fashioned easy pass at a highway toll booth permanently implanted in our bodies."

Jason gripped my arm as we stood in the dim hallway. "Don't raise your voice Christy. It was all done in the name of national security. I read about that era, when the revolution of the masses overthrew the rights of the individual." Jason looked beyond the corner of the hallway before we slipped around and into the final hall. "If you're going to have mass rule, you better be prepared to live with mob control. That's us. People aren't living lives of freedom, to pursue our loftiest individual plans," he whispered. "We exist on the lowest plane possible for all to attain, the level of mediocrity through chemical control."

Just then I recognized the double doors at the end of the hall. "Here we are," I said with great relief.

"Wait," Jason spoke softly. "Come here," he smiled.

He kissed me tenderly, sweetly and looked into my eyes. "You're amazing, Christy."

"Jason, I don't even know how to express all the new feelings I'm experiencing. There are no words left in our meager vocabulary."

"The old novels expressed it well," he reminded me.

I knew authors would have used words like *thrilling* and *desire,* but I hesitated. "I know, but I don't think I have the courage to use those words yet."

"You have more courage than you know, Christy," Jason assured me. I wondered if his words would still be right, over the long course that lay ahead of us.

There was one thing I was sure of. This feeling between us could be the kind of love that lingers and lasts, the kind of love that lives are built on—the kind of never-ending love that lasts beyond our present Length of Days.

CHAPTER EIGHTEEN
Stoner's Encounter

After leaving the Capitol, one of Tombstone Stoner's next stops was the hospital. Ever since his Miriam died, he didn't like anything about the place, especially the antiseptic odor that permeated through the never-ending halls of deceptively beautiful marble. It smelled corruptly clean—like all the life had been scrubbed out with a substance so strong it stung his eyes. He shuddered and moved past the front desk into the wide hallway to the right. He knew where the records' office was. Not the current patients' charts. Those electronic documents were at the nurse's station located near each room. The official records' office held information on discharged, discarded, and deceased patients and the necessary data on each citizen to determine their Length of Days.

Stoner knew that each citizen had credits—factors that make them more valuable—that added to their Length of Days, to calculate the exact birthday at which they would enter the never-ending-sleep. In addition, a health record was maintained to determine the viability of each citizen unit. His Blue Guard training also emphasized that every damage to the body was itemized with a specific point value, and the running total was maintained until it reached twenty-five points. Defective persons were eliminated, just like pre-birth masses that needed no points to justify their termination. The family was notified to bring the unwanted and useless to the sleep chamber at an appointed hour. If they failed to show up, a squad of Blue Guardsmen was sent to bring them in. Stoner's mind raced and tumbled with all the faces of those he had forced into the limousine that took them to the sleep center. His head swam a little and he thought he was going to be sick.

Shake it off Stoner! What were those people to you? Then another voice echoed in his head. *But she was.*

"Yes Sir, may I help you?" A nurse in a white uniform with a round, pleated nurse's cap, approached the inspector.

"No," Stoner snapped when he glanced at her cap. "I want to see your supervisor." Ward Stoner dealt only with the person in charge, no matter where he was.

"Yes, Sir. Certainly."

A woman wearing a smooth, white, nurse's cap with a black band along the upper edge—identifying her as the head nurse—came out of the inner room. "Inspector, what may I do for you?"

"I'm here to place a camera in the records' office. Please lead the way." Short and to the point, Stoner used no more words than were necessary.

"A camera, Sir? I don't understand"

"You don't have to understand, Nurse," he responded gruffly. "Understanding isn't a requirement for you to lead me to the records office."

"This way, Inspector." The nurse's tone showed little respect, but she led the way and said no more. They walked silently to the elevator, rode down to the lower level, and proceeded along the corridor. "May I ask if there has been a problem that we're unaware of?"

"No, you may not," Stoner snapped. "This is a precaution. The files must be protected. Without each citizen record, we wouldn't be able to administer the never-ending-sleep fairly."

"Yes Sir, the endless sleep. We must know exactly when we can legally kill someone, mustn't we?"

Stoner was outraged. He gripped his fists to control his temper. "Hold your tongue, Nurse. We are very fair. You should know that a common cold doesn't carry any point values unless a pattern of chronic upper-respiratory distress becomes evident. Only then is each additional incident noted in the patient's records. That, combined with other indicators, determines the health of an individual. That seems quite fair. I'm sure you'll agree."

"Yes Sir," she reported dryly.

"Nurse, furthermore, it's only the loss of a limb during an accident, or blindness that could automatically reduce a citizen's Length of Days to age twenty-five," Stoner scolded. "You know, if there is compelling evidence of a citizen's ability to contribute to society, well above any financial drain caused by their injuries, their Length of Days can be reinstated with a proper court hearing. Surely, you learned that only a coma of more than three days, or a back injury that results in paralysis, could trigger an immediate placement in the sleep chamber." Stoner gritted his teeth in anger. "I fail to see why I'm explaining myself to you."

"Here we are, Sir. I'll be happy to help you further if needed," the nurse offered as they came to the records room.

"No, Nurse. Just leave. Silence will be the only help I require."

Stoner quickly installed the camera facing the entrance to the large humidity-controlled vault-like records office and slammed the door closed. He didn't look back. He was glad to get out of that dreary place.

Stoner took the elevator down and had stepped off near the lobby entrance when he heard shouting. As he rounded the corner, he ran into a gang of five young men who were waving old, last century, guns in the air. Laughing and stumbling over one another, they were behaving in a strange and hysterical way.

"Look, Benny," one of them laughed as he pointed his weapon at Stoner. "We found us a little soldier boy."

"Get that thing out of my face," Stoner ordered with a controlled, calm voice.

"Whoa, man, listen to the little chief," one of the other young thugs yelled. "You tell one of the nurses, they'd better get us some of those little white pills or we'll find them ourselves," he shouted.

"You've had enough pills already, Mister. I'm going to give you the greatest Gift-giving present you will ever receive. I'll give you a chance to leave this hospital under your own power," Stoner barked.

To Stoner's instant analysis, the men appeared to be intoxicated. Stoner had no idea how that was possible, since alcohol and most other substances were controlled. There had been rumors of a huge increase in the production of an old substance called moonshine. What he saw before him was an out of control mob, of out of control young men, who continued to wave guns erratically in the air and shout obscenities and taunts to everyone who came near. They obviously had no respect for the authority of the Chief Inspector of the Blue Guard and that was intolerable to Stoner. When the young thugs didn't run, he pulled his sting ray from its holster, aimed, and fired in rapid, Gatling gun fashion, sending laser point shots of contact-anesthetic directly into their faces. All five dropped where they stood.

"Clean this mess up," Stoner barked at the head nurse as he stepped over the body of one of the young men. He resisted an impulse to kick him in the ribs.

"But Sir," she responded with an expression of bewilderment and fear. "What do we do with them? Can't you arrest them?"

"Scan them for their names, addresses, and contact information while they're still out. You'll be able to get closer to them while they're still unconscious. When they wake up, if they can get themselves under control, send them home to their mamas for the holidays. If they give you even the slightest resistance, call security and the Blue Guard will put them in jail for the holidays, and they'll stay there until the courts reopen."

"But Sir," she tried to protest, "we are used to caring for people in a near comatose state. Most people are in their own world of mumble thinking. We've had little preparation for handling erratic, uncontrolled patients."

"Are you saying you're not up to your job's requirements, Nurse?" Stoner growled.

"No, Sir. I am not saying that at all."

Stoner turned crisply, leaving the nurse standing in the hallway with the anaesthetized bodies of five drooling young men at her feet. As Stoner rounded the corner, he saw a young woman push through the doors of the adjacent hallway.

Well, well, the same female again ... or she's one of the triplets I've been seeing around town all day. He slipped back around the corner and waited for her to pass. *Now, why is she ahead of me everywhere I go?*

CHAPTER NINETEEN
Dahlia's Secrets

8:30 p.m.

Jason and I had slipped cautiously through the large double doors into what appeared to be an empty outer hall of the hospital. We had been in the off-limits library, but were still not totally out of danger of apprehension. I thought I had heard noises coming from that area but now I only heard Jason sigh deeply. It must have been a situation around the corner, in the adjacent hall. I wanted to get out of there.

Jason motioned that it was clear to come out. "I'll take the stairway and you go down on the elevator," he whispered. "If there's a problem, I'll meet you back at the coffee shop."

Jason moved silently to the doors that led to the stairwell and disappeared. I stood there for a moment then pressed the down button for the lift. My stomach tightened with a growing awareness of the danger we were in. My thoughts went to Silas Drummond's note. Surely, he had lied. All that he described was so grotesque and beyond my mind's ability to take in; it couldn't possibly be true.

"Lady Applewait," Dahlia called to me as I stepped from the elevator car on the first floor, still wrapped in my concern over Silas's warning. "You're here late," she smiled as she came toward me.

I thought fast. "Just doing some research for someone and then realized that I didn't really have the time." I looked at my watch, hoping Dahlia would recognize the social cue to move on. "I'm to meet someone at the Demitasse."

"Really? I love that place. I've finished teaching a seminar and I'm ready to leave. I'll walk over with you." Dahlia didn't wait for a response but fell into step beside me. Her manner was strikingly different from the morning's encounter in the office.

I saw Jason start to emerge through the stairway door. He stopped and turned to descend the next staircase to the lower level of the hospital. Neither of us was ready to be seen together. We had only been *together* for a matter of hours and had no idea ourselves, where it would all lead, if anywhere.

I didn't look back as we darted across the damp streets. It hadn't been raining, but a fine December mist had settled over the pavement beyond the brightly lit hospital. The water drainage system under the heated streets evaporated moisture as soon as it landed on the pavement, leaving only a wet glaze that sparkled in the holiday lights. The night had grown cold. We moved quickly into the coffee shop and claimed the last remaining booth by the front windows.

"May I join you until your friend arrives?" Dahlia questioned as she slid onto the bench seat.

"Sure." What else could I have said? She was already seated. I knew that Jason wouldn't come in if he saw his nurse with me. Too many questions spoil the mystery. I was glad we had found a table in the front, close to the window. Jason would be able to see us before he came in. But, how was I going to politely get rid of her?

"You look tired," I began. "Did you have a busy day ... more than usual? I know you're always busy." I tried a professional tactic.

"Yes, very. Even the mammas with the little kids seemed more stressed than usual. One said she had been herding chickens all day."

"More of those suicides and attempted self-annihilations?" I kept my voice low so the people around us couldn't hear, but clearly enough so Dahlia would know I intended to pursue my line of conversation.

"Suicides?" Dahlia gasped in a hushed voice.

"Yes, Dahlia," I lowered my voice to a crisp whisper, "suicides."

"People don't suicide anymore," she denied.

"Most don't, but there is a growing epidemic of young people who are taking their own lives. It's a strange topic for all of us, Dahlia. Most people have never even heard the term, suicide."

"How do you know what it's called?" Dahlia wasn't asking. She seemed surprised that I knew.

"As a Legacy Citizen, I've begun to delve into the wisdom of the ages, to immerse myself in the history of our people." I pressed on. "Suicide is a sin, Dahlia."

"A what?" Dahlia's eyes frantically scanned the room.

"A sin, you know. It's against Devine law." I heard myself saying words I didn't know that I knew, much less understood. "Life is precious, Dahlia. It's a gift."

"A gift from whom?" She whispered incredulously. "Like a Gift-giving present? A gift implies a giver."

I tried to appear relaxed, but I was a witness, bearing testimony about someone I didn't even know. Dahlia was asking *who*, not as an inquisitor, but as a seeker, and I had no answers for her. I had hoped our conversation would cause her to leave but instead she stayed, and it made me want to flee. "There are things I'm not at liberty to talk about Dahlia." I saw the disappointment in her eyes. "We'll talk about it when we can. This isn't the best place" I picked up my bag and started to leave. If she wasn't going to move, I would have to.

"No, Miss Applewait, I'll go. You're waiting for someone." Dahlia drank from the water glass the waitress had placed in front of her and added, "Don't forget your detox pill."

I saw Jason cross the street just as Dahlia stood up. Behind him, two blue guard officers pushed past him and entered the restaurant. The room hushed as the men slowly scanned each table.

"Wonder who they're looking for." Dahlia whispered nervously.

"Dahlia, you're afraid? Of what?"

"I'm always nervous when the Blue Shirts show up and lately, I've seen them more often."

"Why are you afraid? If you've done nothing—"

"There's a group of people that ..." she stopped as the guards came closer to our table.

"What group? Dahlia, what's wrong?"

"Hush," Dahlia begged as she looked down at her water glass and avoided the men who drew closer with each step.

I asked no more as the officers stopped at our table and eyed Dahlia as she slumped and pulled her coat around her. I raised my chin and confidently looked at them both. "Good evening officers. It's a beautiful night isn't it?"

"Yes, Ma'am," one of them mumbled and then they moved on.

"They're gone," I nudged Dahlia on the sleeve. "What is wrong? What group were you talking about?"

"I can't talk now." She jumped up to leave just as Jason entered. I didn't want them to meet at the door so I touched Dahlia's arm to turn her away from the windows.

"Yes, Dahlia, not now, but we'll talk more later. It sounds like we both have some information that needs sharing. I'm just not ready to talk and it seems you're not either."

"Thanks. Lately it seems, I've had the feeling there's more, and I don't even know what there is *more* of. Those of us in my group are aware of ... something. I sense a change in you, Miss Applewait. You know what I'm talking about even if I don't." Dahlia sat back down on the edge of her chair and spoke quietly. "Miss Applewait—"

"Please, Dahlia, call me Christiana. Very few people do, you know. Even in school I was Miss Applewait. Since I am Legacy, I was set apart. And, please talk to me when you see me in the apartment building. I may be in my own world, but you are welcome there." I touched her arm to reassure her of my sincerity. Then I thought, *Legacy people don't touch others, and they aren't contacted in return.* The old rules now sounded strange.

"Yes, Christiana," she said with a tremble in her voice. "I would love to sit down with you soon. Maybe we can talk about the *knowing* that's inside of you sometime over the Gift giving Holidays?" Her voice was pleading as she touched my hand.

"Yes, that would be nice."

"There's a fresh glow in your face, Christiana. When little Hector Montoya fell down the stairs and broke his leg, you showed love and compassion for him. Most people just accept the inevitable."

"Maybe the inevitable doesn't have to be the inescapable."

"My great-grandmother used to say, 'Bless you child,' and for some reason that seems to fit. Bless you, Christiana Applewait."

I watched as Dahlia stepped out into the night. The serving woman came over to the table, paused and stared at me.

"Are you staying?" she asked and slouched with a hand on her hip. "Do you want to order?"

"She will have a cup of cocoa and a glass of water." Jason touched my shoulder as he sat down opposite me. "And I'll have cocoa too. Oh, sorry, do you want anything to eat?"

"I don't think so."

Jason sat back and waited until the serving girl walked away. "How did you do with Dahlia? Did she ask too many questions?"

"No, she didn't ask much. She started to tell me about a group of friends. Two blue guardsmen came in, and she became really frightened." Christiana paused as the server put the hot chocolate before us.

"Friends? What was she talking about?"

We paused again as the server placed spoons and napkins on the table, then left. Jason repeated, "What friends?

"I don't know. It sounded like a spiritual quest she had recently embarked on. Then she brought up the friends and quickly stopped."

"Spiritual?" Jason covered his mouth with his hand and whispered into his palm so no one could read his lips. "Like, in God?"

"God?" My words were nearly inaudible. "Do you know about God?" I couldn't believe what I was hearing. To speak the name of the deity of old was forbidden years ago.

"Christiana ... we haven't known each other very long. I'm afraid

I'm dragging you into dangerous —"

"It's all right Jason. If you hang, I'll hang right there beside you. They would need two executioners. Besides, our punishment would not be severe, since we're ... well, you know. We would be in a reeducation program." We kept our voices low, but my excitement was hard to conceal. "Tell me Jason, what do you know about God?"

"I have a book." Jason hesitated, but I wouldn't let him stop.

My breath caught in my throat. I was nearly unable to speak. Then I whispered, "Is it ... black?" Could it possibly be that Jason had a copy of Grand-père's book?

"Yes, it's black. It has letters on the front." He paused as if he were gathering permission to say the words. "It says, Holy Bible."

"Where did you get it?" I could feel my heart race to embrace the words I longed to hear again. How could Jason have a Bible?

"I found it in the hospital library. I had never heard anything about a Bible book, so I didn't know what it was." His eyes shone as he talked. "When I read it, Christy, it was like truth had been unfolded in my soul. I don't know how, but I knew. I just knew."

"I know what you mean, and I haven't even started reading it. I have a copy of that Bible book, Jason. I just got it today. It had been Grand-père's. He gave it to me since I've come of age, and they are nearing the end of their Length of Days. He said the Bible book had to be passed on, to be kept safe." I studied his face. I was feeling strangely empowered. Somewhere, in an old text, the haunting words, *and the truth will set you free,* echoed in my mind. But, what truth? Silas' truth ... or had he lied? If he hadn't, how safe was all this talk of forbidden books and old truths? I was learning that truth had power, but I didn't know what truths would be found. Should I drag Jason into all of this? Could I trust him with things I didn't know about ... yet?

CHAPTER TWENTY
Chalky Boone

Over in a part of town Christiana rarely visited, Ward Stoner charged into the headquarters of the Blue Guard, ignoring the Desk Sargent's, "Evening Inspector," as he dashed to his office. Chief Inspector Stoner was in his own world of anger with a purpose. *Why do I have to micro-manage this unit?* He sank into his desk chair and snapped around to look out the window. He saw no holiday lights or happy shoppers scurrying about the city looking for a special Gifting surprise for their loved one. In his wounded spirit, he saw greedy children trying to drain another precious dollar from their overworked parents. Through his own anger and pain, he saw overindulgent parents who wanted to pile presents under the Gift-giving tree to buy the love of their selfish children.

Chalky Boone, Stoner's first assistant, poked her head around the corner of the half-opened door. "Is there anything I can do for you, Boss?"

"No," he snapped and then asked. "Where is everybody? The place looks empty."

"Some people had put in for vacation days months ago, Boss." Her comment was an over the shoulder afterthought as she started to go back to her desk.

"Chalky," he shouted after her, "bring me the daily roster."

There was never a *please*. To Stoner's mind, *please* implied a request. He was not asking for anything. He was giving an order and that didn't warrant *please* or *thank you* for having done what was expected in the first place.

"Here you are, Sir." Chalky smiled and laid the file on her boss's desk. After working for Stoner for several years, she had skin as thick as tanned hide, though it masqueraded as young and supple.

The Inspector didn't look up but reached roughly for the file. Only a handful of the guard was listed for that day. Perhaps because the roster was so sparse, one item, that would have been buried in the dearth of other activity, glared at Stoner. A special contingent of guard was working that day. It mocked at him from the page. There were far more guardsmen on the streets than he had scheduled. He certainly had not ordered a special detachment of personnel. One, two, there were five men at work that day, locations unknown. Beside their name were the words, *Confidential Assignment.*

"What's this?" Stoner yelled as he jumped to his feet. "Boone!" he shouted to anyone beyond his office door. It didn't matter to him who responded.

"Yes, Sir," Chalky stuck her head around the door again, but this time her manner seemed apprehensive.

"What is this ... this *Confidential Assignment,* some arrogant joke?" His eyes flared with the fire of rekindled anger.

"*Confidential Assignment,* Inspector?" Chalky Boone eased carefully into the gladiator's arena with nothing but her fountain pen to protect herself from the lion.

"I have brought the most modern law enforcement equipment into this office," Stoner bellowed. "Aren't our people outfitted with the latest in light weight, oxford cloth upper torso body armor that wears like your favorite shirt? Didn't I fight for and get the best communication device on the market, the Tiny Fleck, a radio and transmitter so small it can look like your Lodge pin or your favorite tie tack your mama gave you as a Gift-giving present? Even the communications implant was my idea."

"Yes Sir," Chalky Boone responded hesitantly to the obvious questions with the not so obvious meaning under the spoken words.

"Then, will you please tell me how we can have an elite, clandestine unit of Blue Guard ..." he paused as the anger rose in his chest and threatened to choke all breath from his raging body ... "which I command!" He seethed ... "And yet, I know nothing about it?" His voice rose and landed on the ground at Boone's feet.

Chalky Boone was usually able to handle his tirades. This time, Stoner's behavior was different. That day, he was the epitome of that which he loathed, a man out of control. Boone could see it in his eyes. "Sir, let's look at the entire week's schedule and see if a pattern emerges that will explain the mystery."

Boone returned quickly with a 281 Palm Device and set it on Stoner's desk. She flipped it on. The picture glowed like a hologram before his eyes. "There," she pointed to the names, "Shiloh Perkins, C.A. ... Clause Zunstein, C.A. ... and there and there. Sir, all five guardsmen were scheduled to work a confidential assignment all of last week. Have they been working undercover?"

"How the blazes would I know!" He shouted. "I'm just the commander. It looks like someone else is giving orders as well." He glared at Chalky for a long minute. Then he grabbed his hat again.

"I'll let it ride for today, Boone, given the season and all. But I'll find out what's going on. You can bet your future on that. And when I do, some careers will fall like downed timber, with a mighty crash." He stormed back out into the world of holiday lights. But, inside him, the only sparkle came from the fire that continued to rage within.

CHAPTER TWENTY-ONE

Christmas – a Word from the Past

9:30 p.m.

Jason and I stepped out of the coffee shop, back into the clear evening air. It was cold. I could feel snow trying to move in on the city.

"I'll drive you home, Christy." Jason motioned to a car parked by the curb.

Jason had an individually owned motor vehicle! I slid into the sleek black car and felt guilty, guilty because an automobile ride was for only a few of Society's most valued citizens. Physicians, police, and those on the fire department couldn't wait for Public Transit before responding to an emergency. It wouldn't be quite so tragic if the fire or robbery was at a low-producing citizens' home. But what if the emergency were in the home of an official of the government or other professional person? Delay wouldn't be tolerated. I shuddered as I heard myself justifying such elitist thoughts. Why were some lives considered more important than others?

I understood Jason's need for a car. As a physician, he expected emergencies, and his car had to in top condition.

"This is nice." I ran my fingers over the hand-sewn leather of the expensive vehicle. "It must be nice to drive such a car."

"Yes, it is," Jason said. "Since they make so few automobiles, the old production lines are a thing of history. Cars are now hand-made, one at a time? If the government didn't subsidize the exorbitant price, I wouldn't be able to afford it."

We drove through the late evening streets where lights twinkled off the glassy surface of the damp pavement. "Oh Jason, just look at the Gifting lights. They are breathtaking. I hadn't even noticed so many of them had been put up."

"They just finished them late this afternoon. We've both been a little busy today."

How could the evil that Silas described possibly exist alongside such beauty? The poor man was mad.

"It's in the next block." I motioned to the large apartment complex on the right. "You can park out front since you're a doctor and I'm ... well, all that and ... never mind ... right there."

Jason parked in the emergency vehicle space and then reached over and took my hand. "You apparently don't like to refer to yourself as *Legacy* either."

"Jason, you're no different. You hide behind your physician's white coat and no one knows you're Legacy." I stopped. I didn't want to be rude or start an argument. "I'm sorry."

"You can flash those gorgeous hazel eyes at me any time." He took a deep breath and looked out the window. "I've read a lot, Christy. I've discovered that no one is better than anyone else. We are all precious in the heart of the Creator." He looked at the brightly decorated tree in the small space in front of the building. "The lights are great though. I enjoy the Gifting season when everything is bright and full of celebration."

"That's why I enjoy this season so much too. I wonder who started the tradition of lights at Gifting time? I have never even thought about it before." Suddenly, with Jason, I was seeing everything in new ways, and my curiosity was mounting about everything around me.

"The lights may have begun with the Sabbath lights around the Jewish family's evening table. Certainly, from what I have read, there was a light from Heaven that shown the night the Christ child was born. That star led believers to a humble manger in Bethlehem; no doubt that is what inspired the lights at Gift-giving time."

"The Christ, Jason? Who or what is the Christ?" I had never

heard that name before.

"He was the promised one, Christy. You'll read about him in the new section of your Bible." He smiled. "The Gift-giving lights are also reminiscent of the lighted tapers in the churches of old, which represented the presence of the Holy Spirit. Look over there at the house across the way," he whispered as if the inhabitants would hear us talking about them. "Those folks are like our early ancestors who put up a tree in their home and decorated it with bright bulbs. See them twinkle," he pointed. "A very long time ago, before people had old fashioned electrical lighting, families carefully placed candles on each branch and lit them only on Christmas Eve. Fire could have taken the tree and the whole house, but the candle light was too beautiful to miss out on."

"Christmas Eve?" I had read about Christmas in some of the novels I cherished the most, but I was surprised to hear the words spoken aloud. The word *Christmas* was forbidden, because it was too exclusive to one group and therefore offensive to a few. "In my books, everyone seemed so happy at Christmas time, so full of love and acceptance." A strange feeling gripped me. The stars of the night were lighting the dark places in my heart. Tears flowed down my cheeks. As I touched my face, Jason pulled me into his arms.

"It's all right Christy. Those are tears."

"Tears? I've never cried before. And I'm not sad. I don't think I have ever been sad enough to cry."

"There were other reasons why people used to cry besides sadness. In fact, joy could bring some people to tears. Also, touch by the heart of God brought many people to tears."

"God's own heart? The Creator is like us? He has a heart?"

"We're like him, Christy, but he is not like us. He's bigger and more wonderful than our minds can ever understand. He is outside of time and outside of our ability to fully know him. If we could understand him, we would be God and ... trust me, we are not God."

We sat there a few more minutes. I didn't want to go in. Everything was so new. It was hard to bend my mind around such strange, unheard of shapes and concepts. I wanted to talk more but, what would people say if I brought Jason into my living space? I thought for a minute and it didn't seem to matter what other people thought any more. Not since ...   Could it be possible that things started to change just this morning? "Jason, do you want to come in for a little while?" Then I remembered, "Jason, your nurse Dahlia lives in my building."

"Maybe we won't see her," Jason laughed.

Even with the cold outside, it was nice in the quiet of the car. I squeezed Jason's hand and felt his warmth. "You follow behind me and I'll check the hallway, but I have to tell you, I'm on the top floor. If no one is in the lobby, there may still be people in the elevator."

"I'm game. I can handle another adventure tonight."

We started to get out of the car. "Wait here." Jason jumped out and walked around the car, opened the door for me and offered his hand to help me to the sidewalk. "My Lady," he smiled.

"Wow, what book did you read that in?"

"None. My father always treated my mother with that kind of respect. He held her chair for her, walked on the curb side of the sidewalk when they were out for a stroll, held her hand, and opened the door for her."

"They remind me of my family, my parents, and especially my grandparents." We hurried along to the front door. The night air was chilled and frost had gathered on the front steps. "Do your parents live here in town?"

"No, Christy, they died two years ago. They were driving in the mountains and the road was icy. They slipped off the pavement and died in the crash."

"Oh, I'm so sorry," I said.

I looked through the large heavy glass window of the front door and saw no one in the hall. As Jason opened the door, I wanted to say words of comfort, but I had no experience to guide me. "Jason, I'm not good at this *feeling* stuff, but I am truly sorry you lost your parents so early. They were Legacy and would have lived long lives."

"Thanks Christy," he smiled.

Few people in 2112 even remembered feeling words. But it didn't matter. The people had no empathy for one another by then.

"The shock has passed," he reassured me, "but the love remains. I miss them every day." He smiled. "I'm glad I found you." The touch of his hand, held warmth that had the power to melt my own loneliness.

CHAPTER TWENTY-TWO
The First Christmas Carols

10:00 p.m.

Jason and I looked through the heavy glass windows in the door to my apartment building. When we saw no one between the door and the elevator, we went in. Then we heard them. To the left of the brightly lit entry, a few people had gathered around the piano.

Jason rolled his eyes in surrender. "Caught," he mouthed.

Dahlia smiled from across the room. She looked like she had just gotten an inside joke or secret. "Doctor," she sang out, "and My Lady." She started over toward us. "Sorry. I remember. It's Christiana." As she came nearer, she threw her arms open as an old friend would prepare to embrace a childhood chum.

"I'm glad to see you two again ... together." She flung her arms around me and hugged me as a friend. "Does *together* have a different meaning for Legacy Citizens than it does for us common people?"

She touched me. It felt good. Except for my family, and now Jason, I was never in close contact with others. People could be arrested for touching me.

"I'm glad to see you too, Dahlia." I looked at my new friend and then at Jason. "Please Dahlia, don't ..."

"I don't tell people everything I know, and nothing of what I suspect." She hugged me again, then stepped back and whispered, "Merry Christmas."

"Dahlia, you know? How?" Jason seemed as surprised as I was. We knew there were only a few Bible books still in existence.

"Yes, Dr. O'Reilly, I know a little bit. I was hoping Christiana could teach me more."

"Me? But, Dahlia, I'm just learning myself."

"But there's something inside of you, Christiana. You glow from within. He's alive in you."

I was shocked, "Who, Dahlia?"

"Come accompany us, Dahlia, so we can sing some more," someone called from the piano.

"They look like they're having so much fun." I watched the people laugh and touch and be together. I had never seen people interact like that before, except for my own family.

"Would you like to join us? We're going to sing more Christmas songs."

"Dahlia, it's forbidden. Aren't you afraid?"

"Not anymore," Dahlia took my hand and led me over to the piano. "Christiana, there are a lot of us now. This is the group I told you about."

"Is Silas Drummond with you tonight?"

"Silas? No. He works nights, but I haven't seen him all day. There were some Blue Shirts in here looking for him earlier."

"Blue Shirts? Why?"

"I don't know. They said he wasn't at work at 3:00 as usual."

I gasped as I thought of Silas's warning. What was going on?

"How many are in your group?" Jason asked. He seemed mystified by the gathering. He didn't yet know about Silas.

Could it be possible that there were many seekers? How could a new spiritual revival have gone undetected by anyone, especially the Blue Guard?

"I can't give you numbers right now, but there are a lot of us who celebrate Christmas rather than Gift-giving Day. The number grows all the time."

"How do you know it's safe to talk about these things? If new people are joining your group every day, how do you know whom you're talking to? Maybe you'll say something and someone will turn you in." Jason was concerned for Dahlia as a friend, not just an employee. Authorities could arrest and jail her.

"We ..." she studied us both very carefully, "we have a way of identifying each other."

"Can you tell us how?" Jason smiled and placed a kind hand on her shoulder. "I really want to know, Dahlia."

"Two ways," she whispered. "First, we say, 'I'm Thomas's friend,' since Thomas doubted until he saw the Savior's hands with his own eyes. We have been in darkness, too. Then we were told a great mystery, which many of us didn't believe at first. But then the truth grew within us, and we knew, we just knew."

"Dahlia," the singer called again.

"Okay, I'm coming," she laughed and walked away.

"Dahlia, what's the other way?" We followed her as she joined the group.

Dahlia smiled at us and pressed her index finger to her lips. "Come join us."

"I don't know any songs," I protested. Few people sang any more. There never seemed to be anything to sing about, no romance, no disappointment, no longing or striving, no inspiration. Besides, they banned most music.

"I've heard you humming when you've stepped off the elevator," Dahlia insisted.

"I have heard you, too," the man from the bus chimed in.

"Do you live here?" I knew I recognized him from the P-T that morning, but I hadn't been aware of having seen him before that. I stepped closer to Jason and took his arm.

"No, I don't live here but I saw you at the university when we were both working on our Master's degrees," the man smiled a knowing smile, like he knew me better than I knew him.

A shiver ran up my spine, and I wondered what else I hadn't been aware of.

"What's your name?" Jason asked.

"I'm sorry. My name is Sean." He offered his hand in friendship, an archaic display of nonviolence, known for spreading germs. I reached out my hand and took his. It was warmer and friendlier than I expected. I liked the gesture. "I got my graduate degree in Communications Journalism." Then he stopped abruptly, cautious but confident. He lowered his voice and whispered, "Dahlia said you two can be trusted." He paused and looked from Jason to me. "I ... publish an underground newspaper."

"A newspaper? I've heard of those," I gasped.

"Where did you hear of a newspaper?" Sean asked suspiciously. Newspapers had been abandoned nearly a hundred years ago when other forms of fast news dissemination flooded the market.

I thought for a moment. "I read about them."

"Come," Dahlia took my arm and led me to the group near the piano. "There is music in your soul, Christiana. Everyone can sing, at least in their own way. Even the angels in Heaven communicate through song."

Angels? My mind was overflowing. I had read about angels and about people who sang when they were happy and sang when they were sad. I had even seen the words of Christmas songs printed on pages of song books I had read, but I had never heard the melodies or felt them resounding in my mind. I didn't know their meaning.

"Your heart will recognize the tunes," Dahlia assured us.

She sat at the piano and ran her fingers up and down the keys, chord upon beautiful chord. I wondered where she had learned how to play.

Obviously, I had seen the piano in the corner of the gathering room before and never gave it further attention. Why had I not wondered about it before? If they banned music, why was there still a musical instrument in the building? Then I remembered what the building manager had said. She had described it as a work of art. Maybe the manager was right in her thinking but only partially. She may have confused the instruments of music with objects of art, like sculpture or paintings. She had said, "Isn't it a beautiful piano?" like it was a fine art statue. How very strange. For a hundred years, people had rejected the sound but not the form.

It was a wonderful evening of music—Christmas carols Dahlia had called them. We sang about a baby who slept in a manger because there was no room for him in the Inn. Angels sang alleluias from the heavens to announce his birth and to glorify God for his precious gift, just like Jason had described. Dahlia was right. The music went deep within me and then streamed forth from the depths of my soul, and ... I knew, but I didn't yet know that I knew.

CHAPTER TWENTY-THREE
Forbidden Singing Heard

Out on the streets, people were going in for the night. As Stoner drove through neighborhoods, he noticed a small group of people sitting on the steps of an apartment building, talking. If he had the capacity for enjoyment, Stoner would have appreciated the solitary quietness of the evening as he drove around the city in the frosty air. Sometimes, he just had to get away from people. For someone who worked with the public every day, he had a growing disdain for most everyone. The truth was, he didn't like himself much. He could only tolerate a short amount of alone-time. He was not his own best company.

The long evening hours had been uneventful, so the silent vibration of his communication device startled him. He tilted his head slightly as a voice spoke quietly in the ear piece buried beneath his skin near the bone behind his ear. "Inspector, I hate to bother you. Your location indicator places you near Indian River Apartments."

"I just passed it," Stoner spoke into the emptiness of the night.

"It's the craziest thing. Someone has reported that they heard singing coming from the building?" the dispatcher reported.

"Singing? You're kidding, right?"

"No, Sir," she apologized.

"Singing was banned a long time ago. No one has sung in nearly a century. How would they know how? Who knows any songs?"

"I don't know, Sir. I'm sorry to have bothered you."

"No, Dispatch. I don't know how they're singing, but I'll check on it." The very thought of music assaulted his ears. Stoner made a U-turn and headed the few blocks back to the Indian River Apartments.

He didn't hesitate. He parked his strata-car in front of the building and stormed to the entrance. He thrust open both double doors and burst into the apartment building lobby. In the large gathering room to the left, a group of people were sitting around on sofas or chairs, and a few were casually lounging on the floor. A piano art piece was present but no one was trying to play it. Who could have? It seemed to Stoner, they were apparently listening to a speaker who was leading them in a chant of some sort.

> "Spending money carefully,
>   my responsibility.
>   Gifting Day is nearly here
>   Raise a cup and shout a cheer.
> Hip, Hip, Hay! Hip, Hip Hurrah!
> Happy, happy, Gifting Day,
>   When I spend up all my pay
>   giving gifts to everyone,
>   is my duty and my fun.
> Hip, Hip, Hay! Hip, Hip, Hurrah!"

"Very good everyone, we ..." the speaker stopped when she saw the inspector who stood listening impatiently. "May I help you, Sir?"

"There was a report that singing was heard coming from this building," he snapped.

"Singing, Sir?" Dahlia questioned. "Song was banned a long time ago. Most people wouldn't even know how to sing, Inspector."

"Someone reported hearing music and singing nevertheless."

"Oh ... maybe they heard our chants." She glanced toward the piano. "People don't even know how to play one of those beautiful instruments any more. They are graceful and lovely, aren't they?" She smiled sweetly. "The chants may sound silly, but I find they're a good way to remember some of Society's important points." She turned to the group. "Let's chant the one we were doing a few minutes ago."

> "Raising children every day,
>   with the help the People give,
>   lets me know they're in control,

giving time to work and live"

"Lady ... shut up!" Stoner shouted as he glared at the group. "Whom do you think you're dealing with?"

"Sir —"

"Enough lady! That sounds like a song to me, a very bad song, but ..." Stoner's face grew red, and his neck was taunt and rigid. "Why am I wasting my time with this nonsense? Chant if you want— just don't sing—or I'm sending a bus for all of you! Got it?"

"Yes, Sir," Dahlia agreed with polite surrender to his authority.

The inspector shot a caustic glance around the room, mentally recording the faces of each participant. Some looked familiar but at the moment, he didn't care. He had to get out of there. He was not going to run around town chasing ghosts and felonious singers.

He turned with near parade drill formation and shot back out the door. He was not retreating. He was leaving. He was too important for such stupidity. "Every minute I stand here, I lose ten IQ points," he mumbled out loud. *On a night like this, somebody always has a complaint or a question to investigated. If they're not griping about something, they lose their reason for living. They wrap their identity in spying on their neighbor. But I will not reduce myself to a baby sitter for these minimal citizens.*

Stoner left the light and went back out into the darkness where shadows provided better cover for his indignant hostility. Back in his patrol car, he tried to remember where he had seen the leader before. Later, he would get the names of everyone who lived in that building.

CHAPTER TWENTY-FOUR
The Spirit inside the Book

11:30 p.m.

That evening, out in front of the apartment building, Dahlia had stationed friends nearby, talking together in little clusters. They watched for anyone the group did not know or trust. Fortunately, someone spotted Stoner's strata-car in time for Jason and me to move to the back of the group, inside Indian River Apartments. After Stoner left, we didn't expect him to waste his time coming back, so, we sang far into the night. There were songs about sleighs and snowflakes, and choruses about a family who had no place to sleep but a barn. Believers remembered that family for thousands of years and the baby was the miracle of the ages.

The lyrics and the strains of music, that had the power to penetrate my soul, were something I had never experienced. Some melodies made me feel like I was riding the wind of the sea, lifting me higher and higher. Other music made me think of home and yet, it was the kind of home I had only read about. I finally understood why the angels sing. Music touched my soul in ways mere words could not express.

It was late when the last of the carolers finally gave up and went off to sleep a few hours before the day would dawn again. Jason and I waited until the others had left, to say good night to Dahlia.

"Well, my new friends," Dahlia yawned, "I will fall off this bench into a sleeping ball, and none of us want that." She stood and stretched, then gave me another hug. "I'm happy for both of you."

"Don't bother coming into the office, Dahlia. Morning starts soon," Jason smiled.

"You're very generous, Doctor. Tomorrow is the day before First-day, our day of rest—which also happens to be Gifting Day. We never work those two days."

Jason laughed and kissed her cheek.

"Night, Dahlia," I added. Then I did something I had never done before. I reached out to her with an embrace. Suddenly, I remembered. "Dahlia, what is the second sign that helps us to identify others who believe? You were telling us earlier. 'I'm Thomas's friend,' and what else?"

She took my hands like one sharing a secret with a friend. "Jesus's friend Peter was often called the Big Fisherman, Christiana. Jesus called Peter and two brothers, James and John, also fishermen, to follow him. As his disciples, they would learn from him, so that they could reveal God to the people as well. Jesus said he would make his followers fishers of men. Christiana, watch for the ichthus. Watch for the ichthus." Then she turned to go up to her apartment.

"Ichthus, Dahlia? Watch for fish?" I called after her, but she only waved her hand in the air, smiled over her shoulder, and walked on.

"Jason, remember those happy, laughing faces around the piano this evening? Somewhere on each one's clothing—a lapel pin, a necklace, a design on a ring—there was a fish, the ichthus." I was amazed. "They recognized each other by their brand—the ichthus."

Jason never went to my room. At the door, we lingered for a moment. It had been a wonderful day and we didn't want to let it end. There had been no joy like this in our time, so it was hard to trust there could possibly be a repeat of this glorious day. We said little, but when our eyes met, volumes lay hidden behind them. Jason kissed my forehead. I watched him turn and walk slowly out into the night. Snow had begun to fall and I remembered a song: something about a white Christmas. I smiled.

· · · · · ·

In my apartment, I pushed the button to ignite the flame in the fireplace, a luxury known only to Legacy Citizens. Workers were forbidden to waste fuel. I started to rationalize how added responsibility should earn special perks and then I shuddered. I hadn't even thought about my elite status before. I had taken it for granted. Now, it all felt pretentious. I wasn't better than others. For the first time, I finally felt I was part of a cluster of friends.

As I sat there in the stillness of my apartment, I felt a presence growing within me, an indwelling spirit. It was mysterious yet loving, beckoning, and calling gently for entrance into my world. It gave me hope and courage. At that moment, I felt emboldened enough to take a stand against the darkness that seemed to be crowding in around me.

I stretched as tall as I could, pulled the leather-bound book from its conspicuous hiding place, and curled up in my favorite reading chair beside the fire.

How could a harmless black book make me feel excited, afraid, curious, and indifferent, all at the same time? If I opened that book, would my life change completely? Why were there secrets inside those pages that were declared unsafe, subversive? *What should I do?* I placed the book on the floor and stared into the fire. *I'll give it back to Grand-père. He'll understand. I don't know why he gave me the dangerous contraband in the first place. What if I'm caught with it?*

Unable to move from the spot, I watched the flames leaping in the firebox and thought of my new emotions. I jumped up, paced back and forth, and stole little glances at the book. I turned my back and walked over to the windows. Sparkling snow clung to the trees and bushes creating a kaleidoscope of color as it danced under the multicolored Gifting lights. I thought about Jesus and the meaning of Christmas. I understood something since I'd heard of him. Without him, there is no reason for gifting.

I looked down at the leather-covered book there on the floor near the hearth. What should I do? *Should I, shouldn't I?* Even that sounded silly. I hadn't just found the book lying in the street. My grandfather had given it to me. If I couldn't trust him, I couldn't trust anyone. I picked up the sacred book, ran my hands over the cover, felt the grain of the leather beneath my fingers, and sat down on the edge of the chair. The old volume fell open to the middle where the heading read *Psalms.* Carefully, I leafed through the pages. Jason had suggested that I start reading alternately from the old covenant and then the new. But, as a reason for my reading, he recommended that I read three passages first. I turned to those selections.

> Genesis 1: 1-3. In the beginning God created the heavens and the earth. Now the earth was formless and empty, darkness was over the surface of the deep. And the Spirit of God was hovering over the waters. And God said, "Let there be light, and there was light."

My breath stopped. God spoke light into being! My mind could not grasp the enormity of what I was reading, but my soul soaked up the words it thirsted for. First there was nothing, absolutely nothing, then God spoke and light blazed forth. I tried to imagine what the thunder of creation from the mouth of God would have sounded like!

Then I turned to the second passage.

> John 1: 1-5. In the beginning was the Word, and the Word was with God, and the Word was God. He was with God in the beginning. Through him all things were made; without him nothing was made that has been made. In him was life, and that life was the light of men. The light shines in the darkness, but the darkness has not understood it.

So, God wants to shine light into all the dark places. He wants us to understand, even though much of life is not understandable. He wants all of us to have wisdom. Jason had said, when we follow God's commands and embrace the wisdom in those laws, we are given promises. He said I will find those promises and the reason for my quest for a solution to my grandparents' fate.

> Proverbs 3: 1-2.
>
> My son, do not forget my law, but let your heart keep my commands, for length of days and long life and peace they will add to you.

Length of days and long life ... what did that mean? The reference explained, enduring days with warm hours, stretched over a lengthy life time, and peace for the heart are promised to those who keep God's laws. All of my worry over my grandparents' fate was stripped away. They had a right to live a long and wise life, just as all of God's created souls had the same right. God had given that promise. Light was shining into what I thought had been the shadowed, empty places of my heart. But I discovered there are no empty places, only foreign lands of the soul that speak another language and have other experiences and customs. It takes time, a life time, an eternity, to travel to the far boundaries of the human soul. Then I knew —and I knew that I knew.

CHAPTER TWENTY-FIVE
Stoner Challenged

Ward Stoner pulled to a stop again in front of the Indian River Apartments. He had been driving around in circles since leaving the building earlier. Each time he passed, the same people sat in conversation on the steps, laughing and enjoying themselves. *How can they stand to spend an entire cold evening together, doing nothing?* His skin began to crawl. Had he known they were spotters for Dahlia, he may have had another opinion.

Stoner felt drawn back to the apartment building, but he didn't know why. Two situations loomed in front of him, the disappearance of a furnace technician and a phantom woman who roamed the transit and apartment complex, with ties to both. Silas Drummond had to be found. He was insignificant, but knew too much.

This time Stoner left the motor running and the heater on. He had no intention of staying long.

Dispatch whispered in his ear. "Inspector, location monitoring places you back at Indian River Apartments. Is there a problem?"

"No, no problem."

"Sir, I heard the exchange before. I think I dropped IQ points too, just listening to your encounter with those people."

"Never mind. I'll build up more IQ points later. I'll not be able to understand people like that. Lack of education is one thing but celebrating ignorance is more than I can tolerate."

"It's late, Sir. Why don't you go home?"

Stoner had used his address pod to check out residents of the building. He made a list of each inhabitant. The inspector vowed to waste no more time that night on ghosts, wayward singers, or on an uppity Legacy Citizen who had the mysterious ability to stay a few steps ahead of him all day. Yes, once he had left the little gathering and cleared his head from the mundane dribble of the chants, he realized he had recognized her standing behind someone else. *Why have you been skipping along in front of me all day, Missy? What are you doing that's so, so important?*

But there was more. Stoner was a man with a personal force of iron. He intimidated people with a frozen glance. Miss Number-One Citizen was different. There was something about her, a growing presence, a strengthening of her will. *Where does her strength come from? She probably doesn't even know she has it.*

He worked in the Blue Guard for years and rose in the ranks, like an alley cat leaping to the top of the backyard fence. One day he was on the ground and the next he was on the top. The rise to power was too heady for him. It affected his mind and sense of his own importance. He struggled with balancing power with his family life. While Miriam was still alive, she kept him grounded. Once she was gone, his equilibrium died with her. All events held equal weight. Everything was an inconvenience. Everyone was an annoyance. Every incident of his long days made him angry.

He stared up at the building and followed the structure's facade to the very top floor. Lights still glowed from the windows in the high penthouse and would have made others feel warm. Not Ward Stoner.

I'm sure you must live up there, Missy, a fairy princess at the top of her castle. Suddenly, he saw the silhouette of a woman framed in a top floor window beyond the shade. He jumped. It forced him to remember she was real, not an imaginary adversary lurking about in his mind, growing larger and stronger with each antagonistic thought. He shook his head to reshuffle the pictures in his deck of mental face cards. *That's enough of you tonight, Missy. Tomorrow, we'll see who has the greater power, you, or me.*

CHAPTER TWENTY-SIX
Silas is Taken

7:00 a.m. Saturday, December 24

I woke up the next morning with Christmas melodies singing in my heart. *I must have been singing them in my sleep.* I stretched and smiled at the morning. Light streamed in my windows and bounced off the beveled mirror above my dresser sending prisms of carnival light across the surfaces of the room. Then I remembered, *And God said, let there be light and there was light.*

Rolling over in bed, I felt a furry body near my foot. "Oh, it's you, Shakespeare." Laying there a while longer, I drew Shakespeare near me, as thrilling images of the previous day filled my thoughts.

Everything I experienced up to that Gifting Season was being over-turned, or up-righted. Not that my life had been a lie. The last generations had not known about the true history of mankind. Purged text books, rewritten many years ago, brought stability to a society full of entitlement demands. We had been proud people, energetic, creative, prosperous, free people, who had forgotten how to think, how to problem-solve, and how to rejoice with what we had. Society took care of everything. Illiterate, uninformed, unmotivated, and volatile, people had just enough energy to be good worker bees. Mind dulling drugs in our water supply now controlled us, but left our emotions flat, our libido restrained, and all creativity thwarted.

I was no better informed. I only read approved text books. My life lacked emotion. When I found the old books in the library, I preferred to read the novels that overflowed with feelings. I neglected books of history, comparative governments, and religions. I was an elective illiterate the same as others.

I shot out of bed with a new resolve. There was still a way to reverse my grandparents' death sentence.

I showered in the open wet area, dressed, and then checked my image in the mirror. For some strange reason, it was important how I looked today. I remembered a red blouse I had bought and never wore, thinking the color clashed with my auburn hair and fair complexion. Today it felt festive. It reminded me of the celebration lights bejeweling the city. I dashed out to greet the day.

Outside, it had grown colder and snow covered the ground. The icicle laden trees looked beautiful. The blue sky was clear. *Maybe God is blessing me with clarity today too.* I hoped I was right.

Another transit ride, I sighed. *I hope there is no stranger staring at me again, like Sean, or no little man to get inside my head with evil dribble.* By the time I got to my stop near the library, my ride had been so uneventful, I nearly forgot about Sean or Silas Drummond.

8:30 a.m.

When I got to the library, it was still early and the sun danced off the window panes. But just as I entered through the main doors, I heard my name and turned.

"Lady Applewait, wait!"

I could not believe it. Silas Drummond called to me again from the opposite curb.

Every word of the awful letter he had written flashed before my eyes and resounded in my ears. I tried to ignore him as I pushed on the door but his words stopped me.

"Look at the glitter of the building Miss Applewait. Believe me, please. Calcium," he shouted.

I gasped in disgust at the possibility that they ground human bones into a fine powder. I gaged and wanted to run but there was something about the man. His beard had grown scraggly and deep lines etched his face. He looked as if he hadn't slept all night and exhaustion was evident in every motion of his frail body. Just as I was feeling a new empathy for him, two blue guardsmen jumped out of a vehicle, grabbed Drummond, and shoved him into the back of their car. I could hear his screams as they sped off.

"Lady Christiana, please ..."

Fear gripped me as I stood frozen on the steps of the library. What was happening? Did they catch him because he was spreading lies or because he was revealing the truth?

CHAPTER TWENTY-SEVEN
Formation of the New Society

The encounter with Silas Drummond left me feeling vulnerable, exposed. I hurried in through the huge library doors and caught my breath in the main lobby. It was the day before Gift-giving Day and the place seemed empty except for security personnel and a few librarians and other workers. I welcomed the sight of Frank, the guard, and sailed through the front inspection barrier where he sat half asleep.

"Rise and shine, Frank," I called out as I slipped through the gate to the safety of the other side. This time I listened for the sound. I had made sure the chip was in my satchel and, sure enough, I heard a faint beep as I walked through the scanner.

"Oh Frank, I left my book over there." It was not an accident. I was setting up my own experiment. I put my bag, with the chip inside of it, on the desk on Frank's side of the gate and walked back through the portal. I picked up the book I had left over there and started back through the gate again. I walked slowly and listened intently. There was no sound. The guard looked up in surprise.

"That's odd," he observed.

"What's that Frank?" I questioned as I scooped up my satchel again.

"You weren't detected. Everyone is detected when they come in."

"Really? How?" I asked innocently.

"I don't know. I just know we all beep."

"Let me see," I stepped back through the gate with my bag securely in my hand. I turned and swung back through the portal like I was executing a dance move, *allemande left,* one of the books had called it. That time, I heard a beep.

"Well, okay." Frank seemed mystified. "I guess I didn't hear you the first time."

"You were asleep, my friend, and we both know it," I teased. I sighed with relief. My experiment had proven my hypothesis. The tagging chip caused the beep - society's methodical counting of souls.

"You sure are different today, My Lady." Frank studied me carefully.

"Am I?" I thought I'd better move on. It wasn't the custom for Legacy Citizens to have lengthy conversations with workers.

I hurried into the back stacks and was surprised to see Marge sitting by the window reading.

"Christiana? What are you doing here? It's the day before Gift-giving."

"I could ask the same of you, Marge." I sounded a little snippy and wished I had phrased it differently.

Marge didn't seem to notice. Perhaps I usually snapped at people. I did not like that possibility. Actually, I wished she would leave. I wanted to go on back into the inner recesses, unnoticed and unquestioned.

"Do you have company you need to prepare for?" I asked.

"No, not this year. I'll be alone."

Suddenly, a wave of loneliness I'd never felt before swept over me. "I'm sorry, Marge."

She looked up from her book. "You are? Why?"

"No one wants to be alone on Gift-giving Day."

"Are you all right, Christiana?" She was still watching me closely. "What did the doctor say about your shoulder yesterday?"

"Yesterday? Was that yesterday?"

"Yes," she drew out slowly. "Was it serious?"

"Was what serious?" She startled me but I had to smile. I wasn't sure if she was talking about the doctor and me, or about my seeing the doctor. "No," I stalled with a chuckle, "it was just like a sliver and the doctor removed it."

"And ... the doctor ... what did you think about him?" Marge closed the book and laid it in her lap.

How could I tell her what had happened? How could I explain my new emotions, my new understandings, my new awakening, my new friends ... and Dr. Jason O'Reilly? I didn't even understand it all myself. How could I explain it to someone else?

"He's gorgeous!" I teased playfully as I turned to go toward the back hallway.

"Gorgeous? So, men are gorgeous now? Christiana, you are bubbling." Marge started to get up and since I didn't want her to follow me, I turned back quickly.

I thought fast and switched the topic. "They have me on a new medication. I am being ... detoxified," I said with a tone of resignation.

Laying her book on the side table, Marge eased out of her chair. "Detoxification?" she whispered.

"Yes."

"With tiny little pills?" Marge moved closer, her eyes darted toward the door and back at me.

I couldn't believe how Marge could have known about the pills? She wasn't Legacy and no one else would have had knowledge of them. "Marge, what do you think you know?"

"I read about them, Christina, about the water and the citizen control ... and —"

"What about ... the never-ending-sleep?" I held my breath. Could it really be that easy? Was the answer that close? "Where, Marge? Where did you read about the pills and all of that?"

"Come back here," she said as she led the way down the hallway and into the back stacks. "Over here. I remember exactly where I had seen it because it was so profound." She ran her finger over the books on the shelf about eye level and stopped. "Here it is," she whispered as she studied the spine. *"Formation of the New Society."*

Marge scanned the index and stopped on chapter eleven. "Here, page one-hundred sixteen, *Citizen Control*. It's all right here, Christiana. They have been putting stuff in our water for years, in order to make us calm and cooperative, but it also robbed us, Christina. Yes, we aren't sad or angry anymore, but we no longer have any joy either. The antidepressants control all negative feelings, sadness, and anger, which should have brought a measure of happiness. But the other chemicals that counteracted the side effects of the additives flattened everyone back out again because their ultimate goal had nothing to do with our best interests. It was all about population control. Their motives were twofold. First, they wanted to ensure there would be no rebellion, and second ... here let me show you this."

She turned more pages frantically. "They wanted to decrease the number of citizens. Here it is, *Population Control*—listen to this. 'In order for any society to support the most productive members, there must be a depopulation policy to legally put down its most disturbed, disabled, and infirmed individuals, as well as the elderly, and those citizens considered not capable of rehabilitation. These individual human units will be placed in a sleep chamber where they will drift off into an endless sleep.' It's right there."

"Population Control? Marge, they have lied all along. Their motives were to build their own power!" I could not believe it, but I knew with my heart it was true.

Marge continued reading. "Since a society in the post-industrialized era requires only a modest workforce, it is necessary to limit the number of children produced in each family unit. Given that children born outside a family unit have little potential for success, they will be terminated before they become viable."

"Oh Marge, those poor babies ... and their grieving mothers ... how could they?" I could not believe our leaders were so cruel.

"Here it is, Christiana," Marge went on. "As a proactive policy, additives in the water supply will decrease the human desire to procreate, which will also eventually depopulate the nation. After a passage of time, this present crisis will pass. Then the policy regarding the endless sleep and these other forms of population control will be reevaluated to see if they should continue. Overturning this law will require a referendum from the citizenry."

"What was this great crisis of the past? What happened?" I felt knowledge deprived and that rendered me helpless to change the future.

"I read the old history books as well as the transitional texts," Marge whispered into the solitude of the back library. "The people had gotten complacent and had no longer participated in the republic. They only wanted to play games and engage in all manner of irresponsible behavior. Gluttony and an insatiable need for riches led most people into a totally self-indulgent, self-centered, and self-destructive life style. Families imploded, financial institutions collapsed and while people slept off their drunken stupor, a political faction of those bent on the total control of others rolled into place and shoved the lazy majority aside where they could continue to wallow in their own self-pity."

"How did this come about? Didn't the people try to stop it?" I questioned.

"No, the people paid no attention to their own government, except to complain," Marge responded and then went on reading. "That anti-democratic political movement had been growing beneath the general population's awareness, waiting for the right moment to take over the government while the country slept in their self-induced fog. When the people finally awakened from their apathy, they began fighting back, but it was too late. The movement had become very strong. The emotions on both sides finally exploded into the streets and chaos rained down. No one trusted the other. Those who successfully won the takeover of the government started drugging the water to control the masses of people."

"Marge, how could it have gotten to that point? It seems impossible that people, who were blessed with the emotions of love and compassion, would give up such jewels for the plastic bobbles of frivolous play?"

"They had become lazy, complacent, Christiana."

"Marge, why hadn't you told me all of this before?" I was both thrilled and disappointed at the same time. Marge knew I had been concerned about my grandparents. She must have known that her information was relevant to my cause.

"I'm sorry." She looked away and whispered, "I was afraid."

"Afraid?" I thought Marge and I were friends. Maybe a Legacy Citizen can have no friends. "Were you afraid of me?"

"No ..." she hesitated, "well, yes ... maybe." Marge touched my hand but would not look at me. "I was afraid of everything. If they had found out I had been reading the old books, I could have lost my job. If they thought I was trying to organize or arouse the people, I could have gone to jail."

"Sedition ... promoting through speech or writing, discontent or rebellion against the country," I clarified out loud, although the warning was meant for me too.

"Yes," she whispered in agreement. "If I lost my job or worse yet, if they put me in jail, I would no longer be a valued citizen. I would have my Length of Days lowered to the status of the common person." Tears rolled down Marge's strained face.

I studied her expression and asked carefully, "Marge, have you been using the pills too? How else could you feel so deeply?" Maybe I was revealing too much. I put my arms around her and hugged her as a friend. "It's okay. But, where did you get the pills?"

"That, I can't tell you, Christiana. Not yet. Please don't ask me again." She was pleading and I couldn't refuse.

"Tomorrow is Gift-giving Day. Do you know another name for Gift-giving Day?" It could do no harm. If she didn't know, she would say so without raising more questions.

She looked at me and smiled. "Christiana ... am I going to get to say it again? I don't usually get to wish anyone a *Merry Christmas*. Not very often anyway."

Joy flooded my heart. Though I'd known about Christmas for less than twenty-four hours, it felt like my soul had known forever. "Tomorrow is Christmas, Marge," I whispered. "I have until the end of the month to find a way to halt the evil euthanasia of the infirmed and elderly." I put my hand on the book Marge had just read from. "I have to get this book out of here today. Grand-père has to see it. Maybe if he knew the true history of our country, maybe he wouldn't be so willing to accept the inevitability of his fate."

"Christiana," Marge's jaw dropped, "you cannot try to remove this book! They'll catch you. We'll both get caught." Panic seemed to have overtaken her as she tried to reach out for it.

"I don't think they'll catch me. I have a plan. If it works, I'd like you to come to Christmas dinner tomorrow at my grandparents' home. It's a family thing, but I'll be inviting a few other friends as well. If it doesn't work, I guess I'll be having my holiday dinner as a guest of the city."

"Christmas in the home of members of the Council of Elders? Christiana, do you think I could?"

I laughed a little, not at my friend but at the joy I saw flash across her face. "You have already been invited. Of course, you can come."

"Wow, what a miracle. Now, we need another piece of gracious luck to get us through the hijacking of library property. How are we going to be able to get this book out of here?" Marge questioned. "You know they'll see us walk through with a book in our hands."

"I want you to walk ahead of me to Frank's station. You talk to him while I slip past. I'll put the book on the other side of the gate, then come back and walk through again." I had a plan I thought might work. "Frank always smiles more broadly when you come into the library, Marge. He watches you. With very few emotions in his quivery of arrows, Frank must save up all day for his brief encounters with you."

"Don't be silly," Marge blushed. "Besides, you'll beep when you sneak through."

"No, I'm sure I won't." I said as I gathered up the book. It wasn't large but it was thick. I was still able to carry it in my left hand, the side away from Frank. "I'll grab my hat but if you'll take my tunic and satchel, I think we can pull this off."

We walked into the hall and through the door that led to the outer library. No one was around. We kept walking, slowly, casually. When we emerged into the lobby, Frank saw us coming and smiled.

"Hi Frank." Marge positioned herself in such a way that caused Frank to turn his back on me to pay exclusive attention to her.

"Hi Marge," he grinned when we came up to his desk. "Are you going to stay here much longer?"

"Are you trying to close up early, Frank?" she smiled.

I took the few steps through the portal. It should have caused a beep from my chip. Nothing. *Good,* I thought.

They no longer tracked books with a bar code system, so the movement of the book alone would have not caused notice. Since people's bodies were now *bar coded* and their every move tracked, it wasn't necessary to know what they carried in and out of buildings.

My heart was pounding when I found myself, uncounted, on the other side of the portal. Then, like a calming breeze, I remembered the words ... *Silent night, holy night, all is calm, all is bright.* Those words blew away my fear and quieted my soul. I stepped back across the line, through the open gate, and slipped in beside Marge as she continued to talk to Frank.

"Thank you for carrying my stuff, Marge. I had almost forgotten. I can take my things now." I smiled and took my belongings from her, including the bag with my chip buried inside. "Walk with me over to the front door, okay?"

"Sure," then Marge turned to Frank, "if you have time to stop for coffee when you leave here later, let me know. I'll be going in about an hour."

Frank looked somewhat confused, so I walked back through the clearing station nonchalantly and beeped obediently. I moved over to the side table, picked up the book I had just placed there, and folded it into my wrap. When Marge caught up to me, we giggled a little.

"Marge, you made quite a sacrifice for the cause back there with Frank," I whispered through my laughter.

"That was no sacrifice, Christiana." She blushed and looked back at Frank who continued to follow us with his eyes. She patted the tunic-covered book. "Are you going home now?"

"I'm going to make a stop and invite another couple of friends for dinner tomorrow." I gave her a hug, and we parted. Out in the bright early winter day, I saw the transit approaching from the east. I hurried along, all the while remembering the calm melody of *Silent Night* that rang in my head at the library checking station. A new, hopeful spirit and calm peace rose and filled all the empty spaces, flooding my soul with joy. God had shown me a way to stop the madness. Then ... I knew, and I knew that I knew why the angels sing.

CHAPTER TWENTY-EIGHT
Stoner Demands Answers

Over at the Headquarters of the Blue Guard, Inspector Ward Stoner was on another rampage. "Boone!" He barked as he charged past Chalky Boone's desk. "Come into my office."

"Right," she responded as she grabbed up her palm-held verbal steno recorder.

The inspector stood at the window seeing nothing. "I need as much information as you can get on Christiana Applewait."

"Lady Applewait?" she questioned.

"Yes, Christiana Applewait. Is she so far above us all that you can't get a dossier on her?" Stoner's body twitched as he hiked up his pants and smoothed his shirt trying to control his seething anger.

Chalky blinked in disbelief. "Yes ... Ward ... she is —"

Stoner certainly knew the law. He turned and glared at her. His valued assistant and First Lieutenant was perhaps the only person left in the city who actually knew him. "Chalky, I don't want to hear that answer."

"I know you don't, but it's the truth." Chalky stood her ground with feet firmly planted. She was the only person who could tell the Chief Inspector, "No."

"Boone, let's not talk about what's true. Let's grind out a little of what's necessary."

"Ward ... she is a Legacy Citizen. You know the laws regarding the Council of Elders and those who will rise to that position. The Law of 2031 purged every file known to Society of even the name of a Legacy Citizen. None of our e-files have a word about the Wise Ones." Boone's tone was calming but firm. Educated as a lawyer, she knew the law.

"What about the little wise crackers, the second and third generations?" He hissed with sarcasm.

"Inspector —"

"Then how do we know she's Legacy? Tell me that." His face was red and the veins on his temples bulged with anger. "Can't anyone do their job around here but me?" he shouted.

"There is a paper file on each of the members of the Council, their ancestors, their descendants, and any pertinent information about them, including education, achievements, and their writings. But there is nothing that we can access from our readers. It is not in the air, anywhere. It's on paper."

"Okay, okay, let's sit down and brainstorm." Stoner sat at his desk, leaned back, and closed his eyes. "Applewait is her father's name. She is Legacy by linage from her maternal grandparents, Oliver and Constance Richly."

"Yes, that's true, Ward, but she is also Legacy through her paternal grandparents, Abraham and Claudia Applewait. They passed into the sleep several years ago following a house fire."

"Those wood frame houses in Oakwood should have been demolished a long time ago. They're nothing but tinder boxes waiting to ignite," Stoner said. "The fancy people think they are so great because they have so much space."

"Space and ambiance. I was in one once and it seemed so warm and friendly."

"Oh please," Stoner drew out his words with indignation. "Those buildings take a lot more maintenance than the newer, high-rise buildings."

"Yes Sir. There was a rumor that the senior Applewait's house was deliberately torched," Boone added.

"Why hadn't I heard about that?" Stoner snapped back. "Arson is a crime you know."

"That was about the time your wife went to sleep, Ward. You were off duty and probably weren't informed."

Stoner made no response. He had barely acknowledged the passing of his wife in his own frozen emotions, locked in a state of grief and anger. He never spoke of her out loud.

"So, by linage, she is a Lady, Lady Applewait," Boone broke the silence.

"I'm not impressed," Stoner snapped back. "So, where are these paper files on the Legacy Citizens?"

"I ... don't know how to access them," Boone said. "But some place I ran across the addresses of a few Legacy Citizens. Those locations are stored here in my palm-reader." She spoke into her reader, "Legacy addresses." She selected a tab and the information was instantly available. "Christiana Applewait lives in the penthouse," she read, "in the Indian River Apartments."

A slight sneer crossed Stoner's lips. "Yes, I know."

Chalky looked up but said nothing about his comment. "Her parents live in the Lee Ridge High Rise and her grandparents, two of the twelve, live in Oakwood, at 721 Primrose Lane."

"That's all we have?" He growled. "That's it?"

"That's it."

"Who has access to the paper files if they're so secret?"

"The Council of Elders, Sir," she stated flatly as if she had just completed a circle. "And those files are stored in the vault at Fort Knox, Kentucky where the gold used to be stored."

"The gold is still there, Boone. It was never moved as they said it had been." Stoner's expression softened from the anger usually stored around his eyes. "I would be willing to bet that not even the current Council members remember what's in those files. We could say anything we wanted to about any of them."

"Yes, but if you spread lies about even one of them, are you willing to bet your career, maybe even your life, on getting away with it?" Chalky asked.

"Maybe not this time. For now, it may be enough to know where I can find them. As long as I know where these people are, they're as good as captured. They're not going anywhere. I'll keep an eye on Oakwood myself. It might be amusing to haunt the good little citizens who never have a worry, never have a care. Maybe I can shake them up a little bit."

"Ward, you just can't harass them." Chalky moved in a little closer and nearly whispered. "It's against the law."

"Boone, I am the law!" he shouted.

"Hold your voice down, Sir. You're sounding out of control."

"Don't you dare talk to me like that," he seethed.

"I'm the only one who can, Ward." She refused to retreat; she did not back down.

"You listen to me Boone, I don't plan to do anything now, just watch and wait. But the time may come when the benefit of creating some chaos in Oakwood might far outweigh the cost. I don't know when. Maybe years from now. But it would be fun if it happened in my lifetime." He spun his chair around and refocused his stare outside his office. "I have the time. Laws or no laws, power is everything. I can wait for the prize — when the golden nugget is ultimate control."

CHAPTER TWENTY-NINE
Gracie's Grief

9:30 a.m.

My conversation with Marge at the library had lifted my spirits. She had revealed her knowledge of the suppressed book and other forbidden documents hidden in the back rooms. I kept the book I had slipped out of the library wrapped in the folds of my cloak. As I rode across town to the medical center, I saw Sean, the man from the sing along—the one who delivered underground newspapers. He was sitting on the P-T side bench, and this time, I wasn't uncomfortable. He smiled but said nothing. I found that strange, since he had spoken out so freely last evening. Then, I saw he was carrying a large bag of rolled up newspapers. I was amazed to see the papers out in the open! News sheets hadn't been printed in years, and were now forbidden. The Government Communications Agency, the GCA, had corrupted the print outlets to the point they were no longer credible.

Sean is delivering newspaper around town! He must have been delivering papers each time I had seen him on the bus. Since people hadn't seen newspapers in our lifetime, there was no danger. They didn't know what he was carrying.

I started to walk past him without acknowledging his presence but he stopped me. He spoke in a dull tone, like everyone else on the bus that day, but his eyes conveyed another meaning.

"I found that special high-mountain coffee we were talking about last evening. Do you know, it is grown at such high elevations, the snow caps look like grandpa's white hair," he laughed lightly. Others looked up.

His cryptic message was not well veiled but esoteric enough to slip past those around us. "Wonderful! Could we enjoy some at the Gift-giving celebration tomorrow?" I asked.

"That would be perfect. I could come by in the afternoon, after dinner." He smiled. We were just two causal friends talking about the little things of life.

"We will be at —" I couldn't mention my grandparents' home. "Well, here's my stop. Why don't you call me this evening and I'll give you the directions?"

Since grandparents no longer existed for most people in our age group, a mention of mine would have drawn curiosity. I saw my stop approaching, so I said no more.

I got off the bus near the huge medical center which housed several physicians' practices, various specialists' offices, and labs. As I walked through the reception area toward the lift, I heard sobbing coming from the Women's Lounge. Drawn to the sound of sorrow was a strange experience. A few days before, I wouldn't have even heard it; or, if I had, I would have walked on past.

Cautiously, I pushed the lounge door open, not knowing what I might find. A young woman lay on the bathroom floor with her legs pulled up to her body. She was rocking back and forth, while moaning and sobbing like a wounded infant. She was gripping a partially opened pocket knife in her hand. I rushed in and knelt down.

"What happened to you? What is wrong?"

She whimpered and opened her eyes a little. "My Lady?"

"I'll get a doctor for you. Just lie still."

"No!"

"But you need care."

"I just came from a doctor's office. They can't do anything." I saw her slide the knife under her body as she closed her eyes again.

I sensed her horrible plan and reached for the knife she had tried to hide under her clothing.

"No, I must have it," she gasped and grabbed at the knife as I pulled it from underneath her.

As she struggled to grab the knife from my hand, the blade popped open and slashed my arm a few inches above my wrist. I flung the knife out of her reach as she struggled to get up.

"Oh no, My Lady, no!" she pleaded when she saw my arm. She sank back to the floor.

I quickly wrapped a clean white cloth from my pocket around the slight wound and then turned back to her. "What has happened to you? Tell me, so I can get the help you need. Can you give me your name?"

"My husband and I love each other, My Lady." She started to sit up. She breathed more freely and the gasping stopped. "We have two beautiful children. Then, I got pregnant again so my doctor said we would have to abort the baby. Then the doctor was sick and my time went on." Her whispers bore testimony to the pain within her.

"So, your pregnancy continued?"

"Yes, there aren't enough other doctors in his practice to cover his patients when he's sick. I was seven and a half months along when they came for me. They terminated the pre-birth mass just this morning." She looked up at me with grief written on her face. "My Lady ... I saw her. She was so tiny and pink and breathing. She wasn't a mass of anything. She was a baby—my baby." Her voice faded to a weak whisper. "It feels like my heart has slipped into a vast abyss. I am so lost and empty."

I felt so stunned that I couldn't find words to sooth her grief, so I sat on the bathroom floor with her and folded her in my arms. "Where is your baby now?"

"She ..." the little mother sobbed in my arms, "she was discarded. They said, since we already had our allotted two children, the third birth mass was unnecessary. They ..." her words drifted off to a whisper, "just threw her away."

"What's the problem, Gracie?" A nurse startled us as she barged into the lounge unexpectedly.

"There's no problem," the new mother whispered with fear in her voice.

"You know what Doctor told you. If you can't pull yourself together, you will have to be hospitalized and that will put a point in your chart," the nurse said.

Gracie looked at me in terror and tried not to look at the pocket knife I had picked up and still held in my hand with the bandaged arm. She glanced quickly away. "No, I'll be fine. I was just a little weak, and this lady spoke to me."

"We've called your husband. He's waiting for you in the hall. Are you coming?"

"Yes, yes of course. Stephen is here? Good," she smiled weakly and got up.

"Gracie, stop by the Main Library after the Holidays. We could have some coffee or something," I said as she started to walk away.

She turned and looked at me with amazement in her tired eyes. "You would have coffee with me?"

"I want to very much," I gave her a little side hug for reassurance. "My name is Christiana."

"I know who you are, My Lady." She smiled and then was gone.

When I got into the hallway, I saw Gracie disappear out the door with a young man. He had his arm around her as though he were both protecting her and guiding her unsteady feet. I stood there and watched them until they were out of sight. Grief was another emotion I was learning. And, sorrow often comes as its opposite, the joy of life. Little did I realize this was only the beginning of the horror stories I would encounter.

CHAPTER THIRTY

An Invitation and a Discovery

10:00 a.m.

I had come to the medical building to see Jason O'Reilly. I looked at my time piece. The encounter with Gracie, the tragic woman in the Women's Lounge, had happened so fast. Still stunned, I walked into Jason's waiting room and looked around. It was empty and quiet. Even the receptionist was absent from her station.

"Christy!" Jason walked through the door from the inner hall and nearly bumped into me. "What are you doing here?"

His surprise would have put me off but when he gathered me in his arms, his reassurance made me feel wanted again. "Well now, that is better," I smiled.

"Oh yeah," Jason ran his fingers across my back. "I'll phrase it differently this time." He cleared his throat with dramatic flair. "I am so happy to see you Christiana. To what do I owe this visit?" He bowed slightly.

"I have come on the happy chance you have no plans for Gift-giving dinner, but I've just had a horrible experience."

"What on earth happened?" It was then that he saw the wound on my arm and the knife I still clutched in my hand.

"My arm will be fine. It's stopped bleeding. I cleaned it in the bathroom. But Jason, there was a woman." The whole incident raced through my mind. "She was so sad. I think she would have taken her own life with this blade if I hadn't heard her crying and found her on the bathroom floor."

He looked at the cut on my arm. "The bathroom? Here in this building? Where is she?"

"She had a pregnancy termination but, Jason it wasn't a cell mass at all. It was her baby they threw away."

"That's why I don't have maternity patients, Christy. It's the law. Thinning out the population has been legal, and even required, for a long time. I can't do it."

I looked around the room to make sure we were still alone and cleared my head of the image of Gracie and her only encounter with her beautiful baby daughter. "We've had the Length of Days policy for a long time, Jason. I'm hoping we can overturn it, including the section on *two for two,* two children for each couple. Maybe it will start a fresh reverence for life for all people. Let's talk about something else. I can't bear the pictures that are stuck in my mind. I have to think about something happy, something full of life."

"I know Christy." He hugged me again. "What would you like for a Gifting present?"

"To have a simple life again, like it was a few days ago. I haven't told you before about this strange little man who lives in my building. He turned up again, rumpled and unkempt."

"You have a lot going on in that building," Jason laughed.

"So it's turning out to be." All of the faces of laughing, singing people flooded my mind. My thoughts were overrun, like an unexpected infestation of vermin, by the foulness that Silas Drummond had described. "Jason, the man told me what really happens to those entering the long-sleep. It was too horrible to imagine."

"What did he say?"

"Their bodies are burned and their ground bones and ashes are used in things like building construction and fertilizer. Jason, today I saw that man being forced into a strata-car. He said that we were all in danger."

"Did you believe him, Christy?"

"I don't know. It all seems so ghastly, so preposterous. I don't even want to think about any of that. I want to think about Gifting Dinner."

"Tomorrow? Christmas dinner?"

"I'd like you to come for holiday dinner," I smiled. "It will be our family Christmas feast. Are you busy? Can you come?"

"Actually, I have no plans at all. Usually, I make rounds in the hospital so those who are stuck there on the holiday have someone to talk to. Right now, I have no patients in the hospital. What did you have in mind?"

"We will all be at Grand-mère and Grand-père's house. I would like for you to come to our family dinner with me."

"I get it, you want a ride in my car," he laughed mischievously.

"I do not need a ride, Sir. The transit will be running tomorrow." I gave his arm a little smack and then buried my head in his chest. "Don't make this so hard, Jason."

He tossed his head back in fresh enjoyment. "I would love to come to Christmas dinner with you. When can I pick you up?"

"Grand-mère serves holiday dinner promptly at twelve noon."

"Oh ... I missed that. Dinner will be at your grandparents' home, two of the Wise Ones. I'll have to confess; I could feel a little intimidated around them." He teased again.

"Don't be. Grand-mère already knew who you were when I mentioned your name, Dr. O'Reilly."

"She knew me or had heard of me?" Jason's chest puffed out a little.

"She knew you. She called you by your first name."

"Perhaps she knew my parents or grandparents," he wondered out loud. "In that case, I would be honored to join all of you for Christmas dinner." He kissed my forehead and lingered there, close.

"Now, here's another thing," I approached the new idea more carefully. "I had thought I would invite Dahlia too. She could talk to my grandparents about the spiritual awakening she is experiencing.

They could give her more answers than I could. I know Society doesn't approve of socialization between bosses and employees. Would you be uncomfortable if I invited her?"

"Christy, she would be your guest, not mine. Besides, joining someone for dinner at another person's house is hardly fraternization."

"Why do you think they initiated the non-mingling law in the first place?" So many laws were beginning to sound strange, now that I was detoxing and thinking with my heart as well as my head. "What could be the harm in enjoying someone's company?"

"Maybe enjoyment of anything was considered taboo. My parents had told me that marital relationships and loyalty to one's spouse had totally broken down in the past, threatening the emotional safety of nearly all of the country's children. Keeping people apart was a way of making sure that new alliances were not begun with people outside the family unit."

The image of Gracie and her supportive husband flashed before my eyes with the agonizing pain and desperate emptiness over the loss of her baby. I shuddered and wanted to crawl closer into Jason's arms.

He gave me a reassuring hug that let me know he was there. "Are you sure you're okay?"

"Yes, of course. I just want to have a beautiful Christmas. I need only lovely thoughts right now."

"Okay, a wonderful Christmas has been ordered for you and if you want to invite Dahlia, that would be fine with me too."

"Do you think she would come?"

"She came in for a few minutes today. Let's go ask her."

I looked around the room again and added, "Wait Jason, I want to show you something first." I pulled the book from under my cloak. I was trembling with excitement and fear. "It's all right here."

Jason pushed the book away, pulled my cloak over it and said nothing. He checked the door to the inner hallway and led me quickly through the complex and back to his private office. Then he turned around and closed the door carefully so as not to make a sound. "We have to be careful with any book in our possession, Christy." He threw his arms around me and drew me close. "Okay, what did you find?"

I placed the book on his desk and it fell open to the page I had marked. I turned the book around for him to read. "Jason, the law regarding our Length of Days can be changed." My voice shook and cracked as I forced out the words in an excited whisper. "A referendum can be scheduled."

"But Christy, how long would that take?" Jason sighed.

I felt my hope plummet again. "I cannot think about that now. The referendum will be in time. It has to be."

Jason looked toward the door. There was no sound, no movement. Then he began to quietly read. "A referendum in our government is usually in the form of a direct vote which is initiated by the legislature, the government itself. There is a second type of referendum, initiated by the citizens. The second type is an *initiative, ballot measure,* or *proposition.* This last form of vote is originated by the citizens as a petition. A *binding* referendum requires only a simple majority of the voters for it to carry. With enough signatures, the measure is brought to a vote by a citizens' referendum. If passed, it is binding."

"Don't you see, Jason?" I begged. "If we can get a majority of the citizens, right here in Capitol City, to sign the petition, perhaps the government will see the need to change the policy for the entire land." I held my breath as I waited for him to answer. He had to agree with me.

"Christy, I think you may have found the solution," he whispered. Then he paused. "There is a small hitch. There is a cover letter that must accompany the petition. If that official document is not with the petition, it won't be valid."

"An official cover letter? Where would we get that?"

"It says that one can be secured from the Office of Government Regulation."

"They won't be open until next Monday, due to the holidays."

Again, my emotions plummeted. "There is so little time."

"Maybe we can intrude on a Constitutional Court judge this evening or even tomorrow. You're a Legacy Citizen. They will have to take your call."

I smiled. "I find it interesting how you can distance yourself from your own legacy, Jason. You are one of us."

"I know, I know," He admitted. "We can ask the judge together. Now ... the next step is the petition. We have to find out how we can get a petition signed by a majority of the voting citizens without raising suspicion from the Blue Guard. I know they would stop us," Jason said.

"There will be a way. I know there will." It was done. "Now, Jason, may I see Dahlia?"

Jason took my hand and led me down the hall to a supply room and small pharmacy. Dahlia, a dark beauty, had her back to us when we entered.

"Dahlia?" Jason's voice was full of disappointment and surprise. "What are you doing?"

Dahlia was stuffing paper packets of the tiny white pills into her pockets. She turned, startled, when she heard her name.

"Dr. O'Reilly!" Dahlia jumped and staggered. Jason eased her onto a chair in the corner.

"Dahlia," I whispered and knelt down in front of her, "you are the one who has been giving the detox pills to the people in town, aren't you?"

"But you reported the missing pills to me in the first place," Jason seemed confused and hurt.

"Since we finally had a patient who needed them, I thought it would soon be obvious that some were missing. I was afraid you would call for an audit of the pharmacy." Dahlia didn't say more. She merely nodded in admission. She swallowed hard then spoke with fear in her voice. "Yes, Christiana, I have started to pass them out too. I couldn't keep feelings of love and other emotions from my friends. Even if caught, the gift of life was too precious to withhold."

"Dahlia, I understand." Not completely out of Jason's hearing, I whispered in Dahlia's ear, "The music stops when you don't have the pills, doesn't it?"

"Christiana, you know? You have heard the music already?" She wiped her eyes on the corner of her cotton office jacket.

"Yes, Dahlia, I've heard it. I wouldn't give it up for anything either." I gave her a hug. "Now, for the reason I came to talk to you. I've just invited Dr. O'Reilly to share Christmas dinner with me and my family. I want you to come too."

"Oh, My Lady ... I am not worthy," she whispered.

"None of us are, Dahlia. I have contributed nothing to earn my place in society. I was born into it. I did not earn it. Please say you'll come."

"Yes," her voice was faint, and I could sense apprehension beneath the surface of her words. She looked at Jason.

Then I realized that Jason held the key to Dahlia's future at that point. I wondered what her fate would be in his hands. I was learning that he was a fair man, a man of integrity, but he also expected the same in return.

He took the pills from her pockets and placed them back in the cabinet. "We'll find another way to detox the people, Dahlia. It will be necessary to do it a little at a time in order to make sure they have no adverse effects." He helped her to her feet. "The chemical additives in our water supply have made illegal drug use a thing of the past. Drawing the police or Blue Guard into this would only raise alarm. No one else needs to know about this. We have to keep our circle small, but I will have to take the key to the pharmacy from you."

Dahlia handed it over with relief.

"For now, why don't you go on home and enjoy the rest of the day. Tomorrow, I'm going to pick up Christiana about fifteen 'til twelve. If you can be ready then, we'll all go together."

"Dr. O'Reilly," she sobbed, "how can I thank you?"

"By being the loving, caring person that you are," Jason said, "and the best healthcare professional I know. No one has been hurt. The pills weren't narcotics. They were neutralizing agents. The patients who became suicidal had abused the tablets you passed on to them. They detoxed too fast. Taken properly, they would have been fine." He took a tissue from the box on the table and smiled. He dabbed at her eyes and added, "You will have to blow your own nose."

CHAPTER THIRTY-ONE
Stoner Waited

Outside the Health Center, Ward Stoner waited in his car for his target to emerge. Her ID tag had told him she was there. He crouched in his vehicle like a thief, waiting to catch his next victim in a weakened state. He had always been able to dominate a situation, to use his mind and the weight of his office, to force his will on others. He could have had any of his Blue Guardsmen follow a young woman around town. But he knew in his gut that this case was different.

A transit car streamed by overhead and he thought again about the ghost who had brought him into the hazy vapor of mystery in which he found himself. It was either one of the biggest cases of his career or someone was making a colossal fool out of him. *It had better not be the latter.* He tried to look at both sides of the paradox he called his life.

He inspected the old-fashioned timepiece he wore on his wrist. It had been his great-grandfather's, and for some reason he enjoyed wearing it. It had a tiny knob on the side of the case that he faithfully wound each night when he took it off. There was no one who would have dared to call him sentimental, any more than they would have called him Inspector Tombstone to his face. Besides, sentimentalism had lost all of it meaning.

Sentiment required emotions and most people had none. But the watch brought a strange sense of continuity, a feeling of family. The hands on the face marched slowly on into the day. He looked again at the doors leading into the medical office building.

He wanted to leave but the whole thing mesmerized him. As he pressed on, in an effort to find answers to the puzzle he had started calling the Princess Case, he felt a strong force pushing back the more he pursued. He had to admit that the challenge made him angry. But, in the greater game he found himself in, he had finally met his match, an equal force to push against. Or was it equal? Still, the watcher watched.

CHAPTER THIRTY-TWO
Many Had No Joy

10:45 a.m.

As I gathered up my things to leave Jason's office, he wrapped me in his arms. "I'll meet you at the *Demitasse* in an hour? We could have some lunch." He gently touched my back, a gallant gesture of ushering someone along.

"Lunch would be fine," I agreed.

I soon walked back out into the wintery day and across the street to the shops I enjoyed so much. I tucked the library book neatly in the fold of my cloak.

The little shopping village was like something out of a Dickens novel, even if most people didn't know who Dickens was. I loved the little cluster of fancy shops and felt at home there.

Since I had an hour before I would meet Jason, I decided to spend my time shopping, something I rarely did. I passed the coffee shop and drifted into the boutique a few doors down. I hadn't bought new clothes in a long time. Clothes never seemed important before. I wandered over to the sale rack and shuffled through the hangers. Legacy Citizens have no need to shop from the reduced section since our personal fortunes and our annual stipend, allow us to live very comfortably, but I enjoyed saving money.

"Good morning My Lady," the sales clerk smiled lightly but her eyes were dull and unresponsive.

"Good morning," I replied then realized the woman was a

classmate from secondary school. "Valley? Is that you? I haven't seen you in several years."

"Yes, Ma'am, it's been a long time. I didn't think you would remember me." Her eyes were looking away but there seemed to be a spark, a new measure of pleasure on her face.

"Of course, I remember you. We managed to survive Mr. Funderman's advanced mathematics class together." I walked through life respected but alone when classmates no longer acknowledged my existence.

"Thank you for remembering," she added. "Is there anything I can help you with? We have a nice selection of holiday green caftogs over here. That color would look beautiful on you with your coloring."

Caftogs were long garments that took their design from a combination of the caftan and toga styles. They had a top with full caftan sleeves, under a wound skirt that then came around and draped up and over the shoulder. The display of fine silk garments, woven with threads that prevented the usual wrinkling, enticed me.

"Yes, Valley, they are beautiful." I ran my fingers over the delicate fabric and down the sleeve to the price tag. It was expensive but certainly not out of my budget. Ordinarily, I would not have considered such an extravagance. I was perfectly satisfied with more modestly priced garments but then I saw Valley's face and understood. She must have worked on commission and a sale of that magnitude, the day before Gift-giving Day, could have made her family's holiday more joyous.

"It is very lovely."

Valley didn't pressure me as it wasn't appropriate to push a sale on a Legacy Citizen.

"I'll take it," I smiled and took the garment without trying it on. "I'll wear it to my grandparents' Gifting Day party." It was bound to fit. The government established a uniform sizing system for all clothing many years ago. If you wore a size six, every six fit exactly the same way.

I casually slipped the library book into my clothing package and started to leave. To continue the comfortable contact I had with Valley, I asked, "Do you have plans for the holidays?" I waited for a response from my old friend.

"Plans?" she questioned with an emotionless expression except for an artificial, painted on pleasantness.

"You know ... are you going to be with your parents for holiday dinner?"

"We always had gotten together but ..." She paused as if she were searching her memory for a happy holiday with her family. "It's been so long since my grandmother was alive. She made the best date pudding."

"I always found the term, date pudding, a strange name for a cake." I hoped to get a real smile out of Valley, a brief reprieve from her dull life.

"What?" Valley blinked and stared. She was no longer with me but had drifted off to a gray existence among the colorless memories of her life.

I took my shopping bag with the book and package tucked inside and wished Valley a joyous Gift-giving Day. Outside, I saw the town clock and knew I was nearing my time with Jason and I smiled. A Blue Shirted Inspector looked at me sharply so I quickly wiped the smile from my face. He darted into the bank on the other side of the boutique and was quickly gone. I thought he looked familiar but dismissed him from my mind and smiled again. I had discovered that my face felt more relaxed when I smiled. And, the annoying pain between my eyes, I used to frequently experience, vanished when the corners of my mouth tuned up. Wow! Life was vibrant and new. But, when would the happiness stop? If I couldn't end the Length of Days terrible policy, my joy, like Valley's, might be gone forever.

CHAPTER THIRTY-THREE
Thackery and the Blue Guard

11:30 a.m.

Inside the *Demitasse,* I found a seat near the back where I could wait for Jason. Rather than facing the wall as I always did, I looked out over the people as they came and went and sipped their drinks. What looked to be a dad and his son were sitting at a table across from me. Even though through stilted emotions, they were obviously enjoying each other's company. The boy, about ten years old, reached over and grabbed the last potato strip from his father's plate, then laughed. Dad rumpled the boy's hair and smiled. A couple in the corner were experiencing the beginning of an attraction neither seemed to understand nor felt comfortable with. He kept averting her eyes and stared into his cup with a hidden grin. I had to smile. Being part of the world was an amazing, new experience. Maybe I had been aloof in the past, just as Jason had teased.

Then, a man entered the café and looked directly at me without glancing away as most people did. He not only kept his eyes fixed on me, he continued to approach me from yards away. I squirmed a little in my seat as the bold, strange man continued toward me. In the present era, men simply do not openly watch a Legacy woman. When he got to my table, he leaned on it heavily with the knuckles of both his hands and whispered.

"Hi, Gorgeous, I haven't seen that beautiful, shiny hair around town before."

I was both irritated and afraid. Men not only didn't talk to

Legacy women; they did not flirt—with anyone. The truth was, in our current age, men simply didn't have the emotional capacity or adequate hormonal level to flirt.

How was I going to respond to him? He frightened me in a way that made me want to run and hide. I thought of my grandmother and the kind words she had for everyone while maintaining a razor back dignity. Looking at the man with Grand-mère's royal authority, I spoke with all the confidence I could muster. "Young man, who are you and what do you want?"

He grinned arrogantly at my response. "Well done, My Lady." Then he leaned in even further. "I wonder if you have noticed how bright the lights are today. The reds and greens are great."

"Yes, but —"

"Thomas thinks the blues are casting dark shadows though."

"Who are you?" I demanded. A cold chill shot across my back and his mentioning Thomas's name offered no comfort. Maybe it was because my world had never been intruded on before and it was now being bombarded with stimuli from every angle. I sipped on the water the waitress had placed on the table, hoping to calm the sickening feeling that refused control.

"I'm Thackery, Ma'am. A friend of Sean's." Then he winked.

His brashness amazed me. "You also have a friend at the medical center don't you," I said. It was a statement, not a question.

He smiled mischievously. "You mean ... well never mind. You may be talking about someone or something else."

"There are others?" I whispered.

"There are many of us, Christiana." Again, he smiled and then suddenly became serious. "Are you with us or against us?"

"I'm just learning who *us* may be, Thackery." My discomfort had changed to interest but a measure of fear remained. I didn't know what to think about the man or of all the new people in my life. "I have one singular goal at this time. Nothing else can get in my way, Thackery. I can tell you that."

"I know My Lady," He whispered.

"What do you know?" I questioned indignantly. I didn't like his smugness. He seemed to know my mind before I knew it myself.

Thackery boldly slipped onto the chair next to me. "I know you have dear ones who will be celebrating their birthdays very soon."

"I don't think I like your knowing all about me and I know nothing about you." A spied on feeling crept in again.

"You and all the Elites, Christiana. We may not be able to print your pictures in magazines that were banned a long time ago, like the celebrities in ages past, but we still know. The underground newspaper announces your every move, each and every event in your life. You are our stars today, My Lady. It's just against the law for us to intrude on your privacy. You must not see us watching."

I suddenly had a need to rub the chill from my arms. "Being watched is just creepy," I said.

"Maybe. I wouldn't know. I'm not the focus of all that adoration."

"Adoration? Thackery, is it admiration? I thought it would be disdain, not respect." My thoughts wandered to the many times I knew I was being observed and my experience was not Thackery's experience.

"You don't have to be afraid of us, Christiana. But, have you noticed the increase in Blue Shirts on the streets? There had been fewer last evening, but now just before the holiday, there is definitely a stronger presence."

"Until the last few days, I don't think I noticed anything going on around me."

"I have. I don't know what it's all about, but you'd better be careful. No smiling in public, no laughter, no display of affection or emotion of any kind."

"That's hard to do." I thought of Jason.

"I know. When you have someone in your life like the Doc, it's hard not to smile all the time. Dahlia gives me the flutters."

173

"Dahlia?" I tried to show no surprise then stopped. What had he just said before referring to Dahlia? "Wait! Have you seen Jason and me together?"

"Many of us have, Ma'am." He lowered his voice to a whisper and looked around the room. "Do you still hear the music?"

My heart stopped its beating and my breath caught in my throat. "You know about the music?" I could not resist rambling on. "Isn't it the most miraculous sound you have ever heard?" Then I stopped.

"What is it?" Thackery asked without turning around. He slowly sat back in his chair, apparently not wanting to give away any urgency in our conversation.

"Some high-ranking Blue Shirt has just come in," I whispered, then unobtrusively dropped a detox table into the water the waitress had previously placed in front of me. I held the glass to my lips, hoping I could block any expression of curiosity or fear. "I've seen him around town several times this morning, and I think last evening as well."

"A lot of people have." Thackery responded nonchalantly as if he were talking about the price of peaches in the winter season. He smoothed imaginary wrinkles from the table cloth. "Is he sitting down?"

"No, he's coming this way." I stopped and replaced my glass on the table.

The Blue Shirt touched his hat but didn't remove it. "Ma'am." He looked at me then at Thackery. "Is this man bothering you?"

I had to think fast. Was he asking me about my association with this man I had just met? I didn't know who Thackery's friends were. If I responded in the affirmative, I may have admitted to an association with those engaged in seditious actions or words. If I said I didn't know him, it might place Thackery in jeopardy.

"We have a mutual acquaintance," I said. "He was asking for a suggestion on a possible Gift Day present for her."

Stoner's facial expression never changed. With his steely eyes fixed on me, he demanded in a frighteningly friendly manner, "And who might it be, Miss Applewait, that you both know?"

"Dahlia Zoobamba lives in my building." I responded confidently, then added. "She is also my physician's nurse."

"Yes, I know. Dr. O'Reilly."

"You know when I've gone to the doctor?" I blurted out. I should have let the comment pass. I was close to revealing an emotion I dare not display. Novels described it as anger.

"No Ma'am. I happen to know that Dahlia Zoobamba is Dr. O'Reilly's nurse." He stared intently at me and then asked? "What have you suggested?"

"About what?" I stammered.

"She thought Dahlia might like a brightly colored silk scarf to wrap around her head in this cold weather." Thackery interjected.

"I wasn't asking you," Stoner glared. Then he turned to me again. "That sounds fine, Ma'am. Just where might one find such a scarf."

"I was just in the boutique down the street. They have a whole display of beautiful, brightly colored scarfs in floral and geometric patterns." Luckily, I had just admired the scarfs as I was leaving the shop.

"Yes, Ma'am. I'll check on that." He looked at me again and stated flatly as if he were reading from a formal report. "You have had a busy schedule this morning, My Lady."

"Yes, thank you for keeping your eye out for me. I'm finishing my shopping for Gift-giving Day."

"Oh, you are?" he stated doubtfully. "And what have you bought this morning?"

I felt uncomfortable. It was as though the hunted had turned and faced the hunter. A chill came over me that threatened to freeze out my fledgling confidence. Again, I could hear the faint sound of angel voices singing their calming songs. Peace warmed my spine and recharged the boldness battery I had inherited from Grand-mère. "I bought a lovely caftog just a little while ago at that same boutique. I'll enjoy wearing it at my family's dinner on Gift-giving Day." Then I added, because I rarely bought anything and had some sudden need to justify my purchase, "I haven't bought anything new in quite a while. Would you like to see it?" I reached for the shopping bag I had stashed under the table. I froze. The book, would the Inspector see it if I opened the package?

"That's not necessary, Ma'am," Stoner replied flatly. He turned and walked away.

I finally exhaled and sat back.

"That was interesting," Thackery whispered.

"What was interesting?" Jason came up to the table while I was still trying to shake the jitters I had just acquired from the inspector's prying comments.

"Jason," I gasped in relief.

"Calmly," Thackery warned.

"I can be calm," I assured him. "Did you see him, Jason? The Blue Guard officer that was at the apartment building last night. He was just in here. He was asking questions and trying to trip us up."

Jason stood for a second and then started to take a seat. "Are you all right?" Then he looked at Thackery. "Who is this man, Christy?"

Thackery jumped to his feet. "Here, Dr. O'Reilly, take my seat. I was just leaving and you two will probably want to be alone."

"How did you —?"

"Dahlia called me last night. I had hoped to get over to see her during the evening but I was helping Sean. I'll see Dahlia later." Then he bowed slightly. "I'm Thackery Swift."

Jason seemed to be shuffling through recent memories in his mind. "Oh," he restrained a smile, "Swifty. Dahlia has mentioned you, one or two or twenty times."

"Yes, Sir," he admitted.

Swifty's cheeks turned red and I remembered the warmth of my own cheeks the day before. *So that's what we look like when we blush.*

Thackery pulled the chair out for the doctor and leaned forward a little as he moved. "Dahlia will be at home on her piano bench again this evening if you want to join us."

"I would love to," I agreed with enthusiasm. "The music was so soul strengthening I long to hear and sing more."

"See you tonight," Thackery waved as he headed toward the door.

Jason frowned as I told him how the Blue Guardsman had almost threatened me. "I see him lurking around wherever I go, Jason."

"We must be careful not to give him anything to be suspicious about," Jason said. "But as Legacy Citizens, we should be free to move about the city, to take a walk, to have an uninterrupted cup of coffee. Are you ready to go?"

CHAPTER THIRTY-FOUR
Story Checking

Ward Stoner had accomplished little at the *Demitasse*. As he stepped out of the coffee shop, he looked out on the street and shook his head. No one had stood up to him in so many years he had forgotten how it felt. Chalky Boone always stood her own ground, but she didn't count. That was her job. Besides, her keen investigative mind and her resistance to intimidation were two of the reasons he had kept her around. Now, there was a new person in his life who didn't flinch in his game of *political poker.*

Well now, we'll just see about you, Missy. He jerked open the door of the store his new opponent had mentioned. *There had better be scarfs near the entrance.*

"May I help you, Sir?" Valley asked as the inspector entered the store.

"I was told about these scarfs you have on display here," he began in his skilled way.

"Yes, Sir," she smiled and picked up one of the colorful pieces of silk.

"Perhaps you waited on her ... Lady Applewait?"

"Yes, she was in here."

"Well, what did she buy?" Stoner had lost his patience years ago and raced through life on raw adrenaline charged by anger, excitement, danger, or any other experience in his day.

"Sir, I'm not supposed to gossip about our patrons and certainly not if they are Legacy Citizens." Valley smiled slightly and pursed her lips tightly.

"She just told me she had bought a caftog," he tried to mask his agitation and managed only a fair imitation of a real person. "That sounded like a good gift for my mother. She's young at heart and would enjoy wearing one just like Lady Applewait's."

"Yes, Sir," Valley perked up with the thought of another generous commission for the day. "They are right here. Lady Applewait chose this gorgeous green. I'm sure it will be lovely with her hair."

"Those things seem to be important to some people ... not my mother." He ran his fingers over the fabric. It was exquisite, with hand embroidered details on the hem. "I'll take it. Wrap it up," he ordered.

"Yes, Sir!" she smiled. Valley didn't mask her surprise or joy. With that additional sale, she had earned more in one hour than she had all that day.

Stoner grabbed the package and started for the door where he passed the scarfs again. *You may have won the first hand, but I will win the game,* he snickered. *You don't even realize you're in a high stakes game with your own life in the pot.* The challenge of each hand dealt to him, invigorated him. No one was clever enough to trump him. He would not lose for any reason. By the time he had reached that hand in the game, he would have marched into hell to win the match.

CHAPTER THIRTY-FIVE

A Dance in the Snow

12:30 p.m.

As we left the café, I shivered as I looked around to see if the Blue Guard might be waiting outside. I was still upset over the contact with the Guardsman.

"Are you cold?" Jason asked as he put his arm around my shoulder.

"No, it was something Thackery said."

"According to Dahlia, Swifty has quite an imagination."

Looking up ahead in the square, I saw a car pull to the side of the street. Two more men from the Blue Guard got out and stormed the area, running in cadence toward the hospital. I tried not to think about them or the cause of their increased activity. I wanted to enjoy my time with Jason.

Focusing on the season rather than the sinister, I turned back to what Thackery had said about Gift Day mentality. "They think the lights cause the little moths to cluster around so they can spend their hard-earned money until they get burned on the bulbs." I snuggled closer to Jason as we walked along in the crisp air of the winter day.

"I guess they think if you have nothing in your life that brings you joy except spending money, you'll spend until you bury yourself in debt you can never repay, just to get a small reprieve from the numbness of your existence." Jason looked to the changing sky and the world around him. "Those who drink the water can't find happiness in even the smallest things around them."

"I understand now what you're saying," I agreed in amazement. "It's like I've never seen clouds before, and I want to take in every glorious image I possibly can, in case the beauty is taken back again. Do you have time for us to walk a while? I want to absorb all the color I see around me."

"I can't think of anything I'd rather do." He patted my hand as it rested on his arm. It fit there like we were made for walking together.

"How much time do you have?" I could have walked all day if I were walking with him.

He checked the clock on the courthouse tower. "About twenty minutes. I have to make two phone calls and do some paper work this afternoon and then I'm going to leave the office for the rest of the day."

"You'll come to the apartment so we can talk and then join the group for singing later this evening, won't you?" I whispered.

"I wouldn't miss it for anything." He patted my hand again.

"If you come about three, I'll have a special concoction for you to try. Then, we could go down to the lobby —" I saw the inspector coming out of the boutique and didn't finish what I was saying. He eyed us suspiciously as we walked arm in arm, but I thought if I pulled away, it might raise more questions. I pretended not to see him. He walked on past us. *Is he checking up on me?* That thought made my skin prickle with fear.

Jason and I said no more for a few minutes until we got to the town square where the old octagonal, shake roofed structure stood in the center. Twinkling lights were artfully wound in and out of the white railing that surrounded it. The afternoon sky was overcast with fluffy gray snow clouds that dropped a linen-like film of shimmer over the day.

"I'm dreaming of a white Christmas, just like the ones I never knew," I improvised.

Jason took my hand and led me up the steps and onto the stage-like platform of the octagon. He pulled me near him and took me in his arms, like dancers I had read about in the books of old. He hummed the melody that streamed under the words, in my ear, "Where the tree tops glisten and children listen ..."

"We'd better stop, Jason." I knew dancing would be just as forbidden as the music and the joy that the holidays had inspired.

"I don't know if I can stop anymore now, Christy. I know I'm moving fast, but I have waited so long for you to come along. Attraction is a powerful thing and without additives, it is like it was in the days of old. They called it *love at first sight.*"

"I've heard of such an emotion, and for the first time, I understand what that means." Being with Jason this short time had awakened me to the new emotions that had the power to make me understand risky behavior. "What will happen if someone sees us dancing, Jason?"

He stepped back and looked into my eyes. "Yes, I know it is best not to draw attention. It's best no one sees us. If our outward behavior gives away our inner emotions, people may notice. That could be dangerous."

CHAPTER THIRTY-SIX

Warmth from a Distance is No Warmth at All

It was too late. Someone had already seen the doctor and his Lady in an embrace. Inspector Stoner sat in his strata-car at a nearby curb. The frosty air was fogging up his windshield so he cleaned it with a small scrapper. It made him even more angry. Every small inconvenience, he interpreted as a personal affront to his worthiness, his intelligence. The gods were against him. *Why does it always —?* Then he would fill in any complaint to complete his protests against life.

Well, well, well, he mumbled to himself as he watched the happy couple dancing in the park. *I may have caught a really big fish. This little mermaid does anything she wants to do.* He sneered into the emptiness around him. *Why do they always think they can get by with breaking the law? And why are they so sickeningly happy?*

He had watched them with irritated interest from the time they left the café. He saw the couple laugh and twirl together in each other's arms. As he watched, he could feel his stomach tie up in its usual knot as he tried to process his loneliness without acknowledging his wife's death. Stoner had no one to smile with. No ear to whisper into. No love to hold next to his heart. His heart had ceased aching. He felt nothing anymore.

Stoner had seen enough. He pulled his car back into the street and headed in the direction of his headquarters. Still, he couldn't resist the need to watch the couple through the rear-view mirror until they disappeared when he turned the corner. He had to acknowledge the reality of his burnt-out feelings but couldn't figure out why the romance between the Lady and the doctor fascinated him. Romance had died in the sleep chamber with Miriam. He preferred feeling nothing. It was easier. His heart beat only by habit. It had become like his name, a stone.

CHAPTER THIRTY-SEVEN
Eyes in the Apartment

1:30 p.m.

It was still early when Jason and I left the town square with the promise that he would come to my place later. In the evening, we would join the singing group again. The city had turned the holiday lights on earlier than other days. Now, it was the afternoon of Gift-giving Eve and the colorful lights seemed to encourage the shoppers to spend more money. Society liked to pretend that it was a time to honor one another with gifts and an opportunity to bring families closer together in celebration. But there was little joy or meaning in any of it anymore, not like the old books had described. It was no secret that Gift-giving was a vital part of our economy and provided the financial support to keep stores and businesses open the entire year, based on the proceeds from gift purchases. So, they decorated the cities to stimulate what fragile emotions remained, to prompt more and more purchases. At least that was my theory. I looked for the blue lights among the precious gold, and I shuddered a little.

2:00 p.m.

I had ridden the P-T back to my building. I hurried into my apartment and threw the curtains open to let in as much of the afternoon light as possible. It was nearly 2:00 p.m. so the long shadows of trees and buildings stretched out across the city. The holiday lights twinkled even brighter than I had previously noticed. I stood at the large wall of windows and looked out on the city I loved. With few private cars and the tremendous cost of air fare and high-speed train tickets, very few people traveled beyond the boundaries of the city, since that was as far as the Public Transit system ran. Besides, it was forbidden to travel to the other zones. Mass communication offered a sterile education about other places but that was different from actually walking in their green woods.

I turned on the large wall mounted communications screen and curled up on the couch. Society reserved one channel that looped a video throughout the day. The scene was of softly pounding waves on a pristine beach.

2:30 p.m.

Suddenly, the doorbell rang. As I turned to respond, I noticed something strange near the bookcase. Was it something that was there that hadn't been there before? Or, something that wasn't there, that had been there before. But ... what was it? What was missing? What had been moved? What had been added? No one could have been in my apartment. It was forbidden to enter the home of a Legacy Citizen unless treason, sedition, or other acts against society were suspected.

The doorbell rang again and interrupted my thoughts. I hurried to answer it, hoping it was he.

"Good afternoon Christy." Jason measured his speech carefully measured there in the public hallway, but his eyes spoke bushels more.

I hung his coat in the closet with mine and then grabbed Jason's hand and almost dragged him into the room. He pretended to be surprised and stumbled in, then regained his balance once the door closed. He whisked me nearly off my feet and hugged me long, with all the emotion his words could not express.

"It is so good to see you and I was just with you a few hours ago," I laughed softly. I found myself whispering in my own apartment. "Come out to the kitchen, I have made something special."

I led him into the food preparation area and ladled a full cup of cold creamy liquid into two cups. I handed it to him and waited for his reaction.

"Looks good. What is it?"

"Eggnog, Jason. I read about it in one of the books. It's made with eggs, cream, milk, and nutmeg. It's a holiday drink they used to serve at Christmas parties. What do you think?" I was too excited to sip mine until I got Jason's reaction. When Jason smiled over the rim of his cup, as he savored the sweetness of the drink, I tasted a sip of my own.

"This is wonderful, Christy!" He closed his eyes. "I want to enjoy the entire flavor of the drink with no other distractions—just taste." He tipped up his cup and emptied the contents.

"Would you like more?"

"You know I would," he admitted as he placed his cup on the counter and dipped out another ladle full.

We took our drinks into the living room and sat them on the table in front of the windows. It was beautiful there. The late afternoon lights were even more magical than they had appeared earlier.

"This looks wonderful, Christy."

We talked and laughed and enjoyed each other, as red and green and gold lights danced across the scene beyond the building.

The events of the last day and a half raced through my mind like a collage of snippets and glimpses into a whole new world of emotions and color. Practicality was no longer the word that would define my life. But I had few feeling-words in my verbal vocabulary to express my experience. I had read them but never expressed them. I was just a mass of sensitivity, and the raw nerves hurt at times.

I finished my eggnog as we sat in the quiet for a while. Later, I smiled at life, love and the cozy shadows that had settled into the apartment as I looked around the dimly lit room.

"Something wrong?" Jason asked as he followed my gaze into the corners of my space.

"I don't know." I looked at the bookcase again. "Just as you rang the doorbell, I noticed that something has been moved or added. I can't put my finger on what it would be."

We both looked around but couldn't see anything out of place. "I must have imagined it," I said. "Or, the kitten may have moved something."

"I am so sorry you've been frightened so many times lately. I wish I could take it all away." Then, Jason paused. "I know we forgot to finish something." He stood up and took my hand, guiding me from the table. "Our little dance was interrupted," he said as he gathered me in his arms in an old-fashioned waltz position. I remembered a well-written chapter in a book that described the dance and the music and the romance of it all.

We moved in a simple step in the silent room, but music soared within me. "The whole world is missing out on so much. I wonder why they banned the music."

"Emotions ride through the air and lodge in the heart on the strings of musical notes. If we couldn't feel anything anymore, they had to ban that which stirs the emotions." Jason twirled me around. Then, like a grand ballroom move in an old book, he bent me back in a low dip.

"Jason!" I whispered a muffled gasp from my upside-down position. It's funny how we see things differently when we view them from another angle.

"What?" he hurriedly pulled me up. "Are you all right?"

"Oh ... yes, but I saw something." Again, I looked toward the book shelves.

Jason followed my gaze, looking for some clue, though neither of us knew what we were looking for.

I walked over to the books and searched up and down the shelves, pretending I was looking for a particular volume. The intruding object was there just as I suspected. I turned slowly and quietly, as if nothing were out of the ordinary. With my back to the bookcase, I winked solemnly at Jason.

"Well, now I'm ready for that ice cream you promised me this afternoon." I was glad I hadn't identified a time when we supposedly talked about ice cream. I had seen Jason during the early afternoon hours but I was so shaken, I didn't remember when. A misspoken time frame would have alerted whoever was watching us that we fabricated a story. Would he take hold of the subtle thread I had tossed out? I could only hope that he had pulled together all the hints I had dropped.

He never missed a beat. "Ice cream it is," he agreed with a smile. I grabbed my hat and our coats from the closet and walked out the door. Jason looked at me seriously, quizzically.

"If we hurry, we can get to the ice cream shop while they're still open. I imagine they'll close early today, since it's Gift-giving Eve," I added to the impromptu conversation.

We hurried to the elevator, hopped in, and said nothing. We rode to the first floor in nervous silence. My limbs were shaking from the anxiety I was feeling. We slipped through the front door and took long strides to Jason's automobile.

When we were safely inside, I began shaking totally out of control. I buried my face in my hands and screamed.

"Christy?" Jason's voice was full of bewilderment and concern as he rocked me in his arms. "What did you see on that book shelf? What was it?"

"Someone has been in my apartment, Jason." I searched my bag for something to blot my eyes. I couldn't believe I was crying again. Jason took a handkerchief from his pocket and tried to blot my covered eyes.

"What? Someone is watching you inside your apartment?" he gasped as he pulled me even closer.

"Drive, Jason, drive, move. I don't know who may be watching us." I was yelling through clinched teeth. I knew I dared not make any noise or draw attention to us but my restraint had dissolved with my tears.

He started the engine and pulled out into the street. "Christy ... what —?"

189

"Jason, there was a small camera of some sort stuck in among my books. I could feel that something was there. Someone must have been in my apartment, probably earlier this afternoon. When I saw the camera, I knew someone had been there. Now, someone may be outside too—watching our every move."

"You felt it? You didn't actually see it?" Jason eased slowly in and out of traffic like any other traveler on the road.

"Yes, I felt it at first, but then, when you bent me back, I saw it. So, when I went over to the bookshelves to get a better look, I saw it clearly, Jason ... like a camera thing I had seen in an old book. It takes motion activated pictures of anyone who happens to be in the room."

"How does something like that, an old camera maybe, continue to operate?"

"I don't know. I just glanced at it and kept pretending not to see it. But, some of the old cameras turned on and recorded when movement activated them. I read about them last week in an old spy novel." I sat back and tried to gather my thoughts. "Motion sensitive, I think they called them. The one in the book took one picture after another as long as there was movement within the range of the lens."

"I see another problem." Jason shook his head as he looked in the rear-view mirror.

"What is it?" I turned around and tried to see what had caused alarm.

"No," Jason snapped and then added, "sorry. We'd better act like we don't notice it."

"What?" I asked but resisted my need to look.

"Maybe nothing but every time I turn, the car behind us turns too." Jason went around another corner to test his theory and looked in the mirror. "I was right. He turned again."

"With that camera in my apartment, if it had sound, they may have heard us. We'd better go to the ice cream shop like we said we were going to do, in case the camera had sound. Marion's Ice Cream Parlor is on North Main Street."

"Right," Jason agreed and turned the last corner to get us back on course.

"Who do you suppose would be following us and why?"

"I don't know but maybe they'll give up once we go into the ice cream shop." Jason said as he checked his mirror again.

Even when Jason stopped the car at the curb, I resisted the urge to look around. We had to pretend we were happily spending an afternoon out. By this time, we both knew it was important to maintain that charade or we might be caught, and tried for crimes against the state.

CHAPTER THIRTY-EIGHT

Ice Cream as an Alibi

4:00 p.m.

Luckily for Jason and me the little ice cream parlor was still open. I started to get out of the car but Jason touched my arm and stopped me.

"I'm not going to let whoever is back there, make me less than a gentleman." He smiled, walked around the car, and opened the door for me. He offered his hand and I slid out. I resisted the temptation to look back to see if the other car had also stopped.

Once inside Marion's, we moved past the other patrons eating frozen treats. Their eyes told the Gifting Day Eve story. There usually was no life, no joy, no gift of Hope, but for the Gifting holidays, there was a faint glimmer of something beautiful. I wanted to find a shadow to hide in. My new happiness may have been dangerous to reveal and hard to hide among the walking dead.

We settled into a small booth in the back. I inhaled the sweet aroma of rich cream and chocolate. I used to think that some wise soul would finally make a perfume from those scents. "No, an aftershave."

"What? We came to the ice cream parlor, and you want to order aftershave?" He smiled but held in his laughter as a precaution.

"No silly. You must have read my thoughts. I was just thinking of a perfume fragrance, then realized the scent would be better put to use as an aftershave. What woman wouldn't be attracted to a man who smelled like chocolate?"

"Chocolate? You design the fancy bottle, and I'll invest in the company." He smiled.

"I would really be in trouble if you started using our new fragrance, *Chocolate Mystery*." I couldn't believe I had said it, but it was already out.

"Wow, that almost sounds like forbidden talk. Remember, women aren't attracted to men anymore. They have no libido."

"Well, most women don't," I teased.

We laughed softly and allowed ourselves to forget. Were we really followed? Was there someone—waiting and watching us?

CHAPTER THIRTY-NINE
The Shadow

From a parked car near a family ice cream parlor, Boone's voice came over Stoner's communication device. "Are you coming back to the office today, Sir?"

"No, probably not. I'm shadowing a suspect."

"A suspect in what?"

"The breach of security case, of course," he bristled.

"Sir, you're not following —?"

"You know who I'm tailing, Boone. And, since you know, you're as much a part of this as I am. Are you going to report the situation?"

"Sir, you're on an unsecured frequency."

"Even the stalker has to take chances with the stalked."

"Your son will be expecting you to come home, Ward," Chalky coached.

"Are you manipulating me, Lieutenant?" he snapped.

"Is that possible?" She feigned an attitude of resignation.

"You're doing it again."

"Sorry ... but I like my job so it's important to me that you ... do well." She sounded cautious. Anyone tuned into the frequency would have been able to hear everything she said.

"A high tide floats all ships Boone and I'm riding high."

"Sir ... you are very brave ... but you have never been careless," Boone whispered, as if only the Inspector could hear the caution in her voice.

"Measuring caution with a larger beaker is sometimes necessary, Lieutenant."

"But a person can drown in a bigger pool, Sir," Boone returned without another word. Stoner had stopped listening. He was confronted with the greater challenge.

He sat back in his seat and scanned the road ahead of him but spent precious little time evaluating his options. The 281 Palm Device was on the seat beside him, waiting for his next bold move. He flipped it on. It glowed brightly; the hologram pulsed in front of him. "Call, Jonathon Fink ... Fort Knox."

Suddenly, his old friend appeared in the middle of the glowing image. "Hi Ward. It's good to see you."

"You too, Johnny. Say ... what kind of trouble would you and I get into if you were to look up some information for me on a Legacy Citizen?"

There was silence, but Jonathon's image revealed a restless man, uncomfortable with his friend's inquiry. "Ward ... you know —"

"You know I know Johnny." Stoner watched the man intently as he shimmered in front of him. "Look Man, this is important."

"I know it is, or you wouldn't ask. What are you needing?"

"The fact is, I don't know. There is a young Legacy woman that is getting under my skin. She cannot possibly be as controlled as she pretends to be. She's brave and growing in self-assurance."

"Sounds like a great woman to me, Ward. How's that a problem?"

"There has been a breach of security here. I know she has something to do with it. If I can't stop what she's doing, maybe I can use some previous history to persuade her to cooperate."

"Persuade? You mean blackmail? Ward, I —"

"I don't see it as extortion, Johnny. I see it as evidence of a pattern of behavior, that's all. What do you say?"

"Okay Ward, I owe you. But this whole thing had better not come back to me." Jonathon stated flatly.

"Thanks Man."

A little fish may drown in a big pool ... but not a shark. Stoner's self-talk dripped with entitlement and confidence. *The great white always circles and waits before the attack.*

CHAPTER FORTY
The Evil at Howard Mountain

5:00 p.m.

Jason and I finished our frozen treats and were cautious in case anyone could see inside the ice cream parlor. I noticed the time. It was five p.m. Marion's was going to close at six. When we finally went outside, the early evening darkness had taken on an eerie glow. The holiday lights had grown halos from bouncing off a fog that had silently crept in, like a panther on the edge of a forest. I felt just as vulnerable as an innocent prey waiting for the pounce of a mighty cat. Eyes seemed to be watching from behind every dark window. It wasn't a curiosity I was used to. This was something else, something profoundly frightening to me.

Jason helped me into his car then paused at the passenger side door when his communications device vibrated.

"Dr. O'Reilly," he acknowledged. "Yes, well, it's late," he apologized. "Yes, I understand. I have someone with me and I'll have to bring her along. All right."

Jason hurried around and hopped in the car. He rubbed his hands as he tried to warm them from the cold.

"Sorry, Christy. I just had an emergency call from Howard Mountain. I'll have to go out there. I think I'd better take you along considering all that has happened this evening."

He looked around, but the parking spaces were empty except for a few nearby. "Must have lost interest in us," Jason said. "But we'll still have to deal with that camera. If the building maintenance man is into spying on tenants, then he's in a lot of trouble."

"That's all right Jason. After a day like today, a ride in the country will be welcomed."

Jason's company blessed me more each time I was with him. Along the empty road to Howard Mountain, the rising moon was trying to burn a hole in the fog and cast an occasional moonbeam along our path. We arrived at the mountain at 5:30.

"Yes?" The speaker at the gate squawked when Jason buzzed for entrance.

"Dr. O'Reilly here. I've been asked to see a patient."

"Dr. O'Reilly, thank goodness you came." There was a rattle and then a screech. "The guard isn't on duty so I've released the lock. The gate will swing inward. Please come to the main entrance."

The gate swung open, and Jason pulled the car up to the front door of the huge stone facade at the entry to the chamber beneath the mountain. A gruff voice greeted us beyond the darkness of the vestibule. Jason assisted me from the car. Ice was rapidly forming on the front steps. He helped me safely over the threshold and inside the door.

"My Lady," the man whispered in surprise.

It was only then that I saw who he was and I shuddered. "Silas Drummond," I gasped. "I am relieved to see you are well. I saw —" I hesitated, not knowing what had happened or why Jason had been called to the mountain.

"Why have I been summoned, Mr. Drummond?" Jason was patient but sounded as confused as was I.

"Follow me." Silas led the way down a dark hall lined with unlit frosted glass display cases and into a brightly lit lounge area. He closed the door and leaned against it.

"We're supposed to be alone. Since it's Gift-giving Eve, I'm the only one here. But I can't take any chances." He moved toward the light on the side table and displayed his seriously injured hand.

"That looks like a very bad burn, Silas," Jason observed.

"I'm sorry to interrupt, Silas, but I have to know what's going on. You tried to contact me several times in the recent days. You wrote an absolutely horrendous note to me and then I saw them take you away in a squad car."

"This is the man you have agonized about?" Jason could not conceal his anger. "Okay, Drummond, what is this all about?"

"The note was true, My Lady, every word of it. I tried to contact you. you were the only person I knew who might be able to get a word about this place to the right authorities." Silas waved his arms to indicate the entire surroundings.

"You mean ... all the people who think they are entering the never-ending-sleep ... are actually exterminated in a crematorium?" I shuddered with the thought of it and what that would mean to my grandparents.

Tears of anguish and exhaustion began to flow down Drummond's cheeks. "Multiple furnaces, Miss Applewait. More than I want to think about. It's my job to keep the flames lit and burning at a steady temperature. The other night, someone delivered a friend, little Mari. You may remember her from the apartment building."

The image of a beautiful young woman, just a few years younger than me, came to mind. "She had an awful limp, didn't she Silas?"

"Yes Ma'am. Her medical advisor recommended a long rest but— there is no such thing, My Lady. It's all the same. Long sleep or extended nap, it's still death by fire." His voice trailed off to a whisper. "And most enter the chamber while they're still alive. I couldn't do it. I couldn't lie to her. I had to get her out of here, so I left before my shift was up. I needed to escape so desperately, I didn't even punch out and ... I took Mari with me. I put a blanket around her, threw her over my shoulder, and carried her out with me. She's hidden near the edge of town at my sister's home. I got her out of the zone quickly. The next day, when I didn't show up for work, the Blue Guard found me in front of the library and delivered me back to this wretched mountain. They didn't even ask me about Mari. Since so few people know about our work here, and the agencies don't communicate with one another, no one was even aware that a soul had gone missing. They won't know someone has escaped until they count the pairs of shoes.

"When they brought me back, I was here alone so I had to hurry making my furnace inspection rounds. I burned my hand on one of the oven doors." He timidly turned the palm of his hand up and reluctantly showed the damage. "I was afraid my injury would be one insult too many to my safety here. I didn't know what they would do to me, so I called the only doctor I knew. Dahlia has talked about you frequently and said I can trust you. I didn't know you would be with Dr. O'Reilly, My Lady."

Jason hesitated for a moment, his jaw tense and a look of disbelief was on his face. "Silas, you mean—people are simply executed here at the mountain?" He clenched his hands as he leaned on the lamp table. "All of them?"

"Every last one of them." Drummond's voice cracked with emotion so heavy it seemed to weigh down his entire being.

"And, my own parents?"

"Your parents, Doctor? Who were they?"

"Charles and Stephanie O'Reilly." Jason's voice trembled to a whisper.

"Oh … " Silas hung his head and averted Jason's eyes. "I don't think I know about them."

"How long have you worked here?" Jason demanded.

"Almost twenty years, Sir."

"Then you would have been here when they were brought in after their accident," Jason pushed.

"I may have been on holiday, Sir." He hesitated in silence. "Can you do anything for my hand?"

Jason stared at the man for a moment. "Yes, I have some cream and a special glove to protect the hand while the burn heals."

"Will I be able to use my hand? If I can't, they may declare me unfit for work. That would be too much. They already gave me consideration for my years of service and the uniqueness of my job when they decided my fate after my absence." He closed his eyes and then added. "No one else would want this despicable position and ... they've taken my car, so now I have no way to leave. I'm stuck here for at least a week, eating out of the food dispensers, during which time I'm supposed to be thankful that I have a valuable job that contributes to society."

"Who else knows about this place?" Jason prodded, as he tended the burned hand.

"Very few citizens, except for me and a handful of other workers, know about the wickedness here in the bowels of the earth. Those who had known about the mountain are gone by now. They left no notes, no files, no trace of anything." Drummond shook his head. He appeared to be in utter resignation to the part he had played in the atrocities under there. "All knowledge of the crematorium's activity has faded into the dust of time, but the Length of Days policy continues to function like a perpetual motion machine, going on and on with no slowing in momentum."

"You mean there is no one overseeing the work down here?" Jason asked.

"Once this horrendous mess was set into motion, it has just kept rolling on?" I couldn't believe it. "How is that possible?"

"That's what I've been trying to tell you, Miss Applewait. The only person who has ever come down here from above is Alister Bedlam."

"What on earth does Alister Bedlam have to do with all of this?" Jason's voice was curt and tense.

"He is the only one that I'm aware of, who has ever been down here or has ever contacted us from the surface."

"Silas, why does he come here? What has he said when he's called?" Bedlam is the richest man in the world, or at least the world with which we have communication.

"He calls to tell us when he has a display for the gallery. And, then he comes to see it once it's there. Sometimes, he just comes to view the collection."

"Collection of what, Silas? No one has ever heard of a museum out here."

"Oh, I don't know. It's Bedlam's private collection."

"Why does he keep it way out here?"

"He wanted to keep it private and since no one knows anything about the process here, I guess he thought it would be safe under the mountain." Silas was growing more uneasy as he shifted from one foot to the other and avoided our eyes. "I'm not allowed to talk about Bedlam's museum. We are supposed to pretend we know nothing about it. Please don't ask me anymore."

"Keep the glove on until the burn is totally healed. Now, let's get out of here, Christiana. The stench of the place is penetrating my skin. But you can be sure, Silas, we will do everything we can to put a halt to these evil practices as soon as possible." Jason took my arm and turned to leave.

"I will do what I can to close this place, Silas. You can count on me," I said. We started to open the door to the lounge, and I blinked in the blackness of the hall. I was a step ahead of Jason.

"Here, Christiana, you need a light." Jason reached for the bank of light switches on the wall beside the lounge door.

"NO!" Silas screamed as the lights blazed in the hallway.

We stepped into the bright hall and found that the cases we had passed were part of a long Galleria where glassed-in exhibits lined the area from the lounge all the way to the vestibule. Lights came on behind the frosted glass display cases as well. The objects of Alister Bedlam's art were grotesque beyond my ability to imagine. They weren't paintings or statues of fine marble. They were human beings, processed expertly for Bedlam's sole possession and entertainment. The maimed, the elderly people, the middle aged, the young, and even children were in the collection: their bodies forever preserved by a taxidermist and encased behind thick glass.

"Christy," Jason whispered in horror, "I know this man." He pointed to a figure in a pinstriped suit with a gray fedora hat perched on the side of his head. "He and his wife used to come over to visit with my parents and play games."

"I know him too, Jason. He was my Uncle Steven. He was one of the Wise Ones before he fell down his stairs and ceased to live." I recoiled in horror at the monstrous display of disrespect for the deceased. "Why would Alister Bedlam do this?"

"Power, Christy. What, or who, he didn't have power over in life, Bedlam gained in their death." Then I heard Jason let out an agonizing groan as he moved up the hallway. He reached out to the case on the right and collapsed against the glass as he sobbed great tears of deep sorrow. "This ... is ... was ... my mother, Christy." Again, he stepped back and took in the fully processed model of Stephanie O'Reilly. He looked with searching eyes for another exhibit and found it slightly behind his mother's glass coffin. "And, this is my father." He gasped as he shot a dangerously wild glance back at Silas Drummond.

"It's not my fault, Doctor. I had nothing to do with any of it. This is Alister Bedlam's total possession. We aren't to touch them or even look at them." Silas looked pleadingly at me with fear in his eyes. "Please Ma'am; get me out of this evil abomination. I had nothing to do with this exhibit. I had to follow orders and—I simply can't do it anymore." Silas dropped to the floor and reached out his hand to us, pleading. "You are the only people on earth who can help stop this evil," he cried.

"Don't look back, Christy" Jason gasped. "Let's get out of here before the vileness of this place corrupts our souls. I don't know if God even knows this place exists. If he does, he must flood these caverns with his own tears." Jason hurried me out of that place of horror and back into the air of the clear night.

As we stepped out into the air, we heard Silas calling. "Please," he begged, "don't forget me." He staggered to the doorway, "Please."

"I won't forget, Silas," I called out over my shoulder as Jason hustled me into the car. "We'll do something. Trust me, Silas!"

Once in the safety of Jason's car, both of us broke down in violent sobs. We grabbed each other and held on while the grief flowed from our spirits like a cleansing rain. Finally, we were able to talk about it. We knew that now, time had reached a vortex, whirling, and churning and sucking all the forces of the world into a point of clarity requiring immediate action. Silas's warning had nearly cost him his life. Now that knowledge rested on our shoulders. It was ours to pick up and carry, or to cast aside.

If we were to keep our promises to Silas Drummond and to my grandparents, we would have to run fast enough to stay ahead of those who followed. Jason and I knew the evil in our society had the power to destroy us.

CHAPTER FORTY-ONE
Stopped

6:15 p.m.

The encounter with Silas Drummond and learning the awful secrets beneath Howard Mountain had shaken us with so much grief, horror, and anger, that we sat in Jason's car, just holding each other for a while. Finally, Jason collected himself. "We'd better go back to your place Christy and think this out. Silas won't be left alone for long."

"You're right. No telling what Alister Bedlam might do," I said. "Jason, we will bring Bedlam to justice somehow."

Jason raced back to the city on a clear and empty road. Just as we crossed the line marking the city limits, the shrill sound of a siren pierced the night, muffled slightly against the heavy air. The squeal of tires followed as three Blue Guard cars screamed to a halt in front of us. From inside the first car, I heard a loud shout. "We have them!"

I saw a tall man in a blue uniform, lumbering toward us and I froze. I could see his jacket, emblazoned with the crest of the Blue Guard, as he stood beneath a streetlight.

"Dr. O'Reilly," he touched his hat brim, "Ma'am."

"Good evening Officer," Jason responded.

Exhausted and shaken with fear, I couldn't answer. The reality that I was being watched, even at my apartment and then the awful revelation of the ghastly murders at Howard Mountain left my emotions spent and numb. Now officials of the government—a government we were in profound opposition to—had stopped us. Had these men been monitoring us? Did they know we had been to the mountain? How was it possible that all of this was happening to us on our very first Christmas Eve?

"Get out of the car and come with me," the man ordered. The Blue Guard turned to leave and seemed to expect us to follow him without question.

"Why?" Jason stayed sitting with his arm holding me tight against him.

"Just come with me, Sir." The officer didn't turn around but kept walking to his car.

"I will know why and where we are going before I expose Lady Applewait to any more unknown situations tonight." Again, Jason did not move.

The man turned back toward us, obviously aware that his orders went unobeyed. "Dr. O'Reilly, there is an emergency. You will have to bring Lady Applewait with you. There is no time to take her home."

"Where? What emergency?" Jason demanded. "Will I have the things I'll need to administer proper care?"

"Sir ..." The Blue Guard's face grew tight and hard. "I will pull my weapon if I have to. Both of you are coming with me. Now, get out and get into my car."

"What is this emergency?" Jason began, again attempting to regain control of the situation.

"Sir, I am ordering you both to get into my car." The Guard placed his hand on his weapon holder and unsnapped the safety grip.

Jason helped me out of his car and into the back of the officer's vehicle without saying another word. I was wondering when we should take a stand. But there are times when, for safety sake, talk is the wrong choice. When we settled ourselves in the back of the officer's car, I saw no handles on the inside of the doors, and I panicked. I grabbed Jason's hand without saying a word, but my mind flooded with fear. What was happening now? Where were they taking us? Were they taking us back to the mountain? Are they aware we know its secrets?

My mind reverberated from the screams I held inside and back to the words of my grandmother. "It won't be in time, Christy. We'll be seventy-five in two weeks."

As I clung to Jason, I kept thinking. How could we reverse the terrible Length of Days policy when no one remembered how it started, or what the terrible processes involved? At the end of the month, my grandparents would reach the end of their Length of Days. They would then endure the vile death process that would only add more agony to their fate. Now, Jason and I knew that Alister Bedlam played a large part in the unspeakable acts and cruel disrespect for life at Howard Mountain. My mind couldn't hold any more. And, still the clock kept ticking.

As the Blue Guard's strata-car sped to our unknown destination, deep down, where fear takes root in all we are, I knew we could be racing to our own deaths. If we were to tell our abductors that we would do nothing to find a solution to the Length of Days policy, would they let us go? What did they know about Howard Mountain? How could we find the solution to unseal the fate of Grand-mère and Grand-père from inside a jail cell, or exterminated like all the rest? I felt helpless and hopeless. I had never experienced those emotions before but recognized them.

I looked at Jason. His set jaw and determined look gave me courage. Together, we would find the solutions. Suddenly, above all the confusion and fear, I imagined that music filling the car with the power to calm my spirit, and I was able to think more clearly.

I had never thought of myself as a brave person, but for the first time in my life, I wanted to stand up for something, to have a cause worth living for. Overturning the laws regarding the Length of Days horror, I vowed would be the single focus of my life. But, while I knew I was willing to live for the principle, and to die for it if necessary, I didn't know if I could sacrifice Jason's life with mine for the cause ahead of us.

CHAPTER FORTY-TWO

Surveillance

Now what is this all about? Inspector Ward Stoner grumbled. *Why didn't I receive the APB first?* He saw the Blue Guard vehicle stop and force two people into their strata-car. He followed behind the racing convoy of heavily marked cars as they sped through the dark night. Stoner gripped the steering wheel roughly and his shoulders grew tight with tension. *Nothing came over the radio.* He couldn't believe the audacity, the arrogant disregard for protocol. *How is it that the Chief Inspector of the Blue Guard could be outside the chain of command, again? People will answer for this breach of policy.*

No one in the department had his finger on the pulse of every artery like Ward Stoner. He was usually the first to know everything, mainly because he was in charge of the unit but also because he never gave up or gave in. If he didn't have the answers, he held on until he got to the bottom of every nuance of the situation. He didn't care how long it took. He sped through the streets, mumbling curses at the colorful lights that twinkled brightly, while he felt dark inside his soul.

Without Miriam to go home to, there was little reason to end a work day. He still had Christopher, but the child only reminded him of Miriam and that made him miss her more. Her golden hair and bright blue eyes shone from the child they had shared. Recently, Stoner had been trying harder to be there for the boy. But, the more he attended to the child, the more inadequate he felt. Then like an exhausting, circular treadmill he could not free himself from, he pushed the boy away again to hide himself from the guilt.

Occasionally, circumstances outside his control forced him to face the reality of his relationship with his son. Now, it was nearly Gift-giving Day, and he wanted to make it special for the boy. Christopher had hinted about a new virtual game he wanted. In the game, the small child could place himself within several environments, like visiting a zoo where he could walk among the roaring tigers and brush so close, he could count their stripes. In another scene, he could walk through a museum where dinosaurs loomed above and around. Within the holographic image, he could find a moment of joy and perhaps a brief experience of laughter. Stoner wanted that for Christopher.

The Inspector worked most of the time and the boy had only his grandmother to read the few approved children's books to him and interact with throughout the day. She was wonderful with Christopher, and Ward appreciated all she did. But Chris was his son, and he knew that he should be more involved in his life.

Now, on Gift-giving Eve, Stoner was chasing around the city following his own men. He had also lost track of Lady Applewait some hours ago, like her chip had simply vanished from the tracking system. *How can that be? She started out toward the country then vanished from the grid,* he argued with himself. *My time is precious tonight, and I don't even know why I'm in pursuit of these cars and not following the little lady who has seemed to evaporate.* He growled on and on into the night.

The Blue Guard's cars flew through the streets at speeds that would have stopped other drivers. However, there was not a single officer of the law with the authority to stop a member of the Blue Guard, much less a posse of them. They sped through stop streets and traffic lights and whipped around corners at break neck speeds. They finally crossed the invisible line into Oakwood.

Well now, what do we have here? Stoner's sneer distorted his face and gnawed at his stomach. *Even the special, fancy people have problems, do they? They're not above needing us, needing me.* His anger rose to the surface again and burst out every pore. *I will find out what is going on. The day after First-day, heads will roll!*

He slowed to the curb a half block down the quiet street from where the other cars had abruptly stopped and turned off his lights. The Blue Shirts got out of the front seat and jerked the curbside back door open. They pulled a man and a woman from the car and nudged toward a large old-style house. Once the authorities and their reluctant captives went into the house, the area was silent again. Stoner could hear the sound of his own breathing. His breath was visible on the chilled air, but he was far from cold. His anger shot hot blood through his veins. In the still of the night, he sat in silence and stared at the old house in the next block. He ground his teeth and clenched the steering wheel with fists of steel.

CHAPTER FORTY-THREE
Rebecca's Husband Michael

7:15 p.m.

Jason had kept his arm around me as the Blue Guard cars sped down the city streets. I knew where we were, and it brought me no comfort. We had crossed into Oakwood, the older section of town. My heart stopped with fear of what that could have meant. *Is this line of boot thumping Blue Guards racing to Grand-mère and Grand-père's house because of something I said or did? Are the dear ones' precious few remaining days at risk because of me? Will they end up on display at Howard Mountain?*

The cars had stopped, however, in front of a stately old red brick house two blocks from my grandparents' home. I felt both relief and dread. I was thankful they were not seeking out my grandparents. But I wondered who lived at that house and what fate awaited them?

The driver stomped out of the car and jerked the door open. "Out quickly."

This time Jason said nothing. It was a command, not a request. We knew we had to play their game to the best of our ability, even though we didn't know any of the rules. A misspoken word or a misperceived movement could be taken as noncooperation, resistance, or even threatening aggression.

I was not sure that my legs would support me as I stepped from the car and staggered slightly. Jason grabbed me around my waist and held me firmly as I regained my footing on the ice. I kept my eyes fixed on the ground and didn't look toward my grandparents' home.

The officers seemed to have more interest in Jason than in me. I didn't want to draw any attention to myself or to my family.

"This way," the Blue Guard leader commanded. "Follow me."

We walked quickly to the front door. The Blue Guard burst into the house without a word of warning. Were we forced into being part of this invasion into someone's personal space, perhaps a government official or a member of the Council of Elders?

"Back here," a man in casual slacks, open neck white shirt, bare feet, and a grim look on his face, motioned for us to follow him. Only professional men continued to dress in the traditional garb of authority but it was easy to see that something had interrupted his attempt at relaxation. I didn't recognize the man. And, I felt a measure of relief not knowing him.

We followed him silently down a bright hall behind a grand staircase and pushed through a set of tall wooden double doors.

"Quickly," the man pleaded as he took Jason by the arm and led him into the adjoining bathroom. I saw a fleeting glimpse of a woman in white trousers spattered in blood, holding a fallen young man's head in her arms. She cradled him close to her body like a mother rocks her sick child, while streams of tears flowed down her cheeks. Her face contorted in desperate fear. For the first time in my life, I could feel her pain, and it was nearly more than I could bear. *Empathy could prove to be a curse, not a blessing*, I thought. *Now, with all I know, my tender new soul will surely wither in the fire of evil.*

The guard held up a halting hand and motioned for me to stay in the bedroom while Jason went inside the bathroom. The sobs and groans of anguish were frightening to hear.

I couldn't focus on the pain. It was too much. I looked around the room and began to separate myself from the agony.

The room I was in was masculine in design, with muted tones of beige and brown. The bed was nothing like a normal bed, even an expensive one from a high-end store. The frame was metal, rather than wood, with shiny bars that came up one side and across and above the mattress. A festive red poinsettia plant sat on the corner of a large bedside table along with a lamp, small bottles with lids, a pitcher and glass of water. *Is someone ill?* A light blue bathrobe was draped across the end of the bed but I saw no slippers.

"Lay him flat." I heard Jason call out orders from the bathroom through a muffled conversation. I could hear frantic movement but nothing more.

Someone was obviously struggling for his life in a society that no longer valued life. The thought came to me that, if they took the young man to the hospital, in his condition, he would have slipped into the permanent sleep. Yet, they captured Jason in the hope of saving his life. Perhaps we were in a home that shared a reverence for life with my family.

The Blue Guard didn't stop me as I walked around the bedroom. A cluster of five pictures hung on the side wall, positioned so the one in bed could easily see them. In the first one, three young men, their arms linked in friendship, appeared to be celebrating their victory in reaching a blue-sky mountain summit. The curly haired blond Nordic type appeared again in the next photo dressed in a fine suit. He held a beautiful young woman in a flowing blue gown in his arms. She looked familiar to me, but I didn't want to stare. Their happiness was written on their faces like a bold and beautiful advertisement of their love. The broad smile appeared again in the next picture, in a playful headlock with an older man. The mature one looked like the gentleman who had led us in through the house. I surmised it might be his father. The young man and the father appeared in the next shot with an attractive older woman, probably the one I saw bending over the man in the other room. The fifth picture was of a cozy log cabin in a deep wood with cloud-covered mountains stretching up toward Heaven. The same blond young man sat on the porch steps and smiled at the one who held the camera.

"Oh, thank God, thank God," I heard the woman shout from the bathroom.

Then I heard what sounded like struggling, grunting, and huffing. Then Jason's voice, "Your Honor let me help you."

Jason stepped out of the bathroom followed by the man I thought must be the father of the injured man. He carried the broken body of his son back into the bedroom. As the man strained under the weight,

I could see his clothes covered in blood. The woman I felt sure was the mother, followed close behind, her hand gripped her chest and her face etched with fear.

I quickly moved aside in the shadows of the room and waited. I wanted to be somewhere, anywhere but there. I was unprepared for the powerful emotions that continued to pour over me.

When he placed the younger man on the bed, I saw the apparatus that spanned above it. Even though he was obviously still weak, he grabbed the bar over his body and helped position himself in the center of the bed. As I watched, I could finally see his face. He was my friend Rebecca Brunner's husband, Michael, and Judge Brunner's son. I remembered that Rebecca lost her life in a mountain climbing accident less than a year ago. Maybe the fall claimed Michael's legs as well. It could have happened near the cabin in the picture. Rebecca was most likely the photographer he gazed at with loving eyes. I stared at the picture again and wondered why he would have placed such a memory in front of his eyes where he would have to look at it every moment of every day.

"How are you feeling now?" Jason asked Michael. "You'll have quite a headache for several days, and yes, that will include Gift-giving Day morning. But, if you're lucky, your stomach will settle by tomorrow afternoon in time for the Christmas feast." He chuckled and patted Michael's leg.

Jason had spoken the word out loud, *Christmas*, and in front of Judge Brunner and the Blue Guard. How did he dare to break the law in such a bold way?

"Vonny will be here at ten a.m. I'll be better by then, or I'll fake it." Michael whispered and tried to adjust his position again. "I wouldn't spoil Christmas for her for anything." Then he looked in my direction. "Christiana, is that you?" He strained as he looked back at Jason. He must have read our feelings. "Wow, Doc, I didn't know." He grinned as his light-hearted spirit seemed to fight through the fog of his pain.

I didn't know Michael well. Rebecca had introduced him to me. She talked about him all the time. Rebecca had said that Michael had a sense of humor, which was a rare gift in those days. One had to feel in order to laugh.

"I didn't know either, Michael, until yesterday. Christy and I just met recently." Jason picked up Michael's wrist, looked at the clock on the side table, and took his pulse.

"I hope you feel better soon, Michael," I offered. "How old is Vonny now?" I approached the bed slowly and stopped a respectful distance away, not wanting to intrude on the family's joy of having their son back from the brink of death.

"She's three years old and looks just like her mother," he whispered.

I could see that Rebecca's death had left Michael's emotions raw and then I stopped and studied his face. Michael was experiencing feelings too, like some of the others around town. How many feelers were there? I wondered what else I had missed while I dozed behind the mask of additives. I had been walking around with my head wrapped in cotton all my life. I wondered if Rebecca too had been able to fully love before she died. I glanced back at her picture in the party dress and suspected that she had been a feeler long before her death.

"Vonny has been staying with Rebecca's parents for a few days since it's the holiday time. They love her so much. It's like having their daughter back again." Michael closed his eyes. It was easy to see his energy was spent.

"Is he going to be okay, Doctor?" Mrs. Brunner rubbed her son's foot, like she was afraid to let go.

"He should be fine," Jason answered.

The disaster had passed, but I still didn't know what had happened to Michael.

CHAPTER FORTY-FOUR
A Little Understanding

I felt relief seeing Jason smile. It had been a medical emergency after all, not a threat connected to Howard Mountain. Jason and I still had to deal with that.

"Michael's fall has done no permanent damage. He will need a lot of rest if he's going to enjoy his Christmas dessert," Jason smiled at Mrs. Brunner. "Let's pull the shades to block the light for a while. Michael, you'll feel better if you take this medication for the pain and close your eyes. You should be better in a few hours."

"Thank God," Mrs. Brunner sighed like she hadn't exhaled for a very long time. "Let's go into the living room, and I'll bring in some coffee. I think a stimulant would be just what the doctor ordered right now." Mrs. Brunner smiled at Jason. "Am I right, Doctor?"

"That would be very nice." Jason sat down on the couch beside me and gave me a reassuring hug.

"May I ask what happened?" I felt like I was intruding into a very private part of a family's tragedy. But I had been dragged into this situation, nearly at the point of a gun. I believed I deserved an answer.

Judge Carl Brunner sank down onto an overstuffed chair and buried his head in his hands. "Wow, that was close," he said when he finally looked up. "Yes, Christiana, you deserve an answer to all of this." He spread out his arms, gesturing toward Michael's room, to include an explanation for it all.

Mrs. Brunner returned with a tray of coffee cups and placed one in front of each of us. Then she turned and served the four guards I had nearly forgotten as they stood at near-attention against the wall. "You could use some hot coffee too, I'm sure." She came back and sat down in the chair beside the judge.

"Who are those men?" I asked. They treated us as if we were kidnaped, and brought here to find that Michael had nearly lost his life.

"They are a very special detail of Blue Guard that are independent of the entire division," Judge Brunner began. "After Rebecca died and Michael was hurt, he would have been immediately placed in the endless sleep. But his doctor, Roy Kundred believed that, given enough time, the nerves in Michael's damaged back could heal with proper stimulation and treatment with the newest procedures. Nerves heal, strengthen, and reattached with the aid of quantum radiation stimulation. But there was absolutely no exception to the rule of termination. So, Michael's Godfather, your grandfather, Christiana, assigned a loyal group of guardsmen to make sure no one got too near Michael or discovered his condition."

"My grandfather?"

"Yes, dear, and Connie, your grandmother, helped us as well. She would stay at home near the communication center to respond to any callers looking for Oliver while he came over here and prayed with all of us. Michael's wonderful guards, who are now his friends, were included." She stirred her coffee and sipped a little. "I would see Oliver walking past the house sometimes. He would pause like he was tying his shoe, and while he was down there, he would pray for Michael."

"He would ... pray with all of you? My grandfather?" Tears came to my eyes as I thought of all I had not known, all of the love I had missed, all of the joy that had flown by while I was asleep in the shelter of my life.

"When you were younger, Christiana, it was dangerous for you to know of our beliefs, dangerous for you and for us. You had to be mature enough to know that you could not talk to anyone about it." Judge Brunner's reassuring words comforted me a little. I still felt I had been left out of the greatest secret ever held.

"Sir Richly handpicked each one of us, Ma'am," said the guard who had driven us to the Brunner's home. "I had felt very privileged at the time. Now, I know I was blessed with a great opportunity, to get to know and serve Michael and to learn about the Master."

"The master of what?" I asked.

"Not the master of just anything, My Lady, but the Master of my soul." As the guard spoke, his face seemed to glow with a mysterious radiance.

While I noticed, I didn't make a comment about the strange light that radiated from him. "And tonight?" I went on. "What happened to Michael that caused the crisis today?"

"Have his treatments not worked?" Jason questioned. He knew Dr. Kundred, but he had known nothing of Michael Brunner and the injuries that left him unable to walk.

"To the contrary, they are working very well," Silvia smiled. "This evening, Michael had swung himself into his wheelchair as he always did. Your dear grandmother had taken his chair from her own attic, Christiana. No one has had a wheelchair for a long time, except in the hospital for very temporary use. Since the severely injured or permanently disabled are not permitted treatment, there is no need for them. It would have brought attention to Michael if we had asked to use a hospital wheelchair. Connie's grandfather had used the chair and when he was done with it, it was stored in the attic and forgotten. When we needed it, Connie and Oliver put it in their own car, drove over here with it, and pulled right into our garage. We closed the door before the chair was removed. No one knows it ever existed. No one knows it's here." She smiled again as the color began to return to her face.

"But what happened to Michael today?" I questioned.

"Today, Michael went through his bathroom door in the chair and tried something he shouldn't have." Silvia Brunner shook her head and closed her eyes. "His treatments have increased the sensations in his legs. They really have, and that's a good thing. This evening, he could feel his legs a little and decided to use his arms to lift himself out of the chair. He thought he could lean against the sink while he washed up for bed. He is improving, but he wasn't ready for that kind of move. His feet went out from under him and he struck his head on the basin on the way down. I heard the crash and found him unconscious on the floor. Blood was everywhere." She finally looked down at her slacks. "Oh, my dear, I am so sorry. I look awful."

"You look like a mother who has gone through a trauma with her son," I reassured her. "I will have to be honest —" I didn't know if I should share my thoughts with her or not, but she knew my grandparents and she felt like family. "I wondered if he had attempted suicide."

Silvia's expression didn't change. The sweetness remained but pain came and mingled with it. "Michael has been through that dark period since the accident." She looked intently at me, and I could feel what she felt. My books called it empathy, but I named it heartache.

"Christiana, several times within the first month following Rebecca's death, Michael attempted to end his life. As soon as he was able to move around the house in the wheelchair, he tried to manoeuver himself out onto the porch. He hoped someone would see him and report the presence of a disabled person in the neighborhood." Silvia Brunner had dissolved into a whisper as fear overtook her again. "Our Blue Guardsmen were able to protect him from himself and brought him back in the house before he was seen. Then, a few days later, Carl found Michael on the floor of his bathroom, covered in his own blood. He had taken a sharp shaving blade to his wrist and, well, that was not the situation today. When Vonny saw her daddy's bandaged wrist and asked him what had happened, it filled him with shame. He vowed then and there that he would never try to take his own life again. Today was an accident, just an accident." Her eyes were pleading with me. "But, Christiana, now that he wants to live, he could have died tonight."

"It was a very close call, Mrs. Brunner." Jason agreed. "If you hadn't been there quickly, to apply a firm compress, he would have bled out before I could have gotten here."

"And thank you so much for coming, Dr. O'Reilly. Dr. Kundred is on a holiday with his family," she whispered, with a voice full of gratitude.

"I'm afraid their coming was our doing, Ma'am. They didn't actually have a choice," the Blue Shirt offered apologetically.

"Oh my," she gasped and looked back at Jason and me. "I am so sorry. I hope you weren't frightened."

"Well, maybe a little," I admitted a partial truth. "But I understand now. The guards couldn't tell us anything in public."

"That's right," Judge Brunner agreed. "I'm afraid their insistence was my fault. I told them to find a doctor and bring him or her here, whatever it took. They weren't to tell anyone the reason. And, they weren't to take 'No' for an answer."

"Carl, you didn't?" Silvia scolded.

"That's okay, Mrs. Brunner. I do understand," I said. "Our family is facing a similar situation. I've been worrying over my grandparents' birthdays coming up in a few days. They will both be seventy-five years old. Their birthdays are only days apart. You know what that means."

"Oh Christiana, not Oliver and Constance," the judge gasped. "I had been so caught up with Michael's needs, I hadn't even been aware that they were coming near the end of their Length of Days. I'm sorry I've been preoccupied. They helped us so much and still support us with their prayers."

I thought of the risks we were all taking that night. I thought about the glass cases of loved ones, Jason's family, someone's family. The images brought a nausea that rose and swelled within me and spoke out more boldly. My insides rattled with fear, excitement, and overspent energy.

"This evil act, the Length of Days policy, must be dissolved. Tonight, Jason and I have learned more about the despicable practice than anyone knew. It's deceivingly called the never-ending-sleep, but it isn't sleep at all. And, I may have found a solution for overturning the policy regarding terminations based on the Length of Days."

"Christiana, praise the Lord! What have you found?" Silvia threw both hands in the air. "It's all so dangerous. Bless you for doing this."

"Grand-mère and Grand-père mean everything to me." As I spoke their names, I felt a renewed strength and reason for the fight. "I used to sit on Grand-mère's lap as a small child while she read books to me. It was magical. She would play out each part, changing her voice to match the characters. Someday, I'd like a child of my own to sit on that same sweet lap while Grand-mère reads to them."

"Ah, my dear, the French word for grandma, Grand-mère. That is lovely."

"And ... Mrs. Brunner," I continued, "I am waking up to a new spiritual awareness and a reverence for life. No one cares about life anymore. It's disposed of like yesterday's trash. And for the rest, life is more endured than lived. Life is ... God given and its worth is God validated." I could feel hot tears gathering in the corners of my eyes and stream down my cheeks. "I will fight for the overturn of that Godless law before it's too late, too late for my grandparents and the unnumbered others who await that fate. Jason and I have just learned some horrible information about the process of termination."

"We'll share more about the process another time," Jason added. "Tonight, is Christmas Eve, a time for beauty and rejoicing."

"That's right, Jason. Thanks for reminding me," I said. "But we will try to stop the policy and put an end to it all."

"You don't have much time, Christiana," Judge Brunner warned. "What on earth can you do with only a few days remaining before their birthdays?"

"Judge, I may need your help."

"Anything," he pledged sincerely. "I owe your grandparents so much. And now, today, I have added another debt, to you and Dr. O'Reilly. Besides, a change in the law could help more people than just your grandparents and my son. How do we do it?"

"Sir, a law can be overturned by a citizens' referendum. I have done the research. With a petition signed by a majority of the population, a law *can* be changed." I didn't know if I dare say any more. But I didn't have time to play it cautiously. I leaned in toward the Brunners and whispered. "I have heard a rumor about a petition that is already circulating, but I don't know yet if it pertains to Length of Days legislation or ... detoxification, or both."

"All of us here have been detoxed for several years now, Christiana." Judge Brunner spoke with the seriousness worthy of our cause. "I said I will do anything, and I will. If you can get enough signatures on a petition before your time runs out, I will institute a stay order, suspending all terminations until you secure signatures from all across the country. This affects Michael too, you know. And Christiana, God bless you and Dr. O'Reilly for your bravery and dedication."

"Thank you, Sir."

"Judge Brunner, we need something else," Jason joined in.

I was baffled. I felt like our cause had been assured if the petition signatures were there.

"The cover letter, Christy," Jason reminded me.

"Oh, Jason." I felt my hopes slip into doubt again, but I shook off the easy way out, of giving up. Maybe Judge Brunner had a solution to the cover letter as well.

"What cover letter?" the judge asked.

"A formality put in place many years ago. You must accompany a citizens' referendum a cover letter. It is an official form that must be filled out exactly according to the directions given."

"And where do you get that?" The judge asked.

"The forms are buried among some old papers in the records office in the Capitol building," I sighed as I thought of yet another hurdle to leap. "The offices are closed until the Monday after the holidays. We'll have to turn it in that day." I got up, feeling I wanted to flee. I was tired of hearing the problem. I wanted to talk about the solution.

Judge Brunner jumped to his feet and reached into this pocket. "The records and forms office is on the second floor of the Capitol. The lift won't be working until after the holidays, but you can go up the steps." He fished out two keys. One looked new and the other was dull and old. It had a scrolled and fancy head and a thick, warn shaft.

"This newer one goes to the door in the back of the building where the judges can enter out of the watchful eye of the public." He then handed me the antique key. "You can get in the records' office with the newer key. It's like a master to all the other locks. But this old one goes to the closed file room where they store old records and forms. Your cover letter and instructions must be in there. Try looking under *Old Order* or simply *Old Forms*. You should be able to find what you need. That's the only place I think, that type of material may have been filed."

"Oh, Judge Brunner, thank you." I flung my arms around him without hesitation or thought.

He patted my back the way my father used to soothe me when I fell. "Your courage tonight will benefit us all, Christiana. God's speed and safety to you both." Then he turned to Jason. "You are going with her, aren't you Doc?"

"Absolutely," Jason assured him and put his arm around my waist.

Then the judge reached out his hand in friendship to Jason. "Bless you, Jason O'Reilly. You saved Michael's life tonight. Tomorrow, when I have pulled my wits together, I will thank you properly."

"I'm glad your Guard contingent could find me, Sir," Jason smiled broadly, "even if your Blue Shirts did kidnap us in the process of getting us here."

We turned to leave then Jason stopped. "I think we will need a ride back to my car."

"One of the guards will take you anywhere you want to go—the moon and back if that's your desire." He waved in wide sweeping motions.

I started toward the door, but I could not let my question go unasked. "Ma'am, I hope this doesn't seem too nosy but—if Rebecca's accident happened near the cabin in the picture, why does Michael have the photo hanging where he has to look at it all the time? I would think he wouldn't want to be reminded of his loss every day."

Silvia Brunner put her hand to her mouth and smiled softly. Gathering her composure, she said, "Let me see if I can explain this to you, my dear. He said, others may forget her, but he will make sure he never does. Michael doesn't have to see the picture every day, Christiana. He wants to see it every day. He told me that it is a privilege. He said it's because ... his heart is buried there."

At that moment, I knew why angels sing. When love overflows the heart, it spills out in song.

CHAPTER FORTY-FIVE
Michael Was Saved

8:55 p.m.

While one of the Blue Guards drove Jason and I back to his car, Jason asked me how I knew Rebecca Brunner.

Rebecca Brunner was my friend. She was older, but we had a similar interest, painting. Rather than talking about my love of words and how authors can paint alphabet pictures that can place the reader in another time, another place, we talked about the breathtaking vistas around us.

Rebecca and I would take our artist palettes, canvases, and brushes out to the foothills of the mighty peaks and paint for hours. I enjoyed painting, but Rebecca was the real artist.

"Christiana, that is a beautiful color," she would encourage my efforts. "How did you see that particular yellow tone in that green? It makes it sparkle like a jewel. You have a talent buried inside you. I see the fluidity, the sweep of movement. You have an inspired gift that you are holding back for some reason."

I only smiled. Now, I wish I could have simply said, "Thank you."

One late-day afternoon, she was talking about Vonny. "She is beautiful. She must get her good looks from her daddy."

"She looks like you, Rebecca," I said.

Rebecca had thrown her head back and laughed.

"Where do you two get all that elation? It must be in the water," I had laughed

"You know, there may be something to that. Michael puts little pills in his water so we keep a pitcher of it in the kitchen. Vonny and I drink it too. It doesn't taste any different, but we seem to have more energy after we drink a glass."

At the time, I didn't know what Rebecca was talking about. Now, Rebecca and Vonny's unheard of happiness made sense. Michael's detox pills, that they all took, were the key that unlocked the flatness of life for them and opened them to a full palate of emotions.

That evening, Mrs. Brunner told us, Michael and Rebecca had built a cabin near where we had gone to paint. The young Brunners would hike and wander through the forested area near the base of the mountain. Occasionally, they would mountain climb with ropes and harnesses and all the equipment. That was how it had happened.

Michael had led the way up the last face of the mountain and helped Rebecca to the summit where her hands grew cold and stiff. She lost her grip and fell. Michael reached for her, lost his own footing, and plummeted from the top. After several days of unresponsiveness, Rebecca's life was terminated.

"That would be awful, to see your loved one slip through your fingers," Jason whispered.

"Oh Jason, maybe being in love isn't so wonderful after all. Maybe, not feeling is better than broken feelings."

"Christiana, you wouldn't want that. Not now," Jason said.

"No, not now. Not now that I have experienced feelings and now that I have met you." Somehow, I knew that Jason was smiling.

"It took a doctor dedicated to life to give Michael the opportunity to live. I'm surprised the hospital went along with it," Jason added.

"The hospital wasn't consulted," the Blue Guard driver said. "I'm sorry, I shouldn't have interrupted," he apologized.

"No, please, tell us," I answered.

"I know the judge wouldn't mind if I tell you. He tells it proudly to those he trusts." He paused. "In the morning of the second day of Michael's stay in the hospital, his physician, Dr. Kundred, came into his room. Michael's eyes were closed; the doctor just patted his leg.

"Good morning, Mountain Climber," the doctor said, then he laughed as if Michael had just responded to him. "Well, that's great," he said to Michael, still comatose in his bed. "Your dad will be here to take you home in a few minutes, so you just rest for now."

"What if they got caught?" I wondered out loud.

"They almost were. A nurse who started to enter his room questioned, 'Home, Doctor? He was unresponsive the last time I checked on him.'

"A few minutes later, Doctor Kundred and Judge Brunner whisked Michael out of the hospital. He began to recuperate in his room on the first floor of the Brunner residence. When he regained some strength and heard that Rebecca was gone, life no longer had any meaning. Later, he knew he had to live for Vonny."

"Thank you, officer," I said. Finally, I understood these new feelings. With the sunshine comes the shadow. If I wanted to experience love and joy, I would have to accept sorrow and grief that accompany them.

CHAPTER FORTY-SIX
The Capitol at Night

9:14 p.m.

It was nearly 9:15 when the Blue Guard pulled up to where Jason had parked his car. The Guardsman opened the doors for us, and I jumped out quickly and into Jason's car. I knew full well that time was precious. My heart pounded in my chest so loudly I wondered if Jason could hear it above the sound of the motor. Would we be able to follow Judge Brunner's instructions with the keys to doors and files in the Capitol? Would we be in time?

As we raced toward the Capitol through the darkened night on our Godly mission, I noticed that Jason kept checking in the rear-view mirror.

"Is someone following us again? Will this ever stop?" I was exhausted from running, from feeling, from being exposed to evil. "Will we be hunted for the rest of our lives for what we are doing tonight?"

My thoughts rushed back to words I had read. The framers of the Constitution risked everything, and many lost it all. I would have to be willing to stand up and be counted among them, regardless of the cost.

"Let's see if this guy stays with us even if we ..." Jason jerked the steering wheel and snapped around the corner just seven blocks from the Capitol. On a side street, we buzzed through a grocery dispensing window where runners picked up food to distribute. Then we dashed down an old alley behind the shops that serviced the inner city and darted into an open, single car garage behind an apartment building. Jason turned off the lights and engine. Everything about the night was still. The traumatic energy in the car felt explosive. We sat there in the darkness so as not to draw attention to ourselves. We nearly held our breath as silence overtook the night. Hyper-vigilant, we scanned the empty alley. We waited in fear, yet prayed in hope.

The black strata-car I had seen around town all day sped through the narrow, one way, one lane passage behind us without slowing. It appeared he was still on the chase, not the careful search.

The night suddenly seemed too quiet and still, as we sat there in the dark. Jason took my hand but said nothing. I was afraid the people who owned the parking space would come home, find us there, and report us as intruders. We already knew the fate of those judged to be unnecessary or dangerous to Society. My eyes darted from the door that led to the entrance of the residence, to the alley behind us. Nothing stirred except my stomach as it churned with anxiety. Strange. I suddenly felt hungry and the humor of that clanged with the reality of the danger we were in.

"Here we go," Jason whispered as he backed out of the parking space and into the back alley. He allowed the downward slope of the driveway to carry us silently out of the garage. Rather than turning left and onto the thoroughfare again, he rolled across the street and continued into the alley. He crept along and allowed the momentum of the descent to carry us forward without gunning the engine. He slowed as gravity no longer propelled us forward.

"This won't work from this spot on," Jason spoke with measured caution.

At that point in the city, all of the roads and alleys took an upward grade. Generations ago, the city planners had placed the Capitol on a mound in the center of the city to ensure the safety of records and other materials in the event of flood. As the need for space increased, existing, adjacent structures were torn down as the Capitol's wings spread out across the city like tentacles that reached out and touched all the areas of the citizens' lives.

A transit bus went silently above the street that ran parallel to the back lane but few other vehicles were on the road. I wondered what had happened to that black car that had been following us. But, thinking about it only made fear rise within me, and that fear could corrode my resolve. I had to calm down or we could lose our cause. Our own, personal fate would also be sealed if we were anything less than totally successful.

"Let me see ..." Jason mumbled, as much to himself as to me.

I saw the back entrance to the Capitol waiting ahead like a refuge from a rolling storm. We eased through the narrow, lower level entry into the huge complex via a valet-hosted entrance to the parking garage. We were inside the basement but not yet all the way in the structure. The entry-bar was down and blocked the way since there was no attendant on duty to raise it. I gripped the keys Judge Brunner had given us tightly in my fist. The mechanism that raised the bar hummed slightly as if it activated. I panicked again as a new wave of fear gripped me.

"Is someone nearby, taunting us with the parking bar?" I whispered as I gripped the key ring more tightly. Again, the mechanism hummed. Then, I realized I had been slightly depressing a button on a tab attached to the set of keys. I held my breath and pressed the button firmly again. The bar jerked and then rose.

"It's a remotely activated, electronic tone to open the garage gate when an attendant isn't on duty," Jason said as he shot through, under the raised bar, and drove around the ramp. I pushed the tab button on the key chain again and the gate lowered. He parked the car in a space out of sight from anyone who might pass in the alley.

It felt a little safer, parked there in the vast cement cavern of the empty garage. Without saying a word, we carefully opened our doors and slipped out. We checked in all directions for the exit. I grabbed Jason's hand as we hurried across the wide expanse of driving area. The sound of our footsteps echoed as we walked. I tried to elevate onto my toes but that only slowed me down. When we got to the door, Jason peered through the glass cautiously and then used the master key to open it. We slipped silently inside.

We were on the lowest level of the parking garage, so we began walking up the two flights of stairs that took us to the main floor. Again, Jason checked for any movement before opening the door into the large rotunda. It looked different at night. No light streamed through from the stained-glass dome above the great hall. But, the wall of windows to the front of the building, which looked out onto the holiday lights of the city, allowed festive beams to shine in.

"Up the grand staircase," I whispered anxiously. We crept up the steps against the inside wall. It reminded me of mice as they scurry through a maze while hugging the walls of the partitions. *I'm endowed by my Creator with a right to life, liberty, and the pursuit of happiness,* I rehearsed in my head. *I am not a mere mouse. I have a righteous obligation and duty to complete the task at hand, not only for Grand-mère and Grand-père, but for Michael Brunner and who knows how many others who may be hiding in back bedrooms of silent homes.* I knew they were worthy of living their lives to the fullest, by virtue of God's precious gift of life.

The second floor, our destination, was a few steps away. I started to move ahead of Jason, when I noticed in the dim light, a bracket attached to the wall near the ceiling. "One of those cameras," I whispered. It was facing the doors on the opposite wall, including the door I needed to enter, and it wasn't stationary. The camera slowly panned the area, back and forth. If we moved, we could be seen. My eyes also caught the now familiar people-detecting device embedded, nearly unseen, near the base of the door, another monitoring portal. Then, I had an idea. I reached in my pocket and removed the chip, still wrapped in the tissue.

"I can't be detected," I whispered and returned the chip to the pocket of my cloak. I took it off and handed it to Jason. "You wait here with my cloak, and I'll take the keys and go inside."

"Christy, no." Jason protested. "It may not be safe."

"Then it won't make it safer if we are both in there and set off buzzers. Besides, we may have already sounded an alarm for all we know," I insisted. I thrust my cloak into Jason's hands and waited until the camera had panned to the left. Then, I darted across the hall, undetected by the people-buzzer and out of view of the camera. I put the newer master key into the lock and felt it turn the tumblers with quiet ease. Once inside the room, I waited until my eyes adjusted to the semidarkness. The room was windowless except for one small window, which, along with the open door, let in enough light for me to move around. I felt more secure in the smaller space. Scanning the far wall beyond the desks and files, I saw another door, an older one. It looked heavy, with raised panels and fancy millwork.

The old key with the ornate head fit easily into the lock, but when I tried to turn it, it didn't budge. I was afraid the shaft would snap off if I forced it. I panicked again. My heart began to pound so loudly, I could feel the beat of it behind my eyes. My hands began to tremble, and I nearly dropped the keys on the concrete floor.

I must use this fear as an ally if I'm going to succeed, I demanded of myself. I translated my panic, to a motivating force for good.

Go ahead and panic, I thought. *The more the panic, the more worthy and justified my cause.* I felt calmness overpower my fear. Now, I had to think of a solution for the key.

I remembered something from an old book. A woman was using fancy scissors called pinking shears to cut some cloth. The sheers were dull and would not cut, so she folded a sheet of material called waxed paper and cut it with the shears. The wax made it possible to cut the fabric. But where would I find wax? I looked around the room and saw a desk with a lamp. I turned the light on and opened the lap drawer and several side drawers until I found what I hoped would be there, a small cube of wax. I had seen file clerks use wax to lightly tip their fingers, making it easier to leaf through a stack of paper.

It flashed through my mind that electronic devices were supposed to have eliminated the need for paper and filing, but when the chaos of the past century hit the country in a vast array of safety breaches, including the crash of all computer servers and systems, it became necessary to file important papers in cabinets again. There had to be a paper trail of the events and contracts we needed to find.

I touched my finger tip to the wax and gently applied it to the shaft of the old key. When I placed it back in the lock ... it turned. *Praise the Lord,* my heart sang, and I smiled as I thought of Silvia Brunner.

Once inside the old records room, the file cases were much

different from the ones in the outer office. Rather than numbers on the end of each drawer, there was a brief account of its contents. I looked for the words, *Old Orders*. There was nothing. Then, *Old Forms* appeared like a miracle.

I riffled through the files frantically, aware of the time. There it was: "Referendum Cover Sheet." I snatched it out and held it to my chest. It had to be in time. It just had to be.

CHAPTER FORTY-SEVEN
Chasing Phantoms

Out in the night, Ward Stoner pulled to a stop outside the Capitol and parked in the security parking space. He stared at the glass fronted building; the interior illuminated by the Gifting lights. He shook his head. *They have to be in there somewhere,* he whispered into the frozen air. *Their chips say so.* Suddenly, he thought he saw a movement inside the building near the staircase. It was fleeting, as a shadow of someone or something ran down the steps. He waited. No one emerged.

At first, the ever-present anger that constantly gnawed at his insides, flared like a fanned flame. He fought with the negative thoughts that bombarded his professional self-concept. *No one will believe this. They'll say, "Old Inspector Tombstone is exaggerating again, casting aspersions on someone as fine as Christiana Applewait." They won't listen to me. Why do I even talk sometimes?*

He shook his head as he tried to clear his thinking. *Stop it Stoner,* he demanded of the demons that haunted him. *They'll have to listen to this tale. This is real and it's happening right here in front of me. They will learn who has the power, and they'd better not cross me.*

As he watched the door to the Capitol, Stoner rolled the old argument over and over in his mind. He had believed that everyone thought he was wrong since he was a young boy and had cowered at the fierce criticism of his stepfather. When he was in his late teens, he had taken an internal stand. *I am not wrong, you worm. You are!*

From that day until the night he found himself chasing phantoms through the city streets, he had done battle with the specter of his stepfather whom he saw in anyone who challenged him. He still fought for power constantly, while he held one of the most powerful positions in society. Only with Miriam was power not part of the relationship.

Stoner continued his vigil, but still, no one emerged from the Capitol. Time seemed suspended. He thought he could hear the tick of a distant clock. He translated the long wait and the loss of the one he had chased, as a personal affront to himself.

So, it's a game of hide-and-seek is it? He jeered. He pulled his car back into the street and drove slowly around the building. Nothing. He shined a flood light into the private parking area, but no one was there. The bar was down, intact, and obviously undisturbed.

"Where did you go, Little Ghost?" he mumbled into the darkness.

Stoner pulled the strata-car around to the side entrance and parked. A set of concrete steps with a pipe-style hand rail ran up to a platform that provided an entry apron for the non-public entrance. With a hand-held tone-controlled master opener, he sent a signal into the lock and opened the door. The inspector emerged into the rotunda. He found it still, silent, and empty. He could see well enough with the glow of the festive lights outside coming through the windows and illuminating the great hall.

From what he had seen from the car window, he believed someone had been on the stairs, so he mounted the steps, and inspected each, one at a time. He searched the marble treads for even a bit of disturbed dust. *The cleaning crew is too good for an investigation like this.* There was no sign of a living soul having passed that way.

Ghosts, he mocked in the dimly lit space. *I guess I'm becoming a ghost hunter rather than a Blue Guard Detective.*

At the foot of the stairs, he pulled back a mirror-like panel that hid a person-sensor. He taped the portal monitor that counted and announced anyone who might step onto the upper floor. Two beeps counted two intruders. Midway up, he tapped another monitor. One beep. At the head of the stairs, there was nothing. He stopped and smiled. *Well, well, little spook. I have found you.*

He opened the door to a supply closet around the corner on the second floor and took out a step ladder. Placing it beneath the camera he had mounted earlier that afternoon, one of several he had placed around the city, he climbed up for a better look. *Well now, we will just see what we have here.*

In the back of the camera was a modest sized viewer. Stoner pressed the rewind button and zipped it back far enough to reveal the activity in the previous half hour. The hall was dimly lit but the screen was bright.

Okay Pluto, let's see who is not here. He watched the screen that showed no activity at first. *If Clyde Tombaugh could find a planet in 1930 by studying the images he took of the night sky, and discovered Pluto by noticing what was not there ... so can I. There is the hall.* The next few seconds of the image revealed the door to the records' room across the hall from the steps as it closed the final few inches. A few minutes later, the lower leg and heel of a woman's shoe were seen as she crossed the hall back to the staircase. He tapped the top portal, no beep. Again, mid-stairs, two beeps. *Well, well, well, she was not there at the portal ... and suddenly ... voila, there ... there she is. So, Miss Daring Spook, I don't know how you did it, but you are my holiday ghost.*

CHAPTER FORTY-EIGHT
A New Emotion - Rage

We had left the Capitol at 10:27 p.m. I had grabbed the paper and hurried to the door of the records room. Jason had given the signal that the camera had panned out, so I could slip past safely. When it was clear, I had darted out. We had carefully and quickly made our way down the staircase, around through the grand hall and out the back door to the private parking garage where we had come in. We hadn't known if anyone was out front when we pressed the button on the key ring and drove back out into the back streets of the city. We had gotten away and had not seen anyone. No one was in the building. No one had followed us.

· · · · ·

"A blessing for your thoughts," Jason whispered once we were back in his car.

We rode toward my apartment in near silence. I was thinking about how much had happened. So many memories stirred. So much pain and horrible evil had been exposed.

"I've been thinking about Grand-mère and Grand-père." I looked out on the ice that sparkled on the trees and bushes. Everything was so beautiful, and yet I felt so ugly and dirty from the filth I had seen. "This is no longer about me and the loss of my grandparents, is it Jason?" I looked at the enormity of the world around me. I had never really noticed it before. If I wasn't checking the weather to determine how it would affect me and my own needs, I didn't even see the blue sky or feel the soft rain. "I don't know if I'm big enough for a task of this magnitude. I don't know if I'm brave enough. I guess I think in micro-bites. I have no big picture panorama inside me."

"You may have seen the smaller picture in the past, Christy. But you have been called to a larger cause, bigger than your grandparents, bigger than any one of us." Jason squeezed my hand to reassure me.

"How is that even possible, Jason? Nothing ever happens to challenge anyone anymore. We live on railroad tracks, never steering right or left, never going backward, never hitting a bump, always rolling toward ... nothingness."

"Christy, there is a strength you can call on. I know how new you are to the Kingdom, but trust me we are not marching toward nothingness. For those who believe, we are always moving toward home. The porch light has been lit, and they're waiting for us."

"Who, Jason?"

"All those who have gone before ... and Jesus."

"I've started reading about him. It's like I'm learning about someone I always knew." Suddenly my eyes flashed on a movement up ahead. A woman and a small boy ran out of a building and across the lawn in the direction of the road. They had no coats and the boy had no shoes. "Jason, what —"

"Hold on," he commanded as he slammed on the brakes just as the two ran to the edge of the road.

I grabbed the safety strap above the door and held on. The road was icy and the surface shone like a giant diamond, beautiful but dangerous. With the help of the DSR 210, Distance Safety Restraint that detected the presence of others in the periphery, Jason was able to control the vehicle and swerve past them to the curb.

"Please," the woman begged as she clawed at my car window. "He's coming."

I left the window safely closed but spoke into the side communicator opening. "What's wrong?"

"He's coming, please let us in," she implored as she checked over her shoulder for what was chasing her. The small boy clutched her leg.

Who was this woman? Was she an operative of the government? Had they found out that we had discovered their evil? Had they come for us, in order to keep their secrets?

At that moment, a large man, sweating, shirtless and wielding a wooden bat above his head, charged out of the apartment building like a raging bull stampeding out of the pen. I eased the door open to let the woman and child climb in, but the burly man pushed them aside and grabbed at my wrist. He jerked me from the car in one fierce motion. Nearly lifted out of my shoes, I struggled to stay on my feet as the man tightened his viselike grip on my arm.

"Christiana!" Jason yelled as he jumped from the car and flew over the hood and landed on the man, jumbling all three of us to the ground in a scrambled heap.

"Charles, no!" The woman screamed and clutched her son close to her body.

The man looked at her without releasing his hold on me. "Ruth?" He looked wild, bewildered.

Then, I saw Jason, unconscious and flat on the ground. Fear seized me when I heard him moan and saw him try to move from under the huge man's foot. He had pinned me down also, and I felt helpless. In that instant, I knew I couldn't reach the man's mind with more struggling.

The man got to his feet and dragged me with him. "Charles," I smiled as casually as I could muster, "something is bothering you. Can I help?" Suddenly, I felt at peace and words came forth I had never known before.

"What?" he stammered, still grasping my arm.

"You were chasing this woman and boy, Charles," I said. "What's the problem my friend?" I patted the man's hand where he held me tight. I hoped he would release his grip.

"No ... that's Ruth, my wife," he stared at me with wide, blank eyes.

"Christy? Are you okay?" Jason gasped as he regained consciousness and tried to get up, but the man had planted his foot on Jason's chest.

"I'm fine, Jason. It's Charles here who needs our sympathy. I want to help him." I swallowed my panic and spoke softly, hoping to calm him down. "I think Charles is just having a really bad day."

"Bad day?" He waved the ball bat he was still holding over his head; his eyes flashed and he raised his voice wildly again. "No. I was showing my son how to play baseball, with a bat like this one."

"Have you been taking little pills lately, Charles?" I asked. "They're great, aren't they? Did you get them from a friend?" I knew this had to be the answer.

"Yeah, from a friend of a friend." He lowered the bat and blinked like he was trying to see everything more clearly.

"Hey, should I call the authorities?" A man yelled from the doorway of the apartment building across the street.

I looked at Charles and his little family as we stood in the snow on Christmas Eve. We were all held by a man who didn't even know he was out of line. "What do you think, Charles? Are you going to be able to calm yourself down on your own? Or, should we have this man call the Blue Guard and have you put in jail on Gift Day Eve?"

"No, no," he protested and stood back a little. He took his foot from Jason's chest. By this time Jason was aware of the situation and slowly got to his feet.

"Should we ask your wife if she wants you to go back in your home with her and your son, Charles?" I asked.

He looked over at his wife. I could see fear on her face. He looked at her in shock and grief. "Ruthie, you're afraid of me? Of me?"

Charles took one step in her direction. She jumped back and dragged the frightened child with her.

The man's face froze with sorrow and shame. "Ruthie ..." he

reached out to her again. She recoiled and tightened her embrace around her son. Charles stopped and looked at the bat in his hand. "What —?" he looked at his family again and then at Jason and me, the two strangers he had threatened.

"That's right, Charles. You're not well this evening. What should we tell your neighbor?" Jason said. "Are you going to be able to get yourself under control on your own? We believe in you. I think you can."

I felt Charles' hand release my arm, but I did not pull away. The touch seemed to quiet him. The medication he had taken may have worn off.

"I'm fine. I'm okay." He turned to his wife with pain in his eyes. "Ruthie ... I am so sorry."

"Charles, I'm a doctor, and I think you will be fine if you get some sleep. We can help you," Jason said.

"I think we'll be all right," I called to the neighbor who had offered help. I hoped we had made the right choice.

"I'll stay at my brother's home tonight, Ruthie. Or, I'll sleep in the jail if you would feel safer." His voice was softer, calmer.

"That might not be necessary," Jason offered. "How many of the white tablets did you take today?"

"Ten," Charles admitted, looking down as if he knew he had overdosed.

"I have some medication in my bag that will counter the effects of those pills, Charles," Jason said. "Take them right away with plenty of water. The white tablets you had taken will dilute quickly and drain from your body immediately." Jason went to get the medical bag from the trunk of his car.

"We'll come in while you calm down," I suggested. "If that's all right with you," I asked Charles' wife. She looked at Jason as he came back with his bag. Then she looked cautiously at both of us as she motioned for us to follow her into the apartment.

Charles responded to the medication Jason administered just as he had predicted. We sat for a while and talked with the family about the holiday. Charles admitted he had been overdosing for days. He had started taking the medication on the promise that he would get back some energy he had been lacking. After Ruth put their son to bed and knew what had happened to her husband, she assured him she was no longer afraid and they would be fine. Soon, he was ready to settle down for the night.

"Thank you both so much," Ruth said as she escorted us to the door. "I don't know what would have happened if you hadn't been here."

"I've taken the rest of Charles' supply of white pills with me. Have him make an appointment right after the holidays. Do not let him go out on his own. He will be feeling tired and may go in search of more pills. He cannot do that."

"Yes, Doctor," she assured Jason. "And, thank you My Lady. You were like an angel. Bless you Miss."

"An angel, Ruth?" I was surprised to hear of heavenly beings again.

We wished each other the happiest of Gifting Days and made our way back out into the snowy night. We were soon back in Jason's car, heading home one more time.

"You are most definitely brave enough, Christy." Jason assured me as we drove through the night. His words filled me with added warmth.

"I was brave?"

"You don't know?" Jason's voice sounded like he was surprised.

"No, Jason. I was afraid, not brave."

"Bravery doesn't mean you're not afraid, Christy. It means you do what needs to be done in spite of the fear or anger you may be feeling. You weren't thinking of yourself this time. You were more focused on that couple and their little boy and making Christmas Day happy for them, than you were concerned about yourself."

I thought about all that Jason had said and held the words close to my heart. Everywhere around me, my life was changing, coming alive. I was now seeing the world with different eyes, and I didn't even know when it happened, when it changed. Regardless of what Jason said, I had not felt brave or up to the task when I was talking to Charles, but I had felt the presence of something powerful in my life that seemed to counter balance the self-doubt. Yet, the thought kept coming back. *Would we win the battle against the evil that had gripped our country for so long? Would we be able to save my grandparents? Or, would the glory of the victory be meaningless without my grandparents to share it?*

CHAPTER FORTY-NINE
Stoner Panics

"I'm done for now," Inspector Stoner stated with finality as he made his way out of the Capitol back to his car. He put the camera on the front seat and slid in out of the snow. The follow-up could wait until morning. Confronting Lady Christiana Applewait and starting an internal probe of the activities of a clandestine unit of the Blue Guard would both come in due time. In the morning, Gift-giving Day would have to share the clock with his never-ending responsibilities. It would be more than just a morning of gift exchanges with his son and family and a breakfast of hot chocolate and homemade pecan rolls. He would have to go over to Oakwood and intrude on Oliver Richly and his family. Never mind that it was a holiday. Stoner shuddered at the thought of the extreme breach of protocol, wound up and bound in the career-ending step of invading the home of one of the Council of Elders. That was not something he looked forward to. He wasn't afraid of Sir Richly. He admired him and, in his mind, there were very few people who deserved his admiration.

He drove along the streets of the city, his streets, and for the first time he wondered how long it had been snowing. He hadn't noticed. Stoner didn't mind spending time in his car. He felt he was surveying all that he owned.

Because of Ward Stoner's job, he was privileged to own a single-family dwelling. As head of the Blue Guard, it was necessary. He could be called at any time to inspect a situation. He couldn't disturb other people hurrying out at all hours as he would if he lived in an apartment building. An efficient workforce required eight hours of uninterrupted sleep. Stoner owning his own home was for the greater good of the collective.

As Stoner pulled onto his own street, he saw that the lights were still on at his house, and he felt good for the first time that day. He had to have nerves of steel and the bearing of a tyrant all day long. His job demanded it. But, if he couldn't lay down the facade of the archfiend of Capitol City at the end of each day, he believed he would turn to dust and blow off into the barren dessert of his own soul. Miriam had helped him shed the mantle of aggression in the past, but she was gone now.

Twinkle lights beckoned him to the front room window, and he smiled. His mother may have let Christopher stay up until Daddy got home. Gift Day Eve had always been a special time of family games and laughter. Even though Miriam had been placed in the sleep chamber, his son deserved a Merry Gift-giving Day. Somehow, he had to pull together the remaining acting talent in his playbill of fictitious characters to create a happy day for his son, and it was late.

He drove the car farther into the driveway. Suddenly, it felt like he had hit a bump. *Christopher, what did you leave in the driveway this time?* He chuckled to himself as he thought about all the toys and tools he had mangled under the wheels of the car in the past. A fairly new wagon, a red tricycle, and a black tool box were recent sacrifices to Christopher's play.

He opened the car door and came around to the walk that led to the house where he saw Christopher laying on the ground near the edge of the driveway. Stoner's heart fell from his chest and landed on the small broken body of his son who sprawled between the lawn and drive.

"Oh, my god!" Ward screamed in agony.

The front door burst open and Stoner's mother ran out into the night. Fear gripped her voice as she tried to scream but no sound came from her throat. She rushed to Christopher's side, fell down on her knees on the snow-covered ground, and gathered him in her arms, rocking him the way she had rocked his father when he was a child.

Christopher must have snuck out to surprise his daddy, thinking he was standing on the edge of the sidewalk. He often got a little too close to the drive and Stoner had warned him about staying back. But it was dark and foggy that night. Perhaps Christopher had not been able to judge his position on the grass.

Stoner's blood froze within him. Damaged children were discarded. He knew that all too well. Christopher's condition was not important to the authorities; an injured child could always be replaced. Stoner had to hide the child immediately.

"Hurry, Mother, hurry! Let me carry him inside. He can't be seen out here like this. The authorities—" Ward Stoner reached for his son.

Sarah Stoner hung onto her grandson's bleeding body and brought his sweet cheek next to her own. "You," she screamed, "you are the authority that you now fear!"

Stoner was stunned by her words—shocked to face the sudden truth of his life. He was the one who hunted people down who were just trying to live their lives as fate had endowed them. He was the intruder. He was the ghost of this life, hiding in the shadows, waiting to snatch away the breath and shorten the lives of others. Now, the broken body was Christopher's. Now it was his family's tragedy. Now, he held the entire span of his son's Length of Days in his own blood-stained hands.

Sarah Stoner would not relinquish her grandson, not even to the child's own father. She struggled to her feet, carrying the child's limp form as she moved. Ward ran ahead of her and held the door while she took Christopher inside and placed him on the couch. Stoner fell to his knees beside his son and listened to his chest. "He's breathing," he whispered.

Sarah soothed the child's cheeks until he opened his eyes. "Hello Sweetheart." Then she turned to Ward. "We have to take him to the hospital to be checked out."

"Come on Big Guy," Ward said as he scooped up his son and carried him into his own room. He placed him comfortably on his bed then turned. "I'll be right back, Christopher."

"The hospital? No!" Ward hissed through gritted teeth as he

returned to his mother in the living room. His face, strained with worry, twisted at the thought of anyone knowing that his son had been hurt.

Sarah's face was ashen and etched with the grip of fear. Suddenly, she raised her arms with hammer-like fists and slammed them down on Stoner's back and head. Blow after blow landed on his shoulders.

She lashed out with her inner rage at all that was evil in the land, embodied in her own son.

Ward did not fight back. He seemed to welcome the attack. Perhaps the mortification of the flesh imposed on him by the little woman who beat him, like a necessary whipping from a devoted mother in the ancient past, might cleanse his soul.

Finally, Sarah let out the raging screams that had been mute when she held her small grandson. Then, completely spent, she ceased the thrashing.

"Mother, Mother, shh." Tears Stoner could not shed when Miriam died welled up within him and broke forth in great sobs and pains of anguish. He cried uncontrollably; his body heaved with emotional pain. Ward's body went limp and weak and the agony drained all life and meaning from him.

When Sarah saw her son, broken and weeping, she called out to him. "Oh Ward, I am so sorry," Sarah sobbed. "I have hated your job from the very beginning ... but I never hated you."

"Daddy? Grandma?" the soft little voice of Christopher called out from the bedroom through his injuries.

"Christopher?" Sarah gasped and hurried to his side. "Oh, thank God."

Stoner wiped his eyes and rushed to his son's room. He put the back of his hand on Christopher's forehead. He wasn't hot. "Where do you hurt, Son?"

"I don't know."

Ward went numb. Was his son paralyzed? Could he not feel his body? "What do you mean?" Stoner ran his hands down the child's arms. "Can you feel this?"

"Yes," Christopher laughed as he started to get up. "Why can't I feel my legs? They feel like they're asleep."

"Christopher, you can't feel your legs?" Sarah's tone was calm but her timbre was weak and shaken.

"Tell me about those legs, Son," Ward coaxed, longing to hear some words of hope.

"I can feel them, sort of, like they're prickly but they're not awake either." Christopher didn't seem to be in pain, just curious. "Why, Daddy?" He placed his small hands on his father's face and patted his cheeks.

Stoner's facade crumbled into rubble at the touch of his son's gentle, innocent hands. With fear and dread he asked softly, "Well ... did Daddy's car run over your foot or anything like that?" Stoner dreaded to hear the answer. How could he live with himself if he had actually struck his own child?

"No, the car bumped me over and I hit my head and bottom on my new wagon," he admitted sheepishly. "You told me to put it away this morning. I'm sorry Daddy."

"You know you aren't supposed to be that close to the car and driveway, don't you?" Sarah smiled. "It's okay this time. Just be more careful the next time, Honey." Sarah looked away, perhaps so Christopher wouldn't be able to see the fear on her face.

"Maybe it's just a pinched nerve," Ward suggested.

"What if it's permanent?" Sarah breathed low. "I know what you said, but maybe we should take him to the hospital, now, tonight."

Stoner turned his back and tried to whisper the words that needed saying. "We could, but let's think this through. Even if he heals, and he's just fine in the morning, this is serious. He would have one strike against him. With very many strikes, he would be declared defective."

"But, if we wait," Sarah tried to keep her voice low and muffled with her hand across her mouth, "what may not be a permanent injury now, may become one without proper treatment."

"I know someone who may be able to find a doctor for us. I'll call him." Stoner reached for his personal communication instrument and touched in the number. It rang several times.

"Hello?" the familiar voice answered. Stoner explained his need for a doctor with integrity, one he knew would have compassion for an innocent child. The person gave him a blind phone number, a contact without a name, and Stoner placed the call. It was a frightening moment. He wondered how much he should tell the doctor. Yet, how could he withhold information the doctor may think could be pertinent to the case? Either way could be disastrous for Christopher. Up or down could be the wrong move. He didn't know which way to bounce.

Stoner knew that physicians had one main object in mind, to protect his own family and career. He didn't know if the person he was calling would be the genuine healer he hoped for, or someone who would place his Christopher's health and needs far down on his own priority list. But, for Stoner, the hunter needed his son to survive before he became the hunted. Stoner's truths, so ridged in the past, could turn into lies in a matter of seconds if necessary.

Stoner placed the call which connected within seconds. "This is Chief Inspector Stoner, here. Someone gave me your number."

There was no sound at the other end of the connection.

"Doctor?" Stoner questioned.

"Yes? What can I do for you Inspector?" a deep voice answered.

"It's my son. He ... fell a little while ago. At first, he was unconscious. When he awakened, he said he had fallen on his head and bottom. Now he says he can't feel his legs like he should. He said they tingle."

"Perhaps you had better take him to the hospital. I could meet you there."

Now it was Stoner who was silent with apprehension and fear. "Do you think that's wise?" He hoped his veiled words were understood.

Again, there was silence. "Are you afraid of ... never mind. If you decide to keep him home tonight, you'll have to try to keep him awake in case he has a concussion. Does he complain of a headache?"

"Does your head hurt Christopher?" Stoner asked his son.

"No, I don't think so," the child patted at the side of his head and paused like he was listening for a slow leak in an inflated ball.

"He said 'No'." Stoner leaned low and covered the mouth piece with his hand. "I would like to avoid the record of an injury if at all possible."

"I understand," the doctor concurred. "If I don't see the boy to treat him, I don't have to make a report. Well, I'm here at the end of this communication line. If you are refusing treatment tonight, there's little I can do. Watch him for twenty-four hours."

"I would have done more in similar circumstances and have already done as much in the past," Stoner admitted like an accused man admitting he had committed a crime. "I would have had the authorities take over the care of an injured child if the parents refused treatment."

"Yes, Sir ... I imagine you would have. But I am not you," the doctor on the end of the line responded crisply.

"No, Sir, you are not. I want to thank you for that distinction. My wife is gone, but my mother and I will stay up with Christopher tonight. We will call right away if he takes a turn for the worse."

"How old is the boy?" the doctor asked.

Stoner's eyes filled with tears as he thought of the possibility of his son being labeled defective. If he were anyone else's child, Stoner would not have valued the boy's life at all. Suddenly, he felt that blood seemed to drip from his own hands, and he wrung them in an attempt to wipe away the guilt that justifiable clung there. Ward Stoner cleared his throat and tried to speak. Finally, he whispered, "Doctor, my son is only five years old." Stoner's heart crumbled into gravel at his feet.

CHAPTER FIFTY

The Eyes on Christy Are Closed

11:45 p.m.

Jason parked the car a short walk from my apartment building. "Hopefully, whoever was following us has gone home for the night," he whispered into the frosty air.

My body felt heavy as Jason escorted me to the door. I wanted to get in out of the darkness and evil that seemed to wait at every turn.

"I know it's late Jason, but can you come in for a while? I'd feel safer," I said.

"Of course, Christy."

We walked quickly toward the door. I felt exposed, like many eyes followed our every step.

Inside the building, firelight danced on the faces of our new friends, gathered again in the large room, like families I had read about in my books. "Look at this, Jason. I hardly recognize it as my apartment building."

"Many of those people are the carolers from the last sing-along," Jason smiled. "Dahlia is still at the piano. I guess I really never knew her at all."

"Do you think it's safe to join them?" I motioned to the group and patted my satchel which still contained the precious lifesaving papers. "What if we're still being followed? I wouldn't want to put these people in harm's way."

"I haven't seen anyone behind us since we came out of the Capitol. Not even when Ruth and her son stopped us in the road near her home, there didn't seem to be anyone around except for one neighbor." Exhausted and filled with fear, Jason and I wondered if eyes would still be watching our every move. He took my hand and led me over to the group who was still celebrating. It was nearly midnight.

I took off my cloak, draped it carefully over my arm, and watched that the paper was secure. Removing my hat, I placed it on the piano.

"Come sit beside me," Dahlia patted the piano bench and kept up the melody with her right hand.

It looked like fun and I needed a peaceful moment before trying to sleep. I knew I would toss all night with all I had seen. I had to bring my soul back from the brink, the edge of utter hopelessness.

Oh, Holy night, my heart soared in ways no spoken words could. *Fall on your knees, oh hear the angel's voices,* the golden melodies threaded the words that linked Heaven with my wounded heart.

After a few songs, Jason and I went over to the coffee pot on a long side table. With cups in hand, we found a place to sit and talk while we enjoyed the group.

"Jason, these lyrics aren't threats to the people's health as Society had said they were," I said. "Look at their faces. Peace and joy shine in their eyes. Their emotional health is not being damaged by the musical threads of these songs."

"I don't see any primal instincts being stirred," Jason smiled. "I do see raw emotions rising. Love is in the room."

Finally, sleep began to overtake me. "I think I need to go to bed," I yawned.

We walked over to say goodnight to Dahlia. Jason stood behind me at the piano. I could feel his warmth on my shoulder. "I'll walk you up, Christy."

"Wait," Dahlia got up from the piano and put her hand on my arm. "I have wanted to talk to you, Christiana," she whispered.

"I know you have Dahlia, but I don't see how I can be of help. I'm newer to these feelings and experiences than you are."

"I realize that, but there is something different about you. You are growing in understanding and love so fast, Christiana. It's like you knew before, somewhere in time. I need to know how you took fire so fast."

"I don't even use feeling words yet," I protested. "I have no idea why feelings are accumulating all around me."

Dahlia smiled. "I remember how that felt. None of us had experienced emotions before, so there didn't need to be descriptive language to talk about it."

"But, I'm a person of words, Dahlia, many words, beautiful words. I have to know my feelings' names."

Jason patted my shoulders in comfort and support. "I think what Dahlia is asking, Christy, if you can think of a pivotal point when suddenly you knew what you didn't know before, on a level where language isn't needed."

Suddenly, I knew. I knew a few of the words that matched my feelings. "I heard the flutter of angels' wings and the breath of their song." I smiled as words poured forth from my heart where knowledge is stored before there is meaning. "A strange warmth filled me, like Jason's warm hand on my shoulder, and a flame was lit deep inside, Dahlia. That is all I know."

"That's all you know?" Dahlia smiled with awe. "I want as much as I can get. Is there anything else you know?"

"I know that, in the very beginning, Dahlia, there was God and that is all I need to know." I wondered if I should cite the source of my certainty. Would I dare? "Dahlia, can I trust you?"

Her expression was pained, but her words were sure and true. "Christiana, you can trust me."

"I have an old book ... a very old book. When it's safe, I'll let you read it."

"When will it be safe enough for me to read a book that's not already on the approved reading list?" She shook her head at the futility of the existence in which we all lived.

"When the time is right ... I will tell you." Then I stood. I was afraid to say more. "I'll see you tomorrow?" I gathered up my hat and cloak. I patted my satchel and compulsively wanted to open it to see if the paper was still there. I had to leave it alone, or risk revealing it to someone who might report that we have it.

"Yes, indeed, I will see you tomorrow." Dahlia's smile was sweet and genuine.

Jason walked me to the elevator and we rode up in silence. It was a comfortable silence in a language that spoke louder than words. There were so many things on my mind, all mixed with a new joy I had never known and a fear I had never experienced.

"The camera, Christy," Jason whispered at my door. "We have to take care of that. I can step inside where I can't be seen by whoever is watching, while you investigate. But I'm not going to leave you alone while that thing is still in there."

I stepped into my apartment. Everything was quiet and still, but I was uncomfortable. My library stepladder still stood against the book case. I knew I would have to do something about the camera that lurked above my head. It seemed to hover above me like a vulture ready to attack the weakest one on the ground. But I was not weak anymore.

I walked past the bookcase, first going to the windows as a diversion to my true destination. Perhaps whoever would view the film later might think my plan was an accident. I stood looking out onto the city and stretched my arms above my head as casually as I could. Then, I walked to the small table beside the couch and picked up a book I had laid there earlier. Pretending to leaf through the small volume, I scanned several of the pages then laid it down as if it didn't hold my interest. I looked up and down my bookcase wall, then climbed the ladder near the camera but avoided looking at it.

"There it is," I whispered as if talking to myself and pulled a book from the shelf with a jerk. Swinging my body wide, as one might if they were steadying themselves against a fall, I flung my arm out and knocked the camera to the floor with my elbow.

"What on earth?" I spoke to myself again and hurried down the ladder. Pretending to trip near the bottom rung, I stomped the heel of my shoe down with a thud on the small camera as I landed squarely on the floor.

"Oh, my goodness," I added in case the camera was still functioning. The object was even smaller than it had appeared while on the shelf. I carefully scooped it onto a piece of paper that was lying on the table and tossed the entire thing into the trash.

"That will be the end of it for tonight. I'll worry about the *who* and *why* another time," I said as I dusted off my hands.

"Good job, Christy," Jason said. "The trash is a good place for it," he laughed.

"Well it certainly is trash," I agreed.

"Are you okay?" Jason asked. "I could stay—on your couch—tonight if you would feel safer."

"Thank you, Jason. I appreciate that but, ... it wouldn't be proper. And—I think that I'll be all right. Whoever placed the camera did so when I was out. I don't think he'll come back while I'm home."

"He seems to sneak around rather than confront," Jason reassured me. "You've been through a lot this evening. We both have. I can be here in minutes if you become frightened."

"I know you can, Jason." We walked slowly to the door. "You would think I would be eager to sleep and free my mind of all that has happened. But—I do hate to see you go."

"Christy, I—"

"I know," I finished his thought with thoughts of my own. "Good night," I whispered as he kissed me. I leaned against the door after he left and smiled.

Alone on the couch, I sat looking out at the city, brightly lit with holiday lights. It was late. The day had been traumatic. Evil was discovered beneath Howard Mountain. A foul, wickedness dwelled there. Tomorrow, Christmas Day, would be as different as joy is from sorrow. Celebrating awaited and the huge task of starting the petition loomed before us. I had to remain positive, or fear and disgust would drain all of my energy. I now knew what vileness lay at the bottom of the souls of some. We would not be safe, and we were only weeks away from my grandparents' final days.

I panicked when I thought of the number of signatures we would need for our petition to stop the Length of Days laws. "Will we have the signatures in time?"

CHAPTER FIFTY-ONE
Christy's First Christmas

8:00 a.m.

In spite of the fact that my energy was depleted from all the joys and horror of the previous day, I awakened on my first Christmas morning, feeling like a child, anxious to open the biggest present under the Gifting Tree. I finished dressing myself in my beautiful new, green silk caftog and looked in the mirror. I smiled and dabbed a little color on my cheeks.

Jason came early. He was going to take Dahlia and me to my grandparents' home for my first Christmas gathering! When I opened the door, he immediately swept me off my feet and into his arms.

"Merry Christmas, Christy." He held me close and added, "You look beautiful!"

"Thank you, kind sir. Jason, this is my very first Merry Christmas," I squealed. "I can't get enough of hearing those words. And, I wish for you a very Merry Christmas as well, Jason O'Reilly."

"We took care of our little spy last night," I said triumphantly as I pointed to the trash receptacle in the kitchen.

"You know that won't be the end of that little chapter in your life, don't you?' Jason put his arm around my waist and kissed my forehead.

"I know, Jason. But, the thought of someone being able to watch my every move on Christmas Eve was more than I wanted to think about."

"Whoever put it there will be back as soon as the holidays are over, looking for their equipment," he whispered and sighed in my ear.

"I know. I realize I've only postponed the inevitable. I also know that they might have placed it here on a previous night when I was asleep. But I will not think about that, not today. I'll think about it tomorrow."

"Now you sound like Scarlett O'Hara," Jason said.

"Scarlett who?"

"You haven't found Margaret Mitchell's book yet? *Gone with the Wind* is required reading in my mind. At the end, a whole race of people was freed."

"Now, a whole nation must be set free." I thought of the enormity and the danger of it all. "Oh Jason, I hadn't even thought about how I've pulled you into all this intrigue. I've only been thinking about myself and my grandparents. I have not meant to be so selfishly unaware of other people's safety and reputation that I would risk a physician's professional standing to help me with my family's problem?"

"This isn't a family problem anymore, Christy. It's a national disaster," Jason insisted. "And, those were my parents in those cases beneath the mountain. They were on display like dinosaurs at the museum. Christy, you have abandoned all concern for yourself. You are selflessly focusing on the needs of your grandparents, and everyone else too, because we are all affected by the Length of Days policy."

I saw the sadness in Jason eyes and felt we needed to focus on the holiday.

"Well, I am certain of one thing. I am not going to think about it today. I am too tired and burned too deeply from the atrocities at the mountain to think about anything." I gathered up my cloak, my hat and bag and squared my shoulders. "I will not think of it today. I am ready, Sir."

"Good," Jason smiled and checked his watch. "It's earlier than we had originally planned, but I got your message about the schedule change."

"Good, I hope Dahlia did too."

"I got the holo-memo but didn't get your reason for the change."

I put on my holiday red hat and Jason helped me with my green cloak. "Wait until you hear about the developments, Jason."

"It's only nine-thirty, Christy. Will your grandparents be expecting us at this hour? Will they be up this early on Christmas Day?"

"Yes, I called Grand-mère and told her that I was expecting someone to stop by their house this morning. She said Grand-père has been up for hours." I laughed to myself as I thought about my grandfather. "He's like a child on Gift-giving Day. He's too excited to sleep. I've seen him sneak into the gathering room and dig around under the tree, looking for packages with his name on them. He shakes them gently and makes sure he doesn't break anything. Then, he'll write down on a small piece of paper, his guess about what's in the gift. Later, after we open the presents, he'll produce the paper to prove he had guessed correctly. He likes to be right." I smiled. Remembering the dear ones was always a joy.

"It will be sad when they die, even from old age. But, Jason, to purposefully cut their lives short while they're still healthy should be criminal, an act of homicide."

I reached in my cloak pocket for the key to lock my door and found the other two keys from the Capitol I had put there the day before as well. "You mean," I gasped as I stared at the keys to the Capitol, "that was just yesterday?" I whispered.

"Just a few hours ago," Jason smiled and shook his head. "It's hard to believe isn't it?"

"Oh, wait," I remembered. "I want to take the book from the library and the paper from the Capitol." I started to dart back inside.

"I have them, Honey. I knew you wanted to take them."

"Honey?"

He threw his head back and laughed softly. "If that's okay with you?"

I smiled and took his arm. "I like it. It is very okay, in fact, it's charming." I nearly skipped along beside him. Then I remembered ... caution ... slowly. "We'll get off on the fifth floor and pick up Dahlia."

The ride down on the elevator was relaxing. Jason stood with his back to the door and we talked. A few minutes later, with Dahlia in our company, the three of us burst onto the morning streets where snow had dusted a powdery white on everything. The day looked clean and pure. Since it was winter and the car windows were up and tight, no one would hear us, so we sang Christmas Carols as we rode through the empty streets.

Everywhere I looked, lights were glowing from holiday homes. Festive, Gifting lights brought more color into most people's lives than there had been all year long. Gift-giving Day had always been a happy day for basically unhappy people. But now, Christmas Day brought a new, holy meaning to my heart and made it a sacred celebration. It all seemed beyond my wildest imagination, outside the limits of all possibilities that a small child could bring such peace and hope to a gray and lifeless people, even though I had read about Christmas in the books I loved. While I had enjoyed the holiday in seasons past, I had never been blessed before by the song of the angels who heralded the Christ child's birth.

CHAPTER FIFTY-TWO

A Referendum, Some Petitions and Christmas Joy

10:00 a.m.

"Wow," Dahlia expressed with awe when we crossed over into Oakwood and drove up to my grandparents' house. "I never dreamed that I would be invited to a home like this. The white clap board is beautiful. Your grandparents' home is a real Victorian." Dahlia sat forward in the backseat of the car and took it all in. "Just look at that wide veranda across the front. It wraps all the way around the side of the house. I didn't know anyone lived in houses like this anymore."

We all got out of Jason's car and started to walk up the sidewalk. Dahlia held back a little as Jason and I moved toward the house. "They are both on the Council of Elders, aren't they?" Dahlia asked in a whisper.

"That's one of the hats they wear, Dahlia. But the chapeaus I like the most, are the ones that go with their grandparent costumes," I laughed.

We walked up onto the wooden porch floor and the boards had a happy, hollow sound under our feet. In my usual fashion, I put my hand to the door latch and pushed it open with my hip.

"Grand-mère," I called toward the great room as we let ourselves in. "I would like you to meet my friends."

I led Jason and Dahlia through the wide entry hall and into the large sitting room, furnished with overstuffed chairs and decorated with wonderful paintings and pottery of bygone days.

"Grand-mère, I'd like you to meet Dahlia Zoobamba and Doctor Jason O'Reilly," I sang out an introduction.

Constance Richly rose with the bearing of a Grande Dame in a royal court. She reached out both of her hands and embraced my friend Dahlia. "Then, this gentleman must belong to you," she laughed. "Mr. Swifty has already arrived."

"Swift, Grand-mère, Thackery Swift," I corrected her.

"Yes, my dear, I know. But Swifty and I have already had an understanding, haven't we young man?" She wrapped her arm in Thackery's and patted his hand.

"What kind of understanding do you have with my grandmother?" I teased Swifty.

"She will feed me part of that goose I helped put in the oven, and I will tell her about my Grandma Rose. It seems your grandmother and mine were school friends." Swifty smiled proudly. Perhaps because his grandparents were now asleep, he seemed to like being close to mine, borrowing some of their warmth.

Then Grand-mère turned to Jason. "And, I am thrilled to see you again, Jason O'Reilly," she smiled. "Your parents were long and dear friends of Christy's parents, Elizabeth and Robert Applewait."

"Yes, Ma'am. They talked of them often," Jason took my grandmother's hand, then bowed and kissed it gently.

"Happy Gift-giving Day," Mother called out as she and my father came through the door.

"We're nearly all here," I said. "When Marge arrives, we will gather in a cluster in the great room." I expected Sean, the newspaper deliverer from the tram, to arrive in a few minutes.

Just then, my father answered the doorbell and Marge came in. "I've asked all of you to come early because Jason and I have some news."

"Jason?" Mother questioned.

"Oh, Mother, Daddy, I would like you to meet Dr. Jason O'Reilly, Marge Cummings, Dahlia Zoobamba, and Thackery Swift,

A.K.A. Swifty." Everyone laughed.

"Jason O'Reilly? I knew your parents, didn't I?" Mother asked.

"Yes, dear," Grand-mère smiled warmly at her. "Jason's parents were Stephanie and Charles."

"Stephie? Oh Jason, I miss her so much." Mother put her arms around Jason and gave him a hug as one comforts the bereaved.

"Yes, Ma'am, so do I." Jason responded.

The vision of Charles and Stephanie O'Reilly, encased in glass in Bedlam's gruesome museum, flashed through my mind. I shook my head to free my mind from the dark memories of the previous night.

As we gathered in what Grand-mère called the parlor and after everyone sat down, all their faces turned in expectation to me. I had called each one to come early, before the meal. Now, the floor was mine.

"You all know by now that Grand-père will turn seventy-five at the end of the month and Grand-mère will follow him a few days later."

Each face in the room grew solemn. No one seemed to know what to say and the silence grew heavy.

"We believe we have found a solution." Jason handed the book and paper to me.

"Any law can be overturned by a citizens' referendum," I began.

"A referendum?" Grand-père snapped to attention and leaned forward to the edge of his seat as he waited for more details.

"Yes. A citizens' referendum requires a petition bearing the signatures of a majority of the population. The petition would call for the eradication of the law concerning the Length of Days policy for termination of life," I explained. "We will also include a reversal of the laws concerning chemical additives in the water supply."

Grand-père stood up quickly and paced back and forth, crisscrossing the room. Then, he sat down on the arm of the chair beside Grand-mère. "Connie, is it possible?"

The doorbell rang and everyone jumped. We were excited and edgy. The government could claim we were practicing sedition right there in my grandparents' home on Christmas morning if the wrong person found us there with incriminating documents.

Thankfully and surprisingly, the new visitor was Judge Brunner. Jason invited him in. Judge Brunner came into the parlor and greeted Grand-père with a hearty handshake and kissed Grand-mère on the cheek. He turned to Jason and then to me. "Were you able to get it?" he asked.

"Yes," my voice cracked with the excitement of our accomplishment. I handed the paper to Judge Brunner and added, "The cover form for the petition."

"Where did you find that document?" Grand-père asked. "I am amazed. I haven't even heard of a special form or a citizens' referendum."

"You don't want to know where it came from, Oliver," Judge Brunner warned. "Just let it be."

"A petition will not be received without an official cover letter or form." I said. "It is a necessity."

"But ... Christy," Mother whispered, "half of the signatures in the whole country ... by the end of the month? How?"

"Well ..." But before I could answer, I heard the door again. I was expecting Sean at any minute.

Jason jumped up and let him in.

"I hope I'm not late," Sean apologized as Jason led him into the room where all eyes had turned to him.

"You're just in time." I rushed to greet him. "And, Sean, I would like you to meet my grandparents and my parents."

"I am honored," he smiled broadly and offered his hand in friendship to all.

Sean carried a black leather valise in his left hand. My love of books drew my attention to the bag and I wondered if the dramatic case testified to the importance of the contents. A character in one of my old suspense novels would have carried such a serious looking grip.

"Sean, I'll have to ask you to respond to my mother's question, because, I don't know the answer. She wondered how we would be able to get the signatures of half the population before the end of the month."

Sean opened the valise and pulled out a tall stack of papers. "The heading on each page identifies it as a petition, or citizens' referendum as Christiana calls it, to overturn the New Bill of Rights, in particular, the policies regarding the Length of Days law and the additives in the water supply." Sean took a deep breath and continued. "We have been secretly gathering signatures for months. We're going after the termination of the entire New Bill. Citizens signed the petition below the heading and included their address and contact information as required. This is a representative sample. We have boxes and boxes of signed petitions, all carefully preserved and filed."

"Weren't people afraid to sign their name, knowing it would be presented to authorities who might misunderstand the petition's meaning?" Grand-mère's words mingled concern for their safety with deep appreciation. "These heroic neighbors who put their name to such a document could be accused of treason." There had been no protests against the government in many years, since words spoken against the current policies or laws were forbidden.

"No, Ma'am, there was no fear at all," Sean said. "They felt privileged to be counted, excited about being able to actually participate in something as large and noble as this." Sean spread the pages on the table. "The petitions we have, account for seventy-five percent of the adult population of Capitol City."

"Oh Sean," I gasped as tears filled my eyes and tightened my throat. "We have the required number of signatures already?"

"But, that's not the whole country." Mother shook her head and her eyes glistened with tears, but they were not tears of joy.

"My wife, Silvia, and I knew that we probably wouldn't have a full sample of the population," Judge Brunner spoke up. "We believed if enough names could be produced to represent a trend, even if it isn't a completed work, we hoped it would be recognized as the will of the people. With the proper signatures, and the required cover paperwork ... we think we can still make this happen. I have no doubt there will be enough signatures when this effort is completed." Judge Brunner cleared his throat and added, "As a Zone Judge, I can issue a stay order on all those who are to be put to sleep due to the Length of Days policy, until the entire country can be canvassed." Carl's eyes fell to the ground and he spoke another truth. "You have to know that I have a conflict of interest in this. My son, my only son, Michael ... is slowly improving from paralysis. But he would have been terminated if we hadn't hidden him. He hasn't been out of our home for nearly a year. Not even the neighbors know that he's there."

"Carl," Grand-mère offered in her own soft sweet way, "Michael is a wonderful young man. He deserves to live ... just as all people everywhere have a right to fight for their own lives, no matter how difficult the strife or how long the battle. It is their own personal battle to fight ... or surrender to ... but it is their decision alone."

Daddy had been silent up until then. He was a man who used words sparingly but when he spoke, his message was profound. "We will stand behind you, all of you, at every turn this cause may take. Together, we will regain liberty for the weak, as well as for the strong, for the sick and broken, as well as for the robust and hearty. This cause must succeed."

Before my father could finish expressing his thoughts, we heard a loud crash coming from the front door. Who would dare barge into a private home of Legacy Citizens—unless? Had he found us?

CHAPTER FIFTY-THREE
Unlawful Entry

10:45 a.m.

I gasped as the front door of my grandparent's warm home burst open and the coldness of the Christmas morning swept across the floor like a flood of ice water. Sean shoved the petitions back into the valise in a subtle, protective action. Then he caught my eye, silently stepped toward the door, and slipped out unnoticed, into the winter morning.

I quickly placed the cover letter back in my bag. I had seen what people were capable of. I knew the danger we were in. My blood froze with the blast of arctic air.

Inspector Ward Stoner stormed into the room; his eyes fixed forward. He didn't even glance at Sean as he quietly slipped out. Stoner shattered the sanctity of my grandparents' home, with one apparent aim—he was looking for someone. "Christiana Applewait, Jason O'Reilly, you will have to come with me, both of you."

"Why?" Jason jumped to his feet and stepped between me and the inspector.

"You were seen in the Capitol after hours." The Inspector's voice was hard, brittle.

"Seen?" I questioned. I knew there had been no one around.

"The heel of your right foot was evident on a surveillance camera, Missy," he hissed, evidently quite proud of his detecting work. "I'm sure a careful comparison of the image we have, with your foot, will reveal a match. You were there, Miss Applewait. Any unauthorized presence after hours in a government building is against the law."

"Unauthorized?" Judge Brunner rose to his full six foot-four inches. "Inspector, these two dedicated people were there under my authority. I am Judge Brunner. I gave them my keys."

I pulled his keys from my pocket and handed them back to the judge. "I'm returning them to you now, Sir," I announced.

Stoner glared at me. Evidently, he was not used to being trumped in the little spy game he played with a tremendous amount of gusto.

"There is also another situation," Stoner proceeded in his game, as if he hadn't lost the previous hand. "There appears to be a secret group within the Blue Guard of which I have not been kept informed. Somehow, and I don't know how yet, but I will, you two have some knowledge of these men."

"I have the information you seek, Inspector," Judge Brunner interrupted again as he squared his shoulders and straightened his back to rebuff the Inspector one more time. "I ordered a small, select contingent of Blue Guard to protect my home."

"It was at my suggestion and authority," my grandfather affirmed.

"Why?" Stoner snapped.

"I beg your pardon," the Judge replied with authoritative indignation. "I owe you no explanation, Inspector. It is well within my authority to do so."

"Perhaps you had the authority, but politically it was not very wise ... Sir," he spit out the words like they had left a nasty taste in his mouth.

"I am not political," Judge Brunner edged toward the inspector. "I am a judge by birth and Legacy by the grace of God," he shouted.

"God?" Stoner yelled back, but there was a change to his expression. "If you are going to hold up a deity as your authority, Sir, can you prove to me that there are gods?" His voice was shrill, not commanding, not controlled. He had lost the moral authority of his position.

Something was stirring within the Inspector. I could see it trying to free itself from his soul. However, the tortured look on his face seemed to be evidence of an evil to come, that blocked the path to freedom.

"I am not defending the gods, Sir," the judge declared with power and strength. "I am bearing witness to the one true God."

"Then call him to your witness stand Judge. Let him defend himself." Stoner was icy in his gaze, but his shoulders lost their square, as one who has already lost confidence in his own argument.

"God does not defend himself, Officer," the Judge replied more softly than before. "We, all of us, bear witness to his existence in our lives and the work he performs in our own hearts. He heals and pardons each one of us. That is our testimony."

Ward Stoner's expression grew weak, and his face was suddenly ashen.

Grand-mère approached the head of the Blue Guard, reached out her steady hand and touched his shoulder. "Inspector Stoner, what is wrong? Has something happened? You were all worked up before, and now you look broken, my son."

Stoner stepped back, out of her reach, as though Grand-mère's touch condemned him, rather than soothed his spirit. "Broken? No never," he insisted with uncertain command. "I am the sole authority in the Blue Guard." His face was twisted and drawn with emotion that seemed to come from deep within his gut, raw and razor-edge sharp.

Grand-mère's love reached out again and would not let him go. She put her hand on his shoulder and drew herself even closer. "But your control stops with your office, doesn't it? Tell me what's cutting your heart so deeply."

"My only son Christopher, Ma'am," he whispered. The Inspector's eyes darted back and forth wildly as if he were looking for a place to hide from the reality of his pain. "My little boy, I ... didn't know he was there in the dark last night. The car bumped him, and he fell." Ward Stoner couldn't hold back the secret any longer, not in the cradle of love Constance Richly was offering him. Then his voice melted. "He couldn't feel his legs, except for some tingling. My mother and I were up all night with him."

"You should have taken him to the hospital or doctor's office," Jason said. The healer's heart within Jason dismissed the inspector's accusations when he first roared into the house and responded only to the need of the man's son.

Stoner's eyes were pleading. He looked at Jason with agony on his face. "I couldn't. He might have been labeled *defective*." Ward's shoulders, racked with pain, heaved under his stifled sobs. "The ... never-ending-sleep."

I knew he was begging for mercy and understanding. "How is he this morning?" I asked.

Stoner rubbed his eyes. His display of grief appeared to embarrass him. "He's a little better, thank you. He's stiff but feeling is beginning to return."

"But he could have gotten a strike placed in his life file if you had taken him to a health professional," Jason said.

"I called a physician. A friend gave me his number—but not his name. He said he wouldn't have to report a telephone call." Stoner looked around the room at all of us, studying each face. "Why do you care?"

"I am that physician, Officer," Jason admitted. "The one you called."

Ward Stoner's face was gray and drawn as if dragged heart first into Hell. He had nearly arrested the man who had shown his son compassion and had helped him during the second horrible crisis of his life.

"Someday soon, Mr. Stoner, I will tell you about the Special unit of the Blue Guard that is attached to me and my family," the Judge offered. "As far as the doctor and Lady Applewait are concerned, they have done nothing wrong. They have simply retrieved a paper that I needed."

"Don't you worry now, Inspector," Grand-mère soothed as she directed him to the door. "You go home and take care of your son and enjoy your Gift-giving Day. We will all be around tomorrow."

"Thank you, Ma'am," Stoner murmured low.

As she guided the inspector toward the door, Grand-mère said to him, "Maybe someday there will be a rescinding of the law about termination through the never-ending-sleep. Perhaps someday, life will be valued again and joy will return to our people." My grandmother boldly stated what was becoming true, even if the inspector wasn't aware of it.

Ward Stoner stopped and took both of Constance Richly's hands in his. "Ma'am, do you think so? Do you know something? Are you all —?"

"We are enjoying Gift-giving Day, Mr. Stoner. Please pass on our well wishes to your son. Perhaps God will bless him with complete healing if you ask him," my grandmother said.

Then Stoner turned, as a small labored smile crossed his lips. "Something strange has been happening to me lately, and I—." He stopped and shook his head. "I just don't understand any of it. I cannot change. I cannot be soft. I cannot bend."

"You can't, or you won't Officer?" Constance Richly asked with a piercing tone of voice.

"I would ... dissolve. I would cease to be," Stoner stammered.

"The you who is not *you*, would cease to be, so the *you* who God intended you to be, could be born again within you." Grand-mère smiled lovingly. "Don't be afraid, my son. God wants only all of you and no more."

Ward Stoner studied the little grandmother as his personal communication device signaled an incoming message. Quickly, he straightened his back with a snap. "What?" he demanded.

His face contorted as he tried to find the side of life he belonged on, the world of power or the world of love. He turned his back to the happy holiday group and hissed into the communicator. "Bedlam is missing? Did someone call in a report or what? How do you know?"

He paused to listen; his jaws flexed with anger. "What do you mean, 'People are looking for him?' Who? What people?" His voice was harsh and full of rage. "I am *the people* who would have been called and this is the first I have heard of it. First it was that Drummond fellow, then Mari, the end-traveler went missing, now Bedlam himself."

Again, he paused. His fisted flexed and clinched as he listened. "He has left the zone?" His voice grew hard and shrill.

"Inspector, please ..." Grand-père cautioned.

Stoner's entire body seemed to be fighting between the spirit that pulled at his heart and the power that dominated his mind. Then, a flash within his eyes changed his surrender to power-hungry anger again. He stepped toward me with a cold, steely gaze once more. "Don't forget to read the handwriting on the wall, Missy." Then he smiled a sinister grin. "Have a very Merry Christmas and may God's richest blessings or his most impoverished curses, be on all of you."

We all stood there in silence. The display of good and evil from the soul of that one man stunned us. I wondered how safe we all were now. Evil stalked the streets and buried life beneath a mountain of blood. There was Silas Drummond's warning and our witness to the evil at Howard Mountain. The monster had escaped to a different zone, so evil was loose in the whole world. Yet, amid all that darkness, the Christ child beckoned us once more to the manger of life, where love was born again in the hearts of those who would believe.

CHAPTER FIFTY-FOUR
The March to Freedom

4:00 p.m.

The Christmas goose had been picked to the bone and the leftovers put away. Some played something that afternoon called *Monopoly*, an odd game of buying personal property and ransoming others' ability to make passage around the game board. If a player landed on another's space, they were taxed with rent payments. The game's rules were old fashioned to all of us since taxes were no longer levied on the citizens. And, for the most part, people didn't own their own homes or property. They rented space in high rise apartment buildings like the one I lived in. Most individually owned homes were in and around the Oakwood area of town, a little oasis where residents enjoyed an expression of individuality.

"Oh, no!" Mother shouted as she and my father tried to beat Grand-mère and Grand-père at the *Monopoly* game they loved. Since that type of game had been replaced with individual, solitary games in past years, we all felt lucky that my great-grandparents had saved many of the favorite old ones of their day and stored them in the attic.

"I want to buy this property," Marge sang out when she landed on a square she coveted.

Thackery and Dahlia were enjoying the lavish grounds that were still beautiful even though it was early winter. In December, the icicle-show on the bushes and trees, sparkled like cut glass and filled their eyes with beauty.

Jason and I spent our time talking. We interspersed our

conversation with comfortable periods of silence in front of the fireplace.

"It's cozy here," Jason whispered, as if we were in an old sanctuary with stained glass windows smiling down on us.

"I have always loved it here. But Jason, even as we relax, I can't help thinking ... in a few days ... well, my grandparents' birthdays." I shook my head. "Their termination just isn't going to happen like the Length of Days law says it must. I am determined that we can win this."

"You are an amazing woman, Christiana Applewait," Jason smiled. "Absolutely amazing."

I thought about my few days with Jason, and imagined spending many more with him, talking, walking, and traveling. "Jason, have you read any of the books that have described travel around the country and even abroad? People used to get in their cars and just drive, for hours, for days."

"Yes, I've read many of them. People would fly in huge air liners across the oceans and take trains to distant towns," Jason answered.

"Wouldn't it be wonderful to travel out of the country and touch the lives of people in other places? I've read about the South Sea Islands, countries on the continent, France, Italy, and the British Isles. Most of us have traveled no more than a few miles from our homes. Jason, I found large picture books in the library with photographs that took my breath away."

"I've seen some too, Christy and ... I've traveled a little." Jason sounded hesitant. "Wouldn't it be nice to go to New York, Boston or maybe Philadelphia? The books say that these are the places our country used to hold in reverence."

"Jason!" I squealed with muffled glee. "It would be marvelous!"

Mother looked over in our direction and smiled. She looked content, even beautiful that late afternoon. She seemed to be enjoying my growing relationship with the son of her old friend.

Jason and I shared descriptions and recreated the word pictures from the books we had read. The firelight sent golden shadows that danced across the room and animated the scenes in my head. The wintery darkness had come on early, gathering familiar forms into her snowy shadows and nestled them there.

"Oliver, dear, please turn on the lights. It's getting dark in here," Grand-mère called out.

"I can see fine Connie."

"Well, yes dear, but I can't seem to see a thing."

I laughed quietly. Those two dear old ones. They fit together like two pieces connected in Heaven, then separated at birth, only to find each other again. I wondered if Jason would be my soul companion, and it frightened me a little. All my life, I had only thought about myself.

"Yes, dear, do you have enough light now?" Jason teased.

I looked at the firelight reflected in his eyes. They were as warm as the flames, and I knew I was home. "Yes, I have enough of everything."

Suddenly, there was a pounding at the door and banging until Grand-père flung it open. "Sean?" He gasped as our new friend stood there in the dim, late day light. Sean wore no coat or hat and appeared to be short of breath. "What's wrong?" Grand-père asked.

Sean burst into the house. His eyes searched each face. "Christiana, there you are," he called out, his voice sharp with excitement.

"Sean? What is it?" Fear gripped me again as the memory of that morning's brush with the Blue Guard flashed through my mind.

"Christiana ... Jason, it's wonderful! You won't believe it. They're marching, right now. They're moving out across this city and gathering more and more people as they go!" He dashed from one side of the room to the other.

"Who, Sean?" I couldn't grasp what he was talking about.

"Everyone, Christiana, everyone. They are marching to the Great Leader's home, President Alexander, to deliver our petitions. They're doing it now, as we speak."

"No, not yet!" I cried.

Sean staggered back. His high mountain of joy seemed to crumble with confusion and surprise. "Why not? Christiana, what is wrong?"

"All petitions require a cover letter, or special form, to accompany them, Sean. You left this morning when the inspector came in. I was showing everyone that Jason and I had gotten the form. Here it is. We have it!" I jumped up with excitement and waved the precious page in front of him.

"Where did you —" Sean darted about the room and bounced off nearby furniture.

"Don't ask," I cautioned as I followed him. I tried to get into his line of view so he could focus on what we were telling him. "Before our Christmas dinner, I filled it out with everyone's help. We made sure there were no mistakes."

"We prayed earnestly for all the courage we could muster, and to know God's will as we put the words on the paper," Grand-père whispered.

Sean stopped pacing long enough to process what he heard. "You have the form? You are very sure you have the right paper?"

"Don't panic, Sean," Dahlia cautioned. She and Swifty had come back into the house in time to hear the discussion and witness the wild emotions.

"Yes, we are positive," Jason assured him.

"Then get your coats and that paper, and follow me to President Alexander's house." Sean shouted over his shoulder as he started out the door. Then he turned. "Well, are you coming?"

Sean had run all the way from the transit stop. Time was vitally important. We had to get to Alexander's house before the crowd handed over the petitions. My parents and Marge rode with Grand-père and Grand-mère. Dahlia, Swifty and Sean were with us in Jason's car. Jason called Judge Brunner and his wife Sylvia on his communications device and let them know about the people's walk to

President Alexander's home.

There were few other cars on the streets at that time of the evening on Gift-giving Day, so we covered the first several miles rapidly in spite of the gathering fog. As we came within the last mile along the corridor leading to President Alexander's home, people were everywhere, in the streets, on the lawns and sidewalks. There was no place, where the citizens of our community had not marched to take back their freedom. Even members of the Blue Guard had abandoned their cars and were walking with the people.

"We might have to go the rest of the way on foot," Jason said as he tried to look past everyone to see what waited down the street.

"We can't." Sean warned. "The people have the petitions. If it's like you said and they give the petitions to the Great Leader without the cover form, Alexander may dispose of them immediately, on the spot."

"We have to get through," I cried. The tension rose within me like a drowning wave. I was worried about my grandparents and the pressure they would be feeling. Finally, I did something I had never done before. I prayed to a God I had only recently heard of, to protect my dear ones, and to make a path through the people so that life could win over death.

"I know." Sean immediately snapped to attention, opened the car window, and pushed back the people who pressed against it. He swung his body, headfirst, out through the window and then used the opening as a stepping stone to lift himself up onto the car's roof where he sat down. "Clear the way," he shouted at the people ahead of us. "We have a piece of the solution. Move, move ..." he called every few feet as both of our cars inched toward the home of Nathan Alexander, the President and Great Leader.

When we got to the president's home, Sean stood on top of the car and held up both of his hands. "Everyone, listen ..."

The crowd stilled. A hush fell over the evening. Lights glistened off the snow and made the spot a hallowed ground where freedom had taken a stand once more.

"Nathan Alexander," Sean called to the house, "President

Alexander, please come out."

"Let me go up and invite him out," I suggested but didn't wait for an answer. "I'll make sure he knows we mean him no personal harm." I tried to squeeze out through the car door, but people everywhere pressed against it. I opened and closed the door inch by inch until I could wedge myself through and started up the walk to the house.

"Christiana," Jason called after me. "I'll go with you."

As I neared the steps, Grand-père had worked his way out of his car. "Christiana, wait, I have an important message for you." He came near and whispered gently yet firmly in my ear with all the confidence I knew my grandfather had.

"Sweetheart, there are some verses from the Bible you must hear. From the book of Luke, chapter twenty-one, verses fifteen through nineteen:

> For I will give you words and wisdom that none of your adversaries will be able to resist or contradict. By standing firm you will gain life."

I hugged the dear man I loved so much, then, I turned. Jason, Sean, and I stepped up onto President Alexander's porch.

CHAPTER FIFTY-FIVE
Accusations Turn to Revelations

6:30 p.m.

My parents and grandparents had maneuvered out of their car, stepped up on the porch, and stood to be counted on that historic night. Even Marge joined us, front and center, no longer afraid who might see her. To the contrary, she was eager to be seen, to be numbered with us as a freedom marcher.

"Are you sure you want to do this, Missy?" Chief Inspector Stoner had pushed his way forward and touched my arm as he whispered in my ear. But his tone was not one of concern or comfort. It felt threatening. I recoiled at his touch.

The President's porch was wired from one side to the other so the president could broadcast from there, both over the communication waves and to throngs of people who might gather there for a special event. I was careful to guard my words that I did not want everyone to hear.

"Inspector, I'm not afraid of you." I looked at him with increasing confidence, my eyes fixed on his. My feet planted firmly on the solid surface of the presidential residence.

"What seems to be the problem?" Jason put his hand on my shoulder. I could feel his strength and knew I was not alone.

"You two have stirred up a hornet's nest of mistrust and rebellion. Look at all these people. We call it sedition," Stoner hissed.

"The people have a right to make their voices heard," Judge

Brunner stated with the authority of his robes as he too stepped onto the porch. "These people are doing no harm. They aren't threatening anyone. They are here for one purpose, to deliver something to the President."

"And what might that be? Is it so important that it has to be done tonight?" Stoner asked.

I wanted to shout, "Yes, tonight!" But I said nothing. I did not want to give away the cause of our sacred mission before it was completed.

"There will be plenty of time to talk about their purpose for being here another time, Inspector. Lady Applewait and Dr. O'Reilly are here merely to present their material to the president," the judge said.

Stoner stared at the judge, determined to not back down. "I am talking to Miss Applewait, Sir. Not you."

"Lady Applewait will talk to you at the first of the week," Judge Brunner stated with firm resolve. "I'll accompany her to your office myself."

The judge's strength gave me courage, and I was determined to press forward. "Excuse me, Inspector." I tried to move beyond the man, but he continued to bar my way. "I have come to speak to the president tonight," I insisted, my eyes fixed on Stoner's.

"I told you to pay attention to the writing on the wall. It may be something you don't want these folks to know about."

Stoner spoke low, as if he were attempting to reveal a secret.

"I don't know what you're talking about, Inspector." I couldn't get past him and had no idea what he was saying.

"There is something in your past that your entire little Legacy club has been keeping from everyone and possibly even from you." Stoner seemed to be getting a great deal of satisfaction from dragging out his accusations against me, whatever they were.

"There is a record of you being involved in a work of sorcery," he sneered. "Do you want these people to hear about it? He studied my face and then added, "Or, nothing needs to be said, if you and your friends and family just go on home."

"Sorcery?" My father advanced and wedged himself between Stoner and me. There was a power in Daddy's stance I had rarely seen.

"Keep it up, Mr. Applewait. If all of you don't go home now, I will tell everyone about your little girl and the handwriting on the wall. Then you can watch how fast these fine people turn into a mob."

"The handwriting on the wall?" Mother moved onto the porch and into the inner circle. "I think I may know what he's talking about. Christiana, we never told you about it and this man should never have found out."

"Told me what?" I couldn't fathom what I could have done that the Inspector would be able to use against me.

Daddy stepped forward to talk to the huge group that had grown silent as they watched and strained to listen to the confrontation. "Ladies and gentlemen," he held up his hands to address the people, "my wife and I have something wonderful to share, not something to hide." A hush fell over the people as they stood in the silent night.

Mother wrapped her arms around me as I turned to face the people.

My father paused for a moment then spoke with power and confidence. "Our daughter, Christiana, is a marvelous young woman. She was blessed with a holy presence since an early age. The inspector would like to call it sorcery, something out of black magic." My father looked at me with the love I had always received from him. "No, what Christiana has, is a blessing from God."

"What is he talking about Mother?" Then, I looked at Jason to see if he had been shaken by Daddy's words. Jason was smiling lovingly, knowingly.

"Let's just listen to him, Honey," Jason smiled and took my hand.

My father looked at Jason and me and patted my cheek. "When Christiana was seven years old, the Council of Elders was meeting in the Grand Hall to listen to requests from many people. The hall was full."

"You'd better think this through." Stoner growled angrily at me as he saw my parents take his ammunition against me and turn it back on him. He tried to move closer to me. "You don't even know what they're going to say. You could be a laughing stock or a freaky curiosity."

I just looked at Stoner for a minute then turned my eyes back to my father. I would not believe that my own father would do anything to harm me.

My father looked at me as he continued speaking to the people. "Your mother and I brought you into the Grand Hall so you could have your first taste of the Legacy you will inherit, Christiana. We sat in the back so we wouldn't disturb anyone. Your mother gave you some coloring sticks to keep you entertained."

Suddenly, I remembered the sticks. I hadn't seen them since I was young.

Mother wiped her eyes. "We thought we were watching you, Sweetheart, but we got caught up in the proceedings."

"I saw it first," Grand-père smiled at me as he stepped forward. "You were standing up on your chair so you could see the proceedings better."

The inspector turned to all the people gathered there and shouted. "It was sorcery I tell you. What are you—sheep? Do you follow wherever these people lead and believe everything they tell you?"

I heard murmuring as a restlessness spread throughout the people. Feelings of fear began to rise within me. Would the crowd turn on me and stop what we were trying to do?

Then Grand-père's voice rose above the throng, clear and strong. "People, Christiana is no sorceress. She is a messenger from God!" Grand-père raised his hands to the people as they gasped in amazement.

"God?" someone asked. Most just listened intently, their voices hushed.

I was stunned, stricken by fear and wonder. A messenger of God? How could that be? I had never heard of God as a child.

"God?" Stoner yelled. His eyes flashed with rage at the name of the Holy One. "There is no God!" He shouted into the darkened sky. "Only the blackness of the night." Then he whirled back to face Grand-père. "Sir Richly, you expect us to accept your statement that this woman is a messenger from God?" He turned to the people and strutted back and forth on the President's porch, as if on his own small stage. "I demand that you produce your god!"

Grand-mère smiled her knowing, sweet smile and opened the locket she wore around her neck so Grand-père could see the contents. She embraced him and waved a calming, royal hand to the people. Then, she kissed my cheek.

"If you will wait a moment, we will produce our God." Then she asked, "Does anyone have a 281 Palm Device with you?"

"I do, Connie," Jason spoke up. "It's in my car. I'll get it."

"Will you all please let Dr. O'Reilly through?" Daddy raised his arms to the people.

Jason squeezed his way through the people and returned with the Device. "Let me open it for you, Oliver," Jason said, as he handed the Palm Device to my grandfather.

Grand-père raised his hands to the people again and they grew silent. "Christiana was very small the day we took her to the grand reception room, so she had to get up on her chair and stretch as high as she could. She took her color sticks and began to draw on the back wall, that's why I saw it first. I was facing her masterpiece and it was magnificent! Little Christiana worked fast, like someone else controlled her creation. What burst forth from her hand was ... the very face of God."

He turned to the inspector and added. "Just like the writing on the wall in the Biblical book of Daniel when a detached hand appeared and wrote on the plaster during a wild banquet. Daniel interpreted the words for the king. He told King Belshazzar that his reign was over. I believe Christiana's drawing and writing, tells us that God's reign is never over, regardless of what government may rule. But you, Inspector, have asked to see the face of God."

Grand-père turned and took Grand-mère's locket. "My wife, Lady Richly, has kept a miniature likeness of the wall art Christiana drew that day, here in her locked. I will project the image against the fog for all of you to see."

Jason helped Grand-père place Grand-mère's locket in relationship to the Palm Devise so it could register on the small device screen and project a hologram onto the wide expanse of Heaven above our heads.

I had seen Grand-mère's locket many times and had asked her what was inside. She always said, "Something holy, my dear. I'll show you one day."

There were gasps and murmurs of awe from the people as the hologram shimmered in the cold night air, then formed clearly against the fog. As it burst forth, the memory of that day took shape in my mind.

"There," Grand-père's voice rang out with might and power, "there is the picture of God you wanted to see, Inspector. Christiana drew it when she was only seven years old. She is seeing it tonight for the first time since the day she drew it, the same as all of you."

Tears flowed like healing waters, as I bathed again in the same spirit of holiness that had touched me so many years ago. Against the canvas of Heaven, like a mighty, holy colossus striding across the firmament, was a completely formed drawing of a being. With the breath of life flowing from his mouth and nostrils, the being looked as if his spoken word had just caused the whole world to leap into creation. His powerful muscles declared his strength and his eyes revealed his love. His hair blew across the night sky like a field of tall wheat in late July. There it mingled with the tails of winter clouds as they stretched across the canopy of our world. The light from his eyes was as glorious as the dawn of a new day. His gaze was as strong as the towering oaks and as sweet as a field of wild flowers after a spring rain. It looked like all of creation laughed and loved within his gaze. There was so much glory emanating from his countenance, it was nearly impossible to look upon him. Across the bottom, under the drawing, were the words and letters, "Ego sum Dominus sum ego"

"What does it say?" a voice called from the crowd.

Stoner kept his back to the sky and would not turn to the face of God illuminated there. "Can't you see what they are doing? It's a trick," he yelled. "There is nothing there you need to see," Inspector Stoner ordered.

"You asked to see our God," Jason reminded him. "Look into an innocent child's magnificent depiction of his face, Inspector Stoner. Go ahead ... or don't you have the courage to look?"

Stoner turned slowly to face what he did not believe in, and yet, there he was. He glanced at the sky and his expression fell like shattered glass. "What does it say?" he whispered.

"The words, 'ego sum dominus sum ego' is Latin. It says, 'I am Lord am I.' And the hand of a seven-year-old child had drawn and written it, my granddaughter, Christiana Applewait. How she knew what God looked like or what words to write, we had no idea. I don't know the mind of God but—he obviously knew her—before she knew him."

I was astonished to hear Grand-père's explanation. I finally remembered the drawing and the words, even though no one had spoken of them since.

"Why didn't you tell me?" I asked.

"The inspired drawing was obviously a miracle, Christiana," Mother reassured me. "We believed the people might not understand your special gifts. We had to protect you from stares, even adoration."

"Christiana, you were a child prodigy." Jason was as awed as I was. His eyes stayed fixed on the portrait of God.

"Maybe that's what Rebecca meant when she said I had a talent that I was holding back." It made sense to me now.

"I am sorry," Daddy apologized. "We were all so amazed. We probably made a fuss over the art and you. Then, we became frightened that people would give you too much attention and adulation that would harm your growing spirit. Maybe you didn't understand our intentions and thought you had done something bad." Daddy kissed my cheek. "We only wanted to protect you."

"I know, Daddy. I have always trusted you and Mother ... and all of you," I added as I turned to my grandparents. "I have always felt safe and protected."

My struggles to paint what I saw and not what I felt came to my mind. I will admit I was aware that I was holding back on my paintings, afraid to express myself through it. I could see wonderful images that couldn't be expressed in words on the blank canvas, waiting for me to bring them forth. Society does not permit creativity. My visions were far beyond Society's approval. I smiled as I thought of some compositions I had wanted to paint but didn't have the nerve to do it.

Stoner turned his eyes from the masterpiece in the sky and stared at the dirt near his feet. He shook his head and added, "I will not believe such nonsense."

As the Inspector turned to leave, Grand-mère touched his arm. He jerked away as if burned. She reached out again, "But, you want to believe, Inspector."

Stoner did not reply nor turn back to the light. Nor did he return the life and love offered him. With his shoulders slumped, he stomped away into the night.

CHAPTER FIFTY-SIX
A Holy Night

Grand-père closed the locket and the vision disappeared. "The people understand that you are not a sorceress as Inspector Stoner accused. As a child, Christiana, you had drawn an impression of a God no one knew anymore." Then Grand-père turned to the people and offered to hold future gatherings to explain and teach more from the scriptures.

Now, we had to confront President Alexander. After calling his name again, the massive front door of the Central Zone president's home opened.

President Nathan Alexander came out into the confines of the clear, attack-proof Ceremonial Reviewing Chamber, a security bubble to the left of the main entrance. Members of the Capitol Secret Guard surrounded him. Alexander stood with closed, folded arms, obviously in protest to what he heard we were doing.

"I was expecting you," he announced through a speaker. "I received a call," Alexander said.

"Sir," I began, "I am Lady Christiana Applewait."

"I know who you are." His voice was edgy as he looked beyond the porch at thousands of people who had straightened their backs and had come here to say by their presence, *No, not anymore.*

The moment was breathtaking as the citizens gathered in closer to be counted before the world. There were so many people with us that cold, yet holy night, the people in the back could not possibly have heard what was said, but that didn't seem to matter. What was important was that they were there. Perhaps they believed, we will stand together or we will fall together, but no one had to stand alone that night, on that very first Christmas Day evening in one-hundred years.

"We have a petition," Sean began, "bearing the signatures of 75 percent of the citizens of this city."

"I don't have to accept them, young man. Things must be done in the proper way."

"We know that Sir," Sean agreed.

"No, I don't think you do. You can have signatures from every person in the entire country, including all quadrants, but if it isn't filed properly, I can throw them in the rubbish pile."

"But we do have all we need," Sean explained. "You have these boxes of petitions."

"And we have the proper cover letter," I added as the glint in President Alexander's eyes faded with my statement. "This citizens' referendum is calling for an end to the policies regarding Length of Days terminations into the never-ending-sleep, the control of the population through chemical drugging, and the reversal of the New Bill of Rights."

"This will still be too late ... Ma'am." Alexander shot a glance at my grandparents. "I understand, Your Excellency, that you and your wife will be seventy-five years old in a matter of days. A few days aren't enough. Your referendum must include signatures from a majority of citizens of the entire country, not just this city or even this zone."

"That's right," Judge Brunner announced with authority as he stepped forward. "I am Judge Carl Brunner and this display of citizen action has been heard. They will expand the referendum they have completed for our city and put it to a vote of the entire population at the next election. Between now and then, freedom loving people will ride out across this land and gather support from every village and hamlet, from every state and quadrant in the entire country. This citizens' referendum will pass. I guarantee you."

Alexander's eyes narrowed and his face grew red with stifled anger. "But it will still be too late," he spit out with a full measure of satisfaction. "The elections you are talking about will take place months after Oliver and Constance Richly are dead and buried. Your little scheme to oust me from office and overturn the entire government will be months past your deadline."

"No, Sir, it will not be too late," the judge rebutted. "We have accepted the inevitable, as if we had no other choice, for far too long. I am issuing a stay of execution, halting the judicial writ regarding Length of Days legislation. I'll file the papers on Monday, suspending the carrying out of all termination procedures and halting the use of chemicals in our drinking water, for the next two years. This will give Christiana and Jason, Sean and the rest of them, all the time they need to complete the task of gathering every signature necessary to make it law."

"It only took one brave man to step out of the silence and testify to the horrors of our society. I see him now." I spotted Silas Drummond as he made his way through the crowd.

Silas moved to the edge of the steps so as not to be seen by the entire group and whispered, "I got your message on my communication device, My Lady. They took my car, so I ran all the way to the transit line. Thank you. Thank all of you for what you are doing."

"You broke the silence, Silas. We all owe you the thanks," I said.

"You won't have to go back to the mountain, Silas," Judge Brunner assured him. "The stay will stop all work there for two years. Come and join us on the porch where your presence can also bear witness."

Silas placed his foot firmly on the first step as tears streamed down his face. Timid by nature and bold by necessity, Silas waved to the people with his bandaged hand, burned by the fire of the despicable furnaces.

Then the judge turned back to President Alexander. "It doesn't matter if you choose to be behind our cause or not. We no longer need you or your government." Judge Brunner took a step forward but still maintained a respectful distance. No one would be able to say that he

289

had intimidated the president of the zone.

"Besides the referendum, at the next election, we will also be voting on a new president," Judge Brunner continued. "We will reconstruct the representative convention system and call for delegates. I plan to help these young people develop a political platform that will drastically change this country, not into something different, but back to the inspired and inspiring nation it was originally designed to be."

"Oh, Judge Brunner that is fantastic," I shouted over the cheers of the crowd.

"Beginning tomorrow," Sean announced, "you will find a free news sheet on every transit car so that all may know of our plans." Then he pointed to the people clustered at the president's residence. "You, here in the front, spread the word to those in the back. They will be informed by the free newspapers available to all."

Those near the front of the group cheered, then turned and passed the word back through the crowd. Each group respectfully stood in silence so the word could go forth to the entire gathering of citizens.

Then, from somewhere among the people gathered on that wonderful night, someone called out, "Christiana Applewait for president! Christy ... Christy ... Christy ..." they began to chant.

I was overwhelmed! And flattered! And for a moment, the thought of power was overwhelming. "Thank you, thank you," I called to the people. "You have honored me beyond any aspiration I could have ever dreamed. But I'm afraid I have read the founding fathers' papers and, my friends, I'm just not old enough."

The people laughed and called out words of teasing and support. "Lower the age!" some yelled. "Kids can make more sense than adults!" another laughed.

I felt loved and accepted. I raised my hands to silence the people and called out above the crowd. "I nominate Oliver Richly to run for office as our new president."

The throng erupted with an uproar of cheers and hugs and laughter. Again, the repeated message of what had just been said spread like a child's party game, from one person and one group to another, beyond the sound of my voice. Suddenly, chants of, "Richly ... Richly ... Richly," rang out above the throng.

Grand-père stepped forward and raised his voice to the people assembled there. He was calm and full of strength. "We are at the dawn of a new day, when free men and women will rise up to say, 'I am loved. I am of value. I am blessed by the Lord our God with the right to life, liberty, and the pursuit of happiness.' Join us, one and all!"

Cheers resounded again with laughter and praise. Even the majority, who had never heard of detoxification, hugged each other, and danced with joy for the first time in their lives. With their hands raised in praise, they frolicked like children, not inhibited from expressing their joy. That night, the human spirit had risen above the evil efforts of others to hold it down.

Jason swept me up in front of everyone, swung me around in a continuation of our dance and kissed me with power and love. I could feel joy and the thrill of the night of new beginnings. The gift of a new life had been offered to everyone on that Christmas Day Eve.

When the people saw our display of tenderness in public, they cheered again and clapped wildly. Such simple pleasures hadn't been seen or felt in many years. Regardless of the laws that had robbed them of joy, there seemed to be a deeper knowing that touched their hearts. They were starved for love, and they didn't even know they were hungry.

A hush fell over the group as someone in the back of the crowd began the words I had just learned, but many of the people seemed to know already. "Silent night ..." they began, "holy night ..." and it was holy. Like the hum of an angel choir, even the trees swayed to the melody as we sang. It all seemed right and good.

It would be hard, but I knew, with Judge Brunner's stay, we had the time to get all the signatures necessary. As time went on and the people overcame their dependence on the drugs they hadn't even known they had been taking, there would be even more support for the cause.

I knew, once people began to feel, they would lay down their very lives to continue in the joy of living. We would all regain a reverence for life. A battle had been waged that day and victory had been declared. On that day, Life had won.

EPILOGUE

Ward Stoner stood in the darkness on the front edge of the crowd on that cold and sacred night, when the country was reborn—and said, "No more." He didn't cheer nor did he sing. A smile never crossed his lips. His job demanded the exercise of power and a total disrespect for life. Silas Drummond had defied the orders of his position, the end-traveler, Mari, was missing, the Legacy one had managed to get by him, and Alister Bedlam had left the zone, illegally, even for him.

Out of the Zone, are you? And, you little petition peddlers are going to try to escape the zone as well? I will reactivate my National credentials and pull my Federal badge out of the drawer. None of you will escape from me.

But Inspector Stoner was torn between the dictates of his job and the distant call of something else. He didn't know what had been pursuing him, what had been tugging at his heart.

That Christmas Day evening, those who passed by or stood near him paid no attention to the stoic figure who hugged the shadows. But the dark figure was keenly observing all of them. At times he jotted down the names of those he recognized or overheard a spoken name. Other times, the joy and display of love actually mesmerized him. But, in the end, even the love he saw for the first time on the streets of his town had no influence on the inspector. In fact, it had an opposite effect on him. The love of his life was gone. There was no more humming in the kitchen or flowers on the table. The scent of her cologne had finally faded and no longer floated on the air of their home, even though Stoner had done all he knew how to do to keep it alive.

Christopher had been the happiest child Stoner had ever known before his mommy went to the sleep. But, after her death, most of the time, Christopher's lethargic gaze looked out on his play yard and saw no joy in any of it. The moments that managed to coax out a little happiness in his day, were the hours after his daddy got home.

Hoping it would help Christopher, Ward Stoner had prepared himself. He had taken a few minutes at the end of each day to reframe his experience. Before going inside his own home, he would sit in his car and try to reconstruct the dirty and evil thoughts of the work he had to do, into upbeat positives that would benefit his small son. He looked for a humorous moment to retell him. But Stoner was getting more and more discouraged with his attempts to bring happiness into his home at the end of the day. Out on the streets, where others saw needy citizens and offered help, Stoner saw lazy slackers who offered nothing to society. When a small child fell from his bicycle the other day, a man stopped and helped him up. Where someone else may have seen a kind man, the inspector saw a child molester, trying to show enough compassion to lure a child from the protection of his home.

Stoner was a man with a bruised soul, who used to come home to a loving wife who had the power to reknit his wounded interior with a smile, the song she sang while cradling their son, and the soft words of endearment that were forever on her lips.

But, now the light in her eyes was gone and the hope in his heart had died with her. All he had left was his son Christopher. What would become of him? Was he now broken and damaged, a flawed child unit? Perhaps Christopher would leave him too. Then Stoner would be utterly alone in a world of anger, fear, and silence.

Blessed by the Lord God, Stoner sneered into the darkness. As with some men of old, he was a man whose own might was his only god. For that moment, he surrendered to the emptiness of his own heart. *Little Lady Applewait,* he hissed, *you will soon learn the true meaning of the word Tombstone. I will chase you to the ocean's tide if I must.*

Stoner watched and listened. He heard the wonderful music, but there was also a whisper of something else. What he heard could make him kinder, or it could make him more dangerous, depending on which voice he listened to.

And, the people sang on.

Page 2 Proverbs 3: 1-2   My son, do not forget my law, but let your heart keep my commands, for length of days and long life and peace they will add to you.

Page 127 Genesis 1: 1-3.   In the beginning God created the heavens and the earth. Now the earth was formless and empty, darkness was over the surface of the deep. And the Spirit of God was hovering over the waters. And God said, "Let there be light, and there was light."

Page 128 John 1: 1-5.   In the beginning was the Word, and the Word was with God, and the Word was God. He was with God in the beginning. Through him all things were made; without him nothing was made that has been made. In him was life, and that life was the light of men. The light shines in the darkness, but the darkness has not understood it.

Page 283   Luke 21: 15 & 19. For I will give you words and wisdom that none of your adversaries will be able to resist or contradict .... By standing firm you will gain life."

297

LENGTH OF DAYS
BEYOND THE VALLEY
OF THE KEEPERS
Doris Gaines Rapp

LENGTH OF DAYS BEYOND THE VALLEY OF THE KEEPERS

Doris Gaines Rapp

The second novel in the Length of Days trilogy

Daniel's House Publishing

Copyright © 2015 by Doris Gaines Rapp

<u>Table of Contents</u>

Prologue		305
1	Howard Mountain	307
2	The Valley of the Keepers	310
3	Chief Inspector Ward Stoner	317
4	A Story to Tell	320
5	The Hospital	328
6	A Place to Begin	332
7	A Pause in Reckoning	341
8	Morning in the Valley	344
9	Through the Mountain of Tears	349
10	The Pretense	351
11	Later That Evening	356
12	Gray Fox and Little Feather	360
13	The Departing	366
14	The Icy Trek	370
15	The Pilgrimage Has Begun	373
16	Revealed in the Desert	377
17	Rocky	384
18	The Western Zone	386
19	Still Searching	393
20	Chalky Boone in Pursuit	397
21	The C-I Board	399

22	Boone in the West	408
23	Simza Bihari	410
24	Late Saturday Evening	421
25	Sunday across the Western Zone	425
26	The Arrival	431
27	The Caravan	433
28	Border–Midwestern Zone	436
29	Headquarters of the Blue Guard	445
30	A Gathering	447
31	Inspector Stoner's Office	456
32	Eastern Zone–Border Crossing	460
33	The Citadel	466
34	The Underlings	478
35	They Came in Search	487
36	A World Below	496
37	Jewels	506
38	Free	516
39	The Gathering	523
40	A Plan	532
41	A Song for the Devil	538
42	Assault on the Citadel	544
43	Bedlam's Humility	555
44	Trapped	559
45	A Surprise Rescue	565
46	Return to the Valley of Hope, The Valley of the Keepers	568
47	Through the Mountain Tears	572

PROLOGUE
Capitol City, Central Zone, U.S.A.

Diary of Lady Christiana Applewait
December 26, 2112

The Blue Guard has been following us for days. We must stay alert every minute, but we are all so tired. I know I have been fighting to keep my eyes open.

I think I saw a strata car behind Silas's vehicle when we made that last turn onto the mountain road. Silas turned off his headlight. I hope the dark of night will hide us.

Even though I'm a legacy citizen, in line for a seat on the Council of Twelve, my position has not protected me from obsessive stalking by Chief Inspector Ward Stoner. But we can't stop. We must place a Citizens' Referendum on the ballot at the next election to overturn the *Length of Days* law. If not, my dear grandparents will reach the age of extermination. They will enter the never-ending-sleep, thus ending their *Length of Days*.

Now, a few of us will try to erase that ghastly law. We will have to cross Zone borders, closed for many decades. Dawn will be coming soon. We don't know what lies beyond the mountains, and there is no road over it or pass at the top. Silas has assured us he knows a way to get past Howard Mountain.

Even though they banned Christmas a hundred years ago, just last night, Gifting Day evening, thousands of our people sang Christmas carols they had never heard before while we marched on President Nathan Alexander's home. We delivered petitions, already obtained in the Central Zone. Judge Carl Brunner ordered a two-year stay on all final-sleep travelers. Now, we have just those twin years of hope to canvas the other three sectors of our country and secure the signatures, then, pass the bill and implement it before our time runs out.

We know no one beyond the Central Zone, but God will be with us. Like the wise men of old, we will follow the promise of Christmas hope. God will be our guide.

Lady Christiana Applewait

Isaiah 62: 6 (NLT@2007)

O Jerusalem, I have posted watchmen on your walls; they will pray day and night, continually. Take no rest, all you who pray to the LORD.

Chapter 1
Howard Mountain

Monday - December 26, 2112

Finally–safety! But we must stay on guard. We had entered Howard Mountain cavern before the sun rose again in the East. We had to stay ahead of the Blue Guard, if they were tracking us. We couldn't risk it. I watched as the light wanted to break on the horizon but was reluctant to hurry the dawn. We had presented ourselves as the end-travelers did, through the big gate that Silas Drummond had opened. He met us in the darkness of the recessed door.

"We'll wait here for the sun to rise," Silas pointed to some chairs on the left of the entry.

We walked over and sat down like strangers on a train, lined up along the wall, all silently facing forward. My stomach growled and gnawed with anxious anticipation. We had fled to the mountain in the dark of night, now we waited for the light we had hid from.

"What is that awful smell?" Dahlia Zoobomba questioned as she cupped both hands over her nose and mouth.

"You don't want to know," Silas said. "That's the crematorium you smell." He got up from his chair and began to shuffle along through the processing area. We followed him deeper inside the huge cave. His gait was short, his step shallow and his pace like that of a banty rooster.

He scurried through the area ahead of us. I was amazed how a stooped man, whose feet didn't seem to lift off the floor, could move so fast. "I can hardly see where I'm going," I said as I pushed the brim of my hat back and brushed my hair from my eyes.

"I switched to the ghost lights just as you arrived," he mumbled but kept walking.

"I'll agree with that," Dr. Jason O'Reilly whispered.

"Why?" I too asked in hushed tones. "To reveal or hide the ghosts? How does that work, Silas?" I groped along the wide hall then realized what part of the cave we were in. I grabbed Jason's hand and clutched it to my cloak. "Jason, we're in the museum," I gasped. "Aren't we?"

"I think so, Honey," he spoke in reverence. The respectful silence was not for the museum that evil power-hungry Alister Bedlam had gathered over the years. It was for the abandoned subjects of his display who deserved our respect.

"Dahlia, don't look right or left, just follow me. The ghost lights may be dim enough to hide the glass cases." Silas said as he obeyed his own instruction and fixed his eyes on the hallway ahead.

I heard Dahlia gasp and moan as she hurried along, but she said nothing. When we got to the end of the hall, her tear stained face glistened with fresh grief. I put my arm around her and tried to sooth her wounded spirit. We hugged for a moment in silence.

"I had no idea," she choked.

"Bedlam has been exhibiting his human taxidermy subjects, the bodies of his enemies, like trophies in a case, after they have ended their Length of Days," Jason explained. "Even my parents are on display in this grotesque museum only he sees."

"Now what, Silas?" Jason questioned as we reached the end of the hallway, where the bare mountain face became the inner exposed wall. He wrinkled up his forehead and searched the ceiling of the cave and the surrounding rock walls for a way out.

Water dripped in a distant finger of the cave as snow melted above. It smelled musty, and I figured it must have been damp for a long time. Perhaps water had actually pooled around one of the down-sloping bends. I really didn't want to know. It just smelled bad.

Silas smiled mischievously. "We'll walk right through the mountain wall."

• • • • •

In Capitol City, Ward Stoner, ruthless Captain of the infamous Blue Guard, gazed intently through the floor to ceiling bank of windows that lined two adjoining corner walls of his office. He had been there all night. Bright red and green Gifting lights blinked from the garden below, but he saw none of it. "I will find you," he seethed through gritted teeth. "You think you are above my laws, the laws that everyone in the Central Zone must follow."

He rocked on his toes and back on his heels as he tried to imagine every place Christiana Applewait could be hiding. "I will release the entire weight of my fury on you ... on Dr. O'Reilly ... and anyone else who dares to side with you and your precious self-determined crusade. You think it's a mission for life. I will make it a fight to the death!"

It had only been two days since Dr. O'Reilly had saved his son from the horror of the Length of Days law. But power-hungry hate remembers nothing of love.

Chapter 2
The Valley of the Keepers

"Martin!" Rebecca called from the house. "Ready for a cup of coffee?"

Martin Spires looked up from his work. Besides the rich smell of freshly brewed coffee that escaped through the open door when his wife spoke, there was something else in the air—an anticipation. The wind seemed to blow more sweetly and whistled down the valley more gently than he had experienced for quite a while.

"In a minute," he shouted back then smelled the air again. He smiled at his own foolishness and turned back to his work. He hadn't had a pre-event-knowing for a long time. *The wind blows wherever it pleases. You hear its sound, but you cannot tell where it comes from or where it is going. So it is with everyone born of the Spirit.* So it appeared in John 3:8 and so Martin knew.

With wide, rough work hands, he spread a deer hide across a wooden sawhorse and began removing the hair with a draw blade. It had been a big buck, an eight pointer. Martin always hated to see the majestic animals fall, but he knew the ways of life and said a prayer in thanks for the gift of the stag and all it would add to his family's sustenance. Besides the venison meat and deerskin hide, the sinew thread would sew winter boots with water tight seams. The December air was clear and cold, just the way he liked it. Dressing the deer was a great reason for enjoying the fantastic morning.

This is a beauty, he thought before he noticed that his wife had come out into the frosty air of the early hour. "It's a real looker, isn't it Sweetie Pie?" he boasted.

"That will tan out real fine, Martin."

"Several people have bid on the hide," he smiled. "Don't know yet if I want to sell it. It's such a good one. I only had to use one arrow to bring him down, so there is just one hole. With the small arrowhead that I used the skin is nearly perfect."

"You're an expert hunter, Martin. But I thought you were going to use the percussion rifle you invented for this hunting season. You told me there would be no hole at all with percussion," Rebecca observed.

"I nearly have the new rifle perfected. I'm still checking on any possible noise a percussive shot might make. In theory, there should be no sound, just a feeling of pressure in the chest. That is, if you aren't in the line of fire. If you're the target, you wouldn't be around to tell us what it felt like."

"I don't think I'd like to be downrange of The Whisper. I like what you're calling it."

Martin officially named it the Spires-C. But he called it *The Whisper* because people wouldn't hear a thing. If struck, you would just drop over. The sudden compression would stop your heart. He ran his hand over the soft deer hide as if he were caressing the smooth wooden stock of the rifle and spoke with the confident facts of the inventor.

"I'm glad it's not dangerous to be near, Martin. With all the children running around here all the time, I don't think I'd like the idea that someone could get on the back side of a shot," she frowned.

"That's what's so great about the percussion rifle. The compression has a very fine focus. The down range danger is nil. It strikes with pinpoint precision on the target. It hits exactly what is in the narrow line of fire."

"Coming through," a small towheaded nine-year-old in a red striped hat and brown leather coat warned as he stumbled between Martin and Rebecca.

"Posse on your trail," pigtailed Virginia cautioned as she burst through the space between the husband and wife, with four other young deputies in hot pursuit.

"Enjoy yourselves while you can, Honey Childs. School will open again, soon after New Year's Day, you know." Rebecca laughed.

"Wouldn't it be great to be able to run wild like that?" Martin marveled then stopped when he felt a tremble beneath his feet. "Something is happening. Did you feel the tremor?" he cautioned as he watched the children disappear down the path that led to the village. "Maybe we should collect all of the children, just in case—"

Suddenly, the earth rumbled and shook. The ice that hung from the mountain outcropping above fell to the ground as the mountain shook. Dust from inside the rubble, filled the cold air and hung like fine gravelly sleet. The icy pebbles hit the earth and rolled down the tiny, dry arroyos that fanned out from the base of the peak. With a great gapping yawn, the mountain opened, as the huge stone that covered the mouth of the cave rolled to the side.

"Silas!" Rebecca called out as the small, wiry man stepped through the giant opening. With wide arms she hurried to greet the cousin she normally sees only a few times a year. On this side of the mountain, family is everything.

"Rebecca," Silas shouted as he approached. Bent over, he skittered more than walked. Behind him came three other people whom Rebecca did not know.

"Silas," Martin gasped, "we didn't expect you. When we heard the noise, we were worried they had found us. But now you have brought strangers into the valley. Why? Who are they? Are they seekers? You know how dangerous it is to reveal our lives to others." Martin clenched his fists, grabbed the back of his neck as if he were trying to rub out the anger.

"I understand your worry, Martin. But I know these people." Silas Drummond turned to the travelers with him. In spite of the cold, he removed his hat as he spoke. "I'd like to introduce Dr. Jason O'Reilly and his nurse, Dahlia Zoobamba."

"Who is the other one, Silas? Who is the lady?" Martin squinted in the bright sunlight of the clearest morning in days and approached the small party of travelers. He couldn't believe that Silas had led adult outsiders into the valley. And, it was Silas Drummond who had breached the rule. He knew better.

"Martin ... Rebecca, I would like to present Lady Christiana Applewait, a Legacy Citizen, in-line for a position on the Council of Twelve." Silas stepped aside and bowed slightly as he presented a Privileged Citizen who called him "friend."

"My Lady," Rebecca curtseyed a little. However, her buckskin breeches didn't gather around her like the fine ball gown she would have worn to greet a person of such stature.

"Woman, get yourself up," Martin insisted. "We are all equals here in the valley." He approached Christiana boldly and extended his hand in friendship.

"Yes, Sir," Christiana replied. "We are all equal in the sight of God." She removed her glove and shook Martin's hand in friendship.

"You are from the Central Zone and ... you know about God?" Martin's jaw dropped.

Lady Applewait smiled as she replaced the black leather glove that protected her hand from the frigid air. "I know about God ... and I know God, Mr. ...?"

"Martin Spires. Call me Martin, Ma'am."

"Only if you will call me Christiana," she smiled at her new friend. "Jason calls me Christy."

The middle-aged man with the long graying beard, looked at Rebecca and shrugged, then gazed with amazement on the small party. "I'll reserve my opinion about you all until I know more. Why are you here?" Martin asked.

"It's been a long walk. I'm tired," Dahlia gasped as she brushed some fresh snow from the edge of the porch and sat down. "Could I bother you for a glass of water? I am so thirsty." She bent down and grabbed her feet that stayed buried inside her winder boots. "Oh," she complained some more.

"We made it all the way from town in the darkened car, and then walked through Howard Mountain, on foot. We couldn't have done it without you, Silas." Jason marveled and slapped Silas on his shoulder in gratitude.

Silas smiled a sheepish grin. No one ever praised Silas and now Jason included him with a nudge to his shoulder. Even the twitter of the birds from the top of the nearby trees was more uplifting than anything he had heard in years. The ghastly cavern had been his only resting place. He couldn't spit out the awful taste of the place.

"You were the only one who knew the way, Silas. None of us had any idea that the valley was still here," Jason said. "The authorities said that the earthquake of the last century had totally destroyed the topography of the area. They said no one survived."

"Actually, we are all doing quite well," Martin boasted as he slapped his breeches with a deerskin glove.

They all laughed and cheered Silas's courage with new, adrenaline-laced energy as they looked out onto the sweetest valley this side of heaven. The morning sun was high enough to warm their faces and dissolve the images of the corruption inside the cavern under Howard Mountain.

"You are all welcome in our home," Martin smiled with a lingering hint of confusion. "Not to sound inhospitable ... but I will repeat, what are you all doing here?"

"Where is *here*, Martin? Silas didn't have time to tell us. He just said, 'Come! Hurry! And, we did," Christiana stated.

Winter birds sang back and forth from the tops of trees as if they would speak if the Squire would not. The more they fluttered, the more tufts of fluffy snow dropped from the branches and floated to the ground, a reminder that it was still December.

Martin studied the small party, but he couldn't take his eyes off the beautiful young woman in the green cape and red hat. Her eyes seemed as though they could see right through him. Then, he paused. He was unsure if he wanted to speak the words not heard in the valley in nearly a hundred years. There had been no need to speak of what everyone in the village already knew, since there hadn't been another traveler through the area in that time, except Silas Drummond. His other tiny travelers were not interested in such things.

"Martin?" his wife whispered. She went to the dear man and took the draw blade that remained in his left hand and placed it on the hide that waited where he had left it on the cross-beamed wood. The aroma of musk from the deer still clung to the air.

The great Squire of the forgotten hamlet beyond the mountain looked at his wife as if asking her for permission to speak. "It is your safety too, My Love," he said.

"Tell them, Martin," she said as she touched his hand. "Silas wouldn't have brought danger to us. You know that."

"You are basically ... nowhere," he began. "This valley was not buried like the outsiders thought, but, sealed off from everything except the passage through the tunnel. Since Silas was all alone and in charge of the despicable activities under Howard Mountain, he had discovered the exit during the long nights of anguish he had spent there."

"We know of the evil there," Christiana whispered. "We have seen it for ourselves. Each of us left all we've known in Capitol City to come here. What is this place?"

"This lovely woman in the leather pants and jacket is my wife, Rebecca. You have joined us in the Valley of the Keepers. All of us here are keepers of the history the ruling elite tried to erase after the great uprising of the previous century. For four generations, every man, woman, and child in the valley have carried a verbal account of the history of this great nation. Different families have in their possession certain books and volumes which they have guarded and memorize, in case there's a book confiscation. We, the Spires family, are the keepers of the Bible, the story of all of us."

"You have never been discovered in all these years?" Dahlia marveled.

"We have skilled and learned people in many areas of life. Our communications people have been able to monitor the outside world without detection or tracking. We know of all dof the world's inventions and innovations, and adapt them to the unique needs of our people who live invisible lives. We simply invent new ways of doing things that won't betray our location."

Rebecca smiled, "Like smokeless fuel. We don't even give off a heat signature. Look above you. You see blue sky, but we have produced a force between us and the clouds. From high overhead, the terrain looks like a rock pile in case anyone should fly too close. But since the borders are completely closed, no one has drawn near for a very long time."

The Squire of Nowhere looked at the four and sighed. "We have been safe here, Christy ... for a long time. We are also Keepers in another way. We have sentries posted on the ridge beyond that far circle of the mountain." Martin pointed to where the outcropping had made a complete ring, which created the valley in which they live. "The guards watch and pray, every moment of every day. We are all watchers on the wall, just like in the days of Isaiah. We rotate duty on those outposts so no one is away from home and family for more than three months." He smiled and removed his broad brimmed leather hat with a bright eagle feather tucked in the band. "Now, I know your names, but ... who are you all, and why have you come into the valley?"

"Come Martin," Christy began, "if we can sit down someplace, I will tell you of a great commission, a miracle, a holy mystery."

Chapter 3
Chief Inspector Ward Stoner

Chalky Boone staggered to the left then to the right as she tried to stay out of Ward Stoner's way. His office was large enough for the Chief Inspector, except when he paced, which he did often. She carried a 281 Palm Device in her hand as she tried to keep up with his erratic movements. "Sir, if you would use the device—"

"Where are they?" he bellowed toward the outer office.

"I'm right here, Sir." Boone's smile was fading and inside, her anger was nearing its flashpoint. "If you would just use the 281, you wouldn't have to yell. I'm—"

"I want to talk to that little snippy Legacy brat or her doctor ... or someone!" The veins in Stoner's forehead bulged and his face grew crimson.

"Sir, you must—"

"I must what?" he demanded as he grabbed his communication device out of Boone's hand. "I do whatever I need to do. Right now, I need to find those two." He picked up his coffee cup, took a sip and spit it out. "This tastes terrible! It's cold."

"I know," she said as the liquid sloshed out of the passing cup and splashed on her arm. Boone brushed the droplets off onto the floor and sat on the edge of the desk as the inspector continued to swirl around her like a life-sucking whirlpool, drawing her into its vortex. "Sir—"

"Get me Applewait's parents' number."

"Sir, they have an unlisted number. You know that." She was growing weary of his unreasonable obsession with the Lady-of-position. Her shoulders drooped, crumpling her jacket. She stood up, straightened her back, and shook the tension from her arms.

"I will find them. If you can't help, get out of my way." Stoner seethed as he dodged Boone's attempts to sidestep his every move.

"Sir, I am just trying to assist you. I'm your assistant," she reported back sharply but with a calm tone rehearsed over many years of working with Ward Stoner.

"Then assist!" he roared. "Find them."

"Inspector, it is 7:30 in the morning on a holiday." Chalky stretched as if to make her taller so she could meet his eyes with strength.

"What holiday?" he bellowed.

"Sir, Gifting Day was just yesterday. The medical center isn't open and the library, where Lady Applewait works, isn't either." Her shoulders slumped again and she eased herself down onto a brown engineered-leather chair.

Stoner paced with wide, pounding strides but said nothing. The room filled with the heavy air of his anger and frustration. He took three deep breaths and held the last one. Then, he let it stream out slowly. With contrived calm, he whispered, "Fine. We will call them both tomorrow at nine ... sharp."

"I'll be at my desk if you need me," Boone sighed softly.

Stoner only nodded once. Then, as Chalky left his office, he added with measured appreciation, "Thanks."

"You are welcome," she smiled weakly as she turned to leave.

"Tell me this," he spit out again, "why can't I reach that wretched little furnace tender, Silas Drummond? Are you telling me the Disposal Center isn't open until 9:00 a.m. either?"

"Ward," with carefully chosen words she outlined one more time, "Judge Brunner issued a stay on all length-of-days terminations. The entire center will be closed for the next two years," Chalky reminded him.

"Well, there is no *stay*—no cease and desist order—in this office.

I will find out just how that fancy pair plans on getting signatures from people outside this zone, when the law against travel is clear. They are forbidden to leave."

"Boss ... wouldn't a repeal of the Length-of-Days law benefit us all? Families wouldn't have to hide every accidental fall and each illness their children have. There would be no limit to medical contacts before their child is labeled *defective.*" Boone's voice strained with indignation. "And, people wouldn't enter the never-ending-sleep just because they lived a prescribed number of years."

"My son was spared a mark in his life chart the other night, I know. And, he recovered," he stated flatly as if it was because of his own doing. "Now, I will uphold every law of this land as long as those laws exist," Stoner insisted in spite of the blessing his family received. "And, those two are going to break the law and leave this zone ... somehow." His anger returned as he thought of Lady Applewait and Dr. O'Reilly. "I will catch them." Stoner stopped and looked out of the window on his town still adorned with Gifting Day lights. He felt no holiday cheer.

"Watch over your shoulders with every step you take ... you privileged ones. I will find you. I will stick to you like fear on darkness. The minute you step over the line, I'll be there."

Chapter 4
A Story to Tell

"Come on in." Rebecca invited us into her home with a sweep of her hand. On the other side of the rugged wilderness door, the frontier stopped. What was inside, revealed a century of advancements just miles from Capitol City, although a mountain away.

The room smelled of Christmas tree pine and warm, freshly baked biscuits. Holiday sparkle, bright colors, and dancing lights hung in swags from the stair banister and adorned a large tree.

She removed her jacket and hung it on a peg by the door. "Let me have your wrap," she said as she reached for mine. "My Lady ... Christy ... your cloak is beautiful. What is this fabric?"

"Thank you, Rebecca. It's manufactured wool, so dense that the wind cannot penetrate it. You don't get too hot in it either. It seems to breathe from the inside out, not the outside in," I said as I looked around. The warm room shone with a golden glow, as the morning sun bounced off the hand-hewn chestnut logs. "I have only seen beautiful, sprawling cabins like this in books, Martin. Did you build this?" I couldn't resist a temptation to touch the smooth log timbers, stacked one on the other and held in place like brick and mortar.

"No, my great-grandfather built this home before the earthquake. It was a mountain retreat for his family until they were sealed off." Martin reopened the door and shook the snow from his hat back onto the porch, then hung the hat on another peg. "Each generation has made their own improvements."

"Well, it is great," Jason marveled as he looked at every detail.

"Martin," Rebecca whispered with controlled excitement. "Did

"With the blessing of a Judge—and his key," I reassured him and smiled. "We didn't break in."

Jason reached over and took my hand. His voice was soft, "The Lord gave Christy the gifts of convincing and healing. And, when Stoner tried to discredit her, her grandmother revealed more gifts, those of discernment and art."

"And the music, Jason," Dahlia added.

"Last night, with everyone gathered around, we sang Christmas carols for the first time in our lives. People who had never heard the songs, who had not even sung before, all joined in with one voice to sing, 'Silent Night, Holy Night', and it was a Holy Night."

I reached down and petted the furry one at my feet. His soft coat was soothing to me. "Judge Brunner declared a stay on all exterminations for the next two years. By then, the entire country, all four zones, will have a chance to sign a petition so the referendum can be put on the ballot at the next election."

"Silas got us this far," Dahlia reached across the couch and patted him on the back.

"We are depending on you and Martin, Rebecca," Silas burst out. He hadn't said much since we came into the house. Forgotten his whole life, he finally spoke out. "I got them this far. Can you and Martin get them out of the valley?"

"There are ways," Martin responded. "Yes, there are ways."

Chapter 5
The Hospital

"We'll go to the hospital first," Rebecca said as we walked along the brick sidewalks and wound our way past quaint businesses in the valley that time had forgotten. It was later in the morning, and the sun was bright in the sky. "Then, if you want to, we'll stop in for coffee. Unless you've had too much of the brew," she said and chuckled.

"There is never too much juice of the bean," I laughed.

Jason and I hadn't had much time alone and I needed to connect. I slipped my hand in his as I studied the architecture of the buildings.

"Look, what do these shops remind you of?" I marveled as I peered through each cross-hatched window.

"The Dickens-style boutiques and coffee shop near the hospital," Dahlia giggled.

"That's it," Jason chimed in.

"Our favorite place, right?" I agreed.

"The coffee or the shop?" Rebecca questioned with a smile.

"Both," all three of us chimed in together.

We all stepped off the curb into the street where patches of ice made a wobbly footing. I pulled my cloak around me more tightly as a light snow began to fall. I welcomed the new flakes that kissed my face. It made the little village seem more real.

"Are you warm enough?" Jason asked as he put his arm around me and massaged some warmth into my back.

"I think my blood is circulating again," I said as a child skittered past me with his coat wide open. "I guess the little ones stay warm by running around in circles."

"It's just here on the corner," Martin encouraged as we neared a large white building.

Silas stood back gallantly as we all passed through the revolving doors of Valley Hospital. Inside, the lobby smelled fresh and clean, not antiseptic. The aroma of freshly baked cookies danced on the air from the small oven at the greeting desk. A child hobbled by on crutches and joined other patients as they clustered around the cookie platter. The children and adults who sat on couches and chairs near the entrance to the examining room looked weak and ill.

"Next time," I heard a father admonish a child whom I guessed to be his daughter, "Watch where you'll land before you swing out over a frozen pond."

"I know, Daddy," the ten-year old responded with a heavy, audible sigh.

"They don't look like they're afraid," Dahlia said in amazement.

"Afraid?" Rebecca questioned. "Why would our children fear the hospital? They are made well here."

"In the Central Zone, each person is permitted only a certain number of accidents before they are labeled 'defective.' Defective human units are placed in the never-ending-sleep," Jason repeated in the mechanical voice he had learned. He paused. "I sound so callous," he admitted, as much to himself as others. "I'm not."

Our group turned to the right in the middle of the wide entrance with its leather covered chairs and approached the lift. The round, glass bullet-shaped elevator swooped silently from above, paused, and opened its doors.

"Kiersten, is everyone all right?" Rebecca asked with concern as a young woman stepped off. "You just brought the baby home a year ago."

The young woman with four little cherubs swirling around the hem of her skirt like a low-hanging halo smiled a patient smile.

"Rebecca, good to see you. Little Hank stopped breathing and became rigid. The doctor said it was another febrile seizure."

"Another?" Jason asked as the rest of the children stepped off the lift and our little party got on. Jason held the door open with his foot while he finished talking to her.

"Yes, this was his third. But the doctor told me he should outgrow them by age three," she said and grabbed the hand of a particularly rambunctious child. "I'd better get these kids home so we can start to prepare for lunch. Children are creatures of habit you know."

"I am so glad everyone is okay," Rebecca waved as the doors began to close.

"We won't take a lot of time, but I really want you to see our surgery theater," Martin rubbed his hands together in glee. It was obvious he was proud of the advancements in medicine of these valley people, even though physically cut off from the rest of the world.

"We're not completely isolated here." He winked as he opened the heavy door to a completely white and totally soundproofed room with theater seats that faced a wall of windows. "Good, a procedure is going on," he whispered.

From our elevated position, we could see beyond the glass as they prepared a patient for surgery. First, the doctor and her assistants draped sterile cloths on the arm and upper shoulder. Then they swabbed a red liquid on the entire area of the surrounding tissue.

"Do they make an incision?" Jason appeared to be shocked.

"No, just a scratch" Martin said. They abrade the surface of the skin so the instruments can make perfect contact with the body. They know, when they disturb the protective layer of the body, infection can get in. Just like the old days when the standard medical practice was to actually open the body, bacteria had mutated to the point that surgery was more dangerous than the condition that called for it." He put his finger to his lips. "Listen," he whispered as the sound of faint whirling came from below.

We watched the surgeon scrape the patient's skin surface and place another instrument, about the size of hand-held sander, on the prepared spot. With a slow firm motion she made small, ever widening circular patterns with the instrument.

"The dislocated shoulder will fall into place like the tumblers on a bank vault. Then, the torn rotator cuff will be fused by the sound waves emanating from the instrument." Martin sat back like he was well satisfied.

"Martin, you can be very proud of the advances you all have made, in spite of the lack of shared science with the other sectors. As a physician, I can say, this is impressive." Jason continued to fix his attention on the procedure that was happening on the operating table.

"I'm pleased too, Martin," I said as I tried to dig for information. "But I am wondering if your isolation is as complete as you claim. You winked. In the books I've read, that usually means the person is not telling the whole story." I suspected that there had been travel between sectors in spite of what Martin had told us.

The squire of the valley paused as another observer came into the observation room. "Hi, Charlie," he said. Then he turned to us and added, "Let's continue our conversation over coffee."

Chapter 6
A Place to Begin

Silas led the way back out into the frosty air. It seemed to me his back was straighter; his stride was wider and his steps more solid on this side of the mountain. Something was very different about Silas. I could see it.

The village square was alive with people, but no one hurried. No one jostled or pushed. From what I could see, everyone had a pleasant expression. The smiles on their faces were a blessing to me. In the Central Zone, no one smiles because no one feels anything. Another thing that amazed me, there were young people everywhere, from the smallest baby to teens enjoying the remaining few days of their Christmas vacation.

"All of these kids, Martin, what about their education and college?" I walked past happy children who played in a sleeping flower garden in the center of the square. The town transformed a little area of dormant flowers into a bright display of lights and bulbs of greens and reds, all decorated for the Christmas season.

"Yes, of course. We have college and graduate school for all of our children." Rebecca said with pride. "Our children are part of our community, and we all participate in sharing the cost."

Suddenly, a loud noise I didn't recognize startled me. "What's that?" I gasped as a large chunky aircraft flew overhead. The noise caused my blood to freeze as cold as the ice that hung from gnarled tree limbs. Instinctively, I knew I should hide ... but where? Not knowing where to go, I slammed my body against the outside wall of the building beside me and tried to recede into its bricks.

"Christy," Jason saw my fear and quickly put his arms around me.

"No, no," I cried and pulled away. I didn't want someone to hold or restrain me. I wanted to feel the cold rough texture of the bricks that faced the building. It felt safer to hug the wall than to stand out in the open. "They've come! They've found us!"

"Who?" Rebecca questioned and tried to comfort me with her hand to my shoulder.

I recoiled from her touch and jumped into a nearby doorway. I sensed I'd be less visible from above if tucked in there.

"The Blue Guard!" I screamed. "I've seen helicopters in magazines I found in the library. Only the military have flying machines. The Blue Guard is here I tell you. They'll be all over this place in a few minutes!" My throat was tight, my voice reduced to a raspy whisper.

Dahlia searched the sky. "Christy, I can see the wavy grid. We're okay," she said.

"Christy ... Honey," Jason soothed and gathered me in his arms again. I finally let go and felt safe there. "Remember what Martin said," he reminded me. "There is a protective force field above the valley. We can see them but all they see are stones and boulders." He hushed my fears with his soothing voice as he whispered, "We don't have to risk our lives, going out into dangerous zones to gather signatures for the petition. You know that. We can go home. I don't want you to go through this trauma." Jason held me so close I thought I could feel the beating of his heart through my cloak.

"Grand-mère and Grand-père," I whispered. "I do have to do this ... for them."

We stood by the side of the walkway, up against the buildings that had reminded us of home. He rocked me in his arms as he spoke to Martin and Rebecca. "She is still terrified ... and exhausted ... and overwhelmed with the enormity of the job. We have been running for many days, chased by the Blue Guard. She hasn't been able to catch her breath."

"Oh, Sweetheart." Rebecca spoke gently as she patted my shoulder. "You won't be doing this alone. There will be many volunteers, including Martin and me. And ... God will be with us. Come into the coffee shop and get rested and refreshed. We'll have latte or cocoa. They also make the most wonderful pastries; pecan sticky buns and bear claws. Almost anything you can think of."

Suddenly, I started laughing. We had a life-saving mission in front of us, but it wasn't the enormous nobility of it that inspired me. It was sticky buns.

"Are you all right, Honey?" Jason asked cautiously. His eyes revealed his concern, and I didn't want to add to his worry.

"Yes, I'm fine now. I just realized what a paradise this is. On the other side of the mountain, they control and measure everything dispensed to us. Here, you can eat as much sugar as you want ... and we will still get a life changing mission accomplished." We all laughed as we entered the shop.

"Six please," Martin told the waitress as we removed our coats. A row of hooks and pegs hung on the wall, some in the shape of small deer antlers and others more like fancy boots and high-heeled shoes where the garment hung on the toe. I placed my red hat on the shelf above the interesting hooks.

Smiling faces were everywhere. It felt like their joy was re-knitting me from the inside.

A server led us to a table in the back-left corner of the shop. We worked our way back, past friendly laughing people. I was glad my chair faced the window. The freedom and energy of everyone I saw in the fresh wintery day was intoxicating. I slowly began to feel invigorated again.

"Our children?" Jason asked. "When we asked about further education, you said 'our children.' You have referred to them in that way several times."

"They are our blessing and our dilemma," Martin admitted. "We have limited space here. Our valley extends from Howard Mountain, across the fertile Valley of Hope, the Valley of the Keepers, to the watchful hills beyond."

Rebecca added, "We ... some ... have ventured beyond the far valley. We have for years. We know how to dress, what their customs are, and their laws."

"Rebecca," Silas gasped, "you never told me you have been to the other sectors. Which ones?"

Martin looked around for ears that might hear. "Some of our pilgrims have been to all of them. Rebecca and I have only been to the west, past the desert and all the way to the ocean. It is beautiful out there."

A small group of children swarmed into the café like a rabble of butterflies, obviously looking for someone, and interrupted our conversation. Then, with glee, they gathered around our table, like they had lit on a garden of flowers. Behind them was a lovely young woman I recognized.

"Mara, how ...?" I was dumbfounded. I couldn't find the words to express my astonishment and my joy. The lovely young woman lived in my building in Capitol City. An injured leg had bothered her and continued to get worse until she could almost not walk. Her doctor recommended a "long rest." Unaware of the true outcome, she arrived at the mountain as an end-traveler just days before Gifting Day, to enter the portal to the never-ending-sleep. She was to end her life's travel at a very early age. But, now, there she stood before me.

"Yes, My Lady. It's me. Silas brought me here, just like he brought you." Her smile was sweet and peaceful. She touched the children who brushed by her, always aware, always loving.

"And your leg? It looks like you can walk again, Mara. How is that possible?" I was shocked and filled with joy for her. Getting her out of there was her salvation. Silas saved her from imminent destruction.

"The rest, My Lady," She chuckled softly. "I rested my leg like my physician said after Silas brought me here."

The children fluttered around Silas like they had found the last flower of summer. "Father Silas," they all squealed.

"Father?" I asked.

"Christ gave them eternal life," Martin offered and tousled a boy's head when he removed his hat. "Their first parents gave them their first life. And, Silas gave them their second life."

Stunned, I tried to make sense of what Martin had said. "Are you saying ... these children are some of the unwanted, discarded babies of the Central Zone?" My heart leaped in my chest.

"We are *the claimed*, Ma'am," said a gangly 13-year-old girl with silky brown hair and hazel eyes. "And Father Silas is our lead wayfarer."

A tear rolled down my cheek, only the second time I had cried in my lifetime. Detoxed only recently from the numbing chemicals, I had just begun to experience true feelings.

"You are beautiful," I whispered to the child.

"Thank you," she said shyly. "All are beautiful in the sight of God."

I looked again at the colorful streets, still adorned with Christmas sparkle. Laughing, playing children were everywhere. I wondered what it felt like to run with the wind in your face and inhale the aroma of life.

"How many children are here?" Dahlia gasped in amazement.

"They all look so healthy and strong," Jason marveled. "And these ... are the aborted?"

"No, I wish I could have gotten to them, too," Silas said softly. Then he turned to the children. "I'm very happy to see you again, kids. Now run and play while you're still on Christmas break."

After the children left, Dahlia whispered, "The aborted are born dead or are killed immediately after birth, aren't they?" The nurse's voice was full of shame. Jason nodded in silence.

Silas pointed to the happy young ones who waved when they got to the door, turned, and bounded out into the snow-covered grass. "These are the lucky ones."

Then Dahlia gasped and blurted out, "These are the third children, aren't they?"

"Oh, my Dear Lord," Jason gasped. "These children are from the three-child-families who are forced to choose which child to abandon—making sure they are left with only a two-child-family as permitted by law," he paused.

Silas watched the happy children through the window. "The third child is sent to the ghastly furnaces for disposal." Silas shuddered. "They're length-of-days is aborted up to age two."

I felt ill. I couldn't believe what I had always suspected but to which I had chosen to close my eyes. "The parents can take up to two years to decide which two of their three children to keep," I realized out loud. My words fell like dead weights around me. I thought I was going to gag.

"Yes, that's true, Christy," Mara agreed." But Silas started claiming them, years ago and brought the children here. Since I have arrived, I've looked after some of the smallest ones."

"That is why you need more space," I realized as I turned to Martin.

"My goodness, yes," Spires agreed. "At first, we tried to find homes for them here in the valley. Many people have included the little ones in their families, but we are outgrowing our space."

Rebecca added, "We have found homes for so many. We had also started finding placements in the Western Zone. Some of the children are ill, some have broken bones ... and we treat them in the hospital here before we send them on. Some children are here a year or much more."

I watched the hazel-eyed thirteen-year-old skate across an ice covered puddled. She threw her head back and giggled with glee. I couldn't ever remember feeling that free. Drawn back into the café, Martin was still talking.

"We have to stop the third-child destruction at the same time we do away with the Length of Days law." I was determined that senseless death would stop.

"Besides the need for larger homes for those families who have taken in as many as six claimed children," Martin smiled as he also looked through the window to see the children play, "we also need larger schools, larger farms and greater acreage on which to graze cattle."

"Then we have come in time," I said, "for you and for the discarded ones."

"Not discarded, Christy," Rebecca corrected gently, "claimed."

"That's right," Martin offered.

"Yes, the *claimed ones*" I agreed and added. "Your work, Silas, has given me the hope I have been seeking. I can see it is possible to accomplish what our laws will not permit."

Jason added, "We have a huge mission ahead of us. After meeting all of these happy children, I can see how our job will help even the youngest among us as well as the oldest. Dahlia will go back to the city and establish a ruse about my absence. She'll say, I'm at home, studying a new medical procedure."

"Jason and I will infiltrate into the three other sectors," I explained. "We hope to recruit volunteers to canvass their own zones and secure names for the additional petitions that we require."

"We have contacts in the Western Zone, Christy. People will be there to meet you, and they'll have a network started for you," Rebecca assured me.

"That will be wonderful! We hope to set up the structure for the volunteers to follow when we move on to another zone," I explained. "We have to have enough names on the line to get a referendum on the ballot at the next election. Then we will be able to meet our two-year time table."

Rebecca patted my hand. "You don't have to do it all alone. That wouldn't be possible. The volunteers will actually do the door-to-door canvassing." She gave my shoulder a little hug.

"So, let me get this right," Martin asserted. "A referendum—is a citizens' bill, right?"

"Right," Jason agreed. "The citizens create it just like a bill drawn up by Congress."

Martin clasped his hands together. "Then we'll make sure that all of the citizens have a chance to sign it."

"We've gotten this far. I look forward to meeting your friends out there on the west coast. Will anyone here be able to guide us into that unknown territory beyond the Valley?" I asked with anxious hope in my heart.

"Rebecca and I can't go, but we will have someone for you," Martin answered. "We'll call on friends to lead you west until we can meet you in the East."

"The East, Martin? You and Rebecca will come to the city?"

"That's our plan. The Eastern Zone will require the most volunteers."

"It will?" I heard what he said about that zone, and I also heard the tone in which he said it. "Have you heard something about that sector? We know nothing," I admitted. "We are venturing into the unknown."

"We know you must feel like that, Honey," Rebecca said.

I smiled because, she seemed to understand. "It feels like a large hatch is opening, and we are stepping out of a space ship onto an alien planet."

"You asked about the Eastern Zone, Christy. We have heard information, but we haven't been there. So, we don't know first-hand how accurate the perceptions are," Martin said. "But we can say with confidence, you will be able to trust your contacts there. In each of the three remaining sectors, we personally know, through face-to-face contact or long threads of communication, the people who will shelter and guide you." Martin spoke with confidence.

Rebecca had been quietly listening. "So ... you are the ones we have prayed for," she spoke in awe.

"You have waited for help? You have wanted to overturn the law all along?" I was amazed. Rebecca's words were the cement for the layers of assurance Martin had already laid.

"I'll be honest. Because we haven't been affected by the Length of Days law, we hadn't thought about fixing it. I would like to say that we weren't aware that it was a problem. But we knew. Look at all of these children in our valley." Rebecca's eyes lowed and revealed the emotion she felt.

The waitress hurried around the room, serving other tables. Dishes rattled and happy voices greeted and laughed, and shared stories with one another. But there seemed to be a respect for those at our table and others gave us space. Certainly, they must have recognized that Jason, Dahlia, and I were strangers in the valley.

Rebecca covered her face with her hands. "Actually, we were just selfish I guess," she said as she then leaned on one elbow. "If the law gave the power to shorten, or take away lives, we certainly should have tried to stop it. And, for that I apologize to all of you who have lived under that evil system. The truth is, we have just wanted to get our lives back ... to restore our country. All of it. We want to repeal unjust laws and stop the madness." Rebecca then tapped her finger sharply on the table. "We just didn't know where to begin. Many layers of corruption piled precariously on top of each other. Like Pick-Up Sticks, we couldn't find the right piece to remove so we wouldn't cause the whole pile to tumble. Now we know."

Chapter 7
A Pause in Reckoning

Tuesday - December 27, 2112

"All right, you uppity pair, Gifting Vacation is over. I will find you and stay on your coat tails with every step you take." Ward Stoner seethed as he maneuvered his strata car through the early morning streets of Capitol City. Since most citizens had no personal transportation in the Central Zone, the roads were nearly empty. He slowed at each stairway entrance to the upper platform of the public transit, or PT.

It was eight a.m.

Snow swirled across the pavement and blew icy chills into the air. People walking to the PT-stop held their heads down to shield their faces from the bitter cold. A woman pulled her coat around her as she slipped on the frozen steps. Everything was white, the ground, the sky—everything.

"Hey, watch out," a man yelled as the women nearly fell into him as she jerked and slid again.

The woman grabbed the stairway railing to the upper landing and held on as the man pushed her in disgust. "Sorry," she gasped as her gloves stuck to the surface of the railing where the snow had melted a little in the morning sun. Her boots protected her feet but there was no one to shield her from the unnecessary rudeness. Her breath hung like a crystal cloud, and she shivered a little in the cold.

Stoner could hear her apologize to the man for what was more his fault than hers, and he thought of his own mother. She was like that. Today, she planned to take his son shopping for school clothes with some of his Gifting Day money.

"Phone home," Stoner spoke into the empty air around him. The lights on his 281-device flashed on. "Mother? You and Christopher had better stay in today. It's very slick."

"I think you're right," Mrs. Stoner answered. She sounded a little relieved. "We'll see you when you get home. Christopher would like to have a game night tonight."

"I should be home in time," he said. "End call," he commanded the 281.

Suddenly he heard yelling behind him. He checked his rear facing mirrors. The same man was now slipping and sliding as he struck the same woman again and again. The Inspector spun the vehicle around and raced back.

"Hey, break it up," he shouted as he leaped out of the strata car and charged at the mob that had gathered. The woman was on the bottom step and still braced herself with the railing. Three men were pounding on the one who had struck her. Stoner grabbed one of the three and tossed him to the side like he was shoveling dirt from a wheelbarrow.

"Okay, okay," one of the three sputtered. "We were just helping her," he bellowed and drew his fist back. Then he stopped abruptly when he saw the Chief Inspector's angry face glaring at him.

"Stand down!" Stoner gasped as he grasped the man's arm with one hand and held off the remaining two with the flash of his Blue Guard badge.

The man struggled and babbled as Stoner held him in his grasp. "Let go of me! You have no right! I am a citizen. I have my rights."

"You have the rights I choose to permit you to have," Stoner growled. The veins in his neck bulged. "What's wrong with you?" He opened his grasp and slapped the man across the face. Astonished travelers on the platform above heard the crack and peered over the railing. "I'm the Chief of the Blue Guard! I write the rules!"

Then he turned to the crowd and ordered, "Be about your own business."

The woman, attacked and trembling, grabbed her scattered packages and struggled to her feet. "Sir," she reached out to the Inspector as she tried to regain her balance.

"You look fine woman. I have no time for you. Now, I have to take this fellow into headquarters. If you had stepped aside and let him pass, I wouldn't have to drag his sorry carcass into the station."

"But Sir," she protested.

"Do I have to take you in too? What kind of trash are you?" The chief kicked at the snow in front of her in disgust. "Get to work!" he commanded.

She said no more. She gathered up her bags and limped up the steps.

"You will regret crossing my path this morning, Mister," Stoner warned with a sneer. He shoved the man into the back of the strata car and slammed the door. "Now, I'll be behind schedule," he muttered as he walked around to the driver's side. "Don't you worry, My Lady Dearest, I will catch up to you yet this morning."

Chapter 8
Morning in the Valley

Tuesday - December 27, 2112

Martin and Rebecca had three birth children and four claimed-children. Our small party of travelers from the opening in Howard Mountain had benefitted from the Spires' large family and home. Now grown, with families and homes of their own, the children's rooms were all vacant. The extra space, used for grandchildren's sleep-overs and Sunday afternoon scavenger hunts, provided the space the extra four of us needed.

I awakened in the fluffy white feather bed in the front bedroom where light streamed through the window and danced across the floor. I watched with childish glee as bright beams waltzed along the walls. Even the sun seemed freer on this side of the mountain. I dressed and went downstairs. As I crossed the living room, I could hear Rebecca singing in the kitchen. "Rebecca, your song is beautiful," I said as I entered the heart of their home.

"Some say, 'Whistle while you work.' I either hum or sing. Can't whistle worth a tweet. I hope I didn't bother you." She smiled as she kept on working.

"It's wonderful! In the Central Zone, singing was forbidden a hundred years ago," I reminded her.

"Not here," Rebecca said. She sounded surprised. "Why would anyone ban singing?"

"Years ago, the government thought the people would be better controlled if they were stripped of all their emotions, no more anger, rage, passion, just flatness," I told her as I sat down on one of the wonderful painted green kitchen chairs. I wondered if Martin had made them. Rebecca had pointed out some of his beautiful wood working craft the evening before. The aroma of crisp bacon and steaming coffee filled the room. My stomach turned a summersault and suddenly I realized how hungry I was.

"But, what does music have to do with it?" she asked as she turned back to the cast iron skillet.

"Good morning. Sorry to interrupt," Jason said as he came in the room then stopped. "This must be heaven. At least it smells like you're cooking food fit for angels." He breathed in deeply and closed his eyes. Then he added, "You asked why no music. If they kill emotions, the things that stir the emotions, like music, need to be silenced too."

"Well, I never," Rebecca breathed in.

"You never what, my dear?" Martin asked as he came in the back door.

"I never heard of such a thing. Martin, did you know that music is not permitted in the city?"

"No. I guess that doesn't surprise me. They practically ban love," he added.

"Martin!" Rebecca blushed and pulled her large, country apron up to her face. She turned her attention to the stove and giggled.

"Good morning," Dahlia beamed as she came in, followed by Silas. Her large brown eyes looked happy and she was light of foot.

Silas yawned and rubbed his eyes as he stumbled to a kitchen chair. He folded his arms across the table and allowed his head to flop down on top of them. "Sorry, I'm fine," he said as he looked up again. "I slept better last night than I have in years. Guess I could have slept even longer ... maybe a year."

"Come on, Sleepy. I have a nice breakfast for you all." Rebecca brought a skillet full of scrambled eggs to the table and set it on a hot pad that looked like a Santa face, complete with rosy cheeks and nose. Christmas decorations still dominated their home.

"Help yourself to some bacon," Martin offered as he passed the platter. "There's a stack of toast made from Becca's homemade bread and her scrumptious strawberry jam. We have a huge strawberry patch alongside the garden on the west side of the house."

"Shall we pray?" Martin began without waiting for an answer. "Papa God," he began. Then he thanked God for the blessing of our presence, our health, our souls, and our safety.

It seemed we all buried our forks in eggs, up to the handle, at same time. It wasn't just how good the food tasted ... and it did ... but my appetite even seemed greater on this side of the mountain. The others were also experiencing the relaxation that comes with freedom. We chattered all the way through our meal then carried our white and wedge-wood blue plates to the sink. With the breakfast dishes cleared and the last of the coffee drained from the pot, Silas spoke the reluctant words.

"Dahlia, we'd better be getting back." He spoke slowly and fumbled with the toothpick dispenser on the table. Suddenly eight or ten of the little slivers of wood tumbled out and rolled across the table. "Sorry, Martin, I know you hand-make all of these."

"You make your own toothpicks?" Jason gasped in surprise. Then without waiting for an answer he added, "I've decided to go back with you, Silas." He spoke to all of us but his eyes met mine.

"Jason, no," I was shocked. "I can't do this without you." I grabbed his hand, hoping I could keep him by my side. And, it was more than that. Jason and I had been inseparable for weeks. I liked it. I no longer felt alone.

"I'll only be gone a few hours," he assured me. His eyes flashed and locked with mine. "I'll come back this evening." He turned to Silas, "Can you get me through again tonight?"

Silas seemed skittish but willing. He made no eye contact, but retreated inside his emotions. "Yes, after it's dark."

"Why?" I still saw no reason for Jason to return to Capitol City. "What if you see Inspector Stoner?"

"You will," Dahlia mockingly shook her head. "He's everywhere."

"Old Tombstone Stoner?" Martin quipped as he tapped his fingertips together.

"You've heard of him?" Dahlia laughed.

"Silas tells us all the happenings on the other side." Rebecca admitted.

Jason spoke in the comforting tones I loved to hear. He traced out his plan with his fingers on Rebecca's festive red and green table cloth. "We can't cross into the western zone until tonight anyway, Christy. And, I want Stoner to see me in the city. I thought about it half the night. It will be easier to establish our story if the Inspector sees me while he hears of my planned absence. It won't seem like we have just disappeared."

• • • • •

The falling snow fluttered down like angel-wing feathers kissing the ground. Voices of happy children from blocks away floated on the crystal-clear air. I wished Jason and I could bundle up in Rebecca's feather comforters and sit on the porch for an hour but it was time for the three of them to leave.

Jason lingered at the mouth of the cave a few seconds after the other two went through the mountain wall. "Christy," he slowly brushed the hair from my forehead that stubbornly stuck out from under my hat. "I promise I'll be back tonight after it gets dark."

"I know." Tears welled up. I couldn't look him in the eyes. If I did, he would surely have seen the fear that was rising within me.

"But?" He continued to press.

"But," I choked on the emotions that caught in my throat. "But, I'm afraid," I admitted.

"You are the bravest person I know," he soothed my fears as he played with a curl near my ear.

"Well, thank you, even if you are full of Irish blarney," I teased.

Jason grabbed me and kissed me tenderly. I felt at home with him, safe, loved. "I'll be back in a few hours," he promised. Then he slipped past the bolder and disappeared into the mountain.

As soon as Jason left and I was alone, fear flooded back in. I felt abandoned. Silas, Dahlia and now Jason had all left me behind, on the valley side of the mountain.

"Come on back in the house," Rebecca coaxed. "The north wind is starting to blow again."

"Will that keep us from traveling beyond the valley tonight?" I asked as we went back into the warmth of the log home.

"We should be all right. The snow and wind might keep others inside. That could allow us to travel pretty far with little interference. Gray Fox will know the best route," Martin assured me.

"Gray Fox?" I hadn't heard of Gray Fox.

"Gray Fox will be your guide. His wife, Little Feather, will go too. They'll be able to get you through anything. But there's a problem," Martin warned.

"What problem?"

"There is a snow storm coming in. We have a small window of time to get you through the pass across the far hills and on your way," Martin said. "It just came across the wire."

"What wire?" I hadn't heard that term in reference to incoming information.

"We have to be very quiet here in the valley. We must make sure we don't draw attention by smoke, sirens or let the outside detect communication devices."

"Then how?"

"Gray Fox sends messages over an old telegraph machine. He uses an ancient Navaho language. Tribesmen in the Western sector pick up the message. Even if someone were to stumble across the signals, they wouldn't be able to understand it. Gray Fox and Little Feather will get you there and safely back. Like I said, there are ways."

Chapter 9
Through the Mountain of Tears

"Hurry," Silas cautioned as he led Jason and Dahlia back through the deep recesses of Howard Mountain, past the ghastly museum, owned and seen only by Alister Bedlam.

"Right behind you," Jason assured him while leading Dahlia through the maze of human relics. The people-statues were all that remained of the elite of the Central Zone who had gone through the deadly portal to the never-ending-sleep.

"Let me know when I can open my eyes," Dahlia whispered as she stumbled blindly behind him.

"We're nearly past," Jason said. "You did it before when we went into the valley. Just a few steps more ... okay you can open your eyes, but don't look back."

Jason saw Silas tremble as they passed the third furnace on their way out of the cavernous cave. The area still smelled of burnt flesh. He wondered if Silas could hear the cries of people from beyond the flames in his sleep.

"Hurry, just hurry," Silas continued to mumble. The man who stood so tall in the valley beyond the mountain, quickly morphed back into the stooped, dejected, shuffling shell of a man he had been before the fresh air of the valley filled and cleansed him. He slumped even more as they neared the exit to the mountain.

Jason grabbed Silas's shoulder before exiting the cave. "You, Silas, are a good man. You broke the silence and made us all aware of the lies of this place. Hold your head high."

"But I was—"

"That's right, you *were*, but you aren't anymore," Jason said as he felt the warmth of the winter sun on his cheek as it filtered through the small window in the door. He had forgotten it was still morning with all the darkness of the cavern and its contents around them.

"Let's hurry to my car before we're seen. We have to arrive in Capitol City early. Those going to work will be there by now. Maybe there won't be too many people still out." Silas burst through the heavy wooden door and nearly ran to his car.

The three piled quickly into the small car and rushed to the gates where Silas entered a code. Slowly it opened like a medieval castle entrance. Then, they turned toward Capitol City.

All three of them sat in silence as they sped along the isolated road that led back to the city. Jason watched the passing fields with steady gaze. "One good thing about all this snow, it's white. We'll be able to see everything that comes upon us from any direction."

Strange, few in the city had personal transportation: the Blue Guard, medical personnel of high rank, the Council of Elders and judges ... and Silas Drummond who kept the furnaces blazing at the Mountain of Woe. He was never to let the fires die out. And now, the coals were cool and the furnaces black and cold. They would remain so, until the people voted on the referendum in support of the abolishment of the Length of Days policy. Jason was determined, there would be a vote!

Chapter 10
The Pretense

"Thank you, my friend," Jason spoke quickly as Silas pulled up in front of his office. He scanned the street from the north and to the south. It was still early, even though the first wave of workers had already cleared the sidewalks and PT stations. "I can't thank you enough for all you have risked by taking us to the valley and back."

Silas hung his head and didn't meet his gaze.

"Look at me, Silas." When the man looked up, Jason said, "You are a good man. You are the hero of our time. You spoke up when no one else knew the truth. That makes you a hero. That's the flat-out truth." They shook hands and Dahlia kissed his cheek.

"I'll be back the minute the sun goes down," Silas reminded the doctor. "I'll be right here in front of your office building."

"Good. I'll not go home. I won't take anything with me. I'll just— be gone."

The three continued to search the street for trouble. It was still empty. Jason and Dahlia hustled out of the car and entered through the glass front doors. No one stirred in the wide entry hall. Their shoes echoed as the heels tapped across the floor. Since many people who worked in the medical office building were still on Gifting Time vacation, the lights only lit the hall. Beyond adjacent office windows and doors, the suites were dark and vacant.

Jason pulled the elevator key from his pocket, and he and Dahlia road up in whispered silence.

"If no one is around, how will you establish your presence today? No one will see you," Dahlia asked.

"I'll make some calls on the communication device in my office and check on a few patients. Monitored conversations and their content are stored in the data retrieval and storage facility at the central repository. Even if no one sees me, there will be a record of my presence in the city today."

They stepped off the lift and it immediately went back to the lobby. The old-style floor indicator above the elevator door registered that the lift car was ascending again. Someone was coming.

"Run!" Jason commanded as the two darted through the outer doors of his office and past the waiting room chairs and tables piled with pamphlets and stacks of government literature that outlined: the expectations of a civil society; the beauty of a two-child home; what to think and what to do.

Dahlia dashed through the inner door, snapped on the lights as she rounded the corner and slipped into the chair at the entry desk.

Jason hurried into his office and grabbed the white coat that hung on the hook on the wall to the left. He could feel his heart pounding in his chest. The medical jacket was more than a piece of clothing. It was a symbol of all he had worked for, of all he had sacrificed—his future position on the Council of Elders, his birthright—for the awesome privilege of practicing medicine, of binding up the broken and curing the sick. Before labeled as *unfit for life,* he could see each citizen a handful of medical contacts.

Slowly, he turned the used clinical jacket right-side-out as he breathed in its essence and exhaled through his mouth. "Calm, calm," he reminded himself and was still buttoning the garment when he walked with measured steps into the nurse's station.

"Dr. O'Reilly," Stoner growled as he burst through the office door.

"Yes, Inspector," Jason looked up casually from the pad of paper he had just picked up.

"Oh ... you're here," Stoner's expression changed from "Got ya" ... to surprise.

"Yes, but then, you came to see me. Did you expect me to not be here?" he challenged.

"Well, it is still the holiday."

"Yes, it is. How did you happen to stop by on a day when you thought I would be out of the office?"

"You and the Lady-girl caused quite a ruckus Gifting Day night."

"Did we?"

"Where is she?" Stoner glared with a piercing narrow gaze. "I'm not here to play games with you."

"If you mean Lady Applewait, she was going to stay with family for a few days." Jason handed Dahlia the piece of paper he had been writing on.

"I'll take that," the Chief Inspector growled as he grabbed the piece of paper out of the nurse's hand.

"Sir, this office has a strict confidentiality policy," she snapped as she tried to grab the slip of paper back from his hands.

"I said ... I'll take it." He ground his teeth in rage.

Stoner turned the small notepaper over and read the words out loud. "Out until December 1, 2113." The officer crumbled the paper in his hand and threw it back at Dahlia. "What's this all about? What do you mean *out*?"

"I'll be studying a new procedure—the non-invasive approach to joint replacement."

"Joints? You have no specialty in orthopedics." Stoner gritted his teeth and his nostrils flared.

"No, you're right. I will be studying at home and at friends' houses as I prepare myself for an internship at an orthopedic hospital." Jason explained calmly and confidently as he met the officer's eyes blink for blink.

"Where, exactly ... where will you be studying?" Stoner demanded shrilly.

"Well, I can't actually tell you that because I will be in many places, depending on my mentor's requirements and my own study needs. I will be checking in regularly with my nurse, Miss Zoobomba. She'll be able to take any messages. Feel free to call her."

"No, Mister, you will contact me regularly! Not some flat-shoed nurse."

"I'm sorry, Inspector. I just can't do that. I will require long periods of uninterrupted concentration. Just call and talk to Nurse Dahlia. She will be in the office each day to handle questions and non-critical matters. She is an independent practitioner you know."

"Didn't you hear me? I said ... you will contact me!" The veins in Stoner's neck bulged and his eyes were large and menacing.

"I did hear you say that, Inspector." Jason's voice was even but his heart was pounding so loudly, he feared the officer might hear it. "I understand your need to make sure a physician is nearby." Jason looked deeply at the angry man who stood before him. "But I'm sure your son will be fine now," he said. "You may not require a doctor on call." Then he added, "Judge Brunner has included Christopher in the stay on the Length of Days policy. Medical contact events will not be counted during these two years either."

Jason faced the man with his own authority. He knew that Stoner had secretly contacted a doctor about his son's accident and subsequent coma the day before Christmas. If he had taken his child to the hospital that day, it would have affected the child's length of days by one less year. Jason knew, because he was the doctor that Stoner had called.

The Chief Inspector said nothing. He stared at Dr. O'Reilly but neither of them flinched. Finally, Stoner pounded his fist on the reception desk with a loud thump, turned and stormed out of the office.

Jason and Dahlia exhaled loudly. "Well, hopefully, he has been appeased for now. It was for this very moment that I returned to the city. Stoner completed his own little charade. Then, he played his part well in my little script. He made it all happen whether he knows it or not. He validated my presence, and the reason for my absence."

"The Lord made it happen whether *you* know it or not," Dahlia reminded him.

"You are absolutely right. I actually gave credit to Stoner, that wretchedly sad little dictator, when the miracle belongs to God."

"What do you want me to do here, Doc?"

"Let's organize the office so you can manage it in the months ahead. You put together new job descriptions for the rest of the staff. I'll look it over when you're finished. While you're doing that, I'll sign drug orders, look through the files and go over policies which will protect you while you practice. Also, you'd better not give out any more detoxification tablets since a few people will abuse the drug just as they had recently. The city will begin to purify the community's water supply as they gradually pour in fewer and fewer chemicals. Some may experience depression because they have been drinking the drug-laced water since they were small. I'll place an order for an increased supply of anti-depressant medication for our pharmacy here in the office so you will be prepared."

"All right, but how will I contact you since Stoner will check our communication lines every day?" Dahlia asked.

"Use the regular lines to send innocuous questions and comments. But, contact Sean for the serious stuff. Silas will bring guarded messages from me to print in the newspaper. You can read my coded words there and ask questions that I will answer ... again, on the pages of the newspaper."

"It will take longer, waiting for the newspaper to be delivered, but okay, we'll make it work," Dahlia paused then jotted the word, Sean, on the pad of paper in front of her.

"No, Dahlia," Jason warned and tore the paper into tiny pieces. "You cannot leave a paper trail. The Blue Guard could come in at any time and confiscate our records. Verbalize your comments and questions directly to Sean with nothing written down except his final news sheet."

"We can do this," Dahlia asserted. "Nothing on paper, but the new structure of the office. It's possible. As Martin said, '*there are ways*.'"

Chapter 11
Later That Evening

"Okay, where is she?" Stoner barked as he burst through the door of the Indian River Apartment building.

Dahlia had just sat down in the large first floor gathering room, just off the entry. She carried a book Christy had given her, a forbidden novel. The clever nurse had put the jacket from a fact-based book on the subject of residential apartment building rules around the novel. The story was about a woman and her four daughters who lived during the nation's Civil War. Authorities had banned the book along with other books of fiction.

"Is there any romance in that book, Dahlia?" Tayton Braxton, a new resident asked as he sat in a facing overstuffed chair.

"Hey!" The Inspector shouted at the two as he stormed into the sitting room. "Can't you two hear me?"

"We can now, Chief," Tayton drew out in his southern drawl.

"Then, answer me! Where is she?" The vein in Stoner's forehead bulged and his cheeks flushed.

"She? Who?" Tayton questioned with a calm voice.

"That one knows who I'm talking about," he sneered as he pointed at Dahlia.

Dahlia had closed the book casually and laid it, title page up, in her lap. "I'm sorry Inspector. Can I help you with something?"

Ward Stoner pulled off his gloves and smacked them across his hand. "Do you want to answer my questions downtown?"

"Sir," Tayton addressed the inspector as he stood up and stretched out to his full six-foot-six-inch frame, "we will be glad to help you if we can."

"Don't I know you, Mister?" Stoner turned to the much taller and more muscular man in front of him.

"I've just transferred into your precinct. My name's Tayton Braxton, Sir. My former Chief, Walter Collier, had written you last month, and I arrived today."

"You're on my team?" Stoner questioned with a mistrusting expression.

"Yes, Sir," he reached out his hand to greet his new chief.

Stoner ignored the gesture of friendship and continued to slap his leather gloves into the palm of his hand. "As I remember it, you asked for the transfer because you didn't like some of the orders old Walt handed out."

"Well, Sir," Tayton wiped his hand on his pant leg, "Chief Collier wanted us to push people around and work outside the law."

"Oh, really," Stoner drew out in mocked surprise. "And you're too good for that?"

"No, Sir," he paused. "Well, yes, Sir. I like to think I'm fair."

"Fair are you?" he paced back and forth across the lounge carpet. "You live here in this building or are you just keeping company with our esteemed nurse here?"

The new man in town blushed. "I would consider myself privileged if Miss Zoobamba would like to spend some time with me," he winked at a stunned Dahlia.

"Okay, okay, I'll call your bluff—"

"Bluff, Sir?"

"I don't know what you know of Miss Zoobamba here and the company she keeps, but if you live in this building, I have a special assignment for you. You stake out this apartment complex," he spit out. "You'll tell me where Lady Christiana Applewait is, when she leaves, where she goes, and when she comes back. You got that, Mister?"

"That sound like a good assignment, Sir."

"Good is it? You are to be rude, aggressive, and violent if necessary, to get the stiff-necked people in this building to bend. And, they will bend," he snorted. Stoner said no more. He jerked his gloves back onto his hands and stormed out of the Indian River.

"Is it true?" Dahlia asked. "You are really a member of the Blue Guard? They are as corrupt as they come."

"I know," Tayton said as he turned back to her.

"If you know, why did you transfer?"

"Sean is an old friend. He asked me to transfer into this precinct so I can protect you and Christy and this mission you're all on. I can run interference with Stoner. But I will have to fit in with the other guardsmen. You may hear rumors about me and think I'm one of them. If you do, know that I have fixed whatever I have broken."

"Why do you care what I think, as long as you protect Christy?"

"Because, I do. I was there on Christmas Day evening. I heard the speeches and saw the crowd. I'm more one of you, than one of them."

Dahlia eyed the man in front of her. There was something that gnawed at her, in a good but surprising way. Something she had never felt before. Deep down where her new emotions felt giddy, she bubbled a little.

"And, the other is true too, Dahlia."

"Other, what other?"

"You were here. You heard what I said to my new boss."

"Tayton, I feel strangely uncomfortable with this game you're playing." She looked down and tried to hide the blush she felt on her cheeks.

"Dahlia, it's called flirting ... and yes, I told the truth to the Inspector. I do want to spend some time with you ... if that's okay with you."

She looked away and tried to hide the smile she could not control. "To your first question, Tayton, yes, there is romance in this book."

Chapter 12
Gray Fox and Little Feather

Buddy pulled himself up from his comfortable bed at the side of the hearth. The large, thick dog cushion, stuffed with Martin's aromatic cedar chips, made the perfect mat. The dog found every excuse to lounge about all day. Now, he pointed his tail and pricked his ears. Something had stirred him from his usual nap.

Dusk had fallen in the valley so Rebecca had turned on the house lights. Martin strategically placed logs in the fireplace to build a fire and quickly ignited it into flame. "That should provide a steady burn this evening," he said as he straightened and proudly reviewed his backwoods talent. "I'd better check on the meat," he explained as he left the room.

The firelight danced across the golden logs of the huge cabin and created interesting shadows on the walls. I sat on the couch and watched the display of amber and light as it moved about the room.

"Do you smell that wonderful meat baking, Buddy?" I asked as I watched the dog sniff the air.

"That's not it," Martin cautioned as he came back into the room and silently pulled down the rifle that hung above the fireplace.

"What is it, Martin?" Rebecca asked from the kitchen doorway.

"Don't know yet," he said as he listened to the night beyond the cabin.

The three of us sat motionless and waited. We held our breath in anticipation. Yet another danger had found us. When would it all stop? It was hard for me wrap any measure of understanding around my doubt. Did God actually place us in this moment as I thought he had? Why couldn't he have made it easier?

"Could be a wild animal, Martin," Rebecca said. "Many still roam around. Especially here in the valley."

"Wild animals?" I didn't like the sound of that. "Is that a problem here? We have no animals at all in the Central Zone," I offered. My heart pounded.

My question fell by the side when I heard footsteps on the porch. Animals don't wear boots. I sat on the edge of my seat as Martin went to the door. Fear mounted within me. Would Blue Guard troopers force their way in? Rebecca motioned for me to hurry to her side and step into the shadows behind the open kitchen door.

Martin hoisted the firearm to his shoulder. With one glance over his shoulder toward Rebecca and me, he jerked the door open. A snow-covered Jason O'Reilly stood in the gathering darkness of the porch brushing the freshly fallen snow from his arms and shoulder. Silas stood behind him. He removed his hat and shook the white icy powder onto the ground beyond the house.

"Come in, friends," Martin laughed as he lowered the rifle and held the door open.

"Jason," I sighed in relief. "You're back." I went to him and threw myself into his embrace.

He wrapped his arms around me and pulled me into his snowy jacket. "You'll get wet on my damp coat," he warned me but didn't let go of his grasp.

"I'll dry in front of the fire," I said and stayed in his arms. When I had refilled my need for him, I unbuttoned his coat and helped him out of it. Together, we sat in front of the burning logs.

"Did you have any problems on the wide-open road out to the mountain?" Rebecca asked her cousin.

"We saw nothing," Silas said as he removed his outer coat.

"The roast beef will be ready shortly. You can relax, Jason, before you and Christy set out on your quest. Gray Fox and Little Feather will join us in a minute." Rebecca went back into the kitchen.

I pulled myself away from Jason for a few minutes and followed her. I hoped to get a few more answers to sooth my fear. This whole mission had developed so fast, my mind couldn't keep up with it all.

"If you go across the ice, you will have to watch every step," she said as she checked the kitchen clock again to time the meat. "Gray Fox is never late. They will be here shortly."

"You said we might cross the ice. Is that safe?"

"It's been frozen for six weeks. The ice is thick enough to walk on or even drive on if you wanted to. Still, I have seen men with their eight-toothed draw-saws this afternoon. They cut holes in the ice so they can fish during the winter months. Many will have small tents over their little fishing site to protect themselves from the wind, but not all of them. Some will leave open holes down through the ice to the frigid water until they return in the morning. Be careful."

"It sounds like large open fishing holes doted across the lake is no real problem," I said.

"It isn't a problem ... unless you don't watch where you're going."

Buddy barked and wiggled as his toenails tapped on the hardwood floor. "Becca," Martin called from the sitting room. "Gray Fox and Little Feather are here."

"Wonderful," she sang out as she removed the large roast from the oven. "If you will grab the rolls and butter, Christy, I'll come back for the mashed potatoes and corn."

"Sure," I said as I turned and saw the large basket of freshly baked yeast rolls and a bowl with a large round ball of yellow butter in the middle. I picked them up as the rolls sent their heavenly perfume into the air.

"Jason, just smell these," I said as I waved the basket under his nose.

"Somehow, I don't think the health department of the Central Zone would approve of them."

"What possible difference would it make to eat wonderful bread if they're going to cut off your life at an early age anyway?" Martin questioned with a mocking smirk.

I turned and stopped. The last two guests to arrive came in, hung up their buckskin coats and entered the dining room. The man, Gray Fox, had long hair that shone as black as the marble in the capitol building grand hall. His skin was much darker than mine and weathered like the descriptions of Native Americans I had read about in books. Obviously, he enjoyed the out of doors. His face was strong and his bearing straight and tall. Little Feather was a bronze beauty whose smile was infectious. She walked with grace, like a deer, with her head held high. Her deep brown eyes scanned her surroundings.

"Little Feather," I smiled back as I extended my hand, "I'm Christiana Applewait."

"Yes, Becca told us all about you. We stopped by when you were napping." Her smile was genuine and friendly warmth poured forth.

"I'm sorry I missed you," I apologized.

"There is no need to be. You have had quite an ordeal." Little Feather touched my arm and made that connection that calls a stranger "friend."

"Come, let us sit and eat," Martin invited. We gathered around the table, Gray Fox, Little Feather and Silas on one side, Jason, and I on the other. As soon as we had finished shuffling our chairs, Martin gave thanks to God for the food piled high on the platters, for friends old and new, and for our safe passage into the unknown zones.

"I heard Becca talking about the animals in these hills," Martin began. "Gray Fox, maybe you can fill them in."

Gray Fox took a bite of meat and thought for a moment. "In times long past, people of the Western Zone had a distorted sense of animal rights. In some cases, they thought the rights of a small speckled bird held more weight than the rights of man. Since they were no longer people of deep faith, they didn't know the natural order of nature, and thought of man as, not the holy protector and benefactor of all that God had created, but the predator. They passed laws that banned hunting and fishing. Then, in 2026, they carried their delusional thinking to the greatest extreme imaginable. They tore down all fences and opened all of the zoos so the animals were free to roam, to hunt and to seek their own comfort. Over the years, bears found their way back into the Northwest where it is cooler. Bob cats roam in packs nearly everywhere. Lions and tigers fought for their own territories and the large animals, like African and Asian elephants, worked again, in much the same way they did in the ancient villages from which they came. Monkeys can be the greatest nuisance. They forage for food wherever they can. They aren't in the trees of their ancestral home. They're in the backyards and on the playgrounds where our children swing and play."

"The health threat alone would be tremendous," Jason said. "Animal droppings would be everywhere and all the germs associated with it."

"The animal advocates didn't care. They believed that man was the menace, not roaming animals," Martin added.

"By the time the folks in the west came to their senses and found a faith in the one true God who ordered all things into their place, the animals were out of control," Rebecca explained.

"You mean the part of the country that gave us, *Do whatever makes you feel good*, now cradles a people of faith?" I couldn't believe what I was hearing. "I read about those who had rejected the morals of their heritage and embraced a freedom from responsibility."

Rebecca chuckled as she sipped her coffee. "The same women, who wore dresses with a neckline that plunged to their navel, now wear long dresses that reach just inches above their ankles, and high collars. The men wear button-up shirts and modest trousers, worn with a belt or suspenders ... or both," she laughed again. "Any male over twelve years old who is caught with their pants drooping down, is taken in to work in the gardens and orchards while wearing wide red suspenders."

"Then, we may find a lot of willing volunteers on the West coast. If they have changed their lives and now respect themselves and others, they may have a love for life that will help our cause." I thought about the task of canvassing the entire country, and I had hope.

"Animals and the empty ones must still be reckoned with," Gray Fox said. He broke his dinner roll in half and spread it with Rebecca's home-churned butter.

"I don't like the empty ones," Little Feather shuddered as she put her fork down and sipped water from the heavy tumbler.

"Who or what are the empty ones?" Jason asked. "Empty of what?"

The valley people looked at each other and then at Jason and me.

"The empty ones are those who are ... empty," Martin tried to explain. "Their eyes reveal no light or life within. They chose to believe the old lies. Everyone around them is supposed to make them happy ... and yet they feel no joy at all. They have no integrity, no steadfastness, and no faith. They exist to take, to consume, and to serve their own needs, although they are unable to name the things that are important to them. They have no inner core. They have no spirit. They have no hope. They are very dangerous because they have nothing to lose. They are the hollow ones ... the lost."

Chapter 13
The Departing

Tuesday Evening – December 27, 2112

"Let's see how this one fits you," Rebecca said as she offered me a long, broomstick pleated, ankle length skirt with deep pockets. "Our daughter, Rachel, often wore this one when she traveled into the Western Zone. It's similar to the clothes the western women wear. She's married and doesn't travel much anymore."

"It reminds me of a gypsy skirt," I said as I thought about the Romani women with their full skirts that swing when they walk.

"You are familiar with the Roma?" Rebecca's eyes widened.

"Only what I have read, of course."

"The women in the west have adopted the dress of the Roma, or gypsies, because it seemed so practical for them. Cool, modest skirts, and loosely fitting peasant blouses that come up to the neck with a small collar, have replaced the scanty shorts and low hanging pants of old."

She thumbed through the hanging clothes and selected a white boxy blouse with blue and red needle art all around the edges.

"But you said the western zone had embraced their faith. Did they choose a pagan religion as the Roma had followed?"

"No. They went through several religions during the first decades following the collapse of their culture. They found them to be the same wishy-washy approach to belief that had contributed to their down fall. Now, they make no demands on others and what they believe, but they have chosen to rebuild their society on the old beliefs of the original founding fathers."

"Wow, how did all of that happen?" I couldn't believe it. "How did they hush the mocking laughter of non-believers, as surely there must have been?"

"Last question first. The public areas will still have Christmas decorations up, since that was the vote of the people many years ago. Various sections of the public parks will have the displays of other beliefs as well. None can be rude or insult the senses of others since they are all in public areas. No one can stop the visual speech of others."

"That is amazing, that they allow other voices to be heard. We can't speak at all in the Central Zone."

"Your other question: how did it happen? It first started as a movement by the evangelist, Francine, Franny Adams, a distant niece of the great Christian equalizer, Dr. Absalom Lucas."

"I've read about her ... Franny Adams," I remembered out loud.

"Then, you are the only one in the Central Zone who has. You may hear more about Franny when you get to the west."

"I'll listen for her name."

Rebecca looked at my shoe coverings and smiled. "Those won't get you very far." She stooped and pulled a pair of low-healed, high-top boots from Rachel's closet floor. "Your low-quarters aren't the best for this trip. Here, these boots are good for walking. They're warm for the desert nights and cool in the daytime. I'll get some socks from the drawer."

I quickly changed into the travel clothes of a Western woman and looked at myself in the mirror. How different I looked. Rebecca plaited my hair into one long braid and fixed it in place with a long piece of sinew.

"Why don't I keep your red hat here? You can get it when you come back through here. I have another one you can wear. In yours, they may spot you as the only cardinal in the woods."

I looked at her quickly as a doubt entered my mind. Rebecca saw my worried expression.

"Yes, Christy, you will come back this way. I know you will," she spoke with the conviction I needed.

I smiled and tried to hide the fear that could betray me if not buried deep inside. I looked at my reflection again in the mirror and hoped I looked different to any eyes that knew me. If I could pass as a Western woman to my friends, perhaps I could pass as a local to those who didn't know me. I checked again, and then stepped out of the room and into my new world.

Jason stood at the bottom of the steps resting his arm on the stair banister. His makeover was amazing. He wore pants made of blue denim material, a red plaid shirt, boots similar to mine, a split leather coat that was both rough and smooth in texture and a polished leather broad-brimmed hat. He smiled as I came down the steps and his eyes lit up my heart.

His hand felt strong when I gently touched it. He grabbed me boldly and pulled me into his arms. "We can do this, Babe," he whispered. "Together, we can do whatever God calls us to do."

I knew he spoke the truth but hearing his words out loud, buried the truth of them more deeply in my heart. I was new to faith, and I was still learning. With Jason beside me, he would be able to reassure me if I became confused.

"I love you, Christy," he whispered in my ear.

"Oh Jason, I love you, too," I responded and drew even closer.

"We must be going, Friends," Little Feather said as she reached for her coat.

"Your green cloak will be perfect in the Western Zone," Becca said. "Here is a smooth leather fedora. The lining pulls down to cover your ears when needed and folds back up into the crown when it's warmer."

"Thank you for everything, Rebecca."

Little Feather looked Jason and me over with a keen eye. "It looks like Rebecca and Martin fixed you two up really well. You won't stand out at all. Let's move out."

"Can we know the route we're taking—what we should expect?" Jason asked.

It had to be Jason to ask that question. Sadly, I usually follow as I have always done. I was no leader and yet everyone on Christmas Day evening called on me to lead them out of the Age of Silence. Truthfully, I would have gone anywhere with Jason O'Reilly, but I didn't know how to get there on my own.

Gray Fox looked at Martin and Rebecca. It was Martin who spoke.

"We met just yesterday, Christiana, Jason. I know you are stepping out into the unknown much like our pioneering ancestors did. But, they had more time to plan and I'm afraid, you do not. The reality is, you will see sights you have never seen. We don't have the time to tell you all of it. Simply stated, once you have cleared the hills, you will be out of the mountainous areas. Then we will cross the desert. Hopefully, the people on down the chain of contact will meet you and take you on by car. There is no time to tell you more. Sorry ... except to say, your mission is holy, and the Lord God will be with you."

Chapter 14
The Icy Trek

"We're nearing the lake," Gray Fox whispered as we silently followed a seldom used path toward the horizon where the sun had already slipped. We could see his silhouette by the light of a three-quarter moon, as he motioned toward the glassy icy that stretched out in front of us. The message was easy. "Watch your step."

We stepped out on the frozen surface of the lake. I thought of Grand-mère's story of Jesus walking on water and smiled. The water, frozen as solid as an old brick road, gave me a little confidence to venture out across it.

Little Feather was in front of me. I tried to walk in the exact footprints her boots had made on the snow. When her right foot slipped out from under her center of balance, she threw her arms out and bent forward as she tried to regain her equilibrium. I wanted to grab hold of her waist and help her, but I was afraid I would only knock her off balance even more and we would both go down.

We all stopped in the middle of the lake and watched as Little Feather tried to steady herself. I could feel my leg muscles tighten and ache as the tension of anxiety gripped me. Finally, she pointed to the other side. There was still ice in that area but there was no water underneath at the edge of the lake. I looked forward to the warmth of the desert that was somewhere ahead of us.

Then, silently we moved from the lake area to the rolling hills. Walking there was difficult. Ruts, buried beneath the snow, and cracks and dips in the ground could break an ankle. We stayed off paths and crept along untraveled areas so as not to draw attention to our movement. Suddenly, I held my breath. Some type of small animal was moving toward us.

I thought it looked like a dog my books called a German shepherd. As it got closer, I saw his bushy tail and froze. It was a fox, but it made no sound. The fox stopped in front of our guide, and fixed his eyes on his. Slowly, the animal stretched out his body to its full length. His tail was stiff, and he bared his teeth. Gray Fox didn't blink and maintained his gaze. Slowly, the sleek animal began to lower his tail until he tucked it between his legs. He turned his head down and slipped off into the night.

I couldn't move. I watched the fox until it disappeared among the frozen, leafless trees. Jason came up behind me and slipped his hand in mine. We walked as one. The snow and sludge were terrible on the upper slopes. My feet slipped backward with every step forward. I grabbed some nearby scrub brush and used it to propel me forward. On we trudged.

Little Feather had pulled her skirt up between her legs and had tucked it into her belt. It created a makeshift pair of pantaloons. I tried to do the same but wasn't as gifted at garment re-purposing as she was. As we reached the top, my skirt tail drooped to my knees.

We met our first challenge. We had crossed the Lake of Hope. Now, we would need to put the distant hills behind us. The walk was easier up the hillsides since the watchers had developed safe pathways with railings and carefully placed pull-rings to assist the hikers to the top. They had walked to the top for decades.

"Orville, anything happening up here?" Gray Fox asked as we approached the last outpost.

"Gray Fox, good to see you." He looked out to the west. "I have seen very little. There is something, miles away. I can see lights in my spy glass."

"We are headed that way."

"Watch your step as you approach the desert," the watcher cautioned. "There are always critters out there." He slapped Gray Fox on the shoulder and we moved on in silence.

Over the hill, the flat lands stretched out before us as far as we could see. On we walked, right foot, left foot, right foot, left foot. I watched the clear night sky out to the west ... and finally exhaled.

Chapter 15
The Pilgrimage Has Begun

7 a.m. - December 28, 2112

The plains spread out like a never-ending table set with scrubs and switch grass. I could not imagine walking all the way to the desert but we would do it if required. I was exhausted. We had walked all night. I thought of the pictures I had seen on the covers of old western novels of dead cattle and chalk-white bony skulls of animals that had died in the blistering heat.

We had only walked another mile when Gray Fox and Little Feather sat down on their haunches and silently watched the eastern horizon.

Jason looked at me and studied our two guides. "Sorry friends. I'm a man, and I need a modicum of control over my life. What are we doing now?"

"Waiting," Gray Fox said with relaxed confidence

"I can see that. Waiting for whom ... for what?"

"For him." Gray Fox pointed to an old red stake truck that approached. It had to be more than a hundred years old.

The truck slowed down as it approached us then stopped. "Gray Fox ... good to see you," the driver said as he rolled down his window. "How did you know I would be coming along?"

"Because it is early Wednesday morning and I knew you would have been heading back from the ranch to be home in time to see your children off to school." Little Feather smiled. "I like that—up, overseeing the ranch for two days, then home for two days so you can see your babies."

"Little Feather, you know how old Alfonso, my *baby*, is now?" Armando laughed.

"I imagine he's older than I suspect," she smiled.

Armando crossed his arms and leaned them on the old window opening. "He is fifteen years old already. Marta is in college. She's going to be a teacher in a few years."

"That is wonderful my friend," she said.

"I wonder if you could give us a ride to the edge of the desert," Gray Fox asked.

"Of course," Armando agreed. "Two of you can ride up here with me and two back there." He pointed to the truck bed behind the cab.

"We'll ride in the back," Gray Fox answered quickly. "This fine woman is Christiana Applewait, Armando, and her friend Dr. Jason O'Reilly." He and Little Feather headed toward the bed of the truck and climbed over the stake sides.

In spite of Gray Fox's generosity, I would have been happy to ride in the back. But he wanted to be gallant, so Jason and I walked around to the passenger side of the vehicle and reached for the door handle. It was a huge step up from the paved road. Luckily a long chrome hand bar was there for grabbing.

I slipped in beside Armando and Jason sat by the door. The view was wonderful, like that seen when riding on the Public Transit as it travels on the ribbons of steel high above the street in Capitol City.

"This is very nice of you," Jason said. "We're fortunate it's not out of your way."

"Your destination could not be out of my way," he said quietly.

"How far do you live?" I asked.

"About five miles down the valley," our driver stated.

"So, not far from the desert?" I asked. When I got no response, I asked, "How far is it to the desert?"

"Twenty-five miles," he stated warmly.

"Then taking us to the desert is out of the way. It's not on your way home at all," I said.

"The way of the Lord is never out of the way for his people," Armando answered.

"You are a believer?" I asked in surprise. Meeting so many who follow the Way is so very different than being one of the handful of believers in Capitol City.

"I am ... and my whole household is as well."

"It is so nice of you to take us," I said, not knowing how to thank him.

"I am privileged to be part of this great undertaking you and the doctor are on."

"Undertaking?" I questioned. How could this man in the Western Zone know of our secret mission?

"Yes, Lady Applewait. We heard of the great walk of the brave people in Capitol City on Christmas Day evening just minutes after your speech on President Alexander's front porch. You are going to get everybody in this whole nation to sign your petition so we can overturn the Length of Days Policy when it comes to a vote at the next election. To be a part of that miracle is a privilege, My Lady."

"Christy, Armando. Call me Christy ... please," I asked. It was important to me that I be equal to everyone else. If not equal, then I would be out of touch, out of reach. Those on a pedestal are very lonely and I had been alone enough to last a lifetime.

"I will call you Christy as you request, but I do so because a woman of God, a Crusader for Life, has asked me to. And I will respect that, My Lady." Armando kept his eyes on the road in front of us.

"But, how did you find out about our cause so fast?" I couldn't believe how quickly information travels from one zone to another.

"The Navajo telegraph," he said.

"Telegraph?" I asked.

"Gray Fox will tell you about it, My Lady ... Lady Christy."

I looked at Jason. The only life I ever sought was an afternoon curled up on the old brown leather couch in the back room of the library, reading a good novel from a century past. Propelled into a position of leadership and notoriety in only a few days? How was it possible? It was all too fast. I couldn't keep up with my own life.

"It's a privilege to live a miracle, Lady Christy," Armando added. "You can't know the way. The telling of it would take the same amount of time as living it. The time spent on your quest will be equal to the people and their stories you meet along the way. The pilgrimage has already begun."

Chapter 16
Revealed in the Desert

9 a.m.

The desert sand was warm under our boots as we stepped from Armando's truck and into the morning sun.

"The coolness of the night has taken some of the fire out of the sand." Armando assured us from his truck window. "It will be easier to walk on now. It'll be hot today." Armando looked at me with a strange expression on his face. He had tears in his eyes.

"Thank you, Armando, my friend," I said as I patted his arm.

"It is my privilege," he said softly.

"I'm honored to have met you," I added. "You have provided another link in our holy journey, and I didn't even get your story as you had promised I would."

"I'm just a humble rancher," he said as his voice cracked with emotion.

"You're the chariot driver who provided safe passage for these papers," I patted the side of the brown leather cross-body, buckled, legal case I carried.

"Those are the petitions?"

"Yes, and the required cover sheets needed to legally file the petitions," I spoke softly and looked around the immediate area for ears that might threaten our mission. "Jason's briefcase holds the same. If we become separated or injured ... the other one will be able to carry on."

"You will be safe," Armando said. Then he reached out and shook Jason's hand as he came over to the window.

I offered my hand. Armando took it, kissed it and said, "My story is: my wife died two years ago. She fell from her favorite horse out on the ranch. She died instantly. I ran in and grabbed my rifle from my gun case and charged out with hate in my heart, bent on destroying the one thing Angelica loved almost as much as her family. My daughter, Marta, grabbed for the gun and it fired, hitting the side of the barn and grazed Alfonso's temple. I fell apart. My father had to manage the ranch for a few months and my mother stepped in to look after the kids. Finally, one day, Marta came into my room and said it was time I pull myself together. She needed me and so did her brother. She said that anger and hate only destroys the vessel that carries it. The object of our hate is only ourselves."

He paused for a moment and wiped his eyes. "I had to learn to lay the anger and fear aside and accept the responsibilities the Lord had given me. Now, Black Lightening is the finest stallion in our stable. I won't let anything happen to him."

"Thanks, Armando. Thank you for the ride. Thank you for your story and thank you for your encouragement. Bless you my friend."

"I am truly blessed," he responded.

I looked around our sand-barren surroundings. Emptiness loomed before us and the last promise of vegetation lay behind us on the plains. There on the edge of all that sand, a few yards from where we stood, was a small, long green building with a sign above the door—Ace's Place.

Jason took my hand and together we followed Gray Fox and Little Feather into the diner. The inside was everything it should be, or as I remembered from my many novels and history books.

"Over this way," Gray Fox led us to the back corner of the small restaurant where a turquoise and cream-colored leather-like fabric covered the cushions of the booth benches. The table was clean but worn from all the elbows that had leaned on the surface. A lunch counter stretched across the opposite side with stools that spun the patron around and deposited him or her back in the isle when they finished their meal.

We took our seats and got comfortable. Gray Fox pointed to a back placard on the wall with white letters. "The specials for today are listed on the black board," he said.

I read the listing slowly, savoring the thought and possible aroma of each of the dishes. Food did not sound as yummy in the Central Zone.

Suddenly, a man entered the diner whose own energy was so vile I could feel his wretchedness from the back corner. The waitress froze when she saw the man and nearly dropped the coffee pot that now dangled limply from her hand. Frozen, I couldn't take my eyes off him.

"Don't look at that one," Gray Fox whispered. "He can't draw energy from your fear if you ignore him."

"Well, is it ready?" the empty one seethed.

"Yes," the woman said. Her voice was harsh with anxiety. She reached behind the service window and brought out a white paper bag. "See, it's all ready. Now, you go on."

She handed him the bag and before she could withdraw her hand, he grabbed her wrist and pulled her forward. She nearly fell over when she stumbled into one of the counter stools. "Raymar ... no! You're hurting me."

I saw it all and heard the fear in the woman's voice. I jumped to my feet but didn't move. The man, Raymar, snapped his glare in my direction and our eyes met. I didn't say a word, but in my heart, I prayed that anger would leave the man.

His eyes were empty. He appeared to be a shell of a man, with only basic animal instincts, like the need for food, still pulling at him. He could have just as easily been a growling bear.

Raymar didn't approach us, but tried to intimidate me with his fierce eyes and hunched attack-stance. Perhaps, it had worked the previous times he had intimidated others. Like a mad dog, he locked his eyes on mine and seemed to be trying to conquer me with fear.

I maintained my gaze on his hollow eyes. For some reason, the longer I maintained eye contact, the less I feared him. It seemed that God's warmth, love, peace, and acceptance, all directed to the creature-man that stood bent over before me, were changing him. Suddenly, the man blinked. Then, his mouth opened as he inhaled a life breath he may have never experienced. He grabbed the bag and backed out of the diner, not out of intimidation, out of something else. It was like he could not stop drinking from the well of life. I watched him all the way out the door. Once outside, he ran out into the street, grabbed hold of the back of a passing truck, swung his body onto the vehicle and was gone.

"Not even the grandfathers of our community have been able to reach one of the empty ones," Gray Fox sighed with amazement.

"Who are you?" Little Feather asked as she looked outside to see if the Hollow Man was really gone.

"I'm just Christiana Applewait, as I said," I answered her.

"What she won't tell you and I just discovered in the last few days, is that Christy is a seer and a healer. She had expressed her *knowing* in artistic expression when she was a very young child. Now, she is only discovering her gifts as revealed to her," Jason explained as he put his arm around me.

"You are a disciple of the Holy One," Gray Fox acknowledged.

I didn't have to respond, and I was glad. I didn't know what I would have said. It seemed I was finding myself at the same time others were discovering me. Luckily, the conversation stopped when a man with shoulder length curly red hair entered, followed by a group of men and women who scattered throughout the diner. The curly haired man slid onto the bench beside Gray Fox and Little Feather.

"My friend," the man said quietly, and firmly patted his forearm.

"Good to see you, Rufus," Gray Fox spoke lowly as he touched his hat.

"These are your travelers?" Rufus asked.

"Yes, Dr. Jason O'Reilly," Gray Fox motioned toward Jason. "And, this is Christiana Applewait."

"The seer," Rufus lowered his eyes as if he were bowing.

"You have heard of us? Here ... on this side of the mountain," Jason asked in surprise.

"Word of Lady Applewait's gifts came to us through the Central Gazette."

"Sean's newspaper?" I couldn't believe how far Sean's circulation extended. Maybe getting the information out about the petitions and referendum won't be as hard as I thought.

"Yes," Rufus said as he smiled. "It comes by truck to my bus and I transport it west."

"Order some food, my friends," Little Feather said as a waitress approached the booth. "We have a long way to go. Make sure it is filling and nutritious."

We briefly scanned the chalkboard again for the daily specials and selected our choices. I chose something called meatloaf and Jason selected fried chicken. Jason and I chuckled over the concept of placing chicken pieces in sizzling fat and cooking it until the skin turned brown. Little Feather, however, assured us that our choices would be delicious. I had read about meals such as these in my books, but I had never eaten them.

"What is our destination?" Jason asked. "I'm still not comfortable with not knowing where we're going."

"Los Angeles," Rufus said. "The new Bible belt."

"Bible belt? Where? What do you mean?" I asked.

"The entire coast, from Baja to Seattle is the new cradle of belief."

"I imagine it's a patch-work quilt of all the world's religions," I laughed. "My books told me of all the many religions and cults that lived in harmony on the west coast, as well the vast number of unbelievers."

"All religions used to live side by side, except the Christian religion. They silenced the followers of the Christ, just like they have in the Central Zone. However, unlike your zone, when a balance returned after the collapse of society, soberness took over the people. Allowed to breathe again, the Christian religion blossomed and grew. While they don't defame the beliefs of others, the Christian religion is in the majority. About 65% are followers and roughly 62% attend church every Sunday. The people have found that accepting love and peace, forgiveness and grace, and eternal life is not a subversive, antiquated concept. It's a life-saving blessing."

"What will we encounter? What will be the dangers?" I knew in every good society, there remain imperfections.

"There is still a remnant of people who believe they hold truth in their hands. Oddly, some are rigid believers who believe they— and only they—are the people at the heart of God. They have been known to ostracize those who do not accept their beliefs or who speak out against Julius, the great Christian Evangelist of the year 2073."

"And Francine Adams ... what about her teachings?" I asked, remembering what Rebecca had said.

"Most people embrace her wisdom. So, those people will be with our cause. We don't know what to expect from the other groups; like the ones who are radical, free-spirits and rely on magic; those who are self-centered, self-importance, and believe in the concept of the self as God. They use crowd hypnosis and aggressive deception to attempt to win others to their way of belief. They and the Julius followers are dangerous and will require watching. If there is to be a return of freedom for all the people, we must try to keep the current balance in society but also bring in the outliers. We want to make sure we don't disrupt the distribution of power, while turning it up-side-down to include the hollow ones."

"Rufus," a woman with a round face and big brown eyes interrupted with an apology. "I'm sorry, but we must be going soon. Raymar may have gotten back to some of those in the caravan of dust heading west. They may try to stop these believers," she warned.

"Caravan of dust?" Jason questioned.

"As the hollow ones travel, their caravan kicks up dust when their wagons pull out. But, when they arrive, it's like no one is there. How can they be so frightening and yet so empty? I'm sure they have all found out there is a saint among you."

"A saint?" I questioned.

"You, My Lady," Rufus smiled. "We all know you have arrived."

Chapter 17
Rocky

We had been traveling for several hours when I woke up from a deep sleep. One of the children on the bus, holding a little stuffed bear, was hanging over the back of the seat in front of me. I smiled and closed my eyes. Suddenly, I felt a fuzzy fabric tickle my nose. When I opened my eyes again, the little boy was straddling the back of the seat so he could reach me with the bear. An impish smile on his face.

"Hey, are ya 'wake? Talk to me," he teased with four-year-old glee.

"Well, I guess I could ... if you will tell me your name," I agreed.

"I'm claimed," he said as he wrapped the words around in his mouth. "I don't have a name."

"Everyone has a name," I said lightly.

The child's traveling companion turned and offered. "Hi, I'm Miss Granger. There are several claimed children on the bus." Then she added, "The family this boy was born into already had two children. They had until he turned age two to decide which ones to keep. This child turned three a year ago on December 15. His first parents kept him too long and didn't obey the law. When the Family Regulation worker discovered him, Silas hid the boy until he could smuggle him out of the zone. In the valley, a doctor treated him for an old spiral fracture of the arm and some problem with his leg. Now that he is doing well, I'm accompanying him to his new family in Santa Barbara, California."

"They'll call me, Rocky," the little boy beamed. "I got to name myself at Hope House."

"Rocky is it? I think you chose a very good name. It's solid."

"Like a rock!" Rocky shouted as he made a fist and showed his muscle.

"Do you want to play a game?" I asked the little man.

"I don't know. I guess," he shrugged, apparently eager to play anything just to pass the time.

"Okay," I thought for a moment. "Do you know your colors? I see something blue," I shot back.

"Sure, Ma'am taught me."

"Ma'am?" I wondered if the boy was talking about someone at the Hope Center.

"The boy's mother," Miss Granger explained. "That is often what the birth mother prefers to be called."

"I understand," I responded and I believed that I did. The first parents would not have wanted to develop an attachment to the boy. The sad truth is, as a baby, he would have had to attach, or bond, to someone in order to thrive and live.

"Blue, that's blue," he shouted as he pointed at the blanket on my lap. "My turn," he grinned and bounced on the chair. "I see something blue, too."

I listed several things in the bus that were blue, Gray Fox's shirt and the driver's ball hat but each time, Rocky threw his head back and laughed, "Nooo."

"I give up on that one," I finally had to admit.

"No, you guess," he giggled.

"I can't think of anything else. I believe I named everything."

"The sky," he shouted.

"The sky?"

"The sky's blue."

"Yes, of course, but that's not in the bus," I protested.

"No, but it's blue," he laughed.

Chapter 18
The Western Zone

December 29, 2112

We had crossed the desert during the night and traveled most of the next morning. We made a few stops but took very little time to eat. Everyone seemed to draw food from their pockets, but mine were empty. I was getting hungry. My stomach growled and churned.

"As a physician, I diagnose your body sounds as symptoms of hunger," Jason leaned over and whispered.

Little Feather tapped me on the shoulder from the seat behind me. "It sounds like you're ready for another pressed food bar."

"Could you hear my stomach rumble from back there?" I was embarrassed. I had lived a life of privileged isolation. Now, I was close enough to people they could hear the growling of my stomach from several seats away.

"I am sure a legacy citizen's digestive system is well under control, My Lady," she said with poise and deference.

"Oh please," I moaned. "No elites can be found in God's kingdom, Little Feather. Everyone is equal in the eyes of the Lord. You know that."

"Yes, Christy, I do. I wasn't sure if you knew it," our guide spoke diplomatically. She passed two condensed food bars to Jason and me.

"Does the little boy in front of me have any food?" I asked Little Feather through the crack between the two chair backs.

"I'm sure he does, Christy," she assured me. "His handler, or guide, is seeing to his needs."

"Is Miss Granger his guide?"

"Yes, his traveling companion is his guide. Silas kept him safe at his sister's house where he stayed for several months. Then he took him to the mountain, hid him in a room behind his own, and then Miss Granger met him in the Valley of the Keepers several days ago."

Jason nudged my shoulder to get my attention. "Look at that wonderful sunrise, Christy." He turned and pointed out the back window. "Have you ever seen anything more beautiful than the sunrise over the desert?"

Together we watched the rosy glow of the sky as it blended with the morning clouds. The desert shimmered as the light danced off the hot sand. When the sun had finished greeting the day and rose firmly in the eastern sky, we turned and faced forward again and I smiled. We were on the last leg of the path that would lead us into the basin and on to the shining City of Angels.

"It is amazing, Jason. The ocean is far to the west, where the city meets the sea. I can almost smell the salt air. I've read about it so many times. It all seems so enormous when compared to the closed-in feeling in the Central Zone."

We traveled many more miles until we finally came to the erector-set creation called the highway system. "They haven't torn down the highways and replaced them with the public transportation system like we have in Capitol City," I observed.

Gray Fox, ever vigilant to all our needs, explained, "The Western Zone continues to enjoy the independence of personal transportation. They have an evolved energy system that produces no carbon," he said.

The nearer we got to the city center, the more it was obvious that the new positive and conservative ethic of the people of the western zone had painted and polished everything in the city, from the trimmed and point-tucked buildings, to the white wash on every rock.

We drove through the city streets and into the neighborhoods of Holmby Hills and Beverly Hills. It was in the latter sprawling community where we finally pulled into the gated drive of a gleaming home that stood tall and stately among the trees and gardens of the estate.

"Who lives here?" I gasped in amazement. "Not even the elite of the Central Zone live in mansions like this."

"This is listed as the home of film producer, Rachel Claudette. She lives on the main floor and the upper floor houses the offices of Claimed-International. Children stay here in the many rooms of the second floor, north wing while they await the arrival of the parents who have claimed them."

"How long do they have to wait?" Jason asked.

"There really is no wait. Call this a meet-up place. The new parents have claimed them before they leave the Valley of the Keepers," Gray Fox said.

"Do the claimed children go to other zones as well?" Jason questioned as he looked up at the massive structure.

"Not yet. C-I is investigating the other zones for their receptiveness to the idea of becoming claimed-parents. The Christian heart of the Western Zone still provides as many homes as we currently need. Some of the families welcome claimed children into their home where three to six other children already live. C-I has placed a few children out of the country, in Canada."

"How can people with six children possibly parent each child effectively?" Jason shook his head in amazement and doubt.

"That is Central Zone thinking, Doctor," Little Feather stated boldly. "A family of six or seven children always has a place of belonging and safety. An only child may actually feel more alone and insecure than a child from a large family, especially if both parents work. I understand all adults are expected to be employed in your zone."

"Point taken," Jason smiled with the sheepish grin of a professional, educated by another.

"Let's go in before you're spotted," a resident from the mansion cautioned when she came out to greet us.

We entered through the massive, eight-foot tall front door. Inside, the children from the bus streamed across the marble entry and into the huge dining room. There, a sideboard, filled with exotic breads, rich meat platters, and fresh fruit and vegetables of all kinds, awaited them. It even had varieties of fruits that didn't grow in the Central Zone. Citrus fruits that abounded in the West were nearly non-existent in the other zones since exportation across sealed borders was impossible.

"Ah, two travelers from Martin and Rebecca Spires, keepers of the Bible," the greeter smiled as she extended her hand in friendship and hospitality.

"You know Martin and Becca?" Amazed by how wide the little circle spread, like eddies in a pool, I followed the others inside.

"Lady Christiana Applewait, Dr. Jason O'Reilly, I would like you to meet Rachel Claudette, the blessed angel who shares her home with C-I," Little Feather said.

"If I cannot help C-I, Claimed International, with all the space I have here, I'm not worthy of the blessings I have received. I do share, with joy. With abundance, comes abundant generosity and abundant responsibility." She smiled and shook our hands.

"Some, who are blessed with plenty," Little Feather explained, "share what they have from an indifferent distance. They pretend generosity. Rachel gives up her own space and solitude to welcome the children and their guides into her own home."

Rachel smiled and turned modestly to the new travelers. "And, yes, of course, Martin and Rebecca are dear friends," she agreed. "During the Great Collapse, the books of the Western Zone were destroyed, as they were in the other areas. When the Evangelical Revolution happened out here, it was all by testimony, by word of mouth. We wanted a real Bible to verify our collective memories. Martin and Rebecca were silent supporters of the revolution and they presented us with a complete copy of the Holy Bible."

"That is amazing," I said slowing. I wondered if I should admit that I had one too. Then I realized that I was past the mountain, through the desert, and in a forbidden zone. If I couldn't trust the people I was with, I was in more trouble than I realized. "I have one," I whispered.

"One?" Rachel questioned. "One what?"

"I own a Bible," I admitted.

"And, so do I," Jason confirmed.

"Two? Two more Bibles have survived?" Ms. Claudette's surprise was evident as her face lit with excitement.

"More than that," Jason offered. "The stash of books in which I found mine has many more bound scriptures."

"This is not the time to discuss a possible sharing of Bibles, since your mission has to be accomplished in a short length of time. Maybe, when all this is over, we can talk about sharing some scripture." Her voice was full of hope.

"And novels, history books, philosophy ... many of them."

"I have spent the last few years in the Library in Capitol City," I joined in. "The books were not destroyed at our facility. Many book lovers simply stored them in the sealed off back recesses of the building. If we can accomplish our mission, you will have more than earned an opportunity to participate in a real *lending library*."

I watched as the children filled themselves with the feast, prepared just for them. As people carried food to and from the kitchen, filling and refilling the serving dishes, I felt a beautiful sense of *enough*. Some fine-china dishes had sterling silver spoons to serve potato salad and mixed fruit. Beside the elegant china and silver display was a sturdy cleaned and stripped tree branch, the children used as a fork to stab an old-fashioned hot dog. It appeared that Rachel Claudette used the tools she owned, not just displayed them like a victor's bounty, or evidence of wealth.

"Thank you, Ma'am," a small one smiled with a tooth-sparse grin. "This is very good. I've never been this full before." His arms were thin and his face gaunt.

"I thank you, young man, for visiting me." Rachel bent down and met the child on his level.

"I bet you get lonely in this big house." The child's eyes scanned the tall ceilings with ornate moldings and center glittering light.

"I would be if children like you didn't come to stay with me for a short while every day," Rachel said.

"Kids come every day?" he gasped. "Are they all claimed-kids like me?"

"Every one of them," Miss Granger informed him.

"Wow! You have saved a lot of lives," he grinned in awe. At the end of the side board were platters of cookies and a giant chocolate cake, which now had a huge hunk carved out of it.

"Yes," Rachel laughed as she saw his longing gaze. "Of course, you can have dessert."

"I've never had anything like that," he gasped.

"Just a small piece then," Miss Granger warned. "It will be very sweet and you aren't used to all the sugar."

As the boy walked away, Mary Granger said, "Many of the first parents don't give treats of any kind to their third child. Sugar is very scarce due to the ban on rich pastries, so they share their finest only with the first two."

As a cherished, only child, I could not believe the cruelty of some first parents. "Don't the children feel profoundly rejected?"

"Indeed, they do, My Lady. See how thin these children are and how gaunt their faces. The opposite is also true, look at Starla over there. She is very overweight. She would sneak into the food storage of her first home and steal food at night, trying to fill the emptiness she felt. In the morning, her first parents would beat her, which made her need to stuff her sadness even more. She is four years old. They had kept her longer than most because they liked to abuse her."

"Please," I begged as I turned my head to the window and the peaceful green garden that grew beyond. "I can't listen to any more."

"I understand," Rachel soothed as she touched my shoulder. "But, Christy, if you don't know, how will you recognize the wickedness of destroying a third-born child?"

"I have seen the evil under Howard Mountain with my own eyes. Those images will be burned in my mind forever," I shuddered as I remembered the ghastly private museum of Alister Bedlam.

"I'm sorry," Rachel apologized. "Now, please have some food. The new parents will be here in about two hours. By noon, they will claim their children. About one o'clock, the army of volunteer C-I board members I have selected will arrive and we can begin. The mission will continue."

My heart leaped within my chest. "We are actually beginning a task some have said cannot be accomplished. I'm as amazed as the rest," I said as anxiety gripped me and tore at my faith. "No, I choose to not be afraid. We will develop a team to canvas the entire country, a country that has its zones sealed. We crossed one zone border and we will, somehow, cross the others. I'm sure of it."

Chapter 19
Still Searching

That same afternoon, Inspector Stoner slowly circled through the streets of Capitol City, trolling for clues to the whereabouts of Lady Christiana and the doctor. Sure, Dr. O'Reilly had helped him when his son was injured, but if the man and his Lady had broken the law by escaping from the Central Zone, he would catch them and see they were prosecuted the same as any law breaker. "Where are you two self-important uppity elites?" he mumbled to himself. "I will have control over this city and that includes you two. I will not be stopped."

He wound around the tree lined streets of Oakwood, the neighborhood in which Christiana's grandparents live. The beautiful old Victorian homes glared at him from the other side of the sidewalk. "Why do two old people, like Oliver and Constance Richly, occupy a large four-bedroom home all alone?" He coasted in front of the white house with the broad veranda, but no one stirred. The icy streets were glassy, which only made him grumble more.

"I would have thought the special-class would have had their roads cleared by this hour of the day."

The winter had been a particularly harsh one. A child from a house two doors down slid across the sidewalk like an ice skater on a pond.

"Hey you, kid," Stoner bellowed. "Why aren't you in school?"

The boy nearly lost his footing when the Inspector yelled. "It's still Gifting holiday," the child said as he froze to the spot.

"Go home," Stoner ordered.

"Mother said I could get some fresh air," the child protested. When Stoner glared him down, he turned to go in.

"Hey, kid," he called out as an afterthought. "Have you seen anybody around this house today?" he motioned toward the Richly home.

"No sir. No one is allowed to hang around in this neighborhood." He squinted at the Chief of the Blue Guard. "You just loitering, Mister?"

"What?" Stoner yelled and reached for the door handle.

"Anything wrong?" Oliver Richly asked as he walked out onto the porch. "So, we meet again, Inspector." He eyed the strata car and the man who commanded a vise like grip on the people of Capitol City.

"Nothing wrong. It seems that your granddaughter and the doctor are missing. Do you know where they are?" Stoner masked his nasty attitude with a vile-sweet smile.

"Of course, ... in general," Oliver answered cautiously. "Dr. O'Reilly is taking a sabbatical while he studies a new procedure—"

"What *procedure* is so important he would be away from his patients?"

"I don't know what he is studying. The doctor is a professional who can take care of himself."

"And Lady Applewait? Is she studying something too?" Stoner grinned, the smirk of one who believes he has trapped another.

"Not that I know of. Her master's thesis has been done for a long time."

"Then, where is she?" Stoner screamed.

"She doesn't live here, Inspector. She did express an interest in the history of the Great Collapse and the social changes in the aftermath of that tragedy."

"What changes would that be?" Stoner questioned.

"Well, now that would defeat her need to write the book. If she told it all before the writing, she wouldn't have to do the telling," Sir Richly said with a smile.

"You are required to tell me where she is," the Inspector growled as he jerked the door open and placed one foot on the snowy ground.

Oliver folded his arms across his chest and rubbed them. "It's getting cold out here. I can tell you this. Christy could be at her work in the library ... she would have the resources there to begin her research. Then, there's her parents' home, her own apartment, the little coffee shop she enjoys, and the many new friends she has been making lately."

"You will get me a list of all her acquaintances, immediately," Stoner gritted his teeth.

"I will do no such thing, Inspector. The Council of Twelve and those who will ascend to one of those positions, cannot be harassed, followed or investigated." He rubbed his arms a bit more and then added, "I think I'll go back in, Inspector. It's cold, and I have wasted enough of my time out here." Sir Richly turned and went back inside, leaving the inspector to shout at the wind.

"Something wrong, Inspector?" Guardsman Braxton said as he pulled his strata car along beside the chief's.

"Not with me, Mister!" he shouted. "But there is everything wrong with these people who believe they do not have to follow the same rules as the rest of us."

"But, Sir," Tayton stumbled cautiously into the line of verbal fire, "they don't have to follow every rule. Special ordinances are in place to protect them and their privacy as well. They can't be vulnerable to possible blackmail if everyone had access to their private information."

"You know too much, Mr. Braxton," Stoner bellowed as he started back to the car. Then he whipped around, "But, do you know where she is?" he screamed.

"Well, I saw her late last evening when she came into Indian River Apartments," he lied. He maintained a sober face and added,

"But, I believe she was gone by the time I left this morning." He continued to fabricate a story that would stall Stoner a little longer.

"You saw her?" Stoner smiled a sickening smile.

Braxton looked corruption in the eyes and did not flinch. "Yes, Sir, I am sure she is safe, if that's your concern. I will be happy to continue my surveillance assignment."

"Oh, you would? You'd be happy? Well now ... isn't that nice," he sneered as he jerked open the door and got back in his car. He clenched the wheel with fists of steel and gunned the engine. The rear tires spun and swerved on the ice, sending broken, frozen puddle shards into the air like an explosion of shrapnel.

Chapter 20
Chalky Boone in Pursuit

5 p.m. - Stoner's Office

"Boone!" The Chief Inspector yelled from his office in the direction of the squad room.

"Ward," Chalky responded with the tone of someone who has repeated herself many times. "If you will use the communication devise, I can hear you and you can save your voice."

"There's nothing wrong with my voice," he bellowed.

"I can hear that," she said as she closed the door behind her.

"I want you to go on a ... special mission."

"Of course," she agreed.

"I want you to go into the Western Zone ... and see if you can get a lead on Miss Applewait," he said her name with distain. "Braxton said he saw her but I think he's wrong. Someone must be impersonating her. I can feel it in my bones. She's no longer in this zone."

"Inspector, you know I follow your orders but ... it is forbidden to ... stalk a Legacy Citizen, especially one who is more likely than others to rise to a seat of authority. You heard the cheers and adoration of the crowd the other evening, Gifting Day Night. You can't—"

"I'm not going to, Boone. You are," he sneered defiantly.

"But Inspector—"

"You will follow that subversive brat. It may be illegal to stalk a Legacy," he screamed until the veins in his neck bulged, "but a sworn officer of the law can follow, in hot pursuit, someone as dangerous as one who would overthrow the government. If Braxton said he saw someone trying to pass as Lady Applewait, then maybe she's in danger. We need to protect her."

"Sir, where will I find her? The Western Zone is huge," she continued to protest.

"Boone, you will find someone who will know something. I can feel it," he said with certainty. He walked behind his desk and opened the drawer. Here," he said as he handed her a small packet.

"What's this?"

"That is your travel permit, the blue one is a border crossing authorization, and the yellow one is a permit to carry one of the new sting-ray laser wands you can conceal in the open, right in your pocket like a writing pen."

"But Ward—"

Stoner's eyes grew narrow and his jaw was tight and clenched. "I better not hear one more word out of you, except, 'Yes, Sir.' I'm not saying it will be easy. You may not find a lead at all if she isn't there, but if I find out she has been in the Western Zone all this time and you haven't at least found a lead, you will be collecting fairs at a transit stop."

Chalky Boone looked at the man she had always respected. Suddenly she saw the bitter shell of the person he used to be. He had turned into someone else, a stranger. Like in the death of an honored statesman, Ward Stoner's flag had slipped on its mast.

Chapter 21
The C-I Board

5 p.m. - In the Western Zone

"In here," Rachel Claudette directed. She had led us past the grand entry, through massive, solid wood double doors and into an office of mahogany paneling, leather chairs, and the scent of peppermint. Rachel pointed to the large jar of wrapped red and white striped candy. "I try to keep a treat in here for the children."

"You are very thoughtful," I said as I took a chair beside Jason around a large conference able. It was good to put my satchel down. Jason and I placed our pouches on the broad polished table.

There was a faint knock on the door and Rachel's assistant entered. "The C-I board is here, Rachel," Kasamar announced. She stepped in and held the door for a group of nine, very different people.

I watched as Rachel introduced each member. A blond man with chiseled jaw and deep blue eyes maneuvered a chair with wheels silently through the door. I was shocked. No handicapped people lived in the Central Zone. The lame entered the portal to the never-ending-sleep immediately after diagnosis of the prolonged disability.

"Friends," Rachel paused as she introduced him to the group. "I would like you to meet Phillip Santiago, a professor of physics at the large Christian University in Berkley."

An echo of "Hellos" followed. Behind the professor eight other members filed in and introduced themselves to our small group.

Annabelle Rodrigues, a judge of the District Court, was a dark beauty with laughing eyes. "I'm pleased to meet you," she smiled. "You are Lady Applewait. We have heard about you."

"How is that possible?" I couldn't believe the story she was telling me.

"The church was praying for you on Sunday. We heard the message of the petitions, carried to the president of your Zone the day after it happened. The Western Zone does not uphold the Length of Days laws. We here die natural deaths. Most live to be one hundred-twenty-five or thirty. They maintain their beloved work as long as their body can do the job."

"A hundred-thirty?" Jason blurted out his surprise.

"Yes, of course. That is our life-expectancy now," Judge Rodrigues said matter-of-factly. "If the Central Zone had not killed their aging treasures, you too would have long life."

The next two people, Faye and Otis Augustine were obviously two of the treasures of whom the judge spoke. "They were both teachers and they retired at age one-hundred," Rachel explained. "They have been wise advisors to many not-for-profit organizations that serve children."

"Happy to meet you two," Faye offered with a strong, clear voice. "You are true patriots and national heroes. We will be happy to do all we can to organize a great citizens' movement to gather all of those signatures."

"Since our Zone doesn't obey the evil law of termination, we will be able to get many signatures and volunteers to cross into the other two zones," said an African-heritage man of mid-life age, about sixty-five.

"As the logistics coordinator of Outreach International, Hermon Lincoln, you would be just the executive to accomplish such a massive drive of people," Rachel agreed wholeheartedly.

Three of the other board members were Chief Zoning Engineer, Deborah Radcliff; author Stephen Seebring; and Young-Life Executive Director, Levi Liu. If nine board members were present, someone was missing.

"Rachel," Kasamar said as she opened the door again. "My father is here. Do you want to prepare the other board members?"

"Thank you. Ask him to wait a moment." She smoothed and stacked a few papers in front of her. "My friends, we have a new, perhaps temporary, board member to replace Shafer Digby who fell and broke his leg and will be out for several months."

"Surely, a mere break wouldn't keep someone down, with the sound wave fusion procedures we have now," Dr. O'Reilly stated.

"True," Mr. Lincoln agreed. "But Shafer is also a world class triathlete. He will have to get back into competition shape. There is an event in a few months."

"I am amazed by all you have accomplished," I admitted. "I feel like such a slacker."

"Indeed, you are not," Steven Seebring bellowed, although I still didn't feel worthy of their praise.

"With your vote and permission," Rachel began cautiously, "I am suggesting that we fill the vacancy while Shafer is out, with ... Raymar Goring."

"How coincidental, I met one of the hollow ones whose name was Raymar," I remembered.

"He is the same," Kasamar said with a cringe to her face and a hesitant voice.

"Raymar Goring is a hollow man." Rachel informed the board.

"A hollow one?" each membered questioned in their own way.

"We encountered him on the journey here," Jason said with a puzzled expression.

"Yes, he has been living in the desert, for the past ten years." Rachel looked at Kasamar and stepped slightly to the side.

"Rachel asked me," Kasamar explained slowly, "if I thought Raymar might be willing to come to the coast and at least meet with you as a whole board."

"Why did you want Raymar?" Judge Rodrigues questioned angrily. "He and his kind have been through the courts more times than anyone can imagine."

"His kind?" I questioned. So far, I hadn't seen a display of discrimination in this loving zone.

"It is not discriminatory to tell the truth," Annabelle snapped.

"No, Judge, it isn't," Rachel assured her. "And, I certainly know why you have informed the board of some of the facts of Raymar's life. It is not discrimination to point out the characteristics of a whole group of people, when it's true. Evil seems to ooze from the Hollow People. Their behaviors are destructive and their history of harming others is legion ... every single one of them ... including Raymar."

"What event happened to all of these people that changed them from being civilized to savage?" Jason asked. I had wondered the same thing but I didn't want to profile a whole group of people.

"The same event was a positive one," Kasamar said and then turned to Rachel. "If I may explain what I understand of them."

"Oh course. Who better to tell their story?"

"When the Evangelical Awakening happened, years ago," she began, "some people didn't accept the beliefs. In fact, some laughed and deliberately chose anything that was in opposition. They became more and more depraved until their soul escaped the evil body in which it lived."

"That was fifty years ago," Steven explained. "And children born to those people were born with no life inside. They breathed and functioned but Life was gone."

"But I think you're wrong, Mr. Seebring," Kasamar protested. "I think they can be reached. I don't think they lost their soul. I believe it hid inside them, away from the horrible experiences the body participated in."

"What do you know about the Hollow People?" Steven questioned.

"A seventeen-year-old Hollow being would sit in the bushes beneath the window of the daughter of his master. There he would listen to the music the girl would play on her piano or her acoustic 723. Sometimes, it was classical and sometimes inspirational. The strains of the music reached inside the boy and rebuilt his soul with the vibrations of the notes. He and the girl secretly married and soon she was pregnant. When she died in childbirth, he abandoned his soul and slipped back into emptiness. Raymar was that boy and the girl was my mother," Kasamar whispered.

"Raymar is your father?" I gasped as I remembered the savage I had met in the desert.

"Yes," she smiled. "Rachel took in a homeless infant and I grew up knowing her as my mother. Raymar would visit me about once a month."

"He had clear rules," Rachel explained. "If he acted out in any way, he would be escorted from the estate and could not return the next month." Rachel spoke with the authority of a protective parent.

"He has moments of clarity," Kasamar insisted.

"What about moments of sanity?" Jason asked.

"He is not insane," she insisted. "He is empty." She smiled as she seemed to remember pleasant times. "Sometimes, I think ... if I had stayed with him, his soul would have returned."

"You couldn't be responsible for your father, Kassie. He was supposed to take care of you ... and he couldn't," Rachel assured her.

"Well, I still don't see what a Hollow one could offer. It would be dangerous to have him around," Judge Rodrigues snipped.

"Statistically, we need him," I chimed in. "I don't pretend to know any of the happenings here. In my library, I have access to the history of the Central Zone since it began. But the history of the other zones was lost when the borders closed one-hundred years ago, prohibiting travel between zones." I thought of Raymar and how he had terrified the serving girl at the diner. But other issues abounded. "Even if we are able to get the signature of every person in the religious majority and those who are in accord with those beliefs, we will still need a small percentage more. The Hollow ones would make up that difference," I concluded.

"Then I say, show him in," Hermon said with resolve.

Rachel nodded to Kasamar. She took a deep breath and opened the office door.

The man who entered was clean and shaven, his hair combed but straggly. His clothes were old and wrinkled like he had used the back of a chair for a closet, but they were clean. He made no eye contact and kept his focus on the floor.

"Raymar," Rachel reached out her hand in friendship, "I'd like you to meet the Board."

Raymar said nothing, but cautiously stuck out his hand in an expression of friendship that seemed awkward to him. The judge sniffed indignantly, but allowed herself to touch the man.

"And, these are our visitors, Raymar," Rachel directed him in Jason and my direction.

"Raymar, I'm happy to meet you," Jason said as he smiled.

"Jason is a physician, Raymar," Kasamar explained. The man looked up and got a glimpse of us.

"Raymar," I soothed as I reached for his hand, then I patted his shoulder with my other hand. "I'm glad to see you are feeling better than when we first met."

His arm started to tremble and his face contorted as I touched him. What was happening? His expression was of pain, but I didn't know why. I took a step forward to steady him, but then everyone jumped to their feet.

"My Lady," Steven gasped.

"I'm okay, thank you. Raymar," I asked while still making physical contact, "am I hurting you?"

"Yes, yes," he cried as tears streamed down his face. I reached out and embraced him. I didn't know why. I just followed the urging of my heart. I could feel the rigid stiffness of his body as it began to relax. Suddenly, his knees started to buckle and I couldn't hold him up. Jason helped ease him into an empty chair but Raymar would not let go of my hands. I knelt on the floor beside him.

Deborah Radcliff and Levi Liu leaped toward him. Jason stepped between them. "Raymar," Jason ordered, "you have to let go of her hands."

"Please ... no," he begged.

I was on the floor at his side and I could see the tears drip from his chin. From within his grasp, I tried to wiggle a finger enough to sooth the back of his hand. As I stroked him, I began singing the only song I knew. "Silent night, holy night," I sang softly. Finally, Raymar looked into my eyes and inhaled a deep gulp of life again and again until he seemed to be full.

His entire countenance changed. The lines in his face softened and turned up. His trembling stopped as he looked deeply into my eyes, and gasped, like one seen for the first time.

"Raymar," I whispered, "God loves you and has been seeking you for a long time."

"Oh," he screamed from the depths of his being as if convicted for all of his crimes, "I am not worthy."

"That's all right, Daddy," Kasamar cried as she bent and wrapped her arms around him. They huddled together for a moment, rocking back and forth.

I took my seat and wiped tears from my eyes and blotted my cheeks. I felt completely drained, like a tea pot, tipped up and poured out of all emotion. Even the judge and fellow skeptics, for that moment, appeared visibly touched by Raymar's coming-alive experience. I wondered about what my eyes had seen. How could a transformation happen like that? Like a wadded-up piece of paper, snatched from the trash and placed in reverse, Raymar unfolded from a life utterly destroyed, to one pristine and pure again.

"Raymar," Rachel interrupted quietly, "thank you for coming. We need your help."

"You?" He looked around the table of impressive people, his eyes wide, then narrow. "You need my help? Why?"

"You are aware of the despicable Length of Days policy, right?"

He looked at Kasamar and back at Rachel with a searching expression on his face. "What policy?"

"Each citizen is allotted a prescribed schedule of life-days. The more value they are to the whole community, the longer their length of days. They even send very young individuals, who provide nothing to the greater good, to the portal of the never–ending-sleep," the Judge made the pronouncement like a sentence of death.

"That is why you have called me here?" Raymar's voice grew hoarse and faint. "You have decided I've lived long enough!" He jumped to his feet, turned right and left, as his eyed flashed like a trapped animal.

"No, Daddy, no!" Kasamar patted his chest to comfort him. "No, we need your help."

"We are a far more compassionate people than those in the Central Zone," Steven assured him. "We are conservative with everything, including the lives of our citizens. We want them to enjoy the most out of their years for as long as they can."

Phillip Santiago smiled and moved his wheelchair back and forth, like a little dance. He smiled reassuringly. "If they were going to get rid of you, my friend, they would have gotten rid of me a long time ago."

"You are an important link to the success of our efforts, Raymar," Rachel spoke quickly. "I told you, we need you and I meant it." She sat back in her comfortable chair like she had used all of her arguments.

"How? Why?"

"We are going to canvass the entire Western Zone," Jason began. "To be more truthful, we need you and many more of the people out here, to contact others and get them to sign a paper that says you all agree that the Length of Days law must be abolished, overthrown," Jason quickly added.

"We hope most of the population will agree with us and sign the petition. But we need many more signatures ... and that means the Hollow People," Rachel explained.

Otis Augustine eyed the man with a piercing gaze. "I'm not a young man," he began, his head lowered. "I have been around the empty ones my whole life. I have never seen them amount to anything. But you, Sir, I must admit ... I don't know what to make of you."

Faye looked him over carefully, "Raymar Goring, you are a puzzle. We are supposed to vote on whether to include someone from the belly of the earth into our small group. To my knowledge, you people have lived in the mountain caves for decades. You come out at night and steal animals like a stalking fox. You attack anyone you think might have something you want. Am I correct?"

"Yes, Ma'am, but is it fair to profile a single example of a group? That is discrimination." Raymar protested.

"When I see a wolf near the hen house, I don't expect the wolf to act like a rabbit. I know it will act like a wolf. I get out my weapon and eliminate it," Otis stated logically.

"But what if the animal has been mistaken for a wolf?" Raymar asked.

"Hollow people do not have your logic, Sir," Otis conceded. "What makes you think you are hollow?"

"My parents were the rejected of man—their parents and their parents. That makes me one of them. That is the way it is."

"But your daughter is not," I smiled at Kasamar. "She is a lovely, educated woman. If my vote counts, I say Raymar is on the Board. He will be part of the canvasing team."

"But—" Judge Rodrigues began.

"And ... I would think some of you may feel better if Kasamar came with us and escorted Raymar around a world he has never experienced. We will see who we have here when he has new clothes and a haircut." I was sure his presence on the Board, and out in the field, would be a blessing to us and to him.

Rachel Claudette stood decisively. "Are we ready for the vote?"

Chapter 22
Boone in the West

Friday - December 30, 2112

Chalky Boone searched the ground below the chopper cruiser. The new silent-ride motors that turned the blades muffled the old sound of the blades above the cab. Still, the cab doors were open so she could lean out and view the space below. The rushing wind was loud. "I see nothing," she hollered as she turned toward the passenger in the back seat.

"I don't see anything but sand out the other side either, Lieutenant." Daniel Washington continued to stretch out the open door. He steadied his reach by holding on to the strap above the door. "We'll be out of the desert soon," he yelled.

"What?" Boone shouted. She smiled as she thought of Ward Stoner and his unwillingness to use the office communication device. She had tried to talk Stoner out of sending Daniel with her. The whole mission was distasteful to her. Following a Legacy Citizen was illegal.

"She is more than a fancy Legacy brat," the Chief had bellowed. "She is breaking the law if she has left the zone. I can feel it inside; it's gnawing at my innards. That Council of Elders wannabe thinks she's above the law." His jaw grew tight and strained. "I am the law! She will not cross me!"

"If she has left the zone," Chalky had said, "she has already crossed you. She's crossed the entire boundary." Boone felt a smirk on her lips and turned away from him. "But why do I have to take Washington with me? I don't trust him."

But that didn't faze Ward Stoner. Daniel Washington was in the chopper cruiser with her. He was the most dangerous Blue Shirt she had ever encountered ... and that's why he was along. While she searched for Lady Applewait and the doctor, he would break bones all around her to see that she got the answers she needed.

"We are entering the city's airspace," the pilot announced. "Close all doors. I will be receiving landing instructions."

They said nothing but sealed up the cab. The silence was louder than the wind. Her mind whirled like the blades. Daniel was brutal and charged many times. She had lost count of the offences. Sometimes reprimanded, his greatest punishment was a week's suspension ... with pay.

One day last summer, Washington dragged a woman into the station. "Help me!" she had pleaded. Boone was with the Inspector in his office at the time. Stoner didn't even look up.

Through the window in the office, Boone saw the woman fall to the floor. As she struggled to get up, the Blue Shirt terror kicked her in the side and then yanked her up by the same shoulder. "Ward," Boone yelled as she jumped to her feet, "that officer just accosted a woman." She started toward the door.

"Boone, mind your own business!" Stoner growled.

"Sir!" She couldn't understand why no one had come to the woman's rescue.

"All of my Blue Guards know the rules, and politeness is not one of them. Sit down."

She lost another measure of respect for Stoner that day. She lost even more respect for herself. She also did nothing. Now, Washington was to accompany her to the Western Zone, but this time he was under her authority. Would she have the steely backbone to keep him under control?

Chapter 23

Simza Bihari

Saturday - December 31, 2112

"Thank you for coming," A woman in a long shaysilk dress with butterfly sleeves said as she greeted Jason and me at the entrance to the huge church, but it wasn't Sunday morning.

"We are very thankful that you were able to contact and gather all the clergy so fast," I said and shook her hand with eager appreciation. "I'm sure those of the Black Robes would have been busy with their congregations. This evening is New Year's Eve, and I hope we haven't kept anyone from their celebration."

She leaned in closer and whispered, "There is a rumor that you have been followed."

"By whom?"

"A representative of the Blue Guard and her enforcer."

Shaken, I questioned, "What will we do? How had they known where to look for us?"

"They may have heard about the gathering of the Black Robes," Rev. Grace Small suggested. "It will be important for you to be able to speak but not recognized. Come with me. I have something for you to change into, a costume of sorts." She led Jason and me quickly into a small room beside the chancel. It had built-in closets all along the eastern wall. She opened one of the many doors and withdrew a garment. "Here you are," she said as she handed me a hanger with an interesting dress on it.

I took it and inspected the design. "Grace, this is something I've never seen before."

"I would think not. This is a Roma transformational dress."

"Gypsy?"

"You know of the Romani?"

"The traveling costume Rebecca Spires gave me was Romani but this looks nothing like that one, well maybe the lines are similar," I noticed as I held the outfit in my hands. The skirt was very full and flowed like a ballet costume. It had a high collared and long, tight sleeves.

"The clergy will be ready for us in a minute." She turned to Jason. "Doctor, I have a vestment for you. Hope you don't mind being a spiritual leader for a little while."

"I can think of worst jobs to do," he laughed as he put his right arm through the sleeve.

"You look very reverent, Sir," I teased. I looked at the skirt and top Grace had given me. "Turn your back, Jason. I think I'd better step out of what I am wearing." I unfastened the bright skirt and stepped out of it, then slipped into the long black silky matching skirt to the black, jeweled blouse. The top had a small capped hood attached.

"Now Christy, I want you to have an open mind." Pastor Small was cautious with her choice of words and I wondered why. "This veil is worn with the mourning clothes because if the widow goes out and doesn't wear it, it is said she will be shunned for up to a year as a provocative woman." She held the veil out for me. "Do you want to affix it yourself or shall I?"

"Please, I would appreciate your help."

"Two little buttons are on the hood," she said as she walked around and placed it on my head. "There they are." She draped the shimmering, sheer veil over my face below my eyes and let it drop to below my chin. Gypsy beads accented the hood and dangled along the bottom of the band below my mouth.

"Christy," Jason started to say then pulled back as he glanced over at Grace.

Rev. Small smiled softly. "I will leave you two alone for a moment. I know what danger you're in. I can only tell you that God will be with you. Perhaps you will want to decide if you are going to go through with this meeting. If you want to continue, we need to begin."

Jason smiled and waited for Grace to leave. "Christy, before we go out there, I want you to know that you are beautiful beyond words. The safe physician in me says we should stop this dangerous mission and slip back into Capitol City in the dark. We can resume our lives just as they were when we left—"

"No Jason, we left a life in which my grandparents would be exterminated soon." I looked at him, searching for the meaning under his words. I couldn't believe I was hearing what he was saying.

He placed his finger over my mouth and smiled. "I know. But I hadn't finished. I started to say, that I know we cannot walk away from this. We ... you are called to such a time as this to follow the leading of the Lord and let our people live. And—"

"Oh Jason," I fell into his arms.

"And ... I want you to know how much I love you. I love you, My Sweet Lady." He held me close and I could feel the beating of his heart.

"Thank you all for coming." I heard Grace speak into the voice enhancer in the huge auditorium style sanctuary. "I am thankful to God that you were all able to make travel arrangements on such short notice. The church where Fanny Adams preached is open to everyone."

"We had better get out there," I said as we hurried out the door that led to the side entrance of the chancel. I slipped inside and slid onto one of the two large pulpit chairs. Jason followed.

Grace turned and gestured to me with a sweep of her hand. "I will turn the pulpit over to Mrs. Simza Bihari. She is a Romani and a real joy to us all. Like Pastor Adams taught us, 'Listen with your heart and the heart of God will draw near.'"

The gathered people of the cloth applauded me as I rose and came to the lectern. I would speak, but, what if someone from the Central Zone was present? Would they recognize me?

"Thank you so much," I said with a feigned raspy voice. "I hope you will all be able to hear me. I apologize for my laryngitis."

People smiled and nodded in understanding. I watched as they settled back in their seats.

"I am here this evening to present a great need—a need that affects the entire country. As you know, some zones do not obey the Length of Days Law, just as you do not here in the Western Zone. There is at least one sector that does."

A murmur rose up in the crowd. I heard whispers of, "What? How can it be?" One of the clergy jumped to his feet in protest. "That despicable law was overturned years ago."

"No, Sir," I corrected hoarsely. "It was never abolished. The people of the Western Zone simply did not obey it. But, our brothers and sisters in the other zones still must live under that evil law."

"All laws are to be obeyed, are they not?" a woman stood up in the back and spoke out critically. "Rev. Julius said that we must obey all laws. Are you saying he was wrong? His teachings are truth," she stated emphatically. "Do you know how dangerous it is to speak against The One?"

"Yes, Ma'am, I understand. We are not denouncing Julius's teachings. We are bringing facts into light about an evil that is still enforced in other sectors. You in the West have been much more compassionate and faithful to the teachings of love, and did away with that law. Laws are intended to protect the people," I said as I tried to maintain my masquerade of one who could barely speak. It was harder now as I experienced gripping fear. I recognized the philosophy of the woman even though we had never met. She was one who belonged to those who believe that they have captured the entire mind of God. Only they know the truth. I couldn't show fear. Fear would have undone me.

"Our laws were changed about one-hundred years ago," I explained. "They no longer reflected the protections that citizens benefited from for so long. We, as a people, are responsible for re-writing laws that are detrimental to the citizens."

Rev. Small came to the lectern and leaned into the enhancer, "Thank you for the question. Those of us who have been clergy for many years know that this body has discussed this law over and over and tried to determine what we could do to over-throw it. We had agreed it needed abolishing, but we didn't know how. Mrs. Bihari has come to me with a solution."

"Will Mrs. Bihari remove her veil? I believe we could hear her better," a stranger in the back asked.

"I beg your pardon, Miss ...?"

"Boone, Chalky Boone. I'm not from here in town."

"I would think not," Grace gasped. "If you were from anywhere in the Western Zone, you would know that a Romani widow woman must hide her face in respect for the death of her husband. If she doesn't, a year of shunning would be her fate. I know you wouldn't want that to happen to Mrs. Bihari. You may sit down and listen, or you may leave. You can make an appointment with my assistant for some time in the next few days. I will be happy to talk with you about the matter at that time."

The woman sat down beside a tall muscular man who seemed foreign to a house of worship. He hadn't removed his hat and his expression was taut and angry. I choked up inside. If these two were from Capitol City, the Central Zone, they would indeed have found the building and its sacred enhancements offensive. They had banned all religious expression and experience a hundred years ago in the Central Zone. But I knew my silence was not possible. Hadn't Silas risked his life by revealing the despicable furnaces under Howard Mountain? I looked Boone in the eyes, squared my shoulders and began.

"We are here to start the process of liberating all of our people from extermination in the furnaces that have burned for one-hundred years. Their flames have never gone out."

I scanned the faces of the good people in front of me. I avoided making eye contact with Boone and her companion. "You, here in the

Western Zone, have not adhered to that law, but it is still enforced in the Central Zone, the Mid-western and the Eastern Zones. I'm here to ask you to inform the people of your congregations of a petition we are circulating. We are gathering life-saving signatures." I watched the expressions on the people's faces. They were intent, but they nodded and followed my plea.

"With the proper number of signatures, this petition will permit a Citizen's Referendum to be placed on the ballot at the next election."

"What is a referendum?" One of the clergy in the front of the room asked.

I was glad for the question. I knew they were processing my message. "A Referendum is like a Congressional Bill, but in this case, citizens by-pass Congress and write the bill themselves."

The people of the cloth were following every word. "After your people have signed the document," I continued, "perhaps they will join us. They can canvass their neighborhoods for anyone who may not have been in church or who aren't church goers. We want to make sure we don't miss even a handful of adults. Our efforts are vital to the lives of everyone."

"I cannot believe you people would undermine the laws of our country," Boone snapped.

"We decide what is best for us, Miss," a man mid-way back snapped back at Boone.

"I thought all of you pray and ask your God to tell you what is best," the Blue Guard woman mocked.

"Many do. God has revealed Himself to some of us," the man smiled arrogantly. "Jesus said only a few will be saved. I am one, but I'm sorry to say, you are not." He folded his arms and sat back, content with his self-serving beliefs.

"You are defaming the body of Christ," another clergyman shouted and pointed his finger back at the self-proclaimed righteous one.

"I am sure these would be good discussions for another time," I said as I felt my hands tremble. "For today's gathering, we need to stick to the topic of the Length of Days law. I'm afraid I won't have a voice left very quickly." I had to change the topic without raising suspicion. I feared that panic would overtake me like the waves of the western ocean and totally take me under.

I began again, "The Length of Days law was never part of the founding fathers' plan for a free people. We have received word from the Central Zone that they terminate each person before the time of their natural passing. Each one is assigned a prescribed Length of Days for their lives, depending on their contribution to society."

The people shifted restlessly with anger and repulsion, their faces drawn up in torment and grief. While in the back, the stranger with Boone smiled a crooked smile, crossed his arms, and settled in with satisfaction.

I ignored the man who had spoken arrogantly and continued. "We have also been told that in the Central Zone, the people have already gathered signatures. They collected them in secret, over time, and were enough to fulfill the quota for that sector. They delivered them to President Alexander's home on Christmas Day eve, or Gifting Day as they call it. We now need full petitions from this Zone, as well as the other two, in order to make the referendum happen."

I heard eager responses. "Yes, we can do it." But there were also murmurs and gossip back and forth about whom does she think she is?

"You ask who I am. I am a woman who has come to speak truth to lies. Will you help our effort?" Most agreed, and those that didn't, listened.

I paused. What I would ask next was risky. I needed people who would be willing to break the law. "Some of your number, or members of your churches, could assist us as we cross the borders into the other zones." I let that reality settle a moment. "You, my friends, are already an enormous body of people who don't have to be convinced of the need for the referendum. You have a reverence for life by virtue of your faith. To make it official ... shortly, Grace will lead you in a vote to record your cooperation in this matter. Time is important. The Central Zone has only a two-year moratorium on exterminations. The collection of signatures here in the Western Zone should go fast, since you are a God-loving people. You value life. The citizens of the Central Zone have never heard of God. Still, they gathered the signatures methodically over time. We don't know what to expect in the other two sectors."

"How do you know all of this, Mrs. Bihari?" Boone asked with a firm, angry tone.

"For the safety of those in the Central Zone, I can't reveal that information," I answered and hoped that she would believe me and cease the questions that could unveil my true identity.

"Have you heard of Lady Christiana Applewait," Boone dug deeper.

"Who is she?" I asked, denying my own existence.

"She is a Legacy Citizen from the Central Zone who had started all of this sedition," she insisted angrily. "If you know her whereabouts, you are aiding a fugitive," she shouted.

Some who were present shouted, "Sit down." Others insisted, "Listen to Mrs. Bihari."

I coughed and actually could not speak for a moment. With most of my face covered, I saw a movement from the corner of my eye and assumed that Grace or Jason had come to my rescue. I was shocked when I saw who had been sensitive to my need. It was Raymar Goring.

"Masters," Raymar began and the entire fellowship of pastors let out a unified gasp. His knees visibly buckled and he grabbed the lectern. "Friends," he began again, "I am not worthy to come before this group ..."

Whispers and uneasiness rose up among those present. Suddenly, a distinguished man with gray hair and beard stood up. "Are you not a Hollow Man?"

"I'm ..." Raymar fumbled and stumbled with his words.

"Do you not have a brand of 'H' on your forehead, under your hair line?"

Raymar's face distorted in anguish. His mouth quivered as he appeared to be trying desperately to control himself. Then, he turned his face from the crowd and I saw that it was not anger he was trying to suppress. A tear slipped down his cheek. Kasamar started to stand up but Raymar put up his hand.

"Fear does cruel things sometimes," Grace spoke softly as she leaned into the podium, but conviction was in the tone of her voice.

"Yes," Raymar admitted as he slowly lifted the hair from his forehead. "I was branded as an infant. My entire life I believed I was not fully human, that I was an outcast, a man empty of all goodness and positive attributes, a Hollow One. When I was a very young man, I met the most amazing girl. She taught me to read and write and do my numbers. She taught and educated me, and filled me with love. Yes ... I was a Hollow Man. When she died, all of that love drained out of me, except for one day each month when love returned." He swallowed hard. "Recently, I met Simza Bihari," he turned and bowed slightly in my direction. "Simza means joy. Just having her eyes meet mine, and knowing she really sees me, has brought joy to my heart. When asked to help in this effort, I said, yes!"

"What can you do?" Boone asked with an indignant tone. "You should be dead. Now you claim to have come alive by a glance from a gypsy woman? Please, do not insult me."

Raymar's expression remained calm. His tone was convicting. "Ma'am, pardon me, but you insult yourself. I am alive, because the same people who considered me—and those like me—to be the walking dead, chose not to put us down. They are good people, a misinformed and ill-educated people concerning those in my class, but good in their souls. I will be honored to bring the Hollow People together and invite them to sign our petition."

"Sign the petition?" Several snorted in disbelief. One woman snickered, "They can neither read nor write. Will you have them make an 'X' on the paper?"

The crowd erupted in a combination of giggles and angry protests. I could see they had no tolerance for this man. I looked at Kasamar, but she was just smiling and remained calm. She seemed to be in prayer.

"But they do," Raymar protested. "They read because I taught them. In a cave in a high elevation, where moisture cannot damage the paper, we have a huge library of books I have acquired over many years. I have read every one of them."

"Did you steal them? Where did you get them?" People shouted from all corners of the auditorium.

Kasamar could not hold herself any longer. "Rachel Claudette gave him the books," she said as she stepped forward.

"Rachel Claudette? How does she know this Hollow Man?" some questioned.

Grace moved to the enhancer. "These are all very good questions. I am so glad you are asking them now, rather than sharing your doubts in small groups after the meeting."

I smiled to myself but said nothing out loud. *Where I come from, no one speaks up and certainly doesn't gossip.*

Grace leaned in closer to the podium. "We have invited Raymar to participate in our critical endeavor, because he is a good man, a man of integrity. Despised and rejected, he did not turn his grief on others. Instead, he educated everyone he knew to read and write. Yes, indeed, these folks can write their own name." Grace explained with firm conviction. "He has read many books. Have any of you enjoyed the novels of Robert Gross?"

Robert Gross? I hadn't heard of him. He must have been a novelist in the last one-hundred years. I knew I hadn't read his works. Since there is no exchange of culture between the zones, I couldn't have heard about him. But, most of those present had read the books. Many smiled and nodded. Some whispered among themselves. Kasamar smiled in agreement.

"My dear friends," Grace said, "I would like you to meet the tender and gifted writer, who only comes alive in the pages of his novels, Robert Gross—Raymar Goring." Grace opened her arms to the gentle shadow that had lived among them all along in the pages of the books they read.

Kasamar's face grew fluid and elastic as she tried to control the flood of emotions that threatened to drown her. "Daddy," she whispered.

The people sank back in their seats, their shoulders drooped with emotion. The room grew completely silent.

Raymar leaned into the enhancer and opened his mouth, but nothing came out but the silence of his life. He cleared his throat and began again. "I know you will not call me friend. And, you won't see me when we pass on the streets. But I want you to know that I have a little less hollowness when I see you laugh with your children or embrace a friend. All I ask of you is the opportunity to serve you, to serve all of us. You need the Hollow Man vote. I can get that for you."

The entire body of clergy rose to their feet. Applause and smiles and cheers burst forth. Some were slow to rise but quickly became infected with the enthusiasm. Raymar Goring was seen.

Chapter 24
Late Saturday Evening

10:00 p.m. - New Year's Eve 2112

Jason and I stayed up late. "Isn't it amazing to walk in the evening on the last day of the year and feel the warmth on your face? The climate of the Western Zone could grow on me," I said as I slipped my hand in his.

Some of our group were planning to stay up well into the night to celebrate the New Year—2113. We had had a long day so Grace Small invited us to stay with her and her husband. Our walk in the garden would be celebration enough. It would be a quiet together time, something we had not had in recent weeks. Although surrounded by others most of the time, it felt like it was just the two of us against the world. We were now alone in a crowded world.

"The backyard garden is beautiful," Jason agreed.

I ran my fingers over the graceful wrought iron poles of the accent lamps that lit the flower clusters and fountain. The iron felt soft and dimpled at the same time. "Just look at that fantastic rock wall around the entire back yard. It looks like it was built out of field stone." The irregularly shaped round rocks varied in tones of rose and beige and held together with mortar. "I feel safer in here than I have felt in days."

"I wish I could have protected you more," he whispered.

"That's your wonderful male strength pushing through," I giggled.

"I'm sorry if I have offended you," he apologized as he came around in front of me and took both of my hands in his. "I have learned you can take care of yourself."

"Offended me? No, Jason. I like your strength. Men are protectors and women are nurturers," I quickly added. "That was amazingly planned. It's not offensive. We were intended to work together, with equal strength in two areas that make a whole."

"What is so sad ... the people of the Central Zone have been drugged out of the very aspects that make them male and female," Jason reminded me.

"Well, I am very happy that you're a true male. I feel safe when I'm with you." I hugged him again.

He whispered, "And I love your leadership and your closeness to the heart of God before you knew his name. If you were President, I would love you and want you to be safe."

I paused and listened again to what I had dismissed as foolishness. We were alone in the garden. I knew we were. But, "I hear sometime ... movement ... over there." I pointed to the far, dark corner of the yard.

We listened together. "I hear it," he whispered so low I nearly didn't hear him. "Stand very still."

That was not possible. I took a step forward and folded myself into his warm arms. I strained to hear what had to be there ... but what?

My mind raced into all the dark corners of fear I had experienced over the last few weeks. Would we ever be safe again?

Then I saw them ... two shinning eyes stared at us from the bushes in the corner of the walled garden. Who was there? He must have known I saw him. We were locked—eye to eye. But there was something wrong. The eyes were a frightening yellow. I thought of the evil beings in some of the old thriller books I had read to take my mind off my master's thesis. I frightened myself there in the lonely back room of the old library, but the books were too exciting to put down. There in the garden, my heart pounded as I gripped Jason even harder.

"I see it too," he whispered in my ear, so close I felt his warm breath on my cheek. "Stand very still. Maybe it will go away."

"What is it?" I couldn't see anything but the eyes.

Slowly, two rhythmic upper shoulder blades shifted and stalked gracefully, menacingly out of the darkness. His full mane blew gently as he moved, step by step closer to us. Suddenly, he threw his head back and roared in a deep tone of dominance. I squeezed my eyes closed and prayed for deliverance. The beautiful rock wall that bordered the entire garden also made it totally closed, sealing us in with the beast.

The warm breeze of the evening stirred the faint aroma of blossoms into the night air and mixed with the musky scent of the wild animal. Why did I smell flowers when I was clearly in immediate danger? Then I caught a strong whiff of petals again and let the aroma relax my body and sooth my mind. A warm wash of peace flowed over me.

In front of us, a lion lay down with his paws stretched out in front of him and roared again a fierce sound—loud and blood curdling. Then ... there was an explosion and the lion dropped his head on the ground. I gasped. Even the sound of my own frightened voice terrified me.

Suddenly the back door squeaked and I caught a glimpse of Grace just as she was lowering the rifle from her shoulder. "Sorry," she said as she walked out and inspected the cat.

"You all right?" Alfred called from the house as he came out into the garden. "What about you?" he asked Jason and me. "You two okay?" He looked down at the lion, spread out on the manicured back lawn. "Another one of those wild beasts the do-gooders set free."

"Is he dead?" I asked as I inched closer to the huge animal.

"No. I got him with a tranquillizer dart," Grace said.

"I called the wild game patrol as I grabbed the rifle," Grace stated matter-of-factly. "They'll be here in a few minutes."

"Wild game patrol?" I asked. My voice was still shaking from the experience of coming eye-to-eye with the beast king.

"The zone had to expand their animal control department to cover these wild animals that are still loose."

I walked nearer and bent toward the cat. "Can I touch him?"

"He'll be out for a while. Sure, if you want to," Alfred said.

I reached out my hand cautiously and touched his coarse mane. He felt differently than I thought he would. I expected him to feel like my soft little kitten at home and laughed to myself.

"And the lion will lie down with the lamb," Grace recited and walked back into the house.

Chapter 25
Sunday across the Western Zone

Sunday - January 1, 2113

At 7 a.m. the next morning, I woke up in one of Small's guest rooms. It was Sunday morning and the church service would start in two hours. I wondered if Jason was up yet. I got up and went into the adjoining bath, took off the night shirt Grace had loaned me and turned on the water in the wet area. The water felt soothing and awakening.

Grace had told us what to expect during the service. Since we didn't know if Chalky Boone and the animal that was with her were still in town, we all thought I had better go as Simza Bihari. The veil would provide a sort of mask. Jason would have to reprise his role as the good pastor.

In the long black costume, I left the room with the veil in my hand. As I walked down the steps, I liked the swirl of silk on my legs. There were stripes of satin ribbon running through it and it felt elegantly modest.

"You look beautiful as always," Jason whispered as we walked down the stairs together. He winked and put his arm around my waist as we entered the kitchen.

"Thank you, Reverend. Make sure your motives are pure," I laughed. Then I blushed when I saw Grace smile broadly.

"Don't mind me, you two. We can always use more love around here." She watched us for a moment then added, "Since my son Charlie died last year, there hasn't been nearly enough love on display."

"I see love every time you smile at fellow clergy and those around you," I assured her. "I see love when you interact with Alfred," I added. Grace smiled.

• • • • •

"We gather this day as we do every Sunday, to worship the Lord. Our sermon, however, will be different than most," Pastor Small began. "We will be linking all congregations in the Western Zone, a connection that has not been used in over fifty years, since the time of the Evangelical Awakening. This time, my friends, we are embarking on a great crusade. Our campaign will be to finally over-throw the despicable Length of Days law." She paused and addressed a man in the front row. "Sam."

Sam rose quickly and pushed a button that brought down an old-style giant screen used at sporting events and huge gatherings. It seemed appropriate in the arena turned church. I had seen pictures of Jumbotrons like this in the magazines I had found in the library. He gave her a hand-held-distance-unit and clicked it on.

Rev. Small pointed the HHD unit at the screen and a series of nine smaller screens appeared—three across and three down. "Good Sabbath to all the millions of you who are connected this morning." She tapped the HHD surface again and hundreds of smaller screens flashed in front of us, one after another in clusters of twelve. "It has been many years since this system has been used, and we thank the wise ones before us who kept it in working order. And now, we are using it for a great mission for humanity's sake, for the glory of God and our reverence for Life itself." Grace faced the screen and turned to acknowledge those in her own congregation. "The Length of Days law is still enforced in the Central Zone, and we believe it is in place in the Mid-Eastern and Eastern Zones as well."

"Pardon me," a voice came over the 'tron. Immediately, the screen filled with the image of a man of ancient far-eastern linage. "I do not mean to interrupt, but I must."

"No, Sir. That is why we are using this form of communication this morning, and not just sending out a message. Please continue and God bless you, my Brother."

"I am sorry, but I find it hard to believe that this evil law could still be enforced," he continued.

"I have some visitors here who may be able to detail our grave need." Grace motioned to me as I sat in the front row. "Friends, I would like you to meet Mrs. Simza Bihari."

I was worried that the woman named Boone and the man with her might be in the audience. Still, I believed that God had called me to this cause, and he would give me the words and protection. I had worn the veil to cover my appearance.

"Good morning to all of you in every sector of this zone. I am here with praises for your love of one another, the grandparents whom you cherish, the infirmed, the young ... you value them all and hold life in reverence."

There was an uneasy stir as Raymar and Kasamar entered through the side door and took seats on the front row. The people seemed to recognize Raymar but, how could they? Then I looked at the screen with Raymar's picture displayed in an image ten feet tall. They could see the brand on his forehead when his hair blew back slightly as he walked.

"I'm glad you were able to get here," I said to the father and his daughter. Then to the people assembled there I added, "Please welcome our dear friends from the C-I Board who have just arrived." I put my hands together to honor their presence.

The congregation relaxed, so I began again. "I have information from a Judge in the Central Zone, who attests to the validity of our position. I have a copy of the stay that Judge Brunner signed on December 25 that put a ban on exterminations for two years. In that length of time, we—you and I—will spread out across this country and get the signatures of all of our citizens. A signature on the petition means that you agree that a referendum should be placed on the voting ballot at the next election." I paused and let the daring plan catch up to them. "A Referendum is a citizens' bill that does not originate in congress and yet it becomes a law." Some of the people nodded and others stirred uncomfortably. Did these people understand the gravity of our situation?

I looked into the eyes of those gathered there and began again. "An underground group in the Central Zone has already secured enough signatures that the referendum will be placed on the ballot in that zone, so Judge Brunner has ordered the stay. We have two years, friends, to accomplish this sacred mission. We must secure the signatures of as many citizens in this whole country as possible."

"North California here," a man said and his image filled the screen. "I don't want to appear hateful, but ... why is that Hollow Man present?" Whispers spread around the room and the 'tron seemed to buzz with the chorus of it.

"Thank you for asking. I was just going to introduce the man, Raymar Goring." I stood back and motioned for Raymar to stand. "Thank you, Mr. Goring. Please be seated. Raymar Goring has a Hollow Man brand, I agree. Since we don't see the invisible ones among us, none of us knew that he is truly a self-educated man. And, not only has he read thousands of books himself, he has also taught his friends to read. And ... we need him. You know him as the gifted novelist, Robert Gross."

This time the crowd was louder than before. I was worried they might become out of control, but I had to stay focused. Did they understand what I had just said? Would the people reject him and turn on me as well? Would the Boone woman rise up with borrowed authority and discover my identity? I said nothing about the restless outburst. I merely raised my arms and lifted my eyes to the Lord. Stillness fell over the arena that surprised me and peace filled the room and filtered into my own heart.

I leaned in toward the enhancer. My voice was barely a whispered. "We need Raymar Goring. Believe me; we need him because he can get the Hollow Man signatures and ... because there is no one with more drive, more dedication and more belief in himself ... for one whom absolutely no one has ever believed in ... than Raymar Goring." Raymar sat down with his back straight and his gaze fixed on the proceedings.

I continued my address and focused on the Jumbotron. "We are embarking on a great crusade that will decide if we, as a people with freedom as our heritage, will have the courage to stand up for freedom in our time. We need every one of you to sign the petition. A currier carried copies to your senior clergy late last night. Contact everyone who is not in your sanctuary this morning, members, family, friends, and non-believers. Raymar will enlist a group of his friends to make sure every name is on a petition." I pointed to a stack of petition sheets that we had placed on a pedestal.

"This next part is up to those of you with the strength and determination of our founding patriots, to chart a new course. We need a team that is willing to cross forbidden borders with us, find volunteers in the Mid-Western and Eastern Zones who will blanket their sectors with petitions and get signatures from every living person." The people in the room, and those in the congregations seen on the 'tron, stirred with excitement. "I know that contact outside the area has been completely impossible, but the impossible is possible with God."

I lifted my hands and voice to draw on the Holy Spirit I felt in the room. "I truly believe that many of you have connections outside of the West that you have held close to your heart. I don't know how you have communicated with them and it doesn't matter. But those connections are what you are going to need to make this work. Be brave." The people clapped with a newly ignited energy.

"Today is the start of a new year. We begin again! Be steadfast. Take courage. You have lived your whole lives for this moment. The time is now! This is the start of a fresh celebration of Life in our country and you are charged with the blessed task of making it happen!"

Except for the sound of tears, there was silence. From the Jumbotron came a sound, a song, from one person in a congregation hundreds of miles away and beamed into the arena like a whisper of the heart. "I have decided to follow Jesus. I have decided to follow Jesus. I have decided to follow Jesus, no turning back, no turning back."[2]

Like a growing, advancing army, the words started coming from each congregation as they joined in the hymn of commitment. "No turning back. No turning back."

Chapter 26
The Arrival

Monday Morning - January 2, 2113

The clatter and banging at the front door awakened Grace long before she had planned. In fact, after celebrating the new life the Referendum would bring, with the visitors from far off, connected at the heart on the Jumbotron the day before, she had not planned to wake up at any particular time. She threw on a cover-up and hurried down the steps.

"What is it?" she barked as she jerked the door open.

"We are looking for citizens of the Central Zone who we believe have crossed the border," Chalky Boone snapped. Her accompanying thug took a step forward.

"Now you just stop right there," Grace ordered and held the door with her right hand and the door jamb with the other, so they would have to go through her to get into the house. "You're far from home Mister ... Ma'am. This is not the Central Zone. You cannot boot-kick your way around here. You got that?" She glared at the pair.

"I am sure you don't want to withhold information concerning a fugitive, Reverend," Boone barked.

"If you know anything, you better tell us." Daniel Washington's gravelly voice sounded like it had rocks in it.

"You don't talk much, do you?" Grace said as she maintained her firm stance. "You just like to let your muscle speak for you."

"That's why I'm valuable to the force," he smirked. "Lieutenant Boone asked you a question. You're here, alone aren't you?"

Washington grabbed Grace's arm and pulled her into the western winter morning.

"Officer!" The Lieutenant barked. "Stand down!"

"You get out of this zone! You have no authority here. You aren't permitted to cross the border either," Grace ordered.

"We have valid travel papers," Boone protested.

"Perhaps, I've never seen travel papers since no one can cross the border. I would have nothing to compare them to for authenticity."

"I'll ask you one more time. Are you hiding Christina Applewait?"

"No one is here but me and my husband."

She didn't lie. She wouldn't have. The travelers had stayed the night at Rachel Claudette's house. For the next week and a half, there would be long meetings every day with the C-I Board and all the volunteers that would be coming and going in preparation for the mission that lie ahead. Grace had told the truth. Christiana was not there.

Chapter 27
The Caravan

5:00 a.m. - Friday - January 13, 2113

"Maybe all of our efforts will finally tear down these borders. It would be a miracle if you and I could travel by car through this forest and stop as often as we would want." Jason took my hand and let me know we were together on this quest for life.

We were taking a longer, but safer route into the Mid-West Zone. Several of Rachel's friends on the C-I Board had arranged for us to travel north along US 101, the Redwood Highway. It picked up its name at the Golden Gate Bridge and ran for 350 miles along the northern part of California. Our bus caravan wound through the virgin, old-growth coastal redwood trees that the state had been wise enough to preserve. I sat back in the lead bus and watched the passing forest. I couldn't nap.

"Jason, just look at those trees. They are marvelous!"

Then, I felt an incline. "We're climbing," I said as we approached a steep stretch between San Luis Obispo and Atascadero called the Cuesta Grade. "Look at the mountains and the view into the valley below. They're breath-taking."

Everything outside of Capitol City amazed me. I wanted to see every bird, every plant ... all that spread out before us. My eyes drank in every sight.

As we descended from the higher altitude, we came into the wide agricultural bottomlands of Salinas Valley. I remembered from my books in the library, this was the area known as America's Salad Bowl. The winters are mild in the area. I watched the sun glance off the rows of mounded dirt, evidence of the last crop of lettuce and other vegetables that had been in the field.

"I wonder what all of this looks like when green is everywhere and shoots push up through the soil?" I asked.

"It is amazing," Raymar offered from the seat behind us. "I've been in this area many times during harvest time."

"You worked in these fields, Raymar?" I asked.

"When someone would hire me."

"Was it hard to find work?" Jason wondered out loud.

"Like the old Romani, people think we are restless and can never stay in one place. We move because the authorities tell us to move on, after we have put in only a day or two of work," he explained. His eyes searched the fields beyond the bus windows, like he was looking for answers to questions that never made any sense to him.

"I'm sorry all that has happened to you, Raymar," I whispered.

"None of us can do anything about the past except learn from it. Maybe people will see our work for the lives of others with this petition campaign and learn to accept us." He watched out the window then added. "We're nearing our stop. Kasamar and I will get off and begin recruiting volunteers here in the northern part of the state."

I turned around and leaned over the back of the seat. "I'm privileged to have met you, Raymar Goring–or Robert Gross. Which do you prefer?"

"I am a child of God. My name isn't important. No one saw me when I was Raymar Goring. Then they loved me when I was Robert Gross, but they still didn't see me."

"I see you, Raymar. You are both, the man—Raymar and the novelist—Robert. I think people will learn to know you as Raymar Goring, the selfless, brave volunteer who, even though a ghost among men worked for the betterment of everyone. Robert Gross is the name you share your thoughts with. Now, we see you both."

Tears ran down his cheeks, and he brushed them away with the back of his hand. "You can see me?" he asked with a voice that cracked under the heavy weight of emotion.

When they stood up to leave, I hurried to my feet and hugged him and his lovely daughter. Jason shook their hands. The two got off in a little town in northern California and waved. I watched them through the back window and Raymar maintained eye contact with me for as long as he could see me. It was as if, once seen, he didn't want to break the connection.

We continued north where the highway again hugged the coast line. "Look, Honey," Jason nudged my shoulder.

I had tried to stay awake and not miss anything but everything had happened so fast. Even when we had time to rest, I didn't feel refreshed. Each day I grew wearier. As we drew near the beautiful placid ocean, Jason awakened me.

"Oh, it is amazing!" I gasped. "We have nothing like this in Capitol City."

"We have nothing like this in the entire Central Zone," Jason laughed and patted my leg.

We traveled up the western coast throughout the night for sixteen hours and crossed into Canada to the north of Washington State. In Vancouver we turned east. Thanks to the logistics coordination of Herman Lincoln, we crossed the provinces of British Columbia, Calgary, and Saskatchewan with no problem. We were all so tired. Luckily, the darkness of the night prohibited site-seeing.

"You are free to sleep now, my Lady," Jason smiled as he pulled a blanket up around my shoulder.

"I know you would stay awake with the force of sheer willpower if the sun were shining. We can thank the good Lord for the blessing of night."

"All right," I agreed as my eyelids grew heavy. "I surrender to the night."

Chapter 28
Border – Midwestern Zone

9 p.m. - January 15, 2113

"Winnipeg," Jason's spoke mechanically, apparently tired from sitting. It was 7 p.m.

We watched as the driver turned south along route twelve out of Winnipeg. "About two more hours," Gray Fox announced quietly for those not sleeping.

I know I drifted off again. I awakened about 9 p.m. when Gray Fox spoke firmly. "We're here."

We quickly got to our feet and made our way to the exit, tapping each volunteer on the shoulder as we passed to make sure they were awake and ready to get off. We stepped off the bus, out of sight of the border, and waited for a nod from Gray Fox to cross from Canada into Minnesota. It was the long way back to the United Zones, but the safest. Canada was still a free country and didn't care who traveled from Province to Province. I pulled my coat tightly around me to ward off the Canadian winter wind.

We were a large party for a stealth operation. One-hundred of us would approach the border. Like Moses leading the Israelites out of Egypt, it was hard to hide. Little Feather said hiding out in the open was our only recourse.

When we had all gathered, the signal came. We moved silently on foot from the buses through a snowy field. Gray Fox put his finger to his lips and withdrew farther into the shadows of the night. We were just inside the Canadian border, where, years before, the runway of the Piney/Pinecreek Border Airport was extended north of the U.S. Midwestern Zone and into Canada at the 49th parallel. With his hand raised, Gray Fox gave a signal for all of us to get down on the frozen ground. I looked at Jason for reassurance. When he smiled, I followed him down.

The freezing winter was thick beneath us. My toes quickly grew numb as I inched across the ground. We were flat on our stomachs on the runway of the old Border Airport, which a century ago had been one of only three Canada/US border airports. Now, with the whole country sealed off from the outside and from within, the airport lay abandoned. The runway, made smooth with tire rubber from thousands of flights, had become overgrown with grass and weeds, until the concrete was completely buried, like an artifact from a long-forgotten civilization, waiting for an archeologist to begin an excavation.

The tall spikey ice-covered grasses camouflaged us there on our bellies. Like frozen stalagmites, the icy blades of grass and weeds poked and gouged at my chest and stomach. I hoped that my coat wouldn't tear and let the cold invade and penetrate to my bones.

The border closed decades ago, and it was dark—the ground and runway lights torn out and sold on the black market according to the C-I people. I reached out and searched for Jason's hand as panic began to well up within me. Although concealed in the dark, I was freezing cold and afraid of what else hid in the black night.

When my hand met Jason's, he held it tightly, soothing my anxious heart. Gray Fox gave another signal—he cracked one finger knuckle and the entire field of prone bodies inched forward another eighteen inches. The journey south to the border took a long time. My elbows and shoulders ached from the strain and the penetrating cold. I was ill prepared for the icy north. Rachel had given us other clothing: denim pants, turtle neck sweaters, jackets with hoods and gloves, but I was cold. My blood still ran with the promise of warmer weather.

I was surprised there appeared to be no guards patrolling the border. Had all the rumors about the danger at the borders been lies or were we too far away to see the detail in the night? Jason grabbed my hand again and nodded at something in front of us. We were within yards of our goal. Luckily, we had neared the border at an old checkpoint.

A laser with a highly amplified beam of radiation protected the boundary itself. They sent the laser beam by capturing it at frequent intervals and sending it along. A black and yellow trefoil sign, displayed on the side of the guard post, caught my breath. There were armed guards present inside the protection of the border house. As we neared, I could see them through the windows of the large building. The special glass allowed the officers to see out but it was only after we were close that we were able to see in.

When the guards seemed distracted by jabbing and joking inside, Gray Fox turned his back on us. At first, I was terrified. Was he saying we were on our own? Then Little Feather stood, turned ninety degrees, and dropped again to the grass-covered runway. We were turning.

We inched along the flat open space and into a large wooded area. No one spoke a word. When Gray Fox gave the order to stand my body felt heavy and sluggish. I ached all over, except the places that remained numb.

Signaled to move, we followed into the woods in the footsteps of the one in front of us. If anyone were to follow, our group would appear to be smaller. We made sure no one strayed or got lost. When no light shone in any direction and darkness completely enveloped us, we knew we were deep enough into the trees. Gray Fox spoke.

"We have arrived at the northern boundary of the United Zones, or United States. The laser beam stretches from the west coast to the Atlantic Ocean. If you break the beam, two things will happen. You will die immediately, and you will alert the armed guards. If our information is correct, there will be three parallel beams. We will have to crawl under, or step over the deadly laser. If anyone believes they can't make it, don't try."

"Gray Fox," Jason began as he seemed to be digging a memory out of his past. "Before the enforcement of the Length of Days law, surgeons had used lasers to excise tumors from the human body. After several major operating accidents, they developed a way of protecting themselves if they were to receive a quick touch. They washed thoroughly. So, I'm thinking, if we roll in the ice until our bodies have warmed the snow, our clothes may be wet enough to protect us from the deadly energy. The huge consequence of soaking in the snow will be, of course, the possibility of slipping into hypothermia. It can happen very quickly. Once we are across, we will have to get inside, out of the night air immediately."

Gray Fox studied Jason very carefully then smiled. "You're the doc. How fast will the frozen death set in?"

"You'll have twenty to thirty minutes from the time you are soaked. That means the lead people cannot wait for the ones behind them. They will have to get to shelter immediately," Jason warned.

"We have to stay together," Little Feather protested.

"Then you will lose the front half of the group who stay behind to wait for the rest. That is for certain," Jason stated flatly.

Gray Fox paced for a moment. "Is there another way?"

"I don't know of any," Jason said.

"Little Feather, you lead the group straight to Musselman's barn. The rest of us will follow."

"We can do it," I reassured Little Feather. "How far is the barn?"

"It is just on the other side of the boundary, about a quarter mile," she answered.

"And, how long will it take to walk it, in this snow with the weight of our soaked heavy clothing?"

"About fifteen minutes, but remember, we will all be freezing wet and may enter a state of shock." Little Feather looked questioningly at Gray Fox.

"We must do it," Gray Fox pronounced, then turned to the group. "Friends, we are going to roll in the snow to get wet, a very dangerous thing to do in the frigid weather. But the laser beams that could kill us will not be lethal through the layer of water. Wet your face or cover it with a scarf and soak that in the ice and snow. Once on the other side, you will have only about twenty minutes to get to the barn on the Musselman farm. We will go in waves so no one is waiting to move."

I looked at the wonderful volunteers who had trusted us this far. Now we were asking them to dance with the angel of death and question nothing. No one protested. Crouched in a cluster of trees very near the line, we waited our turn. We were all depending on Jason's knowledge and medical expertise.

"The first twenty-five of you need to step forward and roll in the snow. Try to get as wet as possible, as quickly as you can. Then you will run across the border and follow Little Feather to a farm with a large barn. Run because your life depends on it." Jason grabbed my waist and drew me to him in front of everyone. There were no public displays of affection in the Central Zone.

I felt the warmth of his breath as he whispered in my ear. "I love you Christy. You don't have to do this."

"And I love you too, Jason, but ... I do have to do this. Our people are being exterminated like insects that have infested the foundation."

"I know, Sweetheart. That's why I love you." He tipped my chin up and kissed me, while all the strangers and new friends looked on. "I want you to go in the first wave. You will be strong willed, a strong runner and an inspiration for others."

"All right." I knew he was right. If I had traveled from a different zone to lead a crusade for our people, I had better be willing to take the first step.

Gray Fox pointed across the border to a dark spot down the road. "There, in the darkest spot on the right, is a large old farm house and a gigantic barn. It is a milk farm so animals will be present and there will be hay. When you get there, crawl under the hay like a feather bed. Warm yourselves as quickly as possible."

I stood for a moment and stared at the ice crusted snow. Images of Mama and Daddy came into my mind. I wondered if I would ever see them again. Then the faces of Grand-mère and Grand-père flooded my thoughts. If I quit now, they would be dead in two years–guaranteed. They had already exceeded their Length of Days.

I could stall no longer. Taking a deep breath, I dropped to the ground, rolled, and broke through the thin ice crust and felt the snow grow damp. The icy cold penetrated my jacket until I could begin to feel the pain of cold on my skin. I jumped up and ran for the border line and tried to crouch down into a ball. Three laser beams could stop us. Could I make myself low enough that only two of the beams would hit me?

I felt nothing as we darted across the border. Not knowing what to expect, I didn't hear or experience a zap or any of the other grave consequences my mind had imagined. Perhaps I thought lightening would surge through my body.

"Run!" I heard Jason in a loud whisper.

Dear Lord, give us speed, I prayed. Panic almost overtook me. *I will trust you, Lord.* I soon discovered, the laser wasn't the danger, the cure was. I ran as hard as I could and had less than twenty minutes to get to safety.

The clump of trees was just ahead but doubt began to take over my will to press on. *I'll never make it.* From behind I felt a gentle push as Little Feather nudged me in the direction of the old barn. She was out running me, and I knew what that meant. I wasn't going fast enough. Will I make it?

My legs felt heavy and stiff and the snow that clung to my boots froze my feet. I had been panting until my breath became so shallow each gulp of air was more painful than the last. I ran through the deep snow and now my lungs couldn't take in more icy air. But the barn was still several yards ahead of me.

Please, Father, give me strength; give me endurance. You are a new friend, but I trust you. Then my thoughts became fuzzy and my vision blurred. It felt like my eyes had glazed over with ice. Then I couldn't think more. I had to stop and sleep. All I wanted to do was close my eyes. What could be the harm in that?

Suddenly, a hand reached out through the opening of a building that smelled wonderful, an aroma I had never experienced before. A large rotund man had grabbed my arm and was pulling me into the warmth and sweet perfume. I didn't care who he was. My legs went limp and every muscle in my body collapsed into the man's arms.

Voices all around me shouted. "Bring her in quickly," one said.

"Put her down over here," someone ordered. "I'll blanket her in the hay. Sophie, run to fetch a feather quilt," she barked with authority, but there was music in her voice. She sounded sure and confident.

The voices rolled and tumbled all around me like the waves of the sea I had seen for the first time at Rachel's house. It was so warm there in the sand by the ocean. Visions of the day Jason and I walked along the beach came into my mind. We had kicked and played in the sand while the frothy tide flowed across our toes. Was I dreaming or remembering? It felt like I was outside my body, experiencing the warm water but knowing it wasn't real. I couldn't hear the voices any more, only the sweet distant deep, rich hum of Jason's laughter and gentle teasing.

"Come on, Christy, I'll race you to that rock up ahead," he challenged.

"I don't want to run, Jason. Suddenly, I feel so tired. I can hardly lift my legs."

"You want to sit and rest for a while?"

"Yes, but I'm supposed to keep moving. It would be easier to lie down and sleep forever."

"Let's walk a little farther, Sweetheart," he said.

"Look, Jason, even in the sunshine there seems to be a bright light ahead. It's more beautiful than anything I have ever seen. It's warm in there. I know it is," I said in a dream, or something I didn't understand.

"Stay here, Christy. The tickle of the ocean around our ankles is wonderful. It's not time to go. The light is pretty, but it's not for you yet. Please, Honey, stay ... stay ... stay with me, Christy," he seemed to plead.

"Stay with me, Christy," Jason was yelling when I opened my eyes. At first everything was blurry but then I felt his dear face.

"There you are," he said as he collapsed beside me. His body was shaking with chills.

"Doctor," the lady in my dreams said. But it was not a dream anymore. She was wrapping a thick downy comforter around Jason's shoulders. "You have to stay warm too you know."

"Jason, are you all right? Were you the last one? Did everyone make it across the line? Have we all arrived in the Midwestern Zone?" Questions flooded my mind.

"I'm fine, Honey. And the answer is yes to all of the rest."

"And now ..." I paused and looked around, "where are we? I'm not familiar with this building. What is this place?" I asked.

"You're in my old barn, Ma'am. Built in 1897. It's been standing for more than two-hundred years. You know why?"

I had heard his voice before. The big man in the overalls and flannel shirt didn't wait for an answer. "It's 'cause this here farm has been in my family for longer than that, and we take care of our own things. Not like some of those other farmers who are afraid to touch anything that ain't theirs. Almost all of the family farms are gone now. All owned by the government, they are. You know how we kept ours?" Again, he plowed on. "Because we kept low. We didn't brag or boast. We kept our mouths shut."

"Silence again," I sighed.

"What say?"

"We are in the Age of Silence, Mr. ..."

"Musselman, Ma'am, Edward Musselman. Glad to meet you. What did you say about silence?" The man slapped me on the side of my arm with the firm hand of someone who worked hard every day and enjoyed the work he did.

"We are in the Age of Silence, Mr. Musselman. But someone in the Central Zone was brave enough to break the silence and we're here to bring a voice to everyone," I explained.

"You must be Lady Christina Applewait. We've been waiting for you for days," he smiled a broad smile. "Maud," he called out, "come over here and meet Lady Applewait. 'Course no one around here has lady or gentleman as a moniker."

"Please, Edward ... May I call you Edward?"

"That's my name, ain't it?"

"It certainly is. We are a team of equals, Edward. My name is Christy," I said as I sat up, "and we have a very large task in front of us. We need equal voices and equal value to our work."

"That's what the government kept trying to tell us, equal everything. It ain't equal if it ain't free. It's the freedom that gives equal opportunity. We can all work for our best but there ain't no need to work if our laziness is our best."

"Can we quote you in the newspaper a friend owns?"

"Breaking the silence here, Ma'am, will cause me to lose my farm." Musselman shook his head and looked over at his wife.

"It isn't your name that has to be heard, Edward. It's your heart and your words. You don't need to mention your name to talk to the people. Like us all, you have a need to hold some treasures close to your heart. You have still spoken. Then, you decide if you can put your name on a petition. That will be a big step."

Chapter 29
Headquarters of the Blue Guard

Central Zone – January 16, 2113

"What do you mean, you lost them? Did you ever find them in the first place?" Stoner roared.

"Well, not exactly ..." Lieutenant Boone stammered.

"Not exactly?" The Chief Inspector's voice was shrill. "Finding someone is a fact, not an opinion. You either did or you did not find them! Which is it?"

"I attended a meeting with a large gathering of clergy persons. A woman spoke who was very much like Lady Applewait."

"Clergy ... you mean religion? Why didn't you arrest every one of them? The ban on even the mention of God has been in force for a hundred years!" Stoner was in a rage. The memory of Applewait and her followers singing Christmas carols in front of President Alexander's home on Gifting Day eve was more than he could tolerate.

"Ward, I couldn't have arrested thousands of them by myself, even with that animal, Washington, along. He could have only growled and bitten so many people at a time."

"Lieutenant, why were you not able to identify her?" He paced back and forth, unable to sit and rest, unable to calm down.

"The woman I saw was wearing a Romani costume with a veil. She claimed to have laryngitis so I couldn't recognize her voice but it seemed odd that she would stand in front of thousands when she was barely able to speak."

"She couldn't speak at all and yet she came to the voice enhancer?" Ward barked in disbelief.

"Well, her voice was very hoarse and raspy ... you know ... laryngitis." Boone explained with impatience in her voice.

"All right, she spoke–sort of—then, where is she? Where is this face-covered, squeaky voiced woman now? Did she disappear under her cape? Was she a magician as well as a gypsy woman? Did she evaporate into thin air?"

"Ward, she was a real person. She's just couldn't talk very clearly. She didn't go up in a puff of smoke. She was there and ... I really thought it was her."

"Okay, okay. Where is she right now?" Stoner demanded answers to his questions. "Boone, the question isn't that hard."

"I ... don't know! Washington and I attended the church meeting on Sunday morning. I have never seen that many people gathered together in one place. There was no crowd control in place. Citizens in the Central Zone cannot congregate in crowds. The woman was there in the same gypsy costume; she still wore a veil and her clothing covered her from her neck to her feet. They connected the church electronically with every congregation in the zone that morning. There were hundreds of links. I couldn't say how many. When they finished with the broadcast, thousands of people in the great auditorium we were in, stood and sang songs of praise with their hands waving around in the air. When I could finally see the front of the arena, the Romani woman was gone. No one, not one person, would tell me that they had seen her, that they knew her, and certainly not where she had gone."

The communication device that connected Boone and Ward Stoner went silent. Neither one said another word. Finally, she heard a deep sigh on the other end. "Come on home, Chalky. Your job is finished there—not completed—just done."

Chapter 30
A Gathering

Mid-Western Zone - Sunday Afternoon - January 22, 2113

"Ed Musselman, you come right up here," a woman in blue denim pants, heavy brown leather work shoes and a thick knit sweater said as she stood on a hay wagon. She amplified her voice with a hand held conical shaped object. It all looked very primitive to me and reminded me of pictures of singers in a long-ago time.

I took a deep breath. We were finally going to speak to the zone. The border had been a dangerous crossing and many of us had caught colds. I had developed bronchitis, and Jason feared it would go into pneumonia. We rested for nearly a week. Most slept in the barn on soft hay covered with donated comforters and quilts. Jason and I had stayed in Ed and Maud Musselman's home. Now, the hour had come.

"There he is," I said to Jason. When I looked around the barn at our group of one-hundred souls, I also counted at least another hundred strangers. "Look at all of these people. They're setting on hay stacks and some are dangling their feet over the side of the hay loft." I had to look closely. Some people blended into the surroundings of the barn. "Look, over at the horse stall. There are two young boys on the back of a chestnut mare."

"You sound like you've been here before," Jason joked. "Are you sure you weren't raised on a farm?"

"You know no farms exist in the Central Zone, just industry and business offices."

"Christy ... no farms exist in the Central Zone?"

"I just said that." Then I stopped. "Where have I been all my life? Why have I never noticed that we have no farms in our Zone? I have read books that painted vivid word pictures, farms from the dust bowl, the old south, the Amish farms, the farms and their families from the thirties and forties. I know what a farm looks like."

"I hadn't paid any attention either. History, neither regional nor zone, is taught anymore. I spend my time in my office, the hospital, and now, with you. We're in town all of the time. With no rapid transit out of the city and few people have cars, very few people travel outside the city limits. The other thing is the drugs that are in the water. Everyone is so compliant; they don't question anything." Jason and I continued to talk between ourselves as we marveled at what we had overlooked all around us.

Edward jumped up on the wagon and waved at the people in his barn. "Okay, my friends, Maud has told you about the visitors to our zone. I know most of us haven't lived long enough to have seen a stranger in our midst. We rarely hear the word, "stranger." And that's what these folks are here to talk to you about."

Maud gestured in our direction and smiled broadly. I could tell we were welcome and perhaps they had heard of our mission already.

"Here in the Midwest, we farm and preserve, we bake and raise fiber for textiles. In the southern part of the zone, we have large mills and manufacture clothing and shoes. We export nearly all of that to the other three zones. We are the suppliers, not the users. Our ruling elites tell us, as farmers and factory workers, it is more virtuous to want little for ourselves. Those of our children who have wished for more, who have wanted a different life for themselves and their families, and have tried to escape across the border into another life, have been gunned down once their feet hit the foreign soil."

Murmurs arose among the people and nods of agreement. But not all were in one accord.

"Ed, that's just not true. The other zones are just like us. They work the land and sweat in the factories just like we do," a man in denims and a plaid shirt argued.

"No, Art, that's wrong. Each zone is different but, in one way, they are all the same. They all live under the Length of Days law that applies to everyone. In the Midwestern Zone, as you near 70 years of age, your food rations diminish slowly. Do they not?"

An elderly woman's expression changed from interest to grief. Perhaps she had recently lost a spouse.

"Their excuse is," Ed continued, "you no longer work the land at your advanced age, so the greater number of calories you had been eating are not needed and would actually harm you. Each year, your rations grow smaller until you starve to death."

"No!" Some shouted from the back.

"What? It can't be. I don't believe that," a woman with a black, hand-woven headscarf snapped back in disbelief.

"You lie, Ed Musselman. You're lying and you know it!" A man waved his fist in the air and pounded the straw bale beside him.

"It's the Lord's gospel truth," Ed shouted into the megaphone. "You want to overturn that evil law?" he shouted. The crowd cheered. "Dr. O'Reilly, please step up here."

The crowd gawked and strained to see the new person in their midst. With no physicians in the middle zone, the people didn't understand his title. Ed raised his voice again. "The doctor is a person trained to cure people of what ails them. He finds medication for people to take, that will make them will again."

Everyone gasped and shifted where they sat. I wondered if there were any doctors in the southern part of the zone where industrial accidents could happen, and those injured would need the help of a physician.

Ed clapped his hands and encouraged others to follow suit. The people stood and became more excited with each cheer.

"I'm happy to be here," Jason greeted everyone. "And, I'm grateful you have all come out to listen. I sincerely hope you will support our mission. Mr. Musselman tells us that everyone in the Midwestern zone quits work when they reach the age of seventy. I understand, at that retirement age they cut your rations, supposedly for your own health. In the central zone, they exterminate people based on a precise scale of their value to the rest of the community. If they don't work at all, they will be put down by the time they are twenty-five." The people gasped and their expressions turned to fear and anger.

"For an elite," Jason continued, "they will use up their Length of Days at age seventy-five, regardless of how healthy and energetic they are." Those listening shook their heads in disbelief.

"We have just come from the Western Zone where they are organizing to support our cause. Even though the law requires some form of elimination at an age when people are still well and strong, just as it is in all zones, those in the West don't obey that law. With all of the advances in food, medicine and spiritual hope, those people live to the age of one hundred forty-five."

"One hundred forty-five?" Someone shouted and laughed among his friends. "Hey Doctor, you mean forty-five, right?"

"No, I meant what I said—one hundred forty-five years. And, you can add longevity to your years as well, with wholesome, healthy living. But first, let me introduce Christina Applewait."

A hush fell over the crowd as I came to the center of the wagon. Then a short lady with long greying hair asked, "Are you Lady Applewait, the seer?"

"I am Lady Christina Applewait. Lady by birth, not for anything I have done for others. I consider myself a *lady* only in my behavior." Everyone chuckled and shifted as they relaxed. "More important to that Lord and Lady nonsense, it is our cause that is a mission from God, not the messenger. There are no Lords and Ladies in the kingdom of God."

"Bless you, Christy," a woman called from the hay loft.

"Thank you. I am blessed ... and I have come to remind you that you are blessed, too."

"We have our work," a man up front said quietly, "but that is all."

"From what Ed and Maud have told me, you are a people with a strong vibrant past. Your ancestors owned the land you now work on," I reminded them.

"But, it's selfish to claim personal land ownership that others can't own," another woman protested.

"We are not elite like you, Christy," someone else spoke up with indignation in her voice.

"Yes, yes, you are. You are children of the King, the Lord God." Many whispered among themselves and snickered at the thought of being a royal anything.

"We have nothing of our own. What do you have?" a man snapped.

"It is not about what I have or may have in the future. It is about what you can claim if you will accept it. Ed told us of the second great *Bolshevik Revolution*. But, my friends, it was not the people who rose up and claimed what was rightfully theirs. It was the government who deceived the family-farm owners into believing that you could not farm on your own. In fact, they regulated the farm, textile, and manufacturing industries until it was completely impossible to do business without government assistance. Then, while you relaxed in your effort to run your business, they stepped in and took them over ... every one of them."

The crowd gasped. Their faces distorted in anger. One burly man stood up in the back and began to pace. Then he turned toward me and shouted, "What happened? You mean our government stole everything our families worked for generations to build?"

"Yes, Sir," I stated flatly, "I mean exactly that. The government stole every single thing your family had. And, they continue to do that. They are now robbing you of your years of life. Years you could have spent with your loved ones."

"What are you talking about?" The big man asked, confused and angry.

"The Length of Days law, Sir. In the Central Zone, when people are injured or reach their allotted days, they are taken to the furnaces under Howard Mountain and are exterminated."

A woman near the middle of the group cried, "No, no."

"You here in the Midwestern Zone are quickly starved to death, once you are no longer able to farm the government land or work in their factories," I paused again as the people struggled to grasp the truths that were bombarding the lies they had been told.

Ed jumped to his feet. "My friends and neighbors, none of what these travelers have to say will make any difference at all ... if you don't believe them. I am telling you as your friend and neighbor, they bring the truth. The truth is hard to hear sometimes but don't say I didn't warn you," he shouted. "I did warn you. This illegal gathering of citizens, which could earn you a flogging, I remind you, we risked for one reason only, to being you the truth. It is up to you to believe the message these people bring from beyond our borders. If you don't accept their message today, you will be condemning your friends and family to certain death ... for treason." He turned to Jason, "Please, Jason, pick up and continue."

"We have come to get your help. We plan to overturn that terrible law," Jason announced with both hands raised. "I will now turn the megaphone back to Christy to give you the details."

I took the mouth piece and stood in the center of the wagon. At first, I felt myself holding my breath. Suddenly, a peace fell over me like a finely made prayer shawl. I knew I felt the presence of the Lord in our midst. The sun streamed through a high window and bathed the room in healing light. "Thank you for listening to us," I began. "I believe you know the truth of which we speak, deep inside. I have chosen to trust you with my life. Now, I need your help. I have brought along some papers, petitions for you to sign. If you believe the Length of Days law is evil and that we must put it down, you will sign the sheet and we will move on. At the top of each petition page is the wording of the citizens' bill. Enough signatures on these petitions will ensure that a referendum is placed on the ballot at the election in two years."

With a petition held up in my hand, I pointed to each section as I spoke. "It's okay if you haven't heard of the term *referendum*. If the ruling class had their way, you still wouldn't have heard of it."

Again, I waited for understanding to catch up to their profound desire to take charge of their lives again. "A referendum is the same as a bill that congress writes to create a new law or to repeal a bad one. The Attorney General of each state prepares a title and summary of the chief purpose and points of the referendum. With our states further divided into zones, we don't have access to a state Attorney General. So, the government constructed a cover letter to accompany it. Dr. O'Reilly and I were able to procure a cover letter." I watched the people's faces as they turned to one another, trying to understand.

When the murmurs calmed, I continued. "A referendum is a law written by the people. It requires the signatures of a vast percentage of the citizens in order to get it placed on the ballot for all to vote on. We need your name on the line."

Again, I felt the information was racing past the people, like a giant snow ball that grows in size as it rolls down the hill. I paused and let the people catch up to our mission. "Besides being brave enough to sign the petition, we need people who are courageous enough to help carry copies of the petition to the entire Zone. A hundred people have followed us from the West to help you with this effort. Half of them will remain here to assist you. The other half will go into the Eastern Zone to help get signatures there."

"You can count on me," a young man called from the back of the barn.

"Me, too," the girl beside him echoed as she waved her hand over her head.

As others said, "You can add me in," I thought of Raymar Goring. Filled with new life only a few days, yet he had agreed to participate and head up a team to get the signatures of the Hollow people in the northwest.

"I will never be empty again," he had said.

"Are you comfortable doing this, Raymar?" I had asked him.

"I may not have talked to others or been in their world, but I have taught the other discarded ones every day." He had assured me with conviction.

I smiled again as I thought of him. He had gone from being a shadow in our world, to a valuable partner in our cause, in a matter of days. I handed Jason the megaphone. I heard him introduce Lomas Karl, one of the claimed children we had brought with us from the west.

"Thank you, Doctor," Lomas smiled as he stepped to the center. "I know I look young. I admit I'm only eighteen, but I have come to bear witness to what you have been told." He paused and looked around the group.

"You're doing fine, Lomas," I soothed. As I walked behind him, I patted his shoulder.

"In the Central Zone, families are permitted only two children. If a third infant is born, the parents have up to two years to decide which two of their three they're going to keep. After the parents decide on the two, the third child is given over to the state for extermination." Lomas lowered his eyes and stared at straw on the floor in front of him. He looked up again and met the eyes of all those gathered. "I am one of those discarded children. But a dear man was brave enough to start claiming the children just before I was born. I am one of the claimed."

Gasps rose up among many in the crowd. They seemed to take Lomas to their hearts. As tears rolled down the cheeks of many, they grieved with him for all he had lost.

"I want to tell you all, don't mourn for me. I'm the winner. In the Western Zone, they took me to Claimed-International, and within hours, a new family wanted me. In my claimed family, I have five brothers and sisters."

"Bless you," someone called from the side.

"I am blessed, Ma'am. You're right. And, I'm asking that you become a blessing to others. We must end this national disgrace, this abomination against God! We cannot let the Length of Days law stand. We must bring it down!" His rallying call filled the whole room. People stood and cheered.

Ed Musselman raised his hands and let out a whistle that rattled the windows in their frames. "Our travelers will be with us for another week and a half. We'll organize by township, with two leaders for each. Christiana will offer encouragement, strength, and motivation. She and Jason will answer any questions we may have. Our goal is to have the structure in place for us to continue by the time they move on to the Eastern Zone. Are there any questions now?"

"Will we make the deadline?" a man shouted from the seat of the International Harvester tractor.

"I can say, 'I hope so,' I answered. "But, I'm sorry, my friends. That is not good enough. We absolutely must be successful and on time. There are deadlines put in place hundreds of years ago and a two year stay of executions. That is our reality. That is our goal," I sang out with certainty.

"We are together!" Ed Musselman shouted. "We will be counted!"

Chapter 31
Inspector Stoner's Office

A Few Days Later

Ward Stoner paced the short distance from his office door to the east window. He searched the parking area beyond the glass. The only strata cars were those that were there ten minutes ago. *Where are they?*

"Alvarez!" he shouted toward the door.

One of the new Blue Shirts stuck his head through the door. "Sir?"

"Have we heard from Lieutenant Boone? Anything?" Stoner leaned on his desk with his fists doubled.

"We received word that she and Washington had left the Western Zone hours ago. Perhaps she has gone home to get some sleep."

"Sleep?" Stoner roared like a pacing lion. "They will sleep when Applewait has been found!"

"But Sir—"

"Do not speak back to me, Officer!" Then in a whisper he added, "Don't you ever correct or challenge what I say."

Alvarez shrunk from the room as Stoner's glare drove him out. "I'll let you know when I hear something."

Stoner's eyes darted to the lot outside as a strata car pulled in. Then he hurried to the desk with a new thought, one he would have to execute quickly. His 281 Palm Device waited for his next message. With minutes to go before Boone would enter his office and reprimand him for investigating a Legacy Citizen, he flipped the 281 on. It glowed brightly; the logo hologram pulsed in front of him. "Call, Jonathon Fink ... Fort Knox," he barked.

"Hi there, Ward," the image greeted. "I don't talk to you for years, now this is the second time in a matter of weeks." Fink's presence appeared in the form of a hologram in front of Stoner. "You're looking good."

"I'm calling you about that Applewait woman again." Stoner looked back out at the lot. Boone and Washington were just getting out of the car. He would have to make the connection short. His impatience mounted.

"Friend, I'm not permitted to speak one word about the members of the Council of Elders, or their families. Not any of the Legacy Citizens. I looked up that one piece of information for you, Ward," Jonathan protested. "That's it."

"You don't have to look up anything in your precious files about those uppity elites, Fink. I just need to find out the activities in general. You're in the Midwestern Zone. I just want to know if you have heard anything."

"About Lady Applewait?"

"About anything," Ward snapped impatiently. "Most of the time, these citizens have nothing out of the ordinary going on. They lead uneventful, do-nothing lives. I would die from stagnation if I lived as they do. Whatever you hear that is not as boring as watching the corn grow, would be something I'd like to hear about."

"Okay ..." There was silence for a second. "There is something going on, but I don't have any idea what it is," Fink said. "There seems to be a new energy among the people. You know how these people are. They are all lazy. We let them live, at very little rent mind you, on the land they work and still they aren't satisfied."

"Have you heard any names ... Applewait or O'Reilly?"

"No. But someone said he heard of a meeting a few days ago. He didn't know any of the details, location, or the names. No one is saying a word. You know, and they know, it is unlawful to congregate in groups."

"Maybe it's nothing," Stoner mumbled out loud.

"That's what I thought, Ward. But ... a report of a meeting is not nothing ... it's something."

"But, is she still in your Zone? The Applewait woman, Jonathan, is she still there?"

"I have no idea, but if I were to guess, I would say no, at least, I don't think so. I haven't heard about another big meeting."

Stoner's shoulders sank with anger and disappointment. "Well, thank you friend."

"Ward," Lieutenant Boone said softly at the door. The hologram shimmered in the room. "We're back."

"If you hear anything, let me know immediately," Ward said as he closed the 281.

"What was that all about?" Chalky questioned as she entered his office and removed her outer coat.

"Top secret," he snapped. "I'll tell you as soon as I can." He stared out the window again at the rapidly accumulating snow. "We're not done, Boone. I will find her if I have to chase her to the ocean's edge."

"You are the one who will drown if you interfere with the privacy of an Elite," she warned.

"Never mind that," he ordered. "Where have you been?"

"Where have I been? Ward, you sent Washington and me out of the zone. I have been to the incoming tide, just as you said, and she wasn't there."

"Not at all?" Ward shook his head in disbelief. "What about that woman in the Romani clothes? You probably had her then. Did she look like the Legacy brat?"

"If I did have her, like you said, there were far too many people present for me to get anyplace near her. She almost evaporated. The woman was guarded and then ... she was gone." Chalky stretched and yawned. "I'm going home to get some sleep."

"Make that a nap, Lieutenant. I've been asking questions, and I'm picking up on some movement. I tell you, it is something." He rubbed the back of his neck in frustration. "I have received word that the Mid-Western Zone has had a little ruffle in their waves of grain. Then everything all settled down again. There doesn't seem to be a disturbance now, but more movement than usual." He paced the floor, then grabbed Boone by both arms and got in her face. "So, you saw that gypsy woman in the West. Then, there was a ripple of something in the Midwest. If the reason for that unrest was her ... she may be going to the Eastern Zone next. That is the only zone she hasn't been spotted in yet."

Boone pulled herself free from Stoner's grasp. "Ward, let it go."

"Let it go? These two fugitives have plotted to change a long-established law. They have thumbed their noses at our President Alexander. And ... they have unlawfully left the zone and crossed several borders, in order to spread their treason."

"Ward—"

"Go home. Sleep a little ... pack ... and I'll pick you up in three hours. I'll drive. Washington will be in the back."

"Must we take Daniel? I don't trust him."

"He'll be our muscle."

"Why do we need added strength? Ward, you cannot lift a hand to a Legacy Citizen. We have gone over and over this."

"Don't lecture me like a child!" he bellowed. "I am the Chief of the Blue Guard! I can do anything I want to, when I want to, and for any reason I invent!" Stoner's face grew red with anger and belligerent revenge, a very dangerous combination.

Chalky closed her eyes and shook her head slowly. "No, I think you are right, Sir. There is nothing I can say that will change your mind."

Stoner looked out at his city as fresh snow began to float down. "It's cold out there, Boone. Dress warm."

Chapter 32
Eastern Zone—Border Crossing

6 a.m. - Thursday - February 2, 2113

"Put everything you're carrying on the table," a stout woman in low, lace-up shoes barked mechanically.

The border post was drab and poorly lit. Shadows lurked in places that needed no shade, except for the dull, monotonous drone of the job there. I wondered if it was the people who worked there or the room that was light-less. The whole room smelled of mold, like an old basement. But we weren't underground. We were in a room with so few windows the dampness could get in but it couldn't escape.

This was the first border we crossed openly. *Openly* for the Eastern Zone. The Midwestern sector didn't even know we were in their territory. But, the border to the East was different. There was a border *understanding*—if you have the price of passage you can cross with no questions asked. The *understanding* was only in force at a few crossings. They shared the bounty collected with those on down a ransom line, that flowed deeply enough into the Eastern area, to make the crossings as safe as possible.

Jason made a slight gesture toward the woman as she opened and searched through my valise. I didn't have much. We had come with very little except what the Musselmans had pulled together for us. The crossing guard groped all the way to the bottom of the bag then forced it closed with the contents jumbled and crumpled. Next, she jerked Jason's carry pack to her without taking a step and rummaged through it in the same way.

Jason and I watched in silence as she dutifully searched every pocket and pouch. She did her work thoroughly, and I wondered what she would have done if she had actually found something. I also wondered what *something* would consist of. It was better that we gave her no information on our own. She didn't even look up when she asked, "Your crossing papers?"

Without saying a word, Jason handed the woman a small, bulging envelope. With it held very close to her chest, she barely opened it, peeked inside, ran her fingers over the contents and motioned for us to pass. Jason placed ten fingers on the cold surface of the metal desk, closed them and held up two fists full again. Twenty of us—twenty travelers passed while the woman pinched open the folder a little wider and counted her money. She didn't look at anyone. I doubt she even saw us at all. We were now the invisible ones, like Raymar Goring had been.

"I wonder if the border is an example of the technology in the east." Jason whispered when we were far beyond her hearing. "She had nothing. She just fumbled through everything. She couldn't even use the old x-ray technology."

"That's the way it appeared," I said, and wondered if things were as they seemed. "Maybe they have so few attempts at border crossing they don't need modern equipment to secure it."

"Let's hope. Ed and Maud were sure their information was correct. We would be able to cross here if we paid the guard." Jason never looked back. We kept walking toward the cars that waited for us in the fog beyond the passing guard post.

Great clouds hung low to the ground and drew a thin veil over all we saw. Suddenly I stopped. A vehicle, like a strata car, sleek with broad lettering down the side, Zone Patrol, went slowly past in the eerie fog. The windows were dark so I couldn't see anyone. A man who stood beside a long, black vehicle suddenly caught my eye and came across the road in our direction. The whole scene seemed odd. The street was two lanes and the grass grew like fringe along the side of the pavement. The ice crystals that had gathered on top looked undisturbed and glistened in the light. Obviously, this was not a well-

461

traveled spot. The man from the stretch car came closer, reached out and gave me a loosely directed hug.

"Sorry, My Lady, act like you know me and you were expecting me to greet you," he whispered while his face was near mine.

I smiled a faint smile. Then I turned and said, "Jason, you remember—"

"Harold, Harold Humphrey," the man said as he stuck out his hand in greeting. "You, Sir, will be called Jason Bogart and you, my dear, Christy Bacall. No one here knows the old cinema stars and if they do, perhaps they won't notice that Bogie and Bacall are together again."

Gray Fox and Little Feather came up from behind me and stopped at a brief distance. Harold stepped around Jason and me and offered his hand. "Gray Fox, I've heard about you. You have been in our zone before, silent and invisible, but the network knew of your presence." He offered his hand again, "Little Feather."

"You have an established network already in place, Harold?" Jason asked.

"Hurry, let's get into the stretch cars and then I'll explain it. The zone has seen cars like these before so we shouldn't be stopped."

"I'll get everyone inside," Little feather offered. Four, six-passenger long luxury cars waited at the side of the road. Little Feather helped five of us into each.

"You four will ride with me," Harold spoke to Jason, Little Feather, Gray Fox, and me.

We all quickly got into the vehicles and Harold led the way down the road. I ran my fingers over the dark leather cushions and inhaled the earthy aroma of the entire interior. I smiled to myself. My usual mode of transportation was the Public Transit of Capitol City, not a luxury limousine. I allowed myself the brief privilege of sinking back into the comfortable seat.

Suddenly, I caught a glimpse of another strata car as it passed by. I felt ill. My hands started trembling and waves of nausea overtook my tired body. It felt like I had been stirred on the inside and the swirling had not yet subsided.

"Are you all right, Christy?" Jason put his arm around me.

"I saw a strata car and suddenly felt overwhelmed," I whispered out of some deep place inside.

"You're right," Gray Fox whispered, validating my experience. "I have seen several, but we are inside a rolling tank with tinted windows."

"I know this is all a shock, Christy," Harold sympathized. "But you are an answer to prayer."

"Answer to prayer?" I asked in surprise. "You know about our cause?"

Harold looked at me through the rear facing mirror. "We are under the Length of Days law, too. But we also have more depravity here than anyone could ever imagine. Those who live in the city are the very wealthy and the moles live underground."

"The moles?" we all questioned Harold in unison. "What are you talking about?" I asked.

Suddenly, colored lights and a screeching siren cut through the morning fog. I grabbed Jason's hand and stiffened. I was frightened and tired. It would have been so much easier to handle all that had happened with rest.

"Put your head on Jason's shoulder like you're sleeping, Christy. Your face will be partially buried when the officer gets to the window," Little Feather suggested with the tone of experience in making her way through difficult situations.

"What's the party all about?" the uniformed man asked through the open window.

"Party?" Harold appeared genuinely confused. He was good at what he had learned to do in order to get around the city.

"This long parade of cars, Mister. What's this all about?" the officer snapped.

"I picked up some friends of Mr. and Mrs. Cornwall. They're having a reunion and week-long private festival," Harold said.

"Reunion of what?" the officer questioned.

"They do it every year and invite the same people. So, they call it a reunion. Other than that, it's none of my business."

The patrolman looked in the car at us in the back. I could feel him staring at me, but I remained silent and rested my head on Jason's shoulder. Flashing his light into the backseat he studied each of us carefully. "Is she okay?" he asked.

"Yes, just tired. We had started the party a little ahead of the others," Jason laughed. "I really need to get her to the house so she can rest."

"The house?" Again, the office pried as he shined the light in Jason's face. "What do you mean, house? Are you trying to be funny, Mister?

"Mr. Bogart is joking. He means the Citadel of course. He is a man of understatement," Harold smiled as if making fun of the comment.

"It sounds like it. It is quite a *house.* Well, none of us keep the Cornwalls waiting and I won't be the first. Here, let me put a flag on your car as the lead vehicle in a procession." His attitude changed once he heard of our destination. He was all business, in the most efficient and pleasant manner. He waved us on and got back in his patrol car.

"I see him in my mirrors. He's going the other way," Harold said with relief.

"Are we actually going to ... the Citadel? The Cornwall Citadel?" I asked. With all the sectors closed, we heard nothing about the people in the Eastern Zone. But I knew. Some of the reference books, available only to me and the Library Curator of old manuscripts, referred to an old New York family by the name of Cornwall. And, I certainly knew what a citadel is. It's a castle on higher ground that protects those around them.

"Yes, we definitely know about your cause. We have two tasks in the Eastern Zone. The second will make the first possible." Harold drove a little further and then added, "The petitions are our main goal, but in order to accomplish that we will have to free the moles."

"The moles?" I questioned again.

"You won't believe it. I don't ... and I live here." Harold said no more. Again, he watched me through the mirror. "Rest, My Lady. We have a long way to go."

I rested my head on Jason's shoulder. I couldn't actually sleep as thoughts of our mission raced through my mind: the Citadel, the moles, and everything we had encountered. I smiled as I thought of the irony of it all. It had only been a few months ago, that all of my exciting experiences came through the pages of the books I read over and over. Now ... I was the adventurer and I still wondered how all of it could have happened. Only God could have called me to such a time as this.

Chapter 33
The Citadel

Late Afternoon

"I think she might have actually fallen asleep," I heard Jason say as I roused. The car was still moving. I knew I could have only napped a few minutes.

"She must have been really tired," Harold was saying as I looked out the window.

Something that sent flashes of light through the windshield at rapid intervals blocked the late afternoon sun. What was it? I squinted as my eyes adjusted to the bursts of brilliance. Buildings were everywhere. It was like driving through a box canyon surrounded by sheer cliff walls I read about. I couldn't see the tops of the buildings so I slumped down in the seat and peered above and out the window. Now, I know what my books meant by skyscrapers.

"We're here," Gray Wolf spoke softly from the back seat.

I strained to see the street sign at the next block. "Park Avenue at Fifty-Seventh Street," I gasped. The magic of New York City had been a reoccurring dream of mine since I found books filled with pictures of the city in the library. The brick and granite buildings rose up from the concrete like a field of enchanted pebbles that had split the pavement.

"The city mountains are almost as tall as ours, Gray Fox," Little Feather marveled.

"How will you guide us here; in a city you have never seen?" Jason questioned.

"Because we don't follow bricks and mortar. We follow people, and their scent is different than motor fuel."

"These are hydro-motors, Gray Fox," Harold said. "They have no sound and no odor."

"We'll see." Gray Fox answered with a doubtful grin. "But I can hear the whirl of the movements," he chuckled softly. Suddenly, he broke the silence again with a gasp. "Navajo," he whispered. "That sign is Navajo. It wasn't until the Great War in the middle of the nineteenth century that anyone wrote down the Navajo language. That sign said, 'Bilh-he-new Huc-Quo.' It says warning, come. Why was that there? Something is coming."

"I'll let Richard and Barbara Cornwall tell you. I'll say you are very important to the success of the second effort." Harold said no more.

The second effort? Then I remembered what he said—*we must free the moles.*

Harold pulled the car up to a huge iron gate. Beyond the fence was a circle driveway. It was dry even in the snowy weather. What appeared to be a large fountain, still flowing with fresh water from which red cardinals splashed and drank, stood in the middle.

"It's all heated Christy, the driveway pavement and fountain birdbath," Harold explained.

He pushed a button on the steering wheel and the wrought iron slowly parted with only the tiniest sound of scraping and squeaking. None of us talked. We drank in all the information the fortified estate in the middle of New York City had to offer. The high iron fence bordered the entire property, with surveillance devices mounted every twenty feet. The home was so large it reminded me of pictures I had seen of the mansions of the gilded era in one of the previous centuries. The Citadel reached up six stories above the street. The entrance area was large enough for all of the long-cars to park on the drive pad.

The doors to each of the vehicles seemed to open in slow motion as people hesitantly stepped out and craned their necks to see the very top of the house. Jason and I, Gray Fox and Little Feather stepped from the long-car.

"Where are we?" Salvador Pérez, a Westerner, asked as he got out of one of the other cars and filled his eyes with the massive structure.

"This is nothing like my vineyard in California," Frank Church agreed.

"Follow me quickly inside," Harold cautioned as he hurried everyone through the massive stained-glass paneled doors.

Inside, the entry hall reached up three stories. A crystal chandelier hung from the tall ceiling by three golden cables. The floors were rose marble and shone in the entry light. The sounds of our shoes made a tapping noise on the stone.

"You are all safely here." A lovely woman in her mid-forties swept graciously down the staircase. She wore a teal dress that brushed around her ankles and moved like sea grass near the edge of the water. "I'm Barbara Cornwall." She extended her hand in my direction. "Lady Christiana Applewait? Welcome."

"Please, Mrs. Cornwall, call me Christy," I smiled and approached her to shake her hand. As she came nearer, I caught the scent of her perfume. It smelled amazing, but I wouldn't have known the name of the heavenly creation. Considered too erotic, there was no perfume manufactured or sold in the Central zone.

"Only if you call me Barbara," she said. Her smile lit up her face. "Come," she offered, "you probably haven't eaten in hours."

"We haven't eaten since early this morning, Mrs. Cornwall." Harold led the way into a dining room the size of which I had never experienced, not even in the books I read.

"Harold, I have told you many times, to call me Barbara. You are my friend first, my bodyguard second."

In the dining room she stood at the head of a wide banquet table and a man in a wheelchair was beside her along one end. "My friends, I would like to introduce you to my husband who is recovering from a fall from his polo pony last month."

With the mention of polo, I saw eyes roll. I knew, not everyone player polo. I didn't know that the other sectors would have followed such an elite sport ... and resented it.

Barbara saw the expressions of disapproval. There was not a hint of embarrassment or offense on her face. She smiled. "I will explain one time that things in this house are not as they seem. We have great wealth inherited from Richard's parents and my own. We seem to live the life of the idle, self-indulgent rich. I hope you will find that we are vastly different from our image. Please sit down. Enjoy your meal."

"Lady Applewait and Dr. O'Reilly, Gray Fox and Little Feather, please join Barbara and me at this end of the table," Richard Cornwall directed.

"I apologize for our cramped seating arrangement. Our table comfortably seats twenty, and with all of us, we have twenty-six. Thank you all for coming. Let us bow," Richard said as he gave thanks for the meal, for those around the table and the cause for which we worked and risked our lives.

Barbara turned as three servants came in and served warm drinks of coffee, tea or cocoa and the soup course. "I'm sorry, Maisie, we don't have enough places for you, Roger and Quinton to sit at the table."

"That's all right Barbara," Maisie said as she placed a soup bowl in front of our hostess.

"Well, that's wonderful that you understand. Please, if you want to make a picnic on the floor with your food, that would be fun," Mrs. Cornwall said with a bubbly smile.

I watched as the three finished serving, then brought in their soup in large cups, sat against the wall and ate. "Barbara," the one named Quinton began, "this is great. What did you use for that special spice I taste?"

"Quinton, that is my secret," she answered with a wink. Everyone was relaxed and comfortable. Although the three served our supper, there seemed to be no unequal relationship in the entire room.

"Barbara, you said that nothing here is as it seems. You preside over this table like a queen over her court, and yet you're a kind woman who seems to think of others before herself. You serve us this wonderful meal that you apparently had a major hand in," I said.

"She made the whole pot of soup," Maisie confirmed as she sipped from the hot cup.

"This is a mansion, styled in a gold, extravagant manner, and ... you do the cooking. I'm confused," I admitted.

"It's not hard," Barbara explained. "It's just out of the normal scene one would expect in a setting such as this."

Without gawking, I tried to survey the room and the entry hall we had first entered. "We don't even have houses like this one in the Central Zone," I said with amazement. "I feel like a school child on a field trip."

Our hostess chuckled and patted my hand. "My dear, you are an elite, not I, and yet you don't set yourself apart from others."

I pulled my linen napkin to my mouth. I was surprised. She didn't accuse me. She simply gave an example I would understand. "Touché," I surrendered.

"I like to cook ... so I cook. If you think we have fallen on hard times and must do the work around here, you have guessed wrong. Richard's parents, and my own, reared us to be selfish, arrogant, and uncaring. We actually lived the life of the above-grounders, the rich and self-absorbed. Then ... our daughter, Phoebe Joy, died and we needed ... something. We didn't know what."

"We walked and walked every day, trying to forget, trying to figure out—*why?* One afternoon we wandered into an old church on Fifth Avenue. It had been a Catholic church but religion had vanished by then," Richard added.

"Religion had been banned in our zone, too. We know what you mean," Jason said.

"No, not here in the city. They didn't have to ban it. Money and prestige have replaced a belief in anything ... except *more*," Richard explained. "Their religion is the god of acquiring—gathering, not just enough—but more than all the others have."

"We went inside the church because we have always found peace in there. We used to wander in on some of our walks with Phoebe Joy. The beautiful stained-glass windows sent shimmering color across the sanctuary, on the floor, the furnishings, and the walls. That day, we walked in and found a prayer group," Barbara beamed.

"A Catholic group of believers was meeting there?" I asked. I had read a little about religious groups. I found them to be interesting yet quaint, deluded people from the naive past.

"No ... I mean yes ... we have no denominations, no Catholic, no Protestant, just Christians in prayer. We have been meeting with them ever since and it has changed our lives ... and our mission."

"Tell them about the moles that attend the group, Barbara," Roger suggested. "They are great. Not what we thought at all."

"You go to the prayer sessions, too?" I questioned.

Quinton tipped up his bowl and finished the last of his soup. "We all do now," he said.

"What do you mean by moles?" Gray Fox asked. "In Navajo, names have meaning. Mole means rodent. It also means the rodent lives underground. But, in this world's terms, it also means someone who is acting under cover. Which is it? I saw a Navajo symbol on this very building. Why?"

"To answer the last question ... the code markings ... there is a leader among the moles who knows the Navajo symbols. He said he is a descendent of one of the Code-talkers, a group of military men who devised a code for secret inscription based on their native language," Richard explained.

"It had never been written down, so the symbols were the first written language for the Navajos. You have one of my tribesmen on your side?" Gray Fox gasped. "He's a mole?"

"He is one of the underlings, the moles, who have lived below ground for more than sixty years. A few decades past the great crisis of the previous millennium, the elites convinced those dependent upon the state: with vouchers for food, medicine, schooling, clothing, public transportation—most all of their daily living supplies—that the surface was not safe. They told them bands of roving marauders slither about and kill just to remove a person's shoes," Richard shook his head in disgust. "During the first year, if an underling came up from below, someone was there ready to shoot them. After that, they accepted that the above-ground world was dangerous, even after the city dwellers lost interest and walked away."

I felt profoundly sad for the gullible people who believed such lies. "Why were they deceived?"

Barbara's face grew tight with grief. "All of the elite ones here on top, didn't want to see the common people anymore. They said they could smell them in their elegant stores and fancy shops. Some said they were like an infestation of common mold. Those with power told them, the only way to care for them properly and safely, was to move everyone underground. They started with the old subway system and converted it to underground lodging. Then they connected the basements of the stately buildings and skyscrapers, but sealed off the underground from any possible contact with the floors above— just business buildings, not residential."

"They haven't had any sunlight down there for all this time? Children are born into darkness and remain in the dark forever?" Jason asked. "Everyone knows that's wrong. With my medical background, I shake to the core. What is their life expectancy?"

Richard opened his mouth to speak and then paused, "Forty-five years." He shifted in his wheelchair and added. "They are convinced, if they come out of hiding, they will be killed. So, they stay below."

"That is actually the truth behind Richard's injury," Harold offered, then looked at the Cornwall's who nodded slightly. "He was not actually hurt in a polo accident. That was his cover. They had to invent a story."

Barbara patted her husband on the hand and smiled. "Richard and I open the roof-top terrace to the underlings for a few hours every afternoon. With so many moles, young and old, it's hard to meet all their needs. The underlings make their way underground to the old manhole cover that opens into our basement. It had been sealed but we released the seal."

"Isn't it dangerous for them to have such easy access to your sub-level?" Jason asked.

"We have been able to trust every one of them," Roger joined in.

"Do they have to come up into your living space to get up to the roof?" I asked.

"No," Richard answered, then added, "But, that would have been okay, too. We were able to construct a special path for them. Not because we didn't want them in our home. Because they have lived in such dark, squalid conditions all of their lives we didn't think they would be able to take all of the color in our living quarters."

"From the basement," Barbara explained as she sipped her coffee and smiled at the faces around the table, "the people can take an express elevator to the roof where they take turns laying in the sun for fifteen minutes every day. Last month, the manhole cover slipped and started to fall on a woman. Richard grabbed for it and fell over backward and broke his hip."

I struggled to understand the vast hoax perpetrated on the masses. "In the Central Zone, the people are kept in a slightly drugged fog that makes them pliable and free from all emotions. Here, it's different. Do they have their emotions down there? Are their riots and chaos in the underworld?"

"Actually, not very often. The severe vitamin D deficiency makes them cognitively dull even in fairly young people—twenties and thirties," Maisie explained. "We provided the brief time on the sun roof each day in the hope their bones will become stronger and they can fight off some diseases and think more clearly."

"You are not a servant girl, young lady," Jason laughed. "You're a smart young lady."

"I'm a surface mole," she smiled, "a former underling who was discovered during one of Barbara and Richard's trips below and brought to the surface."

"She is studying medicine right here in our home library," Barbara said and motioned with a wide sweep of her hand in the direction of the large library across the hall.

"A library right here in your own home," I marveled at the privilege of it. "So, the moles are taught to read in the underworld?"

"No, all of that work will have to be done when they are emancipated."

"Well Barbara, that's not completely true," Maisie stumbled through her explanation. "Barbara taught me all I would have learned in the primary and elementary grades of school in the first six months after I arrived in the sunshine. With my tools for learning, reading and numbers, I have studied all the rest on my own and ... I have gone below and trained others to teach still more of them."

"Maisie, I didn't know that. That's wonderful," Barbara cheered. "Why didn't you tell us?"

"I didn't want to put either of you in danger. You would have gone back down, and then perhaps caught. Traffic between the under and upper worlds is forbidden except for the motormen who deliver the goods and supplies to the people below at the rail head," Maisie explained hesitantly.

"Well, I think what you have done is wonderful, Maisie," Richard said.

Barbara nodded in agreement, then she added, "We're trying to prepare all those below for the shock of learning that they have been deceived in the vilest manner. Their lives and the lives of their distant families sixty years back have been stolen from them."

"Are the moles of one race or similar beliefs or identified by some other grouping?" I wondered how this could have happened. Then I remembered our citizens who were also deceived, just in different evil ways, all for the purpose of control.

"None," Maisie said, "except wealth and position. They had no power. They were the receivers of society, like Richard said, those who received multiple benefits from the State. They were of every ethnicity. Now, living in such close quarters, they are a blend of many."

"They must be beautiful," I added, thinking of the gorgeous blending of cultures I had seen in our sector. Our beautiful friend Dahlia is of African, European, and Native American heritage.

"They would be amazing if they were well," Maisie added.

Barbara continued. "The really hard part will be in preparing them for emancipation. We have no idea how they will accept the truth of their wasted lives. How will they believe that they will be safe on the surface if they have been told all of their lives that they will be executed if they come through the barrier between top and bottom?"

"What do you think, Maisie?" I asked the only one among us who had experienced the transition.

"You climbed out of the darkness. Were you afraid?" Jason asked.

"I could see small rays of light that streamed through the grates and manhole covers." She spoke softly as if she stood in a sanctuary of the deep. "I loved the steam grate over near the old Rockefeller Plaza, on Fifth Avenue outside of Saint Patrick's Cathedral. Although there were no services any longer, if I got there at just the right moment, I could hear music from the church. I didn't know who was in there or who was making the music, but it was beautiful. My soul knew there was more than the darkness. When I came up, the light was … I'm sorry, I don't know a word more powerful than breathtaking."

"So ... you don't think they will be afraid?" I pressed a little further.

Maisie smiled with wisdom gained from experience. "They won't know until they climb those steps up out of the underworld, that they will be leaving fear behind—that they will be stepping into a world of freedom, freedom from fear. There are far worse things than fearing a violent death. Fearing you will live your whole life without ever being seen in the light is far worse."

"We watch Maisie bloom in the light every day." Barbara blew Maisie a little kiss. "Her unselfishness in teaching some of the others makes me say more confidently that they are the key."

"The key?" I asked.

"You are here to get signatures on a petition to over-turn the Length of Days law," Barbara observed. "Here in this huge city, we believe that the only people, who could get around unnoticed, are the moles. The above-grounders don't even think about them anymore. They'll never notice a few moles, traveling as a duo. So many moles live down there now they may come close to fulfilling your quota of necessary names. Richard and I can work on the elites."

"They will be very pale when they come above ground. How will you camouflage them?" Jason asked.

"Camouflage? Jason, women have been wearing skin covering for hundreds of years. Do you have any make-up, Barbara?" I asked with a chuckle.

"I have plenty and we can buy more. Men wear it sometimes too, so the male underlings will fit in quite well," she replied.

Little Feather had been listening, then asked, "If your goal is to have them all live above ground, where will they all stay when they come into the light?"

"The stores around the city are all on the first floor, occasionally a department store is scattered among them with multiple floors. Still, most of the levels above the ground used to be the apartments where the moles' parents or grandparents had lived. We don't know how many are down there. Since their Length of Days is very short, due to starvation, malnutrition, or Vitamin D deficiency and the diseases they cause, there may not be as many as there could have been if they lived in a healthy environment," Harold informed us.

The volunteers who came with us listened intently, with nods of agreement and displays of emotion.

"It may be possible, that a family could reclaim their ancestral home when they come up," I suggested. I pushed my empty dishes back, leaned my elbows on the table and folded my hands together. I wasn't disrespectful. I had finished eating and I was tired.

"That's true," Richard responded. "The records of apartment and condominium owners are still available in the county property tax records office, since the power-hungry elite never expected the underlings to be seen again."

"So, it might be that my family could owe many years of back property tax?" Maisie asked.

"They would not dare!" Barbara growled. "They have enslaved nearly three generations of people," her voice rose with indignation. "And, they would try to charge them back taxes for being absent and unavailable for payment?"

"That won't happen, Sweetie. As an attorney, I'll make sure that it won't," Richard assured her. "I'll start to prepare the necessary counter-documents for any argument the political ruling class may try to impose on them," Richard encouraged. "I have my job to do, and I can work here in my office. Barbara and I would like to offer a suggestion for how all of you may proceed."

"Any ideas would be helpful." I was thankful for anything they had to offer. We were in a strange world with customs and beliefs that were evil and deadly to those who were not in control. And yet, the masses had gladly given up all that they had in order for others to take care of them. It all made me more tired than I was. I needed rest. My body demanded it.

Chapter 34
The Underlings

Monday - February 6, 2113

Barbara insisted that we rest all weekend. On Sunday, we attended a church service but, other than that, we didn't leave the Citadel. It simply wasn't safe. We sang songs around the piano in the gathering room, but most of the time we shared our stories and got to know one another. It felt like we had known the Cornwalls for years. On Monday morning, we gathered for breakfast.

"When everyone has finished eating," Barbara began, "I'll take you up on the roof to meet some of the moles. Then, if you feel ready … tomorrow, I'll go with you into the bowels of the city and see first-hand what you have to deal with."

"The underworld?" *Already?* I was afraid, but I couldn't let anyone know. For whatever God had seen in me that I had not seen in myself, he had called me to these people and the forgotten and discarded ones beneath their feet.

We had all finished our food and went into the entrance hall that stretched elegantly, high over our heads. I was amazed by the house and was learning that it sheltered many secrets.

"Christy and Jason please follow me," Barbara said as she led the way to a door beside the grand staircase. It opened into two areas; one was the door to a private elevator that provided access to the floors above; the other was steps that led to the basement. She flipped the lights on. "Richard can't do the steps with the wheelchair, so he'll join us on the roof. In the basement, there is another elevator shaft that is an express to the roof," she said. "When they renovated the house, many years ago, the access from the basement to the main

478

floor was sealed off. It isn't possible for underlings to get onto any of the floors except the roof. Since the people we invite into the sun get to the top, straight from the basement, I thought we would take their route."

"You have never created a new opening in the shaft, so they can come into the residential floors?" Jason asked.

"No," she said with a sigh, "and it's not because we don't want them in our home. We have to be prepared. If authorities were ever to come in and search the house, they must not find an access from the tunnels below the house to the living spaces. The underlings must be protected from the above-grounders."

Everything about the above-ground people was new to me: their twisted vile philosophy, the grand homes, and mansions all along the streets with devastation below, everything. Wherever I looked there was beauty, but it hid ugly lies. Now, I had to go into the basement, just steps away from the underlings dwelling place. I thought I was learning my way around my own country, and here, I stumbled down a rabbit hole where I couldn't believe anything. I hoped we hadn't been wrong in trusting the Cornwalls.

The steps were wide and made of concrete. I had never been in a basement before. I was surprised. I expected to see junk in every corner and rats running around. Even though it was black as pitch when we started down, once Barbara flipped on the lights, everything I had feared was absent. Just a few boxes and storage crates were present and all of them organized and tidy.

"This is a great space down here," I said. "If there were natural light down here, someone could call it home."

Barbara pointed to the walls. "The windows are covered in black cloth because that is a city-wide law. The authorities tell the underlings that there are coverings on all of the openings so the roving packs of human-animals cannot see them. But the truth is, the good and proper people on the surface don't want the moles to see that the city is actually safe and clean and the sky is blue and the sun is shining." Barbara's tone was that of rehearsed disgust.

Suddenly, there was a screech and the sound of heavy metal scraping across concrete. The cover to the manhole slid to the side and a man climbed up the ladder and into the basement, followed by a woman who appeared to be with him, a boy and a girl, and several others.

"I am so glad you have come," Barbara smiled and embraced them, even though their clothes were tattered and dirty and their odor was putrid. "We have installed a shower up on top, in a warm wet room," she explained. "Since it is still winter, you will want to get wet quickly, dry off and change into clean clothes we have hung up for you. If you are quick, you can still turn your faces to the sun for another ten minutes."

The elevator was large enough to hold us all, those of us who were *fine and fancy,* the little family, and various strays. It was tight inside the lift car. I gaged from their stench and buried my face in my hands which also provided a cover for my nose. When the doors opened on top, I burst out into the cold fresh air and breathed in as deeply as I could. Jason grabbed me around the waist as if to hug me, but placed his hands on my diaphragm to steady the spasms.

I watched as the others stepped onto the roof. They grabbed their eyes in obvious pain and held their hands there. It took several of their precious minutes on top to adjust their eyes to the brilliant winter light.

"Your glasses ..." Barbara coached, "the glasses I gave you, put them on quickly. Look at me, I'll put mine on." She forced the frames open and pushed them onto her face. "Quickly ... quickly."

I felt dazed and had to snap out of it. I dashed from one person to another and helped them to shade their eyes with the dark lenses.

Richard came up on the elevator and brought jackets and caps in his lap. "Up here, it's cold. The heat pipes under the city make the under-world pretty warm. Here," he spoke as he handed out jackets and blankets, "take these. You won't get as much sun as you will in the spring but we will build up to that as time goes on."

Barbara helped a child wrap a wool blanket around her. "I hope it's all right that we left the contingent of volunteers from the west downstairs." She spoke to me in a whisper. "I wanted you to get to know a few of the moles before we overwhelm the underlings with so many of you."

"That's probably a good idea."   I was the one already overwhelmed. I could not begin to imagine what it would be like to live all my life underground. In the Central Zone, we live in the dark, but that's because we choose the dark over the light, not because there is no light at all.

"Is it too blinding for you?" I asked one young woman, about my age. She stood frozen to one spot as she held her hand over her face.

"Yes, the sky is brighter than I had ever imagined," she said through her fingers. "But I want to open my eyes so much." She spread her fingers just a crack to let in the smallest stream of light possible. "I want to see it all ... even the bad parts."

"The earth is full of beauty," I told her as I helped her with her dark glasses. "See? Drink in the color of God's world."

"Lacy, Honey, there is so much to tell you ... all of you from below," Barbara put her arms around the young woman. "Now, enjoy the sun, shower and change your clothes, and then those of you here today will come below to the living area."

"In your house?" Lacy stammered. "But, we will all be shot or put in jail if we come out from the caverns." Her eyes welled up in tears and her expression grew tight with fear. She wrapped her arms around her body as the only protection she had for herself.

"It will be all right, Lacy. I'll prove it. This woman is Lady Applewait; she is a daughter of the ruling class. She won't let anything happen to you ... and neither will I," Richard assured her.

"The rulers?" Lacy recoiled from me and drew herself into the smallest ball of humanity that she could. "You are dangerous," she accused.

"I'm not dangerous to you, Lacy. Mrs. Cornwall is right. My grandfather is Sir Oliver Richly and my grandmother is Constance Richly. I ... I will protect you." I gathered her dirty hand in mine and patted the top. It was surprisingly soft. Her skin was thin to the touch.

How am I going to calm her, to reassure her? If I were her, I can't imagine I would trust anyone.

I opened my heart to Lacy and tried to comfort her. "This is a lovely garden up here, above the city. Enjoy the blue sky. When you come down, perhaps the inside rooms will not seem as bright."

The garden on the roof, above the streets, was wonderful. There was a section of out-door chaise-lounge chairs where sunbathers could rest and drink in the sunlight. On the long edge of the balcony, along the surrounding wall, ran an unending dark brown bench with soft blue padded cushions. The Cornwalls had taken the seasonal cushions out of storage and placed them on the deck/roof minutes before the visitors arrived. An outdoor cooking area with grill, cabinets and bar with chairs was up against the interior wall, protected from the elements.

"Barbara, it is wonderful up here. How long have the cavern people been coming up?" I asked.

"We started in the fall. Then when it got cold, we didn't have the heart to close the basement entrance. The underlings are amazed by the sky and the light." Barbara's voice trailed off. "It breaks my heart that they had never experienced it all before."

Jason had been circulating among the people with the eye of a physician. "I have seen some with the beginning of rickets from the Vitamin D deficiency, and they are all pale with probable eye conditions, but when you think about how they have lived ... it is amazing how healthy they seem to be."

Barbara patted the youngest child as she squinted in the light. "The old subway train runs to the mouth of the caverns that branch off in several directions. It brings only a very small portion of meat, some vegetables and fruits that didn't sell in the stores. The underlings have to share with everyone down there. Diseases due to obesity are certainly not a problem for them. Richard and I would love to take candy and desserts to them, but we were afraid to."

"I'm glad you didn't. I'm not sure how their bodies would have reacted." Jason smiled and then put his hand on Richard's wheelchair.

"Can I take you back down? You will only ache more if you get too cold."

"Let's all go back inside," he agreed. "Barbara will bring the rest of them down in a few minutes."

Jason and I walked over to the elevator and I turned for a moment. Lacy had showered, dried, and dressed. She stood facing the sun with her eyes closed and her chin up. She reminded me of a delicate flower in a spring garden that turns its petals to the life-giving sun. When the elevator car reached the roof, Jason, Richard, and I went down to meet the other volunteers in the dining room.

We walked across the marble floor of the hall and onto the hard wood. Inside the dining room, the other volunteers were laughing and enjoying each other's company.

"We might as well stay in here," Richard suggested. "In a matter of minutes, Barbara will bring in a few underlings who have been enjoying the sun on the roof. Everyone, please remember to stay seated when they enter. I know it's the usual courtesy for men to rise when people enter, but this case is different. You will discover that many things are out of the usual. If you stand, the underlings will feel threatened."

As the house elevator doors opened, Barbara stepped off and invited the moles into her home. They were all very awkward. Their eyes darted back and forth, not only because they appeared to be taking in every sight, but because they seemed to be very hyper-vigilant, watching for any threat, real or imagined. A man, who appeared to have the thin bones of one with rickets that would cause him to struggle with walking, entered with distorted, bowed legs. The handicap that was the most visible among many of them was the shock and terror on their faces. Would they be able to hear or believe anything we had to say? Would they be able to adjust to a completely opposite view of life from the one they had lived under all of their lives? Would fear rob them of the ability to adjust quickly enough to seize this life-changing opportunity?

My impulse was to whisper, like one would sooth a frightened child. "Lacy, there you are." She was the only one whose name I knew, so I started with her. "You look so nice, Sweetheart," I assured her. "You have a little sunlight on your cheeks. Those clothes Barbara gave you are great."

I gently took her hand and led her further into the room. Surprisingly, her muscles had seemed to relax already from the shower and sun. She was compliant and easily led. "I would like you to meet some of my friends from far away, where the ocean is calmer than the one here."

"Ocean?" Lacy questioned.

"They have not seen anything above ground," Barbara reminded me.

"What about the view from the rooftop? Were you able to see anything up there?"

"With the dark glasses I could open my eyes for a few minutes. We have lights below, so we adjusted to some light—but not the bright sun. And, yes, My Lady, I did see a little of the view from up on top."

"Out beyond the buildings there is a wide patch of water that goes on and on," I tried to explain. "You couldn't see the other side, just water. That's the ocean."

"It was all so beautiful," Lacy said softly and smiled.

Well, there is another big ocean, miles, and miles on the other side of our country. Many of the people here in this room are from that coast," I explained in a tone I hoped did not sound condescending.

"All of you ... come on in," Barbara invited the rest of them. "You can sit along the floor with the others." She pointed to floor space on the far side of the room. "Yes, there and there." Then she seemed to blush. "I'm sorry we don't have enough seating."

"I would like to give Lacy my chair, if I may," Little Feather offered as she slowed got up.

"Oh no," Lacy said. "I can't take your place."

"You aren't taking it, Lacy. I'm giving it to you. It is my privilege to offer you what I have." Slowly some of the other travelers got up from their seats and insisted that one from the underworld take it. They then took the floor space along the wall.

"Thank you all for having a generous spirit." Barbara smiled as she watched the moles hesitate then slide onto the velvet upholstered dining room chairs. They felt of the soft fabric. Their eyes lit up with some of the light they had just seen and were now experiencing in a different way. "Let's begin," Barbara announced. "Christiana, please sit at the table with our guests," she gestured toward an empty seat at the head of the table. "Most of you had met Lady Applewait and Dr. O'Reilly up on top."

The newly freed outcasts nodded and smiled. Some whispered between each other.

"Please, call us Christy and Jason," I urged. "We have a very important job that requires our equal ownership for it to succeed."

"Equal?" The man said who now sat on a real chair for the first time in his life. "Equal has never been used in our language. What does it mean?"

"It means—" I started to give a definition and then scrambled to think of words that were so simple they escaped explanation. "Equal means that I am no better than you, and you are no better than me."

"Oh ... yoke-sharers," he said as his face spread into a grin. "I'll carry the bucket on my shoulder if you'll carry the other one on your shoulder."

The underlings smiled and giggled.

"Exactly," I agreed, amazed by his ability to grasp a concept I had trouble putting into words.

"I don't want to offend any of you," Jason began cautiously, "but can those in the caverns below read and write?"

"Yes, nearly all of us, except the weakest ones. And even those can write their name and read short pieces. They get tired so fast it's hard for them to pay attention to anything for very long. They sleep a lot."

"But, could they learn?" I stumbled into the question without thinking about who might get hurt. "I'm sorry. What I guess I meant was, who taught them?"

"We have very little down there," a man of about thirty said with a set jaw and downcast eyes, "but we had loving parents who taught us to read and write. They would scratch in the dirt and sludge on the ground. Together, we would make up stories and Mum or Da would write them down on paper we found in the trash at the railhead, then we would read them back to them. Our history was learned through story-telling."

"And remember, Maisie has gone down to teach some of them and they would have taught others," Barbara reminded me.

"Yes, Maisie, I'm sorry. I did forget." Then I looked at the small group of moles and realized all they had done. "You have created your own society down there, haven't you?" I observed. "I don't know how to tell you, but the history of the world on top has been far different from what you had been told. What I mean is we are no longer the free society that you may have learned about."

"Yes Ma'am. We are not free," a woman said.

"That is true. But the reason for your living below all of these years ... was a lie. Not one word of what you were told was true." I felt so badly for them. They looked at me like I had switched my language into the native tongue of a distant world.

"What part of it was a lie?" Lacy asked. "We have all lived below because they said there are mutant human-animals that would stalk and kill us."

"None of that is true," I whispered. The underlings looked at me, then at Maisie, Jason, and the rest of us with glazed eyes. I wondered if they would be able to absorb the deception they had lived.

Chapter 35
They Came in Search

We all heard some commotion in the entry hall. Richard Cornwall snapped his wheelchair around. I saw he was a man of strength, the protector of the house, and wheelchair or not, he would fulfill his duties. He slipped away from the rest of us and quickly made his way to the door. Just as he got there, the door flew opened. "Harold, what seems to be the problem?"

"Is this Mr. Cornwall?" A man at the door questioned and took a step inside the house.

"Stop there, Sir," Richard ordered. "This is my home, and you have not been invited in."

"Invited?" the man grumbled. "I am Chief Inspector Stoner of the Blue Guard," he announced brashly and took another step. "I have a right to enter wherever I decide."

"Not in the Eastern Zone, Chief Inspector. You have no reason to enter my home. We don't have our homes invaded—and certainly not here in the city. We are in charge of our own fate here. We enjoy certain privileges."

Stoner stood his ground but did not take another step. "Oh, you do, do you?" he smirked. "It has been reported that several long cars pulled into your driveway and dropped off quite a few people. Congregating in one spot is illegal. We are on the trail of some who have crossed into your zone. They could have been in the party."

"We are coming in," a big burly man thundered.

"Hold your ground, Daniel," a woman ordered.

"You have no authority in this zone, Sir," Cornwall pronounced with clear determination.

"I have national papers, Mister. Now, move aside. In the Central Zone, we would *exterminate* you. We don't have men in rolling chairs ordering people around." Again, Stoner edged his way forward.

"Well, we do. Your national papers only allow you to cross the border and observe. You cannot pursue anyone or interfere in citizens' lives. And, you certainly have no right to enter my home."

"Who I am in pursuit of ... Mr. Cornwall," the Inspector spit out, "is not a citizen of the Eastern Zone."

"But he is ..." Richard spoke with measured tones, "he is a citizen of the United States ... before he is a resident of any zone."

"He who?" Stoner bellowed.

"He is the collective *he,* Inspector. *He* would refer to anyone who lives within the borders of the United States," Richard schooled him in American history.

"These are detached but United Zones—Mister. I do not recognize the United States," he yelled as his neck veins bulged.

"Sir," the woman spoke insistently to the inspector, "let's go. We can watch this house to see who comes and goes."

"Boone," Stoner seethed, "do not correct me," he shouted.

"I'm not, Sir. I'm suggesting another strategy."

"If you stay at least one block away, you have the right to observe any house in the city." Cornwall smiled with confidence. He didn't add that the underworld was vast catacombs deep beneath their shoes that connected all of the areas of the city.

"What do you want me to do, Boss?" Daniel asked; his face rock hard with anger. "The Blue Guard can go anywhere we want to."

"But, not here," Richard stated firmly.

Stoner stood back and looked down his nose at Cornwall. "You haven't won, Mister. Believe me, we will research our facts. If we find out that you are harboring illegal immigrants, you will be arrested."

"There is so much injustice in our land right now, Inspector, someone crossing a border within their own country, surely is not that important to you."

"She is not just *someone*." Stoner stormed out with Boone and Daniel Washington on his heels.

Richard sat silently in his chair and listened for the footsteps to fade on the front walk outside. Then he threw the dead bolt on the door. "Harold, be sure to keep the door lock set, even when we are home. It seems we have an overzealous police officer in our zone."

"Sure, Richard. Hopefully, he'll find who he's looking for and leave the zone."

"He has already found her. He just doesn't know it."

• • • • •

Richard wheeled himself back into the dining room where we all sat and waited in stunned silence. Lacy trembled beside me. Maisie had quietly come over and patted Lacy's shoulder and stroked her hair.

"Didn't Richard tell you that he wouldn't let anything happen to you?" Barbara began. "He didn't, did he? We will be as careful as we can be ... but it's true, there will be those who will try to stop us, all of us. I won't speak about the other zones, but the ruling elite in the Eastern Zone, want things to remain as they are."

"There isn't a lot of time for you to catch up to the truth," I started to explain. "For that, I am sorry." My words seemed completely unworthy of the situation. I had no idea how to tell these people that they had been enslaved underground all of their lives for no other reason than that the elites didn't want to see them in their world.

"We have come here from the Central Zone to get your help on overturning a law that you may not know anything about," Jason began.

489

"I'm Lincoln Jeffrey," the thirty-something underling spoke up as he straightened his back. "No, we haven't heard of any of your laws but—"

"We don't mean to insult you. There are things you haven't been told. That's what we need to explain. It is not my law. It's the law of the land. Some zones obey the law, others do not, or they adjust it to meet their needs," Jason said.

"The law is a despicably evil law, Lincoln," I explained. "In the short version, people are not permitted to live out their lives until they finally die of natural causes. A hundred years ago, the government worked out a formula that dictates how long a person can live, based upon how valuable they are to society." I looked around at the moles and I saw something, a connection in their expression. Some place within them, they understood.

"We didn't know about the law, but there's been a rumor for a long time, that people above ground live a whole lot longer than we do," Lincoln said.

I looked across the table at everyone who had gathered there. "We are here to get people's signatures on special papers called petitions, so we can vote to get rid of the law. We will need your help to call on other friends down below to try to get everyone's signature, and bring them to the Citadel, here at Richard and Barbara's house."

Suddenly their faces contorted in fear. "Will we come up through the basement? We can't come out in the open," Lacy gasped.

"There is something else, Lacy," Barbara began. "You don't have to live below ground. The town is safe. No bands of murderers roam the streets."

"That can't be true," the young woman barked in anger.

"Yes, it is true, Lacy," Lincoln agreed. "You know I've snuck into the church services in the big cathedral on Fifth Avenue." He turned to Jason and I. "I retell the sermon when I get below again. Isn't that true?" he asked as he addressed his friends. He wore sadness on his face like a shroud of tears.

The moles whispered around the table. Their voices became flat and despondent. Their tones grew grayer as they listened.

"Listen to Lincoln," Maisie pleaded. "You know him better than me. I was an underling too."

"That's a lie!" A man exploded as if his heart would burst if he remained silent any longer.

"No, it's the truth. Valery and Albert Zimmerman are my parents." She held her head high, as a dual citizen–one foot in the underworld and one foot on top.

"Maisie?" Lacy gasped. "You're my cousin. How is that possible? You went up into the world and everyone said you were killed."

"I wasn't killed. I'm here," she said as she laughed.

"After church," Lincoln began again, "I would go outside, onto the sidewalk after the service and watch the fine people going for a walk in the sunshine, laughing and loving their families all dressed up in fancy clothes." His eyes shone like he was seeing the fine parade of families passing by in their summer whites.

Some of the moles sat dazed by what they heard. Others gasped in stunned desperation, "What happened to us?"

Richard explained, "Those in the government with elected authority, some in entertainment with pseudo influence and many in business who had wealth—began to believe they were more important than those they hired. They believed they were entitled to live their lives away from the common people. They started to separate themselves from the people who worked for them by putting up high walls around their estates. They demanded abundant generosity from those whom they walled out, and lavish ownership for themselves. As time went on, they felt so guilty about their growing wealth, they believed they had to take care of people with handouts of food, shelter, education, health care and, finally, nearly all of their daily needs."

"They made us all like their children," Lincoln realized.

I watched as their eyes welled up with tears, as grief over their lost lives began to pour out. Leaning my elbows on the table, I continued. "Then, they said, if the masses can't take care of themselves, why should we have to look at them every day?"

"Look at us?" Maisie asked, her voice filled with disgust.

They had to hear the truth. I continued. "They built high rise apartment buildings and gave the people a schedule of hours when they could be outside. They claimed it was the way to keep the population on the streets and in all of the stores at a manageable number."

"Manageable?" one said with a gasp. "We were managed–like the rat population?" His voice sounded strained and shrill.

"Then, one of the fancy people said, they shouldn't have to see any of you at all. That's when they started the big lie." Tears rolled down my cheeks as I tried to explain how selfish, evil people had robbed them of their lives.

"So ..." Lincoln tried to speak but his voice cracked, "there was no reason at all ... none ... for us to have been born, lived, and died in the sewers, basements and subways of this city?"

"Absolutely no reason at all," I whispered. "It's like a political prison my grandmother told me about." Tears streamed down my face. "You all have been prisoners, too."

"You can all come out from the underworld," Barbara said. "Everyone can come into the light. For many of you, your ancestral home has been vacant since you or your loved ones left it. The dishes are in the cupboards, the books are on the shelves." Barbara said. "I have been in some of those homes."

"You mean we could walk right out your front door?" One of them asked as he fought tears and anguish. One woman laid her arms across the table and sobbed into the fold.

"Yes, you could. You can walk out of here and not come back." Richard stopped as the facts of their kidnapped lives soaked in. "You are all emancipated." He rolled his chair a few inches back from the table, as a gesture of freedom-giving.

"I feel like a slave being told they are free and can leave the plantation. But I don't know where to go or how to get there." A middle-aged woman's face, etched in pain and sorrow, twitched with emotion. She angrily brushed a matted curl from her brow.

"You have heard about slavery and the old plantation system of generations past?" I ask. I couldn't believe what I heard. "How would you know, with no one to teach you?"

"But we do have teachers, Ma'am. Lincoln taught many. Our grandparents taught our parents, who taught us. Where there's a wish for knowledge, there's a teacher," the woman spoke with pride.

"And, as for places to live, we can help you find your home," Barbara offered.

Suddenly, anger welled up inside the woman with the curl on her forehead as she set her jaw and spoke in tense, chopped words. "What if I leave and never come back? What will you do then?"

"Nothing," Richard spoke softly, comfortingly.

The woman got up and started to walk out of the room, then turned. "You really aren't going to stop me?"

"Of course not," Barbara assured her. "Like we said, you have always been a free person ... but, none of you knew it."

"None of us?" She stopped. "My daughter is still down there. I can't go anywhere until I get her out. I have to get her out," she cried. "I have to get her out!"

"May I tell you the plan the Cornwalls, Jason and I talked about?" I asked. I was careful to make no statements but to ask her permission.

"All right? Do I have to sit back down?"

"You may do anything you want to do," I offered.

"Okay," she said hesitantly and moved against the wall without sitting.

"The volunteers from the Western Zone will go down with some of you to talk to the people and tell them that they're free. Jason and I will go, too. We will lead the people, your friends and family out, and up the steps through one of six subway exits so that we can help as many as need our assistance. I know there will be many, but Dr. O'Reilly believes we need to help the sick when they emerge," I added.

"There aren't as many as you would think, after all of these years," Lincoln reported angrily. Then he added with a sorrow-filled whisper, "They all die so young, so very young."

Lincoln's words stirred me so much it was hard to continue. "I am so sorry, Lincoln." Then I turned intently to all of them. "At the opening from the wretched bowels of the city, people will greet each one and ask them if they want to sign a petition to stop another evil perpetrated on the people, the Length of Days law. It wickedly limits a person's number of years of life. Under that edict, people don't just die of disease or old age. When they reach a certain age, extermination is the law. We are trying to over-turn that abomination."

"Give me a pencil," the woman snapped to attention. "I'll sign that paper."

"Thank you for volunteering ..." I waited for the woman to give me her name, so I could add her to my mental list of heroes.

"My name?" she asked with wide eyes. "You want my name?"

"Yes, Ma'am," I said gently.

All eyes turned to her as she shifted a darting glance from one of us to another. "My name? ... My name is Jennifer."

"What a beautiful name, Sweetheart," Barbara said and gently accepted the woman from below.

"Stewie?" one of the moles gasped. "I thought your name is Stewie."

Jennifer smiled sheepishly and nodded as she said, "They all like my stew."

"If I may, I'll call you Jennifer," I said. "The name is as pretty as you are." I couldn't help but notice the sparkle in her blue eyes, in spite of the conditions under which she had lived her whole life.

"Yes, please do." She smiled a smile that filled her face.

"The people collecting the signatures will not force anyone. They will not tell anyone that their signature is their ticket out of the darkness, or anything like that. They need no ticket. All they have to do is walk out. The people will just be asked if they want to sign it."

"Just like that?" she questioned. "We walk out on our own and no one will stop us or harm any of us. That sounds nice, but how in the world will we be able to cope, in a world of light we have never known?"

"One day at a time," Barbara said.

"I don't' pretend to understand how you feel," I assured her. "I can tell you this—in the Central Zone, the water the people drink is laced with drugs that dull their emotions. They don't feel anger or anxiety, but they don't feel joy or love either. We have started to detoxify them. They have to learn how to relate to each other all over again, to know the feelings of attraction, to feel the love of their families. They have to walk that journey one step at a time, too."

The woman squared her shoulders and drew herself up to her full height. "Then I can do it, too. You can count on me. I have no idea how to do this, but I won't be helpless anymore. They can keep their free food and their free cast off, ill-fitting clothes. I will earn my own."

Chapter 36
A World Below

Tuesday - February 7, 2113

Very late in the morning of the next day, when the sun was nearing its peak above us, Jason, the Western Zone volunteers, and I accompanied Barbara Cornwall, Lacy, Lincoln and some of the other underlings as we approached the opening to the belly of the city. It used to be a subway entrance. But, since the only transportation the wealthy enjoyed was their own personal flash-cars, limousines, or aerial lifts from rooftop to rooftop, the mouth of the River Styx was now nothing more than gum-blotched cement steps and a dangling bronze hand railing.

"It'll take a while for your eyes to adjust to the dim light," Lincoln explained as we descended into the unlit subterranean maze of tracks and tunnels. "Torches are placed on the walls at the entrance to the various areas. Then once you have gone deeper into the underground communities, you'll begin to see crude connections for electric lights. We still have to keep the light dim so we're not seen above-ground."

He sounded so educated, I was amazed. I said nothing. I had no words for this whole experience. It was so far from my own world on the top floor of the Indian River Apartments, I couldn't wrap my mind around the dank existence here. I was surprised I felt no disgust as we descended down further into the troll-like world below the streets of the beautiful city of parks and monuments. Lincoln was right. I saw the faint glow of light, but my eyes focused on the darkness all around me. I wondered if the underlings gazed more intently on the light than the dark. We inched our way through the below-world.

"Oh," Lacy moaned as she bent over.

"What happened?" Barbara asked and put her arm around Lacy's shoulder.

"I stepped on something and twisted my ankle."

Barbara looked apologetically at us. "I am so sorry. I'd better take Lacy back to the house and check her for any scratch or cuts. Infection can so easily get in. Their immune system is very low. She can rest her ankle for the afternoon."

"I'm glad you're going to take care of her immediately, Barbara," Jason said. "And, the rest of us—be very careful where you step. Inoculations for the diseases that may be down here, stopped a hundred year ago."

"Put your feet up, Lacy," I said as they left. "Thanks Barbara."

"Take care, Lacy," Lincoln said before he turned back to us and continued. "We'll be going above and sometimes below the sewers. Where they're below, we'll have to drop down through some manhole's, to follow those trunks," Lincoln explained as he looked both ways into the dark recesses of the underworld. "Some of the large-trunk sewer lines were too large to change when the subway was built, so there had to be a large adjustment of the gradients of the subway in order for the line to pass them," he smiled with satisfaction. "I often spend time in the library and try to figure out what stands over our heads in the world above," he said. "At Canal Street and Broadway and at Duane Street and West Broadway here in Manhattan, the subways were built to go under the sewer. At Brook Avenue and 138th Street, in the Bronx, they actually raised the surface of the street by five feet so the subway could pass over the sewer."

"That's amazing that you found out about all of this, Lincoln. You're so valuable to us," Jason encouraged.

"Over the years, I've been through every inch of this maze down here," he said as we walked and climbed and maneuvered through it all.

"Are you going to make it, Christy?" Jason asked as we both looked at the obstacles in front of us.

"I have to," was all I could think of. And, it was true. I couldn't stop before I had even begun.

As my eyes adjusted, I found myself in a large tiled space with a train track running through it. People were everywhere: on steps that led to nowhere but another sealed opening; leaning against the walls; and even on the narrow walkway across on the other side of the tracks. Some children were playing a game drawn on the floor in which they tossed a pebble into a square and then proceeded to skip along, jumping over the square occupied by the small stone. I panicked a little until I heard the others climb through the opening behind us.

I had led a very sheltered life. Just a few months before, no one could even approach me because I was and am, a legacy citizen. I smirked at my own silly thoughts of privilege and position, while these people lived their lives buried under the ground.

"Oh, Jason, I'm so glad you're here." I felt like a child as I grabbed him and clung to his arm.

"I know, Honey. It's all so strange and different. But, remember, we have our depravity too ... under Howard Mountain." Jason assured me, "You are one of the strongest people I know. You can do this."

"Friends," Lincoln began addressing those who clustered near us as he closed an opening to the stale sewer on the other side. "I want you to meet some new friends. They're from the surface, but it's okay. You're safe."

The people huddled together while the children ran to some adults for reassurance. "The surface?" one of them questioned.

"Yes," Lincoln said quickly, "but they mean us no harm. Their message is the most important news you will ever hear."

Suddenly we heard loud voices and the sound of heavy boot thumps from a trunk line that intersected the one we had just come through. I held my breath. The faces of the underlings around us grew tight with fear and terror filled their eyes. The angry world above had found them.

"Where? Where are the man and woman? I don't know how they got down here but someone reported invaders in your midst." We heard a distant voice from the other track line. "Answer me!" the voice shouted.

I grabbed Jason's hand and drew it to my lips. My kiss was not gentle. It was urgent and full of the panic I felt deep inside.

The underlings around us clutched one another with fear etched on their faces. The older ones gently put their hands over the smaller ones' mouths to caution them to be silent.

We listened to the demands from the distant shouter. I recognized the voice. I knew who was down there. He had followed us to the gates of purgatory. I listen as another man spoke.

"What are you doing down here?" A different male voice bellowed from a short distance farther into the subway trunk. "You three, get out. We may be afraid to come to the surface, but I guarantee you, we'll protect our safety down here!"

"Mama?" one of the children whispered.

The woman made no sound. I wondered how she had caused the child to be silent. I couldn't see them, but I knew that staying in the shadows would be the only thing that would save us.

"I am Chief Inspector of the Blue Guard!" the man bellowed.

My breathing stopped. I was right. Stoner was here. My presence could bring harm to the people who had already suffered more than they even knew.

"Ward," a female voice urged, "let's go. The Lady wouldn't be down here."

"A woman said, those scum from below were meeting at the Cornwall house," the Chief demanded.

"We went there, Sir. Nothing was out of the ordinary. Besides, the citizens of this zone can be anywhere they want to be," she stated flatly.

"But they choose to live in this wretched place. Can you imagine? They gave up the light for this sunless place," his voice was angry and erratic. "That is why we kill the feeble minded in our zone."

"Did you hear me?" the underworld protector hissed. "Get out of here!"

"All right, all right, we're going. But, if strangers are in the tunnels, you will let us know, won't you?" the growling inspector coaxed.

"Sure we will, right away," the voice agreed flatly. "I will escort you out of the lower reaches."

"That won't be necessary," Stoner barked.

The man stood firm. "Yes, Sir, it will be very necessary. No one, and I mean no one, comes down here on purpose."

We all remained motionless, silent. A small child squeezed his eyes shut, balled up his fists and held his breath. We froze in place, regardless of how uncomfortable our position had been. My back stung with pain as I tried to balance myself with one foot on the train tracks and one on the concrete pathway that ran beside and above it. We didn't move until we couldn't hear the footsteps and voices any more.

Lincoln spoke first. "That was Jefferson, my brother. He was the one who ordered them out of the tunnels. He'll join us here in a minute, as soon as he has thrown those three out. They were probably harmless, but we take no chances."

"They aren't harmless." I stated firmly.

"You recognized their voices?"

"Oh yes," Jason agreed. "We know them. They are very dangerous people. But you are not their target."

"They aren't after you," I assured them. "They're after us, Jason and me. We will talk to your people, recruit those who can help and try to tie things up as quickly as possible." I looked at the faces of the little ones around me. I couldn't allow them to be hurt or even frightened. As I adjusted to the dim light, their sweet faces became clear. I didn't want my presence to bring harm to others.

"Okay, they're gone." Jefferson smiled as he backed into our area, not turning his back on Stoner and his crew.

"Lincoln ..." I smiled as I put the two men together. "You have had history books down here, haven't you ... Lincoln and his brother, Jefferson."

"No books, but we have wonderful oral histories and keepers of the stories," Jefferson explained. Then he added, "Is Gray Fox here with you?"

"Yes, he and his wife are traveling with us. You know him?"

"Yes," he agreed.

Gray Fox and Little Feather emerged into the train passage once the ruckus had cleared out. His countenance was stoic and calm.

"I have a message for you." Jefferson offered a piece of folded paper to Gray Fox.

"How did it arrive?" the Navajo asked.

"It came across the Cornwalls' communication device. She wrote it down exactly as it was told to her."

Gray Fox took the paper and unfolded the sheet. "AL-NESHODI UL-SO ... Mission Accomplished," he translated, and then he smiled. "Rachel Claudette had worked with a tribesman of mine to get the message through in a language that could not be translated by others."

"So, the Western Zone has completed their petitions with an adequate number of signatures?" I questioned.

"Mission Accomplished," he pronounced again.

"They are finished with their canvass of citizens?" Lincoln asked. "Already?"

"The Western Zone has a vastly different demographic than the other zones," Jason explained. "There are a huge percentage of Spirit-filled people there. They signed petitions as they left worship services on the Sunday morning that we were there. Connected by the Jumbotrons, we reached a multitude of people in a matter of minutes. That left the collection of names by the Hollow People."

"Hollow? What does that mean?" Jefferson asked. "They're empty?"

"That's what has been said for many years. They don't circulate with the regular population. They can't work, participate in education or receive any benefits of citizenship, including the right to vote."

"Like us," Jefferson said bitterly.

"Yes, I suppose ... just like you," Jason agreed. "And, like the underlings, they are very much misunderstood. One of the Hollow Men, Raymar Goring and his daughter Kasamar reached out to the unseen people in their society and told them they were needed."

"They were needed?" a woman with pale skin and lifeless eyes repeated.

I watched the woman's face as something turned on inside of her. "And you are needed as well," I assured her. "Raymar told his people that they were vitally important to the cause of humanity and our reverence for life. We need signatures from as many of our citizens as possible to overturn the Length of Days law. A return to the old way will let people live as long as their body can," I added. "Life is so precious. You here in the under-world, live to be about forty-five years old. In the Central Zone, people live until they reach a pre-determined number of years. For my grandparents, because they are on the Council of Twelve, they reach the end of their Length of Days at age seventy-five."

"Ah," the woman gasped. "Age seventy-five?" She shook her head in disbelief. "How can that be? They would be old and decrepit by then."

Now that I had informed them, I wondered if they would even believe. "In the Western Zone, people live to be about one-hundred forty-five."

Her expression was not that of disbelief. It was of pain and sorry as she added, "Except for the Hollow Ones," she whispered. "They have no reason to live many years."

I knew she understood the tragedy of the Hollow Ones' lives because she had lived it in her own way. Her face fell in sorrow and her eyes rimmed with tears. "Except for the Hollow People, you are right. We will make sure they can live fully in society too and enjoy long years of life. You all can," I assured her, "with the elimination of the Length of Days law."

"Why would you do that?" someone asked.

"Because you all have a right to life, liberty and the chance to pursue your own happiness," I quoted. "You have a right to reclaim your ancestral homes, find jobs and seek your own joy in life ... above ground where the sun shines and the sky is a beautiful blue."

"I have seen the sky," a boy about twelve years old blurted out.

"Frankie, don't tell people that," a woman warned. Fear escaped her eyes as she clasped her hand to her mouth. "Hush, hush. It's very dangerous to speak out."

"But it's true," the boy said. He became excited as he revealed a secret he may have held for a long time. "I stand below the street grate when the sun is high in the sky and the colors are bright and beautiful. I can see that blue color you talked about. It's super," his young eyes shone with a heart that has seen the color of hope. "That's its name? Blue?" he asked. "But I never knew that I would be able to walk into the world of light, the world of blue."

"It's so dark and dull here," his mother said as she put her arm on the boy's shoulder and gave him a hug. "We had forgotten the names of the colors, or how to explain the shades to our children. In the dark, we only see shades of black and gray. Blue is only blue when you can see it."

"Frankie," I said as I reached out and touched his shoulder, "yes. The color of the sky ... and your mother's eyes are blue."

Frankie reached up and touched his mother's cheek, as if he were trying to open her eyes even wider and inspect the new color of blue.

I wondered if the mother and son saw the tears in my own eyes. "Frankie, would you like to be one of the liberators ... one of the many who will tell others that they are free? We could use an important young man like you."

The boy's eyes filled with tears that made salty streaks on his dirty face. Finally, he was able to choke out a whisper. "Could I do that?"

I smiled and let the enthusiasm I felt inside, slip out into the open. "I'll bet you have been all over down here. I knew every alley, field of wild flowers, and pile of re-usable *good* trash in the neighborhood in which I grew up. You probably have inspected and investigated every nook and cranny in the underground. This is your world and you are comfortable down here. You know the tunnels, the subways, and the sewer line. I can just imagine you inching up manhole openings and darting down dark passages with no fear. Yes, you are needed."

"I am needed? Just like the Hollow Man?" he asked. "He had been all over everywhere, too, because they wouldn't let him stay anywhere very long."

"You would be just like that man. He is full of life now."

"Can we start today?" he asked. "I want to help. I want to be needed." He looked up and his eyes met his mother's. She nodded with pride and mouthed, "Thank you."

"We sure can," I agreed. Then, to all those gathered around, I explained, "Barbara and Richard Cornwall have placed trusted volunteers at several subway exits. They each have petitions and pens so we can get that law overturned. We hope everyone will sign one of them." As I looked around at all the eager faces, another thought came to mind. "Be sure you sign the petition only once. I appreciate any enthusiasm, but it will make the petition invalid if there are false signatures on them."

The people smiled and nodded. They understood the need for honesty, but their expressions revealed a thought that might not have been too far from some of their minds.

I wanted to laugh but thought they might not understand. "It will be important for everyone to come up from the underworld through the subway exits, not the manholes, so they can have an opportunity to put their signature on one of the documents. When they sign the petition, it will also give the Cornwall's a list of all those enslaved on Emancipation Day. They have a committee ready to help the people relocate."

"I can take you all through the world of slime and darkness right now, if you're ready. Can we start now?" The boy reached for my hand and urged me along. I could feel the excitement through his fingers. They trembled with urgency.

"Frankie ..." the woman cautioned. "Be patient. The lady will tell you when she's ready to begin contacting all our friends." She grabbed his hand but he pulled away from her, not in rebellion but in anticipation of the amazing task we had in front of us. I was surprised at how quickly a young child could pick up on the importance of our work. Then I laughed when I learned his motive.

"Please Mama, please!" Again, his eyes filled with tears. "Don't try to stop me. This is my chance to be somebody."

His mother brushed his hair from his eyes and cupped his chin in her hand. "Always remember, Frankie," she soothed. "You have always been somebody, and you will always be somebody. Not somebody else, but the very best you that God has ever created."

"I know Mama," he said.

"All of you are somebodies," I said softly. "No one can be a better you, than you."

"You can go, Frankie, but I want to come along," his mother stood tall and strong. She squared her shoulders and inhaled deeply, filling her lungs with a new life. "I want to join in the enthusiasm. I want to feel like somebody, too."

"Follow me," Frankie squealed as he skittered off and led the way through the dark halls and tunnel-ways of his world, beneath the city, under the very feet of the ruling elite.

Chapter 37
Jewels

We had been groping our way through the underground passageways, basements, sewers, and subways of New York City. I was amazed how readily the people accepted the fact that they were a free people. Frankie and his mother joined another group and followed off in a different direction, a location where many children lived.

One man told us, "In this corner of the underlings' world we had always known that we were lied to. We went up-top to get the truth ourselves. Nothing happened to us. We didn't talk to people, and they didn't talk to us. It was safe." He stopped and sat down on an old up-turned barrel. He looked around at the old friends he had lived with and smiled. "But our family lived all over down here, in various areas of the world below, and they had either not heard the truth or had refused to believe it. We stayed down here so they wouldn't be alone."

"That's a great sacrifice," Jason told him.

"It isn't a sacrifice when it's family," the man said.

"Will you come with us and find the rest of your people, Mr. -?"

"Abraham Felding."

"I must tell you, Abraham," Jason warned, "we will be going deep into the darkest, vilest part of the caverns. It could be dangerous and full of disease."

"Then we must get them all out," Abraham said as he turned and started to walk into the dismal areas. "Some of my people are burrowed way back in there." Suddenly, his eyes welled with tears and his jaw was tight with anger. "What in the world happened to our country? I have a couple of history books that I have read over and over. We were a people blessed by God. How could all of this have happened? Were people that dumb?" He started to pace back and forth in the narrow passage we were on. "They had no right to be that stupid!"

What could I say? He was right. I tried to comfort him but he pulled away so I tried information, a path into him that he had taken on his own in the past. "During the great upheaval of the previous century, some leaders became frightened. Not that the country was endanger of losing its treasured spot in the heart of God, but they feared they would lose power, they would lose control," I answered him with truth. "That is what I understand from my study."

"All of this," he stammered in disbelief mixed with grief, his eyes wild with anger, "all of this horrible existence is because a few of the ruling elite didn't want to lose their power?"

I wanted to tell him that everything had been lost in a great war. Or, a natural disaster had turned society upside down and they took extreme measures to save the little that remained. That would have been kinder. A huge lie would have made more sense than the truth. But, that's not what had happened. It had all slipped away years before Raymar and Kasamar and others called Hollow, or Underlings, and those called Moles, had their lives stolen from them by the imposition of a label. It was all so unbelievable.

The entire population of the Midwest, including the major cities like Chicago and Indianapolis, had allowed a Socialist government to seize everything people made with their own hard work. They then shared it with no one, but allowed only the ruling body to own it. Sure, new land cooperatives had permitted the farmers, shop owners and industrialist to eke out a miserable living by working for them, the government ... deceptively called, The People. But the people were no longer "we the people."

Here in the Eastern Zone, those who were unimportant people with no power trnd wealth were duped into hiding, into not being seen any more as they lived out desperate lives under the fancy feet of the ruling class. But I couldn't lie to them again. I looked at the man squarely in the eyes and said, "Yes, that is exactly what happened."

"What a stupid, lazy-thinking bunch of people they were," Abraham said, shaking his head in disgust. With his arms folded tightly around his body he paused and rocked on his heels. Then, he quickly announced, "We must be totally silent as we pass through this next sector. It is the entry for the Engineer," he explained.

"Who is the Engineer?"

"Shh, he is at the head of the stairs," he whispered. "I hear him and it sounds like others are with him."

"Why?" I whispered. "Who is he?"

"The Engineer comes down the dangerous steps and waits for a pretty girl or a strong man to go by. He asks them if they want to work above-ground. He will protect them, he says, and he'll make sure they never have to go outside again once they're in a new job. They'll be completely taken care of in exchange for food and shelter and a comfortable bed." He watched with widened eyes in the direction of the stairs.

"Slavery, Abraham that is the same as slavery. What color are the people?" I could not believe the lies upon lies told to these sweet people.

"Color? You mean the color of their skin? They're any color. What difference does that make? What matters to the Engineer is if they are pleasing to the eye. Skin color has nothing to do with it. But it can't be slavery," he shook his head in disbelief. "I've read in the history book about slavery and these people are not sold. They are glad to go to the surface." Abraham pressed his body against the wall in the darkest part of the entrance.

"But they can't leave their employer," Jason concluded.

Abraham nodded. His eyes searched the floor, lines of pain visible on his face. Then he stopped and listened intently.

"I told you not to follow me," they heard the Engineer say.

"We are looking for Lady Applewait and Dr. O'Reilly," the man barked.

I almost gasped out loud. Inspector Stoner had continued to follow us into the underworld, the world of mortal pain. Would we ever be free of him? I clutched Jason's hand as we hid in the dark shade of gray below.

"You are looking in the sewer, Mister!" the Engineer laughed as he shrugged and threw out his arms in a demonstration of disbelief. "Just look around you! Where are you? You're looking down here for a fine lady and a physician—in the filthy underbelly of the earth? Now that's what I call intelligent!"

"How dare you mock your superior!" Stoner yelled as the veins in his neck bulged.

"You aren't my superior ... in anything ... Sir," the engineer spit out through clinched teeth and glaring eyes. "I'm not the one looking for gold and fine silk in a filthy crypt."

"Ward, what are we doing down here? She isn't here, not in these tunnels and ghastly places," Stoner's female companion pleaded.

"Boone, you ... so we should just go back home? And leave Miss Uppity to cross borders unlawfully and whatever else she is involved in."

"Yes, Sir, that is what I'm thinking," the female answered.

"Home? Lieutenant what is wrong with you? You have known me for how long now? Have you ever seen me retreat from a case just because it's difficult?" He didn't wait for an answer. "Well, forget it. I will never sound retreat on this mission."

"Nothing is wrong with me, Ward," Boone said with her head held high. "Just think about it. Look around you," she looked at the underlings who clung to the walls and bottom steps. She lowered her voice to a whisper. "Do those faces look like the kind of people Lady Applewait would call *friend*? You aren't thinking clearly, Ward. Think about your pension if nothing else."

I could see the woman from deep within the shadows as she pleaded with the Chief Inspector. She may have been the woman who interrupted the church services in the Western Zone, I couldn't tell. But, I knew I recognized her voice as the woman who came with Stoner to the Citadel. She sounded reasonable but she was arguing with an irrational man. Then, I quickly drew my head farther back when a third Blue Shirt stepped around the lieutenant and began to inch further down toward the subway platform.

"Washington!" Stoner barked. "Get back here. We've seen all there is to be seen down here," he looked around at the squalid, lifeless conditions. "Unless you like derelicts and packs of dirty kids running around."

Little ones had come into the station platform when the above-grounders came down the steps and had stayed to watch the commotion. Now, they scattered like stray kittens when Stoner roared. I couldn't blame them. I was frightened, too. They had slipped into the area in silence and now they had slid out just as quietly. Instantly they were gone.

"No, I won't believe that our friends are walking into captivity on their own," Abraham argued after he watched the Engineer close the opening to the above world. "They just want to earn a little money and get out of this ... place."

"But, once they are above ground, they can't go anywhere, can they? Abraham, that isn't freedom to work. That's bondage," I insisted.

"I can't think about that," he whispered and then said little more as we pushed on through the debris and the garbage. In the recesses of the tunnels, there was less light and less of everything else.

"I'm sorry," he apologized. "It's going to get even darker. But we're lucky that the moon is full tonight. But, remember, with a bright moon, people above will take walks in the night air. Be quiet. Be unseen. We will get some light through the grates above."

"It reminds me of a prayer I read. *God Bless America.*" I said out loud but actually, it was a thought that slipped out.

Suddenly, Abraham began to hum a few notes of the melody to the great old song. I recognized it. "Music had been banned in the Central Zone, but a few of us had gathered in our building to sing," I said as I thought out loud. It was my way of stemming the fear that gripped me.

"That one does sound familiar. I can't remember the words," Jason added. Although he was right beside me, his voice sounded as distant as mine. Perhaps we were dissociating ourselves from the horror of everything around us.

As we passed under an open grate, moonbeams danced through the flat bars above and cast streams of light along our path. Then I heard Abraham softly hum again as we made our way through the dim paths.

"Through the night, with a light from above[1] ..." he sang to himself, like a hymn of faith and encouragement.

The words came back to me like the waves of the sea, one line folded in on top of the other. I clung to the song like Abraham did. Then Jason joined us in our melody of hope and praise in this most unlikely blessing of a home.

We moved on through the darkness and talked to the people who hid there. "The petition will let you live out the lives God has given you." We told them of their right to freedom and happiness.

"What room is this?" I gasped and gaged on the stench of it.

"This is where the gatekeeper to the garbage room stays. See the large, metal door over there? That leads out to the river where barges line up at the dock. The gateman opens the hatch when it's time to dispose of trash, and dumps it into an even larger room. At some point, the entire contents of the room on the other side, is loaded onto a barge and hauled to a dump site. The gatekeeper must stand guard to make sure no rats escape into the underworld."

"This is the disposal for everyone down here?" Jason asked with his hand across his mouth and nose. "How big is the space beyond the wall?"

"I don't really know," Abraham admitted. "There actually isn't as much garbage as you would think. These people have so little, they use everything they get or find. There is not much thrown away." Then he spotted a woman near the door and stopped. "It's all right Jewels. They mean you no harm."

The woman crouched on her haunches against the wall near the floor. A staff with a crook on the end of it was in her hand and stood erect on the concrete. She froze when we came near her, her eyes wild with fear.

"Jewels?" I cautiously approached the thin, young woman who huddled near the door. "Hi." I reached out my hand to touch her dirty hair but ... I was surprised, it didn't seem repulsive. My heart went out to the young woman who would have been beautiful on the surface. Down here, she had dark sunken eyes, a vacant stare and pallor complexion.

At first, she pulled away from my touch. Her eyes darted from side to side, as hyper-vigilant as anyone I had ever seen.

I stooped and crouched in the filth around her. "Jewels, please look at me."

Her eyes flashed back and forth, then they met mine and she stopped with a gasp. It was like she finally recognized the presence of another person. Someone had stepped into her world and saw her there. "Jewels, you keep watch very good. You have a very important job to do."

"We're thankful you're here," Abraham joined in the conversation, welcoming Jewels back into the family of the living.

"I do?" She looked puzzled. "An important job?"

"You keep everyone down here safe from rats and the diseases they carry," Jason encouraged her. "You do a great job. Any rat that comes your way, you push away with your staff." He waved his hand in front of her eyes. She was able to lock on and track his movements as her eyes followed his hand.

"Jewels, these people have a very important message for you," Abraham said. "Everyone down here receives the message and pass it along to their family and friends. By morning, everyone will know," he said with pride. "We're doing something wonderful, Jewels. We're setting everyone free."

"Free?" Jewels stumbled over the word, like she had never heard it spoken.

"All of you down here can leave. You can go to the world above. You can go anywhere you want to go." I watched her expression and reached out my hand to her.

"No!" she shuddered. Suddenly, she pulled back from me like someone burned. She coiled herself into a ball and rocked her body back and forth.

"Jewels," Abraham coaxed, "we're all leaving. We're going home."

"Home?" she whispered, "I am home." She looked around her filthy squalor with lifeless eyes. "When you all leave ... will I be here alone?"

"No, Sweetheart," I urged her. "You are coming with us ... to the surface."

"We will all die," she breathed out with a weak sigh. "We will all die."

"Jewels, you've been told a lie!" Excitedly, Abraham paced back and forth. "We have all been lied to. You can live with your family in the other home your parents' parents grew up in ... up top. Come on Jewels."

"No, Abraham. No. I have no parents ... no one."

"Yes, you do," he stopped his anxious roaming. "Why would you say that?"

"No, I don't. I should know. They are all gone. They died." Her voice trailed off and fell on the floor at her feet.

"Baby, I just talked to your brother, Sonny, a few hours ago. He made me promise to bring you out of this hell hole."

"Sonny? Sonny is alive? But ... how?"

"May I ask you a few questions, Jewels?" Jason asked gently.

She nodded her head. The dirty blond curls bounced on top.

"When did you last see any of your family?"

"I don't know. Before I was told I had to do this job."

"Who told you that?"

"The Engineer," she looked back and forth from Abraham to me.

"So you haven't seen your family in all this time?"

"I haven't seen anybody. No one comes down here." Tears rolled down her face and dripped in the dirt below. "They say it smells so bad they can't breathe. I don't notice it any more. I stopped breathing a long time ago."

"Then, who told you that your family had died?" Jason asked.

"No one. But ..." Her speech broke down into great sobs of grief. "They would have come for me if they were still alive. It's been months and months." Her face distorted with anguish and the filth of the place.

"They couldn't come for you, Jewels. No one is allowed to be down this far in the tunnels." Abraham pronounced each word distinctly, as if a better enunciation would bring understanding to a confused and grieving girl.

I took a step toward her. At first, she started to raise her staff, but then lowered it slowly. Finally, she didn't pull away. I put my arm around her shoulder in spite of her terrible odor. "Jewels, people are waiting for you at the entrance to the world of color and music and hope. They will ask you if you want to sign a petition. We are getting signatures from everyone, so we can overturn the law that limits the number of years a person can live. Sweetheart, you don't have to worry about that. We have volunteers from the body of believers on Fifth Avenue collecting signatures from exit sites all over the city. You will have a chance to sign sometime in the next week or so, if you choose to." I waited while Jewels absorbed what I was telling her.

"We will try to have your family at the very opening to the underworld from which you will emerge. Your loved ones are far more important than the petition right now." I wanted her to know she was of more value than anything else we were trying to do.

"You said everyone will be signing the petition?" She looked me in the eye and seemed to grow a little stronger as she spoke. "Every single living person?"

"Yes, they are."

"Then, I will sign it too," she stated decidedly. "People have a right to live, don't they? And, people have a right to be called a living person."

"Yes, they do," I smiled. "Now, let me help you off the floor," I offered as I stood and held out my hand. She reached up and let me help her to stand, slowly, but with new strength. Together, we walked back through the tunnel, past abandoned cooking pots and snuffed out fires, and up the steps the Engineer used to lure those who longed for light and an escape from the darkness. But, this time, the underlings were setting themselves free, not into the back of a truck that would deliver them through the back door of a residence or business. They walked boldly up the forbidden steps and into the light the moon cast on everything around them.

Chapter 38
Free

This was a walk I had lived for. Although I had been in the Eastern Zone for a short time, the exodus seemed like emancipation for me as well.

We came out from the underground at the far end of Manhattan Island. Abraham put his arm around Jewel's shoulder, but even safe in his grasp, she held the heavy staff firmly in her hand.

It was night, but the moon illuminated the darkness of the hour. The street lights shimmered on the backdrop of the night-time sky. There had been a little rain while we were down below. The air was clear and clean, the freshness like unmatchable cologne. My lungs ached as I sucked in the miracle of life ... the breath of God.

My eyes searched the crowd for any sight of Stoner or his small group of Blue Guard. "Are they here?"

"I don't see them, or any city police either," Jason assured me as we continued to scan as far as we could see. "There are many official exits, with sign-up tables for the underlings at each. Maybe they are at the main one, the Engineer's Entrance. Stoner probably thinks we want a large audience as we emerge, and we would get it at the main opening."

Harold Humphrey waited for us beside a small group of volunteers. They had gathered around a portable table they had set up for the underlings to sign the petition when they emerged. Small, wireless heaters warmed the feet of those who sat at the tables and those who came near to sign the papers. Nearly every soul who came up those steps from the dungeons beneath clustered around the table to sign the paper that would increase their lives by one-hundred years.

Jewels and Abraham walked as boldly as they could, on the feeble legs of malnutrition. They leaned their grimy hands on the table and drew their names on the petition slowly, as an artist would draw a masterpiece. They also put their name and the names of as many relatives as they could remember on the register that would eventually reunited them with their family, and relocate them to their ancestral home.

"Jewels?" a voice from behind called out softly.

Jewels gasped when she turned and embraced her brother at the liberation table. "Sonny, oh Sonny," she sobbed.

"Jewels?" a woman who looked years older than the stated age on the papers she had signed, touched the young woman's shoulder timidly.

Jewels turned and stared at the woman who had touched her, the warmth of the contact still remained as she touched the spot with her hand. "Mommy? Is it you, Mommy?" she wept and fell into the arms of the mother she had not seen in over six months. A man and the young man, Sonny, embraced them both. I watched with my eyes and my heart. A family reunited, rescued from beyond the River Styx.

I didn't want to intrude on their reunion, but I had to make sure each of them knew what was next. I approached them carefully. "A volunteer will take you all to the processing center where you will be linked up with all extended family who could claim your home of origin. Go slowly, be generous and kind, and know that God loves you all."

When I turned again, there was a young woman, immaculately groomed in a soft blue shaysilk dress, with real pearls sewn at the oval neckline, like in a Vogue Magazines of old. I could see snatches of the lovely garment beneath her evening coat when it flapped as she moved along. The dress fell to mid-calf, just above matching pumps with chunky heals like in the movies from the 1940's I had found in the library.

She curled her lip as she looked around at the people, the table, and the volunteers. "What are these inferior ghosts doing on the top?"

"Ghosts?" I questioned in disbelief. Had she heard of the underlings? Did she know of their plight?

"Of course, ghosts," she snapped back as she tossed her long, golden hair over her shoulder. She put her hands on her hips and strutted closer. "Ghosts are unreal beings. They are in your presence but they aren't really there, are they?" she explained with a smirk on her face and her jaw thrust out.

What a brilliant explanation, I thought to myself but didn't want to give her the satisfaction of responding to her. She couldn't have been more than nineteen or twenty, and I wondered what she was doing out in the evening alone. We couldn't have done that in the Central Zone.

She continued to stand in front of me, leaning her whole body in my direction in an aggressive stance. She let out a long string of obscenities and stomped her foot on the ground. "Well, my daddy will see about this! I should be able to walk all the way home without seeing anyone or anything that would offend my eyes," she whined in a spoiled baby voice.

"So, if you see someone on the street, in your path, it would offend you?"

"If they don't look like me, of course it would," her hands flapped in a feeble gesture of tired frustration. "Get those ghosts off my street," she demanded and walked on.

"They aren't apparitions, Miss," Jason called after her. "They are real people."

"They are not!" she yelled. "They are no-bodies. Their carcasses belong in the other place, the garbage dump of the under-world," she shouted back. "No one should offend me. I have rights."

Jason and I stood motionless in disbelief. "She has a right to not be offended? And ... she gets to decide what offends her," I shook my head. "Oh Jason ..." my head was swimming with questions that had no answers and grief that had no justifiable cause.

"We'd better move on quickly." Harold nodded in the direction of the block south of us. "That man, Stoner, and the others are here looking for you two. They moved on to the Engineer's entrance.

Some of the freed people have seen you. They may say something in their excitement."

"But, not many of them heard our names," Jason reminded him.

"It only takes one," I sighed.

We moved back against the buildings where the street lights would not be as bright. How many shadows had I found over recent months that I didn't even know were there? My heart pounded and I was getting tired. It felt like I was racing inside. Would life ever be normal again? And, was the life I had left behind in Capitol City really normal? Normal for whom? For me ... Lady Christina Applewait? Normal for these forgotten of the world, the underlings, and the Hollow Ones ... what was their normal? Lives of slavery, of being outcasts or scapegoats ... sent out from the city to bear the sins of the *nice* people.

"I'm parked up here, in the next block," Harold took my elbow and guided us toward a block to the north. "We'll have to be careful. That man, Stoner has been up and down Manhattan, from the Battery to Harlem."

We inched along through the growing crowd of the newly freed, with our eyes fixed on the long car ahead of us. Then, we spotted them. Stoner and the woman he called Boone were going from one freed refugee to another. They held a 281 Palm Device and a hologram likeness of me shimmered on the sidewalk beside them. One of the women I had talked to earlier looked over at me as I hid in the darkness, and shook her head, "No." Then she walked around the hologram as she moved on down the sidewalk following the others. Her movement caused Stoner and his minions to shift position as well, which took Jason and me out of their line of sight.

With Stoner positioned with his back to us, we quickly darted across the wide sidewalk and got into one of the black long cars with the heavily tinted windows. Harold got in and slowly pulled into traffic without looking back, so as not to draw attention to us. He drove us back to the Citadel. Maisie greeted us at the door.

"It's all a miracle," she chattered as she led us into the large living room. "My family was liberated an hour ago. The Cornwalls invited them all to stay here with us until they research their claim to the family home. They're upstairs showering and resting." She continued to babble with excitement as she led us into the parlor. "Barbara will join you in a moment and then I'll hurry back upstairs to be with them again."

"You go along Maisie," I offered. "You have waited for your family for a very long time."

Barbara rushed to embrace us the minute she entered the sitting room. "You are all back and safe. I know the underworld has two extremes. It is very violent in some parts and quite safe in most of the other areas. I'm glad you found the safest areas."

"I don't think that trash hole is safe for anyone," Jason shook his head in disgust. "They don't live very long because death is waiting everywhere." Then he asked, "How is Lacy's ankle?"

"She's resting it. The skin wasn't broken so I don't expect any infection."

"Oh, thank goodness," I said.

Richard wheeled his chair into the room, applied the brake, braced himself on the arm rests, pulled himself out of the chair and reached out in friendship to Jason and me. "You are our Moses, Christy. We had been gathering volunteers to provide the safety net for the liberated underlings. It has taken a long time, and we didn't know how they would receive us. If we brought them above ground with no shelter for them, that would have been a cruel consequence of trusting us to free them. They not only had to trust us, they had to feel worthy of freedom in order to muster the courage to leave the only existence they have known. You were the one for whom we waited to provide the catalyst for the emancipation effort. You provided another cause, a noble reason for them to come above ground."

"Thank you, Richard," I said. "The real praise goes to those brave souls who are stepping into the fresh air for the first time in their lives."

Suddenly there was the sound of hurried footsteps in the outer hall. The racket startled me. Too much had happened. The Inspector had intruded on our lives so many times before, I expected him around every corner.

"Christy, it is so good to see you," Martin Spires burst into the room with outstretched arms, followed by Rebecca.

"My dear," Rebecca said as she embraced me. "Barbara told us what you have been doing. How can we help?"

"How did you get here?" I was shocked. "How did you get out of the valley without being seen?"

"We are all a network, Christy," Barbara explained. "Sean has been sending his newspaper across the border into all of the zones for a long time. Gray Fox has buried code into the page heading. It looks like an abstract picture but the code is silently waiting for another code talker to translate it."

Martin smiled. "In the last paper, we received word from Barbara to come to the city to help re-locate the ones from below."

Barbara reached for a tray that Quinton had brought in. "It has been a very long day. You all need to get some sleep, and cocoa is just the right prescription to help you." She poured the hot chocolate brew into fine china cups. "Maisie took some up to her family as well."

I laughed a little as she handed the cup to me. "I'm sorry, I was just thinking. The underlings have had absolutely nothing. They lived like cave people in the ancient past. Tonight, they will sip cocoa from translucent, white china cups and sleep on silk sheets. Wow ... none of this could have happened, if you and Richard had not prepared a way for them."

"Tomorrow morning, Raymar, Kasamar and Rachel Claudette will be here from the Western Zone," she brushed away the compliment and dwelt on the service of so many others. "Also, Ed and Maud Musselman will arrive about the same time. We will review the work thus far. We'll make sure the planning for gathering all the signatures for the petition is perfect. The work must be able to continue when you two go back to the Central Zone." Barbara paused and drank the warm sweet brew from her cup.

When she put her cup down, she added, "And, we must begin to plan strategies for getting out the vote when it does get on the ballot."

My heart pounded with excitement. Was it all possible? Would they overturn the evil law? We had traveled far and were tired. We had even dug people out of their burial in the earth, to bring them into the light ... not so they could add their signatures to the petition ... but because they belonged with the living. Maybe it was all possible.

"Yes, Christy, it is possible," Martin laughed. "Don't ask me how, but I believe I know what you are thinking. Maybe it's because it's all so miraculous, I have also wondered about our success." He thought for a moment and added, "But, that is wrong. We couldn't have come this far if the hand of God had not helped us. It will happen, Christy. We will get the signatures needed."

Chapter 39
The Gathering

Wednesday Morning - February 8, 2113

"I will come in!" the voice of Chief Inspector Stoner growled at the open front door of the Citadel.

"No, Sir," Harold stood his ground. "As I told you before, you have no authority here. You will not come in. Now, go back to your fancy strata car and be on your way."

"This officer has authority," he snapped his fingers and shoved a New York policeman into the open space at the door.

"Good Morning, Officer Cardoso. It's a beautiful day today." Harold greeted the neighborhood officer while standing his ground in the expansive doorway.

"Hi, Harold. This Central Zone Blue Guard Commander seems to think that travelers from his zone are here. He aims to take them back and charge them with crossing the border illegally."

"That, and plotting to over-throw the government," Stoner seethed.

"Yes, the Inspector was here the other day." Harold added no more to his statement. The least said the better.

Cardoso turned to Stoner, his jaw tight and his eyes fixed on the man who tried to push himself into a world in which he had no power. "You bothered the Citadel before this? And, now you're back with the same demands?"

"Sir, you hold your tongue. I out rank you by many promotions." Stoner's teeth gritted in anger.

"Not in the Eastern Zone you don't," Cardoso insisted.

The yelling at the door filtered into the dining room where we had all gathered to plan the next phase. I was setting near the end of the table, and I could see the three that Harold appeared to be blocking. I froze. It was Inspector Stoner of the Blue Guard ... again. He had pursued us all over Capitol City, and now he had disturbed the Citadel again. He seemed to pop up behind every building and sewer line.

"From the activity in the house, I would say you have guests," Stoner bellowed as he craned his neck to try to see farther into the house. I slowly turned in my chair so my back would be toward the door.

"Actually, we have a lot of people in the house today—"

"Many people ... they're the ones I'm talking about. Boone, go in there and see if Lady Applewait and Dr. O'Reilly are here."

"You will not," Harold blurted out before the woman could take a step toward the door. "The Eastern Zone has had moles, underlings living in the subways and basements, passing through one area to another along the sewer and subway system lines. It has been a tragedy beyond words to express." Harold spoke with compassion and determination. "These people have just been emancipated from a lifetime of isolation and slavery. A few of them are staying here at the Citadel. They have been through a lot. They will *not* be disturbed." I liked Harold's forceful handling of Stoner and his crew. I turned a little to peak at the reaction.

"Under the city?" Boone asked with astonishment on her face. "We had started down an old subway entrance. You mean they have been living in the sewers? How long have they been down there?"

Harold whispered and nodded toward the stairs that led to the refugees in the rooms above. "Most of them were born in the underworld. Since their life expectancy is only forty-five years, they would have died down there as well. Their parents have all suffered a miserable existence in the underworld and have died without ever seeing the light again."

"Oh, how awful," Boone muttered.

"Don't take pity on them, Lieutenant. They probably are paying for crimes they have committed," the inspector sniffed with superiority.

"They are not," Harold stated firmly. "They were tricked out of their entire lives with lies and deceit by evil people who cared for no one but themselves. The lie that was perpetrated on their ancestors is still in place."

Boone looked over in my direction as she scanned the whole area and the rooms she could see from the door. When she caught my eye, she didn't turn away. She said nothing. She didn't smile. She just gazed at me with what seemed to be warmth in her eyes. "These people have been through enough, Inspector. We had better leave and let them try to pull their lives together." Boone put her arm gently on Stoner's shoulder and steered him in the direction that turned him away from the room in which we all waited in silence. "It sounds like these people have been hard at work, freeing a group of people they didn't even know. I call that pretty wonderful. Let's get back to Capitol City and look for the Lady and her doctor there."

"Maybe we can figure out what road they took out of the zone and put up a road block," Stoner agreed, although his voice sounded like his heart wasn't in retreat. "When they come back, we can grab them at the border."

As they walked out the door, Boone turned and smiled at me. She nodded a gesture that seemed to me like mutual respect, and left the house.

• • • • •

One by one, the chairs in the dining room filled with people we had met since we walked through Howard Mountain, key people in the other zones. Rachel Claudette, the Musselmans, Barbara and Richard, Raymar Goring and Kasamar, Gray Fox and Little Feather, and Jason and I, all sat around the table and summed up the progress we had made in a very short period of time. The other volunteers went from room to room upstairs and tried to answer questions and meet the refugees' needs.

Rachel handed me a large package. "I brought your beautiful cloak with me from the west."

"Thank you, Rachel," I said and was so glad to get it back.

The beautifully polished table shone, and the exquisite seventeenth century floor-standing clock in the corner, pulsed—ticking like a metronome keeps the beat of a song. No one said anything about the authorities who stalked us. That was a frightening reality none of us had an answer for.

"Never forget," Richard began, "you are not breaking the law by gathering the signatures. That doesn't mean that those who want things to remain as they have been won't look for ways to try to stop us. So far, the only law you have broken is crossing the boundary lines between zones."

"What you are saying is we have become wanted criminals because we have traveled around our own country." It all seemed so ridiculous to me.

"Those pompous, self-righteous, power-hungry, ruling elites thought the people would be more manageable if they were confined to smaller sectors. It doesn't make any sense. Each of the states used to have a unique quality all their own," Rachel added. "Now, most of that diversity is gone."

"But, we can get it back," I jumped in. "We have seen such unique characteristics of each of the zones in the short time we've been here. And, since people don't travel more than a few miles from their homes in order to preserve fuel, those distinctions could still be present. They weren't free to go anywhere. If anything, hopefully, the sweetness of the uniqueness may still be there."

"So, you're saying that we can get the Length of Days law over turned and put our country back together, too?" Ed Musselman asked. "I've been waitin' for this moment all of my life."

"The Citizens' Referendum will be on the ballot at the next election and ... we hope to run my grandfather, Sir Oliver Richly, for

President of the re-United States. I know he can bring our country together again."

Everyone around the table stirred with hope and enthusiasm. Maud announced with energy, "We in the Mid-Western Zone have enlisted a huge body of farm people to help. They have friends or family all over the zone, from rural farm life, to the cities of Chicago, Indianapolis and Cincinnati." Her excitement spilled around the table. "Another great aspect of mid-western living is the connectedness they have maintained with those family and friends." She sparkled as she continued. "They had recently started or continued an old practice of family round-robin letters. They use them to make contact with each other on a monthly basis. Drivers of milk tankers, grain semi-trucks and anything else that continues to move on the highways carry the letters. Family is as important to them as their country. You should see the excitement in the families we have already contacted."

"Perfect," Barbara said as she smiled. "The army of volunteers will grow. The wonderful people in the Mid-west listened to all of the fancy speeches about sharing everything one has with those less fortunate. They forgot that you can only give away all you have once. Then there is no money left to help yourself or anyone else." Everyone around the table either nodded or spoke words of agreement.

Maud added, "In the present system, no one can strive to be the very best that they can, because, the best that they can be is no more than the least among them can become. Now, the government has all the power, all the wealth, and all the future. Those in control, the elite, never gave away anything. The people in the Mid-western Zone are more than ready to get their lives back."

"Wonderful," I agreed with relief. "How did you manage to keep the dreams of the past alive?" I asked as I thought of the stilted emotions of those in the Central Zone. They had no memories of yesterday, let alone images of their family's history, the story of their lives. They were flat in the present, and walked a path with no destination or starting point.

"We kept hope alive, 'cause we're country," Ed explained. "There are few of us. Large groups of urban people could not corrupt our stories. Those in the cities don't even think about us out in the country. We were left alone with our traditions, our family histories and our beliefs."

"I'm sure that's right," I said. "I wish more of our large country had been left untouched."

"That is wonderful, Ed. I'm wondering how the Western Zone has fared?" Richard inquired.

"There was a huge percentage of people in worship services that morning Christy and Jason were there," Rachel smiled. "With Grace Small's help, we were able to contact all of the worshiping groups in the entire zone with the use of the Jumbotron. Raymar Goring organized the Hollow People. He is here with us today, to map out the next step in reclaiming our blessed country."

"The moles have been freed from their slavery that was forced on them by the ones who hold the purse. Nearly all of the molls signed the petition as they left their vile underling squalor," Quinton said.

"But how will you convince those who have it all, that some others have nothing?" I questioned as I thought again of the monumental task ahead.

"Not all of the influence peddlers, ruling class and elite business owners have hearts of glass. There has been an Age of Silence here in the East as well. Most have been afraid to speak truth to lies and deceit, even the most despicable, vile injustice perpetrated upon a group of people." Barbara eyes filled with tears. "The underlings thought they couldn't make their own happiness on their own. The more they depended on others, the more they lost respect, until they were stored away in tunnels like useless old paintings no one wanted to look at any longer. But many who were above ground thought that was wrong. There was no way to speak out in the past. If we did, the label of dirty underling-lover followed us. We can get their help to gather signatures."

"But they didn't appear helpless below," Jason said. "It looked like they had carved out small communities, unique villages, down below."

"Isn't it ironic? Once separated from the ones who provided for their every need, they began to take care of themselves and each other. They became creative as they found ways to make things out of stuff considered trash to others and sent to the caverns below. But they couldn't leave that dark life, buried beneath the feet of others." Barbara added.

"We have decided to dress them in fine clothes," Richard laughed. "Barbara will teach them to apply make-up to their pale, sunless complexion, and introduce them to New York Society as royalty from abroad."

"The above-grounders will believe it because they will want it to be true. Nobility in their midst will make them feel even more important than they already think they are. If Baron Oakridge tells them that signing the petition will give them knight-like valor, they will arm-wrestle with one another to be the first to hold the pen."

"Is that honest?" I asked. "I'm not judging. I mean will the signatures be valid based on a lie?"

"Everything they tell the people about the petition: the over-turning of the law by a citizen's referendum, the facts of the paper itself, will be as true as true can be. The only fabrication will be the name and position of the one who asks them to sign it," Richard explained.

Barbara quickly added, "The name and position of the underlings have already been taken from them. Their existence blotted out of current history, even census records. If it weren't for the old property tax records, their names would never be found."

We sat in silence for a moment as the full tragedy of the underlings' lives penetrated all the way to our heart. In the quiet of the room, I felt a sudden breeze from the entry hall. The doorbell had not sounded, but I looked to the area to see what might have caused the gust of wind. The woman, Boone stood silently in the entrance and quietly closed the door. My heart pounded.

"Christy, what's wrong?" Jason asked when he saw my expression freeze.

"Jason, I—"

"I am so very sorry, My Lady. I would not have dreamed of entering a private home uninvited a few months ago. But I was there. I was there on Christmas Day evening when the whole city sang for the first time and you and the others brought the signed petitions to President Alexander's home. And ... I saw it, Christy, I saw your drawing." She paused for a moment as her eyes filled with tears.

"You are Boone?" I asked.

"Yes, Ma'am, Lieutenant Chalky Boone." She shifted her balance as the snow dripped from her shoes and made a small puddle on the marble floor. She glanced down and gasped, then stooped to wipe it with a cloth she pulled from her pocket.

"Lieutenant," Harold placed his hand under her elbow and helped her to her feet. "Please, I will be happy to take care of that for you."

"Thank you, I—"

"How did you get past the alarm at the gate?" Richard was impatient but controlled his emotions.

"The Litchfield Master Lock Company springs every lock of any kind with a tonal frequency that sets up a vibration." She pulled it from her pocket and embarrassingly revealed it in her outspread hand. "My Lady, please, give me a few minutes, I beg you. I mean you no harm. I would have told the Inspector and that creature, Washington when we were all here a few minutes ago if I did."

"Where are they, the two men?" Raymar questioned. "I know a dangerous man when I see one and those two are both dangerous."

"They are at a nearby restaurant. I excused myself for a few minutes. Please, let me speak."

"They will come looking for you." Fear rose up inside me. "When they find you, they will find all of us as well."

"I'll leave. I just wanted to tell you that Ward Stoner is not the man you have been seeing. Before his wife died, he was kind and even funny at times. But now, you have become the focus of his anger and resentment. I have seen nothing but good in you and what you are doing. I'm sorry I judged you differently when you were in the

Western Zone. Then, I saw all that you did today to help others. I'll stay close to Stoner and try to divert him away from you," she explained as she backed out of the room. "I've got to go so I don't lead him back here to you."

"Thank you, Lieutenant," Barbara said as she rose to escort Boone to the door.

"Please stay seated, Ma'am," Boone motioned with her hand and quickly slipped out the door.

"Regardless of Stoner or Boone or whoever, we must continue to help the newly freed underlings find their families and their homes," I said. "I would like to help get it started. I know we can take a few days more to do that. I would not miss the beginning of a new life for so many."

Chapter 40
A Plan

Friday - February 10, 2113

"Christy?" Jason called up the staircase.

"In here," I said from the sitting room. I had found a comfortable chair near Barbara Cornwall's floor to ceiling library shelves of books. I placed the leather-bound book that smelled as good as it was beautiful, on the table beside me.

"Can you imagine having a personal library of this size in your own home?" he marveled.

"My few shelves wouldn't hold a full box of books and these cases are ... well, they're wonderful!" I scanned the books that filled two sides of the room and ran like a river of words across the top of the doorway.

"Honey ..." he paused, came to me, and rubbed my shoulders. "You don't have to go if you don't want to, but ..." He stopped caressing me and seemed to be at a loss for words. There was heaviness in the room I didn't understand.

"But ... what, Jason? You're worrying me."

"Richard has invited me to the opera this evening."

"The opera?" I stammered. "People are upstairs who have only been free from their prison of fear and slavery for a few days ... and you are going to the opera?" I couldn't believe it. This was not the Jason I had come to know. "It's sort of like the French Revolution, 'Let them eat cake.' How can you be so disconnected from their suffering?" I stood up but felt trapped. I didn't know if I should run away from him, beat on him as hard as I could with all the confusion and sudden anger I felt, or fall into his arms for the honest attempt at putting his mind on pleasant things for a few hours.

"No, Baby, it's not like that." He touched my arm but I pulled away. He didn't try to hold on, but his voice held all the love we had been feeling and I stopped.

"Then, why?"

"Richard said that Alister Bedlam would be in his box tonight." He nearly whispered as if a gentle tone would make a kinder man of Bedlam.

"Bedlam?" I gasped. "He's a monster."

"That's why I have to see him. We know the things he has done and I ... I have to see the Devil face-to-face." Jason's fists clenched and has jaws grew taunt with anger. "I want to know who our enemy is. I want to be able to recognize him if he comes near you."

"Oh, Jason," I sobbed with dry, exhausted tears.

"I know you're tired, Honey. I don't expect you to go. It'll be all right."

"No, Jason. Can Richard get another ticket?" I felt more worn down and worn out than I could ever remember. My arms were too heavy to lift, but I had to go. "Is Barbara going?"

"Yes, they have a plan."

"A plan? For the opera?"

"No, a plan for the elite and it will start at the opera." Jason held me in his arms, and I felt warm again.

We stood for a moment in our togetherness. "A plan for the elite? I don't' know what that means."

"There is absolutely no reason for the elite to help the underlings and the underlings are going to help get out the signatures for the petitions."

"They have the same reason to put an end to the law as all of us. I thought the Eastern Zone upheld the Length of Days Laws. They and their loved ones are terminated at a prescribed age, too." It made no sense to me.

"Yes," Jason said, "Richard told us the law is enforced in the Eastern Zone, but not in the city. The wealthy can buy extra-year credits."

"Credits? You mean they can purchase addition life-years for themselves? Under what law?"

"The law of the affluent, Christy. Here, in the city, it's all about who you are and what you have. At least in the Central Zone, everyone is under the same law, as corrupt as it is."

"If they can escape all of the consequence of the laws they create, they would have no reason to help anyone else. How can we stop that?"

"Richard has a plan to expose Alister Bedlam." Jason raked his hand through his hair with nervous anger.

"Expose him for what? Do they know what lies beneath Howard Mountain?"

"I don't know ... maybe." Jason looked out to the hallway, around the room and beyond the English Tudor glass panes of the windows. Then he whispered, "Richard said that a huge, secret network of world-wide, cross-hatched connections filter, launder, and hide all of the money that comes in across the whole country for life-credits. And ... it is all paid to Alister Bedlam."

"I don't know if I can look at him, but I will go to the opera. That is, if Barbara has something I can wear." I thought about what Jason had just said and I wondered. "How can Bedlam hide all of that and how could Richard have found out?" I still couldn't wrestle it all around in my head.

"Richard ... is Bedlam's son-in-law, Christie. Barbara's father is Alister Bedlam." Jason stood in front of me, his eyes danced with a mixture of so many emotions I didn't know whether to shrink in fear or shout with joy.

"Barbara? Our Barbara ... here?"

"Yes, Christy, our Barbara."

"Does she know about the *plan*? Is she part of it?" I thought about my own parents and my dear father. Would I be able to turn on him?

"Honey," Jason caressed my arm. He surely knew I was thinking about my family. My love for them was the catalyst for all of this, everything. "Barbara came up with the *plan*. She hasn't seen her dad in over ten years because of his corrupt ways, his corrupted soul. But her mother stayed with him so she could get to the bottom of what she had suspected for years. Barbara and her mother have collected the final nails for his cross."

"He's no martyr. He is the vilest of crucifiers." I wrung my hands in frustration and anger. "How can one man have so much power?"

"He holds life in his hands, Christy," Barbara said as she came into the library.

"But how?" I asked as Barbara walked over to the fireplace mantel. "One cannot have power over another unless that other relinquishes their own."

Barbara pulled back a large portrait above the broad oak beam to reveal a heavy, old-time wall safe. She spun the dial right, then left, back and forth, then pop, it was open. She reached in and withdrew a tan envelope. "Mother gave this to me weeks ago, before she went into hiding."

"Hiding?"

"From him ... but, she won't be able to hide for very long. He won't even know she's gone for months. In their home he lives on the first floor and she lives on the second. He uses the back entrance and she uses the front."

"Why hasn't she left? Is whatever she was looking for, worth it?" I put my hand in Jason's and connected to my anchor.

"She was afraid to leave. The only way I got out of there was to marry my Richard. He's from a wealthy old family with quiet money and elegant power. While Father is the wealthiest man in the world, he is feared not revered." She sat on the edge of the sofa and tapped the unopened envelope in her hand. "When Mama took the document, she fled from the house, came here, and gave me the envelope, slipped through the passage in our basement and has been staying above the underlings. No one would look for her there. But, once we start our campaign of discrediting ... him, he will start searching for her. We won't have a lot of time."

"And the underlings are above ground now. Where is she?"

"I'm afraid to say it out loud." She scratched at her hands and then dropped them in her lap.

"You can trust us, Barbara. If we can't trust one another, we'll all hang." We sat in silence for a moment.

"You've been in the basement. Under the stair steps, behind a set of shelves that used to hold canning jars, there's a door that leads to another staircase. Those steps open only into the kitchen near the old chimney and do not have access to any other floor until you get to the attic. We fixed up a comfortable suite of rooms for Mother up there. She just can't have a light on after dark."

"Your family has sacrificed so much. I hope it all works out." I smiled and looked at my watch.

"What time is it," she asked, then checked her own time piece. "Oh my, I'll have to hurry. You too Jason if we're going to get there in time for the curtain."

"Would it be alright if I went too?" I asked.

"I'm sorry, Barbara," Jason jumped in. "I assumed she would be too tired to go."

"Oh, My Dear, I would love for you to come. We have plenty of room in the box." She checked her watch again. "Now we're really going to have to hurry. I'll ask Maisie to hang the dress Rev. Small sent with Rachel in the closet in your room, along with some shoes. Gotta run," she rattled out as she jumped to her feet, replaced the document in the safe, the shooed us out of the library and up the steps to get ready.

Maisie brought in the dress and shoes while I was freshening up. As I dressed, an energy I hadn't known I could call on rose up within me. I had no idea what was in the envelope Barbara had, but if she believed it could move that evil man off his throne, then it would be so. I prayed that God would reveal the horror that our whole country had been living under, each in our own zone, each in our own way.

Chapter 41
A Song for the Devil

7:00 p.m.

I felt like a Lady of old as I stepped out of the Cornwall's long car and my fancy shoes hit the sidewalk. I wasn't sure how we would make this work. How could we see Alister Bedlam without him seeing us when we were with his daughter and son-in-law?

"We'll take the stairs to the upper floor. Our box is on the left facing the stage. The Bedlam box is directly across from ours. He will be there with whatever concubine is current in his life."

"Barbara, won't he see us? He probably watches you, his only daughter." I insisted a little nervously.

"I know I have never seen him before. I don't know how he could recognize me," Jason added.

"We are both legacy citizens, Jason. He probably knows every one of us." I shuddered at the thought that someone could recognize me while I had no idea what he looks like.

"Christy, people aren't even allowed to approach you on the street," Jason reassured me. "Theoretically, no one is in the ethereal world of the Council of Twelve and the Legacy Citizens. To my knowledge, no pictures of you ... of us exist. It is forbidden to even try to find our addresses, except perhaps our office and work," Jason said as he put his arm around my waist and drew me closer.

"Besides," Barbara reminded me, "since you are dressed in the Romani mourning clothes of Simza Bihari, one of your alter personalities, the veil will shield you when we walk in and take our seats. You can unbutton the veil and set it back once you are in the shadow of the box." Then she tuned to Jason and added, "You look passable as a vicar."

We stopped outside the door to the box. "Four chairs are in the front row of the box," Richard explained, "and another four behind them. My parents are coming tonight as well as my sister, Valery and her husband, Oscar. With your permission, I have placed you two in the row behind us along with Valery and Oscar. My parents will sit in the remaining two chairs beside Barbara and me. I mean no disrespect, My Lady. My parents are against seating you two in the rear, but I thought you would be less visible in the back row."

"Disrespectful? Richard, I hope I'm not an arrogant princess. I think you're brilliant." I felt a weight lift from my shoulders. I could see everything from the shadows–see but not be seen.

"Thanks, Richard. I was concerned I might not be able to protect Christy in this great theatre," Jason said.

"Protect me?" I felt my chest fill with a feeling I hadn't experienced before. Detoxed for less than three months, many emotions were still new to me. Since we had been outside of the zone for those months, we were fairly sure the other zones didn't drug their citizens. The drugs were probably out of my system by now but I was still taking the small white detox pills. That may have accounted for my anger and apprehension at times. I quickly added, "I know I have been pampered all of my life, but I'm learning fast to take care of myself."

"You sure are," Jason agreed. "You amaze me."

"Maybe that observation is not just the small white tablets," Richard added, winked, and pulled the door open to the fabulous private boxes of the first tear of the five level surrounding balconies.

I had hoped that we could enter the box with little notice. I had forgotten how much attention those who sit in pretentious elite seats can draw in a huge gathering. We had been traveling around the country incognito for months, in simple clothing, except for Simza Bihari, silently crossing the borders in the dark of night with no attention paid to our passing at all. As we entered the theater box, the entire gathering rose to their feet as if royalty had entered.

"These people here in the city need their pseudo-aristocrats in order to make their own pretense more real," Barbara whispered. "They lead make-believe lives of self-importance and must have a few people to act as those they worship in order to find meaning in their own lives. The closer they are to their demigods, the more important they believe they are." She turned and waved to the crowd.

"My dear," Mrs. Cornwall, Richard's mother, offered, "put the opera glasses to your eyes and you can look around the entire auditorium. They will provide another layer of anonymity. Even if Bedlam has seen pictures of you two, he will not recognize you behind your costume and veil or glasses."

We took our seats and I checked my time piece. The curtain would go up in five minutes. I leaned forward and whispered in Barbara's ear. "You said you were going to launch your program to gain Bedlam's cooperation this evening? How?"

Barbara put her hand to her mouth to cover her words as she spoke. "Basically ... he will never cooperate. He would lose power if he relinquished an inch, at least in his mind." She paused and nodded slightly in the direction of the opposite side of the auditorium.

A man with graying dark hair strutted into the opposite box, followed by a glitzy woman in flowing gown and dangling diamonds. He flipped his opera cape lined in red satin from his shoulders with a fanfare and flourish. When he took his seat, the woman fluttered like a swan into the one beside him.

I watched him through my small binoculars and suddenly felt suffocated by fear. The face of the man was so full of evil I trembled. Hate and anger had carved deep lines around his mouth and drew it down into a tight scowl. But there was an attractiveness that was frightening. The aura of the magnificent power he emitted could suck one into his vile cunning.

"Are you familiar with the opera, *Diablo*?" Richard asked with a friendly smile, behind which he hid the cunning plan.

"It's much newer than the traditional ones, maybe seventy-five years," I said. "Not that I have ever heard it sung before. They banned singing in the Central Zone a hundred years ago. But I've read about it. A banned book turned up in the general stacks of the library. They were going to destroy it and they gave it to me to dispose of it."

Barbara handed back a manuscript bound in colorful leather binding. "Here is the libretto. The words are in Spanish. You can follow along if you want to. I want you to pay particular attention to Act II scene four, not to the stage as much as the opposing box. I want you to enjoy his full expression as we get near the end of that scene. Bedlam knows this opera. He will recognize that some lines have been changed."

"Will everyone know they're different?"

"Most of those here are familiar with the opera, but I don't know if they will hear the change in lyrics." Highly animated, she seemed to relish the thought of his first hearing. "He is so self-centered he will assume that everyone will know the meaning of the changed words. He'll think that the entire city will know the secrets of all he has done. I certainly don't think he'll miss it. He liked to play the music at his home and sing to the top of his lungs—if one would mistakenly call it singing.

"What has he done?" I asked as the lights dimmed and the opening curtains revealed a village in South America. I sat back. This was no time to talk. It was time to fill my heart with song and hope.

I reveled in the beauty of the Latin melodies, the flashing dances, the exotic charm of the people depicted on the stage. I followed the libretto in snatches, but mostly, I let the music flow through my pores like the parched earth drinks up a spring rain. There was an intermission at the end of Act One but we all stayed in the box.

"Mother was able to finally get into Bedlam's safe a few weeks ago." Barbara laid out the introductory phase of the plan. "The man loves to hold on to trophies of his many sins."

"We know," Jason said with grit in his voice. "We have seen some of his handiwork."

"Tell me about scene four. What has changed?" I needed to know. I wanted to be able to see Bedlam's reaction and I might miss it, if I reacted in shock as he did.

"Act One has been about the Alvarez family in Columbia. They are part of one of the leading South American families. All admire Don Alvarez, but he controls his family with an iron fist. His son, Javier, has fallen in love with Angelica, a peasant girl. He is against the union. His actions to discredit her and imprison her family are evil. The whole community loves Javier so they're on his side. They begin calling the father Diablo, the Devil. Some have jokingly labeled Javier, Pequeno Diablo, Little Devil because he has turned on his father. So—" The lights dimmed and the auditorium grew silent. Barbara faced the stage as the footlights glowed and the coloratura soprano began her aria.

Act Two, Scene One flowed melodically into Scenes Two and Three. The story built as Angelica's sensuous love wooed Javier and tried to coax him out of his personal hell, as a son of the king of evil.

"You are my love, Alister. You do not have to follow evil," she sang in Spanish.

My eyes snapped from the stage to the dark box across the wide expanse of unaware people. Like someone struck by a stray bullet intended for his heart, Bedlam's posture immediately changed. He covered his eyes with his hands and I wondered if he was suddenly ill. Then, he stole a glance past his trembling hands as if searching for those who had made the connection and were staring at him. I looked through my opera glasses as well, still directed on the stage but with enough peripheral vision to see that no one else seemed to catch the change. Bedlam's reaction was as Barbara had predicted. He looked like a guilty man caught in his own evil, like one so self-centered he would believe that all eyes were on him.

Bedlam continued to search the auditorium, the general seating, and the reserved boxes. All eyes appeared to be on the growing climax to the opera on the stage.

The baritone stretched out his stance, stage left, stage right and began his grand pleading in low tones that built to a crescendo, then to an angry request. "Diablo is what they call you and Diablo you are. Release me from my prison of lies or I will release the Alister menagerie for all to see," he sang. The singer aimed his gaze into the Bedlam box.

Again, Bedlam seemed to shrink inside himself. His shoulders slumped and his posture recoiled into the plush opera chair. Amazingly, no eyes but ours watched the emotional melt-down of the powerful man. The audience seemed interested only in the story on the stage before them. They were unaware of the drama inside his mind.

Just as the last scene was nearing its finale, I saw the door to Bedlam's box open. A man stepped through and handed him a note over his shoulder. He unfolded it and gasped loudly enough the audience was finally aware something was going on. They stirred and whispered as Bedlam gathered up his cape and his woman and exited the box. The curtain closed.

Chapter 42
Assault on the Citadel

11:00 p.m.

We sat in silence as the long car pulled into the stream of traffic and headed back to the Citadel. A light, chilling rain peppered the windows. We had left as soon as we felt that Bedlam and his friend would have cleared out of the large marble lobby. I felt giddy with excitement. The evil one had finally received a direct hit without body-armor. The rain seemed to baptize us with a holy mission, rather than soak us with droplets.

I couldn't hold my question any longer. "What was in the note?"

"Yes, Richard, was that part of the plan?" Jason asked. "What caused him to bolt out of there before the final curtain?"

"I wondered when you two would ask about it," he laughed. "The small note read, 'Like distant grandfathers, like Grandpa, like Father, like son. Don't block the petitions to change the Length of Days law.' Bedlam knew what that meant. What was at the bottom of the note sealed his fate."

Barbara spoke with whispered disgust. "He didn't even hesitate to figure out its meaning. He knew immediately. The note was bordered with 23-66-62-31-51."

"And he knew what that meant?" On the first telling, it made no sense to me.

"Oh, he knew," she stated decidedly.

We watched the buildings pass by for a few blocks then Jason asked, "Okay ... we can't ride in effervescent silence. We have to know. I know that note would have meant more to him than to anyone else or you wouldn't have revealed it out in the open. What did that note say to him?"

"Bedlam likes, no he is compelled, to collect trophies from his evil actions," Barbara explained. "So did his father, his father's father and back two more generations. Evil must have flowed in their veins like acid. Every one of them was corrupt of heart and soul. Back in the thirties, my distant grandfather was the head of one of the largest mafia families here in the East."

"The mafia?"

"You have heard of the la cosa nostra?" Barbara gasped. "How is that possible? They have been underground, completely invisible, for well over a hundred years. Some said they began to engage in legal businesses, but that's just silly. They never changed. How have you heard about them?"

"The back stacks of my library," I said flatly.

Richard lowered his voice. "Every kill, every bribe, every profit from human trafficking was written in ledgers and journals. Photographers who worked full time for the mob photographed it all. Can you imagine the evil arrogance of it all? They had no real need for that information. It's not like they would be audited so they had to keep copies," Richard added. "They didn't need proof."

"They kept it all so they could revisit the crimes; re-experience the thrill of the kill. They were evil men." Jason explained then looked at Barbara. "I am so sorry, Barbara."

"No place near how sorry I am to be a part of his family." She stopped and watched the traffic light beckon the cars to proceed. "Christy, he had a huge, walk-in vault, full of shelves with all that data orderly placed in files and ... a statue or something of a chubby man in a three-piece suit, sealed behind glass." She grabbed her mouth as if she felt ill.

"We have seen similar trophies in his secret museum in the Central Zone." Jason and I said in unison.

"Oh, precious Lord, deliver us from this evil one," Barbara whispered.

"Diablo is his name," Richard stated with finality and reached for his wife's hand.

"Now ..." she stopped and directed her words to the driver, "Harold, hurry to the Citadel. I'm worried about Mother. He will know she is the one who gave out the information."

"Yes, Barbara, I'm hurrying. I can run the blue flag up the standard. We can go as fast as necessary," Harold offered.

"No, if we were watched, our urgency could give away our knowledge," she answered nervously.

"We're almost there," Harold announced.

"I have to tell you," Barbara cautioned, "no one knows about the attic apartment but those of us in this car. I cannot express enough how afraid I am ... for Mother."

"They wouldn't have to enter the house. They could bomb it or burn the whole place down," I thought out-loud, and then wished I hadn't spoken the words she probably already knew.

"No Christy," she said as we turned into the driveway of the Citadel, "the whole place is a giant bunker and totally fireproof. We had prepared for Bedlam's appearance when we renovated it."

This time, we didn't get out at the front door. Harold pulled the bullet-proof vehicle around the building where he punched in a numerical code on a panel inside the car. When the door opened, he drove down into a parking structure that went under the building. The door slammed shut as soon as a sensor detected the back bumper.

"Let's hurry. I expect Bedlam to arrive in a matter of moments." Barbara opened the door before the wheels stopped moving. "I need to ask you two to disappear upstairs for the reminder of the evening. I hope that's alright with you."

"Of course, Barbara," I agreed. "Would you want us to go up and visit your mother?"

"There isn't enough time for me to warn her you'll be coming, but that would have been nice."

As we stepped from the car, a flashing red light above the elevator door blinked feverishly. "Oh no, someone is at the front door already."

"What do you want us to do?" I felt a little panicked and didn't like the feeling.

"I have to get upstairs. If you go up on the lift with me, we will open onto the main floor. You won't be able to get to the grand staircase or continue up on the elevator, since both are in the entry hall." She glanced right and left then caught Richard's eye with a look of indecision.

"We have to go up. Walk over there behind the steps," he began as they got onto the house elevator. "Do you remember what we said about the hidden express elevator?"

"Yes, yes," I agreed as my eyes flashed to the corner.

He stopped the elevator with his hand and added, "Behind the shower on the roof is a door to another staircase. You can walk down from the roof to the attic."

"I guess you will visit Mother after all," Barbara whispered.

Jason and I hurried to the darkness under the steps. We had to hurry since we didn't want there to be any noise from the basement if Bedlam made it into the house. "There it is," Jason gestured with a silent mouthing of the words.

I nodded. With trembling hands, I opened the door to the lift. "Hurry," I whispered but was surprised at how loud my voice sounded. "I don't want Bedlam to hear the sound of the second elevator. Maybe we will get past the first floor before Harold opens the front door. The express is faster." I grabbed Jason's hand and we stepped on.

"I'm here Baby," he said and held my hand.

The elevator swept us up to the roof, out of the reach of anyone below. We would find the stairway door with only the moon to light our way and walk down to the attic and Mrs. Bedlam's apartment.

• • • • •

"Mrs. Bedlam?" I called carefully through the slightly open door.

"Come on in, Christy," she called, her voice low.

We walked into the large comfortable apartment. From the doorway, I could see a small kitchenette appointed in sleek glass-fronted cupboards and glistening appliances. The furniture in the sitting room was mid-century overstuffed chairs and sofa, upholstered in a spring flowered fabric. I could see a bedroom through an opened door. "This is lovely, Mrs. Bedlam." I felt immediately at home.

"Please, call me Ms. Sondra. I detest the name—Bedlam."

"Yes, certainly Ms. Sondra," I replied, confused. "Do you know this guy's name too?" I pointed to Jason.

"Dr. Jason O'Reilly—yes, my dear, we haven't met, but I know you all. This is a very busy house," she added as she waved her hand with a broad sweep, and gestured to the wall of video screens. She giggled a little and added, "What a cast of characters we have here."

"Wow," I gasped as I saw Raymar Goring in the hallway of the second floor on one of the screens. He moved swiftly, slipped down two rooms and knocked on Kasamar's door. "What is all of this?"

"This is my present home, Christy, here in the tower of this beautiful house. Barbara and Richard installed these screens many years ago. She has known what her father is for some time now, so they prepared a watch room. See over here, those are live shots of the city. There is Fifth Avenue and beautiful Central Park. They just tapped into the surveillance cameras that network the city." She pointed to the screens on the far right.

"And these?" I didn't recognize the images on several screens.

"Those are locations outside of the city," Jason observed as he studied them. He pointed at three. "That is the art district in Albany," he smiled and moved on. 'Look Christy, that's a horse farm in Virginia." He turned to Ms. Sondra. "I have read about amazing country places like that, but I didn't know they still exist. Christy, look at the horses!"

"I have seen no animals, except my small cat, and Martin and Rebecca's dog, Buddy. The Central Zone has no animals. The authorities claimed they polluted the air." I loved the beauty of the rolling hills. "And, this one? Where is this?" I pointed at the third image. There was something familiar about it.

"That is a rotation between Philadelphia and Boston and the scenes around the two cities, the historical sites we Americans hold dear," Ms. Sondra answered and smiled. "The Liberty Bell, Betsy Ross's house, the Old North Church."

"Those aren't just pictures. It's in present time. People are walking around." It was all so amazing.

"Everyone is tracked and monitored." She picked up a pointer the size of an old fashion fountain pen. No one writes much anymore, so few pens are actually around. "This is a PID, a point and isolation devise. I can enlarge anyone on any screen and listen to their conversations."

"The screens would emit light that could be seen from outside," Jason observed. "I thought there could be no light up here after dark." Then he stopped. "Oh, I see you have black-out shades on the windows."

"I just press a button and they go up and down." She smiled sheepishly. "I have the screens on all the time. I like to listen to some of the conversations. It feels like I'm part of the community, when I'm not."

"It's scary to think about that, but it is wonderful for you, Ms. Sondra." I surveyed each of the screens and then stopped. There was a camera in the main hallway down stairs, where a new drama was unfolding.

"He's here," Sondra whispered. She used the PID and immediately we were able to hear the frightening words.

"Who do you think you are, Missy?" Bedlam roared as he charged through the front door.

"One of the many differences between you and me is—I do know who I am," Barbara asserted with a calm voice and a spine of steel.

Bedlam pushed himself over the threshold and into the opulent entry. "Is she here?"

"Who?" Barbara questioned.

"Your mother, my wife," he demanded. "You know who I'm talking about."

"My mother," she spit out, careful not to refer to Ms. Sondra as his wife, "is probably at home. We were at the opera, Sir," she announced defiantly. "Richard and I know you were nowhere near my mother's Park Avenue residence." Barbara's chin was firmly set.

"Who I go to the opera with is none of your business," he shouted.

"What are you doing here?" Richard questioned with a tone of superior force.

"You had better tell me where she is or I will call out my personal muscle and over-turn every inch of this town until she's found."

"Your *muscle*?" she mused. "My, my, your sophisticated charm in slipping, Daddy Dear."

He glared at Barbara with a steely gaze. "You ain't seen nothin' yet, Girlie."

"Again, what are you doing here, in our home?" Richard insisted.

"There was a note ..." Bedlam stopped.

The video images on the screens in the attic were clear and sharp. I could see Bedlam's fists clench inside his exotic leather gloves.

"What note?" Barbara jumped into the battle of power and words, as if Bedlam had to prove to her there actually was a note.

"It doesn't matter 'what note.' A man passed a small piece of paper over my shoulder just as the opera ended. Some numbers were neatly typed on it that only your mother and I know."

"Have you forgotten her name, Old Man," Barbara sneered. "Her name is Sondra."

"I know her name," he bellowed. Then his expression and his voice changed. Vulnerability showed in the creases on his face. "The numbers are a very important code. If ... Sondra didn't write that note, then someone else knows the code." His shoulders slumped and his energy wilted with his sunken body. "Barbara, this is serious." He paused and his voice changed to pleading. "I have to find her."

"You lost her long before this dark night," she fired back with quiet furry. "But ... we might be able to help you ... if you help us."

The muscles in Bedlam's face contorted as his manner switched from pleading, to that of a cornered mountain lion. "What's all this about, Barbara? Did you know about the note?"

"I did not touch any note," she stated honestly. She had not touched it. "As for Mother, if she wants to talk to you, I will help you find her ... on one condition."

"Here it comes, Babe. The old Bedlam squeeze," he sneered. "Your great-grandfather and each grandfather Mafia Don who followed built their empire of power and money by blackmail or intimidation ... and now, Miss Goodness-and-light is following in their footsteps. What do you want?"

"Mafia?" I gasped as we watched the screens in the attic apartment above the drama below. I hoped to spare Barbara's mother that humiliation. "Ms. Sondra, did you know?"

"No ... well, not Mafia. I don't know what that is. But ... after the many years I had lived with that man, I certainly knew that evil was at the core of his being. He shared the little bit of love he could dredge up from the depths of his soul with one flashy woman after another. We got none. I kept Barbara away from him as much as possible." Her tired eyes turned again to the screen. "And, now she knows."

"She already knew," I said, feeling the weight of all Sondra's losses in love and family. We turned back to the video transmission.

"You may be surprised, Don Corleone," Barbara enunciated with bullet precision, "but, I have read some of the old gangster books, and now," she squared her shoulders and aimed her eyes like daggers, "I know who you truly are. I will tell you this; I am nothing like you."

He shrunk from the accusations in her eyes and focused his gaze on the marble tiles of the floor. "If you are holding information over my head in order to get me to do what you want me to do ... then you are exactly like me."

"I know nothing of your precious note. I am only offering you my assistance in communicating with my mother. But there is an urgent matter we are dealing with and I am sure, if I help you, you will want to help us."

"Help you do what?" He growled the sound of someone not used to having the power shift from his own hands and slip into another's.

"While we search throughout the city for where Mother has taken refuge from your abuse, we will accomplish another goal. We'll also gather names for a petition, so a referendum can be voted on to over-turn the Length of Days law." Barbara was firm and confident. I could see her stand so tall she seemed to stretch her spine to its full stature.

"Length of Days law? What do you care about how long people in other zones are permitted to live?" His brows furrowed as he tried to understand someone, unlike himself, who had character. "Besides, I would buy as many years for you as you would want."

"Thank you, Daddy Dear, but I wasn't thinking about myself. I was thinking of all those people who cannot buy years for longer lives. And ... remember the underlings? They have to have their lives restored. Richard and I will be very busy assisting them. We need for you to put your blessing on these petitions. Of course, you won't block the effort in any way. The elites of the city have nothing to gain by giving freedom to the moles or letting people live full lives. They won't want to see those beneath them walking the same sidewalks where they stroll to show off their fine clothes and jewelry. You will use your influence and power to convince the above-grounders of the merits of our cause so we can get this job done as soon as possible. It will come up for a vote at the next election."

"Why will the wealthy ruling class want to have the moles in their world?" he asked again and shook his head, evidence that kindness made no sense to him.

Barbara crossed her arms in front of her and flipped her hair impatiently. "With the underlings safely restored to their homes and old family businesses rebuilt, there will be more people for the elites to sell their goods and services to. The bankers will have more depositors and the clothing manufactures will have more people who need clothing–I think even you can understand the wisdom of a prosperous middle-class."

"I will do all of that so ... you will help me find your mother? That doesn't sound like a fair trade to me." Bedlam's eyes narrowed into reptilian slits.

"A balanced barter is in the eye of the beholder. You know that. You want to talk to Mother about something. I can't promise you anything. She may not want to talk to you. But you will have to decide if that conversation with Mother is equal to what I am asking of you." She rubbed her folded arms and planted her feet firmly on the floor. "Well, is my request worth your assistance?"

"How do you expect me to convince the elites of anything?" he stammered.

"You're a bright man. I'm sure you'll think of something," Barbara insisted while Bedlam shifted from one foot to the other.

Upstairs, Ms. Sondra smiled as she watched the screen. "Look at him squirm. I can't think of a time when someone has gained the upper hand on Alister Bedlam. He doesn't know what to make of it," she chuckled with satisfaction. "Oh, how he does not want to admit that he will be getting more out of the bargain than the millions of people it will affect."

"What are those numbers, Ms. Sondra?" Jason asked. We had both wondered but no one had offered the information. Should we ask?

"They are the numbers to his safe—his huge walk-in safe that holds all his family's secrets. He displays them like trophies. Can you believe it?"

"We can believe it, Ms. Sondra," Jason agreed.

"We have seen his atrocities. We have touched his trophy cases," I said and thought of Howard Mountain and all of the evil Bedlam had caused. "It must have been a miserable life living with him."

"Trust me, My Lady; there is enough evidence in that safe, of his family's vile acts of violence, to convince anyone. There's murder, manipulation, corruption, bribery, racketeering, malfeasance, money laundering, human trafficking—Christy, it goes on and on. But the pain and grief of his life and the work of his, and his family's hands, is too much to speak about."

"Will he help us, Ms. Sondra?" I asked, hopefully.

"Watch him leave. He has his orders and, like a school boy in knickers, he will follow them in every detail. He'll do anything to make sure people show him respect. He has so little respect for himself he must get it from others." She watched the screen as the front door closed.

"Doesn't he know that people are only putting on a show? Has he no idea what they say about him behind his back?" Jason and I had the same thought, the same unbelievable question.

"He has masqueraded as a benevolent man of honor for so many years, he's come to believe it himself," Ms. Sondra whispered in silent acceptance. "Now, it's his daughter who has pulled back the mask." She shook her head as we learned more of the futility of their marriage. "Oh, he'll cooperate. What hides behind the false face he wears is too grotesque for even him to look at."

Chapter 43
Bedlam's Humility

Saturday Morning - February 11, 2113

In the morning the Citadel was alive with people. The underlings who had taken refuge in the Cornwall's home shared several of the rooms on the upper floors. Rebecca and Martin were on the second floor, down the hall, across from Ed and Maud Musselman. Raymar Goring and his daughter were in each of the small rooms toward the end of the hall.

I listened as I stepped out into the hall. The video screen in every room was broadcasting the same message. Even the hum from the lower level had a cadence that matched the voice in the rest of the house. Every screen displayed a special announcement.

I pounded on Jason's door as I hurried toward the stairs. "Hurry, Jason. Are you hearing this?"

I listened as I ventured down the steps with several others. Jason was right behind me. Like water seeking its lowest level, we all moved into the flow that ended in the library. We found Barbara and Richard listening intently to the television, with a pot of coffee and white sculpted cups. We smiled and nodded at each other, received our steaming cups, and sat quickly on the edge of our chairs.

"Good morning everyone," Barbara welcomed.

Everyone nodded and smiled in response. Several sat on the floor, while I chose the beige wing-back chair. Martin and Rebecca were on the sofa; Ed and Maud stood by the fireplace. Jason came in and sat on the arm of my chair. Maisie offered flavored cream and sugar for our coffee. We nodded a thank you but no one spoke. We sat in polite silence with our eyes fixed on the screen. The intensity of the live activities testified to the importance of the upcoming announcement.

Harold checked the front door for security and joined us in front of the screen.

"Everything okay, Harold?" Richard asked.

"Yes," Harold commanded with fierce determination. "I was just double-checking. Those three may be in the vehicle parked down the street. At least they are keeping the required distance. They don't know that the Eastern Zone brought back the old frontier laws from centuries ago. I can shoot them if they try to come in. They had already violated the sanctity of the home. They have no idea it is the house of the daughter of Alister Bedlam." To Jason he explained, "The Citadel has twenty-four-hour private police on duty as well as surveillance cameras, connected with the police station."

I wondered if we were really safe. Questions bombarded my mind as I sat back in my seat, shaken but relieved. Jason put his arm around me and caressed my shoulder. There seemed to be no time for me to catch my breath. It was all happening so fast.

"We interrupt the regular service programing and yield to our distinguished guest, Alister Bedlam," the professional talking figure stated. "Mr. Bedlam," the monotonous drone continued, "thank you for being here."

"Thank you for having me," Bedlam smirked with puffed up self-importance.

Bedlam smiled and stiffened his neck in an arrogant pose. "My fellow New Yorkers, I am sure most of you will rejoice with me when I tell you that people, who had been lost to our city many, many years ago, have returned. Thousands of our citizens have been living beneath our city in the tunnels, sewers, subways and basements for more years than some of them know."

If there had been an audience, there would have been a mix of disbelief, discomfort, and rebellion at the news that no one wanted to hear. If they were interested in them at all, the underlings would have still lived in their own apartments and homes. I closed my eyes and felt a uniform gasp from all over the city.

"These people will be restored to their former residences and businesses. There is a committee to facilitate their relocation, and I have guaranteed them I will pick up some of the bill. I'll buy the food for their pantries, the clothing for their closets, and pay their utility bills ahead for one full year." He paused, smiled, and looked around as if cheered by a crowd, but no one else was there.

"There is another grand and glorious effort I am sponsoring. The rescued people will need to earn some money until they have their businesses up and running again. I will pay them a generous wage to complete a huge project, not just here in the city but in the entire Eastern Zone. I have discovered that the old Length of Days law, which established a prescribed number of years for each person's life, still stands in some sectors. I am hiring these poor, misfortunate, and mistreated people to organize the various communities and get every single citizen's name on a petition to over-turn that despicable law. Please, welcome these people into your home and," he paused and pointed his finger right into the face of each person viewing the broadcast, "and, every one of you ... sign that petition."

"Thank you, Mr. Bedlam," the public voice said. "I believe we will hear this message repeated many times throughout the day?"

Bedlam stepped forward again. "Yes, I am underwriting the entire get-out-the-signature effort. This announcement will run every hour on the hour until every citizen has signed the petition."

Then the screen switched to a pre-recorded program of a woman who was showing the proper way to wash your hands. "Remember," she said, "for those of you who have been underground all of your lives, you may not have had the opportunity to wash properly. In order for you to stay healthy and for the safety of the people with whom you will come into contact, proper washing will prevent the spread of germs that cause illnesses we, above-grounders, have not had in decades."

"I wonder what Bedlam has to say about all of those germ carriers?" Jason asked.

Suddenly, Bedlam stepped back into the picture. "My friends," he cunningly coerced, "don't be afraid of the underlings. They are carrying no diseases. I will be having a full team of physicians check them thoroughly." He smiled at the speaker with a stern eye, "Now, Miss Garrison, I can personally vouch for the health of these newly discovered citizens." He looked at the camera and back at Garrison, "I am sure you will prepare the people for the canvassers who will come. You will repeat my message of welcome and ... take note ... I did say ... you will personally pass on my message ... the citizens are not to fear my new employees. Do we understand?"

Garrison stared with glassy eyes, "Yes, Sir. I will be happy to reassure the people on your behalf."

The eleven of us sat in the library for several minutes before anyone spoke. "Well, he did it," Barbara smiled wryly. "He managed to force the people to sign the petition or they will have their programs interrupted every hour-on-the-hour. And ... he managed to come out as the people's savior in the process."

"The mission has begun," Rebecca Spires whispered. "I find it all absolutely amazing."

"We'll stay and help organize the underlings. They'll need a lot of encouragement," Ed stated.

Raymar and Kasamar sat on the floor near the window. "I've been an outcast most of my life. I think I can help with the moles, too," Raymar added.

Kasamar smiled, "You will be great at it, Dad. Barbara, I can help you if you need me."

"That would be perfect," she said.

"Jason and I will go back to Capitol City, through the opening in the mountain, Martin." I thought about the trip back and the border we would have to cross. "We brought nothing with us. You all have provided generously for all our needs. I want to thank you so much. We must leave within the hour," I stated. "You are right Rebecca. It has begun."

Chapter 44
Trapped

Saturday Afternoon

The afternoon sun was low over the spikey outline of skyscrapers. The canyons below grew dim in places where the shadows met the pavement. It was time to go. Jason and I were to meet Harold at the front door. Barbara waited in the hall to say goodbye with my cloak draped over her arm. It was the end of phase two of our mission.

"Well, Christy, the petitions from the Central Zone were delivered on Christmas Day eve, and now the process to obtain the names from the other zones has been put into place," she paused. "We're ready and well-staffed with volunteers. I can guarantee you we will have the petitions turned in on time. We'll vote on the referendum at the next election ... as well as for a president for our newly unified country."

"Praise the Lord," I sighed as the words spilled from my heart.

"I can't believe you have been here for these few days and I already feel close to you, Christy," she said as she placed the wrap on my shoulders. "I know a lot of people in this city, too many to count, but I think I know you best and I've known you for the shortest amount of time."

"I know. I've found many friends since this whole thing began. At home, it is forbidden to even approach a Legacy Citizen." I thought of everyone I had met on our journey to the other zones. "I have begun to realize how much I have needed friends. I plan to keep the new friends I made on this adventure."

Jason and I, ready for the weather, stepped out into the clear air of the late afternoon. Harold held the door as we got in and settled in the back of the long car. Martin and Rebecca sat in the facing seats, Little Feather was beside me and Gray Fox sat up front with Harold. We all looked both ways for evidence of Stoner's presence. We saw nothing by that hour on a Saturday as he pulled into traffic.

"I can take you all the way to the border," he offered. "Richard has arranged to have you picked up and taken back to the Valley of the Keepers."

"Thank you, Harold. It'll be good to see my family on the other side of the mountain, but I'll certainly miss the freedom you have in the other zones." I watched Harold through the rear-view mirror. He fixed his eyes on something in the street behind us. "What is it?" Jason and I both turned and looked back.

"I don't know, Christy," Harold said with measured speech. "Richard told me to zigzag through the streets. I have been, and that car behind us has matched every turn," he said as he careened around the corner, the last turn more sharply zipped than the other.

I checked the side of the car as it followed us around the bend. "That's no strata car. There's no signage on it at all."

"I've heard of the strata cars of the Central Zone," Harold said. "We have few official cars on the streets here. Since the middle and lower classes were still under-ground and the upper class put on great pretenses about being honest, the streets are safe. Our police cars are actually quite old. We've had them for thirty-five years. The motor, tires and running gear are up-dated every quarter." He looked again. "That isn't one of those, but then Stoner is not here under the auspices of the police authority. That looks like a hired coach."

"I don't like this," Jason said. "Harold, is there anything you can do? If that's Stoner, he'll follow us all the way to the border and arrest us there."

"These long avenues run for miles, like open racetracks. He's so close behind us, we won't be able to outrun him but we might be able to out maneuver him. He doesn't know his way around the city." He checked again in the rear-view mirror. "Hold on."

Jason grabbed my hand as we shot around the corner at the next light. There was an assistance strap by each door to help one get out of the car. We both grabbed onto the one nearest to us.

"Sorry, but I think it's better that we shake this guy. The traffic isn't too bad at this time of the day—just enough to hide in but not too much to become trapped," Harold said as he snapped around the next corner to the left just as the light changed. We breezed through on red. For a flash in time, we were out of sight of the car behind us.

"Barbara," Harold said into his communication device. "We're enjoying this ride times two."

"Wonderful," those in the car heard her shoot back.

Harold raised two fingers and pointed behind him with his thumb. Easily, he meant there were two cars traveling together.

"That sounds nice. She's a lucky lady tonight," she sounded back in a code I didn't understand.

Harold checked the mirror again, zipped to the left on another red light and pulled to the curb. "Jump out here at the Lucky Lion Pub, hurry down the subway stairs and turn to the right. Barbara will have someone meet you to take you both back to the Citadel."

We asked no questions, leaped from the car, and dashed down the snow-covered steps. I grabbed the railing after slipping a little on the way down, but I had to get to the bottom before our stalker caught up to us. I looked back to see Gray Fox pick up a handful of snow and toss the crystals across the treads to cover our steps. We disappeared into the eerie darkness of the rusted tracks and dripping, melted snow from the occasional grate above. As we moved deeper into the bowels of the city it became darker with each step.

"I don't like this, Jason," I said as I grew apprehensive in the dark silence below.

"Harold said they were sending someone to guide us out. Let's keep moving. I have no idea how many blocks we had traveled before we got out of the car."

"We made several turns. We're not as far as it seems," Gray Fox said.

561

"Down here, in the dark, everything seems distorted," Little Feather added.

"We were down here yesterday. It seems so different now ... dirtier, scarier." I knew we had to press on but my eyes couldn't adjust to any more darkness. We were rapidly walking into blackness, without enough light to cast a shadow.

"Hold my hand, Becca," Martin offered. "Maybe together we can see something."

"You need new glasses, Martin. You can't see in broad daylight," she reminded him.

"Eek," I screamed as a large rat ran across my boots. "Ugh," I gagged. "Oh Jason, I don't know if I can do this." I stopped in the middle of nowhere. I couldn't touch the walls. They dripped with ooze I couldn't see. I grabbed Jason's arm and buried my head in his chest.

"Christy, we have to move on. I believe Harold. The Cornwalls are sending someone to bring us back to the Citadel," Jason assured me.

"But, how do we get back home if we're trapped in the city?"

"I don't know, but there is a way," he assured me.

"This is a large city. We can contact some of our Native American friends if we need to," Gray Fox added.

Suddenly, an animal of some kind jumped out from a left running passage and pierced the blackness. It leaped on Jason's back and pushed him a few feet down the darkened passage to where a beam of light streamed in from a man hole above. Jason turned and whipped himself in every direction until the thing flew against the wall and fell to the floor. In the dim light, I could see it was a small man, who jumped to his feet and grabbed me with his forearm around my neck. The stench of him was nearly unbearable.

Jason turned sharply and was ready to lunge when he saw the six-inch blade in his filthy hand. "Now, calm down," he said softly to the underling. "We mean you no harm."

"Where are they?" the man whispered, his voice trembled with fear.

"Who?" Jason asked.

"Are you trying to find your family ... your friends?" I asked hoarsely, the man's arm still pressed against my throat.

"Mama?" he gasped.

"She's on top," I tried to reassure him. Although I didn't know him or who his family was. Clearly, it seemed no one else was still below.

"No!" he screamed. "She wouldn't. She would be killed or jailed up there." He drew his arm more tightly around my throat. "Where is she?"

Another figure appeared in the tunnel, hunched and menacing. He stared at the mole with empty eyes and the evil that exuded was more than I could look at. Who was the hulk of a man who leaped into the breach and jerked me from the mole's grasp as the underling weakened with the new one's gaze?

"Raymar," Jason cautioned. "Hold him but don't hurt him."

"Raymar?" I gasped as I whipped around to see these two utterly abandoned souls. The mole's eyes were empty and the void went all the way to his soul.

"He won't hurt you," I said to the underling. "He is here to protect us, to guide us out of this forlorn world." I touched the man's shoulder and felt an electric tingle of love pour forth. "They are above. We released all of them from this prison of slavery yesterday. Where were you?" I could feel the man relax his muscles under my fingertips.

"I snuck up to the park and hid beneath one of the bridges. The air up there is so clear. When I came back late last night, everyone was gone. I couldn't find anyone." The man put his dirty hands to his face and sobbed the grief of the frightened and abandoned.

"They are on the surface, I tell you. Go up the steps at the next subway entrance and find the nearest church. That's a building with a cross on top," I told him and made the shape of the cross with my hands.

He looked at us and back at Raymar. His body grew limp as he stepped back, with fear still written on his face.

"It's all right," I said as I watched the man's eyes still fixed on Raymar, like a hungry lion maintains eye contact with its prey. "He won't hurt you. He was just protecting me." He backed away, then turned and ran off into the darkness.

My hand on Raymar's shoulder, I could feel his tension and fear. "You are good, Raymar," I soothed. "You came just in time to save us."

Tears rolled down his cheeks and he wiped them away with the back of his hand. "I felt so hollow again," he wept.

"You were feeling anger," Jason said.

"You're afraid the bad feelings will take over your life and leave you with that empty feeling again," I told him. I wondered if I should have said more. I looked at Jason for a sign and he nodded.

"You aren't hollow and never have been. Abandoned to a life of isolation, your spirit grieved for the loss of contact with others. When you came to help us, you lapsed into survival mode again but, Raymar, you weren't fighting for your survival ... but mine."

Chapter 45
A Surprise Rescue

Raymar led us back through the tunnel to the opening below the basement of the Citadel. "See how close we were?" he said. "You were only three blocks away and Richard said to turn left and go straight."

"Why did he send you since you're not from the East?" Jason asked.

"No one but the underlings had been below and they were afraid to go back down. I volunteered," he explained.

"That's wonderful," I said with amazement and patted his shoulder again. "You're not a hollow man. You're our hero."

Raymar pushed the manhole cover with his shoulder. With it open we scrambled up the metal ladder to the basement of the Coldwalls' home. Barbara was just hurrying down the steps from the main floor when we emerged.

"Come, the Blue Guard has been diverted to the Battery, down on the south end of the island."

"How did that happen? The police wouldn't help them, that was evident," Jason said as he helped me hurry to the stairs.

"I called Bedlam. I told him to leak a message to Stoner and his group that someone had seen you in the Wall Street area. He was so sure you both are wealthy, it would be logical that you would have gone to Wall Street, even on Saturday." She laughed as she thought of Stoner. "I've only known you a few days, and I already know you wouldn't be interested in the Stock Exchange."

We emerged through the basement door into the grand entry hall. "Hurry," Richard cautioned as he wheeled his chair to the elevator door.

"I'll say good-bye here," Raymar said as he offered his outstretched hand. "And, I want to thank you both. You will get the Length of Days law overthrown. I know you will. But you've also saved thousands of lives, the underlings ... and mine. You are a blessing to us all." He came over to me and touched my shoulder.

With opened arms I said my farewell. "Raymar Goring, you have come back from the living-dead on your own. You let love fill all the hollow places. It is an honor to know you. I'll look forward to reading the novel you make out of all of this—"

"Do you think anyone would believe it?" he laughed. It was so good to see his eyes light up and joy enter his soul.

Richard rolled over to the elevator. "Bedlam has ordered his old-school Osprey to fly you back to the Valley," he said as he maneuvered his chair onto the lift and waited to press the button. I waved to Raymar as the door closed. Richard and Barbara rode up to the roof-top garden with the six of us.

"Fly us?" I asked. "Where will they land the airplane?"

"Not too many airplanes are made anymore," Richard explained. "Since people are confined to small geographic locations for control, air craft aren't needed as much now. You will be flying in a refurbished Osprey. It has vertical takeoff and landing, and the long-range, high-speed cruise capability of a regular airplane."

When the doors opened on top, the roof garden was vastly different. A great wind from the Osprey blades had been blowing, forcing the plants and some of the smaller pieces of furniture up against the wall.

"So that's the Osprey," I marveled. Stunned by how fast life was flying, I turned to say goodbye. "Jason ..." I reached out for him and grabbed his arm.

"I know," Jason whispered in my ear. "We can't slow down life, Christy. Right now, we'll have to run as fast as we can go, but it won't always be that way. I promise."

I held onto my hat as I hugged Barbara and Richard then boarded the flying machine. "Hurry," a woman inside the aircraft called. "We want to be out of the city before your Blue Guard officer gets back to this part of town. If he doesn't see us take off, he won't know you have left. You'll be a little ahead of him for a while."

"He isn't my Blue Guard officer," I insisted as I sat back and closed my eyes. I reached for Jason's hand, brought it to my lips and fell asleep on his shoulder.

Chapter 46
Return to the Valley of Hope, the Valley of the Keepers

6 p.m. - Saturday Evening - February 11, 2113

The Valley of Hope appeared like a magical hamlet as the Osprey flew over the ridge cap. From above, the valley below looked like piles of jagged boulders awash with crawling green moss. But I knew better. Hidden below a projected image of rock covered mountains was a hidden treasure.

"Look, Jason, it's just as you told us, Martin." I had watched the ground from the aircraft window when we were high up and as we came closer to landing.

"It does look different from up here," Gray Fox added. "Look, Little Feather, I'm not sure our braves could have tracked us here."

"It is amazing," Jason agreed. "Martin, you said they release a harmless gas into the area above the valley and project the one-way image onto the backdrop the gas produces. Like a one-way mirror, it's transparent from the valley side and it looks like the projected picture from above. In this case, piles of rocks."

"There is an approaching aircraft about five miles out but still below the ridge line. Are you expecting company?" The pilot questioned.

"What about a radio signal?" Jason asked.

"We've had that off the whole way. There are so few big birds in the sky these days there isn't any real chance of running into anyone up here."

"So, we really don't know if we were followed," I asked as I looked back to the vacant sky we had left behind.

"I can turn it on for a minute, if you want me to. We won't be broadcasting ... so ..."

"I can't stand not knowing," I admitted with a gasp. "Will they hear us too?"

"If they do hear us, it will only be on for a second. The open channel will hear any sound around us, and if we point the receiver in the direction from which we came, we should hear if something is there," the pilot said as she reached over, hesitated a second and then flipped the switch.

Schhh, schhh, the rushing wind broadcast its monotonous drone over the receiver. "Ha_e yo_ _icked up an_ thin_?" the radio squawked. *Schhh, schhh* "Try it _gain," an order barked.

I froze. I knew that voice. The sound blasted a scar on my mind in the spot where fear is stored. "Stoner," I mouthed to Jason, careful not to make a sound.

The pilot threw the radio switch in a flash. We all sat in silence for a few seconds. Finally, I asked, "Can they see us? Do they know we're here?"

"They can't hear us ... but if they break that ridge before we duck under the veil of invisibility ... yes, they will certainly see us," the pilot said as she sat up straighter. Her eyes darted from one gauge to another.

My thoughts raced, and I couldn't control the tangents my mind raced down. I grabbed Jason's hand and willed myself to breathe. Would there be a problem for us to fly through the veil of gas? Will it be bumpy? Could the gas affect the engine?

Suddenly, the Osprey fell rapidly a few hundred feet as the pilot forced the craft into a dead drop. Just as quickly, the descent slowed and the flutter to the ground gradually lowered all souls on board safely to the valley floor. Just as the wheels touched the ground, the pilot flipped the switch to silence the engine. We sat frozen. No one unbuckled their safety belt. No one spoke. We waited. Rebecca mouthed words to Martin, "We're home."

In a confused mix of freedom and captivity, I looked out beyond the window onto the sweet valley we had left months ago. Large patches of soil pushed up through the moist earth on what must have been several really warm February days. But it was not Spring. Crocus did not dot the valley. There was a patch-work quilt pattern of old snow and bare winter grass. The sun bounced off the puddles left after a winter rain, and sent ripples of sunshine on the surface. I wondered how I could even see the beauty while I feared for my life. Then I realized—God had given me the grandeur around me to calm my fear within.

The sound of an aircraft overhead shattered the silence within the Osprey. Instinctively, we crouched in position and gazed into the sky, as if ducking would conceal our hiding place. A silver metallic, roaring monster bird-of-prey flew directly overhead. The craft swooped above us, like a flying dinosaur in a science fiction novel. It roared with a scream of death across the expanse of the heavenly space above. Then, the noise faded into the distance.

Air escaped in one unison exhale. Jason smiled and grabbed me in a great bear hug. "They're gone."

Still, we crouched low in the craft and waited for a sense of security to return. Finally, Martin whispered, "Let's go."

We slipped silently from our hiding place and inched across the lawn a little below the Spires' place. There the terrain was flat and large enough to hold our flying angel under whose wings we were sheltered.

"Buddy," Martin laughed as the dog bounced down the road in leaps and bounds. There was no stopping him. "Hi there, boy," Martin said as he scratched behind the dog's ears. The animal dropped to the ground, rolled over and presented his tummy for proper scratching. "Come along," Martin said as he stepped over the dog and motioned for him to follow.

People emerged from their homes at the hour when children had started settling in for the night in their pajamas and selecting their bedtime stories. There, in the middle of the square sat a grounded flying machine the likes of which no one had seen before.

"Hey, Mr. Spires," red haired Gabriel gasped with widened eyes, "what ya got there?"

"Well, Gab, this here is a fancy flying machine, just as you probably saw," he winked and rumpled the boy's hair.

"A flying machine? Wow, can you take me for a ride in it? That would be streaky!" he shouted with excitement as he tried to inch toward the Osprey.

"Well, now, I just can't do that, Son. It was dangerous for us to land here in the first place, but we made it. We'd better not put God to the test to try it again."

"Test God? What ya mean?" Gabriel wrinkled up his nose.

"When a person does something, they know good-and-well they shouldn't do ... and then ask God to protect them ... that's putting God to the test. We shouldn't do that. It's like sayin', 'I dare ya God to protect me.' They might as well add that they're smarter than God."

"I know I'm not," the boy admitted.

"I can testify to that, Young Man," Mara said as she came up behind them. "I saw your last test score." She laughed as she put her hand on his shoulder. "Come on now, I'll walk you back to your house." She smiled at all of us. "I am so glad you are all safely home."

"Bye," Gab waved, actually more at the Osprey than at Martin.

"Martin," Rebecca called after her husband as she, Little Feather, Gray Fox, Jason, and I walked ahead toward their house. "Come along. I'll fix some coffee. Then, Christy, we'll have a bite in town before you and Jason rest before heading back—"

"Home," I whispered before she could finish her sentence. I really wondered if I would ever feel at home again.

Chapter 47
Through the Mountain of Tears

Eventide

"We have quite a job ahead of us," I thought out loud as we sat on Rebecca's front porch and waited for the night to gather around us a little more. Silas had not yet returned. I wasn't really worried. But I did wonder. I wondered about so many things. Mostly, would our country ever wake up in time to save even a remnant of what we had before, long before ... before the silence?

"Smell the winter rain?" Jason inhaled deeply as he closed his eyes and sucked in the aroma of the earth around us. "It came down over an hour ago, but the sweetness remains."

"Why is everything more enjoyable on this side of the mountain?" I asked. "I could just sit here and relax for hours." Then the memories of home rushed back in, and I answered my own question. "The drugs."

"The coded messages Silas has gotten through Sean's newspaper are very hopeful," Rebecca said as she rocked in the ladder-back porch rocker.

"We've been gone for two months," I said. "I feel guilty that I hadn't kept up with what has been happening at home."

"How could you, Honey?" Jason reassured me. "There is no communication between the sectors."

"Rebecca has stayed in touch," I sighed.

"My Dear," she explained, "I didn't catch up to you two until a few days ago in New York. I've talked with Silas a few times as he was able to sneak, unseen, through the mountain opening. Since we were gone, he left a note for me on the kitchen table and that's what I wanted to share with you."

"Thanks, Becca." She did manage to make me feel better when I didn't feel sorry for myself. "Did Silas' note tell you anything about what's going on over there?"

Rebecca pulled the piece of paper from her pocket just as Martin joined us on the porch.

"I see you got the note," he said as he sat down.

"Did you read it?" she asked her husband.

"No, I didn't have time. I checked on the animals in the barn. Dixie is about to drop her calf."

"She's awfully early, isn't she?" Rebecca questioned.

"Seems she likes the idea of more freedom too," he laughed.

"How wonderful, Martin," I thought out loud. "A new beginning all over the country and a new calf to celebrate new life for everyone." My thoughts clung to the promise of new life and the wobbly calf that would soon come into our strangely divided country. Life was still going on as planned.

"Rebecca," she began reading the letter, "I had to come through to tell you what's going on over here. Tell, Lady Christy, if you are with her, that her grandmother had been very ill this winter—"

"Oh, no," I gasped and sat up straight in the chair.

"Wait Christy, there's more," she cautioned, "... very ill this winter ... but is doing much better. The Blue Guard Chief told Sir Richly that they captured My Lady in New York and shot her during the arrest. Her grandmother collapsed under the grief of it."

"He what?" I gasped as I pounded the arm rest of the porch chair. "The liar!"

"Christy," Jason soothed, "you know Stoner can't be trusted with anything. He probably thought the news would make you drop your guard."

"Where that man is concerned, my guard will always be up!" I said as I ground my teeth. "Did Silas say more?" I hoped for a better outcome than I had heard so far.

Rebecca continued. "Rumor has it that Lady Richly was so upset by the news, her health took a downward turn. But I was able to get word to her that you were okay. Tell Christiana and Jason that they must be doubly cautious when they get back. The people's emotions are really uneven due to detoxification. Some have gotten hyper-excited about putting Christiana's name up for President at the next election. That could be dangerous for her."

My eyes jerked to attention. "I told them I'm not old enough to run."

"But Honey," Jason patted my knee, "your supporters don't sound reasonable right now. You cannot apply logic to an illogical argument."

"You're right. I know you're right but Jason ... it's Grand-mère ... and it's this election ... that will continue to keep us running. Now ... maybe some are unaware they are putting our lives in danger."

"I know, Baby. I understand." He took my hand and squeezed it for reassurance. "Is there more Rebecca?"

"The word is that Alister Bedlam has put a bounty on Christy's head. Maybe they should stay on the valley side of the mountain. Sincerely, Silas ... p.s. I will check if you are back at 9 p.m. on February 11."

"A bounty?" Jason bellowed as he charged out of his comfortable chair.

"What does he mean by a bounty?" I gasped.

"It means anyone can catch you and turn you in to authorities," Gray Fox barked as he rocked harder and faster.

"On what charge?" I asked. "I know Jason and I crossed borders, but Stoner doesn't have proof that we did, and Bedlam doesn't either."

"Bedlam's power has been threatened. He has no one to blame but the visitors at the Citadel, and he has decided to blame you since Stoner is after you anyway," Martin figured.

"I have to get back home," I insisted.

"Then make sure you aren't caught before you reach your apartment," Martin insisted. "He can't say you're missing if you're there in front of him when he arrives. It'll be dangerous. Watch yourselves."

"I'll go in and get your hat. You've already changed into your own clothes. Although, Christy, you look so much thinner than you were."

"I know my clothes are really loose." Then I thought, "But, maybe that's good. I can say I've been sick and have been regaining my strength. Now that the Length of Days law has been suspended until after the election, I won't even have points placed in my life file."

"I'll go get my things, Honey. It's nearly nine," Jason said, then stopped and gathered me in his arms. "With God's help, we can do this. Look at all that has happened. Now, it's time to go home."

"Next week will be Mid-Winter Bash," I said but didn't feel like celebrating.

"Bash?" Martin asked.

"To make the winter months a little brighter after Gifting Day, they have continued with Mid-winter Bash. You know: gifts of candy, jewelry, lite entertainment." Then I thought about that word. "They are so rarely entertained, or have the capacity to enjoy life at all."

"When is the Bash?" he asked.

"February 14—wait, that's in a couple of days. I guess it will be nice to be home after all."

"Christy," Rebecca began with a crooked smile on her lips, "February 14 is Valentine's Day."

"Valentines? I've read about Valentine's Day," I gasped.

"Yes, Dear," she chuckled. "It's the day of love. The gifts they share are to show their loved one that they care." She patted my hand.

"Wait right here, Christy," she said as she stood up. "There is nothing I can give you since you would have no way of explaining where it came from. You must travel with nothing in your pockets, not even an extra wrap. But I want you to have my grandmother's necklace. It's a cross and you can hide it under your clothes. If there is any danger that they could catch you with it, you have my full permission to cast it aside. It is only a symbol." She turned to go. "I'll be right back."

"You don't have to give me your grandmother's necklace, Rebecca," I called after her.

"Of course, she doesn't Christy," Martin agreed. "And ... of course she does, My Dear." Martin got up and followed his wife in the house.

"I'm going to run in and get my own shoes, Honey," Jason said. "I still have on the boots they loaned me."

"Here it is," Rebecca said as she returned, holding her hand out reverently. "It's simple because I was very little, maybe five years old. Later, I had a longer chain made for it." She dangled the beautiful gold cross in front of me. "Let me fasten it for you."

I turned and lifted the back of my hair so she could secure the clasp. Once fastened, it dropped into place, long enough for me to see it and to hide under my clothing. I ran my fingers over the delicate design. "Rebecca, it is beautiful. I will cherish it."

"I know you will—that's why I gave it to you." She smiled and kissed my cheek. "Bless you Christy. May the Lord keep you safe."

"Thank you, my friend," I whispered.

"I'm going to run in and make sure you haven't left anything in the house." She went back in the house, but I knew the goodbye was hard for her. It was difficult for me, too.

Alone on the porch, I looked beyond the valley to where we had been, to where the setting sun met the distant ridge—and suddenly I had hope. It felt like the lunar glow was resting on my face. Everyone had sacrificed so much for me I could do no less than return the trust. Hope never sleeps. We form our lives around it. It may nap for a while, but it always makes its way to the brim of the Eastern hill and soars in the spirit of the new morn. We were going home, to whatever new challenges awaited us. I refuse to be afraid.

Reference:

[1] "God Bless America" by Irving Berlin © Copyright 1938, 1939 by Irving Berlin © Copyright renewed 1965, 1966 by Irving Berlin © Copyright Assigned the Trustees of the God Bless America Fund International Copyright Secured. All Rights Reserved. Reprinted by Permission.

[2] "I Have Decided to Follow Jesus." Unknown. Folk Melody from India

John 3:8 (NIV © 2011).

LENGTH OF DAYS
SEARCH FOR FREEDOM
Doris Gaines Rapp

LENGTH OF DAYS
SEARCH FOR FREEDOM

Doris Gaines Rapp

The third novel in the Length of Days trilogy

Daniel's House Publishing

Copyright 2016 Doris Gaines Rapp

Zone Borders

Table of Contents

Prologue												587

Chapter 1	April 2113									589

Chapter 2	Home										594

Chapter 3	New Information								599

Chapter 4	An Intrusion									606

Chapter 5	Jason is Back									611

Chapter 6	May 2113									614

Chapter 7	June 2113									626

Chapter 8	The City of Angels								632

Chapter 9	Suddenly									643

Chapter 10	January 2114									653

Chapter 11	Evening Meal									664

Chapter 12	Attacked									668

Chapter 13	Another Kind of Healing							673

Chapter 14	2pm - May 2114								676

Chapter 15	Pulling it Together								684

Chapter 16	Inside the Bubble								688

Chapter 17	Looking for Answers							694

Chapter 18	A Gathering									698

Chapter 19 Flash-train to Texas   703

Chapter 20 Research   707

Chapter 21 Stoner in the Southwest   711

Chapter 22 The Organ Mountains   719

Chapter 23 Old Mesilla   724

Chapter 24 The Basement   729

Chapter 25 Late June   737

Chapter 26 Down the Hall   741

Chapter 27 Escape   744

Chapter 28 Worn-In   754

Chapter 29 Still Late June 2114   759

Chapter 30 Doubt   764

Chapter 31 The Lie   772

Chapter 32 The Last Week in October   779

Chapter 33 The Event   788

Chapter 34 November 3, 2114   794

Chapter 35 The Grand Ballroom   799

Chapter 36 The Promise   803

Chapter 37 An Unknown Hero   809

Epilogue   813

PROLOGUE
Return to Capitol City, Central Zone, U.S.A.

Diary of Lady Christiana Applewait

2113

My heart is breaking and fear has flooded the craggy fissure. Dear, sweet Grand-père is missing. Dr. Jason O'Reilly and I must find him quickly, not only for his safety but because he is the presidential candidate for the newly formed *1787-Constitutionalists Party*. He is our only hope for freedom and a return to the original Constitution. My precious Grand-mère is in constant prayer.

It has only been four months since Silas Drummond broke the silence about the atrocities buried beneath Howard Mountain. Judge Carl Brunner issued a two-year stay on all those forced into the never-ending-sleep, thus ending their Length of Days, including my grandparents. Jason and I sneaked across all four closed zone borders, establishing a network to secure enough signatures to place a citizens' referendum, to overturn the Length of Days Law, on the ballot at the next election.

I am in a panic over Grand-père's disappearance. Who will help us? We can't ask Chief Inspector Ward Stoner, the head of the corrupt Blue Guard; he has stalked our every move. I cannot trust him. It isn't safe to get help from mass communication journalists; if word of Grand-père's abduction gets out, those who took him will surely kill him.

We will search for him with the few clues we have. I am willing to go all the way to the beautiful Pacific Ocean, wander through the hot and barren desert, cross the lofty Blue Ridge Mountains and tunnel again below the streets of New York City seeking my grandfather. When we find him, and we must, we will find freedom as well.

Lady Christiana Applewait

Luke 4: 18-19 (NIV©2011)

The Spirit of the Lord is on me, because he has anointed me to proclaim good news to the poor. He has sent me to proclaim freedom for the prisoner and recovery of sight for the bind, to set the oppressed free, to proclaim the year of the Lord's favor. (Book Three)

CHAPTER 1
April 2113

The year had rolled over from 2112 to 2113 while Jason and I were out of the Central Zone but I had not forgotten the evil buried beneath Howard Mountain. When we arrived back at the heavy door on the Valley side of the mountain it thudded and scrapped open on rusty hinges. Once inside the hollow rock chambers, the darkness of the subterranean lair ahead of us was as black as the evil that clung to the cold, damp, stone walls. I knew what waited there, and my stomach churned violently. With my friend, Dr. Jason O'Reilly so near to me I could smell the scent of him, I inched up as close behind Silas Drummond as I could. Sandwiched between the two men, I shuffled along with my eyes tightly closed, not wanting to see the frightening reality around me. I had seen it all before.

"Are you okay?" Jason asked.

"I just don't want to see them again," I said in a whisper. Then I shuddered. Would I ever get over the memory of seeing each body grotesquely stuffed and displayed like lifeless figures in a wax museum? Once the images burned a hole in my mind, I knew they would cling to me like black bats hanging from the walls of every safe sanctuary I would ever have.

Even though Silas had opened the massive door to the cold, vile cavern beneath Howard Mountain, I felt like I couldn't move, or keep up with the little stooped man in front of me. Jason moved up beside me and clutched my hand. I was desperate for comfort and cringed with every step we walked.

"They're just ahead, My Lady," Silas cautioned in a whisper. "The glass cases—they're in the next room."

I thought of how Jason must feel and tried to set aside my own fear and loathing. "If you want to pause for a moment in front of your parents' display cabinets and pay your respects, I can cover my eyes," I said as chills ran down my arms. "I can't look at them. The very fact they're on display for Alister Bedlum's bizarre pleasure, is reprehensible."

"Christy, there is no respect anywhere down here. And, certainly not in the glass coffins of the bodies Bedlum stole away from their loved ones." Jason paused a moment. "I don't need to see the violated, taxidermy displays of those I loved in life on display in Bedlum's despicable museum."

"The furnaces are just in front of us," I gagged. "I can still smell the burnt flesh."

"Remember, Christy, it is over," Jason reminded me. "No one will enter the never-ending-sleep just because they have reached the end of their Length of Days—thanks to you and Silas."

I pulled a cloth square from my pocket that Rebecca Spires gave me and covered my nose. "For two years, Jason. The stay is for two years—not forever—not yet. We have to finish the task."

Silas had said nothing since we entered the cavern until that moment. "Then breathe deeply, My Lady. Inhale the stench of death so you will never forget the wretchedness of it. All of our lives depend on the work that you and Dr. O'Reilly will do while the stay on exterminations remains."

I knew he was right. But I was so tired, drained of every ounce of energy I had just a few days ago. The thought of so few of us overthrowing a corrupt and heinous government seemed impossible. But I knew impossible was not a word I could use. "I know. Grand-mère and Grand-père's lives depend on us."

"We all do," Silas said again. "All of our lives are cut short so we never live out our full Length of Days."

"I know," I said again, but inside, I thought about the very short time I had even thought about these things. Drugged with chemicals the government put in our water supply, robbing all of us of our emotions, our energy, and our libido, I hadn't even thought about the Length of Days Law, terminating a person's life when they reached a pre-determined age, until my own grandparents arrived at their termination birthdays. Since I was a Legacy Citizen, my detoxification pills allowed me to begin to feel, to think clearly, and to recognize, not only my loss, but the loss of everyone around me.

Bedlum's private museum of the bodies of people-of-power was in the next hall. I had seen them once. I knew I couldn't see them again. I kept my eyes tightly closed and allowed Jason to lead me through.

As we came to the other side of the mountain within the peaks, my pulse quickened. "Do you see anything, Silas?" I whispered hoarsely; my voice raspy from exhaustion. We had entered the crypt-like space through the secret opening in the mountain-wall, walked on the nearly forgotten old road through the mountain, passed Alister Bedlum's despicable museum with averted eyes and emerged into the grand entry hall on the other side. There we waited.

"There's no one in the entry foyer." Silas's voice was gruff and weak. I could hear the pounding of his heart in the spacing of his words. He cracked the door open a little more, craned his neck and looked beyond the entry to the windows that flanked the front door. "I see nothing," he whispered. "I'll leave it up to you two. If you want to make a run for my car, that's fine with me. If we hurry, I can get you back to town before the city stirs."

"Let's run for it, Christy," Jason instructed.

"I'm ready," I agreed.

The only sound was that of heavy breathing and the crackling gravel beneath our running feet. Since few people owned personal cars, Silas's vehicle would be easy to spot. We would have to hurry. In silence, we all piled into the front seat of the old, broad vehicle of yesteryear.

The first blush of morning had already touched the eastern sky when the doors slammed closed on Drummond's car and we turned toward the city. The sweetness of the spring morning air filled my senses like a strong tranquilizer and my body relaxed. The empty road back to town stretched out like a magic carpet along the Devil's hideaway.

"Do you suppose Chief Inspector Stoner is up and out?" I finally questioned through a sluggish haze.

"He could be," Jason agreed. "But he shouldn't be out on the streets just because we're back. There would be no way for him to know we've returned, or that we were gone for that matter. He had his suspicions, but no evidence."

"He, or his minions, tracked us from the western ocean to the subterranean pits near the eastern shore," I insisted. "I don't think we were spotted, but Stoner *knew* we were beyond the hidden valley. He just *knew*."

Suddenly weariness overtook me beyond my words to express. My eyes grew heavy and refused to stay open, until my head came to rest on Jason's shoulder. It remained there the entire trip into town. It was too early for the *P*ersonal *T*ransit to swish above the streets below. All was quiet.

Later, Jason nudged me gently when Silas stopped the car in front of the Indian River Apartment building. "Honey, you're home." He kissed me softly on the forehead.

"Home?" I questioned. The word *home* had not been part of my vocabulary for months, only my dreams.

"I know. It sounds strange doesn't it?" Jason agreed.

I leaned over and kissed him tenderly. "I wish you could come in."

Silas said nothing but smiled shyly.

"I wish I could, too," Jason admitted. "But each second is important. You have to be in your apartment and ready to come to your door if Stoner were to show up. I have to be at my house or in my office if he were to go there. We have each given plausible excuses for our apparent absences. You claimed you've been sick and have been regaining your strength. Since we no longer have illnesses, there aren't medications for some of the previous medical problems. Even influenza is a dangerous disease and requires a lot of bed rest."

"I feel like I have a serious illness right now" I sighed. "I know— it's called extreme fatigue." I knew Jason was right, but I was too tired and too frightened where Inspector Stoner was concerned to think clearly.

"Thank God your real condition isn't serious. Just remember, rest will be important," Jason said. "Dahlia helped me support the story that I've been studying a new medical procedure, Orthopedics. Now, with the Length of Days Law suspended, people no longer get points against them for injury or illness, so bones can be set and heal properly when an accident occurs, rather than leaving them untreated with the resulting bent backs and limping legs. I need to come out of my lengthy study time and be available too. My nurse can only cover for me for so long."

"I love you, Dr. Jason O'Reilly," I whispered in his ear.

"And, you as well," Jason replied in response.

I got out of Silas's car and stood on the sidewalk. Leaning in through the car window to embrace Jason, I stroked his face. Then, turning toward the apartment building, I didn't look back. My heart pounded as I walked up the sidewalk and reached for the door handle.

Before I opened the door, I looked around the bushes and trees, and down the street in both directions, for eyes trained on me. I turned the knob and was thankful the hinges didn't squeak. Pushing the door open, I entered the building into the huge entry hall and turned to close the door behind me. I was home.

CHAPTER 2
Home

Once inside the Indian River Apartment building, I realized I had been holding my breath. With my eyes closed, I exhaled slowly. That was when I heard him.

"Welcome home, Lady Applewait," a deep voice announced from the large, common area to the left of the lobby.

My heart raced in my chest and once again, my breath caught in my throat. I grabbed at my shirt and pulled on the fastener to release its grasp on my neck. Could I get enough air? Slowly I turned in the direction of the voice I had never heard before and saw a stranger standing near one of the over-stuffed chairs in the large room.

"I'm sorry," I smiled politely, but inside, my stomach churned, knotted, and turned sour. "I'm at a disadvantage. Have we met?" I started to reach out my hand in a gesture of friendship. When I couldn't control the nervous tremors that rattled my body, I quickly put my hands in my pockets.

"No Ma'am, we haven't met."

"Then—" slowly I began again and stopped. I felt trapped. Was the man a member of the Blue Guard? Did he answer to Ward Stoner? I nearly choked.

The man took one step in my direction and spoke quietly, calmly. "I'm sorry. I don't mean to frighten you, Ma'am." The tall, muscular one squared his shoulder. "My name is Tayton Braxton. I'm a friend of Sean's. He asked me to transfer into this district, get an apartment here in the Indian River complex and protect you and Dahlia Zoobamba. Stoner found out I was living here and made my stay a special assignment. I'm supposed to tell him every time you leave and return." He looked toward the windows that faced the front of the building. "We'd better get you off the first floor and into your apartment. Stoner shows up here at all hours."

I said nothing. I was simply too tired. My homecoming could be my undoing if not found in my apartment. Our mission was too great to risk it all. Yes, Judge Bruner had ordered a stay for the Length of Days Law. Death wouldn't come to anyone in the furnaces under Howard Mountain just because they had reached a pre-determined number of years and lacked a significant value to society. But our work had only begun. Jason and I had crossed borders illegally to get signatures on petitions that would make the stay on exterminations permanent through a national referendum. But it wouldn't come to a vote for almost two years.

"Hurry," Tayton urged as he checked his time piece. "Stoner has burst in here at 4 a.m. and 4 p.m. He never shows up at the same time twice."

Following him obediently, I stopped at the lift door that opened immediately. The doors swished open and we hurried on. The doors closed again before there was any movement near the front of the building.

"Are we safe?" I whispered.

"Yes, Ma'am," Tayton responded.

I stood rigidly, facing the front of the car, and stared at the crack between the doors. Afraid and exhausted, I couldn't force my mind to stay in the moment. At first, I wondered why. After all, I was finally home. With a review of the last few days in my mind, even the previous months, the cause of my weariness was no mystery. Jason and I had literally covered the entire country.

"You're a friend of Dahlia's and Sean's?" Finally, I asked the big question, as I tried to pull together a measure of safety through questioning.

"I know Sean better. I just met Dahlia recently." He paused as the lift door opened on the top floor. We stepped off and Tayton followed me to my door.

With my hand placed on the door knob, the identifying markers in my palm released the lock. I turned and placed my back to the door, blocking the stranger called Tayton.

"Thanks," I smiled a little and waited for him to back away.

"I know you just met me, Ma'am. I understand that my assurance of trust may not be enough for you. All I can say is time will prove my loyalty to you and to your cause. It is a cause I believe in too." He took a few steps backwards and bowed slightly at the waist.

"Thank you, Tayton." I paused and watched his face for changes of expression that would give away his true feelings and meaning. "If we're going to become friends, Tayton, I must ask you not to bow."

I thought for a moment and cleared my head. What should I tell this stranger? "Tayton, Jason and I started an adventure months ago, one we had not even considered a possibility just weeks before that. I was, and am if I choose to be, Lady Christiana Applewait, a Legacy Citizen, privileged by accident of birth." I searched his eyes to see what clues hid there. "Now, I see myself as an equal to everyone. We met Raymar Goring, Kasamar's father, one of the hollow people of the west; the underlings in the sewers and old subway passageways of the east; and all those who lived in the forbidden zones in- between."

"Yes, Ma'am," the double-agent began again, but I interrupted.

"We each have a job to do, Tayton. And, if you are true to your word, your task will be equal to mine." I still didn't turn my back on him nor open the door. I wasn't ready for that. I would have to talk to Dahlia and Sean first. I stood firmly, with my feet planted, and watched as he backed down the hall, got back on the lift and started down.

With a deep breath, I opened the door to my flat and a life I had left behind came rushing back in. The room was silent. I didn't hear the sweet sound of the coffee maker that was always humming on the counter or the toenail tapping of my little kitten. Then, I remembered

I had left the furry bundle with my parents before Jason and I left the Central Zone. Still, I half expected to hear the little feline playing near the window.

First, I needed to empty and stash my carry-all bag on the floor of the sleeping-room closet. I was not going to make that obvious mistake. If Stoner were to come in unexpectedly, he shouldn't find a packed bag, evidence of my absence, when my cover had been a lingering illness with confinement to my apartment.

I hurried into my room and opened the closet door. While there in the wardrobe, I pulled out a lounging suit and slippers, removed my clothes and hung them up. I slid the clothes I had been wearing in place along the pole, inviting a sense of casual organization, and went back into the sitting room. Flinging the window fabric back, I welcomed the rising sun. I even opened the window sash a moment to let the stale air out, and then went into the kitchen to put on a pot of fresh coffee. The morning air was crisp and fresh. I was reluctant to re-close the windows, but wastefully letting out all the mechanically treated air would have been irresponsible.

Over at the bookshelf, I ran my fingers over the books that had gone untouched for months. *"To Kill a Mockingbird,"* I read from the book spine as I pulled the volume from one of the shelves. This was one I hadn't read. It was one of the paperbound books Jason had given me from the huge stash of books in the hospital library.

Following the great uprising of the previous millennium, the government banned all books, so I thought the only books that had survived were the ones in the back stacks of a closed section of the public library. The curator of the library and I were the only people who had access to those books. My key to the back room was because I had been working on my Graduate Degree in Library Science. I smiled as I took *Mockingbird* to the couch and lay down with a pillow under my head.

Suddenly, I heard a tapping at the front door. My book fell to the floor with a muffled flop when it landed on a small rug. The intrusion on my greatly needed rest set my pulse racing. I jumped upright with rattled and jangled nerves. My hand trembled as I picked the book off the floor. Would I ever be safe again?

"Stoner," I gasped silently, pronouncing the fearful name with my lips. Then I thought again. *The Chief Inspector would have beaten down the door, if necessary, not gently rapped. But, if it isn't Stoner, who could it be? Who's here?*

CHAPTER 3

New Information

Did I have the nerve to open the door to my penthouse? What if I had forgotten something, a detail left unattended? Was there some tiny leaf, grown only on trees from the Eastern Zone, still attached to my shoe? But my shoes were in the closet and no time to run in there and check. The crack I permitted between the door and the jamb was minuscule. My hands trembled as I peeked out and then flung it opened. "Mother, Daddy," I squealed, like an Academy school girl with a coarse and raspy voice.

"We thought you might be home." Mom and Dad embraced me as they hurried into my apartment. Mother stood back quickly and held me at arm's length. "Honey—your voice. Are you really sick now?"

"No, I don't think so, just exhausted." I hugged her again. I couldn't get enough of her touch or the fragrance of her hair. Even though I was an adult of twenty-four, she smelled like Mama.

"Well, you look like you haven't slept in days. Let me make you a nice cup of tea." Mother patted my cheek and turned toward the kitchen. "How's Jason?" She asked over her shoulder.

"Resting, I hope," I said as I yawned. "He plans to go to the office today."

"Oh my," Mother said. "He is really pushing himself. I hope he has a nice cup of tea, too."

"I imagine he will." Then I added, "We won't need tea. The coffee pot is already on." I smiled and sat down at the table. Mother was eager to take care of me and I wanted to honor that. I had been gone for many months.

"And—we brought a friend of yours," Daddy offered as he placed a brown paper sack on the floor and then reached under his sweater.

"Shakespeare!" I smiled broadly and reached for the feline that had grown since the last time I saw her. Careful to keep the cat's paws off the table, I snuggled her in my lap. "She seems to recognize me. I can't believe it."

Daddy reached for the sack he had brought in. "You rescued her, Christy. You brought her in out of the winter cold months ago. She was fed and loved," he reminded me. "And, here are her water and food dishes and a box of food only half eaten." He put the dishes on the floor of the kitchen, filled them and put the rest of the food box in the cabinet under the sink. "There cat, enjoy," he chuckled.

Mother took a small plate from the cabinet. "We brought some orange juice and salt crackers. Good food for eating lightly," she assured me. "And, I'm embarrassed to say, we brought some of your grandmother's best cookies. She made them yesterday." Mother arranged the sugary treats in an artful display. "I'm sure the government health department would say they are too rich for healthy eating, but we'll enjoy them anyway." Her chin jutted out in defiance as she placed the plate on the table.

"Mother, you would be amazed by the pastries and other foods I ate while I was away. We had home-made noodles at Martin and Rebecca Spires' home in the Valley of the Keepers, with wonderful smashed potatoes and butter and large chunks of beef." I closed my eyes and could taste the warm melted butter that oozed over the top of the bowl. In Rachel Claudette's fine dining room on the far west coast, she loaded the sideboard with sweets of every kind, some with names I had never tasted and some I had never heard of. The memory of the platters of meats and other finger foods makes my mouth water." I cleared my throat and smiled at the thought of all that cuisine. Then I remembered I hadn't eaten in a long time.

Daddy's voice lowered and grew coarse. "Do you think that Chief Inspector Stoner knows you're back in town?" he asked. He sounded worried.

"He has posted an officer here in the apartment building," I said as I swallowed hard. "I met him when I came in. He seemed to be waiting for me. He said his name was Tayton Braxton and claimed to be a friend of Dahlia and Sean's. Stoner shows up here at frequent but random times Tayton said. The Chief could bang on the door at any moment."

I was surprised at how confident Mother was as she stated resolutely, "Then we'll do what's natural. If he comes in unexpectedly, we'll be caught being us."

"The most natural thing in the morning is coffee. Would you like some?" I asked as I watched Shakespeare. The little creature wasn't an inanimate replica of a cat as others in the Central Zone had, but the real thing.

Daddy agreed with eager anticipation. "I would love some coffee," he said as he gave me another hug. "We sure missed you, Angel."

"Let me pour the coffee," Mother offered. "If Stoner comes in, I would love to be caught in the act of being a normal family." She also poured a small glass of juice. "Here Christy, drink this quickly for medicinal purposes."

"I missed everyone on this side, too," I responded, exhausted but full of feelings only possible since I started my detoxification. I sat and watched Mother do her motherly thing, while I emptied the glass of juice. "How are Grand-mère and Grand-père? I thought of the dear ones often during our travels to the other zones."

Mother finished pouring the coffee. "They're fine now. Your grandmother had quite an episode when Inspector Stoner told her of your capture in New York and the gunshot wound you received at the time. Your grandma collapsed, but when she found out it had all been a lie, she was too furious at the Inspector to stay down any longer." Mother laughed and added. "Can you imagine your grandmother not seeking the truth behind anything Stoner had to say?"

"I can't imagine Stoner ever telling the truth!" I joined in the fun as I watched her take three cups from the cabinet and pour our coffee. Far below the window I heard the *thunk* of a car door and jumped. All sounds startled me now. There were few vehicles on the roads and I knew that strata cars, of the infamous Blue Guard, were some of them. I had to calm down. I didn't want to alarm Mother and Daddy. I snuggled Shakespeare closer and began to relax a little as I stroked the cat's soft fur.

"We have to tell you what's been going on since you left," Mother said as she took two of the filled cups and placed them on the coffee table in front of the couch near the windows. She went back to the food prep-area and brought the plate of Grand-mère's amazing cookies and the third cup.

Daddy sat on one of the side chairs and Mother joined me on the sofa. "It feels so 'same,' having you both here—and yet so different, like I have been gone for years." I looked around the room with heavy eyes and glanced up at the Bible, hidden in sight near the top of the bookcase. *It's there. Stoner didn't break in and confiscate it. Neither did Tayton. I don't know if I believe him yet.*

Daddy sipped a little from his cup but when it was obviously too hot, he drew back. "The Council of Elders met many times while you were gone, to discuss the direction of our country. Christy, you and Jason are close to having enough signatures already to place a citizens' referendum on the ballot at the next election here in the Central Zone. By the time the other three zones have finish canvassing their people, there will be an abundance of names. We will vote to overthrow the Length of Days Law for good on Election Day November 3, 2114."

"Election Day? The Presidential Election should be in 2116," I thought aloud. "I've read the old documents many times."

"The Council is aware of the old documents," Daddy reminded me. "The new Constitution changed the presidential election date. They had to hurry to get everything passed as quickly as they could. Christy, it was a coup. They acted fast."

"A coup d'état," I whispered. "A sudden strike against the State." My stomach began to churn. The thought of an uprising to bring about change was overwhelming.

Mother drank her coffee with excitement. "People will no longer be placed in the never-ending-sleep, ending their Length of Days." As she crunched her cookie, she dropped crumbs onto the saucer. "Everything is coming together so fast, Christy. As volunteers sign up to travel all over the country to put the campaign in place, Sean will continue to keep us all up-to-date with his underground newspaper." She shook her head in disbelief. "Your friends had started to establish a network before most of us even knew there was a need for one."

Daddy added, "And—in Sean's newspapers, the topic of a truly *elected* president continues to be the center focus of the articles." His voice was giddy with excitement.

"No more seizing of power? A real presidential election—isn't that amazing?" My head was swimming with the pace of the life I had returned to.

"That's right," Mother assured me.

"November of 2114 will be the Presidential Election day?" My memory went back to the display cases in the old part of the Library where historical documents had been laid to rest.

Daddy scooted to the edge of his seat, his hands in full expression. "Judge Brunner explained that even the date for the election was changed when they re-wrote the Constitution. Those who seized power had their own agenda and needed to rush things past the citizens in order to accomplish their devilish plans," his jaw ground in anger. "So, the presidential election is now in November of 2114. Actually, that's why Judge Brunner issued a two-year stay, to coincide with the next National Election. So, besides voting on over-turning the Length of Days Law, we will elect a new president at the end of next year."

Mother placed her cup on the table and clasped her hands together. "Christiana, your name continues to fall on the short-list of candidates for president."

"But, Mother, constitutionally I'm too young to run for president. You have to be at least thirty-five years old."

"Yes, I know," Mother relinquished. "But it is an honor to be asked." She smoothed the skirt of her dress and brushed the crumbs to the floor again. "The Council pulled the original constitution of 1787 out of storage and—they got rid of the new one."

"What?" I gasped. "They just threw it away?"

Daddy leaned in closer as if there were others around that may hear. "With a careful re-reading of the history of the time, following the great upheaval of a hundred years past, your grandfather discovered that the new constitution had not been ratified."

"It's not legal?" I squealed silently as I mouthed the words with exaggerated movements. "Not binding?"

"No," Mother agreed as she jumped to her feet and began to pace. "It's not legal at all." She swirled around and faced me again. Then, she threw her hands up and buried her face in them.

"What is it?" I asked as I turned and looked out of the large window. Below, on the wide street that ran in front of the building, a strata car hadn't even pulled to the curb. Inspector Stoner leaped from his vehicle where it stopped in the middle of the road. "Oh no!" I felt truly ill.

"We'd better leave," Mother whispered.

"Why?" Daddy questioned. "We're Christy's parents and we're checking on her following her illness. It's perfectly natural. We'll relax and it'll all appear to be quite normal."

Shaken, I stepped back from the window, as if Stoner could see through the tinted glass. So much had happened I didn't know if I could handle more. Morning had started on the other side of Howard Mountain, in the Valley of the Keepers. It was now hours later and I was only half awake. I wasn't sure if I was ready to face Chief Inspector Ward Stoner.

"Go ahead, Mother. Tell me more about the Council's decisions." If rested, I would have refused intimidation. In my current state of exhaustion, I was just stubborn, and that would have to do for today.

"Okay—the other big news, Christy," Mother continued. "They want your grandfather to run for president. It looks like the current Zone President Nathan Alexander will run in opposition."

"Oh, Mother!" I leaped off the sofa and gave her a hug. "Grand-père has agreed to run?" I sat back down on the edge of the couch and waited for the answer that would change everything.

"Yes, Honey," she said as she sat next to me and threw her arms around my shoulders. "He didn't hesitate a moment."

"What about the primaries?" I asked, excitedly.

"Primaries? What are primaries? Mother asked.

"That's when the citizens vote on which candidate they want to represent their political party," I explained.

"There aren't multiple candidates, Christy," Daddy reminded me. "For more years than I can remember, the government selected a successor to the one in office without the waste of time of an election. They did away with the primary process. And, since there is just one candidate in each of the parties at this election—again, there is no need for a primary."

I thought for a moment. "I imagine the entire election process will have to return to the previous system eventually, or maybe an improved one."

Daddy smiled and groaned at the same time. "There will be a lot of work to do."

"Then—" I said as the truth of what I had heard sank in and recharged my tired body by igniting my spirit. "In spite of Ward Stoner and any of the negative forces that have strangled our country, a rebirth of freedom has begun."

CHAPTER 4

An Intrusion

To my mind, it was both amazing and logical. My own grandfather had become a candidate in the first presidential campaign in decades. Of course, no one could be better.

"What's the plan for getting Grand-père elected?" I asked as I sat back and took in the enormity of what we were talking about that morning in my living room.

Mother was excited as she talked about her own father. "He's filled out and filed the paperwork to register his intent to run and has named Judge Carl Brunner as the chairperson of his election committee," she said in amazement. "Your grandfather is working on a schedule to visit the other three zones. The courts ruled that a candidate for a national office cannot be prohibited from crossing the borders and visiting the entire country in which he is running."

"I'm going to have to sprint to catch up on what's going on here in the Central Zone." My head was swimming with exhaustion. I still had not slept. "Does Stoner know about Grand-père?" I asked, flooded with new information and challenges that seemed insurmountable to my tired mind. There hadn't been a real election in our country for so many years I doubted that the young people would remember it was a normal practice in the past. I had read all the documents in my secluded spot in the back room of the city library. I knew what the founding fathers intended but the re-written constitution had changed everything.

"We—" Mother began. Her words quickly fell on the floor as the door to my apartment banged open and slammed against the wall that flanked the opening.

Startled, I jumped and grabbed my forehead. My nerves, frayed and raw, caused my thoughts to swim frantically like one caught in a riptide. Would I be able to stop the waves of confusion that threatened to overtake me?

"Well, well, well," Stoner drawled, like someone who finally found his coveted four-leafed clover. He strutted through the door and mocked, "The little princess is home, looks well and is surrounded by her loving family. Isn't that sweet?"

"Inspector Stoner," I said and coughed, unable to think of a cleaver thing to say. "Thank you for your concern. I continue to improve."

Daddy extended his arm, a gesture of invitation. "What can we do for you, Inspector?" He asked. "It's really quite early in the morning for you."

Stoner only smirked. "I'm fine. It's you and your wife I'm surprised about. What are you two doing in town so early?"

"Listen to the man, Bob," Mother cooed. She replaced her coffee cup on the table beside her and casually watched Shakespeare cross the room, chasing a stream of sunlight that had managed to stay ahead of her. "We enjoy getting up early. Besides, we wanted to check on our daughter. She's been sick for a long time."

"Yes, so I've heard." Stoner observed the cat for a second and then followed her into the kitchen. He watched her eat from the bowl Daddy had placed on the floor. Popping the lower cabinet open, he mused, "Half a bag of food, huh?" He shook the bag and replaced it where he had found it. "I'm sure you must have run out of food during the time you've been confined to the house."

My stomach churned. My body ached with weariness. As I lifted my cup to my mouth, I couldn't believe how heavy it felt. How could I cover my exhaustion and how could I explain it? The coffee sloshed in the cup and spilled into the saucer.

"I'm sorry," I apologized automatically. "I guess I haven't improved as much as I thought I had. I'm still pretty weak." I coughed again and the depth of the raspy sound and scratchiness in my throat was evident. Was I really getting sick?

Stoner stepped back, out of the path of flying pathogens. "I can't waste my time here any longer," he barked as he stumbled into an overstuffed chair. Quickly, he straightened himself with anger and gathered his dignity. "Missy," he hissed, "you'd better get yourself well real fast. I hear your granddaddy is running for president. He's going to need a smart little lady like you to front for him."

"Lady Christiana is a Legacy Citizen, in line for a seat on the Council of Elders," Daddy said as his jaws grew stone hard with anger. "You will treat her with respect."

Stoner started to speak and then closed his eyes. "You're right. Lady Applewait, please accept my apologies." He bowed deeply from the waist. Then, he raised his brows and darkness like a raging storm crossed his face. "Or is it, Simza Bihari?" he asked. Contempt dripped from his voice, evil from his eyes.

"Who?" Mother asked with a blank expression.

"Ask your daughter," Stoner seethed.

Lieutenant Chalky Boone burst through the door Stoner left open. "Inspector?" she shouted, her breath short and her tone urgent.

Stoner snapped around, his shoulders were taut and drawn up to his ears. "Boone, do not interrupt me."

"Sorry, Boss," she apologized and brushed off his reproach like an annoyance. "I had to let you know that your mother messaged the office. She was taking Christopher to the doctor."

"The doctor?" His eyes flared and his brow furrowed deeply, like ruts in a muddy, warn road. "Why?"

"Mrs. Stoner said Christopher's legs were numb again."

"Boone," he growled. "Hold your tongue. Don't talk about my son in front of others."

"You asked, Inspector," she shrugged and stood tall. "Besides, citizens no longer have to fear every scratch and damage to their body. The government doesn't keep a running tally of life points, until it reaches twenty-five. Defective persons are no longer eliminated."

"A short reprieve in that policy," Stoner snorted. "This obsession with freedom will be voted down at the election. Sanity will be restored soon." He paced across the room with wide, pressured strides. Then he stopped abruptly and spun around with rage pouring from his eyes. "Well, Missy Applewait, is your precious doctor seeing patients again?"

Shaken by his glare and anger, I didn't know what to say or how to say it. My mind raced to the safety of words that would conceal my fear. "He said he wanted to return today," I drew out slowly, like someone searching their mind for a lost conversation. "I'm not sure if he's going to the office this morning or this afternoon." I couldn't help but smile a little as I thought about how tired Jason and I were even hours ago. The only place we wanted and needed to be was in our beds sleeping. Then I remembered his words and knew why I didn't know for sure where he would be right then. *I have to be at my house or in my office if Stoner were to go there.* I couldn't know where Jason would be because he hadn't made up his mind before he and Silas let me out in front of my apartment building a short time ago.

"It's about time he got back to work." Stoner snorted.

"He has been studying orthopedics, Inspector." Daddy spoke with firmness and yet a full measure of compassion. "If there is something wrong with your son's legs, you may be very thankful Dr. O'Reilly has been learning that branch of medicine."

Inside, my muscles froze. Jason may have to put his "study" into practice immediately. He had taken a 281 Palm Device along on our canvas of the country. It projected holograms of orthopedic procedures onto any background that was handy, including the space between Jason's lap and the back of the bus seat in front of us as we traveled through northern California. He studied every available moment with dedication and serious intensity. But was his time of study enough to learn all he needed? I quickly side-stepped Jason's involvement and focused on the Chief Inspector's son.

"Is Christopher okay?" I asked, intending to speak to Lieutenant Boone.

"How would I know?" Stoner roared. "Boone just got here." I watched his face draw up tightly as he continued to pace.

"Sir, if you think you should leave, we will pray for you and your son." Mother's offer sounded sincere and compassionate.

"Pray?" Stoner thundered. "Madam, do you know you are committing treason? Prayer is a forbidden act. And using the names of God and the Christ is treasonous. If the people were to rely on God, why would they cast their lot and loyalty with the government?"

"Surely, you don't believe that?" I asked him. I remembered when he accidently struck his young son Christopher with his strata car on Gifting Day Eve. Dr. Jason O'Reilly was the anonymous phone number, a physician contact without a name, Stoner had called.

"Do not challenge me, Missy!" he shouted.

"I am Lady Applewait, Inspector—not Missy anything," I stated firmly with my jaw set. "The New Constitution is clear about the need to treat all members of the Council of Twelve, and those who will rise to that position, with respect. I am sure you are aware of your added responsibility to protect Legacy Citizens."

Stoner gasped and gritted his teeth. He slapped his hands together as one would who was brushing the dust from his hands and moving on. As he left, he pounded on the door with his fist and stomped out of the room.

CHAPTER 5

Jason is Back

"O'Reilly?" Stoner bellowed as he burst into the doctor's waiting room. He pressed the heels of his hands to his temples that pounded with hours of anger and thwarted determination.

"Yes?" Dahlia Zoobamba hurried through the door that led from the back hall. She stopped abruptly and stared at the Chief Inspector; her eyes wide. "Oh, it's you Inspector. What can I do for you?"

He worked his jaw in anger; his eyes flashed. "Nothing! I believe I called out for O'Reilly if you were listening." He marched back and forth a few more steps. "I hate to repeat myself."

Nurse Zoobamba swallowed hard. "Sir, I'm sorry. I was in the back office."

"What were you doing back there? What if a patient were to come in?"

"I know the morning's schedule, Inspector. There are no appointments until after lunch." She stepped around the partition from the waiting room and into the receptionist's area.

Stoner sneered. "Do you need a wall between us, Nurse?" He lowered his voice to a whisper, placed his arm on the opening's wide writing surface and leaned into her space. "Are you afraid of me?"

She straightened up and crossed her arms. "Should I be?"

Stoner grinned but his joy soon faded. "Have you heard from my mother?" he questioned as his eyes darted to the entrance.

"Inspector?" Dr. O'Reilly asked as he breezed through the door. "Was I expecting you this morning?"

Stoner's mouth dropped and his eyes bulged. "Doctor—you've finally arrived."

"Yes, Inspector—this is my office." Jason reached out his hand in greeting with a self-satisfied expression on his face. "I'm glad to be back."

"What's the smug expression for?" Stoner scoffed and flipped his hand at the doctor's offering of friendship.

"It seems like a glorious day," Jason said with measured enthusiasm. "Wouldn't you agree?"

"I know this is your office, Doctor. I wasn't sure that you knew it." Stoner ignored Jason's positive attitude. He preferred to intimidate and dominate. That's not possible with someone with a smile on their face.

"Did you want something?" Jason asked the inspector as he reached through the receptionist's window and handed Dahlia his briefcase.

The outer door opened again and Inspector Stoner's mother hurried in carrying his son Christopher in her arms. "Thank God you're here," she mumbled under her breath.

Stoner's eyes darted toward her, then to the doctor. He said nothing, unspoken surprise written on his face. He had never heard his mother evoke the name of the old Deity before. He wondered if the other two heard her.

"Ward," Mrs. Stoner gasped. "Take him." She smiled at the child, but concern was evident in the drawn lines on her face. "You're a big boy," she said. "And, heavy," she added as she kissed the recently turned six-year-old on the forehead as she passed him over to his father.

Stoner grabbed Christopher and drew him close. Since his wife died, Christopher was all he had. "What's wrong, Son?" he asked gently. Turning to Jason he flared, "You're lucky you decided to come back into the office."

"My leg doesn't want to work," the child said, a look of wonderment on his face.

"Did you fall again?" Jason asked him as he ignored the Inspector's prodding. "Remember when you were hurt on Gifting Day Eve?"

"No, he didn't fall," his grandmother said, her eyes searching for answers.

"Yes, I did," Christopher corrected her.

"You did?" she questioned.

"Yes, I fell on the front steps when you were in the house," the little one explained.

"Well, we'll have a look," Jason offered and continued into the inner hall. "It could be as simple as a pinched nerve. Follow me." As he held the door open for the three to pass, he finally answered Stoner's intended question. "I was out of the office long enough to learn new procedures to treat your son, Inspector." Reaching out, he patted Stoner on the back with a firm and confident slap. "I'm sure we are all happy about that."

Stoner was silent but, in his heart, contempt festered like a seeping wound. *Well, well, well—the rats have crawled back to their nests.*

CHAPTER 6
May 2113

"Are you ready for this?" Jason asked one evening in May as we hurried from my apartment building and got into his car.

"Yes, I guess I'm ready—why?" At first, I thought it was a strange question. I follow my agenda carefully. The meeting that evening was the next event. "Holly reminded me."

"Holly?" Jason asked.

"Holly," I stated. "That's what I call my holographic avatar. I programmed her to appear to me when I have upcoming appointments. I have her set to not appear if there are others around."

I watched the colors of spring pass by as we drove toward Oakwood and my grandparents' home. I didn't want spring to be so busy that I'd miss the pastel daisies, pink snapdragons, and the opening leaves on the budding trees. I missed the end of winter crawling around in the old subway system and sewers of New York. Not that I minded helping all the underlings. Tricked out of their homes, they lived underground for decades. It was just that time had slipped through my fingers like the sands of the desert and I didn't know where the months had gone.

"You didn't answer me, Honey," Jason urged as he started the car and pulled onto the street. The solar powered vehicle hummed as we moved into traffic.

"Did you think I might be anxious about the meeting?" I asked and then added. "Are you asking as the man in my life or my physician, Jason?" I was still in doubt about what he was getting at.

"I'm asking as the man who loves you, Christy." His eyes revealed both concern and a little disappointed.

I nuzzled in closer to him and felt his warmth. "I love you too, Jason," I said as a new reality sank in. "You know, this year could be hard on us, at least on me."

Jason rubbed my knee gently. "Why?"

"All of this political stuff is flooding in faster than I can possibly hold back the waves. If Grand-père asks me to help him on his campaign, I could be gone a lot," I whispered as I watched the passing scene. I couldn't take in enough of the glowing colors as the setting sun cast golden rays on the greening grass.

"*If* he asks you?" Jason chuckled in a teasing tone. "He will definitely need you—and he will certainly ask you," he said as he took my hand. "Christy, do you not know that it was your brave confrontation of President Alexander and your willingness to believe Silas Drummond that started this drive to overturn the Length of Days Law and openly elect a new president? If your grandfather wins the election, you will be single handedly responsible for our return to the original Constitution and a rebirth of freedom."

"Oh, Jason," I protested. "I'm a librarian, not a revolutionary."

He squeezed my hand warmly. "I think it's wonderful that you're naive to the impact you have on the events of the day." Jason sounded serious. "But, Honey, you will have to be aware enough of your importance to the cause, to stay safe."

"I'll remember," I said. "We all went through a lot in the other zones. We just got back, so I do remember the gripping fear and my pounding heart. But the Lord was with us."

"Yes, he was," he agreed. "But he gave us the ability to sense danger. We have to use our heads too, Christy. And—I won't always be there with you. I used a plausible excuse to be gone before, but I won't be able to convince Inspector Stoner of the same need this time."

"But, Jason," I sat up straight, "it's not going to be illegal to travel into other zones for purposes of campaigning, so we won't have to sneak out of this one. We won't need excuses."

Jason laughed and added, "And—you have Holly." The smile in his voice sounded sweet. "I'll have to program my Hank to keep me straight about where you are—when you aren't here by my side."

"Hank and Holly, I like that." I laughed at the thought of two holograms crossing beams in the night. Before we went into Grand-mère and Grand-père's house, Jason pulled me to him, kissed my face and brushed back my hair. I felt his tender lips on my eye lids and melted in his arms. Though loved all of my life, by my parents, my grandparents and all those around me, with Jason it was so much more. He filled in the micro-slot of my life that had been incomplete. Not that I wasn't strong on my own. I was—and I am. Jason completed the love-particle, that earthy completion that God had intended. We were almost as one.

• • • • •

Jason pulled the car into the driveway at my grandparents' home. The stately, turn-of-centuries-past, two-story house had beds of yellow tulips around the porch, like colorful lace at the bottom of a fine lady's skirt. I didn't knock but walked in, my usual custom for many years.

Judge and Mrs. Brunner had already joined Grand-mère and Grand-père. Even the Brunners' son Michael had improved enough following his accident to be able to enter with the aid of two canes. Sean, the underground newspaper publisher, and Dahlia, Jason's nurse, Silas Drummond, my parents—Elizabeth and Robert Applewait, and Jason and I all gathered around Oliver and Constance Richly's ample, oak dining room table. An assortment of doughnuts, artfully arranged on an old bone china platter, sat next to a tray holding a coffee pot and last mid-century pink Depression-glass cream pitcher and sugar bowl. Each place setting boasted a matching china dessert plate and a small crystal glass filled with orange juice.

"Christy, dear," Grand-mère stood up and gave me a hug. "I am so glad you are back safely."

Grand-père took my hand as I walked by. "Welcome home, sweetheart."

"Thank you, Grand-père," I said and kissed his forehead. When I saw Silas, I added, "It's so good to see you, too, Silas." I reached over and gave him a little hug. "You have a small bandage behind your ear. What happened?"

"I was bitten by a bug," he whispered as he looked around, his eyes darting from one person to another.

"Do you want me to look at it?" Jason offered.

Silas covered the small spot on the left near his hair line with his fingertips. "No—no, I'm fine."

"You're looking tired," I said as I observed the circles under his eyes.

Silas's gaze fixed on the large cut glass platter in the center of the table. "Thanks for your concern, but I'm okay."

Before the meeting began and each one around the table had their turn at the huge doughnut plate, Judge Brunner bowed his head in reverence. He raised his eyes and studied each member seriously. "Good evening everyone, and especially you two, Christiana and Jason. We are so glad you've returned safely and without detection. Your venture into the three other forbidden zones was amazing and your safe return, a miracle. I am convinced of it. Bless you both."

The judge turned to Sean. "It wouldn't be safe for you to write about their silent movements right now. The network of freedom-loving people they have established to secure the signatures necessary to overturn the Length of Days Law, freely elect a new president, and place freedom at the heart of our country again is vital to our future."

"Absolutely!" Sean agreed. "I've started writing rough drafts of articles, and in-depth stories about all they did, so it will be ready when we do want them published."

"Perfect," Carl Brunner agreed. Members shifted their feet as they leaned forward, their arms rested on the edge of the table.

I saw Silas open his mouth to speak and then close it again. "What were you not saying?" I teased him.

"Nothing really—well—" he said as he stumbled through his thoughts. "I just wondered why we can't brag a little about your adventures."

"It's for their safety, Silas," Carl assured him. "Christy has some arena speaking events and a big trip east coming up."

"East too? Again?" he asked.

I smiled but felt nervous inside. "New York and Maine are some of the venues on my grandfather's agenda."

"Perhaps some added protection would be in order," Silas suggested as he sat back and seemed to relax a little. Still, I worried about him. He looked tense.

"Carl," Grand-père began, "I'm sure we're all anxious to hear what you've found out so far. How do we stand in the process of identifying zone chairpersons?"

Carl placed his elbows on the table and rubbed his hands together briskly. "It's amazing, Oliver," he said as his eyes flashed. "We started by contacting the Western Zone, since Christy and Jason had gone there first. Within a few days after they left the coast, Rachel Claudette, the head of Claimed-International, contacted me and volunteered to spear-head that zone's efforts to place Oliver Richly in the office of the president."

"Claimed-International?" Silvia Brunner asked. "What's that?"

I looked around for someone to answer Mrs. Brunner's question. *Of course they don't know,* I thought.

"Since the four zone borders were sealed years ago, none of us knew of the work of C-I until we arrived," I explained. "In our Central Zone there is a 'two-child-per-family-law.' If a couple accidently has a third child, the parents can choose any two of their children to keep. They have up to two years to decide which two they want. The rejected child is sent to the furnaces under Howard Mountain for extermination."

"Oh, no," Silvia gasped. "It can't be." Her face wore the same grief I had seen when her son Michael was injured.

"Yes, Mrs. Brunner," I insisted kindly. "I'm sorry, but it's true. We have met many of those children. When they arrive at Howard Mountain—Silas Drummond here," I gestured to Silas, "the furnace keeper, spirits them away on weekends, in the dark of night into the Valley of the Keepers, on the other side of the mountain. From there, Martin and Rebecca Spires find homes for them. Some families may already have two or three children of their own, but they 'claim' at least one bright, precious child from the cast-aside ones, and cherish them as their own." I was so excited about Silas's work with the kids, my voice trembled with emotion. "Now, the Keepers' village has grown so crowded they transport many of the Claimed Children to the West Coast and even cities out of the country. Rachel Claudette, a very wealthy Western Zone woman, has chosen to dedicate her life and fortune to these children."

"They are beautiful, bright, and loving children," Jason added. "They're healthy in body, and in spite of everything, their spirit isn't broken, even though their first parents try not to bond with the third child in case they don't want them."

I couldn't hide my smile that spread so wide I thought my face might crack. "One of the children told me proudly, 'I am not rejected. I am claimed and Father Silas is our lead wayfarer.' She was so beautiful, and I told her so. She said shyly, 'Thank you. All are beautiful in the sight of God.'"

"Ah!" Silvia gasped. "Then, somehow, someone has told those children about God, the Holy One. Here in the Central Zone the name of God has not been spoken for so many years!"

Silas was silent but then spoke. "I didn't know God's name either, since there was no one to tell me. But, forced to work in the vilest place on earth, beneath Howard Mountain, I had to hold onto the hope of a God who cares and loves and forgives, or I would have withered and died."

"Bless you, Silas," I offered as I patted his arm where it rested beside me on the table. "Once Silas rescued the rejected children and took them to the Keepers, the people of the Valley taught them about God."

Jason smiled at Silas and added, "It was through Silas's work of rescue, that we met Rachel and stayed in her beautiful home in California."

Mother was sitting beside me. She straightened and put her arm around my shoulder. "So, we have Christy and Jason to thank for Ms. Claudette's quick response," she boasted.

"That's true," Sean agreed. "I was there when Christy spoke to a huge group during a church meeting."

"You were there?" I gasped in amazement. "How did you get there? I didn't see you." I couldn't believe what Sean was saying. Forbidden to cross zone borders, there was no mode of travel.

"I go to the other zones all the time," Sean smiled sheepishly. "I have newspapers to sell."

"At the rally, were you dressed in a disguise?" Jason asked Sean.

Sean laughed. "Simza Bihari was the only one there in a costume."

Dahlia's nose wrinkled in surprise. "Simza Bihari? Who's that?"

"A woman in a gypsy dress and veil, as all women in the Romani culture must be when they're in mourning." Sean was serious. "What do you say, Christy? Do you know who Mrs. Bihari is?"

I laughed and blushed. "Yes, Sean. I am Simza Bihari. Covered in black clothing and wearing a veil was the only way I could speak to the people and go undetected. My face, spread across the Jumbotran, would have been recognized if anyone were in the audience."

"And, someone was in the congregation," Jason chuckled. "Stoner's right-hand assistant, Chalky Boone and her thug, Daniel Washington, were in the back of the arena-turned church."

Grand-mère threw her hand to her mouth in astonishment. "Didn't she recognize you?" she stammered.

"Lieutenant Boone questioned me, or I should say questioned Mrs. Bihari, about my veil. Grace Small, the pastor, explained to her that a Romani widow woman must hide her face in respect for her deceased husband. If she doesn't, a year of shunning would be her fate," I explained. "For that Sunday morning, I was a Romani—or a gypsy widow."

Silvia put her hand to her chest. "Sometime, I want to hear all about your trip around the country. I'll look forward to Sean's newspaper articles."

"Certainly, when all of this is over, we'll have long talks," I agreed and then turned to Grand-père. "Now, as I understand it, you have filed out all of the papers necessary to be a legitimate candidate in the next presidential race."

"That's right," Grand-père said and smiled. "It's hard to believe that we will actually vote on a president again, just as the founding fathers intended more than three-hundred years ago."

Judge Brunner wiped doughnut filling on Grand-mère's colorful napkin and sipped his coffee. I smiled because most people didn't use cloth napkins in 2113. But, Grand-mère is not most people.

"Christy," the Judge began, "as we said, Rachel Claudette is heading up the Western Zone election committee for your grandfather. Edward Musselman is in charge of the Midwestern Zone. And, that's very dangerous for him."

Jason agreed. "The Musselmans are one of the few families that didn't have their farm confiscated through laws designed to confiscate every crop-growing acre. The government owns the farms in the Midwestern zone. Edward and Maud managed to keep theirs by staying out of the spotlight, by hiding in plain sight as they called it."

"And, if Ed steps out of the shadows to spear-head the election committee in their zone, his family could lose their farm?" Mother's expression fell as she put it all together.

"He knows that," Daddy spoke up.

"Like the underlings in the bowels under New York City, believing the lies the elites told them, they lost everything. They crawled into the old subway and sewer systems under the city and didn't come out for decades." My eyes filled with tears that spilled over the rims.

"We were really clear about the dangers involved when Ed contacted us." Carl rolled the corner of the paper he had written notes on. "He insisted he wanted to stand and be counted this time."

"That is so brave," Dahlia whispered. "I don't think I could do that."

"Dahlia," Jason's jaw dropped, "you were the only one in the office every time Inspector Stoner stormed through the door. You had to stand firm, to take his insults and questions and act as if I were a 281 Palm Device hologram away. If he had demanded that you contact me, he would have seen that I wasn't within reach. Now, that is brave."

"I hadn't thought about that," she mused.

Daddy listened and then offered, "Oliver will need all the time we have left until the election, just to get into the other zones and meet people. No one even knows who he is in the rest of the country, although they should be aware of the Council of Elders in general. He'll have to canvass every major city and all the small hamlets in between."

"Do you have a leader for the Eastern Zone yet, Dad?" Michael asked the judge. "There's a lot to do," he observed. "This is the spring of 2113 and the election is November 3, 2114. How will Oliver be able to get to every region?"

"I'll get to the large venues," Grand-père said slowly, "but the entire election team will have to help out. There will be a committee in each zone to set up speaking opportunities, interviews—all the things that candidates for president used to do. They can't rig this election. We will carefully monitor it. The people will have to get to know me fast so they can make an informed decision regarding their vote. Christy, the people like you. You will be able to make speeches where I can't go."

Sean tapped his fingers on the table and jumped in. "A hard part of getting Sir Richly's message out to the people, will be designing the logistics for travel outside the zone. I know because I've taken my newspapers to distributers all over the country. But this campaign is different. We have no connections, no trans-zonal airlines, not even maps from the other areas."

"Yes," I smiled as I remembered. "But there are maps within the other zones outside of ours." With the sound of bus wheels and Raymar Goring's deep voice in my ears, I added, "Even the children on board the bus that wound along the beautiful stretch of highway between San Luis Obispo and Atascadero, California poured over the maps they had along with them. It is just this Central Zone that has no maps since most people no longer have cars, and the Public Transit only runs up and down the rail."

"There are ways to connect with people, "Carl said. "And, where there are none, we will create them." He folded his hands on the table and took a deep breath. "Michael, to answer your question, we have a volunteer for the eastern zone; the woman Christy and Jason stayed with at the Citadel–the Cornwall Citadel on Park Avenue and Fifty-Seventh Street. It's the home of Richard and Barbara Cornwall. Barbara is the one who volunteered." He paused again and looked around at every face at the table. "Since we are so isolated here in the Central Zone and forbidden to travel beyond the closed borders, we have no idea who some of these people are. I don't know who Barbara Cornwall is. What do you think, Christy? You and Jason stayed with the Cornwalls; you know them. What is your opinion of her?"

"Barbara and Richard were wonderful to us and to those less advantaged," I said slowly, articulating each word carefully. "They took in some of the moles and underlings when they came out from below the city after years of living beneath the feet of the elite ones who lived above. The Cornwalls filled the rooms in their mansion with people they had never met."

"It was Mrs. Cornwall who volunteered to head up the process in the East. When she contacted me, she didn't say a lot. She did tell me that her husband would join her as co-chair when he recovered from an accident. Mrs. Cornwall insisted that she had to be of service. She said she has a debt to pay. Christy, will she be strong enough to do this?"

"Yes," Jason offered. "I'm sorry to interrupt, but, as a physician, I observed Barbara a lot. She is strong enough to do anything she chooses to do."

The Judge paused; his eyes focused on the ceiling. "Jason, did she do something that she needs to pay penance for? Will her former actions come around and embarrass our efforts to elect Oliver as president?" He looked at Jason and then at me. "Now is the time to tell us of any possible legal action against her."

I chuckled silently. Barbara Cornwall—in trouble with the law? "No Carl, there are no charges against Barbara. She has no criminal record. She is a very strong person. She stands up to her father often, and she does it with a straight back and clear eyes."

Carl breathed deeply. "Standing up to one's father is not necessarily a brave thing to do. Does that account for her need to pay off a debt?"

I looked around at all those gathered there. Then I lingered on Silas for a moment. "It is not her debt," I explained. "She is trying to repair the moral obligation of her father, to restore a measure of respectability to the family name."

Silas adjusted his position in his chair and continued to hold his eyes on me. "My Lady—Christy—who is her father and what did he do?"

"Silas, I know what you have been through." I patted his hand again and tried to reassure him, as his eyes darted left and right like a trapped animal. "The evil under the mountain and the museum of horrors you had to live with down there were unbearable for Jason and me to see—and we just passed through. You had to live with it all." I lifted his hand and kissed the top of it. "Silas—Barbara Cornwall's father—is Alister Bedlam, the richest and most evil man in the world—and the source of all your fears and sorrow."

Tears rolled down Silas's cheeks. "Then she has been in more pain than I. She's a perfect zone leader," he stated as he slapped the palms of his hands on the table.

The judge folded his hands and looked at me intently. "Christy, with a line-up like that, we are going to need you in Oliver's campaign office. You'll need to travel with him to be his liaison with these people in the other zones. Are you ready for this?"

Then I really knew why Jason had asked me the same thing on our way over to Oakwood. He was preparing me so I could answer the question when the judge asked it. I didn't have to think about it.

"Yes, sir, I'm ready," I said without hesitation. "And, where I'm not, the Lord will go before me and prepare the way."

CHAPTER 7
June 2113

The lettering was bold and black–*1787-Constitutional Party*–with red, white, and blue stripes and full fans of bunting surrounding it. I knew the signage hanging over the door was a little too ostentatious for Oliver Richly's liking. It must have been a decision made by the Richly Election Committee. In the window of the storefront-turned massive office space was a two by three-foot photo of Grand-père with the caption, OLIVER RICHLY FOR PRESIDENT.

I opened the door and walked in to more bustling energy than I had seen since the Claimed Children bellied-up to Rachel Claudette's dining room sideboard. People were laughing, having discussions in small groups, some had pulled their small ear deflectors out of their pocket to work quietly and independently.

Spring had dripped into early summer and still the rains continued. Water droplets gathered on the window panes and together formed a stream that ran down the glass to the sill below. Someone had placed a bucket beneath the double-hung sashes to prevent puddling on the floor. I watched a young man swap out a half-full pail for an empty one and smiled. Grand-père would never have had such a make-shift scene in his own home or office, regardless of the need for election funding.

"Lady Applewait?" a thirty-something woman with bouncing curls questioned as she approached me.

"Yes, I'm Christiana Applewait." I watched the room with excitement. Before the government removed the anti-emotion chemicals from our water supply, no one would have had the energy or interest to forge up this much enthusiasm.

"I see you are amused by our antiquated building," the woman who had greeted me said. "Starting yesterday, rapidly awakening campaign contributors started to drop off fists full of money for this renewed concept of free elections. The people want full freedom. We might also be able to make a few needed repairs to the building with some of the campaign money."

"What is your name?" I asked as she led me to a vacant desk behind a glass partition.

"My name is Ivy, Lady Applewait," she answered. Then she turned to the area in front of us. "This is your desk—if you want it."

I looked around and sized up the space. Complete with a small vase of flowers and a few books on the desk top, it looked homey. I would be able to help my grandfather from this small cubby of an office. "Yes, Ivy, thank you. I believe I do want it."

"I understand you will continue to monitor the progress of each zone campaign organization. That's great," she looked around the small space again. "And—I heard the signatures are all in place for the bill to come to a vote to overturn the Length of Days Law. It has secured a spot on the election ballot."

"Yes, Ivy, that task is complete. Now—" I paused and took my place in the chair behind my new desk. "Those same volunteers are working on the Richly Election Campaign Committee."

Ivy smiled as she sat in the facing leather chair. "We have a full agenda for you, Lady Applewait."

"Christy," I corrected her. "If the office is going to run smoothly, let's not complicate the conversation with cumbersome titles. Please, call me Christy. Everyone does."

Ivy blushed a little with cast down eyes. "I heard that. But I didn't want to assume anything. I—I was in the crowd on Gifting Day Eve. I heard it all. I saw it all—and it filled me with awe. You are—"

"I am a campaign worker, the same as you, Ivy," I protested.

"You are the seer, Christy," she beamed. "I heard you described as a disciple of the Holy One. The Lord has blessed you with—"

Crack! The moment was shattered and the glass partition fractured by something that whizzed past my head.

Screams rattled through the air as everyone in the outer office hit the floor in self-protection. But I was frozen. I experienced no shock, helplessness, or hopelessness. I wasn't confused or disoriented. Rigidly fixed in a state of focus I had never known before, I didn't move. The last months raced through my mind like the fleeting images of a drowning person. Jason and I had experienced dangers of many kinds, under filthy city streets or crawling along frozen ground in order to avoid detection. But we had never been the target at the end of a firearm, actually fired on in broad daylight.

Ivy flew across the desk, threw me to the floor and dropped her body on top of me. Pinned down and dazed, I waited for an all-clear signal.

"Is everyone out there all right?" Ivy shouted to the pool of volunteers in the front office.

Ivy and I scrambled to our feet. She started out of my office and I followed close behind. We both were on a mission to determine what had happened.

"Yes—I think we're all okay, just scared spitless," one volunteer gasped as we approached. Others just stared with wide eyes.

In the larger staff office, Ivy began at the windows where she slammed heavy storm shutters closed. The room grew eerily dark without natural light pouring in. She inspected the area all around the broken glass. "It appears that a long range rifle round pierced the street window," she began as she walked through the room, "lanced the tight spaces between campaign workers here in the outer office," she continued as we walked back into my small space, "and then embedded its lethal projectile in the wall just over your left ear," she concluded.

Then it occurred to me as I stood behind her, Ivy hadn't dodged any flying projectiles by falling to the floor like the rest of us. She had actually leaped onto my desk and placed her body between me, any additional bullets and the flying glass from the window that divided my office from the outer general work area.

From behind her, I could see something in her hair. I placed my hands on her head and felt hard, sharp fragments that nicked my hands. "Ivy," I gasped as shards fell from where they had clung to her curls. "Here, let me help you."

I guided her back to the chair she had been sitting in and carefully parted portions of her hair and began to remove the glass. At first, I worked silently, my mind full of possibilities. Who would have shot at me? Stoner had many opportunities to murder me in cold blood if that was his intent.

"Christy!" Grand-père shouted as he dashed into my office, with both arms spanning the entry. His eyes quickly darted around the small space and then rested on the gaping hole in the wall. "Are you all right?" He hurriedly put his arms around me as I stood over Ivy.

"Ivy, how are you? Are you hurt?" he asked when he saw the broken glass.

"I'm fine. Just itchy with fragments in my hair I don't want to scratch." She carefully picked at some remaining pieces that had eluded me.

"If you're sure you're okay, I'll check out front again on the rest of them," he said as he headed back out the door. I could see him going from one volunteer to another.

Ivy started to get up from the chair, but I touched her shoulder and asked her to stay, gently running my fingers through every blond wave and curl. "Your hair is very thick. It looks like the depth of your curls caught some of the glass and wouldn't let it slip away."

"I always knew my thick mane, that I can hardly get a comb through some days, would eventually cause a problem." She patted my hand and inched to the edge of the seat; her eyes fixed on the hole in the wall. "Thanks, Christy." She didn't look at me but crooked her finger for me to follow her direction. "Look at this," she whispered as she inspected the end of the failed attempt at murder.

"What?" I asked but eagerly followed her lead.

"This is not the projectile from a 750-Z or any of the other Blue Guard weapons," she mused as she fished in her pocket. She pulled out what appeared to be an old-fashioned pocket knife I had seen pictures of in some of my books. With determination, she opened the blade and began to dig out the lead.

I watched as she pried at the shattered area, seemingly careful not to damage the bullet. "Ivy," I finally began slowly. "How do you know about a 750-Z and any of its ammunition?"

"Oh—I read a lot," she answered as she worked on the spot.

I continued to watch her extricate the bullet. "You probably don't know, Ivy, but I have a master's degree in library science. With book burnings in decades past and book banning of our current era, there are no weapons of any kind or pictures of weapons in the current literature. That information was eliminated a very long time ago."

As Ivy pulled the bullet from the wall and inspected it in her hand, I asked, "How could you have known about any of this—and where did you get a pocket knife? They aren't manufacture anymore?"

"Christy—there are some things you don't know," she began, stumbling as she searched for words— "yet."

"Okay," I said as I sat back down and motioned for her to return to the chair. "Let's talk."

"Well—your grandfather—"

"Grand-père? What does he have to do with this shooting?" Now, I was really confused. But one thing I did know, "That bullet comes from an antique long rifle. I do have access to books of all kinds and that round looks familiar."

"I won't lie to you, Christy. You're right. I have never seen ammunition like this. Where would it have come from?"

"I once overheard Ward Stoner say, 'We have a well-stocked arsenal of weapons and instruments, both new and vintage.'"

My head was swimming with dreaded possibilities. "I still say, Stoner would never attack me or Grand-père. He would chase me to the ends of the country, but he would never attack me. He's too loyal to his precious rule book and wants to carry out every new law that was created under the New Constitution."

"Then, there has either been a breach of security at the Federal arsenal—or there is a rogue Guardsman who can get really close to us," Ivy thought aloud.

"Ivy," I began cautiously, "just who or what are you? And, tell me now, what does my grandfather have to do with all of this?"

"Sir Richly hired me to pose as your assistant—but in reality, I'm your bodyguard." She winced as though she expected me to reject her.

"Sounds like a good idea to me," I agreed. "I hope I never need you to protect me with your own body again. "And—" I began as I looked into her eyes. "I want only honesty between us," I insisted. "I know I'm young, but I'm not a child. I have proven that I can help implement changes and take care of myself. I will allow you to be my partner-in-safety. Today has proven that life has become even more dangerous than before." I reached out my hand and eagerly shook hers as a gesture of warm, equal friendship. Then I added confidently, "We're in this together—as friends."

CHAPTER 8
The City of Angels

October 2113

Unable to take my eyes off the ground below us, I watched as our plane closed the space between the landing gear and the runway. "Look at the colors on the tree tops below us. I can't believe this is early autumn already."

Months ago, Jason and I were smuggled into the Western Zone on a cool winter day. It was early evening this time, bright enough to see the landscape below and dim enough to bring up the sparkle of the night. The lights of the bright City of Angels glowed in multi-colors, with shimmering hallows around the beams. Gray Fox and his wife Little Feather weren't here to guide us this time, but that would have to be okay.

"Grand-père," I began, slipping my arm through his as the plane descended, "you won't meet Martin and Rebecca Spires on this leg of the campaign. There're wonderful, and I really want you to meet them, but—they'll be with us in New York."

"Martin and Rebecca—keepers of the Bible," he nodded, remembering what I had told him.

Ivy mostly remained silent and stayed in the background, ever present, ever watching. Not this time. "I'm sorry to interrupt, but what are the keepers of the Bible?"

I smiled as I watched Ivy lean in and listen to the story of the wonderful people of the valley on the other side of the mountain from

Capitol City. "Their valley was hidden after an earthquake but not destroyed as people on both sides of Howard Mountain believed. All the families in the Valley of the Keepers are responsible for different books the ruling elite tried to erase after the great uprising of the previous epoch. For four generations, every man, woman, and child in the valley have carried a verbal account of the history of this great nation. Because their existence in unknown to the rest of the world, they can live in seclusion and their secret activities go undetected. Different families have in their possession certain books and volumes which they have guarded and memorize in the event of book confiscation. You're right. The Spires family is the keeper of the Bible, the story of all of us."

Ivy's jaw dropped. "Families memorized whole books?"

I was thrilled to say, "Yes, they did," as if the knowledge of it was as stupendous as the act of it.

Ivy began to gather up her belongings as the plane taxied. "I have recently heard of the Bible, but I've never read one, or held one in my hand for that matter."

Not sure of how much to tell her, since the confiscation of Bibles happened years ago, I wanted to say something, since she seemed interested. "I think we can get you one out here in the Western Zone while we're in the area. This zone follows the rules they agree with, not the rules written down. The Western Zone is the new Bible belt."

"That would be great," Ivy beamed. Then, as if she had just noticed, she asked, "Why isn't Jason with you, Christy?"

My last moments with Jason when he dropped us off at the airport, flooded back. I felt my cheeks grow warm, and I hoped my blush wasn't evident to others.

"I love you so much," Jason had whispered in my ear. "I'll miss you more than I want to think about."

At the gate, checking out my grandfather and Ivy Trudeau's diverted gaze, I leaned in and kissed Jason goodbye. "I didn't think I could do this without you."

"You are so strong, Christy. I know you can," he assured me.

"I love you." My lips formed words I shared only with Jason.

I smiled again as I thought of him, picked up my cross-body satchel and slipped the strap over my head. "Jason was out of his office for so long when we were gone during the winter, he thought he had better stay in Capitol City. He'll join us in New York."

"I may be a member of the Council of Elders, but I have never been to New York—or L.A. for that matter." Grand-père reached under his seat and pulled out a leather bag. "Odd, I'm willing to come to the coast, but my worthy opponent, President Alexander, chooses to call his presence in from Capitol City."

Ivy thought for a moment. "Alexander is a zone president, now he wants to be president of the whole country."

I chuckled a little. "He's afraid to have his face enlarged to gargantuan size. Everyone will see what he really looks like," I said as I rolled my eyes. "They'll use the Jumbotron. He'll be bigger than life. When you see your own face enlarged by tens, you get a sense of your own presence. It will be the same for Alexander," I added as we began to disembark the plane.

"Jumbotron is it?" Grand-père asked, but it sounded more like a statement than a question.

"Just remember, Alexander may be the Zone President but you are on the council, and that's national. They will recognize your position, if not your face."

I paused when I arrived at the cabin door. A jetway from the previous century was still in use and waited in front of me. With travel between zones, even from town to town, forbidden, lack of use ensured that most of the equipment of air travel would never wear out.

Now, here we were, legally flying into the Western Zone. I smiled at the miracle of my awakening country and then thought of my grandfather's participation in it all. "Regardless of Alexander's size on the huge screen, the image would still just be little-old-him."

Grand-père hoisted up his bag, like a man intending to make a point. "Maybe that's why he will only be present electronically. He needs to feel larger than he really is."

We walked quickly down the jetway ready to take on all that the west had to offer. "Raymar!" I shouted to the man who waited with a small American flag in his hand. He was the only one in the terminal with a flag. When they partitioned the country into zones, they banned Nationalism. The American flag was one of the first emblems to go. With so many nationalities coming to our country, it offended the immigrants that they could not fly their own flag. Therefore, to be fair, none was visible.

Raymar stood there—clean shaven, dressed in appropriate clothing, with a calm and peaceful expression on his face. "I didn't know if you would recognize me," he blushed. "They tell me I look different."

"You look wonderful, old friend," I smiled as I reached up and gave him a hug. Then I turned to my grandfather. "Grand-père, I'd like you to meet Raymar Goring. He is a man of many identities. He was one of the hollow people. But he is also, the famous author, Robert Gross."

"I'm still one of the hollow people. The government said the hollow ones will always be second class citizens until a law is written, specifically overturning the previous law." His expression was dark and defeated.

"I am so pleased to meet you," Grand-père assured him as he shook his hand. "I've read your books. As Robert Gross, they can't call you second class anything." He gave Raymar's shoulder a hearty pat. "And, as to creating a new law, we are going to overturn the entire New Constitution and reinstate the original one. A plan is already in place." He gave him a friendly slap again. "There was no mention of the hollow people in the Constitution of 1787, and to be precise, there is nothing in the new one about the hollow ones either. Some may treat you like a second-class citizen, but you are equal under the law. And, all of you can vote—so get out there and register everyone."

"Thank you, Sir," Raymar said with sincerity. "Come," he stated briefly. "Rachel Claudette will have a late supper ready for us when we get there."

"Wonderful!" I said out of appreciation and a hungry stomach. "It will be good to see your daughter, Kasamar, again." Then I paused. "I hope she'll be there."

"Rachel had me drive one of her cars. It's this way." Raymar directed us toward the door that led to the parking structure. "Indeed, Kasamar will be there. Rachel has put her in charge of Claimed-International. Since Rachel will be heading up the Western Zone committee for your election, Sir Richly, she knew she would need dependable help."

Grand-père stopped in mid-step. "Raymar, there will be no class-system in the renewed USA. Call me Oliver."

Raymar smiled. "I will try to remember. But know, in my heart, you are my friend."

"Stated like an accomplished writer," Grand-père bowed at the waist, laughed, and preceded out the door.

Since the sun had set, the parking structure was dim and full. The west wasn't like the Central Zone where the government prohibited citizens from owning personal transportation. Those in the Western Zone would kick and scream if anyone were to attempt to take their car, so vehicle owners crowded every parking facility.

I watched with caution as my grandfather and my friend bonded—and smiled. I wasn't cautious because I feared Raymar, but there was something eerie about the surroundings. The smell of the old gasoline engine cars that dotted the garage reminded me of the wonderful time we spent in California just months previously, and yet it was so different. Something was wrong.

I tried to brush off the feeling of danger with conversation. "Did Rachel send her personal flash-car?"

"Rachel had me drive her last-century minivan." Raymar laughed as he approached a funny car that looked to me like a pointy nosed sausage. "She said we would all have more leg room." He smiled at Grand-père. "I guess she already knew how tall you are." I watched him measure Grand-père's six-foot five-inch height with his eyes.

"Sir," a large man in a black suit and white shirt intruded in our small group as he took Grand-père by his elbow and tried to lead him aside. "I must speak with you, Richly."

"Not now," I urged the man to move on, acting as Grand-père's handler.

"No, he will come with me this minute," the man insisted with a near tourniquet grasp on Grand-père's arm.

"Release him, mister," Ivy said as she stepped between the man and me trying to reason with him.

With his free hand, the robust one drew back his fist and delivered a direct punch to Ivy's face, knocking her down and out. He tightened his hold on my grandfather with white knuckles and tried to pull him away.

Raymar snapped around with a hollow stare and faced the man. I saw him try to conquer the man with the same mad-dog eyes I had seen when I first met him, when Raymar was still a hollow man. He moved in close to the man's space with no fear or hesitation, his teeth bared, a sign of unspoken but fierce aggression.

The man in the suit withered and averted his eyes, but he did not back away without one last word. "I have a message for you, Richly." He raised his eyes and cast a hostile gaze at Grand-père, holding his ground. "We have certain information you wouldn't want shared. Drop out of the race or drop dead."

Raymar grabbed the man's throat with one hand and pried his grip from Grand-père's arm with the other. Raymar didn't use words, but throwing back his head and growling like a rabid wolf, he headbutted the assailant. Then, like a nasty piece of spoiled fruit, he flipped the assailant to the ground. With one last evil glance at the three of us, the suited man picked himself up, limped and stumbled off.

I wished Jason had come with us. I felt safe with him around. Raymar and Ivy would have to fill in for him until he arrived. Turning to Ivy, I bent over and helped her stagger to her feet.

"Are you okay?"

"Yes," she said as she shook her head and reached for her sidearm. "Did you see where he went?"

"No," I said as I looked off in the direction to which I thought he escaped. Overwhelmed by the danger, the attack on my grandfather, and the instantaneous change in who I thought Raymar had become, the truth was, I couldn't think about anything.

Now, with Raymar's return to the screeching persona of a hollow one, I wasn't sure what he was capable of. Torn between fear of the possibility of Raymar's actions and relief that he was able to turn the man away with the power of his will, I reached out and patted Raymar on the shoulder.

"Thank you, my dear friend. Are you all right?" I was worried. I didn't know if he would be able to drag himself back from the edge of the dark abyss again. Could he step in and out of his hollow man behavior?

Raymar had lived in the world as a wild man all of his life. Along with others like him, a hollow one was his label. Seen as half animal, people supposed the hollow ones had little civilized nature within them. It was only Raymar's relationship with his wife and then his daughter that cooled his savage fire.

Then, there was his other side, his inner life as a beloved philosophical author that the world loved but did not know. Who would win this new battle between the light and darkness?

Raymar straightened his hunched shoulders and rose to his full height. He shook his head like one would shed lake water after a swim. Then, he smiled a smile that filled his face. "I'm okay, Christy. Thank you for worrying about me."

"You are really in control!" I marveled.

Grand-père followed the suit-man with his eyes until he was out of sight. "That one was not in control," he said as shades of anger crossed his face like I had never seen before. Grand-père did not get angry—ever.

"And, thank you Ivy for your efforts to protect me," he added.

Her jaw was red from the fist jab and set rigidly in disgust. "But I didn't protect you."

Grand-père patted her shoulder, "But you stepped into harm's way. That's all anyone could do."

She muttered as she walked ahead to the car. "But it wasn't enough."

As we hurried into the safety of Rachel's vehicle, I wondered aloud. "What did he mean about having information about you, Grand-père? I cannot imagine anything negative about you. What do you think he has?"

"I have no idea," he shrugged off the question. "I do know I have nothing to hide."

• • • • •

"Rachel, I'd like you to meet my grandfather, Oliver Richly," I said as Rachel Claudette led us into her beautiful home in Los Angeles. "It is wonderful to be here again."

"I'm happy to meet you, Sir Richly. I recognized you from the posters that are already dotted around the city."

"Please, call me Oliver," Grand-père urged.

"If you'll call me Rachel," the movie producer and director of Claimed-International said as she showed us into the dining room.

The table, covered with a cream-colored cloth with hand painted golden birds of paradise artfully placed on it, already boasted a wooden server with a huge loaf of steaming bread on it. White porcelain dinner plates, placed at each setting and flanked by shinning silver flatware waited for us.

"Oliver," Rachel directed, "please sit at the head of the table. I'll take the foot. Christy and Raymar, please sit facing each other. Ivy, please take the seat beside Christy."

As we sat down, I noticed there was still an empty seat beside Raymar. "Your home is as lovely as I remembered it," I admired as someone came through from the kitchen with a platter of steaks.

"Kasamar!" I said as I jumped up and hugged Raymar's daughter as soon as her platter touched the table.

"Christy!" Kasamar squealed as she turned and embraced me. "I'll be right back with the rest of the food," she said. "Then, we'll catch up."

I started to follow her into the kitchen. "Let me help you," I offered.

"No, My Lady," she protested. "Let me serve you."

"Kasamar," I chuckled and followed along behind her. "I went from Christy to My Lady, practically in one breath."

"I'm sorry, Christy," she apologized. "With your grandfather's campaign for president and his presence here, I guess I'm a little star-struck."

"No stars here," I said and laughed. "Just us."

In the kitchen, the large six burner stove held several pots. She hurried over and ladle out a serving bowl full of small red potatoes. She dabbed a large dollop of pure creamery butter in the middle. I watched it melt and soak in. Into an oblong serving dish she placed long spears of asparagus to which she topped with more butter.

"In the Central Zone, the dietary police would arrest you for butter indulgence and throw you in jail without a trial." Laughing again at the silliness of it all, I marveled at how good it felt to just laugh. "Okay, what can I do to help?"

"Well Christy—I think I may have forgotten the steak knives," she nodded her head in the direction of a cutlery drawer that remained open from the last piece she removed. "It would be wonderful if you could take them in. There's a narrow basket there on the side counter. It would look better if they were passed around rather than plopped down." Kasamar picked up the vegetable bowls and turned to me again. "Thank you, my friend."

Picking up the small basket and placing the knives inside, I couldn't help but anticipate the hot juices running into the bottom of the meat platter that already sat on the table. My mouth began to water and I wondered when I had eaten last—perhaps a breakfast bar and a half cup of coffee in the morning?

As I went back into the dining room, I saw Grand-père's eyes, still widened, as he continued to fix them on the meat platter. "Oh, my goodness, Rachel, those steaks look amazing." He sat back in his chair and patted his stomach. "Wouldn't Jason love one of those, Christy?" he sighed. "Your grandmother would say, 'Now Oliver, remember your heart.'"

I stopped abruptly as I placed the knife basket on the table. My words caught in my throat. "What's wrong with your heart?"

"Absolutely nothing." He grinned as he continued to eye the meat.

Rachel rolled her eyes and smiled. "You're healthy because your wife continues to be proactive and reminds you—before you eat."

We all laughed at the logic of her simple statement. "I was contemplating a diet that would eliminate meat," I said as I looked again at the platter. "I'll consider it again sometime in the future."

Rachel placed her elbows on the table and folded her hands. "Many here in California were vegetarians in the distant past." She shook her head slightly and a faint smile crossed her lips. "Then the government changed, and they re-worked all the facts about nutrition and how certain foods act on the body. Most people decided to go back to the plain eating of our farm ancestors, only we eat in moderation. Common sense people—common sense." With her hands still folded in prayer, she turned to my grandfather. "Oliver, would you please bless our food while it's still hot?"

Grand-père bowed his head and reached for my hand. Then I reached down to Rachel and took hers. Around the table, we held the warm hand of the one near us while Grand-père lifted up words asking God to bless our food, gave thanks for our safe trip and the profoundly important assignment we had been tasked to accomplish.

"Eat up," Rachel encouraged after the Amen, "and then we'll talk about the political rally at the arena tomorrow. There will be thousands present. The Jumbotron will pick up President Alexander in the Central Zone and send your images out across the old public airwaves of previous years."

"Who will ask the questions?" Grand-père wondered aloud.

Rachel passed the meat platter and then cut thick slabs of yeasty smelling bread. "I will, Oliver."

"Great—I guess," I said as another thought rushed in. "Will anyone wonder if you had fed Grand-père the questions ahead of time? You are managing his campaign out here."

"They shouldn't," she stated flatly. "Actually, I haven't seen the questions either. A committee, made up of three political analysists, created the questions. They are in a sealed envelope and will be presented to me at the debate."

"That's a relief," I sighed. "It's been so long since there has been a presidential debate, I wasn't sure how that would be handled."

"I'm glad they chose you," Grand-père said as he began to cut his meat into bite size pieces. "I'll welcome a familiar face."

"They didn't actually choose me," she smiled sheepishly. "I own the production company, the communications network and the studios."

Grand-père placed his steak knife and fork on his plate and beamed. "I'm glad to know you, Ma'am."

"Don't Ma'am me, or I'll Sir you," she said and laughed.

It was a good supper and a great evening.

CHAPTER 9

Suddenly

The next evening, the Los Angeles Memorial Coliseum sparkled like a precious jewel in the night. It was full to capacity. Increased two decades back, the seating capacity now held over one-hundred thousand spectators. The Central Zone had no such arena, so I was taken aback by the shining bowl that glowed with multi-colored flood lights.

Capitol City would not have drawn one-hundred people, let alone thousands. With the chemically treated water, citizens simply wouldn't have had the energy to go out again after work. Since emotion-numbing chemicals no longer cloud the old water supply, I'd seen a few people out walking in the evening and tossing a ball with their children.

Ivy and I stood at a distance to the center of the arena and watched. "This is astounding," Ivy gasped in awe.

"As compared to the Central Zone, where it is illegal for more than two or three to gather in one spot, it is indeed astounding. I agree."

"I am amazed," a voice whispered in my ear.

"Jason!" I yelled as I turned and threw my arms around him. "I thought you couldn't get away," I gasped.

He kissed my forehead and held me close as Ivy smiled and stepped a few paces behind us.

"I couldn't stand not seeing you." The fire in his soft eyes said it all. "Besides, it's Friday evening and the weekend is ahead. I would have had an intern on-call for me anyway."

I took his hand and didn't let go. My heart felt full to overflowing. "Rachel asked about you. She'll be happy to see you when we go back to her place later."

"Ladies and gentlemen," an announcer interrupted as he bellowed across the booming speaker system. "Please greet our moderator, Rachel Claudette."

The crowd jumped to their feet and cheered as Rachel came into center field. She turned to face the four corners of the massive arena and eagerly waved to everyone. Her smile lit up the Jumbotron.

"Now, please welcome President Nathan Alexander, who is with us on the screen," the voice announced and waved in the direction of the Tron. There was relative silence from thousands of spectators. Alexander cast his eyes down in embarrassment and then shot them back to the camera in a defiant smirk. A few called out questions I imagined he would rather have not heard.

"Why aren't you here?" a man yelled on the clear evening air.

"Are you afraid to show up in person?" another shouted. Loud, inaudible mumbles followed, along with the sound of those who shifted in their seats and shuffled their feet in discomfort.

"And now," the voice drew out slowly, like a pitchman for a new kind of communications device that customers had to rush to purchase immediately, "please show your appreciation to Sir Oliver Richly, who traveled all the way from the Central Zone to our sunny coast."

The stands went wild, cheering and clapping and throwing their hats in the air. "Richly—Richly—Richly!" they chanted feverishly.

Grand-père walked briskly and confidently out to the middle of the arena, where all attention focused on him. Turning, he waved to all those present. The cheering didn't stop for eleven minutes. On the Jumbotron, the producer had split the screen, with Grand-père's smiling, strong, humble image on the left, and Alexander's scowling, bitter face glaring down on everyone below on the right. The cheering turned to laughter when the crowd watched and then pointed at the vast difference between the two expressions.

The contrast between the image on the screen and the miniature size of the one person in the middle of the excitement was powerful. Grand-père didn't have to puff himself up. Even though he appeared small to those in the upper seats, he filled the arena with his presence.

"The order of speaking has been determined by a toss of a coin," Rachel began. "Our first question begins with you, Sir Richly." She touched the air in front of her and read from the screen that was invisible to everyone else.

She paused, "This question is about the Constitution. Sir, your campaign slogan is the *1787-Constitutional Party*. Exactly, what is the 1787 Constitution?"

"I'm glad that this is the first question because it will set the theme for everything else I say." He raised his arms to the sky and clasped his hands as a sign of triumph. "My friends—this country of ours was a miracle from its making." His voice echoed off the bleachers, high in the stands. "People had left their homeland for the promise and hope of freedom here in the new world. When the time was right, our forefathers wrote a Constitution, creating a government like none other in history, a place of equality. It took many years for all of those who lived here to secure that freedom for themselves— but it happened when we rectified those flaws.

"We as a people were the shining light in a dark world—an experiment in freedom never experienced before. When the chaos of the previous millennium created a security gap through which the revolutionaries sneaked through, like thieves in the night, they sat at the desk of our forefathers and wrote a new Constitution. In that new document, they stripped freedom from all of us. The government took over every decision in our lives.

"Your own Western Zone banished a group of people to the forests and caves of the mountainous regions. As those people languished in exile, you began to call them the hollow ones."

Murmurs of unease and discomfort rose up from the assembled body. But the crowd saw Grand-père's eyes of love and forgiveness on the huge image of the Jumbotron.

"Some of you are loving them back into the human family." Shouts of joy floated across the air like the melodic sounds of music. Grand-père started again.

Alexander's face appeared on the right side of the split screen. He looked hard and red with anger when he interrupted. "Wait a minute. How long does he get to talk?"

"There is a ten-minute limit on these introductory remarks, Mr. President," Rachel Claudette soothed. "Sir Richly, you have more time on the clock if you want it."

"Thank you," Grand-père bowed to Rachel and ignored the interruption. "In the Midwestern Zone, they confiscated all the crop-growing acreage, and made the farmers tenants on their own land. In the Central Zone, they drugged the water so the citizens didn't really care about anything nor have the energy to rebel."

He paused while the crowd jeered the audacity of those currently in power. "And, the Central Zone obeys the Length of Days Law. When people reach a prescribed age, based on a formula that is determined by their value to society, they are taken to the extermination center and placed in the never-ending-sleep, thus ending their Length of Days."

"What?" angry voices belched from the distant seats.

"It is true," Grand-père insisted with his arms lifted in power. "My granddaughter, Christiana Applewait exposed the atrocities under Howard Mountain!"

The crowd erupted in chants and cheers, "Christy—Christy—Christy!"

"Thank you—thank all of you," he shouted and waved his hands in the air.

Still he continued. "In the East, the elites told the citizens that there were roving bands of marauding plunderers who would steal everything they had and kill them and their families, just for the thrill of it. Thousands of the citizens escaped to the sewers and old subway systems under the streets, thinking that would save their lives. For generations, those fine people lived in the filth and utter darkness of the caverns beneath the feet of those who lived above. Called the underlings, just recently they have been set freed." Again, those in attendance jumped to their feet and shouted for joy.

"When I am president, the first thing I will do is overturn the New Constitution and reinstate the original one, the Constitution of 1787, which will also completely erase the Length of Days Law." Thunderous applause and cheers rose up from the stands and they pounded their feet on the floor, creating the sound of thunder.

"I'll have to admit, he does look like a powerful man," Inspector Stoner grudgingly admired from behind us.

At the sound of his voice, I jumped and grabbed Jason's arm. "Inspector, you startled me." Then the impact of his words caught up to me. "Is the head of the Blue Guard admiring my grandfather?"

Stoner didn't look in my direction but kept his eyes on center field. "I would not have believed it, but there is something there." He planted his feet squarely and firmly beneath him. "I always admire power," Stoner rumbled, his eyes narrowed.

Jason crossed behind me and stood between the Inspector and me. "What are you doing here?"

"I am tasked with protecting Sir Richly and, by association, both of you." He folded his arms across his chest like one with no intention of moving from the spot.

"How can you protect him in the middle of all these people?" I asked, genuinely worried about the number of followers and fans in the arena and the thunder of the applause. I remembered the man in the parking structure at the airport.

"There is a force field around him, Lady Applewait." Stoner looked around the mammoth structure.

Then, in a strange comparison, the gently moving air blew in a sweet autumn fragrance on the evening breeze. The aroma reminded me of the orange-red serpentine columbine that grew in Rachel's flower garden. I smiled. It was a stark contrast to my own perception of Ward Stoner—a black rose.

"He is protected," Stoner insisted.

I thought for a moment and wondered if I could trust him. Stoner was a conundrum and I didn't know what to do. "If you are truly here to protect my grandfather...."

Jason seemed to know what I was going to say. "It's all right, Christy. Tell him about the airport."

"What about the airport?" Stoner asked, his brow furrowed and his face deeply lined.

I watched as the crowd continued their loud agreement with all that Grand-père said. Finally, I explained, "After we got out of the airplane terminal and entered the parking garage, a man approached my grandfather and threatened him. He grabbed his arm and told him to drop out of the race or he would reveal certain information. Grand-père had no idea what he was talking about."

"Yesterday, right here in LA?"

"Yes, Sir," I said as I turned to hear the question posed to Alexander.

Stoner spun around and looked at me intently. "You mean a man was able to get close enough to accost the Center Chair of the Council of Elders?"

"Yes, that's exactly what happened," I agreed. I worried more for my grandfather's safety now after I saw how concerned the inspector was. "Ivy tried to stop him but got knocked down. Raymar's near rage chased the man off."

Stoner bristled. "Where are Raymar and Ivy now? I thought Ivy was assigned to protect you, Miss Applewait."

"Raymar is just out of the spotlight near Grand-père." Then, I smiled and nodded off to my left. "Ivy is right there. Near me and yet giving Jason and me some space."

Stoner sniffed and rubbed his nose, seeming indifferent to anyone's need for privacy. "Tomorrow, at first light," Stoner shouted to me over the crowd, "I want a full description of the man from the parking garage. Write down everything you can remember, his facial features, his possible age, what he was wearing—everything."

The loud speaker squawked open again as Rachel's voice filled the air. "And now, President Alexander, your first question." Again, Rachel touched the open space in front of her and read from the invisible tablet. "Please tell us your theme for this campaign and for the first months of what would be your administration. What will you hope to accomplish by this advancement from zone president to national president?"

"Theme? I need no contrived message," he spit out. "My theme is to continue to maintain this great country just the way it is." The veins in his neck began to bulge and his face reddened. "My army will not allow an insurrection." His cheeks glowed like two blotches of over-ripe purple plums. "And, I will defend the New Constitution from all those who would attack it. The New Constitution was written to provide food for the workers, love and guidance for all of our children, protection from one's emotions and sexual appetites, and to maintain a lean census by discarding those who cannot or will not work and those who have outlived their usefulness to society." He thumped his fist on the desk in front of him. "These are noble causes." He straightened the front of his suit and pulled himself up as tall as he could reach. "The next question please."

The crowd said nothing but sat in stunned silence. Stoner said little more.

"Who is protecting Alexander in Capitol City?" Jason asked as his eyes scanned the thousands of restless people in the seats.

"His bodyguards," Stoner said as he gritted his teeth. "And, the strength of his entire Zone Guard."

"Since he has nothing to offer," I breathed out slowly, "I doubt he has anything to fear."

"Oh no, Ma'am, he has everything to fear," Stoner said as his eyes scanned the angry faces of thousands of people. "With your grandfather, it is the man in a parking garage and those like him that he has to fear."

I pondered deeply the words Stoner had just used. Fear for Grand-père's safety flooded my heart. But there was something else Stoner said. He referred to Grand-père as 'your grandfather,' not just a name or title. He didn't keep him at a distance. He drew Grand-père closer, and made him real. I felt better, more hopeful. Perhaps Stoner would put more effort into his task of protecting us.

"Hey, Richly," someone yelled from the stands with the help of an old megaphone. "The Council of Elders is powerful. Why didn't you stop the Length of Days Law?"

Grand-père didn't apologize or hesitate to answer. "The Council doesn't make laws. They only interpret them."

"Isn't it true that a change in that law would mean that you and your wife will get to live longer? Weren't you and your wife scheduled to surrender your Length of Days? Why didn't you just change the law?"

"As I said, we don't create new laws nor amend the old ones. The Council only interprets the laws."

"Interpret this," the man yelled.

Suddenly **ka-pow, pow, pow, pow** echoed across the top of the arena. Stoner reached for his holstered weapon and ran in Grand-père's direction.

I grabbed Jason's arm and buried my head in his shoulder. "Is Grand-pere okay?" I gasped. My body shook in terror.

Ivy ran to my side and grabbed my arm. "Come Christy. Let's get out of the open." She tried to pull me off to the side.

"No, Ivy! I have to see how my grandfather is." My hands trembled and my throat tightened.

"I know, but we have to move—now!"

"Wait," I demanded, looking to the infield and then back at Jason. "What do you see?"

"I can't see anything," he said, his breath short and choppy. "There's like—smoke—in the infield."

"Smoke?" I asked as I flipped back and forth to see the chaos in front of us.

The people in the stands didn't stampede as I feared would happen but sat stunned where they were. A few screamed, but for the most part, the thousands of Richly followers and fans only seemed to hold their collective breath while experts assessed Grand-père's safety.

Blue Guardsmen streamed out of the side entrances and flooded the grass with weapons drawn. From our distance, they looked small but mighty, ready to devour everything in their path. Some of their number came out of the box-seating area and ran in the direction from which the gunfire came.

"Let's go!" I yelled and grabbed Jason's hand.

"No, Christy!" Ivy ordered and took my arm again. I wiggled free and stared back at her in disbelief.

"Wait!" Jason protested and tried to rein me in.

"Why?" I turned to him and stammered. "Grand-père may need me."

"You cannot put yourself in harm's way. That won't help Oliver." He stopped and look toward the field. "Look, Christy," he said as he pointed to the middle of the arena.

The smoke was clearing enough to see a transparent dome over Grand-père. The pungent odor of Nitroglycerine hung in the air. Dust particles that landed on it defined the dome.

"There is a force field around him." I said as I stood and gazed on the scene in amazement.

"Christy," Jason grabbed me and pulled me to him. "Honey, if you go down there, you could be in the sharpshooter's crosshairs too—and without a bubble to protect you."

The Jumbotron revealed an encapsulated Oliver Richly on the left side of the screen and a smirking Nathan Alexander on the right. Finally, the president asked weakly, "Is Sir Richly all right?"

At first there was silence. Then, the announcer assured everyone. "Ladies and gentlemen, Oliver Richly is safe. Blue Guardsmen pursued, found, and eliminated the gunman. Everyone is safe. We will continue."

I looked down at my grandfather. His huge image on the screen told me a lot. His face was neither drawn nor strained. Then I noticed something. He winked, as he often did at me, and mouth, *I'm hiding in plain sight.*

I laughed and wiped tears from my eyes. "'I'm hiding in plain sight,' he just said, and winked at me." Turning, I grabbed Jason's jacket lapels. "It was a code, a secret message."

"Code?" Jason questioned.

"When he gave me the—" I looked around to see if anyone was near enough to hear me and lowered my voice to a whisper. "When he gave me the Bible, he told me to hide it on a shelf, *in plain sight.*" I turned back to see Grand-père smiling and waving at the crowd. "He means he is fine and can continue. He told me—he is trusting in God."

CHAPTER 10
January 2114

The campaign continued through the Christmas season, or Gift Giving season as we were required to call it in the Central Zone. No one mentioned the name of Jesus Christ, Christmas, or God the Father.

Gifting Day Eve of 2112, a little over one year ago, was the day we challenged President Alexander with a march to his home. We delivered thousands of petitions, signed by most of the citizens in the Central Zone. When all zones had the required number of names, they would place a citizens' referendum on the next election ballot to overturn the Length of Days Law. Thousands sang the Christmas carol *Silent Night* though they had never heard it before. The longing of their souls knew the words.

I couldn't believe it. With all of our travel and speaking engagements, I wasn't totally exhausted. The harder we worked, the more energy I had. I felt the Lord with me at every turn.

Now, Jason and I were in New York City again. Ivy had accompanied us as my bodyguard. We had all been staying with Richard and Barbara Cornwall at the Cornwall Citadel; it felt comfortable and homey. Richard's broken hip had mended and the limp would eventually work itself out. The truth is Richard's injuries occurred when he helped a woman crawl up out of the sewer through a manhole. The heavy cover had fallen on him. He considered it worth the price for the underling to see the light of day, even for a short time.

"Richard, no wheelchair?" I marveled the next morning at breakfast.

"I am free at last," he said as he laughed. "Now, come. Let's eat."

The table was set with steaming mugs of coffee and the most delicious looking coffee cake imaginable. Cinnamon and butter oozed from the pastry and puddled on Barbara's yellow-handled California Art Pottery serving platter.

"Barbara, this serving plate is amazing," I admired. "In the Central Zone, no one cares about fine dining or how food looks."

"The platter is very old, but I love using it. Mother had it before me," she said.

"Does she still live up stair?" I asked.

"Yes, but she is visiting family in California right now. She will be so sad she missed you."

"Hence the California connection?" I asked and nodded at the serving platter.

"Exactly," Barbara agreed with a big smile. "I'll cut the pastry while it's hot but save room for scrambled eggs and sausages."

At that moment, Maisie, the surface mole we had met when we were guests of the Cornwalls months before, brought in a large bowl of fluffy eggs, moist and scrambled to perfection. "It's so good to see you two," she squealed. "I'll be back with the sausages." Then she added, "We'll catch up."

She whisked back in with mounds of deeply browned sausage patties, sat the platter on the table and then whirled around to collect a hug from me. "Christy, you look wonderful!" she said as she stood back and studied Jason and I. "Dr. Jason, you always look good." She laughed out loud.

"Maisie, I'd like you to meet my friend, Ivy Trudeau. She's traveling with us."

Maisie put a generous spoonful of eggs on Ivy's plate. "I'm happy to meet you."

"Thank you, Maisie," Ivy beamed as she looked at her plate.

"Speaking of doctors," Jason teased, "how are your medical studies going?"

Maisie talked with her hands and drew out an emphatic, "I am loving it."

Barbara patted Maisie on the arm as the young woman served her and then she waited while Maisie sat down opposite me. "She is working hard and doing great," Barbara said as she beamed.

I could barely believe all I had seen as we drove in from the airport yesterday. "I noticed lights were on in the apartments above the street-level businesses. I hope that means the moles, the underlings, have reclaimed their vacant family homes and apartments."

Richard started to reach for his fork and then stopped. "I am so excited about what has happened. The underlings not only relocated from the sewers and old subway system when you were still here in New York, the elites accepted them aboveground. Even Alister Bedlam put up the money to make it possible for those who wanted to reopen family businesses to do so."

I stuck my fork effortlessly into the lightest eggs ever placed on my plate. As I took a bite, they melted in my mouth, if eggs can melt. Turning to Barbara, I began hesitantly, "Your fa—"

"Yes, my father, although I'll have to admit the title 'father' still doesn't really apply to him. But—we have found a measure of peace." She cut her sausage patty with the side of her fork, closed her eyes and seemed to savor the richly browned flavor.

Richard smiled and reached for his wife's hand. "I am so proud of you, Sweetheart," he said. Then he turned back to Jason and me. "Her father has even been coming to the church services Barbara and I started over on Fifth Avenue, where the old Cathedral had been."

I thought of Barbara's mother, hiding in safety in her upper floor apartment. "What about your mother? It sounds like she is coming out of her apartment to be part of the world again."

Barbara's eyes welled up with tears as she put her fork on her plate. "Yes and no. No, Mama won't come out of the tower, under most circumstances. But—her sister Rebecca is dying—so—we arranged for a private flash-flight to California." She sipped at her coffee and then added, "I hope her stay in the attic apartment isn't permanent. She has been traumatized by my father's previous activities and doesn't trust that he has changed." Replacing her cup on its saucer, she added, "She may never return to any normal life. Perhaps, as the wife of the richest man in the world, she never had a normal life."

Richard blinked and swallowed, obviously concerned for his wife's pain. "Christy, tell us a little about what you plan to tell Oliver's supporters and fans tonight."

I wiped my hands on the linen napkin and paused for a moment. "Since the borders to our zones have been closes for decades, no one in the other areas of the country has heard of Oliver Richly."

Jason smiled and added, "The most time-consuming part of Oliver's campaign is introducing himself to the people as one of the candidates." He reached over and massaged my shoulder. "That has been Christy's job—since she knows him the best."

"Part of what I'll be doing tonight is taking the starch out of Grand-père's title. Because he sits on the Council of Twelve, he is Sir Oliver Richly. It is the 'Sir' that might frighten people. They may think his elite status sets him apart from the average citizen. That's not true. Grand-père isn't rich, and he doesn't live in a mansion. His elite status just affords him protection by the Blue Guard and keeps him safe from harm."

Jason shook his head in a gesture of disbelief. "In California, a gunman fired at him from the stands at the Los Angeles Memorial Coliseum. Oliver was in the center of the field—surrounded by an electronic-vapor force field, so he wasn't struck."

"The gunman got away, but—so did Grand-père."

"I thought they said he was 'eliminated.' Is that not correct?" Richard asked.

"He got away," Jason repeated. "They were careful with their words. Because they eliminated the danger when the gunman got away, they borrowed the term and stretched it to include the physical presence of the shooter."

Richard thumped his index finger on the table. "Certainly, the people must know that all candidates will receive ramped up security after that attempt."

"They know," I sighed. "But knowing and being inside of the knowledge are two different things."

"I understand," Barbara admitted. "People see all that my father is doing for the previously oppressed people in New York, but they don't seem to own that knowing."

I smiled at her and tried to place myself in her shoes. Her father had been so evil it was hard for me to believe he had changed, just like the others who hear the story. "When someone has broken a trust, it takes years of exemplary behavior to rebuild that trust." I broke off a corner of the coffee cake and pierced it with my fork. How could I not think about the grotesque private museum Bedlam hid under Howard Mountain—taxidermized bodies of the deceased leaders and elite of the Central Zone—when I had already seen them? Those images seared a brand in my mind. "It will take time, but if your father is truly sincere, he will take joy in doing what is right, even without the recognition and approval of others."

Barbara placed her hands in her lap and looked deeply at me. "I hadn't thought of it that way. You know, he does seem happier now." She picked up her cup and added. "Time will tell. Is he truly a changed man or is he duping the people—and his family again?"

• • • • •

Jason, Ivy, and I joined Barbara and Richard in the library after our brunch where we relaxed and listened to music. Since the government banned all music in the Central Zone years ago, I closed my eyes and soaked up the beauty of the melodic themes that had the power to lift me out of myself. I thought about how our government believed that

657

people would not be able to keep their emotions in check when under the influence of music. They thought, since music had the power to stir one's soul, the government would control the people's emotions by silencing the music. How silly, how very sad and silly.

Finally, Jason woke up from a brief nap, rubbed his eyes and said, "Christy, how about a walk? Maybe some shopping?"

I couldn't belief the suggestion. I rarely went shopping in Capitol City. Now, he was offering a chance to shop in New York City.

Barbara sat straight up in her chair; her eyes wide. "Do you think it would be safe to go out on the streets after your grandfather was fired on a few months back?"

"But, I'm not a candidate," I said as I brushed off Barbara's concern.

She nodded in agreement. "I know, but you're the granddaughter of a candidate. Someone could try to get to him through you."

"I hadn't thought about that," I denied.

Jason looked at me in disbelief. "Christy, you were shot at in Campaign Headquarters last June." He shook his head. "I should have thought before I spoke."

"Not exactly," I corrected him. "The office was shot at, not me personally. It just happened to go past everyone else and get embedded in the wall beside me."

"But—"

"Jason," I stood my ground. "I wasn't targeted. I know I wasn't." I had to believe that. If I didn't, no place was safe.

"Okay," he agreed. "Technically you're right. But, a few more inches and you would have been hit, target or not."

"Factually I'm right," I insisted and stood up. "The bullet was embedded in the wall."

Ivy rolled her eyes. "I was there. Everyone in the office was targeted, Christy. You are a member of Oliver's campaign team.

You're the warm-up act to his major attraction. Maybe going out isn't the best thing to do."

"Well, come with us if you want to, Ivy. But I refused to be a prisoner, regardless of how beautiful the prison." I turned to Jason. "Let's go." As I grabbed Jason's hand I said, "Barbara, would you and Richard like to join us?"

"I don't think so," she answered slowly, indicating she may still have concerns about our leaving the Citadel.

"How about you, Maisie?" I asked. "Would you like to go shopping?"

"Maisie," Barbara chimed in enthusiastically, "that might be nice for you. You have had your head in your books for months." She turned to Ivy. "If you think it will be safe for them to go out, Maisie would benefit from the walk if not the shopping."

"Thanks, Christy," Maisie said. "If you don't think I'll interrupt your time with Dr. O'Reilly, I would love to go."

"Ivy is going too, aren't you, Ivy?" I teased. I knew she would have to. A bodyguard would have to be with the body they were guarding. The plan was set. The whole city waited just beyond the front courtyard.

• • • • •

We put on heavy coats, hats and gloves and went out the front door. The previously manicured front courtyard now boasted a light dusting of snow. I had brought the same winter cape I wore last year and pulled it around me as the winter chill whistled up under the folds of the unique fabric.

Ivy went out to the gate first and checked the street for anything or anyone that looked suspicious. With a wave of her arm she motioned an all-clear signal and gestured for us to move forward. I felt free as we walked through the Citadel gate, left the grounds, and walked along Fifty-Seventh Street over to Fifth Avenue where we stopped for coffee at Trump Tower, a mid-century old building from a hundred years past. Jason stood back and let us enter first. It seemed hard for Ivy to not pull up the rear, but she acquiesced.

As we went in, Jason started laughing. "Honey, this is not our quaint coffee shop at home."

I took his arm and snuggled close as I remembered happier, simpler times from a year past. "The Demitasse Coffee Shop," I said as I smiled to myself.

Inside the Trump Tower, we sat at a small table. "Maisie," I included our young friend, "the little shopping area where our Demitasse Coffee Shop is located looks like something out of a Dickens novel. Ivy, you know the Demitasse, don't you?"

"I love the place," she answered.

Then I paused, "Maisie, do you know the writings of Charles Dickens?"

"Yes, of course," she said. "I've read many of his books."

"Somehow, I knew you had," I said as I ordered a chocolate flavored mocha. We looked around the room. "I wonder if this place looks the same as it did when Trump built it."

"Builders don't put this kind of marble and brass in today's buildings," Jason observed as his eyes caught the details of the place. "The floors are foot-worn, like all elegant antique buildings, but buffed to a high sheen. My guess is the finishes are original to the building."

"They are beautiful," I admired. "Everything gleams and shines. We have nothing back home like this."

"O'Reilly," the lady behind the counter signaled that our order was ready. Jason went over and brought back the tray with four cups.

I took mine off and placed it in front of me on the table. First, I inhaled the perfume of the chocolate in the coffee. "I think God created chocolate just for me." I blew across the steamy surface and then took a tiny sip, waiting for it to cool. "Now, tell me about the shops we'll find along Fifth Avenue."

Maisie tipped up her mug to savor the cup. "Jewelry stores, high-end fashion clothing, so much to see, and so much to buy."

Ivy's expression was serious. I smiled and wondered if she was a no-nonsense shopper. "What is security like in the city?"

Maisie started to speak and then seemed to gather her thoughts. "While only the elites lived above ground, physical safety was not an issue. But their haughtiness caused financial corruption and defamation of the character of others."

What I heard, saddened me. "It sounds like the underlings have created a problem now that they are above ground."

Ivy listened intently and asked, "Have they become dangerous?"

Maisie sat back in disbelief. "Oh no, I'm sorry. I didn't mean that. Actually, the elite only thought the moles would be dangerous when released from their purgatory so they hired more guards and police. The underlings are very honest. They had to be above reproach. Living on top of one another underground, they would have killed each other if they weren't trustworthy."

Ivy smiled and concluded, "So you're saying, it is even safer than before."

"Yes," Maisie laughed, "stated succinctly, the city is safer."

"Of course," Ivy added, "bad things can happen. Christy, you have inherited the target that is now on your grandfather's back."

"I understand," I agreed, although deep down, I'd have to admit, I didn't want anyone telling me what to do. I tipped my cup and watched the last drop flow to the rim.

Jason also polished off the rest of his coffee and stood up. "Lead on, Miss Maisie," he directed.

We were having fun for the first time in so long, I smiled and my face muscles hurt from lack of use. I walked out onto the sidewalk backwards, laughing and talking to Jason and Maisie behind me. The sky was a winter blue, so bright I wished I had worn dark glasses. My joy was so great I wanted to dance in circles. "Oops," I said as I nearly fell over backwards when I felt someone grab my shoulder. It could have been a masculine hand or a very strong woman, I couldn't tell. They spun me around fast, and I saw a man in a knit face mask for just a second. He gathered me completely off my feet and headed to a waiting large vehicle at the curb, with me forcefully thrown over his shoulder like a bag of trash.

"Hey!" Jason shouted. He slid low in the abductor's direction and swept the man's lower legs with his feet, knocking us both to the concrete. Ivy and Maisie piled on top of the man and started pounding him with their fists. Suddenly, I heard the sound of a strata car's siren. Even though I needed help, I hated that sound. I felt my eyes grow large as Inspector Stoner pulled in front of the large van, blocking the driver into the curb. Stoner jumped out like a blue beret trooper on an assault mission.

My abductor tried to get to his feet as I lay in the scrambled mess. The concrete of the city sidewalk was hard and rough. I felt the crunch of every bone in my body.

I lifted myself up on my elbow there on the sidewalk and reached out my hand in a blessing. "May the Lord forgive you," I called after the assailant. Surprised by the weakened sound of my own voice, I sank back down again.

The man turned back and looked at me with an expression of disbelief and pain on his face. He held up his hand like he was trying to block any good will I might send his way. Lunging into the van through the open sliding door, the assailant desperately tried to crawl in as the driver backed up and maneuvered around Stoner's strata car. Left to flounder on the sidewalk, I was bruised and aching.

Jason helped me to my feet just as I saw Stoner hurrying to my aid. "Inspector? Where did you come from?"

"Are you alright?" Jason asked as he looked me over. "Your leg is scraped. We'd better go to the hospital so you can get a tetanus shot. We haven't needed those precautions for years, but since the underlings came up out of the sewers, there may be greater danger of infection."

"I had a tetanus shot when we were in New York months ago," I said as I remembered the barbaric needle. "I don't need another one of those do I?"

"No, it would still be effective," Jason said as he gathered me in his arms. "I'll just clean and dress the wound for you."

"You'll do that back at the Citadel," Stoner demanded. "Get her back to the Cornwall mansion. What were you four thinking?" His face was rock hard. Then he looked at Ivy. "I thought you were supposed to protect her."

"I thought you were," Ivy snapped back.

"Touché," he bowed. "Now—get off the streets. It's too dangerous." Then he shook his head in anger. "Last year, I knew you were here in the city when everyone said you weren't." Then he just waved us off. "Get going. Get out of here."

I steadied my feet and turned to leave. Jason put his arm around my waist and brushed some snow from the folds of my cape.

"Are you people on foot?" Stoner shouted and opened the back door of the strata car. "I cannot believe this," he belched. "Get in the car!" Ivy got in the front; Maisie, Jason and I sat in the back.

I didn't care who saw us as I leaned into Jason's shoulder and he wrapped his arms around me. I felt safe there as a new reality sunk in. "The fun is over, isn't it?"

CHAPTER 11
Evening Meal

Barbara had arranged a marvelous dinner. The first course was Manhattan clam chowder, followed by London broil with fried onion rings, broccoli, and mushrooms. A basket of assorted breads graced the table, with pure creamery butter and a ceramic jam pot of orange marmalade and another of honey.

I used the little ladle inside the marmalade pot to slather a generous amount on a yeasty fragrant thick slice of Italian bread. "I cannot believe the flavors and textures of all this wonderful food." I took a bite and inhaled the aroma. "You would be heavily fined or detained for re-education by the nutrition police in the Central Zone, Barbara." I closed my eyes and savored the taste and texture of it all.

Richard passed the colorful pot of honey, with a tiny spoon that stuck out of the sculpted opening. "Be sure to add a dollop of honey on a corner of your bread," he turned to Ivy who sat beside him. "If you eat a little honey from hives in your own county, you won't have allergies to the things that grow in the area."

"That sounds almost decadent." Ivy chuckled as she took the honey and put a little on her bread.

Dessert was an extraordinary espresso crème brûlée. I swooned as I scooped out a spoonful and licked the spoon. "Barbara, this dessert is amazing, but then, anything with coffee in it would be awesome."

Jason laughed, "You may tan even more easily next summer, Christy. The coffee beans may darken your skin from the inside out."

I held my hands out in front of me and checked them carefully. "Do you think so? I've been so pale a little more color would be wonderful."

Maisie was more serious than Jason and I. "It will be time to leave for the rally soon. Will Inspector Stoner pick you up?"

Barbara stopped abruptly. "Inspector Stoner? What does he have to do with your speech tonight?"

"We didn't want you to worry," I explained apologetically.

"Not worry?" she blinked rapidly. Her eyes darted from me to Jason.

Jason chose a calm and quiet tone. "We had a problem when we were out today."

Barbara blotted her mouth on the linen napkin. "I wondered why you came back so soon, Christy," she said slowly as she turned to me. "You said you had fallen and needed Jason to treat the scrape." Her tone sounded hurt. Maybe she thought I had lied to her.

"I did fall," I admitted openly. "I'm sorry I didn't tell the whole story."

Barbara turned to Maisie for answers. "What happened?"

Maisie looked a little restless, like she didn't want to be the one to tell Barbara all of what had happened. "A man tried to abduct Christy as we came out of Trump Tower."

"What?" Barbara and Richard's jaws dropped at the same time.

Jason seemed embarrassed. "I'm afraid the lack of information was my fault. We didn't want to worry either of you." He reached over and took my hand where I had placed it on the table. "It happened, and we all took care of it. I tackled the assailant, knocking him down and accidently taking Christy out along with him. Both Maisie and Ivy pummeled the would-be abductor. When Christy fell, she scraped her leg. Inspector Stoner pulled up to the curb before she was even off the sidewalk. The attacker wore a mask so we couldn't identify him. Stoner brought us back. That's the whole story."

Barbara gasped as she threw her hand to her mouth. "Oh Christy—maybe I'm glad I didn't know. But—you are all home safe." She smiled warmly at Maisie. "Maisie, you're like a daughter to me. If you hadn't come to us from the world of the underlings," she paused as her eyes welled up with tears, "we would still be two middle-aged souls rattling around in this big house."

Maisie blushed. "Barbara, they weren't after me."

"Exactly," Richard added. "They didn't need you at all. They could have just erased you as unnecessary without a second thought." He clasped his strong hands together and lifted them above his head. "I thank God for your safe keeping—all of you."

Ivy cast her eyes down. "I am so sorry. I'm supposed to protect her."

Barbara tapped her finger tips on the table. "There will be no blame, Ivy. But perhaps we can find a way to keep this from happening again."

"With everyone's cooperation," Ivy began diplomatically, "I do have some suggestions." She cleared her throat. "When we left the Citadel, I walked out to the sidewalk first and looked for anything out of the ordinary."

"Everything in New York is out of the ordinary," Maisie stated.

Ivy smiled but remained professional. "I did check, but you all followed me and entered the sidewalk area beyond the courtyard before I gave an all-clear signal," she said. "In every future instance, I'll need to check each area before any of you enter." To me she added, "Especially you Christy."

I nodded in agreement, embarrassed that I had ignored an obvious safety protocol.

Ivy sipped from her cup and added, "Once the area has been cleared, and only then, do you proceed."

"Agreed," Jason and I said in unison.

"We're lucky," Ivy said with one corner of her mouth turned up, "whether we like him or not, Stoner is good at what he does. He is also here to protect you Christy. But—"

"I know," I admitted as I traced the rim of my water glass with my finger. "I have to take my safety, our safety, more seriously."

"You will," Jason assured me, his voice soft and certain.

I smiled in wonder as I looked around the table. "Until a year ago, people weren't even allowed to talk to a Legacy Citizen on the street. They couldn't so much as touch me. Now, with my grandfather's presidential campaign, there is so much activity around me, it's hard for me to sort out anyone who might want to do me harm. I'm right down there on the ground level." I shook my head and smiled at Jason. "But, you know, the excitement is intoxicating."

Barbara threw her head back and laughed in resignation. "Okay, we get it," she said. "But for tonight's rally, will Ward Stoner pick you two up tonight and drive you there?"

"He will be there to head up security," I said.

"Richard, Maisie, and I are going. We'll take the long-car. It's bullet proof and our driver is a very good bodyguard. You can ride with us." She stopped and added, "I have had to have security for many years—considering who my father is."

I scrapped the last bit of crème brûlée from the dessert bowl and put down the spoon. "Then, it's settled. We'll all go together and together we'll all be safe."

CHAPTER 12

Attacked

Though I'm a Legacy Citizen, I have just as much stage fright as the next person. I know I appear relaxed. That's because I know who stands beside me. The Lord calms me and makes it possible for me to talk.

If you remember, before all of this happened, I spent my days in the back stacks of the library reading everything I could find. Some would call me an introvert but that doesn't mean I'm shy. I just get my energy from the thoughts inside myself and drained of energy by interactions with others. Stage fright is another thing. My fear of speaking in front of others is probably due to a half-belief that my opinions are not worthy of all the fuss. I was never the center of attention, except in my own family. Never criticized as a Legacy Citizen, now I wouldn't know how to handle it. If I had received a little criticism when I was young, it would have sharpened my ability to speak in front of others and honed my ability to defend my own positions. It was family love that has made it possible for me to get up in front of others.

Now, I stood in theater wings, hidden by the leg drapes behind the grand stage curtain of New York's old opera house. There hadn't been a performance in so many years those in attendance had never been inside the ornate walls with its colorful trappings. Only the campaign message of Sir Oliver Richly could bring out a crowd large enough to require this kind of space to house his political supporters. While Grand-père wouldn't be there until the next night's rally, I was to give the audience his background and outline the points on which he was running. This was a night of political conversation and enlightenment.

The crowd hummed and buzzed with excitement. When I walked to center-stage the rise in clamor from the assembled-throng startled me and the glare from the spotlight flashed in my eyes. I could see figures surrounding the stage in what would have been the orchestra pit but I couldn't make out who they were. All I saw were dots from the lights. I looked back to the wings for Jason's smile. He nodded and gave me a victory pump of his arm.

"Christy—Christy—Christy—" the crowd chanted in a loud cacophonous rhythm.

Holding up my hand in both greeting and a plea for order, I felt helpless to calm the people. On and on they cheered until my eyes cleared a little and I could see who stood below the foot of the stage. Blue Guardsmen were shoulder to shoulder, alternatingly facing the crowd and the next one facing the stage. *Who and what are they guarding—the speaker—or searching for a possible assassin in the audience?* I shuddered as chills crept down my arms. What could I do?

Closing my eyes, I lifted my arms in prayer and praise. The Lord had blessed me beyond any words of my own to express. How many times had I dodged danger in the last months? With my eyes closed in reverence and my head turned to Heaven, I waited for the words of God to lead me.

Suddenly, a hush fell over the auditorium as one by one some in the room also lifted their arms heavenward. In the standing-room-only area in the back, a wave started as a hum. *Silent Night, Holy Night* they sang, not because it was still the Christmas season, but because it was the only song the people of Capitol City knew and these New Yorkers knew the amazing story of our Gifting Day Eve event of 2112. It calmed the soul.

Ward Stoner, near my feet to my left, put his hand on his weapon and didn't remove it as I stood there. I guessed that he had been convinced of my danger after the abduction attempt that afternoon. I also saw Lieutenant Boone at the base of the stage. She faced the footlights and could see Stoner move for his weapon.

Although she caught my eye and acknowledged me with a small smile, rather than continue watching me, she kept her eye on her boss. Then, I remembered what she had secretly told me on our previous trip to New York when Stoner was out of earshot. "Ward Stoner is not the man you have been seeing. Before his wife died, he was kind and even funny at times. But now, you have become the focus of his anger and resentment. I have seen nothing but good in you and what you are doing." Somehow, I trusted her to keep him at bay, although I could see he had changed. Even though I knew he was there to protect and serve, it was evident he was supportive of Grand-père and the campaign.

"Oh Lord, God," I implored. "Please, come and fill this place with your peace and love."

Crack, crack, crack, Pop! Odd, I not only heard the sound, I felt the pressure of it. In an instant, Jason leaped into action; Ivy jumped out of the wings; Boone charged up onto the stage, followed immediately by the Inspector.

What are they doing? What's going on? They're going to interrupt my speech?

I felt so strange. *Where had my energy gone? Why did I feel so weak? What's wrong with me?* My shoulder felt tender so I automatically reached up to massage the upper right portion of my shoulder and chest.

"What is this?" I whispered breathlessly as my knees buckled under me and blood dripped from my hand. I slipped to the floor as Stoner scooped his arms under me and lowered me to the hardwoods of the stage.

"Off to the right!" I heard Boone yell as feet scrambled and leather pounded.

"Boone, over there!" Stoner ordered as I felt him lift my head and stuff something under my neck.

Jason immediately became both physician and my love. "Grab that cloth from the dais," he ordered a Blue Guardsman. "Put it over her before she goes into shock." More feet shuffling, and I felt the air stir as a man ran past me and into the wings. There was a scream and more frightened voices joined the rumble around me as the sounds began to fade. Through blurred eyes, I saw that Ivy had fallen where she stood in the wings. *Why is she on the stage floor? Why isn't she moving?*

Jason pulled my lower lids from my eyes and looked intently. His eyes showed concern but his hands were steady. "Christy, can you hear me?"

I nodded slowly and touched his hand.

"I'll be right back. I'm not leaving you, Honey. I'll be right over there, checking Ivy." He pointed to Chalky and said, "Quickly, cover her up."

I nodded again and tried to see where he was going. What had happened to Ivy?

As Boone covered me with the cloth, she leaned close. "Laying his hands on each one, he healed them."

"What?" I questioned. I knew I heard her, and I knew the words she said, but—how did Chalky know what Jesus of the Bible had said and done?

"What did you say?" Stoner growled. It didn't sound like anger as usual. It sounded like astonishment.

Boone said no more but reached out and took my hand. *What is she doing?* Rather than holding my hand, I could feel her pry it open. Then, she gently moved the trembling fingers of my right hand and placed them into the sticky blood. I could feel her touch my hand to what felt like a gaping hole in my shoulder. The pain I experienced was nearly unbearable.

"What are you doing?" Stoner shouted.

"I'm not hurting her," I heard Boone's voice off in some distant place.

I heard very little more—no buzzing crowd, no words from those around me—but it wasn't silent. There was the deep sound of a man's voice saying, "Stay with me, Christy. Stay with me." I drifted off again, in and out of a white mist.

Then, there was a sound of—something, like the rush of a mighty wind. My face felt warm, like a window had opened and the sun had streamed in. I heard them—the crowd was singing again, "… holy night, all is calm …." Energy seemed to flow through my arms and I knew—I had been healed.

CHAPTER 13

Another Kind of Healing

Stoner was the one whose wound still festered—in spirit at least. He could feel anger rise within him. Or, was it something else he couldn't identify? He was conflicted by emotions which he didn't understand or even know the feeling-names. One was the familiar anger he always felt, and some other emotion he thought he had not experienced before.

"What happened?" he questioned. Although just shot, Christy's strength was increasing. He looked from Boone to Christy in full detective mode.

"You saw it, Ward," Boone answered in awe as she brushed Christy's hair from her forehead. "I know I saw it," she said. Then as Christy began to stir, she added, "Lay still for a few more minutes. Dr. O'Reilly is over there checking on Ivy. You'll soon be in good hands."

Ward stared in disbelief. "I saw what happened, but still find it hard to believe. What did you just do?"

"I didn't do anything, Ward. I merely guided Christy's hand to the gunshot wound," she explained.

His eyes darted over to his Blue Guardsmen and then back at Boone. She looked up at him with more warmth in her eyes than he had experienced since his wife died. He felt uncomfortable, embarrassed, and wanted to look away. But the responsive feelings it gave him were intoxicating. "Then, how did she improve so fast?"

"It was the Lord who healed her, Ward, not I, and not Christy by herself," Chalky said gently and then stroked Christy's forehead again, brushing back her hair.

Stoner touched Boone's hand as she continued to sooth the wounded brow. Suddenly, Christy stirred a little and turned her head toward Jason as he attended to Ivy.

"Don't worry—rest for now," Boone assured her. "It looks like Ivy is moving. She's sitting up. Your friend Maisie is taking care of her now."

Stoner felt like a distant spectator as he watched Jason hurry over to where Christy lay. The doctor kissed his Lady gently and began to examine her wound. Ward watched as Chalky finally let go of Christy's hand. His lieutenant was so comforting, so loving.

Then, the eyes of Ward's heart opened. "Boone, look at the blood stains on your clothes. It's oozing from your fingers." And then he looked again, "Your hands are trembling."

"Ward, I ...." He saw both fear and wonderment on Chalky's face. Her eyes welled up in tears and spilled over the rims. She began to tremble violently.

Stoner stared at Chalky for a second and then quickly grabbed her to him with strong and massive hands. Wrapping his arms around her, he rocked her back and forth intent on soothing her, warming her—but maybe something else he couldn't admit even to himself. Suddenly, he realized he was looking at her, not with the eyes of her superior, despite his need to hide his own emotions.

Ward Stoner was truly overwhelmed with it all. How could one brief span of time see so many life-changing events?

Someone shot Christy Applewait in front of thousands of spectators and yet healing came through the touch of her own hand. God sealed her wound and the bleeding stopped. The gunman who shot Christy got away by jumping from the nearest theater box and onto the stage, just like John Wilkes Booth after he shot President Lincoln. All Blue Guard cadets studied that investigation. In the escape of Christy's gunman, he knocked Ivy down. She bumped her head resulting in unconsciousness. But Stoner had to admit to himself, something that also pleased Christy's Lord, was that on that miraculous night of healing, the searing fire of love had cauterized the hole in his own heart.

CHAPTER 14
2 pm - May 2114

It was a new beginning for Jason and me. My body had healed from the gunshot wound and my energy returned. We had been working the small towns and big cities along the New England coast. The crowds had grown larger and more enthusiastic with each event, like the wild flowers in the meadows we passed. As the days sprouted into weeks, blossoms filled the fields and spilled over into the ravines and the banks of the fresh flowing streams. Spring had opened its ample paint buckets and splattered color everywhere.

"Grand-père is already in Caribou," I said as Jason drove along old US 1 north in Maine. "He'll speak tonight at 8 pm. We should get to the hotel in another half hour, rest and clean up, then eat a light supper before the gathering."

"Sean said they built a huge ice hockey arena at the Maine Winter Sports Center years ago," Jason said. "Oliver will speak there."

"It's May. I doubt it will be cold in there?" I thought of a floor of ice in the middle of the room and shivered. "I think I'll take a light jacket."

We drove a few more blocks. "There's the hotel," I pointed to the twenty-story building on the right.

Jason pulled into the drop-off zone and released the door on my side. I stepped out and started into the building when a man in a dark suit approached me.

"Lady Applewait?" he questioned.

I studied his face for a glimmer of familiarity. "Do I know you?"

"We haven't met—but I know your grandfather." His eyes darted back and forth and he clutched at his hands.

Jason got out of the car and came around where the stranger and I stood. "May I help you?"

The man smiled an awkward smile and held out his hand. "You must be Dr. O'Reilly."

"I am," Jason said as I watched him take in the full length of the man. "Again, how can I help you?"

"I'm sorry—is Sir Richly with you two?"

My heart leaped into my throat. "With us?" I suddenly couldn't see or think clearly. I felt rattled. "He got here yesterday."

"He was supposed to," the man said as he continued to look around the front parking lot and entry area.

"Who are you?" Jason questioned, his jaw set and his brow furrowed.

"I'm sorry," the man apologized. "My name is Malcolm Merrick. I work for your grandfather's campaign. Actually, I'm part of his Advance Team. Some of us got here two days ago and began setting up everything for Oliver—but he never showed up."

I felt ill. My mouth was so dry I could barely form words. My lips stuck to my teeth. "He never got here?" I gulped. "Well, Malcolm Merrick, I don't know you at all, and I'm part of his campaign, too."

Merrick looked at me with a worried expression but confident tone. "I know you are Ma'am. I joined the Eastern team a few weeks ago. My specialty is logistics and, I am so sorry—but Sir Richly has not gotten here even though I know he was due yesterday."

I looked up and down the street as if half expecting him to show up. "I don't understand."

"Again—I'm sorry," Merrick apologized. "I don't know what else to say. Oliver is simply not here."

Jason put his arm around me and drew me close. "Let's go inside. Maybe there's a logical answer." Jason opened the car boot, gathered up our bags and handed them to Merrick. "Here, please take these and I'll attend to Lady Applewait."

We hurried inside and looked around the lobby that sparkled with polished marble and brass. Over at the check-in desk the clerk was busy with another customer. My hands trembled. I reached out and steadied myself on the dark marble counter. As I leaned heavily on the broad desk, my knees began to buckle underneath me. Jason scooped me off my feet and carried me to a nearby silk brocade chair.

"Wait here, Honey," he said. "Merrick," he directed the campaign worker, "find Lady Applewait a cup of coffee." Jason kissed my forehead and whispered gently, "Don't leave yet, Christy. Your grandfather will show up at any minute. I'm sure."

I could not stop shaking. "Jason, I am so frightened. What if something has happened to him?" I thought of the danger he could be in. We had our share of close escapes. "I wish Ivy were here."

Jason smiled and patted my cheek. "I know. It would be wonderful if she were around to help protect you. Something could be brewing with Oliver's absence."

"I talked to Ivy before we left. She said there would be a man here to guide us. Her mother is really ill." I understood and was glad she had chosen family. "I told her I wanted her to attend to her mother. After that attack in New York, she knows the danger. Her shoulder was slashed too as the attacker ran by." I looked over at Malcolm. "Maybe she was talking about Merrick, but she didn't call him by name."

"Some of Oliver's bodyguards are here,' Merrick said.

"That's good, but I wish Grand-père was here."

"I know, Honey—I know," Jason whispered. I felt his warm breath on my face when he held me close.

Looking up, I smelled the hot coffee Merrick waived under my nose. "I guess it's as good as smelling salts," I said and smiled weakly. As I sipped the hot brew, I let the steam warm my face.

Jason looked at Malcolm Merrick up-and-down, taking in the full measure of the man. "Merrick, I'm going to step over to the check-in desk, and I want you to stay here with Lady Applewait. I'll not take my eyes off you. I'm sorry. You've not been vetted according to anything that we're aware of." He kissed my cheek again. "Drink some more of your coffee, Honey. I'll see what I can find out."

Jason stepped to the desk, not more than six feet away from where I sat. He looked near, but I needed his touch. I watched him over the top of my coffee cup and heard every word.

"Has anyone left a message for Christina Applewait, Dr. Jason O'Reilly, or any of Sir Oliver Richly's Advance Team?" he asked.

The clerk blinked his eyes and waved his hands in an empty gesture. "No sir. We are still expecting Sir Richly." He looked over at me and a wave of sympathy crossed his face. "Is something wrong? Can I be of assistance in some way?"

Jason continued to study my face and smiled faintly. To the clerk he added, "Sir Richly is never late—ever."

The man in the black pinstripe suit and white shirt could not have been more sympathetic. His expression was almost pained. "I will let you know as soon as he gets here." He looked over at me and added, "Will you be checking in? Rooms are waiting for you; everything is ready."

"Yes, of course," Jason continued. "Lady Applewait could use some rest."

A young woman in a black jumpsuit placed our bags on a four-wheel cart. I had seen pictures of hotel luggage carriers in old magazines in the library at home. I smiled at all I knew mentally and yet had never seen.

Jason helped me over to the desk so I could place my hand on the palm reader for room 721. He did the same for room 723. I walked to the lift, feeling like I was in a daze. I heard others talking and laughing around me. It was like the buzzing of bees or the clicking of locusts. We rode up to the seventh floor in silence, Jason and I, the hotel worker and Malcolm Merrick. I wondered about the confusing energy I was getting from Merrick. On the one hand I felt like I could trust him, and yet there was an unsettled feeling between us.

Merrick seemed to be aware of it. Halfway up in the lift car he said, "I will help you settle in, and then I'll go back to Campaign Headquarters here in Caribou. I don't think they know anything yet or they would have contacted me. But I'll see what I can do."

"Thank you, Malcolm," I said. I wanted—no—I needed for him to be an ally. With Grand-père missing, I had to trust those around me. I said no more.

The lift car was small enough, I began to feel claustrophobic. My heart was racing so hard I could feel it pounding in my chest.

The lift doors swished open and everyone paused for a moment. "After you," the hotel worker offered.

We all hurried from the elevator and started in the direction of the 720 room numbers. Jason started to put his hand on the doorknob and then stopped, "You'll have to open your door, Honey."

My hand was trembling as I touched the shiny chrome knob and twisted it in my hand. The hop reached around the open door and flipped on the light switch. The light from the windows on the opposite side of the room let in a deceptively friendly glow. I crossed the room and sank into one of the overstuffed chairs near the desk.

Merrick walked over to the communication device that sat on the desk. It was an old-fashioned instrument with a funny round dial on the front in keeping with the mid-twentieth century decor of the hotel. He picked up the piece that sat on the top, placed his finger in the hole on the dial marked "zero" and spun it around.

"Yes, operator, please connect me with Sir Oliver Richly's Campaign Headquarters." He paused for a moment and waited. Then he began again. "This is Merrick. Have you heard anything about Sir Richly's whereabouts?" Again, he waited for what seemed like a lifetime. Suddenly his shoulders dropped and his countenance fell. "I'm with Lady Applewait right now." He took a small pad and pencil from his jacket pocket and scribbled a few words on a piece of paper. "I'll tell her."

Jason looked at me and then back at Merrick. "Okay, man, what is going on?"

Malcolm Merrick's eyes darted from Jason to me and back again. "Christiana—I cannot spare the words or the impact the message will have." He walked over to a bar area, put ice into a small glass, poured from a water pitcher and came back to me. "Here, My Lady," he offered. "I need for you to drink some of this."

"Why?" I gasped as my stomach knotted, and my hands began to tremble again.

I took the glass and sipped on it mechanically as my eyes fixed on nothing out in front of me. Fear had frozen me rigid. Then, a new determination welled up inside me. I stiffened as a new power filled my body. I could not sit there knowing that Grand-père was missing; I couldn't and wouldn't. The glass thumped forcefully from my hand onto the table beside me as I stood up. "I am not a victim here," I demanded. "Malcolm Merrick, you tell me right now what was said."

"Christiana—a message came in to Campaign Headquarters a few minutes ago." He raked his hand through his hair and shook his head. "The message was strange. It wasn't long, but Ben Summersall said the creep who called it in still managed to say it in a mocking tone in the few words he delivered." Merrick stopped and pumped his fist up and down on the palm of his hand. "And, yes, headquarters said it was from a man."

I couldn't stand it any longer. Now I was getting angry. "And—what did he say?"

Merrick didn't even look at me. He took a deep breath and stared out the window. "The man said, 'You will be enchanted to know—I have taken Oliver Richly—'"

"Taken?" I gasped and grabbed the top of my head, for fear I would explode. "You mean Grand-père has been kidnapped?" How could I believe what he was saying? Helplessness caused my strength to vanish in an instant. With my head buried in my hands, I collapsed into Jason's arms. He helped me to the edge of the bed where I went limp and crumpled onto the bedspread.

"Yes, Ma'am," Merrick said softly, his voice shaking and course. "Oliver Richly has been kidnapped."

"How? Where? He is surrounded by bodyguards." Disbelief flooded my thoughts. It couldn't be possible.

Merrick turned in my direction without meeting my gaze. "I am so sorry, Christiana," he apologized. "I don't have that information." He looked at the floor and then out the window. "The man also said, something like, 'If not you, then the big man. You would have stopped his campaign and now he's just gone.'"

Jason grabbed me and put his arms around me with the force of a warrior-protector. "So, the failed kidnapping attempt on you in New York was his first effort in trying to get Oliver out of the race."

"They tried to get you?" It was easy to see the shock on Merrick's face and beaten body posture.

"I didn't want to upset anyone so I had said nothing. Ivy, my bodyguard, was there—she knew. Jason was with me, too. And friends, a couple in New York, knew about it," I told him, reassuring him that I had not kept it a secret. "And—Chief Inspector, Ward Stoner, the head of the Blue Guard knew it, also."

"I see," was all he said.

I wondered what he was thinking. Maybe, he thought of all those people around me and still someone tried to snatch me. But I wasn't really thinking about me. I whispered, "Now—they've taken Grand-père."

Then Jason and I repeated in one voice, "Enchanted?"

I shook my head. "He said, 'Enchanted?' That's so strange," I added as my mouth went dry again. "How could the heinous act of my grandfather's abduction be enchanting?" Outrage continued to grow within me and became weeds that take over and drown out all healthy living plants.

"Then, the man said," Merrick continued, "'Find him if you can. But it will take you beyond the election date. You got away, but you still lose.'"

I breathed heavily; my chest was aching. "I'd better call Grand-mère."

CHAPTER 15

Pulling it Together

"Yes, Grand-mère, I'll be careful." My voice cracked on the antique telephone and I was nearly unable to finish my call. "I'm sorry that I didn't call you immediately. But I was utterly destroyed when I heard about it." Tears welled up in my eyes and rained down my cheeks. "I'm glad the Campaign Headquarters had already called you. I was feeling so guilty. Thinking that I had let you down, I couldn't talk." I looked over at Jason who was napping on the bed and felt my face contort in emotional pain.

Grand-mère's voice was calm but full of emotion. "Oh, my dear, you are my joy. You couldn't possibly let me down. I'm just happy you're all right." I could hear the tears in her voice and it broke my heart.

"Grand-mère—maybe if I had gotten here earlier"—

My grandmother continued. "What could you have done, Christy? Nothing, except, perhaps, get yourself kidnapped with him." She was quiet for a moment and then added, "I will pray for him and I want you to as well. His kidnappers do not know what they have done. They have kidnapped the Constitutional Party's presidential candidate and the Chairman of the Council of Twelve. But, more important than all of that, they kidnapped my Oliver, a man of God, and he will have them converted before this is over." She laughed a little; but her voice choked with tears.

I smiled to myself. "Yes, Grand-mère, I think you're right." I thought for a moment and then checked the clock. "It's getting late," I added. "I'd better go."

"Christy," Grand-mère coaxed, "I need for you to promise me a couple of things."

"Sure, Grand-mère—anything."

"First," she whispered, "you must be very careful. Our family would wither and die if anything happened to you."

"I will be careful. I promise."

She cleared her throat and added, "Please, Christy, do not worry or feel guilty. There was nothing you could have done. If Oliver Richly couldn't have fought them off, you would not have been able to either."

"I'll remember, Grand-mère," I promised. I hung up the phone and crawled up beside Jason on the bed, aching everywhere. I backed up against him, a glowing fireplace on a cold night, and felt comforted by his warmth.

Two o'clock slid into five p.m. like sap dripping from a maple tree. What could we do? We had no more information than we had the three hours previous. I tried to rest but couldn't sleep.

At 5:15 I said, "I've been Grand-père's voice up until now. I guess I'd better go to the Sports Arena. They will expect to see him center stage at 8pm. It's after five now."

Jason curled his arms around me more tightly and spoke from his physician's voice as well as his heart. "You'd better eat something first."

"Eat?" I questioned, a little irritated. "I wouldn't be able to eat anything."

"I understand," he said. "But, Honey, you may collapse from fatigue and worry if you don't support your body with nourishment. You haven't eaten anything since that cup of coffee. We waited to eat lunch until we had settled into the hotel. That didn't happen."

"Oh Jason, I don't—"

"I know." He paused and then continued. "How about some soup? We could go down to the restaurant—get out of our rooms for a while, and sip soup. They might have New England Clam Chowder."

I perked up a little. We don't have anything like fish soup in the Central Zone. "That sounds interesting. I might be able to keep that down."

Before we went downstairs, I stopped in the bathroom to splash some water on my face while Jason went to his room to freshen up. Shocked by the image I saw reflected in the mirror, I gasped. My eyes sunk in their sockets and the dark circles under them made me look like I had a second pair of tired eyes. I chose to ignore the rude replication of my former happy, carefree self, and instead, ran a comb through my hair and forgot the rest of my appearance.

My luggage still lay on the luggage rack, unpacked. I quickly flipped up the top, pulled out a light sweater, and met Jason in the hall. "I am dreading this," I admitted. "What should I say?"

Jason put his hand on the small of my back and sent caring warmth up my spine. "It's up to you, Honey."

When we got to the lift door, he pushed the button. As we stepped on, he added, "Since Oliver can't be here, you can explain what happened to him or you can give a campaign speech on his behalf. As I said, it's up to you."

• • • • •

Down in the hotel's first-floor restaurant the mixture of sweet and spicy aromas from the kitchen made me nauseous. Waves of queasiness flooded over me and threatened to pull me under. "Jason, I don't think—"

"I know, Honey. Is there anything that sounds even *okay* to you?"

"A cup of tea would be nice," I thought aloud.

686

"Would a little honey in it taste good?" Jason asked without pushing me.

Honey struck a sweet spot. "That would be great."

We placed our order with the serving girl. Her name badge had "Tara" printed on it. Jason ordered tea as well. We sat in silence for a moment until Tara returned with a fancy porcelain teapot of hot water and a loose tea diffuser's chain dangling out the side. I smiled at the quaint display. "This looks good. I think it will taste okay too."

"How about some toast?" Jason suggested. "In the old books in the hospital library, people used to eat toast when nothing else might stay down." He looked up at Tara and placed two orders for toasted bread.

"Toast?" I questioned. I, too, had read the wonderful old novels that had survived the book destruction of the previous century. I spent hours in my comfortable brown leather chair in the back room of the library at home, inhaling the fragrance of the novels no longer permitted for mass consumption. I laughed for the first time in hours. "Can you imagine the reaction of the Nutrition Authority if they saw me eating toasted bread with mounds of dripping butter?"

Jason joined in my mental picture with his own offering. "Buttered toast is even better with strawberry jam piled on top."

"Oh, Jason," I said, "what would our lives have been like if we had lived in the country that the heroes and heroines of the great books had lived in—under the original Constitution of Freedom?"

"I don't know, Honey. Maybe that's what you want to focus on when you address the people tonight."

"I'll turn that over in my mind," I said. When Tara returned with our food, the steam rising from the bread filled my nostrils with delight.

CHAPTER 16

Inside the Bubble

Our driver pulled the car up to the side alley door of the Arena. I put my hand on the car door handle but, stopped by someone from the outside, I waited. I tried to peer through the tinted window but the person stood so close, all I could see was a blue shirt and belt buckle. The person was small and I assumed they were female.

"You can get out in a moment, My Lady," our driver said calmly while searching the area that was visible through the windows and mirrors of the long-car.

"What's going on?" I asked as I twisted around to look out of the back window.

"A threat came in to Campaign Headquarters, Ma'am," was all she or he said.

"A threat against me?" I asked.

Jason put his arm around me and held me tight. "It will be okay. I'll stay right beside you."

"Even in center stage?" I asked.

"Of course—I can be on stage, too, if that's what you want," he stated with strength in his voice that made me feel safe. "We can do this however you want to—or not do it at all."

"Jason, I don't know what I would do without you," I admitted.

"Yeah, me too," he said as he kissed my forehead. "I love needing you to complete me."

"Okay, My Lady," the person on the outside announced and slapped a hand twice on the top of the car. When the door opened, I was surprised.

"Ivy," I said and smiled broadly. "I didn't know you were going to be able to make this trip."

"I flew up a few hours ago," Ivy said as she gave me a side hug. "In light of recent events, the campaign insisted."

"Thank you so much for being here." I said as I smiled. "How is your mother?"

"Actually, she is doing better, Christy," Ivy answered. "Thank you for asking."

I looked up and down the narrow alley. With the high side walls of adjacent buildings, it felt like a canyon, nestled in a safe valley. Then I remembered books of the western expansion of our country, and the visual image of marauders firing from mountain tops—or the roofs of the buildings above. It all came rushing in. I cringed as I grabbed Jason's hand and darted from the alley toward the door.

Ivy had her arm around me from the other side and shielded me from any danger as Jason reached for the arena door handle. Once inside, I felt safe, at least less conspicuous.

"Lady Applewait," a man in blue work clothes and matching ball cap said as he approached me.

I felt like a small child as I slipped behind Jason a half-step. This had to stop. I squared my shoulders and lifted my chin.

"Wait, Christy," Ivy said as she put her arm out in front of me. "Who are you?" she asked the man.

"Charles Lewis," he said with a smile and touched the tip of his fingers to his hat.

"Let me see your identification," Ivy order, seeming to be in no mood for friendly conversation.

The man's face turned ashen as he reached for his ID. "I'm sorry," he apologized as he looked from Ivy, to me, to Jason. "I didn't mean to—"

Ivy did not respond but studied the man's card. The small pocket size ID was complete with the required hologram, that when activated, created a holographic image that testified to the man's vital statistics. "Okay, you can move along," she said with a brush of her hand.

"But, Ma'am, I'm an employee here. I need to get Lady Applewait to the force-field bubble and secure her inside." His eyes batted and he appeared suddenly jumpy.

Jason stepped between Charles and me, still in full protective mode. "How much room is inside that bubble?" he asked.

"It can be as large as you need it to be." Then he looked at me, up and down. "She's a tiny little thing, isn't she?"

"I'm normal," I corrected him, insulted by any reference to being *tiny*.

Jason was insistent. "I will be at her side, within the bubble."

"Oh, sure," Lewis agreed and started off toward the tunnel that led to the center of the arena floor.

Ivy touched my arm and held me back. "Wait, Christy." She called after Charles Lewis who had already moved quickly. "Stop, Mr. Lewis."

Looking back over his shoulder, he seemed surprised that no one was following him. He stopped where he was and limply turned his palms up.

"We need to have a plan," Ivy insisted, "before Lady Applewait is going out there."

"Oh," Lewis paused and waited for us to catch up to him.

Ivy held her hand up to stop Jason and me, and then walked to the end of the access tunnel. "If the force-field can be expanded to include two people, can it be positioned over here, at the entrance to the arena, to let Christy and Jason walk into the bubble and then cover them while they move to the center?" She finally stopped and waited for the man to answer.

Mr. Lewis looked to the floor and then smiled. "Sure, I can do that."

All three of us exhaled loudly. Cautiously, we moved toward Mr. Lewis who waited at the opening. He stopped us there, and then moved into the arena on his own. With a small, shiny tool, he adjusted a mechanism that sent two laser points onto the floor and a flickering light bubble around it. He motioned for Jason and me to enter.

I experienced no change: no zap, no chill, no sound of any kind as I entered the field. Inside the bubble, it seemed like I was looking through an old glass-bottom boat window at a park my parents took me to as a child, named Life Beyond my Sphere. When Jason reached over and took my hand, I began to feel calm again.

Suddenly, the lights flooded the center of the arena and a voice on the loud speaker announced, "Ladies and gentlemen, please welcome Christiana Applewait, Oliver Richly's granddaughter and exciting spokesperson."

The crowd got to their feet and roared. I felt humbled but not frightened. The bubbled seemed to glow like a holy light was surrounding me.

"Thank you," I called to the crowd. Turning to Jason, I added, "I'd like to introduce you to Dr. Jason O'Reilly, my good friend. A physician, he provides medical advice and assistance to the entire election committee."

Jason squeezed my hand and waved to the people with his free one. He, too, seemed at ease. I was amazed at how quickly both of us had adjusted to being in the center of the light.

"Jason has joined me here to give me strength and a feeling of security." I paused and smiled as best I could.

My stomach churned as bitter acid rose up in my throat, but I knew I had to carry on. "I wasn't sure what to tell all of you." I looked around the room at the sea of shadowy, blurred faces and gathered my thoughts. "My grandfather, Oliver Richly, has been kidnapped, sometime between the late evening hours of yesterday and early this morning. When Dr. O'Reilly and I got here today, we discovered that he did not arrive at the hotel here in Caribou when expected."

There was stone silence. It was like all the air had been sucked up through a small hole in the ceiling and everyone had gone limp, gasping for life.

"I could have told you all about the wonderful things my grandfather stands for—and he does. I could have told you about the importance of returning to our original Constitution—and it is. I could have told you about the Central Zone's adherence to the Length of Days Law and how they kill children, the useless to society and the elderly—and they do. I could have told you how we must stop that un-godly practice—and we do. But, that's not why I am here."

I swallowed hard, trying to hold back tears that had finally seeped through my terrified heart. "I'm here to ask all of you, thousands and thousands of you, to become Oliver's eyes and ears. So far, we haven't heard that he's in physical danger—not yet. We just know he has been taken." More gasps rose up from the midst of the crowd.

"We have received one message from the kidnappers. I'm going to read it to you and—if anyone understands the encrypted message under the words, please call Campaign Headquarters in Capitol City. It reads: 'You will be enchanted to know—I have taken Oliver Richly.'"

"Enchanted?" Some mumbled in the great arena.

"Then, he said, 'Find him if you can. But it will take you beyond the election date. You lose.'"

Angry outbursts erupted around the room. "Lose?" one man shouted from the left. "Not hardly!"

My own rage seethed inside me. "How dare anyone grab a presidential candidate? That part of the message is clear. The kidnapper intends to disrupt a constitutional election!" I could feel my temper boil under the pot of my new emotions. Before my detoxification, I would have done very little—except where my grandparents were concerned. I wouldn't have had the emotions to care or the energy to do anything about it. The chemicals the government put in our water supply would have robbed me of the ability to raise the anger necessary to motivate me to do something about it.

"Every one of you who are here this day, are drafted into an army for freedom's sake. Talk to friends and family in other zones, track down every lead, listen to every conversation beside you on the PT, and watch for anything unusual or out of place! I will fill in for my grandfather during debates and public appearances, but we must find Oliver Richly before election-day!" My voice had risen to a near scream. The energy and magnitude of our task frightened me. Would I be up to the job I was asking everyone else to do?

Then from the middle of the stands, off to the deep right, I heard one voice. "New Mexico!" he shouted.

"What?" I heard him, but I didn't know what his comment had to do with anything.

"New Mexico," the man repeated. "The Land of Enchantment!"

CHAPTER 17

Looking for Answers

The sidewalks along the edge of the alley outside the arena were still fragrant with fresh rain when we came out. An occasional drop continued to fall, but for the most part, the clouds were beginning to part. It smelled fresh and clean.

"We have to get back to New York, Jason," I said as I yawned. I wandered if my exhaustion was physical or emotional. "I called the Citadel and talked to Barbara Cornwall. The other zone leaders will arrive tomorrow morning."

Ivy checked the shadowy doorways and behind trash dumpsters for anything or anyone who didn't belong there. Safety was always important but now it had become a life and death obsession. There was no place for mistakes. With the door handle in her left hand, she motioned for us to hurry and get into the hotel long-car.

"Get inside quickly," she ordered.

I knew that the power had shifted. I was used to having everyone obey my wishes. Now, it was the safety professionals who ruled the day. I got in and slid across the seat. Once Jason was inside, I said no more but leaned my head on his shoulder. I could tell that the lights and buildings of the city moved past the car windows; I didn't look up. Still, they appeared like flashes of light behind my eyelids.

When we returned to the hotel, we silently got in the elevator lift and rode up. Turning the knob, I opened the door to my hotel room and turned on the light.

"Honey, it's a ten-hour drive back to New York City," Jason said and put his arms around me. "You need some rest—and so do I."

"If we leave at 8am, we'll get to the Cornwall's at 6pm." I didn't like that assessment, but I had no other solution at that point."

Jason snapped his fingers together. "I know," he said, smiling, "Barbara and Richard have a helicopter. All above-grounders have one. I'll call them and ask them to send it in the morning. We can freshen up, get a good night's sleep, and then leave."

"What about the car,' I asked, unable to think the situation through clearly.

"Someone from the campaign can drive it back. If you want Ivy to come with us in the chopper, then someone else can drive the car down the coast," he offered. "There is a way to do this."

I sighed and threw my sweater onto one of the chairs. Slipping off my shoes, I curled up on the bed and pulled the corner of the spread over me.

Jason smiled softly and sat on the edge of the bed next to me. Brushing away the hair that had fallen across my face and eyes, he opened his mouth to speak and then stopped. "I'd better let you sleep," he said. As he pulled the covers around me, he kissed my forehead.

"Jason," I said and took his hand. "Please, don't leave."

"Christy—"

"I know. I really do—but—" I couldn't stop tears from welling up. "I can't be alone, not tonight."

Jason caressed my cheek with the back of his fingers. "Christy, I love you. I can't just—"

I understood what he was saying. We had been traveling together for months, but we had rarely been alone. In the night glow of my hotel room, it was so different. It was quiet enough I could hear his breathing and still enough to catch the faint fragrance of his aftershave. If I listened with my heart, I could hear the thump-thump of his pulse as well. I said nothing else.

Jason turned to go to his own room, paused but said nothing. I watched as he went over to the light switch and turned it off. The room was dark except for the light that filtered in through the drapes. He didn't leave. In the darkened room I saw him remove his jacket and tie and lay them across a chair. I could still hear his breathing and the thud of each shoe as it hit the floor. The sheets swished as he raised them and got into bed still partially dressed. We were nested spoons in the silver chest as he wrapped his arms around me and held me close with warm and gentle hands. "Good night, Sweetheart," he whispered.

I felt safe and loved. Where a moment ago I was unable to shake off the trauma, anxiety, and panic of Grand-père's abduction, with Jason close, I was able to close my eyes and quickly fall asleep.

• • • • •

Morning rose like the flowers of spring, with the color of light, and the sweet aroma of coffee which had brewed in the automatic maker. I hadn't moved all night. I awoke just as I had fallen asleep, in the arms of my Jason.

"Can you smell the coffee, Honey?" Jason whispered.

"It smells like ambrosia, the drink of the gods—or so the books in Greek mythology called it," I swooned.

"Does it smell good enough to get up and get some?" he asked as he laughed. "I programmed the coffee maker last night before we went to sleep."

"Almost," I admitted and then rolled over to face him. I snuggled my head in his shoulder and pulled as close as I could get. "Jason, we—"

"I like that. 'We' means a future together." Jason put his hand under my chin and tipped my face to him. Moving his hands with the caress of a lover, he placed his finger tips on my cheeks and kissed me tenderly. "When this is over, and Oliver is the newly elected

696

president, we will think about the future." He looked deeply into my eyes. "Won't we?"

"Yes, Jason, we'll talk—but for now, I can only think about today." I kissed him again, passionately. Suddenly, I stopped. The seriousness of the day's task and our commitment to the cause of restoring our country's freedom were too important for talk of "us". God had trusted us to see His power in the plan and not abandon our promise to it.

"Where's the coffee?" I laughed and jumped out of bed.

CHAPTER 18

A Gathering

The helipad landing on the roof of the Citadel in New York was as thrilling this time as it had been in the past. Jason and I had first been on Cornwall's roof months ago when Barbara and Richard had permitted a few of the underlings to bask in the sunlight of a glorious day, away from the belly of the city underground. We had ridden to the top on the home elevator. Today, entering the familiar lift, we whisked down to the entry.

Harold, the Cornwall's every-man, met us in the grand hall. The rose marble floors shone in the crystal chandelier light. "It's good to see you again, Christy." To Jason, he nodded, "Doctor." Turning, he motioned for us to follow him. "They have all gathered in the sitting room."

As we walked, Jason's hand at my back was the knot on the mooring line that secured me to safety. "Why am I so afraid of everything?" I felt like I had changed so much, even I didn't recognize myself. "I was so brave, so independent, just months ago."

He pulled me back before we entered the sitting room. "Christy, your life has changed a lot in the last few months. Gunmen managed to take shots at you twice. You have a gunshot scar in your shoulder. Someone even tried to snatch you off the street, and now, with the kidnapping of your grandfather, your world is no longer safe."

"How am I supposed to feel strong and safe, when I know I'm not?" I asked in a hushed but anxious tone.

"We live in a dangerous world, Honey. We always have. But before, in our drugged state, we didn't know we were supposed to fear everything."

"Gracie knew she wasn't safe." I remembered the young woman I found on the bathroom floor of the medical center in Capitol City. "No one said anything, complained or spoke the truth. We lived in the age of silence, Jason. Now, reality is hitting us hard."

Jason drew me close at the entrance to the sitting room and whispered, "Would you rather live your life with buried thoughts, drugged emotions and unspoken love, or risk the dangers of really living?"

"I choose life, Jason," I announced and knew I was sure of my choice.

"Come in you two," Barbara called from her chair by the fire. Richard stood beside her, his arm resting on the marble mantle, the same beautiful rose color as the entry floor.

Inside, Kasamar and Raymar Goring sat on the sofa. The Spires couple, Martin and Rebecca, enjoyed the two wingback chairs near the windows. Edward Musselman sat between his wife, Maud, and Rachel Claudette around the game table with its fine leather top.

"I can't believe it," I gasped when I saw all of the lovelies Jason and I had met and depended on for our lives, just months before. "I get to see all of you, at one time, in one room."

I went around the room and hugged each dear friend, catching up on the immediate past. But, the activity for that day was not fellowship. "I don't know who is aware of the events of the last twenty-four hours."

Each one looked to the other. It seemed by their facial expressions, and the few words of condolences they offered, that most of those gathered there knew that Grand-père was missing; but I had to say the words again.

"Yesterday, when Jason and I got to our hotel in Caribou, Maine, we discovered that Grand-père hadn't gotten there yet as he was supposed to. Later, we received a call that he had been kidnapped."

Some nodded in acknowledgement while others gasped in shock after hearing the terrible words spoken out loud.

"How could it happen?" Martin asked in anger. "Where were his bodyguards?"

"Malcolm Merrick, a member of his Advance Team, said he hadn't even arrived in Caribou." I looked around at each one. "The team in Maine could not have protected him since Grand-père hadn't gotten there. There was no flight logged into any airport. Right now, we don't know where security broke down."

Richard ran his hand through his hair and slapped the back of his neck. "Are there any clues at all?" He shook his head and set his jaw hard. "There has to be something."

I knew Richard was right—but, the fact was, there was nothing. Nothing I could think of.

Jason's eyes snapped to attention. "Wait, Christy—remember? The note said, 'You will be enchanted to know—I have taken Oliver Richly.'"

"Enchanted?" Richard barked, his eyes narrowed and his mouth set in a scowl.

"That's what I said," I admitted. "Then someone at the rally last evening yelled out from the side seats, 'New Mexico–it's the Land of Enchantment.'"

"New Mexico?" Rachel protested. "What is this, a treasure hunt? You have to be able to read the clues to find the buried treasure?"

"It feels like it," I admitted.

"New Mexico?" Barbara asked. "New Mexico," she shrieked in one gasp. "My father has investments in New Mexico—hotels, ranches, all kinds of stuff."

"Alister Bedlum is behind this?" I couldn't believe it. "I thought he was going to try to be a positive force. Not the most hated man in the world."

"That's what he promised," Barbara said as she twisted her hair. "He said, if he could talk with Mother, he would repent and become a better person."

"Did Mrs. Bedlum agree to talk to him?" Jason asked as he controlled his anger but not his body language. His fists were white knuckled and the veins in his neck bulged. "With the way Sondra had to drastically change her life, it's hard to believe she might even consider it."

Barbara squared her shoulders and smiled a wry smile. "She told me to tell him that he'd have to prove himself. If he would set up some sort of foundation to distribute part of his wealth to those in need, and prove to her that he has done it and has started giving it away, she would talk with him."

"And?" Raymar asked.

Barbara's eyes flashed with strength and assertion. "He hasn't set up a thing. Mother would know, because the foundation was to be in Mother's name and she would have to sign papers to put it in place." Tears welled up in her eyes. "Not a single paper has been drawn up."

"Barbara, I am so sorry," I said as my heart boke for her disappointment. I thought about my own father, his integrity and honesty. I could not imagine how I would feel if my father were Alister Bedlum.

"Don't be sorry, Christy," she said as her voice grew stronger. "I'm not. I have dismissed him. He's a monster, not my father." Then her eyes grew sad and tired. "I remember once, when I was very small, my daddy and momma took me to the tree lighting program at Rockefeller Center. We were happy, a family." Tears rolled down her cheeks and she wiped them away with her fingertips. Richard handed her a handkerchief. "Thanks," she said and kissed his hand.

"Then, that next year," she continued, "his business took off with the use of dishonest and gangster-like activities and my world crumbled. I knew then that Daddy had died that year and the Alister Bedlum the world knows was born."

"So—Bedlum has a New Mexico connection?" Jason asked. "Then, we need to contact Campaign Headquarters out there and see what clues may have been dropped."

"Barbara," I held my breath, "your chopper?"

"The little city helicopter won't make it that far, Christy," Barbara quickly added. "The flash-rail!" she clipped with enthusiasm. "You can board here is New York at Grand Central Station and disembark in El Paso, Texas. A car can be waiting for you at the station-terminal."

Everyone was silent for a minute. "How does that sound?" I asked.

"You're still packed," Kasamar reminded me.

"We might be rushing off thousands of miles away, with very few cues," I said, anxious to find Grand-père but terrified of wasting time and what that could mean to my grandfather.

"The trip will take about eight hours," Richard said. "Part of the tracks runs underground and some lines are far above the roads. Both of you will have your 281 Palm Devices with you for research and messaging." I could see his mind work as he paced back and forth, his hands motioning in the air.

"As an attorney, I have built many criminal cases," Richard added with enthusiasm. "We will build a case against Bedlum here in New York while you find Oliver." He beat his fist on the satin finished mantle. "Every step you take, every person you talk to, every clue you find can and will be used against that monster."

"You can do it, Christy," Maisie assured me. "You are my hero."

"Hero?" I blurted out loud. "My grandfather is the hero," I said as I looked at each person there. "Those of you from the other zones, stay in close contact with your campaign workers. Reassure them that Grand-père will be back soon and encourage them to spread my grandfather's message to everyone they meet, in small groups and large gatherings. We will find him—before it's too late. And, he will win."

CHAPTER 19

Flash-train to Texas

We ran along the boarding platform to the last car from the front, the exclusive private coach Barbara had arranged for us, and hurried up the steps. My pulse was pounding as I fell into the seat. Panting, I gasped with relief, "We made it."

"Are you all right, Baby?" Jason asked as he plopped into his seat and laughed.

I couldn't catch my breath enough to answer. I tried not to laugh since laughing seemed like a series of exhales and I thought I had none in me. Then I smiled. Even though someone kidnapped Grand-père, Jason and I had enough hope within us to laugh at the events of the day.

I grabbed my chest and willed myself to breathe slower. That would slow my pulse and let me catch my breath. "I talked to Grand-mère before we left the Cornwall's Citadel."

"How is she holding up?" Jason asked as he adjusted the pillow at the back of his head.

As I began to gather my thoughts and look around, I quickly saw that our rail coach was a penthouse luxury experience. The seats were sleek, with hard poly-infused sawdust frames, bright red deeply tufted seats and reclining backs with pillows. Raised, they sat at a broad table for work and dining.

I sighed as I thought about my dear grandmother and the years she and Grand-père had spent together. "She prays constantly and is leaving Grand-père's life in God's hands."

"And your parents?" he asked.

I closed my eyes and saw my family. "Mother and Daddy are spending their nights with Grand-mère. I think she's the one comforting Mother. But I'm relieved they're all right and that they are together."

Barbara had arranged the private flash-rail car for us so we could rest, research and study in quiet. It was mid-morning when we came up for air and pulled our chairs up to the table. A rail steward came in with a tray.

"I hope that's coffee," I swooned when I saw the steaming decanter.

"Yes, Ma'am," he said and smiled. "I also have a plate of cinnamon rolls. Enjoy."

"Thank you," Jason said and reached for the plate with both hands. The steward poured two cups of hot coffee and excused himself to the door.

"There is a button on the arm of each chair. Just push it if you need something. Lunch will be served at 12:30." He bowed and backed out of the car.

I looked at my palm device and waved it back and forth. "How do we begin?"

"Okay," he started to process as he opened his own device. "The only clue we have is New Mexico. Well, two. Bedlum has a connection with the state and owns ranches, hotels, and other properties."

Just then, a hologram of Barbara Cornwall rose up from my device. "I'm on my secure Cooper-line," she began breathlessly, "so no one can cyber-hack into our conversation. This is very dangerous, Christy. Bedlum is a very dangerous demon."

"I know he is, Barbara," I agreed. "My own grandfather has been kidnapped, and I was shot. I know how dangerous he is."

"I asked my mother about a New Mexico connection," Barbara started.

"Of course," I threw my hand to my chest and gasped. "I hadn't even thought about asking her."

"Mother said that Bedlum owns a hotel in Las Cruces, New Mexico. He was investigating the possibility of buying more properties in the area before he got reconnected with the mob."

"Reconnected?"

"Remember Christy," Barbara whispered, "my father, his father and his father's father were each the head of a crime family. They were mafia kingpins—godfathers."

"I remember your mother, Sondra, telling Jason and I."

"That note that was given to Bedlum at the opera when you were first here, had the combination to his safe written on it." She paused. "I have to trust that this information is safe," she said with a deep sigh. "When Mother left the mansion, where she had lived with Bedlum for years, she took the scrapbooks and ledgers from the safe that covered the first years of their marriage and that also merged into his la Cosa Nostra era. That's really why Bedlum is looking for her—not because he cares about her."

"Oh, Barbara—I am so sorry."

"Mother is safe for now. I'm not concerned unless Bedlum finds out she's here. Then—I don't know." She was silent for a moment.

I could see from her shimmering holographic image that she was thinking. "Barbara—what?"

"Those scrapbooks—pictures and ledger entries," she said slowly as she rubbed her forehead with her hand. "Mother, Richard and I will pour over those books as quickly as possible for any clues about Bedlum's holdings and interests in New Mexico so we can get back to you as soon as possible." She took a deep breath. "I called to say that you could research the mafia and any connection they may have had to the Southwest, based upon old books and documents you could find on your palm devise."

"Old books and manuscripts?" I immediately thought of Marge Cummings, the curator of the historic documents at the main library in Capitol City.

"I know most books were burned or destroyed during the devastation of the last epoch." Barbara was a reader and she well knew of the loss to mankind of all the books published before the mass destruction. "And, I don't think there are any electronic data bases of previous books and manuscripts."

I looked over at Jason who was busting with excitement. He grabbed my arm and held on. "Barbara, yes," I reported, "there are not only data bases, there are books: the classics, novels, TV videos and copies of the original Constitution, Bill of Rights—everything, in the old back stacks and warehouses of our library in Capitol City. I can call the curator and ask her to do some research as well. She is part of the *1787-Constitutionalists* Campaign team." I reached over and hugged Jason, my life-line to reality.

"Great, Christy! I'll talk to Mother and we'll get busy on scrapbooks and other papers. You contact the curator. You and I will talk again before you get to El Paso."

"Barbara—you have brought some hope to Grand-père's disappearance." I choked up and had to pause before going on. "Grand-père will be found. He will win the election; we will overturn the Length of Days Law. God bless you."

CHAPTER 20

Research

"Marge?" I spoke into my 281 Palm Device.

"Hi, Christy. You look tired. Are you all right?"

"Marge—something has happened." It was hard for me to form the words. "Grand-père has been kidnapped. I need your help."

Marge said nothing for a second. "Sir Richly? How is that possible?"

"We don't have the details yet. And, we have just a few clues." I was sure Marge could find something regardless of how small. "Marge, we need for you to do some research in the back rooms and in the old files."

"Of course," Marge offered. "Anything."

Waiting for her to calm down and focus, I counted to ten in my head. "We need whatever you can find about the old mob, the mafia, la Cosa Nostra and any connection they may have at all with the state of New Mexico."

"Wow, how esoteric. The mafia?" Marge seemed to stumble through the request as if saying it over and over would bring clarity.

"Right—and look for any mafia dons with the name—Bedlum," I asked and held my breath, waiting for her to melt down again.

"Bedlum? Like in—Alister Bedlum?" Marge sounded like the concept was incredulous. "How—"

"It's a long story and we have very little time to spare," I apologized. "I'll catch you up later. Alister Bedlum is Barbara Cornwall's father. Enough said."

"More than enough," she agreed as her image shimmered in front of me. "I'll let you know what I find."

As Marge's hologram dissolved, I closed my device. "I should call Grand-mère." I felt tired and defeated. I stole a glance out the window at the flying scenery. "But I don't know what to say to her," I admitted.

Jason reached over and patted my knee. "We don't have any new information, Honey. It would be hard to call and report nothing."

"I know—but I still feel guilty."

"Christie, I think you could use a nap. Your voice is weak. Your body is slumped. You're not yourself. I know that Oliver—"

"It's that—and more." I stopped, unable to find the words to express feelings I also couldn't identify. "I feel like everyone is expecting me to find an answer to everything, and I can't even find my own grandfather."

"Honey, if any of us have made you feel responsible for all the solutions, I am sorry."

"You, Jason? I didn't say you—"

"I know you didn't. I guess I'm really the one who thinks you can do everything," Jason admitted. "You healed the man who was out of his mind with drug intoxication. And again, when Jewels felt abandoned and without hope, you used words of encouragement that really made a difference." He took my hand and whispered. "I'm sorry if I made you feel overwhelmed."

I smiled at him and began to stack up all the events of the last year. "It wasn't just me, Jason," I admitted. "It was so many of us. And, it started when the whole town gathered to sing, *Silent Night*, on Christmas Day Eve, at a time when no one heard the name of Jesus. In order to not make a few people uncomfortable, millions lived their lives in silence."

• • •

We continued researching for hours using our 281 palm devices. With all the books confiscated and burned years ago, it was hard to know where to begin. It isn't like there was a list of books somewhere, until—

"Eureka!" Jason shouted.

"What did you find?"

"Here—listen—I found it on something called the dark web. Authorities thought they had shut it down years ago, but the websites that were located there just dug in deeper," Jason said as he sat up straight and waved his 281 back and forth.

"The dark web sounds sinister," I said with a shudder.

"Some of it was." Jason stood up and walked back and forth. "But, it was also a way to post something anonymously. Like, reporting a crime but not wanting anyone to know who called the Blue Shirts. Or, reporting an industrial or governmental mismanagement and keeping the whistle-blower's name a secret."

I said nothing but waited for the information he had uncovered. I knew I was becoming very impatient and it was best to stay silent.

"Christie, someone, or many someones, put massive amounts of information about the mafia on the dark web." Jason concluded.

Just then, my 281-device flashed and Marge shimmered forth. "Christie, Jason, I found something!"

"So did Jason," I said eagerly. "Tell me first what you found."

"Okay," she began. "Back in the middle of the last century, before the great collapse and before they banned speaking up, there was a story posted about Bedlum's grandfather, Mafia Boss Charles Bedlum, or Lucky Charlie as he was called by the press. He slipped through authorities' fingers a lot."

"That sounds exactly right, Marge." I was so excited, I thought I would hyperventilate. "Is there any connection to New Mexico?"

"Yes," she said with anticipation. "Lucky Charlie bought an old ranch in the foothills of the Organ Mountains near Las Cruses, New Mexico. He liked the legend that Pat Garrett's mother stayed at the ranch when she came to the area. Sherriff Pat Garrett captured Billy the Kid, so Charlie thought he had one-upped Garrett by owning the ranch or something like that."

"Oh, Marge, thank you so much! I'll stay in touch." And, with that Marge dissolved.

I stood up, reached out and hugged Jason as we jumped and danced around the room. As he swirled with me around the rail-car, the steward came back in with a huge silver tray.

"Lunch, Ma'am—Sir," he said as he placed the tray on the table. He removed a silver domed lid from the platter with smaller dishes arranged on it: savory slices of roast beef, small red potatoes dripping in butter and sweet-smelling tender carrots. An assortment of desserts waited on another plate: dark rich chocolate tortes and white cakes with raspberry filling.

"Thank you," I gasped. "It all looks wonderful."

The Steward turned to leave and then added, "If you need anything else, just ring for me."

Grabbing the steward's elbow, Jason asked. "We will be getting off at El Paso, Texas. A car is waiting for us. Then we'll drive into New Mexico." He paused and seemed to choose his words carefully. "We heard of an old legend that says Pat Garrett's mother stayed at a ranch near Las Cruces. Have you heard of that story or where the ranch would be located?"

"Yes, I know that story." He smiled and relaxed his professional posture a little. "Follow the War Road out of El Paso and you'll come to the entrance to Dripping Springs Ranch. It's beautiful up there. They turned it into a National Park but in recent years it's become a little overgrown. But you'll find it."

"Fantastic!" I shrieked. "We have food and a destination! Perfect!"

CHAPTER 21

Stoner in the Southwest

Ward Stoner could not believe the events of the last few days. His trusted Blue Guardsman, Daniel Washington, had followed him to New Mexico. Why? The man knew the Chief Inspector's rules of conduct. And, number one on the list was, *follow all rules*, written and spoken. Stoner had told him to stay back in Capitol City and watch the Richly Campaign Office. Oliver Richly was missing, and it didn't matter how distasteful Stoner found the new "Freedom March" of the *1787-Constitutionalists,* it was his job to keep the peace and protect the people, in whatever fashion or method he deemed necessary.

Yet, when he and the lieutenant got off the airplane, Ward had seen Washington dash past him and Boone, and slither behind a colonnade in the terminal. Certainly, the man didn't think anyone had seen him. That would be childish. Did he think, "If I cover my eyes, the world goes away?" But, enough of that.

With his dash-bag firmly in his hand, Stoner darted toward the door. He never even glanced over his shoulder to see if Boone was behind him. He assumed she would be there. He always assumed.

In front of the terminal, a car waited from the El Paso, Texas Police Headquarters. Quickly whisked into the vehicle, Boone and Stoner barely saw the passing buildings on their way to meet the police chief.

They came to a stop in front of the two-story flat roofed, tan adobe style building of police headquarters. Nearly running, they darted from the car, hustled through the doors, and made their way with fixed gaze to Chief Montoya's office.

"Please, take a seat, Chief Inspector Stoner," Montoya offered with a smile.

"We have no time for pleasantries," Stoner barked without the slightest trace of a smile. "You would not know yet. It's important that the upcoming presidential election is not compromised." He paused making sure the chief heard the seriousness of his message, not just the words. "Oliver Richly has been kidnapped."

"What?" Montoya gasped as he rose from his desk chair.

"It's done, Sir." Stoner said with a crisp clip of his heals. "We must move on. We heard that his kidnappers brought him into New Mexico. This stop at your office is just a formality. Since we flew into your airport, we stopped here to let you know we're in your area." He turned to Boone. "Let's go."

Montoya rushed from behind his desk with a unique car door key in his hand: a finger-simulator lightning etched into an aqua-plastic card. "Take any car from our fleet, Sir." He handed over the sim. "This master finger print simulator will open and start any vehicle in storage."

"Thank you, Chief," Stoner snapped, in his assumptive manner. With that and a handshake, he and Boone left the office and went into the police garage. They selected a SPV within minutes, slipped the simulator near the lock, opened the door, and got in. The vehicle responded to the fingerprint sim with a hum and they quickly pulled onto the road.

"That was nice of the Chief, don't you think?" Boone asked.

"What else could he do? Of course, he handed over a car. The man who might be the next president has been kidnapped and may be near El Paso." Ward said no more.

Stoner followed the old I-10 highway out of El Paso toward the Las Cruces, New Mexico area, heading north. An underground inter-zonal informant told him about some unusual activity at the old Dripping Springs Ranch, in the foothills of the Organ Mountains that rose like the majestic peaks of a mighty pipe organ. The rising of the immense full moon behind Organ Mountains lit the sky like a blazing wild fire.

"Ward, it is breathtaking," Chalky whispered as she gazed with amazement at the brilliant red sky above the mountain ridge.

Stoner said nothing at first. He had been driving the small police vehicle, or SPV. He felt like he was in an alone-place, at peace with the gathering night around him. He had nearly forgotten that his lieutenant was in the seat beside him. He found that odd. It had been harder and harder to forget or ignore Boone in recent weeks. He could feel her near him, even before she spoke. He found it distracting and enjoyable at the same time. And, Ward Stoner was rarely distracted.

"Yes," he admitted as he gazed skyward. "Beautiful, I guess." But his mind was not on the magnificent sky or the majesty of the mountains. It was on the uppity legacy brat, his name for Christiana Applewait, and her insistence on disregarding the rules.

"Ward," Chalky began diplomatically, "the prohibition against travel between zones was lifted. What has she done?"

"I told her that I would find her grandfather. She should stay in Capitol City. But did she? No!" he seethed as he gripped the steering wheel.

Chalky looked out of the side window at the passing desert sand, creosote bushes, yucca plants, and desert grasses. "Which one makes you angrier," she asked in a controlled voice, "Washington or Applewait?"

"That's another one. What does he think he's doing?" Stoner snorted, like a challenged bull moose.

"I received a message on the flight out here," she said boldly. "Daniel has accepted a large assignment from President Alexander."

"What?" Stoner shrieked. "You're just now telling me?"

"Ward, I was waiting for the right time."

"The right time?" Stoner's neck veins bulged.

Boone set her chin and jaw firmly. "You have been more difficult since Sir Richly was kidnapped than at any other time in recent years."

Ward's knuckles turned white on the steering wheel. "Washington has agreed to another job while on my watch?" He pounded the wheel with his fist and paused. "Now, what's this grand and fearful assignment?"

"Alexander refuses to consider failure at the election, Ward. And, while the Blue Guard has been a staunch defender of everything about the new government—Alexander no longer trusts the Guard. Call it paranoia. Call it mistrust of the developing interest in spirituality as re-introduced by Christiana Applewait."

"Oh, you cannot be serious!" he thundered.

Boone reached over and patted his hand, causing him to flinch. "Ward, whatever the reason, someone told me that Alexander has hired Washington to take you out, since you are the head of the Blue Guard."

Ward Stoner drove on in silence. Darkness would have been a blessing. It would have hidden the rage that was building within him. "How dare he!" Stoner hissed.

"The road up to Dripping Springs is off to the right, past the University," Chalky directed. "Why is the University still here if there are no books?"

"My sources tell me doctors, teachers, and other professionals are taught my rote memory since there are no books," he paused. "Isn't that stupid?"

"Christy Applewait told me about a community of people called, the Keepers. They—"

"Never mind that, Boone," Stoner barked and said no more. He turned east on University Avenue and followed it until it turned into Dripping Springs Road.

The scenery hadn't changed much according to those who had given directions in El Paso. The great upheaval of the previous century had halted progress everywhere. What did not lie within the great cities, deteriorated alone in the dry deserts and windswept prairies in many zones. There were no buildings along the road that could cast light from their windows or open doors, creating shadows and contrast. Stoner and Boone's only blessing was the brilliance of the moon that lit the path.

As they neared Dripping Springs Ranch, both of them stiffened. Old adobe buildings lay in rubble with gaping holes where windows and doors had been. Weathered earthen bricks cluttered the area. Most structures didn't have all four walls or roof. Overgrown hiking trails, once enjoyed by walkers willing to trudge the walkway from the La Cueva rock outcropping to the rugged spires of the mountain peaks, were barely visible.

"I don't like this, Ward," Chalky spoke. It sounded like she wasn't breathing.

"Don't be silly. If Richly is imprisoned out here, they wouldn't have blazing lights to give away their position."

Chalky's eyes darted from rocks to ruins, like an animal that sees no escape. "The Park Service used to keep this area up, but money hasn't been allocated for park upkeep for decades." She rigidly clutched the door handle. "Ward—who gave you the tip to come out here?"

"It came through a third party," he said with measured speech. Nearing the structure with the most promise of habitation— it had walls and a roof—he slowed the SPV and turned off the lights.

"Ward," Chalky whispered as she searched the area around them from inside the car, "I don't think we should get out. There's no one around. And, if there is—I'm not sure who is hunting who."

Stoner opened the vehicle door with disgust. "Harrumph," was the only sound he made, and an occasional snap of a dry plant underfoot. With only lunar light, he approached the building that appeared to be the most intact and pulled out his sidearm.

Boone was slower to emerge from the impenetrability and safety of the SPV. She unfastened the clip that held her firing arm securely inside its holster. Then, she stopped in place.

Stoner heard nothing. But—he could feel a presence in the thicket at the corner of the crumbling building. Turning with a snap, he aimed his weapon.

"No! Ward!" a familiar voice snapped. "It's me, Boone."

Stoner lowered his weapon and searched the long shadows cast by the bright moonlight. "What are you doing? You nearly got yourself killed."

"Ward," she rushed toward him. "You know that Washington followed you here. I told you—you are his target! This feels like an ambush!" she whispered hoarsely.

"A what?" he bellowed like a bull elephant protecting his territory.

"Let's get inside something. It's—" Instantly, the blast from a 980 short-distance firearm drowned out her voice.

With the crack from the weapon, Ward Stoner hit the ground like the falling of a giant timber, strong, full of life and now face-down in the dust and the sand of the desert.

Stoner saw Boone crouch low and whip around, with her 980 in her hand. He could smell no tell-tail sign of smoke like from an antique weapon. Then the sound of running crunched and rattled down the path and disappeared. He watched through blurry eyes as Boone holstered her weapon when the whirl of a motor started up in the distance. Ward felt her kneel beside him as she snapped on the light mounted like a broach to her upper, left shoulder. In the flash of the light, he saw little but felt her hands run along his back. His shirt felt warm and sticky.

"Ward?" she whispered; her voice sounded desperate as he felt her roll him toward her. The light from her shoulder flashed on the dirt as it fell from his face. He saw her eyes fix on the upper left quarter of his body. "Oh Ward," she gasped.

"Miriam?" Whispering, his eyes blurry with pain.

"No, Ward," Boone sighed. "It's Chalky. Miriam died—a few years ago." He heard her choke on the words that separated her from the ghost of his dead wife and then she swallowed hard. Tears drip down her face and gather in pools where she caught them on the back of her hand.

He gripped his chest and thought of his son Christopher. The boy had already lost his mother. He could not lose his father as well. Not tonight. Grabbing Boone's hand, he brought it to his lips.

"You have followed the words of the healer, Christiana Applewait." He gasped for breath as he lay with his head in Boone's lap. "Heal me," he pleaded.

"Ward!" Her hands trembled and her voice cracked. "I can't. I'm not—"

"You are, Chalky," he said as he clutched at her more desperately. "I have seen the love in your eyes."

"But, I—" Tears choked her words. She wiped them with the tail of her shirt.

"Now, Chalky, now!" he insisted, his voice growing weak and thready.

Boone bowed her head and prayed to the God of other people, those she had chased to the great waters of the west. The moon light that lit the evening seemed to focus a beam on her hands, on Ward's gapping, bleeding wound. Suddenly, she thrust her hands, her left palm pressing on top of the right, into the opening in the shoulder of the man she had admired, feared, loathed, and lately—loved. Stoner knew that but could not admit it to himself or to her.

He could hear the thumping of his pulse in his ears. At first, he feared, with each beat, his life-blood was pumping out of his body. Truthfully, if he could have thought clearly, he would have known it was, but he preferred to think of it differently. Through the growing delirium of his pain, every thump, thump reminded him of the people's march, a year ago on December 25, when Christmas returned to Capitol City on Gifting Day Eve. He let go of the agony that tortured his body and saw himself walking with the faithful, singing songs of love and joy. No one knew the words that glorious evening, since singing had been silenced. But there was a knowing, and a sharing of musical phrases, one beat behind the next. That's where Ward Stoner mentally crawled while Chalky forced life back into his body.

The compression beneath her blood-soaked hands slowed the escape of his blood, beat by beat. When Ward gasped, filling his lungs to capacity, Chalky eased up, her face shining in wonder and amazement. "Praise the Lord," she sang with a joyful sound on her lips.

"How did you do that?" Stoner asked, aware that he was in the arms of his lieutenant.

"I didn't Ward. I followed a—an instinct, a knowing I didn't hear or understand. It just came to my heart that I should place my hands in your wound and stop the bleeding. Just like with Christy." Chalky shook her head in seeming disbelief although she had seen the glory of it. "Amazing, yet I believe it came from God."

Ward Stoner searched his soul for another answer. The name of God and his son, Jesus, banned so long ago, still came to mind when needed. How could that be? How could anyone know the name of a friend they had never met? But he could not deny the fact. Touched by the King of a kingdom he never knew existed—he had been healed.

CHAPTER 22

The Organ Mountains

The night moon still hung in the star-peppered sky, a garden lantern in a bejeweled tree. Jason and I followed the War Road out of El Paso and into New Mexico.

"There it is," Jason pointed. "The sign says, Dripping Springs Road that way."

Jason turned our rented vehicle toward the Organ Mountains. Since individually owned cars in the Central Zone did not exist, except for medical and police personnel like Jason and Stoner, it was exciting to ride in a really fancy vehicle anyone could buy in the southwest.

"This is beautiful," I admired as I ran my fingers over the ebony leather covered dashboard. "Look," I pointed at the headlights of an on-coming car, "so many people have their own transportation here. Just like in the Western Zone."

"It sure is dark out here," he said as we both searched the sides of the narrow road along the path out to the ranch. "Watch for anything, a clue, a warning that might tell us something about where they've taken Oliver."

"I'm looking," I whispered, almost afraid to speak, "but—I see nothing."

"I know, Honey," he said. "But it feels better to look for something, anything."

"What is that up ahead?" The lights at the foot of the mountains looked like a cluster of emergency vehicles, with red and blue lights spinning around, flash—flash.

As we neared, there were so many lights, they were blinding. "Do you think they found Grand-père?"

"We'll see," Jason said as he slowed and prepared to talk through the window speaker.

"What are you doing way out here at night?" A southwest version of a Blue Guardsman clipped; his brow deeply knitted.

Jason shielded his eyes from the man's bright lapel light. "What's going on?"

The guardsman put his hand on his weapon. "Sir, I asked you a question. First give me your name and then answer me. What are you doing out here?"

"Certainly," Jason began slowly. "My name is Dr. Jason O'Reilly and this is Lady Christina Applewait. We're looking for her grandfather, Sir Oliver Richly."

"Out here—in the dark?"

"Sir," my words came hesitantly. Could I trust him? "My grandfather has been kidnapped." I watched as the man's expression turned from stern-man-in-control to a person of true concern. "We received a clue that led us out here."

"I'm sorry to hear that Ma'am, but this area is deserted."

The lights of the emergency responders flashed in my eyes. "What are all the lights and storm troopers about?"

"An important Inspector of the Blue Guard was shot. We received an emergency beacon signal from the SPV he drove out of El Paso."

"Inspector Stoner?" I gasped. Flooded with feelings that tore at me left and right, fear finally won. Ward Stoner was nothing if he wasn't a staunch fighter for what he believed was right. Lately, he had been on my grandfather's side—and mine. Had we lost a valuable alley?

"Yes, Ma'am," the Stormtrooper acknowledged.

Jason gripped the steering wheel and cleared his throat. "Have they caught the shooter?"

"No, Sir. He apparently got away."

"I'm a physician," Jason offered. "Does the Inspector need my help?"

"Go on through, Doctor," The trooper said as he waved us past.

The dirt road, lit by moon glow in spite of the nighttime hour, left a cloud of dust in our wake. "I wonder if Chalky Boone is with him." I thought of the time she tried to "explain" Ward Stoner to me, saying that he is actually a nice guy. "I think she really likes him."

As we neared the source of all the lights and activity another trooper held up the palm of his hand. "This is a crime scene. You'll have to turn around."

"I'm a physician," Jason offered again.

"Good," the guard said. "First Attenders are here but no doctor."

Jason pulled off the trail and stopped. He opened the door, jumped out and headed over to those gathered around a man on the ground. Getting out of the car, I looked down to make sure my feet were on stable ground and noticed some sparkly stuff under my shoes. "What's all this?" I questioned, although not to any one in particular, just a question I spoke aloud.

One of the many troopers gathering clues in the area, smiled and said, "That's crystalized jalapeño granules. A store here in the area is marketing the powder as a night-hour substance to identify a homeowner's property lines. The fire in the peppers mixed with other chemicals causes the product to glow after heating all day in the New Mexico sun. It's made in Old Mesilla, a very, very old historical village around here."

"That's nice," I whispered. "Few people in the Central Zone own property." I didn't wait for a response and turned to walk over to where Jason was in attendance.

"My Lady," Lieutenant Boone called out as I approached her.

"Lieutenant—"

"Call me Chalky," she asked.

"It's Christy, Chalky. How is he?"

"Better—he was shot, Christy."

I gasped at the thought of the stern warrior, shot down in the dirt of the road. "By who?"

"We think Daniel Washington was the shooter," she said, her breath short and choppy. She seemed overcome by events that brought down her friend. "He got away, but he can't hide. He'll want to go home sometime."

Boone and I walked closer to Jason and his patient. "It looks like the bleeding has stopped," we heard Jason say. "The bullet will have to be removed."

"I understand," Stoner said—his voice not as clipped as usual. "But Chalky stopped the bleeding."

Jason's eyes widened, "Lieutenant Boone?"

"Yes—" Stoner paused. "Doctor," he whispered, "I need to tell you—my lieutenant believes in the things your Lady believes in. And—I guess I must too—because I asked Boone to heal me like Christiana would if she were here."

Standing in the background, close but yet not, my heart seemed to stop beating and still pounded harder. Had I heard him correctly? Did he say, he believes?

Jason stopped and felt the pulse in Stoner's wrist. "What did Boone do?"

"I told her I knew she could do it," Stoner began. "Then she placed her hand in my wound and the bleeding stopped." He grabbed Jason's wrist and leaned toward him. "I could feel the life in my body return." He grabbed Jason's arm, hard. "Doctor, I know I could."

I watched as one of the First Attenders tapped Jason on the shoulder. "Doc, we're ready to transport the patient."

"Stoner," Jason corrected him. "His name is Ward Stoner." Jason stood up and motioned for me to come closer.

The attendants placed a lift board on the ground beside Stoner and transferred him onto it. Reaching out, I took Stoner's hand in mine. I could feel energy transfer from my body to his and my knees felt weak.

Stoner smiled. "Thank you."

As they moved him onto the patient transport, Chalky reached out and threw her arms around me. "Christy, I am so glad you brought Dr. O'Reilly to us."

I looked into her eyes. "We were following the same lead you were on," I explained.

"Be careful," she warned. "Daniel Washington, that animal, is on the loose."

"We'll watch for him, thanks, because, we can't leave. We came here following a connection we found with the mob of many years ago, and Dripping Springs Ranch. Sheriff Pat Garrett's mother would stay there when she came to visit."

A First Attender standing nearby chuckled a little. "If you want more Sheriff Garrett flavor, he put Billy the Kid in jail here in Doña Ana County."

"Where?" I questioned, excited about a possible new lead.

"Old Mesilla, Ma'am."

CHAPTER 23

Old Mesilla

The adobe village of Old Mesilla lay just off the highway that ran southwest out of Las Cruces. The road would continue past the old pecan groves and on toward La Mesa and the Texas border if you didn't turn off into Mesilla. The world of Las Cruces in 2114 was fast and sleek with only patches of real estate saved for the past, but the color and flavor of the southwest splashed over everything. Old Mesilla was one of those preserved treasured jewels of yesteryear.

Once we turned off Route 28, I felt transported from the present, twenty-second century, back to when the Butterfield Stagecoach stopped at La Posta where the Corn Exchange Hotel and restaurant provided an oasis for tired salesmen and visitors as they climbed out of the coach and rested or stayed for a while. I could imagine cowboys I had read about riding in on dusty horses to refresh themselves at the cantina and enjoy the beautiful terracotta Mexican-American culture. Flat roofed adobe buildings with rough dressed viga logs projecting through the roof to the outside were still the architecture design after hundreds of years.

"Jason," I whispered in reverence to the years of history the village represented, "is it possible that Grand-père could be hidden in one of these small buildings without people in neighboring stores and homes knowing about it?"

"I don't know, Honey," Jason said, his voice full of amazement peppered lightly with doubt. "But we have to check it out." He pulled into a parking space in the lot behind La Posta Restaurant where we sat in the car for a moment.

"We have to have some sort of plan," I said, knowing we had followed the sparkle-lead with nothing more than the name of a small village to go on.

We got out and walked along the sidewalk in front of the stores where the aroma of scented candle and strings of hanging red peppers mixed into a delicate southwestern perfume. The old Saint Albino church anchored the plaza at the opposite end and the stores flanked the square.

"Jason, look," I said as I pointed. "Some of those crystalized jalapeño granules are scattered there on the edge of the brick and concrete walk. They must have been swept off the walkway."

"That's right, Christy," Jason said as he studied the particles under his feet. "Good eye. I would never have seen them."

"Where did they—?" I drifted off as I traced the path the granules had taken.

"There's some more," he added as we inched along.

The last store where there was any trace of sprinkles boasted a window full of gleaming silver and turquoise squash-blossom necklaces. "I read," I smiled to myself at how many times I prefaced a statement with "I read...."

"What, Honey? You read what?"

I pointed to the beautiful jewelry. "The upside-down crescent is what the Navajo called the 'Naja.' It's said to protect the horse that has it on its bridal as well as the rider who wears one. First mentioned in the Bible in the book of Judges, the symbol found its way from the Middle East, through Spain and to the early native peoples in the new world."

"That's amazing," he said as we both stood and admired the display.

"Why would the crystals lead us to a jewelry store?" I wondered aloud.

"The trooper said some shop owner here in the village makes the crystalized jalapeño granules. Why not this store?" Jason studied the store front and reached for the door latch.

Inside, the store hummed with customers searching for a Charles Russell print of a fearless cowboy gripping the reigns of a bucking horse; the gleaming nuggets of Navajo jewelry and the fine crafted needlepoint bracelets of the Zuni tribe; or the woven Native American rugs and blankets draped over wooden sawhorses.

"May I help you?" a woman behind the counter asked.

"We're looking for someone," I began.

"You're Lady Applewait, aren't you?" she whispered, diverting her question from listening ears.

"Yes," I mouthed with a nod of my head. I touched the woman's hand and she came from behind the counter. I leaned my head in her direction and whispered, "We're looking for my grandfather."

"Sir Richly?" she questioned. "Why would he be in New Mexico? Our telecommunications messages have stated that he's in Maine. You're a long way from the Down East coast."

I looked at Jason and knew what I had to say. "My grandfather has been kidnapped. We had a lead he may be in Old Mesilla."

"Here, in my store?" she gasped, her faced turned ashen. "Are we in danger here?"

"I wish I could say you weren't," I said slowly.

Jason quickly added, "We just don't know, Ma'am. And, my name is Dr. Jason O'Reilly."

"I'm Faith Rodriguez," she offered with her hand to her chest as in a pledge of honesty.

"Does your name have any significance?" I asked her, hoping there was real faith behind her name.

"My family and I are Christians. My ancestors have been for hundreds of years."

"I was hoping you would say that. We are people of the Word as well, Faith," I told her. "I wish I could tell you that none of you are in danger, but the truth is, we have no idea who is involved, how many there are, and how dangerous they may be."

Faith took a deep breath and asked, "What can I do?"

"Are these the only rooms you have here? Where do you make and package the crystal product?" I was confused. How could they have another business out of this space?

Jason looked around as well. "Do you have a basement?"

"My husband, Manny, invented the **crystalized** jalapeño granules and makes them in a garage-factory near our home. As he has orders, he brings them in here for bookkeeping, tracking, packaging, and shipping since my staff handles those services all the time."

"So you have no basement?" Jason asked again.

"We don't mean to pry, Faith," I reassured her.

Faith smiled and patted my shoulder. "I know you're not prying. You're worried and I understand."

"No basement?" I chimed in.

"No—and yes," she began, her brow furrowed. "We were approached by the owners of the adjacent store. They wanted to rent our basement. Since we weren't using it, Manny said, 'Yes.' That was a few years ago. How long has your grandfather been missing?"

"Just a couple of days," I told her and turned to Jason. "How can a space rented years ago, have anything to do with all of this?"

"I don't know, Christy," Jason admitted his own bewilderment. "But remember, this is a mob connection we're following, not political."

"What's a mob?" Faith asked with a wide-eyed, innocent expression.

"Never mind that," Jason brushed off. "I shouldn't have brought it up."

"I'm sorry," I interrupted. "What is the store that rented your basement?"

Faith's eyes welled with tears. "It's has had many names over the years but has always been known as the store with the Billy the Kid connection."

I closed my eyes and shuddered. "Lucky Charlie's favorite outlaw."

CHAPTER 24

The Basement

The store that consistently boasted a relationship with Billy the Kid, sat of the southeast corner of the Plaza. It was the jail and courthouse in 1881, where the Kid, tried and sentenced to hang in the wild west of the eighteen-hundreds, actually walked.

"Jason, look," I said as we entered the old building made of adobe-mud bricks. "The windows are set into eighteen-inch thick walls. The lower level would be completely sound proof and isolated from the rooms above."

"This place was the capitol building when Mesilla was the capitol of the Arizona Territory," Jason offered. "A book in the hospital library told of men hammering out aspects of the Gadsden Purchase here."

"Yes, Sir," a man said as he approached Jason and me. "I heard you two talking about the Kid. After his sentencing they took him to the courthouse in Lincoln where he escaped. Doña Ana's sheriff, Pat Garrett, later tracked him down and shot him."

"Pat Garrett?" My head swirled as I tried to take in all that had happened. I studied the man for just a second. I had no time not to trust him. "You have a basement—right?"

"A basement?" he asked. "Look around. We have enough space; we don't need a basement."

"It looks wonderful," I soothed the clerk, not wanting to arouse his anger or suspicion.

The man brightened a bit but remained tense, his jaw clenched. "The display of hunting knives in front of you was made by a local man," he offered as he opened the case without taking his gaze from mine.

I tried to take his mind off our question about the basement for a moment. "This one is beautiful," I said.

"The handle is made of petrified bone with embedded accents of opalized wood." He ran his fingers over the hilt as if caressing a baby. "Every one of these superb blades is unique. No two are alike."

Jason joined in the admiration with a twinge of honest appreciation. "They are all magnificent."

Temporarily caught off task by the shinning swords and exquisite cutlery, I quickly refocused. "Do you store the additional inventory in the basement?"

The man looked at me, hard; his eyes seemed to bore a hole in mine. "The basement is not open to the public," he growled, his expression growing dark and flat.

Jason stepped in the gap between me and the man, like a wedge protecting me from the dangerous world. "We don't want any trouble. We just want to look around."

"Look around? The boss would kill me."

"Boss? You don't own this store?" I asked.

He looked around the room, like one searching for a hidden informant. "This whole place was purchased years ago by an organization out of New York, Charlie somebody is the CEO."

"Was the—CEO's name, Charles? He died years ago." I corrected and thought of Bedlum and his seeming legitimate and philanthropic group. "There's a new leader—or Don."

"Don?" the clerk said with a question on his face. "His name is Don?"

"Something like that." I stopped and thought of Barbara Cornwall. "We talked to his daughter just a few days ago, and she gave us permission to go into the basement to look for something that's missing."

"There's a staircase that goes down off the back workroom and another one that enters through a bunker or shed in the back of the building." The man seemed to shudder. "I never know who—or if anyone is down there."

"Thank you," I said as I finally exhaled. "Which way?"

The man made a small, silent gesture in the direction of an exit into a back hallway. Jason and I approached cautiously, slowly turned the door knob and looked down the stairs.

"The light is on," I whispered.

"The light seems to be on all of the time," the clerk said quietly behind us.

I jumped. I had anticipated something unexpected from the basement below us, not from the man behind us.

He put his index finger to his lips and motioned for us to continue on downstairs—silently. With hand gestures, he indicated he would remain on the retail floor.

The old, narrow wooden steps were uneven and steep, each tread a little different in height than the other. I felt unbalanced as I made my way down the sixteen rungs to the hard, polished earthen floor. We stopped and listened. The very thick walls were good insulators for heat, cold and sound. We heard nothing. Jason pointed left then right and shrugged.

I had no idea which way to go. I knew it could be dangerous in either direction. To the right, there was an alcove that led into a dark windowless room.

"The bunker," Jason mouthed and pointed to the left. He motioned for me to get behind him as we slowly moved on.

The lower level was a maze of rooms that stretched out under several of the stores above. It smelled dry and dusty down there, not at all like a musty old basement of the Midwest. New Mexico's semi-arid desert left no moisture for mold.

It was eerily silent down in the hand carved caverns of the underworld. The pounded dirt of the floor made for silent steps as we moved back deeper into the cellar. Rickety wooden shelves lined the walls scattered with dust-covered boxes and cans.

I stopped. Did I hear someone behind us? Who? How? There was no one to the right of us after we had descended the steps. We waited for a few seconds but heard no more. There was still no sound from the left.

I listened hard. I couldn't hear anything that sounded like Grand-père. Was he alright? Until a year ago, I had lived in a safe world. Down here under the desert floor, all sense of safety was finally shattered.

As we inched through the dust, our pace didn't match my rapidly pounding heart. I felt as terrified as I did the first time I walked through the gapping cavern of Howard Mountain and witnessed the atrocities there. How could any place so silent, scream at me so loudly from the dark corners?

Creeping slowly, the muscles in my legs began to ache. I was tense, with every inch of my body readied for fighting or fleeing. Suddenly, Jason raised his hand and signaled for us to stop.

When my anxiety settled a little and my heart stopped pounding in my ears, I was able to hear distant muffled voices.

"How long are we supposed to hold this guy?" A deep gruff voice asked.

"Let's just kill him," another voice snapped. "He cannot turn up before the election and that's still a long time from now."

I threw my hand to my mouth to muffle the screams of fear that wanted to escape. With only my grandfather in mind, I suddenly felt a fierce determination grip me and I stepped forward taking the lead. I could feel the presence of people not too much farther ahead.

Jason touched my arm and motioned for us to step into the shadows under a stairwell that led down from yet another store. There was a rustling behind us that stopped almost as abruptly as we did.

I knew we had no weapons with us. That hadn't really occurred to me before I was there to find Grand-père. I had anticipated calling authorities if we found him, not staging a heroic rescue. As I strained to see around the dimly lit space, it occurred to me, we were as trapped as Grand-père.

"Hey, Old Man," one of the men taunted. "In a minute, we'll find out what to do with you."

At that moment, a dark figure blocked the light from the window that was high in the room, near the ceiling. I nearly gaged on my own surprise. It was Daniel Washington.

"There you are, finally," the first man bellowed when Washington charged around the corner. "What're we supposed to do with this guy?"

"He really looks important, doesn't he?" Washington jeered. "Caged like a mad dog and drugged out of his mind."

I gasped. They drugged Grand-père?

"What's that?" The second man asked.

"Nothing," Washington barked. "You've been down here so long; the rats are talking to ya."

"No," the man protested. "It ain't nothin'. It's somethin'."

No one said anything more. Jason and I waited.

I felt movement—behind me—around me—where? The silence was deafening.

"Well look what I found," Washington hissed as he grabbed my wrist and dragged me out from under the stairs. He held a Henry long rifle, barrel pointing down, in his left hand.

Jason grabbed the animal's arm and pulled, trying to free me from his grip. Washington swiped Jason with the back of his hand and sent him smashing against the wall. He slid down the adobe surface and landed unconscious on the floor.

"Jason—no!" I screamed as Washington pulled me into the next room where Grand-père lay slumped on the floor.

"Screech!" What was that? A nonhuman sound filled the space down there, so many feet below the surface. An animal in strange clothing leaped between me and Washington, its eyes full of rage. He slammed my captor to the floor and leaped, his feet forming wide arches that spanned all the area around him.

"Raymar!" I shouted in amazement and relief.

The former hollow one crouched low; he was a mountain lion readying for attack. As Raymar held them at bay, Ivy Trudeau rushed in with her weapons drawn. Washington raised the rifle into firing position while the other two captors jerked their pistols from their belts. Ivy shot Washington in the knee before he could get a round off and delivered well-placed bullets to the other two evil ones in their shoulder and thigh. They dropped to the floor in astonishment.

"Where—" the mad dog, former Blue Guardsman began in fear and amazement. "Mr. B. said there would be no interference. He said no one would think of New Mexico."

The ugly little one with the shoulder wound, glared at Washington's humiliation and began to smirk. "So smart, no one will find him down here." He doubled up the other fist and lunged in my direction.

Raymar pounced on the man in one leap, a great cat with sharp and powerful reflexes. He tore at the man's bloody arm and opened his mouth as if to devour what remained of the loathsome one.

"No, Raymar!" I screamed, unable to face what he was about to do.

Instantly, Raymar stopped, looked at me and smiled. Ivy covered us with her firearm as Jason came to. I rushed to his side and threw my arms around him.

"Jason, I was so worried," I gasped.

"I'll be alright. I'll probably have a headache but—" he stopped as he looked over at my grandfather. "Let me check on Oliver."

"Grand-père," I called to him as I hurried over, knelt on the floor, and eased his head onto my knees. "Grand-père," I repeated.

He rolled his eyes slightly and a faint smile crossed his lips. "Christy, I—"

"Shh, shh," I urged for fear his words would use breath he didn't have to spare. "I don't want you to talk, Grand-père—please."

"Your grandmother—"

"I'll call Grand-mère—I promise—just as soon as I get back up on top again." Hugging him close to me, I tried hard not to cry and frighten him more than the whole experience already traumatized him. But, since I found him, I didn't want to let go, not even to call my grandmother.

Grand-père started to speak and then nodded weakly in agreement.

Jason felt my grandfather's pulse and lifted his eyelids to check his pupils. "They said he was drugged. His pulse is weak but seems to be rhythmic." He looked around at our situation, then at the mud brick walls of the rooms under the stores of Old Mesilla.

His eyes were sympathetic but insistent. "Christy, hurry back up to the store above and get help—police and an ambulance for Oliver."

"Ambulance?" I whispered and cast a darting glance at my grandfather. I couldn't pull myself away from him, even to call for the help he needed. I stood up and started to leave, then looked back. How could I leave them there?

"Tell them we need a transport for three gunshot wounded perpetrators too, Christy," Ivy added. "And hurry, Washington will probably lose his knee."

"Oliver will be all right, Honey," Jason assured me. "Your grandfather needs your help. I'll be here with him while you run upstairs for a few minutes. Just remember, it's really a miracle that we found him. That was the hard part."

I hurried back through the shadows of the cellar to the stairs and started up. It seemed darker and more sinister now than it had before. Then, I smiled to myself. I was beginning to feel again, to think more clearly and not out of fear, or as a response to danger. All the numbness was beginning to wear away. It was true. "Praise the Lord—Jason was right," I said aloud. "He has been found."

CHAPTER 25

Late June

Grand-père's room at Memorial Medical Center in Las Cruces was bright. Warm, bold splashes of color replaced the all-white décor of previous years.

I slipped into his room hoping not to awaken him. Ivy and Raymar were with me. When Grand-père's eyes opened to slits, I spoke to cheer him on. "You look better," I whispered close to his ear.

"Hi Sweetie," he began. A faint smile crossed his lips. "I may look better, but I feel crumpled, like an old piece of paper."

"I could lie just to make you feel better," I laughed. "But, an old piece of wadded up paper pretty much describes you."

Grand-père took my hand, "I talked to your grandmother already. She'll be here soon. Barbara Cornwall is flying her out."

"We could have no better friends than the Cornwalls," I agreed.

"We have so many good people around us, including you two," Grand-père said to Ivy and Raymar.

"Thank you, Sir," Raymar said as he offered his hand. "It is a privilege to serve you."

"You have already served me for years, Raymar. Your poetry and writings lift my spirits every time I read your works—Robert Gross," he said as he placed his hand on top of their handshake.

"Again, thank you Sir," Raymar said blushing a little. "It is strange for people to know who I am. As a hollow one, they didn't even see me unless I threatened to attack them."

My grandfather's eyes grew large. "I know I was drugged, but seem to remember a wolf-man flying through my dungeon cell."

"That was me," he admitted. "But I wouldn't really have devoured anyone. I just wanted them to think so."

"Even in my dazed state, that's what I was hoping," Grand-père's eyes twinkled. Then he turned to me. "Speaking of loyal friends, where is your doctor?"

I looked toward the door. "Jason is talking to *your* doctor."

"Is he going to spring me out of this place?"

"You're not in prison, Grand-père," I assured him.

"Funny, it feels like it," he said with a wry smile.

At that moment, the door popped open. "Are you still lying around here in bed, Oliver?" Grand-mère asked as she breezed in.

"Praise the Lord, the cavalry has arrived," he pulled the edge of the bedding back, sat up and started to put his feet over the edge of the mattress.

"Hold on there, Oliver," Jason warned as he came in the room behind my grandmother. "The results of all of the tests aren't in yet. There's still the Cranial-Graph feedback, to determine if Oliver's hit on the head, which resulted in his unconsciousness, will leave any lasting damage."

"When will that report be in? I have a campaign to get back to." Oliver Richly was a man of determination and acceptance of the role he played in history. Nothing would stop him for long.

The door opened again and a woman in a light blue, bamboo fabric business suit waked in. "Doctor, I have the results. Do you want to meet me in my office?"

Grand-père pulled himself up again and planted his feet flat on the floor. "Absolutely not," he demanded. "It's my head. I want to hear the outcome before you two physicians have a chance to spin it, making me out to be some invalid or something."

"Oliver, now get back into bed," Grand-mère ordered.

Grand-père glared. "I want to say, 'No, I will not,' Connie." He added in mocked surrender. "But I know you'll win anyway."

Grand-mère gave him a love pat on his knee. "Oh, stop and pull the covers up." We all assumed he would do as she asked.

"Sir Richly," Dr. Gayle Raddin began.

"Oliver," he insisted.

"Oliver, I just thought you'd want some privacy," the doctor began. "That's why I suggested my office."

"Privacy from my wife and granddaughter? Why?" he growled. "And, this fine woman is my granddaughter's bodyguard. The gentleman here," he pointed at Raymar, "can be the bodyguard to the world." Everyone laughed.

"It's your choice," she concluded, not seeming to hear all he said. She finally opened the patient record tablet in her hand. "The results indicate a small area of swelling which we can control with a skin-wicking application of Vascular Repair. We can teach you to treat any headaches with icy water and fist flexion therapy."

"No lasting damage?" I asked to make sure I had heard her correctly.

"None," she said and smiled a little, like her face had lost its elasticity. "You may want to take the flash train back home rather than fly. The pressure on your head will be less." Closing her tablet, she added, "If you have any questions, I'll be available. I'd like you to stay the night and get plenty of rest."

Grand-père waved her off. "I'd like to check out right after lunch. They say the food is good here."

"I can sign off on that—if you agree to call me this evening and again tomorrow afternoon." She sort-of smiled again. "That's for my own peace of mind. I won't have to explain how I let the next

President of the United States out of the hospital too soon, and he collapsed at one of his speaking events."

Jason put his hand on my shoulder and gave me a reassuring squeeze. Then to Dr. Raddin he added, "Thank you, Doctor. Remember, I'll be traveling with Oliver."

Ivy patted her sidearm in a habit of assured authority. "Dr. O'Reilly will be there for Oliver's medical needs, and I will be there as well." She grinned a little. "Raymar will be there to cover our backs."

"And, I'll be there, too," I said as I looked at my grandparents with love and pride. I am so thankful that I still have them. If Silas Drummond hadn't broken the silence, they would have entered the never-ending-sleep at the end of December 2112 and never awakened. If we hadn't had friends like the Cornwalls, Jason and I would never have reached Grand-père in time. I could see the Lord's hand at work at every turn.

CHAPTER 26

Down the Hall

Five colorful rooms down the hall, Ward Stoner also lay on his hospital bed, itching for release. A young doctor with dark hair and large glasses came in. He was tall, with down-turned lips that made him appear to wear a perpetual frown.

"Hey, Doc, when do I get out of here?" Stoner barked as usual.

"Mr. Stoner—"

"That's Chief Inspector young man."

Doctor Martinez's expression didn't change. "There are no inspectors in here, just doctors and patients."

Instantly, Stoner came up on his elbow and glared into the physician's eyes. "Mister, wherever I am, there are only Inspectors and suspects."

"I'm under suspicion for what?" the doctor managed to raise one eyebrow.

"For being arrogant," Stoner snapped back. "Now, discharge me, or I'll walk out on my own recognizance."

The doctor rolled his eyes. "You're not posting bail, Sir."

"No, but you will be if I don't get out of here soon." The veins in his forehead bulged and his eyes grew large.

"Well, well what's all the yelling about," Chalky Boone called out as she breezed into the room.

"I am not yelling," Stoner bellowed.

"Then protest at a lower decibel, please," she said as she smiled. Turning to the doctor she added, "Could I please talk to the Inspector—alone?"

"My time—"

Stoner looked at him beneath hooded eyes. "Your time is no more important than my time, Doctor."

Dr. Martinez only stared for a moment and then added, "I have to see a patient across the hall. I can be back in five minutes."

"And charge them for a visit, I'm sure," Stoner sneered.

Dr. Martinez only smiled in his unique, starched way.

Stoner didn't look at his lieutenant, but he directed his question in a mellow tone. "What are you doing here?"

"Nice of you to ask," she said and smiled. "I'm here to check up on you and see how long the doctor thinks it will be before you can get out of here."

"If you can get that information, you're a better man than I."

Chalky's cheeks flared. "In case you haven't noticed, I'm not a man."

"Oh, I noticed," Ward said as he allowed his fingertips to touch Chalky's hand. A warm silence, like an August breeze, filled the room.

She placed her hand on top of his. "Ward, really, how are you feeling?"

"Did you change the subject for a reason?" He said and actually smiled—something he rarely did unless his son Christopher was around.

Flustered, she babbled as she smiled. Embarrassed, she turned away. "No, no—of course not. I just—"

"I know—I haven't been very warm and friendly, let alone—"

"Warm and friendly?" she said as she whirled back to face him, although she seemed unable to look into his eyes. "No—no one could accuse you of being friendly. But—Ward," she groped for words that didn't seem to flow freely. "I don't know what I'm allowed to say." Her hands were shaking and tears gathering in the corners of her eyes.

"Allowed to say? Chalky, you've never needed permission to say what you're thinking." Ward reached for her hand again.

"About work, yeah, but—Ward—never about anything personal." She permitted him to take her hand in his and not pull away.

"Can we change that rule?" he asked, still mellow even when the doctor came back in the room. "Ah, the great healer." He actually smiled.

Dr. Martinez stopped in full stride. "Well, it sounds like you're feeling better."

"I am," Stoner stated as politely as he could. "So, when can I expect to get out of here?"

"I will sign you out now," he said as he pulled a pen from his lab jacket pocket. "The wound is healing nicely and your blood count is good. If you take it easy," he stopped and looked hard at the Inspector, "and I do mean easy, light desk work only, you should be okay. Check in with your doctor at home."

"Yes, Sir," Ward said and saluted. "Boone," he barked in his usual way. "Make flight arrangements for us. We're going home."

CHAPTER 27

Escape

My grandfather was still a little weak. But with Grand-mère's help and coaching, we were able to arrive at the flash-train station twenty minutes before departure.

Grand-père's eyes brightened when he saw Jason and I prepare to board with them. "You two are going to take the train with us?"

"Oliver, I told your physician I would travel with you. So—here we are. We hired more bodyguards. They'll travel in the next car. Ivy and Raymar will be with us."

I tried to joke and treat all that had happened with some humor. "You certainly didn't think I would let you two go by train with Jason while I flew home, did you?" I said, but inside I knew the danger Grand-père had been in, that we all had been in. "This is a family trip back to the Central Zone. I even brought some cards—if you want to play."

"Maybe, Sweetheart," Grand-mère patted my hand after I helped her up the train steps.

I noticed Raymar's usual constant hyper-vigilance. This time it made me feel safe. Ivy scanned the front and back of the car, apparently checking each exit.

As we walked through the passenger car, I studied each face and wondered if any of those on board were a further danger to Grand-père. I had to be vigilant and not worry at the same time. How was I going to do that?

The porter directed us to a private car much the same as the one Jason and I took to El Paso. "Here we are, Sir Richly," he said as he opened the door and carried in a pitcher of water which he placed on a side bar. "The glasses are there for your use," he pointed to the gleaming glass shelves behind the bar.

"Thank you," Grand-père said and reached in his pocket to tip the man.

"No, Sir," the porter said as he put up his hand to decline the gratuity. "I don't have extra money to contribute to your election campaign, but I can help by serving you at my pleasure."

I saw Grand-père look at the porter's name plate. "Thank you, Ronald." He patted the man's shoulder. "I really appreciate it."

Ronald smiled broadly. "It is the least I can do for freedom's sake."

"It sounds like the most you can do," I suggested. "And, we do appreciate it."

We settled into the comfortably sleek, poly-infused sawdust framed chairs, the same as in the south-bound car a few days past. Ivy sat off to the side. She seemed to be with us and on guard at the same time. Raymar was silent and sat at the bar. We were all quiet, almost like we were afraid to speak for fear the peaceful moment would go away. At least, that was my experience.

"What is our next event?" Grand-père asked. "I've been a little tied up."

"Oh, Oliver," Grand-mère moaned. "That was awful."

"Sorry about that," Grand-père said as he grinned, seeming to return gradually to his former jovial self.

I glanced at my 281 Palm device. "You've missed several rallies, but that couldn't be helped." I felt my head begin to pound from the stress of the last days. I rubbed my forehead and closed my eyes.

"Headache?" Jason asked. "Go over to the sink at the bar and run your hands under the cold water like Dr. Raddin suggested. Then come back over here, sit by me and close your eyes for a while."

"That sounds like a great idea," Grand-mère agreed. "We should all rest and start again in a little while."

Ivy crossed her arms and settled in with a healthy measure of alertness. "I'll keep my eyes open for all of you," she offered.

I did as instructed. Raymar ran the water for me until it was icy cold. He put his fingers under the stream and nodded in his silent way. Putting my hands under the frigid water, I held them there until I could no longer take the cold. When I pulled them back, my fingernails were purple.

"My head does feel a little better," I admitted and let Raymar dry my hands with a towel made warm in a special small heater mounted on the wall. When I went back over to where we were all sitting, I snuggled up in the chair beside Jason. Leaning back, I let my feet lift off the floor as I cozied into a tranquil space in my head.

A few hundred miles passed in a streak. I kept my eyes closed, hoping I wouldn't disturb anyone else if I stirred.

Suddenly, our whole world was shattered. Tossed out of my chair, legs and arms flew around me by the percussion created by a large impact. We were on the floor but the floor wasn't where it belonged. We were more on the side or wall than down. I heard the moans of my loved ones around me and smelled the distinct odor of sweet hot metal. The ssss of hissing steam came rushing into my awareness.

"Out!" I shouted with the small amount of voice and breath I could rouse. "Get out! Smoke!"

"Christy?" Jason whispered with a faint raspy voice. "What happened?"

"I don't know," I said as I tried to clear my head. "But it sounds like something is still escaping. It smells like gunpowder or dynamite, as my books described it. There's also something leaking. Maybe gas but I can't smell it."

"I know," Jason said as he tried to standup in the tilted train car. "The odor of gunpowder is overpowering. I learned to identify it in medical school. We'd better get out of here just in case something blows."

Ivy shook her head and pawed at the air for something to grab hold of. Finding the edge of a chair, she pulled herself up and quickly checked for her firearm.

"My grandparents?" I gasped, realizing that I hadn't heard their voices.

Then, I heard Grand-mère's voice first. "We're here, Christy." She was silent for a second. "Oliver, are you all right?"

"Yes, Connie," he groaned. "This sure has been a challenging trip."

"Okay," Jason said urgently, "let's get out of here, but be careful. Where you step may not be where it's safe to place your foot. We seem to be tipped over."

I struggled to my feet and worried about my dear ones. How were we going to get them safely out with everything on its side?

"Grand-père, can you stand?" He was not only my beloved grandfather he was the candidate for president in the *1787-Constitutionalists* party. I was overwhelmed.

Grand-mère's voice was both loving and insistent. "Oliver, you must stand so you can help me get up."

"Coming dear," he agreed as he struggled to his feet.

The hissing sound had increased. I looked at Jason and Ivy. They both nodded. Raymar tilted his head like an animal stretching his senses beyond their range.

"Let's move out of the train—" Jason began and seemed to be searching for words. "They will have to get this car, and maybe many cars, back on the track. We might be able to help others who are struggling, so, let's hurry."

I looped my arm around both grandparents as they wrestled with upturned chairs and broken glass. Jason shepherded all three of us as we groped our way toward any outside opening we could find. Ivy went ahead of us with her firearm ready. Raymar, as usual, fell in behind, protecting all of us from anyone or anything that might approach us from the rear. The door at the side-end of the car would have opened out to the entry but it was now on the bottom of the upturned railcar. Our next hope for escape was a window. I wondered if we could push one of the tempered panes out. We had to do something. I could hear shouting coming from other cars.

"Listen," Grand-père said as he stopped and listened.

"Screaming," Grand-mère agreed.

"No," he insisted. "I heard gun fire."

Ivy didn't look back but added, "I heard it too, Oliver," she said. "Let's just keep looking for a way out."

"Here, Ivy," Jason shouted. "I think we can break this window out." Immediately, he pulled himself upside down by the decorative bars that flanked the window and began to kick at the shatterproof glass. When it popped out, he stuck his head up through the opening.

Crack!

"Jason, no," I screamed. "Get down!" When I heard the sound of the same round that had pierced the window of Campaign Headquarters I began to panic.

Ivy grabbed his pant legs and pulled him down. "You're struck." Her eyes calmly scanned the opening created by the kicked-out window.

I felt sick. Blood was dripping down Jason's forehead and soaking into his shirt.

"Christy," Ivy spoke firmly. "See if there is any water still in the sink pipes and a clean towel. Then she grabbed my arm, "Christy— he'll be okay if the wound is cleaned right away."

Jason patted my arm. "She's right, Honey. Get a couple of clean, wet towels and one to pat the wound dry."

"I'll help you," Raymar volunteered.

"What happened out there?" Grand-père demanded. "What in the world is going on—again?"

"Someone doesn't want you to be the new president," Ivy stated flatly.

I was trembling but had to help clean Jason's wound as he asked. The bar was lying on the end of the car. "I hope I can drain out some water," I said aloud and then wished I had been silent. I had to stay strong for everyone, or at least appear strong. I was so afraid; I didn't know if I could convince myself. We were all in serious jeopardy. If we didn't know who was firing at us, how could we stay safe?

With a towel bunched up under the faucet, Raymar turned the faucet handle. I held my breath. A stream of cool water flowed out and soaked the cloth so much I had to gather another clean towel beneath it.

Ivy blotted the towel on Jason's head with the rest of the cleansing water, in obvious haste. Finally, Raymar gathered up the wet cloths and tossed them in the corner.

"Okay," Ivy announced with a firm booming voice. "We need another quick plan."

Grand-père climbed over the chairs and fallen table. "We had just passed over a bridge just before the dynamite and crash." He looked back and forth along the side of the car but there was no way to see out. "It just might be—." He hurried into the lavatory at what had been the back of the car and forced the folding door open. "Yes!" he shouted. "All of you come here quickly."

We all crowded into the small bathroom, just large enough for a stool and corner positioned sink. We all looked up.

"Don't look up," he insisted. "Look down!"

Beneath our feet, the scene from the overturned window, the one that would have been on the north side of the car, was now of the tracks and the river below. "We're still over the bridge. I knew it. Force that window open, if you can Raymar."

Raymar squeezed into the tiny room and studied it quickly. "I think it will just open, since there's no pressure from below holding it closed." He quickly slid the sash to the side. The aroma of gunpowder, mingled with the peaceful sound of river birds, drifted into the car.

"Quick—down and out," Ivy threw up an arm to block our path. "You'll have to drop into the water. Can anyone not swim?"

"We have all been swimming all of our lives," Grand-mère reported. "How about you Jason? Raymar?"

"Sure, I can swim," Jason agreed. Raymar, the quiet one, nodded in agreement.

Oliver looked at my grandmother and then at me. "Jason, you'll have to jump in first, then Connie, and then you, Christy, so you can both help your grandmother if necessary. Then Ivy, because she has the gun—then I'll jump."

"It all sounds good except the last part," Ivy said. "Oliver you go before me, just in case someone storms into this car."

"No—"

"Yes," Ivy insisted firmly. Her tone indicated no compromise.

"Go Jason, fast," Ivy pushed. "Christy—Ma'am," she called out as the next jumper stepped up.

Raymar, then Grand-père followed in a matter of seconds. Ivy dropped in last. The water was warm, but we all splashed wildly, probably from the shock of jumping and hitting the water from high over the river.

"Swim!" Ivy ordered. "To the opposite shore," she redirected.

"Oliver," Jason said as he swam beside my grandfather. "I'll swim with you, and Christy will swim with Connie. Raymar and Ivy will pull back-up detail."

We splashed and swam and made our way to the shore. It wasn't far, but after the crash our energy had drained from our bodies. As least, mine had. I hoped no one had seen us escape. If they had seen us jump in, they could be waiting for us when we waded out of the water.

As we neared the opposite edge, we came up in the shadows under the bridge. Panting and panicked, we looked at each other for any stress and obvious reassurance.

Jason went over to Grand-père, lifted his wrist, and took his pulse. "I think we're pretty good, considering all." Shaking his head and smiling, he added, "Oliver, you are amazing."

"And, to think," Grand-mère chimed in, "they wanted to do us in over a year ago. They said we were too old to live."

"How about you, Connie?" Jason asked as he reached over to check her pulse as well. Then he reported, "You two are unbelievable."

"Maybe we should be safe and call Dr. Raddin and report in," Grand-mère suggested. "I know you're okay Oliver, but I'd feel better if we told her about all of this."

"No," Ivy snapped. "We don't know who else knew that the presidential candidate was on the flash-train, but we do know Dr. Raddin knew it. She's the one who suggested it."

"Ivy," I gasped, "you don't suspect the physician of anything do you? How could she have caused a train wreck?"

"I don't like to think about it either, Christy," Jason stated. "But our main concern is for our safety. We're soaked. We'll have to find dry clothes as soon as possible."

"We can't all go into the stores," Ivy stated emphatically. "Oliver, I am sure your poster is all over town. It pops up on mass communication screens every fifteen minutes. But, no one will recognize me. The village is right over there, past the bridge." She turned in the direction of town. "I'll go buy all of us some clothes. You might have to wear wet shoes. If I bought six pairs of shoes, it would be too obvious that we just walked out of the river."

"Okay," I agreed. But. inside I was scared, for myself and for my loved ones. If I couldn't trust Dr. Raddin, I doubted my ability to know who to trust.

Ivy looked around the side of the bridge abutment again. "It looks like the building on the left side of the street, just over the bridge, is empty. Make your way there, one or two at a time. I'll bring the clothes there."

"All right," both of my grandparents responded in unison.

When Ivy left, I suddenly felt cold, vulnerable. Maybe my helplessness was because she had taken the sidearm that protected us all with her. I had seen pictures of guns in the books I had read, but had never seen one in person. Could the very idea of a firearm make me feel safe?

Jason took my hand and massaged the soft spot between my thumb and index finger. I felt some warmth return and began to feel safe again. Holding my hand tightly, he stretched up tall and looked past the bridge. "It looks safe—but then, we thought the train would be safe too."

Grand-père squared his shoulders and reached out for Grand-mère's hand. "Connie, hold your head up high. Walk with dignity and not like your drawers are soaked."

We all laughed as they started up the little hill to the pavement. I counted to twenty. Jason kissed me and, with my hand still in his, we walked up the little embankment to the street above. There was much more traffic on the road in that little village than in Capitol City, where few people owned their own cars. We cautiously darted across the street, walked casually along the sidewalk, then slipped in through the worn, faded door that Grand-père had left ajar.

Inside, the large, empty room was dark. I hate dim, dark places and have a need to shine light on it all. A few paces more and we stepped into a room with a wall of large windows. The sun was shining brightly in there, creating a greenhouse effect. My grandparents were standing in the brightest sunrays, hugging, and rubbing warmth into each other's backs with gentle strokes, like kittens warming themselves in the sun. It was almost like scenes from years past, so familiar to me, of Grand-père protecting Grand-mère and she nurturing him.

Soon, Raymar slipped in the door. He said nothing but began the restless and stealthy prowl he always exercised in new spaces.

Raymar was the same as always. I wondered if life in general would ever be the same as before for him or for any of us. But then, maybe the same is not what was best either. I didn't want to go back to a life without feelings. And, Raymar would not have wanted to go back into the hills and forests and live as a hollow man, with anger as his only emotion. To feel, to love, to be free to make our own choices requires a lot in return. The past was free from concern, by being free from fully living. I was learning that true freedom comes at a very high price.

CHAPTER 28

Worn-In

It seemed like hours, but it really wasn't. Ivy came into our little hothouse with bags of clothing within a half-hour.

"There was a re-sale shop up the street so I got our things there." She stopped with a sheepish expression on her face. "I am so sorry to give you used clothing, but I thought there would be fewer questions at the Worn-In Shop," she apologized.

"Not worn-out—worn-in," Grand-mère mused. "I like that," she added and reached out her hand. "I'll be very happy to wear them."

"You've given so many clothes to the needy," I reminded her. "Now you get to be the one on the receiving end."

"I couldn't be more blessed," Grand-mère said as she smiled. She took the clothes and stepped into the next room.

"Thank you, Ivy." I too was thankful for dry clothes and joined my grandmother in our private changing room of pealing walls and the stench of rat dropping.

"Isn't the boudoir lovely?" my gracious grandmother said as she waved her arms around like a model displaying her products.

I changed quickly, zipped up my pants and smoothed my hair with my fingers. "That's the best I can do."

"You look lovely as always, dear."

"You're just saying that because we're related and any comeliness may be inherited," I teased.

"You're right on that, Christy," Grand-père agreed as we came out of our "fancy" changing room.

Jason and Raymar looked dry at a minimum. On the other hand, "interesting" may better describe their appearance. Their clothing was so miss-matched, I wondered if their strange attire would soon give us away.

"I'm not saying you two look bad, but Jason if you and Raymar would switch shirts you would look less like escaped prison inmates who had just stole clothes off a clothes line," I offered as a strong suggestion.

"A clothes line?" Ivy questioned.

"We still hang our clothes to dry on a rope stretched between two trees out in the mountains," Raymar said quietly. "Hence—a clothes line."

Ivy smiled briefly at all of us. "Clothes line is it?" Then her expression fell as she addressed the serious issue at hand. "We'll have to keep moving—fast. They must have discovered by now that Oliver escaped."

I sighed and resigned myself to the situation we were in. "Actually, for one minute, I had forgotten about all of that."

"A nice vacation from the mess of our new reality," Jason sighed as he put his arm around my waist and squeezed.

"While I was out," Ivy began as she pulled hats out of another sack, "I contacted Barbara Cornwall. She was the only one I could think of with the financial means to help us out of this—and someone we can trust."

"And?" I asked. I hadn't thought about how we were stuck in the empty building. The walls had seemed like a solution. Now they were part of the problem. Once we would go outside, we would be at risk of capture again.

"Obviously, she can't send an airplane from New York in time to get us out of this one."

"Therefore?" I asked again.

Ivy looked around at each of us "She has business connections here in New Mexico. A helicopter can land on the roof of this building in twenty minutes."

Jason's eyes snapped to attention and studied Ivy hard. "She has a business relationship with people down here?"

Ivy nodded. "Yes, that's right."

"I imagine she has business contacts all over the country," Grand-père added.

Suddenly, I knew what Jason was getting at. "The head of the New York mafia, Alister Bedlum and his ancestors have done business in New Mexico for nearly two centuries. The mob seemed to like the idea of rubbing shoulders with the ghost of Billy the Kid. It somehow gave them power by association. Ivy, the mafia bosses? That's Barbara's family."

"But Christy," Grand-mère protested. "You said that Barbara is a true patriot. She wants to blot out the mistakes and mayhem caused by her father and all the Bedlum fathers in the past."

"I know—I know." None of it made any sense to me either.

"Christy," Jason reminded me, "that has been Barbara's problem all of her life—living down the sins of her father. Her mother has to be in hiding from him."

"You're right," I agreed.

"Christy," Grand-père came over and put his arms around me. "There comes a time when we could run out of friends if we begin to trust no one."

Raymar had been silent, but he too had sat around the table at the Citadel in New York City. He had an animal's sense of danger and the intuition to identify a friend. "Barbara Cornwall is a good woman," he stated decidedly.

I heard the quiet whir of a six-blade helicopter overhead and realized that Jason, Grand-père and Raymar Goring were all correct. "Okay, we take the flight home. I'll trust again."

Ivy snapped her fingers. "Listen up. I don't know how much time we have, but I'll just say—very little. While you all changed out of those wet clothes, I poked around for another way out. It appears that this building had been an old furniture factory. There are huge freight elevators in the center of the building. The elevators operated on electricity. There are also smaller lifts that operate manually, like old dumb-waiter systems, used to move small amounts of goods and material from one floor to another."

I felt a surge of hope creep up from the center of my being. "Dumb waiters don't need electricity or other means of energy?"

"Just muscle," Ivy said. "We can manually pull the ropes and lift each other to the roof." She clapped her hands together. "Now, let's get at it."

We quickly fell in line behind her and followed as she led us to the center of the building. She lifted a three by four-foot door in the wall and stepped aside. "We'll have to have the women go first because we'll need the men's upper-body strength below to lift the men last."

"What about the last man?" I asked. "Who will get him out?"

"Oliver and I can pull Jason out last from above," Ivy said as she motioned for Grand-mère to crawl up into the little lift.

"No," Raymar countered, "I will go last. I can shinny up the rope on my own if I have to. I do it all the time back home."

"Thank you, Raymar," Ivy said as she patted him on his back. Turning to my grandmother she said, "I guess I'm most worried about you, Connie."

My grandmother looked at me and winked. At seventy-five years old, she and Grand-père still danced together, walked several miles daily and ran up and down their stairs at home many times a day. Preparing to crawl into the lift, she stepped on Jason's knee as he knelt on the other, grabbed hold of the inner top of the lift and pulled herself up and into the small space of the dumb waiter. She crawled around on her knees, turned, and sat down on the floor of the lift with a big smile on her face.

"Fantastic!" I yelled and gave her a big thumbs-up. "You showed us how to do it Grand-mère."

One by one we slipped into the little cubby and rose to the roof. Lastly, Raymar grabbed the rope, and hand-over-hand he lifted himself to the tar paper covered flat area above. A large copter waited on top with the blades till spinning. We crouched, hurried to the open door, and quickly boarded. Before we could lift off, the sound of bullet fire shattered the sky.

"Close the door!" the piolet shouted.

Ivy slammed it close. It was easier to hear without the sound of the motors from outside. "The sides and glass are bullet proof," she assured us.

Ting, ting—two more rounds glanced off the hull. I held my breath as we lifted off and rose into the sky, first a few feet, then, the copter became God's might hand, snatching us up to Heaven. I exhaled.

CHAPTER 29
Still late June 2114

The helicopter was flying high, far above any ability for gun fire to pierce the cabin. I felt relieved for the moment. The sky was a color of blue rarely seen on the ground where a canopy of clouds blocked the beauty overhead. I couldn't help wonder what else would happen before Election Day.

November 3, 2114 was a little over four months away when our great country would vote for a new president. We had been living under a quasi-right-of-succession to the presidency, not under constitutional law, just a ruling-class decision of what they thought was best for the "little people." People we talked to were excited about the election, but I wondered how much they really knew about any of it, the election process or even their own rights as citizens.

"I am way out of the stream of things," Grand-père admitted. "I have no idea what our next political event is."

"The dates are a little tentative," I told him. "You were missing and we had no idea when—or if you would be found," I answered cautiously and studied his face. "You do know the danger you were in, don't you?"

Grand-père scratched his head. "Yes—in retrospect I do. Drugged when they grabbed me, I remained under the influence of chemicals the entire time. Now, hearing all you have told me, I see I was in a lot of danger."

"Oh, Oliver," Grand-mère whispered as she linked her arm in his, "you could have died."

"But, I didn't Connie," he said as he patted her hand.

Raymar sat in hyper-aware silence then asked, "Did you see their faces when they first took you?"

My grandfather's face grew taut and an unfamiliar scowl crossed his face. "No—none." His brow furrowed, "But—dots. I saw three dots on a man's hand, between his thumb and forefinger. It looked like they were punctured into the skin with ink."

"Tattoos," I gasped when my words tumbled out of my mouth.

"Tattoos?" Ivy asked. "What are tattoos?"

Raymar rolled up the sleeve of his T-shirt. An angel, drawn in blue and white ink with outstretched wings, descended from his shoulder to about four inches above his elbow. "This brand on my arm distinguishes the hollow people who want good for our people and those who just want to destroy everything in their path."

"Raymar," I said as I lightly touched the drawing, "I had no idea."

Jason studied the ink carefully. "Does anyone ever get infection from the punctures?" Rubbing his fingers over the emblem he added, "It looks like tiny puncture wounds."

"They are Dr. O'Reilly," Raymar said with a slight smile. "Yes, you didn't ask, but, yes—they do hurt as the needles go in, but we don't get infected. Infection is prevented with the reintroduction of the old medication, mercurochrome."

"Mercurochrome?" Jason asked in surprise? "Where could you have possibly gotten mercurochrome? The government banned it over a century ago. The mercury can be deadly."

Raymar smiled again. "There is an old hospital, buried now in the bramble and overgrowth near the foot of the mountains I lived in. In the old pharmacy, I found medication, bandages, and splints—all of the things my people have needed."

"But Raymar, some of those medications would have expired," Jason's eyes were wide. He appeared startled.

Raymar pulled his shirt sleeve back into place. "It was our belief that expired medication was better than none at all."

Jason shook his head. "Not always."

Raymar sat back and closed his eyes. "Then, the spirit that hovered over the valley beneath us and whistled in the caves we sought shelter in, surely must have been with us."

"So—" Grand-mère drew out slowly, "the three tattooed dots represented something to the evil ones who captured you. Some sort of club or fraternity."

I didn't like the sound or idea of a fraternity, as if the gangsters who kidnapped my grandfather were just young men interested in an education and a good time. But there was something I could do.

"I'll contact Marge Cummings at the library and see if she can find out something for us." I checked Holly for the time in Capitol City. "Marge will be there. Maybe we'll have an answer by the time we get home." I pulled my 281 Palm Device from my pocket. "I hope the river water didn't damage it," I said holding it up to the light. Instantly, I brought Marge's hologram into the helicopter's cabin.

"Hi everyone," Marge shouted out with enthusiasm. "I hadn't heard back from you Christy, but the news has already broken that Sir Richly was rescued."

"The news?" Grand-père shouted. "They knew about my abduction?"

"Yes and no," Marge began. "They found out that you had been missing, at the same time they learned you had been rescued."

"Oh, good," Grand-père said with a deep sigh. "People may have doubted the strength of my campaign if they had heard that I was only taken."

Jason nodded in agreement. "And, if they found out there was no trace to your whereabouts."

I shuddered at the thought. "The story now comes from a position of strength. Even though you were taken, you're coming out as a superhero that broke free from your captors, and captured them in the process."

"Wow," Grand-mère grinned, "I've been living with Superman and didn't even know it." She grinned sheepishly. "Well, maybe I suspected it when I would occasionally hear the telephone booth door fly open."

All of us who had access to books, films and graphic novels laughed; Marge joined in on the stress-relieving fun. I felt a moment of relaxation. "Ivy, I'll loan you my stash of comic books."

"Comic books?" Ivy asked.

Raymar smiled. "You'd be surprised at what we found in the old hospital."

"No, I wouldn't," Jason joined in. "I have an old wing of a hospital too, with a well shelved library."

"Marge," I got serious again, "I need some research."

"I would be honored to help," she agreed.

"Marge, Oliver here," Grand-père chimed in. "I saw three marks on one of my captors. Raymar Goring here tells us it's a tattoo and has a special meaning."

"Robert Gross is there with you?" she asked with the enthusiasm of a reader encountering her favorite author.

"Yes, Ma'am," Raymar laughed. "I'm here, too." Then, he quickly rerouted the conversation back to the need for research. "Marge, we need some information on a very small but unique tattoo."

"Yes, my friend," Grand-père leaned forward and rested his forearms on his knees. "The tattoo consisted of three equally spaced dots, in triangular formation, inked into the soft spot between his thumb and index finger."

"Okay, I'll get right on it," she agreed. "Anything else? I am here to serve you."

"Thanks, Marge," I added. "Get back to us when you know something."

"Agreed." Her hologram dissolved leaving the cabin dim again.

We were all quiet except for the silent hum of deep thoughts that screamed in my ears. The energy level was mounting as strained energy erupted.

"I'm going to be grandma to all of you now," Grand-mère spoke softly. "I know we are all wound up, but like old watches our mainsprings will snap if we don't unwind a little." She smoothed her hair and leaned over on my grandfather's shoulder. "Let's try to rest. There will be plenty to do when we get home."

"Once we pull into Capitol City and gather again around our table in Oakwood, we'll have to hit the ground running," Grand-père added.

Each person settled into their own comfortable spot. I leaned back into the seat and curled myself into the cozy security of Jason's shoulder. I felt at home there and in a foreign land at the same time. How long had it been since Jason and I had been able to snuggle up together? It didn't matter that I understood the reasons for our growing distance. We had both been through so much and we went through it all, right out in the middle of the action, with no privacy.

He wrapped his arms around me and pulled me close. I felt safe for the moment but—there was something so different. His skin still smelled like expensive men's cologne but now, mixed with river water and the stale odor of used clothing, it was different. In his arms, he felt like a familiar stranger. Had we left our relationship wilt from lack of time just for us? Would we be able to nurture what had started to grow, or was it too late? Maybe the roots had not run deep enough to stand strong during the hard times. As I pressed deeper into Jason's arm, I wondered and worried before I finally gave up and fell asleep.

CHAPTER 30

Doubt

It was so good to be back home. And yet, home was different, smaller than I had remembered. Jason and I had been from one coast to the other and states and their zones in between. Now, we were enjoying the warm July day, with the sky so blue it took my breath away. Summer flowers bloomed everywhere in the town square and around the parameter of the gazebo. How could I put my finger on the difference, when it had no name and resisted description? It just was. Ever since Grand-père's kidnapping; my being the target of a gunman; our train wreck; and our escape by jumping into the river, my safe-and-same world was shattered.

Jason had picked me up at the Indian River Apartments and we rode the few miles to Oakwood, to my grandparents' home, mostly in silence.

"What's wrong, Honey?" Jason asked as he pulled up in front of Grand-père's house with its wonderful large porch. "You've been so quiet."

How could I tell him how I really felt? "I don't know," was all I could say. I was telling the truth. I didn't know myself what was wrong, or if anything was. Things had changed. Jason seemed distant, or I was the one who was distant from him. I didn't know that either.

"Do I need to worry? Is there something wrong—with *us?*" he asked as he took my hand.

"Us? Are we an 'us?' We haven't talked about you and me for a long time, Jason." I didn't physically pull away but felt withdrawn within myself.

Jason released my hand and looked out of the window. "I guess I assumed—" his voice sounded heavy and hurt like it came from a place inside him I hadn't heard before.

"Christy!" Grand-mère called from the wide front porch. "Hurry, we're about to begin." She waved her large white apron at us. "Your grandfather just took steaks off the grill."

"Steak? Wow! I think Rachel Claudette must have inspired your menu," I said as Jason and I got out and walked up to the house.

My conversation with Jason stopped. But, deep inside, I had so many questions—so many things I needed to sort out. My internal conversation had only gotten started. But it would have to wait.

Grand-mère shepherded us up the steps and into the house with a wave of that apron. "There's a lovely salad and cookies for dessert."

"Sounds wonderful, Connie," Jason said as we walked through the entry and living room.

The chairs around the table in my grandparents' dining room were full of friends and family. Ivy and Raymar sat beside my parents, then Jason and I. Sean McDermott. Carl and Silvia Brunner and their son Michael were opposite us, with my grandparents at the head and foot of the table. Everyone seemed to be in their place. However, one chair was empty beside Michael.

"Ah, the last one," Grand-mère announced as she jumped up when the doorbell rang.

"Who else?" I asked. As I turned, I saw a stooped and shuffling Silas Drummond drag into the dining room. His eyes were dull and sharply etched lines dug into his face.

"Silas!" I was shocked and could not hide it. "Are you well?"

"Yes, Christy, yes, I'm fine," he answered slipping into the empty chair across from me.

When Grand-père announced that he would offer prayer, Jason reached for me. His hand felt warm in mine. When everyone else had their head bowed, I watched Jason. He finally opened one eye and winked. As Grand-père said, "Amen," Jason squeezed my fingers gently. I felt my cheeks grow warm and rosy. I wondered if anyone else noticed. What was going on with me?

"Oliver," Silvia's eyes sparkled with wonder, "these steaks look great. I know the food police don't patrol in Oakwood, so we're all safe. We haven't had steak at our house in months. Carl is on a chicken binge."

Raymar didn't look up from his plate, but cut his meat, placed a forkful is his mouth and closed his eyes in a swoon. "It is very good, Sir." He sliced slowly into the meat again and watched the juices run onto his plate. "We are used to eating berries and fruit in the forest and mountains, and what rabbits we can catch."

"Even Robert Gross?" I asked without thinking.

"Yes," he answered as he looked up, "Robert Gross has been locked in the body of the hollow one, Raymar Goring, all of his life."

I wished I hadn't spoken so quickly. "I'm sorry Raymar. I don't know what's wrong with me lately."

Smiling at me, he waved his hand before cutting into his steak again. "There's nothing wrong, Christy. You have honored me over and over." He stuck his fork into the meat and popped the piece in his mouth.

Silas cut his meat but then pushed the bites around on his plate and sighed. His arms rested on the edge of the table and his fork seemed heavy in his hand.

"We can begin our meeting while we eat," Grand-père started.

"Oh, Oliver," Grand-mère interrupted, "we have all been through so much. Can't we just have a nice meal?"

The corners of Grand-père's mouth turned up slightly. "Well, okay. We'll begin in—" he checked his timepiece, "thirty minutes." He looked at Grand-mère as he glanced up from his plate. "Is that enough rest, Connie?"

"Actually, no," she stated firmly. "But, I'll take what I can get." Then she laughed a little and we all joined in. Grand-mère had a way of taking a rough situation and smoothing out the wrinkles.

· · · · ·

Jason and I helped by clearing the dishes as Grand-mère refilled the coffee cups. There was no more stalling. We had to get back to the work at hand, electing a new president. Strangely, I didn't have the same fire for the election as I had before Grand-père's kidnapping. It all seemed mechanical, like I was just going through the motions.

Judge Brunner began the meeting. "It goes without saying that we are all happy that Oliver is back, safe and unharmed." He looked around at all of us. "The report said that all of you were in danger. Even Inspector Stoner was shot trying to find you and in pursuit of those who kidnapped you, Oliver."

"We haven't had any news about him," I stepped in. "How is he doing?"

Carl rolled his eyes. "The acting Blue Guard leader told me that the Inspector is back in Capitol City. He'll rest a few days and then return to the office."

"A few days?" I gasped. "How will he be able to return to work in a few days if he was shot?"

"Well Christy," the judge said looking straight at me. "Stoner is alive partly because of you."

"Because of me?" I blurted out loud. "I thought he was shot because of me."

"Lieutenant Boone said she heard of your healings and experienced your touch when you stopped the hemorrhaging in your own shoulder," Carl began. "So, when Stoner was shot, she prayed and then put her fingers in his wound and stopped the bleeding, as she believed you had done. So, the Inspector didn't have to recover from blood loss, just the wound."

I was stunned. "What a blessing," I whispered. But, deep inside it was almost more information than I could take in. Good and bad bits and pieces piled on my shoulders until I felt weighted down under it all. Jason reached over and took my hand again.

"As for the election—" Carl pulled a leather-bound notebook from under some other papers on the table and opened it. "We just rolled into July the other day. There are four months left until the election."

"Rallies, debates, town hall meetings, and a lot of ground work shaking hands, meeting people, and answering questions," I sighed. "Will you have enough energy for it all Grand-père?"

Jason leaned on the table. "We'll have to plan a lot of rest into the schedule." He smiled at my grandfather. "If you will follow medical advice, you should do okay. Rest, then talk, then rest again. No one should even be aware of your down time. Politicians for generations have had to pace themselves."

I wondered aloud, "The people know he was kidnapped and that we had to escape from the wreckage of the train. What has been their reaction?"

"We're not sure about all of that," Carl responded with a frown. "We know the mass media had gotten hold of the story, but after first posting it, the information outlets went black. That may mean that someone has blocked more information from getting out. On the other hand, if we pose the question to the people at town hall meetings, we've already told them what happened. Will Oliver sound stronger if we don't say much about it? It's tricky."

Sean pulled some newspapers from his large brief case. "Oliver, if you notice these last four or five papers, I haven't expanded the details about the recent events in your lives beyond the initial public notification. I assure you, no one has gotten to me. I simply thought the information about your kidnapping would have suggested a weakness in your campaign and perhaps endangered your lives even more. The public had a right to know the event happened. I will not be a part of making Oliver look weak, however."

"And, their escape would indicate strength," Carl added. "So, you made sure that was reported. Good."

"I say we go with the truth," I suggested. "If we get ahead of the story with complete details, we can present it all from a position of strength."

As we told Sean the entire story, he jotted down many notes about the kidnapping and escape. "This is amazing, Oliver," he said. Then he added, "I'll get it all in the next issue if that is your desire."

"Go with it," my grandfather stated with a pound of his fist on the table.

Grand-mère twisted her napkin between her fingers. "How do we make sure the visual media won't get their version of the story out first and twist it another way?"

Sean looked up and shrugged. "How would they possibly know that I'm going to run the story? And, how and where would they get the details?"

Bam, bam, bam—someone banged on the front door. I jumped and my skin crawled. Confused by the reaction of those around the table, I saw they were amused.

"Stoner," they all laughed out loud.

Neither startled nor amused, Silas's lack of reaction shocked me. His expression was so flat, I couldn't stop watching him.

Grand-mère jumped up and hurried to the door, but Stoner had already walked in. I heard my grandmother's usual gracious welcome. "Inspector, it's good to see you are able to get out and about."

"And why not?" he bellowed.

She smiled sweetly and led him into the dining room. "Well, with having been shot and all."

His eyes scanned those present at the table. "Oh yes, that."

Jason stood up and brought over another chair that sat beside the antique buffet hutch. "Here you are Inspector. Have a seat."

"I do not need to sit down," Stoner growled.

Grand-mère placed a cup on the table in front of him and started filling it. "You'll be more comfortable while you drink your coffee if you'll sit."

Stoner rolled his eyes. "Yes, Ma'am."

No one said a word but, in my mind, I thought, *Grand-mère can charm anyone.*

Jason actually reached out and patted Stoner's shoulder. "We're all glad you're healing, Inspector."

Stoner stared into his cup for a second, then mumbled, "Thank you."

Grand-père cleared his throat. "To what do we owe this visit?"

"Sorry," Stoner blustered as he placed his cup on the saucer. "You weren't kidnapped in my zone, but you're a citizen here. Is there anything my department can do to help keep you safe? I know you have your own body guards." His voice sounded mellow.

"I would welcome anything you can do," Grand-mère said sweetly. She ran her hand across her hair and smoothed some stray wisps.

Stoner lifted his cup in an informal salute to his new general, "I will double my people on campaign duty." His gaze drifted down and he added, "Lieutenant Boone and I will work very closely with your people to keep you safe, Sir Richly."

"Oliver, Inspector. Call me Oliver."

"I'm not sure I can do that Sir. But please—call me Ward."

"I'm not sure I can do that, Inspector," Grand-père said as he smiled.

"Tell me this," Ward said as he placed his cup firmly in the saucer with veiled anger. "Did any of you recognize any of the kidnappers?"

Did Stoner actually not know? I couldn't believe his question. "I thought you knew, Inspector. Daniel Washington led the men who kidnapped my grandfather. But he was not the brains behind this whole thing."

Stoner jerked his gaze in my direction. "The brains?"

I felt my face grow hot again. "That's an expression used in old mystery books."

"I suppose they used to talk like that," the inspector blustered. "You're saying there is still someone above Washington."

"Yes," I stated. "But we don't have any idea for sure who that is."

"For sure?" Stoner's eyes leveled on me hard. "Do you have a guess?"

At that moment, my Palm Device glowed and Marge appeared in the midst of us. "Hi, Christy, I have the information you asked for."

"What information?" Stoner snapped as he leaned in the direction of Marge's glow.

Jason touched Stoner's shoulder again. "Let her talk at her pace, Inspector."

Stoner sat back and gave in to Jason's request. "Of course."

I was so excited I felt my stomach quiver and my heart pound. However, I'll have to admit, I would have preferred to get the information in private. I didn't know what Marge was going to say and I guess I feared it might involve the Cornwalls. "It's okay Marge. Inspector Stoner has joined us at our campaign meeting. Please, just give us what you have found."

"It's very interesting," she began. "The three-dot tattoo on the hand was known in Turkey as Görmem, Duymam, Söylemem. It means, 'I hear nothing; I see nothing; I tell nothing.' In that country, the tattoo meant that the person took an oath to a given society. The one tattooed is willing to sacrifice his or herself for the sake of the society. It's like a la Cosa Nostra tattoo–the mafia."

A unified gasp rose up around the table at the sound of the old gangster group–the mob. Silas gagged and grew pale. But Jason and I knew something else. It meant for sure that Alister Bedlum was behind it all.

CHAPTER 31

The Lie

I awakened the next morning, yawned and stretched. The July sun sparkled high on the horizon. I knew I must have overslept. Jumping out of bed, I hit the shower, then dried off and quickly dressed. Shakespeare wrapped her furry body around my legs, in and out as I walked over to the window and looked out on the morning. My palm device hummed on the table. When I answered the page, Mother's holo appeared.

"Are you watching the news?" The pitch of her voice rose and sounded urgent.

"No," I stammered. "I just got up. Why?"

Her voice shook with worry. "Quickly, turn it on."

The huge screen danced alive but what appeared could have marked us all for death. "The details of Oliver Richly's kidnapping have been kept secret up until now," the news reader said. A large picture of my grandfather, weak, beaten and lying in his hospital bed, flashed across the screen. "Perhaps his campaign is worried that his age will prevent him from completing his presidential race. Contests of speed aren't for old men."

"What?" I shrieked.

"Now, for the latest in the progress of the Public Transit station at Mulberry and Main Streets. The PT Board has asked resident to walk the mile to the next station at—"

"PT stations?" I yelled at the screen. "Mother," I turned to the hologram, "where is the redeeming follow up, how the train was sabotaged and how we all escaped using our own intellect and strength?"

"They ran this story about fifteen minutes ago and there was not a single word about the escape there either," she said through gritted teeth.

"It's not only the story," I barked. "Where could they possibly have gotten that picture?"

She shook her head. "I have no idea, but the image would worry me if I didn't know better."

"Mother," I turned and pointed at the screen that was still devoting more time to the PT story than the kidnapping of the head of the Council of Elders and a candidate for president. "That's it. You and I do know better and—I think the people do too. They've wised up to the lies and tricks perpetrated on them by an elite controlling media. I think they'll believe Sean's story over the mass communication fable."

Mother's excitement was obvious. She nearly jumped up and down. "When will Sean's exclusive report hit the streets? Will there be enough papers for everyone to get one?"

I laughed when I thought about Sean's operation. "Sean started his newspaper distribution by hand-carrying copies of his paper right out in the open on the PT. Then, truckers would pick up stacks and stacks of them at the zone borders and transport them further into the forbidden areas. No one suspected him of producing and distributing contraband alternative news. Newspapers finally met their demise a century ago in order to silence an alternative voice to the state visual mass media."

"And—?"

"And, yes there will be plenty of newspapers for everyone. But—no trucks this time. Sean worked out a digital copy to send to underground printers in the major cities. The papers will be in millions of citizens' hands an hour after he pushes the send button."

"Everyone?"

"It will also appear on people's Palm Device—instantly."

Mother's face brightened. "When will he push the button?"

I checked Holly. "About forty-five minutes ago. Everyone will have a paper in a matter of minutes. And, it should be on your device—now."

We both pushed the split-screen button on our devices. A hologram of Sean burst forth on my device in duo with Mother's image. "I'm going to have a full living room of virtual-people soon," I said and laughed.

"I'm Sean McDermott," Sean's holo began, "columnist, editor and publisher of The Free Voice Newspaper. Our feature story today is about the recent kidnapping of presidential candidate, Oliver Richly. Drugged and dragged to where he was held in the cellars under adobe buildings in New Mexico, he was rescued by Christiana Applewait, Dr. Jason O'Reilly, Ivy Trudeau and Raymar Goring."

A selected picture of my grandfather, smiling and well, with all of us gathered around him, appeared on the device screen. Sean's holo shimmered again. "After a day or two in a hospital, he and those with him took a flash train to travel back to the Central Zone. However, terrorists attacked, derailed the cars, overturned the train and injured many in the forward coaches."

An inserted photo of the wreck appeared next on the device, with smoke billowing up and twisted metal poking their tentacles toward the sky. "Oliver Richly organized those with him and found a way to escape the wreckage. They all jumped into the cold river below the bridge on which the last cars still remained and swim for the shore. It was Oliver Richly's strength and leadership that saved the entire group."

Sean had placed a photo of a strong although wet image of Grand-père, smiling, tanned from the New Mexico sun with his wet sleeve draped around my laughing grandmother's shoulder. "It takes strength, intelligence and maturity to solve the very real problems in our country. Oliver Richly is our man for that job."

"Mother," I sang out. "Sean did it!"

"Wait! Wait, Christy," Mother hushed. "There's more."

"I have with me," Sean continued, "Inspector Ward Stoner of the Blue Guard."

I looked at Mother's hologram and we both opened our mouths in surprise at the same time. "Stoner?" we mouthed in unison.

Ward Stoner's hologram appeared before us. I winced at the thought of the Inspector standing in my living room before I had my morning coffee. "Perhaps I should put on a fresh pot for our little party."

"My friends," Stoner began. I covered my mouth so my laughter wouldn't drown out his words. The thought of him having friends was too humorous for words.

"I am Inspector Ward Stoner, the head of the Blue Guard. I want to reassure everyone of Oliver Richly's safety. He has a private group of body guards around him now and I have doubled the number of Blue Guard normally assigned to protect a politician." He looked down and gathered himself, an action I had never seen before.

"Oliver Richly is a man of honor, a quality of esteem I have never seen before. He is a brave, honest, brilliant and masterful leader." Stoner gazed with steely eyes. "Know this, I will catch those who kidnapped Oliver, then tried to kill him a second time by wrecking the train that endangered all those on board, whoever they are. If you are the terrorists, know that you will not slip out of my grasp. I will follow you to the ocean's edge." With that, Stoner's hologram dissolved and Sean spoke again.

"Thank you, Inspector. A full story of Oliver Richly's capture, rescue, and escape again is the feature article in my newspaper, The Free Voice. You can find a copy in stores around your town. Pick up the current issue." Then, Sean's hologram was gone too.

At that moment, I heard a knocking from the hall. "Gotta run, Mother. Someone's at the door."

"Love you, Christy," Mother sang out before her hologram dissolved and left the room darker than it was.

Hurrying to the door, I caught sight of my image in the mirror at the entry. "Oh my," I gasped as I ran my fingers through my hair, pinched my cheeks for color and pressed my lips together firmly, raising the pink a little. Any harder and I would have drawn blood.

With the door knob in my hand, I slowed down and opened the door cautiously, remembering all the warnings about acting smart and staying safe. "Jason," I said with relief. "I'm glad you're a friend, not a foe."

"I hope I'm more than a friend," he said and pulled me to him once we both closed the door. "Did you check the security feed Ivy had installed before you opened the door?"

"I did," I lied. How could I admit that I had forgotten the surveillance camera so soon?

"You did not," he teased.

"You're right," I admitted and buried my head in his chest. "I forgot." I grabbed him by his shirt and pulled him over to the couch. "I'll make some coffee."

"No need," he said as he offered a tall cup of coffee from the Demitasse Coffee Shop.

"Jason," I gasped, "from my favorite place in the world."

"I know. I remember." He placed our cups on the table in front of the couch, took my hand and pulled me next to him. "I think you're right, Christy, about not having enough time together. We have had almost no time alone since all this began. We had only begun our relationship when we were thrown into the chaos around us." He wrapped his arms around me and snuggled close.

"Thank you for understanding, Jason."

"Now, I won't keep you from your coffee any longer," he said. As he handed me my cup of the steaming brew he added, "What have you been doing this morning? You look great."

"Oh you are a good guy," I said and laughed. "I have been watching Sean's Palm-cast."

"Sean?"

"Here, let me show you." I reached across Jason for my Palm Device from the side table, went back into the archives and brought up Sean's hologram again. Sitting on the couch, sipping our coffee, we entertained our guests in hologram form. The morning felt comfortable.

When the hologram evaporated, I leaned back into the crook of Jason's arm. "I was only detoxed for a few weeks when our running began, first to the west coast, the Midwest Zone and then the east. I hadn't even learned the names of the feelings that the chemicals had robbed from all of us. At least, as a privileged citizen, Jason, you were able to prescribe the detox pills for me when I turned twenty-four. I truly don't know how I feel because I had only begun to feel just before we lost all of our privacy."

"Well," he drew out, "there is like, dislike, and then there's love." He chuckled a little. "I've been detoxed longer than you."

"Oh, so I'm with an old man."

"Old—no. Older—yes." He kissed me on the nose. "Now, let me educate you, young one."

"Grasshopper?" I laughed as I remembered an old movie Marge and I had seen in the library.

"Grasshopper? If you like that. In the love category: there's the love of family-familial love; the love of friends-platonic love; the love of God-Agápe love, and the love between a man and a woman-a mix of eros, familial, and unconditional love."

"And, what are we?" I teased.

"Well, I'm no god and you're not my sister."

"Are you my best friend or—what?"

Jason leaned down and kissed me, tenderly, passionately. "I want it all, Christy."

I said no more. The words and feelings were all too new, too unpracticed, too raw. I caressed his cheek and my mind was at rest in our new understanding with the naming of our relationship. I guess I had believed it wasn't a relationship if I couldn't identify it by its name.

I won't say Jason and I had enough time to bond together, but we had a little. I was thankful for that but wondered if it was enough.

CHAPTER 32

The Last Week in October

In the next weeks, we were all *toes along the starting line of the fast lane.* I wondered if I would be able to catch my breath and run a good race.

We had meetings stacked upon more meetings. It helped to divide up the work among all of us. Even quiet Silas Drummond agreed to meet people in coffee shops and diners, shake citizens' hands and answer questions about my grandfather's position on many issues. I did worry about him. He looked sick and weary each time I saw him, but he denied ill health.

Everyone made sure Grand-père rested frequently. No one was more diligent at policing his sleep, diet, and exercise than Grand-mère. As the months stretched past, the pace picked up.

It was early in October when Grand-père had a major speech at the restored McCormick Place along Lake Shore Drive in Chicago. It was a Friday evening event. My grandparents had gone to the city the day before the event to meet people and acclimate to the city's wind and change in weather in the colder climate. Jason and I stayed at the same hotel, arriving at the Blackstone, about a mile and a half from the event center, early on Friday.

The hotel was on South Michigan Avenue. It felt good to be among the tall buildings. I remembered how much I liked New York City when we were there.

Jason, Ivy, and I went to the check-in desk and waited our turn. The desk clerk was busy. Her expensive silk jacket and the flower in her button hole identified the finer care the hotel put into each detail. As we waited, I leaned a little on Jason. He planted his feet firmly on the plush carpet to allow for the pressure of my arm to drape across his shoulder. I looked up as he smiled softly and put his arm around me.

When we got to the head of the line the clerk covered her mouth, "Oh, no. Lady Applewait, I am so sorry you had to wait."

A little embarrassed by the favoritism she was displaying, I responded, "That's fine. I can stand in line just like everyone else."

"But the hotel security team will have my job when they find out."

"Then, let's not tell them," I whispered.

"Yes, Ma'am. Thank you."

Ivy's brow furrowed but she spoke softly. "Please, move them out of the lobby quickly."

"Of course, Ma'am," the clerk responded politely as she looked down at her booking list and glanced up. "I have you down for three rooms on a secondary, secure hallway," she looked from Jason to me.

"Yes, three rooms," I agreed. "I believe they were booked as adjoining."

"Yes," she agreed, consulting her booking notes again. She looked around as if checking to see if others were close enough to hear and explained, "There is the public hallway for that floor, which opens by palm ID to a smaller, private hallway that connects the three rooms, plus Sir Richly's rooms. None of you will have to walk out into the public space to move between the rooms."

"Perfect. We all have a lot of work to do," Jason explained.

"Yes, Sir," the clerk agreed and pointed to the palm scanner on the desk. "Please, check in."

We each placed our hand on the scanner and stepped back while vetted bellhops gathered up our luggage. Following them to the lift we soon arrived on the executive floor with the hallway the clerk described. I opened the door with my room number on the outside and walked into the second hallway with multiple doors, just down from my grandparents' suite.

I opened the door and was pleased with the relaxing setting. There were massive windows overlooking a park and Lake Michigan in the distance. As I unpacked the few things I brought for the evening's program, I heard a tapping on my door. Reaching for the knob, I then remembered the safety precautions. A light touch to the keypad to the right of the door allowed an image to come into view on the small screen above the coded numbers. Touching the O, a picture of the empty outer hall appeared. The "I" key brought up Jason standing in the inner hall just outside my door.

He was not going to catch me unprotected so I called through the door, "I see you Mister." On the other side of the door, I saw and heard Jason laugh.

I flung the door open and Jason gathered me in his arms like a movie clip I had seen in the library of banned romantic films. Feelings fluttered through me and emotions rushed in that had been drugged out of existence all of my life.

Laughing, I threw my head back. "Maybe it's been good that we have had no time alone together."

He nuzzled his head in my neck and then said breathlessly, "I am positive of it, Baby."

The buzzer on the door interrupted us as usual. The "I" key brought Ivy's image to the screen. When I opened the door, she dashed in and began pacing back and forth.

"I didn't like the choice of hotels from the beginning," she began as if she were in mid-thought. "We should have been booked into the hotel adjacent to the event center," she said as she bounced from one side of the large room to the other. "We could have gone to lunch in the hotel and later walked over to the arena/center in the underground passes."

"Ivy, stop." Her pacing was making me nervous. "Sit down and tell me the latest news. Something is bothering you."

"We have received some intel," she said as she sat on the edge of one of the chairs at a round table near the window. "There are at least three assassins in the building with their cross hairs fixed on your grandparents—and on you too, Christy."

"Ivy, we can have someone bring our lunch to the room. We won't have to go out."

"And getting to the program this evening?" she asked.

"I asked Marge to research this old building," I admitted as I sat with Ivy and gazed out on Grant Park below and the cold water of Lake Michigan out beyond.

"And?"

I leaned in toward her as if there were "bugs," as my old mystery novels would call them, secretly stashed in the light fixtures. "There is a tunnel under this building."

"Yes, of course," Ivy agreed.

"No, no," I shook my head. "Yes, there's the tunnel everyone knows about. Then, about thirty years ago, a very powerful man, a recluse really, secretly had another tunnel dug under the original one. Access to that second one is through the walk-in freezer in the kitchen. A car backs in through a grove of trees in Grant Park and coasts down a long ramp to the tunnel below."

"Are you sure?" Ivy gasped.

Jason sat with us and added. "Of course. Marge is able to find almost anything."

"Okay. We'll eat in our rooms and then use the sub-tunnel to get to the arena." Ivy slapped her hands across her knees indicating a decision was made.

Grand-père and Grand-mère joined us for lunch; we ate at the table in my room. The hotel brought up a platter of shrimp, cheese, small pieces of fruit, and little sandwiches made with ham, pepperoni, salami, and pizza sauce. No one was still hungry after the leisure time we took over our feast.

Lunch and an afternoon of planning did interrupt the time that Jason and I had together. I had to recognize that we weren't in Chicago on vacation. Grand-père would give the most important speech of his life and the lives of every citizen in our country that evening. Jason and I were there to help him polish it. Ivy was there for all of us.

I changed into black wool slacks and a festive top of spun gold and silver threads over a tight shirt of silk. The creation moved with ease like a shimmy dress I'd seen in an old movie depicting clothes of the 1920's.

"Wow," Jason gulped when he came into my room before we left. "You make my eyes water, Honey." He started to put his arms around me. "Maybe I'd better not. I might bend the shirt or get stabbed by precious threads. I don't know which."

"Thank you, Sir. I'll take that as a compliment," I said as I feigned a small curtsy.

Ivy came in the door behind Jason and immediately growled, "That door was not latched. I'm serious about assassins in the building people."

"All right everybody," Stoner said as he followed Ivy into my room. "Here's the way we're going to do it." He swaggered over to the large windows and peered out. "Boone, take a look at this," he ordered.

Chalky walked immediately to the floor-to-ceiling windows that faced the park. "Down there," she pointed.

"What?" I asked. I had no idea what they were looking at except the beautiful crimson and gold leaves that I had sat and watched, filling the color-loving part of my brain.

"The two men on the park bench below," she pointed.

"So—two men. There are people all over the park on a wonderful fall day like this." What was she talking about?

Stoner was firm but somehow kinder than before. "Christy, those men are carrying long duffle bags. The three could have come from the gym down the street or the bags could conceal rifles."

I didn't know what to say and mumbled. "I didn't notice them."

The inspector actually placed his hand on my shoulder in comfort. "I know you didn't, Christy. That's what I'm trying to teach you." He turned to the park below. "You have lived a privileged life. That's good for you but bad for your safety. Even the people around you, who weren't allowed to approach you or touch your garment, were so drugged they didn't notice anything around them either. That was the government's plan. You and Dr. O'Reilly have been through a lot in the last year, but you haven't learned. You still trust people. You have come to a point in your life when, if you don't watch the actions of everyone around you, your life and the lives of your loved ones could be in mortal danger."

I felt my heart sink and my hope waver. "I don't want to live a life of doubt and mistrust."

"Then you might not live a life at all," Stoner stated with firm resolve. He turned to Chalky and snapped his heals. "It's time to go. Boone, I'll take the lead and you and Trudeau take the rear." He threw out his arms to shepherd each of us out of the room on his time and by his plan.

Another moment of precious time with Jason burst, a lovely soap bubble—that hits the wall and breaks.

• • • • •

All of us crowded into one elevator car. Dividing our party would not have been safe. Ivy pushed the button for the ground floor. Stoner faced the front, his hand on his sidearm.

As we rode down, someone pushed the call button on the fourth floor. Ivy over-road the elevator call and we passed by.

"I went down and walked through the kitchen while you all changed for the event" she announced. "I didn't go near the freezer. I couldn't give away the escape route."

"So, we don't know if the access is even in the freezer," Grand-père said.

Ivy was facing the lift door and didn't turn around. "No, we don't, Sir."

"It will be there," Stoner stated decidedly. "I trust Christy's research."

"Marge's research," I corrected.

Grand-père did not hesitate. "Then, assuming it's there, we will have quite an adventure."

When the door opened on the main floor, Grand-père's security staff met us before we stepped off. The men, many of them over six feet six inches tall, surrounded our party like a picket fence. We walked in rhythmic dance, always with Grand-père at the center of the march.

I could barely see past the bodyguards so I had no idea if anyone was stalking us. Suddenly, I heard the crack pop of gun fire. The guards, with many angel wings, swooped low and hovered over us, pushing us all down to the floor.

"Stay down," Stoner ordered when I started to lift my head. Suddenly, more shots rang out.

I heard my heart beating so loudly, I thought I would lift off the ground. My breathing was short and labored. I worried about Grand-mère but I couldn't see her. With one eye fixed past a dark blue suit that was laying heavily over me, I saw the bloody body of two people on the marble floor to the left of us. Just as quickly, a suited arm jerked me not-so-gently off the floor and whisked me down the hall. I tried to look around to see if Jason and my grandparents were following but all I saw was navy blue. I did hear Stoner's voice barking orders.

After what seemed like too many steps, I could smell the aroma of fine gourmet cooking and knew we were either in or near the kitchen. Frazzled and mussed, I soon stumbled into the walk-in freezer.

Strangely, I wondered if my clothes were torn or damaged and if my hair was still in place. I was embarrassed by my egocentric obsession and glad no one could read my thoughts. We were in a gun battle and I wondered if I had remembered to bring a comb. My life had become so used to danger that nothing seemed dangerous.

"Christy," Grand-mère called out from inside a gathering of guards. "Your granddaddy is with me."

"I'm here Grand-mère," I sighed deeply in relief. "Jason? Where are you?" There was no sound in return.

"Christy?" Finally, he asked as he entered the freezer.

"Okay, we are all here," Stoner announced. "Ivy called for the cars to pick us up in the sub-tunnel. How do we get there Christy?"

As the giant guards stepped back, I moved through the crowded walk-in freezer to the back. "Here it is." I ran my fingers along the wall, momentarily forgetting my manicure. "Behind this wall-size poster of the various cuts of meat—it should—"

My hand felt for anything that seemed different, until I finally touched a tiny spring lever. When it snapped, a fourth of the poster sprang open revealing the handle to a heavy door. I jerked it down and a large portion of the wall opened like a normal door. Inside, wide grey terrazzo steps descended to the right and flowed to the tunnel below. With a guard's hand under each arm, my feet barely touched the ground as I slipped and slid down the old steps. The only thing that kept me from falling was the heavy coating of dust, dirt, and mouse droppings on the unused treads.

The descent was a blur as they hustled us along. Once we got to the first tunnel, we found another elevator in the corner of the space off to the right and entered it silently. I pushed a button simply marked with a dot inside a circle and the car went down again. We all turned toward each other and smiled.

"Thank goodness it still works," Grand-père said.

"I'll bet it hasn't been serviced in twenty or more years," Ivy winced.

When the door slid open, the rush was on again. Guided, pushed, and jostled toward waiting long-cars, I grabbed Jason's shirt to make sure we would end up in the same limousine.

"Thank God you're all right," he said as we slid onto the leather seat and he threw his arms around me.

Suddenly, I started shaking uncontrollably like someone chilled to the bone. But I wasn't cold. Feeling completely out of control, I started to cry.

Jason rubbed my back gently and hummed "Silent Night" softly in my ear. It wasn't Christmas or Gifting Season, but it was the song we loved. I slowly began to calm down but felt so very tired. My arms were nearly too heavy to lift.

"Less than a month to the election," Jason reminded me quietly. "Then all of this will be over."

"Will we all make it until then?" I asked and laughed wearily but truly saw no humor in any of it. The question was real, and I knew it.

CHAPTER 33
The Event

The roar of the crowd at the event center was deafening. Energy seemed to hang from the catwalk. A band was actually playing a rousing song. I wondered where they found a group of people who could still play instruments in the Central Zone. Then, I thought of Dahlia Zoobamba's beautiful playing on the grand piano in the sitting room of the Indian River Apartments. Music seemed to be buried in people's hearts even though banned decades ago.

A stage was set up at one end of the arena. I could see that it was within a force-field security bubble. The Jumbotron, hung from the ceiling, showed multiple images of the audience as it panned around, in and out of the roving spotlights. It was hard for me to take my eyes off the giant screen. Perhaps I expected to see a slithering assassin taking aim in some corner of the arena and trapped in the image on the Tron.

Chants of, "Oliver—Oliver—Oliver" filled the place. My eyes scanned the entire area of ten thousand people. All seemed smiling, full of energy and happy, but then, so much of the scene was a blur.

When I heard, "Christy—Christy—Christy," my blood froze. I wondered how long I could stand in the center of an adrenalin flood and not completely burn out.

Ivy studied the lay of the arena, turned and talked to Grand-mère and me. "Nothing has changed from the early setup. I checked it over this afternoon." She pointed at the area to the right and said, "Oliver and Christy will come out of entrance A1A, just as the athletes do when they enter the arena for the True Warrior vs Avatar Games. Your only vulnerable spot will be where the low ceiling of the entry hall meets the open secure area of the arena. While the security bubble extends from the stage to the hall, there is no overlap at the entrance. Space yourselves wide apart so you're not a waiting target. Hurry through the void," she instructed. "Any questions?"

My mind was a dichotomy of emptiness and flashing ideas all spilling over one another as they crowded in for attention. "No," I whispered.

Looking up at Grand-père, I nodded. Grand-mère and Jason kissed us for luck as we started toward the arena and out of the shadows of the hallway. Grand-père stepped back to position me so I would enter the bubble first, since I should arrive on stage before him. I would say a few words of thanks and then introduce him.

Looking at the bubble, I could see the wavy haze that demarked the entrance and the gap where there was no protection. Then I did the very thing I wasn't supposed to do. I stopped.

"Move!" Ivy yelled.

Behind me, Grand-père nearly stumbled over my heels. I jumped which threw me into the gap between safety and danger. Inspector Stoner grabbed me in a great bear hug and lifted me past the unsafe zone.

Crack, pop, pop! Shots rang out from the stands in the section above us. I heard a projectile glance off the floor in the spot I just stepped out of and chip the concrete. A small piece of flooring hit the back of my leg and nicked the wool of my pants. Several bullets struck Stoner's protective vest. I felt the impact through his arms. *Thud, thud, thud,* the bullets jolted us there in the gap. Stoner slumped in stride. I wondered how weakened he was from the previous attack in New Mexico that had only begun to heal. Other shots struck the force-field which sent off ten-foot high rockets of flash, sparks, and fire like an erupting fountain of flames.

"Go!" Stoner demanded and shoved me into the safety of the force-field.

Looking back, I saw the inspector grab his chest, his face drawn and pinched. "Are you okay?" I shouted.

"Yes, yes, go!" He bellowed with the wave of his hand toward the center of the stage.

Some of the people didn't understand what had happened and cheered on what seemed like a brilliant entrance for their new leader. Others screamed in fear and started to stampede out of the arena. Retaliating fire pinpointed with laser accuracy the source of the shots and nearly shoved the bullets right up the barrel of the assassins' firearms. An announcer came on the microphone.

"Calm, please everyone. The authorities have taken out the terrorists. Everyone is fine. Let me assure you, you're safe." The noise of the crowd lowered to a mumble from person to person.

"Now, let's give a hand to Christiana Applewait!" He roared into a hand-held mic.

I thought for a moment I might vomit. My hands trembled and my knees barely held me up. I looked back at Jason who still stood on the edge of the hall reaching out for me with fear written on his face. Finally, he straightened his back, smiled, and blew a reassuring kiss.

A microphone hung from the catwalk on a cable so thin it was nearly invisible. Now was my time. Now was my hour. I closed my eyes in prayer, a prayer for strength, courage and the words that would inspire the thousands there.

"Ladies and gentlemen," I began and wondered if I sounded like the ringmaster in an old circus. I heard my own internal voice remind me, *It's not about you Christy. It's not even about Grand-père. It's about our beautiful, blessed country and the wonderful people who have only begun to awaken from their deep, dark sleep.*

I continued with new energy. "On behalf of Oliver Richly and the entire *1787-Constitutional Party* I thank you all for coming tonight. You are the last great hope of our nation."

The crowd roared with enthusiasm and fidelity for our cause. They stood and stomped their feet, waving their arms and whooping in joy. It sounded like thunder on distant hills.

Their response filled me with a power I had never experienced before. "Now is the time to listen with open ears and an open mind. Now is the time for each of us to learn of our blessings, our privilege, our obligation, and our responsibility. Now is the time to have the courage to stand and be counted." Again, the people shouted and cheered.

I looked out and into the bright lights focused on me as the granddaughter and warm-up act for Grand-père's speech. "You may not know this man yet, like I do. Oliver Richly is a man of honesty, steadfastness, and honor. His dedication to our country and our people is based on his knowledge and love of the country we used to be, when the Constitution of 1787 was ratified and was the law of the land, and who we can become again."

Then I paused and added, "Now is the time for us to awaken in a new land of hope and opportunity—and the time for me to introduce my grandfather—Oliver Richly."

Grand-père stepped into the center of the stage as the spotlight glowed on him like the sun from a near-by galaxy. The arena went wild. He bowed from the waist, a true servant of the people, and dipped his head in respect to all those gathered there. Finally, he raised his hands to the people in a plea for quiet and held his eyes on them until they all grew calm and still. It was like each one had moved to the edge of their seat and waited in anticipation. Grand-père opened his mouth.

He cleared his throat and placed his hand across his heart. "We gather here to make a decision, a decision about our future, the future of our children and our children's children. The good news is, what we decide today and what we do next week will affect every man, woman and child in our country and those people who used to depend on us around the world." A hushed silence washed over the arena.

He continued. "Let me be very clear, there is no argument between the freedom we as a people would enjoy under a return to the original constitution and the alternative of spending the rest of our lives under a cloud of drugs and dying on the government's schedule. I am here to proclaim freedom for the prisoner in this government's prison of life. There is only one way to guarantee life and a life worth living, and you can have it in one week—vote."

I studied the faces of the people I could see in the first rows. Some were in tears but all were in rapture of the man and his words.

Grand-père raised one hand in affirmation. "I know there's a risk in showing up and being counted at the polling place. But more danger exists if you don't vote and we fail in our efforts to return the country to the people.

"There is a risk in following a course toward a restoration of freedom. We saw it played out a few minutes ago when assassins tried to take us down right here in the arena. But history has taught us that this great nation and the freedom she promised and provided decades ago, is the one great hope of the world. That hope is nearing total extinction. It flickers in a window left open by those who went before us. Are we going to be the generation that lazily blows it out?"

"No!" The people yelled.

Grand-père held up his hand again. "The greatest risk and danger lies in turning our backs on freedom and giving in to the fear that the new constitutionalist spread like a cancer, eating at our resolve and killing our dreams. The current government's policy is total control and it gives us no choice but to escape the bonds they try to hold on us."

"Oliver, Oliver, Oliver!" voices rang out.

As soon as the noise level lowered, Grand-père went on. "We must fight to the death or surrender. If we do continue to yield to their ideas of government, we give our children no hope of freedom.

"Nathan Alexander has told you that we are weak and afraid. He has told you that we have no right to live beyond the days they decide—those wiser and better than we number our Length of Days. I tell you that is a lie!" He shouted. "Alexander believes it because he has heard some of us say, 'Take care of me. I cannot do it on my own.' My friends, you cannot do it at ALL under the new constitution. The ruling elite have decided your education, your work, the strength of your relationships and your ability to love. They have robbed you of the joy of Christmas and the name of your Creator.

They even have the date of your demise written in their book of death.

"We are not weak: not morally or spiritually. We speak out of the wisdom and faith of the Word. In Proverbs it's written, 'My son, do not forget my law, but let your heart keep my commands, for length of days and long life and peace they will add to you.' How can we know the law if the book has been banned? We don't even know the commandments of God any more.

"Those voices of surrender do not speak for me, and they don't speak for you. Your current leaders tell you that fighting isn't your job. They say, 'Sit back, watch the flickering screen that dominates your home, play your games and let those above you tell you when to put yourself into action.'

"My friends, there are things worth fighting for. Freedom is first on the list. Your God has been hidden from you; the music of your life has been silenced; the joy and meaning of Christmas have been cauterized out of your celebrations; the history of your own country has been stolen from you, along with her stories of honor and valor."

He raised his voice in a call to action. "You can decide what is best for you and your family. You can say to the government, there is a price to be paid, and I am willing to stand and pay it. We must have the courage to trace our finger in the sand and say there is a line over which the government cannot cross. President Reagan, a president you have never even heard of said, 'We have a rendezvous with destiny.' He was right. We either step boldly and courageously into the light of freedom's beacon or we will live forever in absolute darkness."

"No," someone yelled in the otherwise silent room.

Grand-père shook a triumphant fist in the air. "Next week is Election Day. On that day, we have an appointment with the future. Do we have the courage to face it boldly, or will we let fear grip us and turn out the light of hope? My friends turn out next week and— vote!"

CHAPTER 34

November 3, 2114

Election Day

I was excited to vote, but didn't want to go to the polls by myself. Not that I would be alone. With Ivy, the Blue Guard and many of the party's security people surrounding me, I hadn't been alone in a long time. My parents' single-family home was not in Oakwood where my grandparents lived, nor near the Indian River Apartments. Since Election Day fell on Saturday this year, Daddy didn't have to go to work as the Director of the Schools in Capitol City, and Mother, the Chief of Staff to the Center Chair of the Council of Elders, was also home. So, they voted at 6 a.m. when the polls opened and then came over to my apartment to accompany me to my precinct.

The Campaign Committee would have provided a long-car to take me to vote, but I didn't want flash and pomp to further draw attention to myself. Daddy's car had two seats so that wouldn't work. We would have taken the Public Transit; I rode it every day before my world turned upside down. However, if Grand-père's bodyguards heard about it, their height and size would have derailed the train when they all boarded at the same time with us.

Ivy had the solution. She pulled up in front of my apartment building at 7 a.m. in her small four- passenger boot-car, the few personal vehicles that had storage. She stashed her weapons in the lockable boot. All four of us were able to fit into her car, which solved my need for a measure of anonymity.

• • • • •

November 3 was a beautiful fall day. Mums of many colors in brightly painted terracotta pots flanked the walkway in front of the polling place where I would cast my vote. Jason's apartment was in another district so he would meet us at the airport after I voted.

That wasn't all that lined the sidewalk and the perimeter of the polling building. Huge men in tan paramilitary shirts and pants with black berets worn low across one side of their brow stood elbow to elbow. The door was the only part of the building that wasn't blocked.

Mother and Daddy walked beside me with their arms linked in mine while Ivy went a few steps ahead, her hand on her weapon. We all said nothing to the tan-shirts, but I'll admit I felt intimidated. Ivy pulled her Palm device from her pocket and pushed one button. Ward Stoner appeared in a haze.

"What's going on?" He bellowed when he saw the background of tan.

Ivy panned the screen so Stoner's holo could see all of the men. "It doesn't look like they're stopping anyone from voting, but voters feel intimidated," she said. "At least Christy does. I can tell."

"Miss Applewait?" Stoner blasted as he talked into the space. "Christy, are you all right? Some of my men are less than a mile way. I'll have them there immediately."

"Yes, Inspector, I'm okay," I answered with my head held high and my chin out. "People better than these have tried a whole lot harder to harass me. But, I'll admit, I don't want them here. They do make me feel uncomfortable. And—many of our citizens are not as experienced in dealing with bullies."

The sickening sound of a trio of Blue Guard sirens whined in the morning air and tires screeched at the curb. Four large men jumped out of each car and the dozen Blue Shirts descended on the sea of tan.

"Break it up and move on," one of the men in blue ordered as he approached the wall of men. I could see it was Tayton Braxton. As in the old behavior pattern of the infamous Blue Guard, he took his prodding stick from his belt and smashed it over the first black beret he came to.

"Hey!" other paramilitary troopers yelled and started in Tayton's direction.

What they hadn't noticed was that the other eleven Blue Shirts had raised their fully automatic handguns at the same time Tayton pulled out the stick. The Blue Shirts stood in a circle, elbow to elbow, facing those who were there to crowd-out voters. The black handguns perched like vultures in the men's hands.

"We are a kinder, gentler Blue Guard," Tayton hissed. "But— where's the fun in that?" He took aim at the slouched crown of the man's beret. "The cute dip that little hat makes creates a perfect target." He smiled, baring his teeth as the red laser light from many firearms marked the kill-spot on the man's head.

"Whoa," the man in the beret pleaded with his palms raised. "We didn't do anything but stand here. We were hired to be a presence— that's all."

"By who?" I heard Tayton ask.

"A friend of Alexander's. No one gave the name," he whimpered as the prodding stick poked him in the belly.

"Out of here—now," Tayton ordered. "Take off those silly uniforms and stay home. The Blue Guard presence is four-fold today, so none of you are going to be able to slip by us. If I catch you out again, you will suffer a fate you don't want to know about."

"Yes, Sir," the man answered and waved off the rest of his group. "Get out of here. Go home."

Tayton turned to Ivy. "We'll stick around to make sure the last one is gone, but then we'll go. If we stay, we'll become the intimidators."

"Fine, clear these hired bullies out and then go. It's early. It shouldn't change the turn out," Ivy responded.

Tayton touched his guard cap at me in a salute and turned away. He was never one of the former guardsmen who beat up on citizens and terrorized children. He was no tyrant, and I knew it. Tayton based his approach on the fact that the tan shirted hired-bullies wouldn't know him.

· · · · ·

I went inside. The polling station was in an old abandoned church and it was amazing. Since speaking the name of God had been banned under the new constitution adopted one hundred years ago, few people knew the reason for the building or the meaning of the emblems and stained-glass pictures. I owned one of the few remaining Bibles that had not been burned years in the past. Grand-père had given it to me and told me to hide it in plain sight on one of my bookshelves. No one would have heard of a Holy book called a Bible, so it was unlikely anyone would discover it and identify it as something precious.

"Look at these beautiful pictures made of glass," Mother whispered in awe.

"They tell a story," I said. Pointing to a picture of a man in a long garment with a flock of sheep around him, I said, "That depicts the truth that Jesus is the Good Shepherd."

"You know a lot about Jesus," Mother said with a wisp of a smile.

I studied her carefully and wasn't sure what to say. "Some, yes—but I thought you did too."

"I found a black book in Daddy's library one day," she said with her finger to her lips. "I started reading it and couldn't put it down. The last fourth of the book told about Jesus. But it didn't have any pictures."

"I know. That's the Bible I have," I said and smiled. "But there were many picture books in the library, of churches and some with pictures of old masters that were representations of Bible stories," I said as I looked past the art and to the voting booths.

"Sign in with your thumb and index finger," Daddy reminded me. "Then—vote."

As I stepped into the voting area, I thought I would burst with pride. Grand-père's name was the second on the list of two candidates. The only other item was the citizens' referendum to overturn the Length of Days Law. I tapped the screen for Oliver Richly for president and a "yes" for the referendum. I left the booth and didn't look back.

After I finished voting, it was time to hurry to the airport. Barbara Cornwall would have a large helicopter waiting for us, one large enough to hold my grandparents and parents, Jason and I, Ward Stoner and Chalky, Silas Drummond, Sean McDermott, the Brunners with Michael Brunner and his daughter—Vonny, Dahlia Zoobomba, Ivy Trudeau and Tayton Braxton. We would wait out the vote in New York.

CHAPTER 35

The Grand Ballroom

We flew over the beautiful Blue Ridge Mountains on our way east. The flight path had to do as much with security measures as anything. It wasn't on a direct path to New York. We were tacking into the east.

The morning sun danced off the copter windows and sent prismatic rainbows across the cabin. It was impossible to see the ground below. The sun shimmered through the tops of the trees, causing the canape to sparkle with morning dew, a wedding veil, kissed with diamonds. I wondered if the people on the mountain peaks and in the hollers knew about the election and the events of recent months. I knew they were bright, well educated people, but I also knew that the mass communications had exerted considerable effort into keeping the citizens uninformed about the election and my grandfather's heroic escape. I closed my eyes and reviewed the events of the week.

It was just after twelve-noon when we got to New York. Barbara had arranged for a sleek chauffeured bus to pick us up. Suddenly, I felt so tired I couldn't believe it. My head keep nodding so I rested comfortably on Jason's shoulder. I drifted in and out and picked up bits and pieces of conversation and the sounds of the city beyond the windows.

"Why did you choose New York to wait out the vote, Sir?" Stoner asked Grand-père from across the side aisle and behind Jason and I as we road through the streets of the city.

"Maybe you'll have a chance to see the underworld of the city," Grand-père said. "Christy and Jason can tell you all about it," he explained. "We'll check in for a minute at the Grande Hotel a few blocks from the Citadel. I'll want to meet and thank all the volunteers. Most of this bus load will stay there. Rooms have been reserved. Then some of us will go back to the Citadel."

"I was in New York before," Stoner smirked. "I saw a few entrances to the subway. But, why this city?" Stoner asked again.

Grand-père nodded across the aisle in my direction. "Christy told us the underlings lived in the old subway tunnels and sewers of the city for decades. They made connections that no one knew about through cellars under many buildings into the world above them. They were told they would be killed if they surfaced." He paused and looked out the window. "If there is a problem, any danger, more terrorists, and we can't travel above ground between the Citadel and the hotel—we can easily get there underground."

"Interesting idea," Stoner mused.

"But," Silas interrupted over the back of the seat. "How do you know that the tunnels haven't been filled in?"

I heard the question, even through my drowsy fog, and turned in Stoner's direction. "There are hundreds and hundreds of miles of subway tunnels under the city, Silas. More than a century ago, there was reclamation of valuable land for construction of important homes. Streets were reconfigured which also changed some old sewer lines. A forgotten manhole comes right up through the basement of the Citadel."

I watched Stoner's face as it seemed to brighten with possibilities and then added, "If we have to, we can walk from the hotel to the Citadel underground and come up in the Cornwall's basement."

Grand-père smiled with satisfaction and closed his eyes. "And that, Inspector, is why we chose New York. With everything that has happened, we need to stay a few steps ahead of those who would do us in."

I watched Stoner close his eyes in contemplation. Instantly, they popped back open as he frowned. "I'm not sure who is ahead in this race to the Inauguration."

I settled back and rested my head on Jason's shoulder again. There was no sleep however. I couldn't shake my worry over the Inspector's last statement. Who was getting ahead of us?

• • • • •

A large crowd of volunteers and supporters were already waiting in the Grand Ballroom of the hotel when we walked in. Grand-père was prepared to walk in ahead of the rest of us. Ivy, Inspector Stoner, and his entire party of bodyguards stopped him.

"Sir," Stoner said firmly as he placed his hand on Grand-père's chest. "You are not taking the lead going into that room. There are too many unknowns: people as well as the layout of the room."

The Inspector motioned for five of Grand-père's bodyguards to enter the room and fan out. Their reconnaissance would be vital to Grand-père's safety and the safety of all of us. They went in and moved to every corner, checking packages, people, and every possibility.

When they had totally swept the room, Tayton reported, "The room is clean."

"Copy that, Mr. Braxton," Stoner responded. "When Sir Richly is finished here, you will accompany the family to the Citadel."

With everything clear, Grand-père held his head high and charged into the ballroom with a burst of energy I attributed to his brief nap on the bus. Grand-mère followed and stood a few steps behind him on the small stage.

"My friends," he began, "I had to stop by. In years past, a candidate often didn't come to the gathering place until it was time to either thank them for their supporters in spite of their loss—or thank their supporters for making their win possible."

The crowd cheered and clapped, shouting, "Oliver, Oliver, Oliver."

"Thank you," Grand-père repeated over and over with his hands raised to silence the people. "You are the reason for my running for president, you and your children and your children's children."

Again, those assembled cheered warmly, enthusiastically.

"Connie and I want to thank you all." Grand-père began again as he stepped back, put his arm around Grand-mère's waist and drew her into the spotlight. "We cannot begin to express our gratitude for your time, your sacrifices and your belief in our message of hope for a bright and free future."

"Thank you President Richly!" Someone called out.

Grand-père bowed and smiled. "Thanks to you, my friend." Grand-père called back. "Because of your dedication, there will be food and coffee and punch here in the hall all day. Any of you who want to drop by and cheer each other on are welcome to enjoy whatever is here. After you have eaten and rested, we would appreciate it if you would go out and encourage all you see—to vote! It is a rare privilege, one that people haven't enjoyed in their lifetime," he rang out. "Thank you all—and we'll see you later."

After the cheering and applause, Grand-père excused himself. Once off stage, he surprised everyone by sweeping Grand-mère off her feet. He swung her around, her feet two feet off the ground as both of them laughed and filled the room with joy. This is the man and woman the government saw no need for any more, even though he was the Center Chair of the Council of Elders and as full of energy as any man I know. Their Length of Days was up at the end of December 2112 when they turned seventy-five. Now, at the age of seventy-seven, he was running for the office of president. And, God-willing, it would be so by the end of the day.

CHAPTER 36

The Promise

The Citadel sat back from the street behind a protective drive, decorative foliage, and artistic statues. In many ways, I was glad to be back. Barbara and Richard were wonderful friends. The city, in spite of the evil we had found under the streets, was magical. Most of all, today was the day the election results would come in. A lovely lunch was waiting for us when we came downstairs from freshening up.

"Maisie," I greeted her with a laugh, "it's so good to see you again."

"Christy," she shouted with glee. "It's great to see you, too. We have a special surprise for lunch."

"Sounds wonderful," I said as I gave her a hug. "Tell me about it."

"Come on into the dining room," Maisy coaxed. "Everyone is here."

"I'm sorry," I said and blushed as I walked in. "I hope you haven't waited for me."

"We just got here too," Grand-mère assured me and patted the seat between her and Jason. "Come—sit."

As I walked behind him, I ran my hands over Jason's shoulders. He reached back and touched me gently.

The table, spread with sliced duck breast and Wagyu beef with assorted sweet and specialty breads and salads, was beautiful. For dessert, there was a lemon tart with blueberries and whipped cream. Coffee, ice-chilled water, and several juices were on the side board.

Richard gave thanks for food, friends, and the faithfulness of the Lord. After the Amen, he said, "Oliver and Connie, we cannot tell you the privilege it is to have you in our home. I guess we can thank the sewer system of New York for that."

"Richard," Barbara scolded. "Not at the table." Then she looked at each of us. "You do know it was a little joke—right?"

"I did," I agreed, hoping to deflect some of the teasing from the others.

"Yes," Oliver smiled at Richard. "I recognized right away that it was a very little joke."

"Ouch," Richard said as he winced. "I deserve that."

We laughed and enjoyed our meal time together around the table, but we all knew we wanted to get to the media reports of the election turn out. Silas excused himself to go to his room upstairs for a short nap. His shoulders slumped and, as I watched him, his feet shuffled so much I was afraid he wouldn't be able to take the next step up the stairs. The rest of the group retired to the sitting room. I joined them once I saw Silas safely disappear upstairs.

Barbara reached for the tray that Maisie brought into the room and placed it on the library table. "I know we just ate, but there will be refreshments here on the tray all afternoon with light sandwiches in the evening. Maisie will add and replace food as we need it."

Then she turned to the young woman and added. "Thank you, Maisie. Why don't you find a little picnic spot on the floor and join us."

"Thanks, Barbara," she said as she sat on the hearth.

Dahlia stretched and yawned. "I'd like a nap, too, but I think I'd rather take a short walk."

A trio of "No!" rang out from Stoner, Ivy and Tayton in one voice.

"There had been assassins after these people, Dahlia," Sean reminded her gently.

Stoner wasn't as kind. "Lady, what is it you don't understand?"

"The Inspector is concerned about your safety, Dahlia," Chalky tried to interpreted Stoner's unique language.

"I'm sorry," Dahlia apologized. "For a moment, I forgot." She started for the hall. "I think I'll take that nap."

"Do some push-ups while you're up there," Ivy suggested. "It'll either energize you or make you tired enough to sleep."

While Dahlia went upstairs, my grandparents settled on the couch. Jason and I sat on the wide chair in the corner. Again, we couldn't say much in private. There were too many others around.

I mulled a question over in my mind and finally asked, "Barbara, how is your mother?"

She wasn't surprised and smiled. "Thank you for asking, Christy. She so enjoyed seeing you when you were both here during your last visit. I see her every day, and she seems to have her eye on us and what's going on around town all of the time."

"I am so glad she's well," I responded and knew what Barbara meant. Her mother, Sondra Bedlum, was still in her attic apartment above our heads, watching life play-out on her many video screens from the surveillance cameras that network the city. She never left her space. Barbara and Richard visited her several times a day. Also, as they moved about their house, motion sensors activate cameras so they could talk to her openly, and they would appear on the attic screens. Sondra would be watching and listening to us even now.

• • • • •

The afternoon sun was lower on the horizon. The tiny sparkling lights in the garden beyond the French doors had come on.

Dahlia, having returned to the sitting room, found a seat beside Maisie on the wide fireplace hearth. "Look at that," she said as she pointed to the screen.

Grand-mère eyes were wide. She threw her hand to her chest as if she were unable to catch her breath. "Oliver, look!"

The pie-charts the talking news head was pointing to were dripping in green, the color assigned to Grand-père. "As you can see," the anchor explained, "with less than an hour left before the polls close here in the Eastern Zone, Oliver Richly has pulled substantially ahead of Nathan Alexander."

"Wonderful!" I screamed, clenching, and unclenching my fists. I fanned my face with a side pillow. "Oh Jason, I don't think I can stand this."

He looked beyond the French doors to the right of our chair and his face softened. "Inspector, I would love to take Christy into the garden. It will be a while before we get information from the Midwestern Zone."

Stoner looked toward the heavy multi-paned glass doors and back at us. Then he did something I had never seen him do before. He smiled knowingly. "I'll go out and do a security run-through first, and then the garden is yours." As he passed us, he touched my shoulder gently.

"Should I accompany them?" Ivy asked.

"No," Stoner said as he rolled his eyes. "Stay in here, Trudeau."

Jason stood and, taking my hand, he pulled me up from the chair. We waited at the doors and watched Stoner walk through the garden, checking every corner of the large, five-foot high, walled-in terrace.

"Take the blanket-throw from the couch, Christy. It's November in New York. It is unusually warm, but it will be cold in the shadows," Barbara said as she offered the small light blue cashmere blanket.

"Yes, Dear," Grand-mère agreed. "And the color looks good on you."

The soft throw felt warm and comforting around my shoulders. When we walked out into the crisp eastern November air, I was glad Barbara had insisted I take it. Jason folded my hand in his as we took in the beauty of the garden.

The gardener had created a winding walk path that flowed past small ornamental potted trees, bushes and planters of mums and other fall flowers. Several artfully placed wooden benches dotted the magic garden under a canopy of city lights and distant neon that seemed to blink at us.

At first, we said nothing. We just enjoyed being together and alone. I looked back at the French doors. There wasn't a single eye focused on the garden and our precious time together.

I breathed in slowly and exhaled the same. "Jason thanks for this wonderful idea. I was feeling so anxious; I hadn't even seen the garden. You've presented it to me as a beautiful gift."

"Are you—still doubtful about us?" he asked, his voice sounded rough and gravely.

"I guess I never doubted *us,* Jason," I tried to assure him. "It had just been so long since we could experience *us* I didn't think I recognized *us* anymore. We had only started being *us* when *us* began to include the Claimed Children, the hollow ones, the entire colony of underlings and hundreds and hundreds of new friends and supporters of our campaign."

Jason said nothing for a moment. "You are absolutely right. But Honey there is a solution."

"There is?" I questioned in amazement. I had accepted the inevitability of our situation for so long, it never occurred to me there might be a solution. "I've been so overwhelmed I could only put one foot in front of the other and soldier on."

"Our time has been spent in the public eye almost since we met," he said.

"I don't think I could have faced the public without you, Jason. You have become my rock."

"Christy," he began as he caressed my arms, "I want to hold you. I need for you to be mine. I need you alone—with me."

I smiled. "That sounds like an old romance novel."

"Just our romance," he said and pulled me to him. "Christy, we have no time alone because we don't own each other's alone time."

"Own?" I questioned in surprise.

"Okay, you know what I mean," he said as he threw his head back and laughed. "I wouldn't own you—any more than you could claim me—except as your husband."

"Husband?" My heart began to pound. "Are you asking me to marry you?"

"You know I am," he bellowed, like a fox howling at the moon after a successful hunt. "Christiana Applewait, will you marry me? We've almost talked about it before. Then my alone time would be spent with you in our alone place."

"Yes, Jason, yes!" I answered. I stepped into his arms in the closeness of the garden and felt sure I would never be alone again.

CHAPTER 37

An Unlikely Hero

How could the day change from sunshine and neon, to the blackness of night, in an instant, like the extinguishing of a candle on a night of the new moon? But, it did.

Crack, pop, pop, the repeating fire from a lethal firearm pierced the silence of the terrace. Jason and I hit the grass, he with his body partially covering mine.

"Stay down," he whispered as he crawled toward the French doors. At that moment, the doors flew open and the edge of the frame hit Jason's head.

"Get in here!" Alister Bedlum demanded. His face was red with anger as his hot 980 waved wildly in the air.

Jason and I got up and eased ourselves around the doors and past the gunman. Blood was dripping for Jason's forehead.

Ivy's body sat rigidly in the chair near the fireplace. Her eyes fixed on Bedlum.

Barbara jumped up and whipped a cloth napkin from the refreshment table. "Jason, here, let me stop the bleeding."

As Bedlum's temper grew, the weapon in his hand began to shake. "Sit down!"

Stoner held his hands up, palms out. "Let's all just calm down."

Bedlum turned again and screeched, "I said sit down!"

Barbara stared into the emptiness that began to engulf us all. "What are you going to do, Father, shoot me, too?"

Bedlum's expression did not change. "If I have to, Missy. We come from a long line of heads of family who have had to do what was necessary to maintain power." He leveled the gun and pointed at Barbara's heart.

"We?" Barbara straightened her spine and stretched to her full height. "No. I do not come from your family at all. Not anymore."

"Barbara, sit down," Tayton warned her.

Ivy had not moved until then. She slowly inched to the edge of her seat and then, suddenly, *pow pow*. Grabbing the arms of the chair, she screamed out in pain.

"Try being the body guard with no right foot," he snickered.

My heart felt like it stopped. What could I do? Nothing. I watched Ivy's face for a sign of how badly she was hurt and was surprised. Her expression was of one in pain, and I knew she was injured. I could see by the damage to her shoe, that the bullet had nicked the side of her foot and no more. She was able to keep Bedlum from taking another shot by feigned more pain and more injury than was there.

"Toss that sidearm over here—and it had better not hit my feet," he said with an evil smile. "That way you won't have to think about it all the time."

Ivy released her weapon slowly and slid it in Bedlum's direction.

Stoner's eyes darted from Ivy to the evil one who held them all at gunpoint. "Can we talk about this?" He asked as he took one step toward the end of the gun.

With rage in his eyes, Bedlum hissed, "Are you stupid?" The end of the 980 exploded and Stoner collapsed onto the floor.

Chalky fell to his side and lifted his head to her lap. "Ward?" she gasped. Blood oozed from his side and began to soak into the carpet.

"Now—you," he growled at Chalky, "pull his service weapon from its holster and push it over here—yours, too."

Chalky did as ordered, reached in past the sticky seepage of blood and lifted Ward's revolver from its holster. She removed her own sidearm and cautiously slid the two pieces in Bedlum's direction.

"What have you done?" Silas asked as he came into the room, his hand covering his mouth.

Bedlum waved the gun around in the air and then snarled, "I did what I ordered that idiot Washington to do. They captured him with a busted-up knee. So, I sought you out, furnace keeper, to do it. And— you botched it up, you sniveling mouse." Bedlum's eyes looked wild. "You only gave me half the information about their where-abouts and then you couldn't even pull the trigger on this piece of elite trash running for office."

"What?" I gasped as I jumped to my feet. The madman waved the gun at me. I flinched, expecting him to fire at any moment. Jason pulled me by the hand, and I fell onto the chair beside him.

"Who do you think has been feeding me your every move? How did I know where you'd be?" Bedlum roared—his voice shrill. "The mass-murderer of Howard Mountain told me," he yelled, pointing at Silas Drummond.

"Lady Applewait—" Silas begged.

"Silas, I am Christy, remember—and have been all these months."

"He forced me to tell him where you'd be," Silas said as his eyes flooded with tears.

"You are a weakling," Bedlum accused.

Tayton didn't move but said calmly. "What do you want? Maybe we can talk about it."

"You want a shot in the head little Blue Guard boy?"

I held my breath and waited. Out of the corner of my eye, I watched Stoner begin to stir and wondered if he would be strong enough to save us. Chalky was going through the motions of attending to him while her hand slowly doubled into a fist.

"You will lose that hand," the inheritor of all the mafia families warned through gritted teeth. "Didn't you learn anything when you saw what happened to your boss, or is he your boyfriend?

Chalky said nothing but stared at him with a steely gaze.

"Christy," Silas spoke only to me, his eyes pleading. "You must understand. He said he would hunt down and kill every one of the Claimed Children I rescued from the furnaces and smuggled into the Valley of the Keepers. Every one of them, Christy."

"I'll still do it, you lazy, weak whiner." Bedlum raised the gun and shot Silas in the shoulder.

Silas fell back onto one of the library chairs and slumped down. I watched him intently for signs of shock. When I saw him adjust himself in the chair, I was encouraged by his ability to move.

"Suffer a little, you butcher, as I work on my favorite target." He aimed at Grand-père's head. "While you marinate in your own blood—furnace-keeper—I'll finish off this arrogant wise-one." This time Bedlum was controlled as he took aim.

Stoner lunged at Bedlum's legs, waving his arms out in a wide sweep. Chalky reached toward the sociopath, but she and Stoner only succeeded in knocking Bedlum off balance. When he staggered, his 980 fired wildly in the air as falling plaster landed on the marble mantel of the fireplace.

Crack! The deep throated sound of a .30-30 shattered the house. Alister Bedlum fell with a mighty thud and rumble, like an ax had just felled a huge tree. His head struck the hearth when Maisie and Dahlia jumped out of the way.

Every eye in the room turned to follow the trajectory of the blast. Sondra Bedlum stood on the third step of the grand staircase; a Winchester carbine still poised in her hands.

"Mother!" Barbara gasped and ran into the entry to her mother's side.

I was as stunned as the rest of those in the room. Would Sondra crumble over what she had done? She had just killed her estranged husband.

Grand-père stood and hurried to her side. "Mrs. Bedlum, you have saved us all."

Immediately behind Grand-père, Tayton gently removed the rifle from Sondra's hands, secured the trigger and checked the gun for additional shells. "You are a hero," he said softly as Barbara put her arm around her mother's shoulder.

Stoner eased up on his elbow. "Ma'am, thank you for your courage. You prevented a blood bath here. I'm sure of it." To Chalky he added, "Boone, contact a removal unit. Have this body hauled out of here—and summon the investigative team who will need to interview the shooter." He looked back at Sondra. "It will be slick, Ma'am. There will be no charges. I'll make sure of that."

Grasping Mrs. Bedlum's hand in mine, I started to cry before I could get the words off my lips. "You have not only saved my grandfather, Sondra, you have played a huge part in saving our country from the prison of fear and hopelessness."

With roaring shouts and cheering from the mass media set behind us, I looked back. I needed to see if there was a second attack in another location.

"Grand-père," I gasped. "The election results are all in. You won!"

EPILOGUE

Inauguration was January 20, 2115. The sun was brilliant on the cool winter day. The crowd stretched out for blocks around the East front of the Capital building. Everyone who attended and those who watched on mass media were filled with new hope. The Length of Days Law had been over thrown and freedom had been found and returned to the people.

The ceremony that thrilled me as much as Grand-père's swearing-in was my wedding to Jason the following spring in the White House rose garden. My dress was long white satin covered in lace at the bodice. The veil was a simple cluster of white roses that fixed in my hair with a comb and draped down the left side of my head. Friends from all over the country came. Even Sondra Bedlum came out of her hiding place to attend. We celebrated life and the living of it; hope and the expectation of it; and freedom and our belief in it.

NOTES

Oliver Richly speech in chapter 27 is inspired by the cadence in Ronald Reagan's speech that includes the sentence, "You and I have a rendezvous with destiny." — Ronald Reagan, <u>A Time for Choosing: The Speeches of Ronald Reagan, 1961-1982</u>

Information on Billy the Kid, taken from, http://www.mesilla.com. Accessed 12/28/15

<u>About the Author</u>

Doris Gaines Rapp, Ph.D. is a writer by birth, psychologist and teacher by education and experiences. She creates fictional characters that live in several centuries and loves the stories she tells. As a psychologist, she understands the people who appear on her computer screen; she laughs with them, cries with them, and triumphs over adversity with them. They are real and full of life. All of her works have at their heart a Christian world view.

Rapp also writes on the non-fiction topics of Self-publishing with an encouragement to promote yourself and your work; as well as Prayer Therapy, learning to pray specifically so God can answer prayers specifically.

She speaks on several topics:
Voices of Assertiveness within My Novels
Prayer Therapy
Promote Yourself
Know Your Own History

Dr. Rapp is a former counseling center director of Taylor University, Upland, IN and Bethel College, Mishawaka, IN. She currently writes and speaks full time. She and her pastor husband have survived rearing six children. They live in Indiana.

Other Books by Doris Gaines Rapp
Available at amazon.com, barnesandnoble.com, and others
<u>*Novels*</u>:
Tucker McBride's Many Live
Tucker McBride
Escape from the Belfry
Escape from the Shadows
Murder, She Blogged – Just in Time
News at Eleven – A Novel (Prequel to *Murder, She Blogged - Just in Time*)
Length of Days – The Age of Silence (1st in the trilogy)
Length of Days – Beyond the Valley of the Keepers (2nd in the trilogy)
Length of Days – Search for Freedom (3rd in the trilogy)
Hiawassee – Child of the Meadow
Smoke from Distant Fires

Children's Picture Book:
Shyloe and the Mayor
Lincoln's Christmas Mouse

Collection:
Christmas Feather, one of eight short stories in *Christmases Past*

Non-Fiction:
Prayer Therapy of Jesus
Promote Yourself
Waiting for Jesus in a Can't Wait World – Advent 2014

Internet Presence
Facebook: Doris Gaines Rapp – Author Page
https://lengthofdaystrilogy.blogspot.com
www.dorisgainesrapp.com
www.dorisgainesrapp.blogspot.com
Activities and discussion ideas available for Tucker:
www.tuckermcbrideintheclassroom.com.

* 9 7 8 0 9 9 8 8 5 9 0 9 5 *